Lord of Reason

Lord of Reason

an historical novel by

Roy Luna

professor of French Language and Literature
at the Key Largo Campus of the Florida Keys International College,

with historical notes provided by

Dr. Theophilus Ralph

professor of History at the University of Münster,
Thunder-den-Drang Campus, Westphalia, Germany

SOLUTION HOLE PRESS

SOL UTION HOLE PRESS

First Edition.

First Printing: 2016

ISBN: 978-0-9967031-0-9

Solution Hole Press LLC.

www.solutionholepress.com

Cover Design: Rowena Luna

Book Design: Jorge Saury

When I first set out to write a novelization of Voltaire's triumphant return to Paris after an exile of twenty-eight years, I did not suspect that this particular rendition would take the form that it did. Footnotes in a novel? Interrupt my dear reader's attention by forcing her or him to descend to the bottom of the page? Well, the reader does not really have to read the footnotes. Besides, those readers who are used to reading literary criticism have no qualms about interrupting the main text in order to read the secondary text which—perish the thought!—at times is at the back of the book. (One keeps two bookmarks in such cases.) I just didn't know how else to provide the reader with information that was taken for granted back in 1778. If the dear reader already knows these facts, I humbly beg her or his pardon. I know most readers will recognize some of the characters who were contemporaries of Voltaire's just before his death and the French Revolution, but lesser known individuals require an introduction.

Please be advised, however, that some of the characters in this novel will not be found in *Webster's Biographical Dictionary*; they may be composites of several historical people, or else they were fashioned from the milieu of Parisian life, be it in the salons or in the streets, or perhaps they came out full-blown from my imagination.

Fiction demands verisimilitude; reality forces no such exigencies. The outlandish historical characters and their not-to-be-believed stories in this novel did exist. I have not even embellished. Their biographies are easily accessible in French or English. None of their actions has been invented. Well, almost none. Juxtaposed with the unbelievable characters are the probable characters who, although they may not have existed as historically verifiable individuals, nevertheless must have existed in order to let the real characters do what they did. I am thinking especially of those who belonged to the servant class. Their actions in the novel are by comparison more logical and timorous since they are subjected to psychological straightjackets, all in the name of likelihood. By the way, any resemblance between these fictitious characters and real people of any other era including our own, is my prerogative as a novelist.

This book would not have been possible had it not been for the arduous research of historians and biographers. In our days, history has become not just a search for people, actions and dates, but also a method of reaching out to another time and figuring out how people lived and loved and coped. My gratitude goes out to the giants in their field: René Pomeau, Jean Orieux, Pierre Lepape, Jean Goulemot, André Magnan, Didier Masseau, Pierre Milza, Wayne Andrews, Peter Gay and Ian Davidson for Voltaire; Maurice Cranston and Leo Damrosch for Jean-Jacques Rousseau; Elizabeth Badinter and Robert Badinter for Condorcet; Otis Fellows for Diderot; Walter Isaacson, Edmund S. Morgan, H. W. Brands, Gordon S. Wood, Claude-Ann Lopez and Stacy Schiff for Benjamin Franklin; Jeffrey Merrick for the Marquis de Villette; Gary Kates for the Chevalier d'Éon; Stefan Zweig for Marie Antoinette; Jean-Christian Petitfils for Louis XVI; Pierre Gaxotte for Paris in the Eighteenth Century; Arlette Farge for living on the streets of Paris in the Eighteenth Century; Daniel Roche for the people of Paris and David Andress for the people of Paris right before the Revolution; J. Q. C. Mackrell for the vestiges of feudalism in Eighteenth-Century France; David McCullough for the flavor of the times in America; and for the chronicles of the time just before the Revolution: Simon Schama, Claude Manceron, and Georges Lefebvre. I also want to thank James W. Lowen for his dramatic eye-popping takes on how history comes to be revised, bowdlerized, transformed, laundered, curtailed, "fableized" and in general "made fit" for current fashions or prevailing political and religious dogmas. (If Voltaire's texts were on American public school reading lists, how much of him would be left scattered on the floor after pea-brained ulterior-motive-minded scissor-wielding textbook committees had finished with him? I venture to say: most of him.)

I wish to thank my friends who either trudged through the working versions of this book and/or sparked the generation thereof with ideas and observations that have truly been equal to the height and breadth of the Enlightenment. They were the prisms who helped me focus and organize the light of the Eighteenth Century: C. M. Clark, Marie-Josèphe Jarry, Aracelys López, Barbara Mihm, Rudy Molina, Miguel Montañez, Maureen O'Hara, Michel Philip, Roselyne Pirson, Jorge Saury, Denise Strauss, Michael Subklew, Mary Ann Talmadge, Guy Teissier, Marie Zurenda and Mark Young. Just looking at their names and knowing their origins make me realize that Voltaire would be happy in the thought that he is still bringing people together from all parts of the globe.

My sisters also were extremely helpful, Rowena Luna for her brilliant design of the covers, and Rossibell Luna for her patience in having to listen for hours while I ran possible scenes by her.

In addition, I wish to acknowledge the most wonderful gift I have ever received for my birthday. It was this that started the wheels in motion: a pristine set of the complete works of Voltaire, the historically important "Kehl" edition, published posthumously in 70 volumes in 1784 by Beaumarchais and edited by Condorcet. This publication by Voltaire's friends was of course a clandestine operation. Five years before the Revolution (but who knew it was coming?) retribution could still befall those who flouted royal and ecclesiastical laws. That I can read these books openly today–and teach my students from them–without fearing reprisals is something that would please Voltaire. I can see him smiling, on my library shelf: inimitable is his intelligent, impudent, cynical smirk. Without him, our life today would certainly be different. Without him, we could easily revert to the mistakes of the past. Without him, many lands on this Earth have already taken that backwards road to intolerance, superstition, absolutism and theological repression. Let us keep Voltaire and all the *philosophes* alive, for our own sake, because nothing less than our very freedom depends on their accumulated wisdom.

Écrasez l'Infâme!

Last, but certainly not least, I wish to thank Professor Theophilus Ralph, historian, biographer, academician, and enlightened *philosophe* in his own right, for his generous and non-remunerated authorship of the footnotes. In spite of the constrictions of time before publication, he has acquiesced to provide details to serve as backdrop for Eighteenth-century life in France, details which no modern reader is expected to know. Professor Ralph's international reputation–the esteem of his colleagues is legendary!–bespeaks the meticulousness of his œuvre, and I have no doubt that the readers will find themselves in good historiographical hands. His has truly been a labor of love.

Preface of the Historian-
author of the footnotes

Bonjour. Allow me please myself to introduce. My name is Dr. Theophilus Ralph and I have historiographer at the University of Münster at Thunder-den-Drang, in Westphalia, for these past thirty-two years been. It is flattering indeed that my expertise in Eighteenth-Century Paris has been judged creditable enough to have invited been to add a few explanatory blurbs to this novelization of the private and public events of Voltaire following his triumphant return to Paris in 1778. The novelist, whom I have yet to meet, has nevertheless with me enough corresponded that I can certify that he has great pains taken to render the historical events of this story with impeccable, and even inviolable accuracy. In one letter, this writer told me that he once spent four hours walking up und down, up und down the Quai Voltaire and the rue de Beaune in an effort to "breathe in the air of history" and to "imagine the scenes of two and a quarter centuries ago." He in addition took the same walks, and indeed, the same runs, that his characters take in the story, in order to make sure that the distances traversed required the time that he says they do. He lunched with an internationally diverse group of best friends at the very popular restaurant "le Voltaire" which has recently on the ground floor of the Hôtel de Villette opened and they drank toast after toast to Voltaire as the hero of the Enlightenment and the voice of those without a voice. They left quite drunk and by accident joined up with the good-natured marchers at the nearby Boulevard de Saint-Germain marching in the midst of their Marche des Fiertés. He wrote to me that he could not help feeling all the while that Voltaire would have of the gay festivities approved. In another letter, or perhaps in an e-mail, he wrote that he once remained in front of Voltaire's tomb in the Pantheon late one afternoon after all the tourists had gone and stood there in quiet meditation, trying to meld his mind with that of the philosopher, but the racket that Rousseau was making in the tomb behind him would not allow him to resuscitate Voltaire's spirit. Ach, I'm not surprised that Rousseau is still envious of Voltaire. I do believe, however, that our writer recounted this detail in jest.

In any case, here, according to the author's wishes, is the first blurb: the Quai des Théâtins is now called the Quai de Voltaire, in view of the old philosopher having there dwelled, twice. The first time it was to visit his old friend the Présidente of Bernières in 1724. The second time was to stay with his friends the Marquis and Marquise de Villette in February of 1778 until his death in May of 1778. But perhaps I should not have this part of the story away given. Ach, but everybody knows that Voltaire died four months after his arrival in Paris, do they not?

Still, I find it befitting that Voltaire's name has that of the Théâtins replaced. This old religious order, founded in 1524 by Saint Gaétan de Thiene, with principal churches in Munich, Turin and Paris, did not deserve a street named after them in the Age of Enlightenment. It is quite à propos that the name of the person who dedicated the whole of his life in the fight against the primacy of the Church eclipsed that of the infamous tyranny.

I profess I leave no doubt as to where I myself stand in the fractious debates of Eighteenth-century Europe. I have never impartial been. Und I offer no apologies. Perhaps this is why I have been asked to blurb this text. In my book of history entitled

The War of the Gods, from Roncevalles to New York, published in 2007 by the University Presses of Thunder-den-Drang, I explained the causes and effects of MIR (Mutually Intolerant Religions) and assigned the guilt to the INRI (Indoctrinated National Religions & Institutions). The crimes in the name of God perpetrated are vast, and until the fanaticism is by tolerance crushed, the fate of the world precarious remains.

But, to get back to the matter at hand, this novel is soon going to press and I have instructions to be pithy received. I promise pithiness in subsequent notes, even though it is extremely difficult German exuberance to subdue. Therefore, remembering the immortal Leibniz, who said that "the present is pregnant with the future," we are able clearly, in the time of Voltaire's return to Paris in 1778, a very, quite visible, pregnancy to witness.

This book is dedicated to the readers of
Voltaire
in the hopes that, through them, his words
will continue to enlighten humans
today and in the future;
to the dix-huitiémistes who toil in the world's universities,
who nurture the light of the torch
as they pass it to new generations;
and to my muse,
Chérie Clark,
whose brilliant insights and enthusiasm
enlighten and energize me.

Warning: This is Not a Novel
Warnüng: Dies ist kein Roman
Avertissement: Ceci n'est pas un roman
Avvertimento: Questo non è un romanzo
Предупреждение: Это нероман

Prologue: Panic at Court

The courtiers in the library of the *Parlement* at Versailles were at wit's end. The restraint, the reserve, the grace, the dignity, all of those gentlemanly virtues which usually reigned in these somber hallowed chambers had been eclipsed hours ago by a sort of frenzy, a turmoil bordering on lunacy. Decorum yielded to pandemonium, and disorder was the tyrant who ruled in the elegant rooms of the King's library, late in the day. On every surface reams of paper and voluminous bundles of documents covered in florid script lay in uneven stacks. Serpentine scrolls swirled to the floor, there to stay, to be trod upon. Ladders were shoved from one bookshelf to another as the King's librarians scurried up and down them like squirrels. Incredible as it may have sounded to their fellow aristocrats, some were even running–running!–from one office to the next. A buckled shoe with a red heel slid across the floor, the man still attached to it! Voices were raised in useless bickering, gasps of irritation were released. There were also muffled oaths and undignified grunts as heavy loads were lifted from the tables and dropped onto the floor. Dust burst in little clouds here and there as the aristocrats blew on the heavy bound volumes of royal letters. The library had never seen such brouhaha, yet nobody had the time to stop, review the unprecedented scene, and feel ashamed. God Almighty! They were working like peasants!

The gentlemen of Louis XVI's court responsible for keeping the royal records were about to come to a terrible conclusion. That this was a matter of national security was undeniable, and it could serve to explain, but not excuse, their altered state. Under their powdered wigs hanging askew, drops of sweat ran down their temples. High up on a ladder, dust made one of them sneeze, but even he hardly realized it as in one motion he used his frilly silk sleeve to wipe his nose and continued, unabated, in his frantic search for the *lettre de cachet*. They were looking for the royal document of exile that His Majesty's grandfather, Louis XV, had signed to banish Voltaire forever from Paris. In spite of their meticulous search in which no paperweight was left unturned, the mountains of sheets of vellum would not relinquish what they so desperately sought. Finally one of them, a count, muttered that perhaps it had never existed.

"Would His Highness have banished the royal historiographer from his court forever?"

"What did you just say?" asked one of his peers, a pinched-nose *chevalier* who looked more like a marmot than a gentleman.

"Nobody ever saw His Majesty sign this *lettre de cachet*. I do believe that it was just an oral banishment. We must conclude that there never was such a letter, let alone one affixed with the royal seal."

"But that was over twenty-five years ago! All the credible witnesses are dead!" cried one of the younger ones, a myopic, and cross-eyed, *vicomte*, whose head shook with the vexation of a mole who has lost his tunnel.

"It is imperative nonetheless that we find it, for without it we cannot impede him from returning to Paris," said another, an older, usually distinguished, gentleman wearing an expression of nervous agitation such as the jittery shrew shows with the coming of the serpent. Antoine Raymond Jean Guilbert Gabriel de Sartine, director of the King's Library, was not accustomed to having difficulties barring his way to success, and in this particular case he was verily twitching with trepidation.

"Haven't you heard what *monsieur le comte* just said?" the *chevalier* asked the director. "This *lettre de cachet* might never have existed. His Majesty simply expressed his wishes orally in Court (as he was wont to do!) and never bothered to put it in writing."

"I remember how His Majesty reacted," said an older courtier, a baron of Savoyard descent whose ancient countenance and grave comportment gave double credence to his story, "the day he was told that Voltaire had received an invitation from Frederick for an extended visit to Prussia, and that Voltaire, great God, had accepted it. Imagine, the King's historiographer gallivanting off to a rival court, and to the Prussian court, no less. To be with that unnatural, unsavory, sexually inverted German speaker. You can imagine His Highness' reaction. His Royal Majesty said absolutely nothing, his expression changed not a whit; he just turned regally away."

"But he must have punished Voltaire's insolence in some official way," retorted the director. "That *lettre de cachet* must exist."

The tenor of his voice was close to that of yelling. When none of the dozen men around him reacted, he did start to yell.

"We must find it! *Nom de Dieu!* It has got to be here! We are all idiots if we do not find it! We'll all be dead if we cannot find it! Worse, we shall be the laughing stock of all of Europe! It will be thought risible that Louis XVI cannot interdict the entry into Paris of a mere writer. We will be deemed ridiculous." That last thought put an edge of hysteria to the expression of his eyes. He sputtered, "Voltaire cannot come back to Paris! We shall not allow him the impunity to return! *Merde, putain, sang de Dieu!* Don't just stand there. Look for it! Find it!"

After the shock of this blaspheming excoriation, the stunned librarians continued working in meek silence, stupefied that their worthy colleague could lose his head over so little. One lost one's head over something of more importance! A quarter of an hour later, the courtiers pulled away from the tables and shelves in dismay. Having searched in the same places numerous times, defeat made them look haggard and pale. Their eyes burned. Indubitably, the yearly royal stipend they received for service to the King's Library was not worth all this travail.

"Where will he be staying?" asked the youngest courtier who was present that evening. He wore one of those outlandish new wigs that ended in a silly pony tail.

The others barely heard the question as they kept up their intense search.

"I mean, who would dare harbor this *persona non grata* in the midst of all these epistles dispatched daily from the offices of the Archbishop of Paris? I would think such a host would be instantaneously excommunicated."

"You mean you really haven't heard?" answered a Lord worthy of the imposing quivering of his several chins. "Voltaire shall be sojourning in the house of the *marquis* de Villette."

"On the quai des Théâtins?"

"The very same."

"The one who just married one of Voltaire's orphans?"[1]

"There's none other."

"The one whose father was a banker and made a fortune as Treasurer Extraordinaire of War?"[2]

"And whose marquisate is of embarrassingly recent vintage."[3]

"But I daresay his fortune counts for something."

"As does his provenance as well," said *monsieur* Chins with a look that bespoke of lurid gossip.

"His provenance?" repeated the young aristocrat who had heard nothing of this. "Do, I pray, tell."

"Well, it was bruited about town that Voltaire was rather charming to Villette's mother around the time that she became enceinte. I remember her well, a ravishing beauty, brought in from the provinces, and she created quite a stir. She stole quite a number of hearts, but she only really cared for one, and that was Voltaire's."

"Imagine that. Villette being Voltaire's progeny. Too bad he won't have any of his own."

It was the older man's turn to pray for more information for he was curious as to why Villette could not sire a child. It was still contemporary to speak of Louis XVI's difficulties at producing heirs, due to a malformation of his penis. Surmising a possibility in the case of the *marquis* de Villette, the Lord raised a rigid finger that slowly relaxed to a state of dangling despondency.

"Oh, no, it's not that at all. The problem lies in the appendage's preferred target, which, suffice it to say, is rather more—how can I put it?—Grecian, if you catch my drift."

Aristocrats knew their literature and ancient cultures. The drift was caught, and the older man stopped to consider how Voltaire would view a son who was more interested in catamites than in his lovely new wife, a wife who, after all, was one of Voltaire's adopted children. Then he thought that the Church should be consulted, for the whole thing smacked of incest. But then, he realized, Voltaire could not care one whit, for he had been a participant in an incestuous relationship for over twenty-five years, with the daughter of his sister. How that man flouted the rules of man and God! How could he be so utterly irreverent when it came to the proper regulations of social conduct? There were principles to be followed, after all!

The old nobleman and the young courtier separated from their gossipy tête-à-tête, and plunged anew into their search for the *lettre de cachet*. Surely it would be detrimental to society to let a man like Voltaire in. He would overturn convention and religion in

---

1   Voltaire was adamant that there be no orphanage in Ferney, the village that was part of the grounds of his château: he would pick up lost children and raise them as his own under the aegis of philosophy. *Mademoiselle* de Varicourt quickly became his favorite, and he was happy to see her become a *marquise* upon her marriage to Villette.

2   *Trésorier général de l'Extraordinaire des Guerres.* He was also Secretary to the King.

3   Older, more established aristocratic families looked down in contempt at the recently ennobled. But the king happily continued the practice of selling titles of nobility because it meant more money coming into his coffers. Villette's father purchased his title from Louis XV in 1741.

a second, especially among the stupid commoners. They were so dupable. He would degrade morals and upend ethics. The young would be ruined, society torn asunder, souls lost, government undermined, the Church attacked. Voltaire had dedicated his entire life to these evil deeds!

A duke with spasmodic facial muscles asked feebly, "When does he get here?"

"He was seen in Dijon three days ago," answered a disheveled *marquis*. "It is reported that young men were bribing the waiters at an inn for the pleasure of taking their places, in order to serve him. Can you believe it? They wished to *serve* him! The following day he left Dijon but his axle broke around Moret, and his party has had to wait to have it repaired."

"Where is Moret?"

"It is a stone's throw from Fontainebleau."

"Fontainebleau!" they cried out in unison.

"But that is only a day away!"

"He should be in Paris tomorrow," said the director, "unless, of course, he arrives later on tonight."

One of the courtiers gasped. "Unless, of course, he is here already!"

As of one mind, invigorated by that impossible thought, they all plunged themselves anew into their task like frenzied rodents, looking for a piece of paper that had never existed. Louis XV had failed to keep Voltaire out of Paris forever. This deep fear of what Voltaire represented, overturning social conventions, reforming judicial institutions, revolutionizing beloved conservative policies, in short, bringing change where change was not wanted, made them recoil with entrenched panic.

The great philosopher would have appreciated the irony: panic in the face of approaching Reason. Voltaire represented Reason, and the two of them were coming into Paris like the unstoppable light of the rising sun. The King had not given his aristocrats the tools to fight his return. He had neglected to sign a *lettre de cachet* to keep the philosopher out of his realm. It never occurred to the tyrant that Voltaire would one day dare to return to Paris, or even that he would live that long! While it was true that His Majesty had died a most terrible death, with smallpox slowly decomposing his body from the outside in, he nevertheless received no small comfort from the belief that the archenemy of his absolutist system would never again set foot in his domain, and because of that certainty he had never bothered to draw up the formal papers. It was the heir apparent, his eldest surviving grandson,[4][5] who would have to deal with the unfinished business of banning philosophers. Once on the throne, Louis XVI, young and inexperienced, found that he could not. He was by far not the smartest of Louis, and he was leagues away from being the canniest. Quite the contrary. He was fat and slow, indecisive, bashful, solitary and secretive. Not a good personality for a king to have in the midst of a hugely public life where his every move, dressing, undressing, eating, defecating, was to be done in front of courtiers, visitors, physicians, witnesses. As luck would have it, this was the Louis who would have to pay for the sins of all his

---

4   One must realize that Louis XVI would never have reigned had it not been for the fact that both his father and older brother had also of smallpox died. Oh, microörganisms truly over the destiny of monarchs rule!

5   [From the author] I respectfully submit to the fact-checker and to the editors of this novel that knowledge subsequent to 1778 not be incorporated into the footnotes of this text.

predecessors. It was he who would have to swim in the deluge that Louis XIV had set in motion so long ago, and go down the drain that Louis XV had unplugged.

For the immediate present, his courtiers knew that it was this monarch who would have to deal with the return of Voltaire. That is why they were at wit's end. *Monsieur de Voltaire* was just hours away.

Candles and lanterns were lit in the library. More wood was added to the fireplaces. They burned through the rest of the night, but all that nocturnal activity which they illuminated, all that fuss and worry and scampering about, in the end, did no good.

Day of Philosophical Rejoicing

It was in the middle of the night that the lone visitor finally arrived in Paris, at the Barrière St-Martin, where no customs worker was even awake. His progressively louder knocks on the huge wooden gate echoed in the darkness but brought nothing but the barking of dogs. Three or four of them gathered their forms in the gloom and snarled through holes in the gate, looking like Cerberus guarding the gates to hell. The visitor drew back, then slowly mounted his horse.

After a rattling of chains and a couple of curses in an accent which the visitor surmised was Parisian, a figure congealed in the doorway.

"In the name of God's blood, who has the gall to wake us up in the middle of the night?"

The cold and the growling dogs were worse than the *douanier*'s[6] irritation, and the man on the horse quickly gave a response.

"In the name of all that is human, allow entry to a wanderer who is come from a long distance and seeks some solace and warmth!"

The *douanier*, too sleepy to offer resistance, proceeded with the customary interrogation.

"What's yer name?"

"Marie-Jean Joseph Zénobe Bosquet."

"Whence come ye?"

"Dijon."

"Carry ye goods?"

"None but my personal effects."

The man opened the gate, kicking the dogs away.

The visitor thanked the man, bade him fall back asleep quickly, and went through. He was glad the *douanier* had been too impatient to check him for contraband, for he was carrying books, most of them listed in the Index of forbidden books, including a few written by his hero Voltaire. It would have saddened him greatly to see those books confiscated. What he didn't know was that he himself would have been turned

---

6   The *douanier* was the customs guard posted at the city gate who not only collected taxes on merchandise being brought into the city but also searched the travelers for contraband.

over to the ecclesiastical authorities in the morning, to face a formal interrogation and possible imprisonment.

The visitor entered Paris for the first time in his life, and he could not see a thing. The candles in the lamps of the city streets had not been lit that night because the moon was one day from being full. Too bad for Zénobe, the cloud cover was thick and ran like milky oats under the moon. He could see nothing of the city. The lonely sound of his horse's hooves alerted him when he was getting too close to walls. In this melancholy fashion, he made his way down, as best he could, in the direction of the Seine. Without realizing it, his horse's hooves were clattering on the cobblestones of the rue Saint-Antoine. The huge form of the Bastille floated by unseen right beside him to his left. When he heard the *guet* announcing three o'clock, he headed towards the voice.[7]

The *guet* was surprised to see a man on horseback at such an hour. He was as amenable as the *douanier* had been unfriendly, as if welcoming the chance to be sociable.

"Where are you headed?"

"To an inn in the Quartier Latin."

"I shall accompany you to the Pont Marie on the Isle St-Louis. You'll need me as an escort to cross the island. Otherwise you would have to go all the way to the Pont Neuf. Nobody's awake at this hour, except for those up to no good."

"Thank you for your kindness, *monsieur*," answered Zénobe. "I would rather have arrived in Paris at a less ungodly hour, but I can't get much of a gallop out of my steed here."

---

7   [From the fact-checker, *Herr* Ralph] I must against an injustice protest. After I wrote to author Luna to remind him that the Royal «*guet*», by Saint Louis in 1254 founded, had been into the Garde de Paris in 1750 fused, *monsieur* Luna responded without much grace and with no gratitude whatsoever. Here is his response, so you can for yourself judge:

Herr Ralph,
You are right, of course, to scour my text in your dogged pursuit of veracity, for in a historical novel the reader needs to believe in the absolute truth of the details. You, however, make it sound as if I did no research whatsoever and allowed fanciful flights of imagination to fill in where I was lacking in historical fact. *Nein, mein Herr, mein sehr gnädiger Herr*, this won't do at all. The «*guet*» had by 1778 long been disbanded, as you take great pleasure in telling me, taken over by the more efficacious *Garde de Paris*, since most of the newer patrols were made up of unemployed soldiers who had the nerve to survive the Seven Years' War and thus needed work. Fortunately, they turned out to be more ruthless than the *guet* ever was. However, I repeat, however–and this is where you must question your own supposed expertise on the subject–the wealthy residents of the Île Saint Louis continued to employ, privately, the leftover remnants of the *ancien guet*, to make sure that no undesirables, including members of the Garde de Paris themselves, penetrated into their exclusive domain.
I suppose that you have been swept away by your role of fact checker, and in your mind you have become another gendarme, patrolling my text like the Garde patrolled the streets of Paris. Nevertheless, think of the image of me that you are placing in front of my literary agent and my publisher; they who have been so nice, helpful and patient, might begin to entertain thoughts that I was amiss in my responsibilities, and for this, I will place the blame directly in your tenaciously Teutonic hands.
                                                                                          Signed, Roy Luna
P.S. I wish mightily that you would your verbs in the right spot place. But who checks the fact-checker, ah, *mein Herr*?

Such anger must indeed something hide. *Monsieur* Luna is very touchy, and he forgets that I am on his side working. And, anyway, what is wrong with the placement of my verbs? Cannot he see that I am trying my very best to do?

"What affairs bring you to our City of Light?"[8]

Zénobe chuckled. "Not much light tonight. However..."

He sprang off his horse in order to converse better with the *guet*.

"However, I am come to meet the philosopher who is the most responsible for Paris deserving this description."

"Ah, we have heard rumors that the Sage of Ferney will soon be in our number."

"You know about it?"

"Well, yes," the *guet* answered matter-of-factly. "News of that nature cannot be kept secret in a city like Paris. We've heard several reports of his approach."

"Allow me to add mine to the testimony. I had the pleasure of serving him in Dijon when he came to dine at the inn where I worked. When I found out he was on his way to Paris, I resigned from my post to come see him here."

"Good enough reason to leave the province."

They had arrived at another massive gate. The *guet* unlocked it, and bade the night visitor keep quiet while they traversed the Isle St-Louis. "You don't want to wake these people up," he whispered. Zénobe understood that these people were of a special class, and as such deserved uninterrupted sleep. Still, as he looked up to the apartments overhead, he could see flickering candlelight through some of the windows. In quite a few of the *hôtels*, he noticed, there was activity, and music.[9] Laughter and moving shadows fell on the street as Zénobe and his escort passed by.

On the other side of the island, the *guet* unlocked a second gate, and instructed the traveler to turn west after the Pont de la Tournelle. "But you better go south first, south and then west. You don't want to remain on the quays. Even we *guets* don't like to linger there. No telling what you may find on the quays, but I can tell you it won't be anything good. With luck, you'll hear the *guet* from the Faubourg St-Victor. He'll tell you where to go. There is a whole slew of inns in the Quartier Latin. Farewell. I hope you get to see your philosopher friend."

"My philosopher friend," Zénobe repeated softly to himself. To his guide he said, "Thank you, thank you very much, *monsieur*. You have been very kind."

The gate closed and Zénobe found himself alone again. But this time, the words *"ami philosophe"* brought cheeriness into his heart. This night would soon turn into day, and with the day he would perhaps be seeing Voltaire again. Voltaire, without whom he could possibly not be able to continue living. Having brought bread and wine to him at the tavern in Dijon, he had seen the man up close. And now he realized that it was Voltaire who brought hope to him.

With such musings going on in his head, Zénobe neglected to go south first, and turned immediately west on the quai de la Tournelle. His reverie was suddenly arrested when he perceived in the distance to his right the considerable mass of the cathedral of Notre Dame de Paris. He could not believe his eyes, supposing the broken moonlight to be the cause of an optical illusion. But there it was, seemingly diaphanous in the

---

8   *La Ville lumière* was a name to Paris given for its fame in being a center of the Enlightenment. In its physical aspect, the city was as dark and somber, and as dirty and malodorous, as if it were still the Dark Ages. Victor Hugo expressed it best. In *Les Misérables*, he states that if Paris contained Athens, the City of Light, it also contained Lutèce, the City of Mud.

9   In the 16th through 18th centuries, an *hôtel* was a private aristocratic town house, usually of impressive dimensions. Not until the 19th century would the word take on its modern meaning of a building with rooms to let.

gloom, floating on the glimmering currents of the Seine. With its backside towards him, its faintly visible towers jutted high and its flying buttresses made him think of a huge insect ready to spring up from bended legs.

In awe, he halted his horse at the sight, peering to get a better look, but something else made him turn his head towards the bank of the river. He heard voices in distress ahead of him. He thought perhaps there was a boat on the Seine, for he heard splashing, and then a woman's frightened moan. He led his horse forward, towards the commotion. Ahead, by the river's edge, he could make out ghostly movements, dark shadows shifting about, and then he could distinguish some of their hoarsly whispered words.

"She's under… can you hear her? …the water's freezing…"

Zénobe left his horse on the *quai* and walked down the riverbank. As he did so, the figures and the words became clearer. It was a trio assembled on the bank, two men and a woman.

"She's gone," the woman was saying. "She's done for."

"'Er mind's gone," said one of the men. "That's for sure."

"Who was she?" asked the other one.

"Who knows? I can't fathom, losing hope an' all. She walked right in. You didn't see?"

"Has there been an accident?" asked Zénobe, startling the three.

"Who are you?"

"A passerby."

"What do you want?" asked one of the men.

"What's happened?" asked Zénobe in return.

"A girl," answered the woman. "She came from up there," she said as she pointed towards the quay behind Zénobe. "She walked right in, all by 'erself. We 'ad nothin' to do wi' it! We'd never seen 'er before!"

"Well, where's the boat?"

"No boat 'ere," said one of the men.

"What are you planning to do?" asked Zénobe.

There was no answer, the still silence of the river had an converse effect on Zénobe.

"What are you planning to do?" he asked in mounting impatience.

"She could be anywhere by now," said the other man.

"We'll fish 'er out when she float up," offered the woman.

"Are you mad?" asked Zénobe. "Something has to be done now!"

Zénobe looked up and down the bank but could see or hear nothing.

He leapt onto his horse and made him run up and down the riverside but Zénobe could make nothing out, except for the cathedral reigning on its throne of the Isle du Palais in front of them, as silent as the Seine.[10]

Zénobe came back to the trio huddled on the quay. He dismounted and reached into a knapsack.

"I have a rope!" he told them.

"Whaddya goin' to do wi' that?" asked the same man as before.

"She woan hold on ta it," observed the woman. "She wanta die."

"But we must do something!" yelled Zénobe. "We have to try! One can't let a girl drown like an animal!"

The woman, as cold as the still air around them, replied, "But she *want* ta die. All the people fished out of 'ere are suicides."

---

10   Today, the island is known as the Île de la Cité.

"What do you mean?" asked Zénobe.

"Well, seeing as 'ow this place is in such proximity to the Fac."

"The Fac?"

"Why, yes, *monsieur*," said one of the men. "The *Faculté de Médecine* has its new amphitheater of anatomy right there behind you."

Zénobe took a quick glance but could see nothing.

"So?" he asked impatiently.

"So," explained the woman whose teeth had begun to chatter, "people commit suicide 'ere so that their loved ones can fish their bodies outa the water in the morning and sell them to the Fac." [11]

Zénobe unleashed his rope and in one crack unfurled it into the Seine. He ran his horse to and fro on the bank, jerking the rope from side to side. The trio disappeared into the blackness, in spite of the fact that Zénobe yelled out to them, "Why don't you want to help me?" He brought the rope in and threw it out again into a different direction. He did this a dozen times, until he was breathing hard and his fingers were numb. Before long, the cold, the silence, and the stillness of the water convinced Zénobe of the futility of his efforts.

If the victim had been saved, no reward would be given. The poor girl no doubt had left plans for the money to be used after her death. Did she have a family? Children, perhaps? Were they starving?

For the last time, Zénobe reeled the wet rope back in and methodically rolled it into a coil around his shoulder and elbow. He couldn't help but continue to pace on the bank for a few more minutes. Finally, he directed his horse west along the quays of the Seine. He looked for the three witnesses but they were gone. Had his shirt and coat not been wet he would have surmised that the whole episode had been a dream, a nightmare of his fatigued mind. Still, every once in a while, he would look into the waters of the dark river as they flowed downstream in the direction he was riding, hoping to see or hear someone splashing in the dark current.

When all hope was leached out into the dark and frozen riverbank, he turned left on the rue de la Harpe, knowing that the Quartier Latin was close by.[12] It was too late to find an inn. Dawn would be coming soon. He needed to sell his horse for whatever he could get for him, or spend another night out in the cold.

Sounds of activity sprang up all around him in the still-dark streets. He discerned wagon wheels approaching. Through his sense of smell he understood that it was a farmer bringing in his produce and chickens into the city. Zénobe bid the dark figure "Good morning" and asked if he had heard of suicides in the Seine. The man answered without stopping his wagon. "Whence hast thou fallen? The moon?"

Zénobe watched the man roll past him.

Indeed I have fallen from the moon! he thought. What kind of city is this, that people kill themselves for money? And that others care not a whit about it? What kind

---

11   The building still stands at 13-15, rue de la Bûcherie at the corner of the rue de l'Hôtel-Colbert. The inauguration of the new anatomy amphitheater designed by Barbier de Blignières took place in 1745. It was part of the new, enlightened way of looking at things. Before that, the study of anatomy had been for centuries by the Church forbidden. The ignorance and superstition that made the Ecclesiastics think that the mysteries of Nature were for God's eyes alone were slowly to scientific curiosity and humanist methodology yielding.

12   The Boulevard Saint Michel did not yet exist. Today, the rue de la Harpe is but a meager shadow of its previous self, having given up most of its length to the boulevard in the 19th century.

of society is this? It must be a city without a heart, wicked and cruel, indifferent to human suffering. Perhaps it is not the City of Light. Perhaps it is the City of Darkness, the City of Indifference. I am come into a place of pain and sorrow, but without pity or compassion. But, I see the light of dawn arising in the east, and it is Voltaire who heralds it. He will make a difference. I know he will. He is the harbinger of hope, of change. If anyone can make these people care about each other, it is he. He has been for years, and continues to be, the conscience of Europe.

Twelve hours later, just an hour before sunset, another traveler was come to Paris. The somnolent *douanier* could have recognized this visitor in his sleep. In an act of exaggerated ceremony, the *douanier* bowed low and bade his lordship's carriage pass through the gates. For a visitor of his lordship's quality, it would be his pleasure to dispense with the customary interrogation and search. The visitor, hanging out of the carriage window, one hand clasping on to his wig to keep it from flying off, yelled in toothless glee, "The only contraband here is me!" as his horses whisked him into the city.

Paris was not to be wicked or indifferent on this day. A celebration had sprung up, like an early Carnival of mirth and festivity, but without religion or masquerade. The whole city was jubilant while gazing fixedly towards the east. *Tout Paris* had learned of his return. Indeed, no one had spoken of anything else for two days. Although, truth be told, not everyone awaited his return with joy. There were those who felt anxiety, even doom. This little visit by a skinny old man, Jean Marie Arouet, whose books sold in the hundreds of thousands, whose *nom de plume, non! nom de guerre*, was Voltaire, might turn out to be the first lever to set off the cogs and wheels that in turn would trigger change. Those who held the mechanism of power in their hands did not want change. The royal family, ensconced behind concentric circles of safety in Versailles twenty leagues away, felt apprehensive. Louis went hunting, since denial was his immediate reaction to difficult news. Everybody else in any position of power, in government or in the Church, was on the lookout, expectant, anticipating some sort of change, but any change would be detrimental to their system, which is why everyone had his eyes (or his spies' eyes) on this feeble octogenarian, once tutor to kings, now a renowned luminary, a magnet, a king in his own right—the King of Cartesia, the Apostle of Notre Dame de la Méthode, the Lord of Lucidity, the Vicar of Veracity—as he entered the City of Light, the City of the *philosophes*, on that dreary, drizzly afternoon at 4 o'clock. As his carriage flew by the Rive Gauche side of the Seine and drew closer to the quai des Théâtins,[13] the old man espied the multitudes and could only smile sadly that everyone was cold and wet.

The crowds had been gathering since noon. A throng had swarmed onto the *quai* as if it were some sort of huge snake coiling and uncoiling its loops, spilling into the rue de Beaune, in the corner of which stood the sumptuous residence of Charles-Michel, *marquis* de Villette. He might have been merely a second-generation nobleman, but he

---

13   Today called the quai Voltaire. On the opposite bank stood the two royal palaces, the Tuileries to the west and the Louvre to the east.

did his best to keep his name in the newspapers, mostly for immoral escapades with actresses and opera singers, at times for his own dilettante writings. As the eldest son of a wealthy banker whose fortune had enabled him to purchase an aristocratic title for himself and his heirs, Villette was able to wear shoes with red heels, carry a foil, and be exempt from all the taxes that everybody else had to pay.[14] His marriage to the beautiful and intelligent *mademoiselle* Reine Philiberte Rouph de Varicourt, one of Voltaire's educated orphans, kept tongues wagging. She was so beautiful, and so good, that Voltaire called her *Belle et bonne*. The ceremony had taken place the previous autumn in Ferney, Voltaire's exile next to the Swiss border. Witnesses said that it had been an intimate candlelit midnight ceremony in the chapel that Voltaire had built. The fact that such an irrepressibly irreligious philosopher had even built a chapel was newsworthy, but the fact that he married people there like the *marquis* de Villette was even more shocking. Voltaire was mocking the Church! First of all, Villette was the son of the exquisite Marie Claire Deschamps de Marcilly, *marquise* de Villette, who was a devoted friend of Voltaire during their youth. Most of the older people of society recalled that Voltaire and the *marquise* had been extraordinarily intimate and that perhaps the little *marquis* had more than Voltaire's friendship to his credit.[15] [16] Moreover, the Paris police on more than one occasion had caught a crapulous Villette in the bushes of the Tuileries Gardens at night, with other men. As if that were not enough, Charles-Michel liked to bring in handsome boys from the provinces and have them function as his personal valets, scullery boys and cellar domestics. His serving staff were the most handsome of those at any aristocratic *hôtel* in all of Paris. And it was to this *hôtel* that the *marquis* and *marquise* had already returned on the previous day. They had preceded Voltaire to ensure that the house was in readiness, but then had decamped early that morning to go meet him in Villejuif in order to make the grand entrance at the same time as he. Everybody would see that they were Voltaire's Parisian host and hostess. Villette was not about to waste the social event of the century. Here he was, in order to debut his new wife's beautiful new *salon*, the only person in the whole land with the wherewithal, financial, familial and residential, to bring into Paris the most enviable of all possible treasures: a five-foot-five bony packet of wrinkled skin who, of all the *philosophes*, had caused the most commotion during the past fifty years.[17]

Yet, for all their precaution, Charles-Michel and Reine-Philiberte, the *marquis* and *marquise* de Villette, were invisible to the crowd. The impatient mob that had been waiting for hours on the streets flanking the rue de Beaune that blustery winter afternoon was there for Voltaire only. In spite of the overcast sky pregnant with precipitation, menacing the populace with its gray foreboding tones, the horde spilled out onto the adjoining quays on the Seine. They filled the windows and balconies of neighboring houses whose

---

14   The punishment reserved for an uppity commoner who wore red heels or carried a foil in public was a fine, corporal punishment, banishment, and/or having to wear for a whole month shoes with no heels at all. The wealthiest class in France, the aristocrats, were immune from paying taxes, purportedly for the services they provided to the Crown. They were so egocentric as to call themselves indispensable: according to them, without them there would be no economy.

15   Allow me please to clarify: The rumor had it that Voltaire was the true father of the *marquis* de Villette.

16   [From the author] *Mein Herr,* I think the readers got it.

17   A word about the word *philosophe*: it denotes not just a philosopher, but a humanist in the most progressive sense. A man of the people, and for the people, whose ideal is the truth, and whose central concern is how this truth should be to the people made known.

proprietors were renting out more spaces than were available. Everybody roared with glee each time there was a report, though it proved to be false, that Voltaire's carriage was approaching. It was towards the ominous sunset, by the time the fine drizzle had started to become a wet slushy snow, that the carriage finally made its appearance. It was a luxurious vehicle, painted sky-blue, decorated with gold leaf stars, equipped with springs for rough roads, and pulled by six prancing white horses.[18]

By the time Voltaire passed the church of Sainte-Geneviève,[19] he knew that once again he was fomenting trouble. People were running towards and behind his carriage, shouting out his name, crying forth in emotional jubilation, "The man who fights against tyranny!" and "The man who is afraid of no one!" As the carriage rushed along the Seine, the roar of the crowd was audible to him all the way out to the Faubourg Saint-Germain. As the fast and shiny *berline* made its way westward like a modern-day chariot of Apollo piercing through the heart of Paris, more and more people pointed to the old man surrounded by the voluminous gauze that had been placed inside for his protection. To his right, across the Seine, he saw the massive Louvre, notorious symbol of royalist oppression, abandoned by the Bourbons for their even more massive palace at Versailles. To his left, the magnificent town homes of wealthy aristocrats whizzed by. Ahead, his faded old eyes discerned in the dying light a multitude such as he had never seen, and his heart leapt at the sight: against the veiled setting sun, a jubilant throng welcoming him back after a 28-year royal banishment. A long time ago a man wearing a crown had forbidden Voltaire's presence among his subjects, but today it was the people themselves who not only grabbed the power, but who displayed the audacity to stand in the streets to welcome him back home.

As he approached the quai des Théâtins, the crowd parted and engulfed his carriage, forcing it to slow down to a crawl. The *marquise* de Villette, seated beside her adored father/mentor, gazed at him with love and respect as tears quivered in her eyes. Facing them, the *marquis* was scouring the throng for faces he recognized, especially those of his sycophant aristocratic equals, when suddenly his eyes fastened in a lecherous instant on the cerulean gaze of a tall, delectable young man with long black hair and broad shoulders.

Amidst the crowd, Zénobe waited for the apparition of his god. He had heard rumors that Voltaire would be staying at the *hôtel* de Villette. Ever since he had married *Belle et bonne*, the *marquis* had wanted to bring Voltaire back to Paris in order to be the center of attention. Zénobe suspected that it was Voltaire himself who finally felt ready to ignore orders of exile. Villette was an idiot and a coward who had fled Paris to avoid a duel that he had provoked. Straight into the embrace of Voltaire he ran, and once in

---

18   By law, only the King's carriages could have eight horses.

19   Today, it is as the Panthéon known. In 1778 it was still under construction, and will be in 1789 completed, just in time for the irreligious Revolutionaries to christen it with its new secular name. During the anti-ecclesiastic paroxysms of the Revolution, the patron saint of Paris will give way to the new nation's need for a space to honor its fallen civic heroes. Without knowing it, Voltaire was at the future repository of his mortal remains looking.

Ferney, he met *mademoiselle* Varicourt who was, indeed, very beautiful, and quite witty as well. Voltaire noticed the effect she had on him. It did not require a philosopher to realize that they should marry. In two weeks it was done, and the gossip papers were full of shocking stories about orgies in Ferney in which the *marquis* held the central role. But Zénobe knew the truth: Voltaire was no atheist, but a humanist, and therefore would not allow immoral acts to be held in his *château*. A great man who had spent his life saving, or trying to save, victims of gross injustice, could not be an evil man. Far from it, Voltaire was known from St. Petersburg to Philadelphia as a harbinger of toler-ance, an annihilator of superstition, and a combatant against political and theological oppression, and his battle cry was *"Écrasez l'Infâme!"* (Crush the Infamy!") in order to squelch the repressive alliance between the Roman Apostolic Catholic Church and the tyrannous monarchical State.

For this reason Zénobe wanted to touch the hem of his hero. He might be a bumpkin from the Savoy village of Annecy who had braved the den of iniquity that was Paris, but he was determined to see his hero again. Zénobe futilely tried to fight his way through the crowd to get closer to Voltaire's carriage, but the currents in the mob pulled him away violently. When he tried to circle back, another eddy swirled him around in an opposing direction. He thought that by forceful shoving he could wedge himself closer to the passing carriage, but to no avail. When the *marquis* de Villette caught his eye, Zénobe raised his hand, palm up towards the carriage, as if the *marquis'* gaze itself could levitate him over the heads of the mob. The carriage kept inching away to the row of townhouses on the rue de Beaune, and all Zénobe found he could do was follow it with his eyes.

He decided on a different tactic. He pulled away from the tumult surrounding the carriage, heading towards the river where there were fewer people. He did this without too much difficulty. Once he was free of the worst part of the mob, he ran along a huge arc whose focal point was the Villette townhouse. By running away from the townhouse towards the quai d'Orsay, he thought he could double back along the row of houses on the rue du Bac, then head back east on the rue de Bourbon. It took him just a few minutes. When he came up from behind the townhouse, he realized with a thumping heart that if he squeezed up against the building walls he might have a better chance of seeing his hero. But by the time he came up to the house, it was only to see the heavy gates of the courtyard close with a thud behind the carriage.

The crowd kept cheering and chanting, with different chants going up in different places: «*Écrasez l'Infâme, écrasez l'Infâme!*» or «*L'homme aux Calas, l'homme aux Calas!*» or «*L'homme aux Sirven, l'homme aux Sirven!*»[20] It was another two hours before the cold finally chased most of the crowd away. Zénobe and a few other staunch supporters of the philosopher kept up a vigil, studying the façade of the house from all angles as they spoke among themselves, an immediate and easy camaraderie springing up among these strangers whose admiration and zeal for an 84-year-old man united them in a strong bond, a fraternity/sorority of sorts. They told each other tales of everything wonderful that Voltaire had ever done. They spoke of Voltaire's efforts to save the Calas and Sirven families, Protestants who had been falsely accused of murdering family members rather than see them convert to Catholicism. These stories warmed their hearts. So, too, did

---

20   The Calas and Sirven families were the most famous of the victims of religious intolerance whom Voltaire saved from annihilation.

the stories of how Voltaire had had throughout his entire life the courage to stand up to the despots of Europe. Voltaire had always fought to undermine their wicked authority with every page he wrote.

But soon enough, they too had to seek shelter from the cold night ahead. In spite of their excitement, it was the freezing wind that was making them stamp their feet. They dispersed. Zénobe returned to the Latin Quarter where he had found a dreary inn more in keeping with his purse, which consisted of the money he had received from having sold his horse that morning. His sole possessions left were now a tiny packet of clothes, and a tiny library of forbidden books. His money would soon run out, but he was committed to staying in Paris and meeting his hero.

February 11, 1778

Waiting in Line

André was exhausted but when he heard the sounds of the *maître d'hôtel* come to wake the servants up with the first of the morning light, he rose with a start. In a flash he was standing by his bed, almost immediately having to sit back down when he became dizzy.

"Calm down, boy. There's time to have your breakfast before you faint," said *monsieur* Maurel.

An innately jovial man, the supervisor of the household had light hazel eyes, a small straight nose with flaring nostrils, and a mouth whose sensual lips hardly ever gave up their curl of amity and co-conspiracy. On his finely shaped head he kept his black curly hair closely cropped, wearing his wig only when the masters were up and about. He must have cut a stunning figure when he was younger. It was memories of Jacques-Henri Maurel during the apogee of his good looks that kept him in the employ of the *marquis* de Villette. That, along with all the secrets that the *maître d'hôtel* kept discreetly to himself. In someone else's employ perhaps the secrets would not be kept so tightly within the confines of gratitude and propriety. But Maurel kept secrets like a tomb. As an enemy, *monsieur* Maurel might be formidably dangerous, spreading gossip all over Paris, so the *marquis* de Villette made sure to keep him satisfied, in spite of having a difficult household to run. Still, Maurel had not yet lost his gallant and debonaire ways. It was he, after all, who kept on a constant lookout for new serving boys to bring into the domestic management. Sharing his master's propensities, he had similar tastes, which made for a strong and lasting mutually beneficial relationship. Maurel's admiration and concupiscence for masculine aesthetics were such that if he approved of a new lad, so would the master. In the *marquis* de Villette's mind, his *maître d'hôtel* could do no wrong. On the contrary, how many times had his finesse and diplomacy worked wonders with the authorities, who otherwise would have received great pleasure in having the *marquis* pay some sort of price for his outlandish immoral escapades.

His finesse and diplomacy certainly were working well when the previous autumn he had located André on a farm in Normandy, in the village of Saint-Saturnin-des-Lignères, not far from where Maurel's mother lived in Caen. At sixteen years of age, surmised Maurel, André might be a difficult subject, given his provincial naïveté, his inexperience, and perhaps his lack of imagination. But Maurel threw his caution to the winds of desire, for André had several redeeming qualities: long blond hair, beautiful brown eyes, high cheekbones, straight white teeth, and a healthy muscled body. This last, Maurel imagined, was honed from seasons in the sun picking the apples to make Calvados. When he went back home to Paris he took several crates of the Normand *eau-de-vie*, many crates of cider, and stashed wherever possible in the carriage, many crates of the biggest and best Normand apples, and sitting on one of the larger crates, the Normand human specimen André Armand Cyrille Corday. He promised the Corday family that he would take very good care of their son, telling them that André would be in the employ of a man who would soon be hosting Voltaire in his Paris home. They were duly impressed. André bade adieu to his parents, and to his sister Marie Anne Charlotte. As soon as their carriage left, Charlotte went back to her chair in the garden to continue reading a book by Rousseau. She did not like Voltaire. How could she be impressed by her brother's future employ in the house where Voltaire would live? It was such at the time that most people who loved to read Rousseau did not like to read Voltaire, and vice versa.[21] She loved Rousseau's naturalness, and disliked Voltaire's sarcasm. Her sadness at seeing her elder brother go was attenuated by the exquisite sufferings of the characters in Rousseau's novel *la Nouvelle Héloïse*. Charlotte loved to tend her garden in the morning and read there in the afternoon.[22][23]

André, however, had always wanted to travel. Not necessarily to Paris, for he had heard about its sinfulness. Still, *monsieur* Maurel appeared to be a nice man, and seemed to be authentic in his desire to educate him. He threw his caution to the winds of adventure. He so loved the imagery of that metaphor which *monsieur* Maurel had taught him that he acted it out physically. Off he went in a beautiful carriage to discover new things. All the while, seated in front of him, Maurel was imagining the new role André would play, or could play. He looked at the lad's shoulders and arms. The youth could make a good equerry, since he was strong. Maurel looked at his long legs. Perhaps a *valet de chambre*, if he proved smart and assiduous enough. In the meantime he could be a lackey or a scullion. If that did not work out he could certainly be an errand boy. He could always be sent back to his province. Maurel hoped he could be a valet. He would personally assume responsibility for his uniform. As Maurel imagined taking André's measurements he simultaneously sighed and smiled. André took this melancholy sigh to mean that *monsieur* Maurel was anticipating difficulty with the education he had agreed to undertake for him, on top of all his other responsibilities. André decided that he would be as amenable as possible to the efforts *monsieur* Maurel would make on his behalf. He smiled to his new mentor with as grateful a smile as he could muster. Maurel could not help but be both joyous and dazzled because of the provincial honesty and freshness of that angelic face.

Maurel knelt down in front of the boy and put his hands on his shoulders.

"You shouldn't get up so quickly. All the blood rushes out of your head." He smiled at André. "Are you all right?"

"Yes, *monsieur*," answered André bashfully. "I think so."

---

21   One's predilection for either Rousseau or Voltaire branded one as being either emotional or intellectual, spiritual or cartesian, revolutionary in an affective way or rebellious in a rational way.

22   I hope I am not any bounds here overstepping. I do not know if the modern American reader knows who Charlotte Corday is. I do not know if it is my place to tell them about her, but, as any French pupil knows the story, I am not any big secret giving away. It is she who in 1793 comes to Paris during the Reign of Terror to assassinate the Revolutionary Marat, by stabbing him in the chest while he is in his bath.

23   [From the author] The kind reader should perhaps not be tempted to read the fact-checker's footnotes. Herr Ralph is liable to give away my most dramatic moments. In this particular instance, he has nothing of importance given away, for I assumed that the erudite reader knows about the historical Charlotte Corday.

"Well, come on then," said Maurel. "Sylvie will soon be wanting you in the kitchen. It's a very important day, today. With *monsieur* de Voltaire staying in the house we are sure to have many visitors. Everyone will want to pay his respects to *monsieur* de Voltaire. That's a good boy. Help me wake the others up."

So it was that with the *maître d'hôtel*'s direction, all eight of the servant staff were up and running the house before any of the masters were awake, and well before any of the visitors had started to arrive.

The servants' quarters were behind the *hôtel*, beyond the garden at the back of the property. They were perpetually in the shade of the Église des Théâtins.[24] Still, André liked the view of the sunny garden from his bedroom window. And *monsieur* de Villette had made sure that the *hôtel* looked as ravishing from the back as it did from the street.

André rushed to the main house once he had taken care of his ablutions and dressed in the crisp uniform that Maurel's infinite patience and exacting measurements had fashioned for him. He realized he was nervous. Numerous visitors were expected.

The previous day the staff had all remained inside the house. Imprisoned would perhaps be a better description. The crowd made it impossible even to open a window. The hubbub of *monsieur* and *madame* de Villette's entry, accompanied by their retinue, along with their prized *monsieur* de Voltaire, had proven to be taxing. Against the backdrop of the constant roar from outside, the servants had to make sure that all the master and mistress's needs were taken care of, in addition to the needs of all their house guests. These included Voltaire's niece, *madame* Denis, Voltaire's two secretaries, *messieurs* Wagnière and Bigex, and four servants who accompanied them from Ferney, who promptly took their places besides their eight city brethren. These four were *madame* Denis' *femme de chambre*, Hélène; Voltaire's cook, le Parnaud; and their two coachmen. Le Parnaud and the two secretaries took rooms on the third floor, next to the *marquis'* own secretary Ursus Papillon Requain; Hélène slept in a cot in *madame* Denis' room on the second floor; and the two coachmen accommodated themselves as best they could in the servants' quarters, sharing rooms and beds with the Villette's two coachmen. The Villette's household help were Sylvie the cook, Suzanne and Marianne the maids, Philippe and Henri the manservants, and of course André, who had a tiny room to himself all the way at the back of the servants' building. There were now four carriages in the courtyard and twenty horses in the stables.

Sylvie took great offense at Voltaire's cook coming to share in her kitchen and having been given his own room in the main house. It took all of Maurel's tact and aplomb to convince Sylvie that le Parnaud was of utmost importance and needed to continue preparing Voltaire's dishes in view of the *philosophe*'s great age and ornery digestive system. Every Tuesday Voltaire had himself treated with a strong purgative, to "wash away his maladies." Starting every Wednesday, Voltaire had to receive specially made increments of sustenance to ease his digestion back into function. The rest of the week, Voltaire's meals had to be just so. Voltaire had a difficult digestion, and the whole household had to be on the lookout and in readiness.

Voltaire's arrival yesterday, having been a Tuesday, had been an exception to his purges. The *philosophe* was in no mood to be purged during his travels. His grand

---

24   This church no longer exists, save for a few vestiges of an oriental façade of the original convent built in 1661, visible in the courtyard of no. 13 quai de Voltaire, even though it originally extended all the way to the rue de Lille. Like many churches, it was sacrificed on the altar of anticlerical sentiments of the Revolutionaries after 1789.

entrance into Paris had to be unencumbered with physiological tripe. Today, Wednesday, he wanted to receive visitors, and as such he wanted an ample breakfast to regain his strength.

Voltaire could have had three breakfasts back to back and he still would not have had the strength to contend with the day's visitors. Thousands of people came to call, but only three hundred, in groups of ten to fifteen, were chosen to be invited to enter the inner sanctum: *madame* de Villette's *salon*, which was being inaugurated in such a spectacular way.[25] The visitors started to arrive at nine in the morning and the last few didn't leave until after ten that night.

André's post for the entire day was at the front door. Pedestrian callers came to the door. Carriages waited in the street while their coachmen also came to the door and presented their employers' visiting cards. From his vantage point, André could not see the end of either the pedestrian queue or the line of carriages. Oncoming traffic on the *quai* had to find detours as best it could to avoid the bedlam on the street. It was André's responsibility to announce the name of the pedestrian, or the name of the carriages' occupants, to *monsieur* Maurel. He in turn would announce the name to the *marquis*, the *marquise*, to Voltaire's personal secretary Wagnière, or to *madame* Denis, his niece, whoever was closest, and they would allow entry, or not. André would wait by the vestibule until Maurel came back with the answer. André would then go back to the front door and with a memorized response, would either invite the guest in, or offer *monsieur* de Voltaire's regrets. Obviously priority was given to the people with the highest credentials. Members of the stratosphere of nobility were allowed in. But so were the *philosophes*, most of whom were considered to be libertines. The nobility were usually straight-laced God-fearing confession-seeking hypocritical reactionary Catholics. Voltaire's intellectual colleagues were usually rakish atheist/deist/agnostic humanists who long ago had exposed the Roman Catholic Church for what she was: an avaricious, power-hungry, hypocritical and castigating slut who sold herself to the highest bidder. The *salon*-fellows were consequently an incongruous group, pitting atheist to pious, intelligent to stupid, cartesian to superstitious. At midmorning the Knights of the Order of the Holy Ghost were allowed in, if anything because they came in full regalia and lent the *hôtel* de Villette an air of pomp. *Madame* du Deffand, who was elderly and blind, sent her secretary in her stead to reconnoiter the place and report back to her. She wisely decided to visit on another day. *Monsieur* Charles-Augustin Ferriol, *comte* d'Argental had an audience with Voltaire, being an old friend, but so did *madame* Suard, who was pretty enough to be asked in.[26] It was she, as a matter of fact, who wrote that very day to all her friends who had not gained admittance into the sanctuary, that Voltaire looked radiant, that "it was impossible to describe the sparkle of his eyes and the grace of his features," and that he would utter the most outlandish things. In effect, she was engendering as much envy as possible in those who had not had the luck to receive the honor of an invitation to enjoy an audience with Voltaire.

As the day wore on, André thought that his feet would refuse to hold him up any longer. There was no time for dinner, no time for supper. At one moment, he made a

---

25   *Salons* were at the center of the social universe in the Age of Reason. Run by wealthy, aristocratic, powerful women, *salons* were a hotbed of activities for the intellectual, scientific, political and cultural élite; someone had arrived if he were a guest at the *salon* of a *madame* du Deffand or a *mademoiselle* de Lespinasse.

26   Besides, the reader needs to know, she was married to the academician Jean-Baptiste Antoine Suard who was the royal Censor of Public Spectacles, and worthy, therefore, of special treatment.

desperate dash into the kitchen for three quick glasses of water and half of one of wine, and thought that he had never felt so much pleasure. A half hour later he had to rush off to urinate into the first chamber pot he saw. (It was Voltaire's.) That pleasure was even greater, not just because of the intense relief, but because of the knowledge that he was using the great man's pot.

But contrary to yesterday's free-for-all street-carnival atmosphere, today the madness was organized, stately, and even. People waited patiently. People entered ceremoniously. People who did not gain entry had no other option but to leave, perhaps in deep disappointment, but graciously nonetheless. People stayed an allotted half-hour, or hour, depending on their stature. D'Argental and the *philosophes* could stay all day, and did. Those who were discreetly pushed out left Voltaire's presence in utmost tranquility, gratitude, and awe, as if quitting the oracle at Delphi. The whole system worked like one of those Swiss watches that Voltaire fabricated in Ferney.

Three things stood out in André's mind that day. The first was that each time he came to announce a visitor and it was the *marquis* de Villette's turn to grant a yea or a nay, the *marquis* would forego the mediation of his *maître d'hôtel* and come speak with André directly. The *marquis* would take one of André's hands into both of his, bend his face towards his to within a few inches, and ask officiously who wished to seek admittance. André would respond, "*Monsieur* d'Alembert" or "*Madame la duchesse* de Polignac," or "*Monsieur* Antoine-Raymond-Jean-Guilbert-Gabriel de Sartine" (the shrew from the *Parlement* library), and then the *marquis* would give André's hand a squeeze, and pronounce his answer. The shrew, by the way, was not allowed in this first day, but *madame la duchesse* de Polignac, the Queen's favorite, was.[27] [28] D'Alembert, a fellow *philosophe* and favored friend of Voltaire's, stayed all day.

The second was that he noticed a young man outside with shoulder-length black hair and startling blue eyes who would hover between the pedestrian and carriage queues, in no-man's land. He was not waiting in line. André could read on his face an expression of both anxiousness and hopelessness, as if he thought that he might be invited in, but at the same time that it was perhaps useless to be waiting around. For most of the day and well into the evening, André's eyes met Zénobe's. But André was much too busy to concern himself with the presence of one man. Still, there was something about this young man's demeanor—perhaps it was his otherworldly eyes—that brought out in André a curiosity that he had never felt before.

The third thing that stood out in André's mind that day was Voltaire himself. Every time that André would come close to the *salon* he could hear snippets of the old man's perorations, and sometimes he actually caught a glimpse of him.

Voltaire was truly enjoying himself. He felt like a lad of twenty again. Only this time, he had the mind of a *philosophe* in his eighties. Oh, the marriage between an experienced, wise and infallible mind, with the vigor and youth of a robust stud! He hadn't felt this sexual in years. A parade of luminaries, celestial court ladies, virile philosophers, titillating knights, renowned countesses, Diderot! (but not Rousseau),

---

27   *Madame* de Polignac did not become a *duchesse* until 1780. In 1778 she was still only a *marquise*.

28   *D'accord, mein Herr Doktor* Ralph, she was still a measly *marquise* in 1778, but she was already Marie Antoinette's favorite lady-in-waiting. And she was in the Villette's *salon* the very first evening of Voltaire's return.

all were there to see him.[29] And he was not about to disappoint them. He kept up a constant chatter, brilliant conversation, and witty retorts. He hardly sat down. He bounced up. He danced. He twirled first to one interlocutor then to another. He punctuated his laconic ripostes and lyrical comments with gestural grace. His grandiloquence could not be contained. People were eating him up.

André would observe this man with awe. How could such energy explode from such a tiny, skinny framework? He could barely grasp what the old man was saying; the vocabulary was strange, as were the ideas. But the people in the *salon* exploded every ten seconds in laughter, or in gasps, but always with keen admiration at the wit and sacrilegiousness of what the *philosophe* would say. Sacrilege was dear to this old man's heart.

Voltaire was not one to shy away from risqué remarks, either. André himself had already observed this on the previous evening. After being greeted by the Villette staff, Voltaire had stopped the pretty Sylvie in her tracks by saying within earshot of his niece, *madame* Denis, who was twice Sylvie's age, "Ah, Sylvie, your tits have gotten bigger, I see." The cook did not know where to put her eyes. "Come, turn around," said the *philosophe*, as the matronly *madame* Denis fled the room in all her jealous rotundity. "Let me see you in profile." And then later on as André was helping the old man to put on his nightgown, Voltaire had said, "You are new among the *marquis'* staff. Has he asked to see your pecker yet?" And then he laughed his twittering guttural laugh. "Ha ha! *Hé hé*! I'm surprised he hasn't asked to see your pecker yet." And then he stood still when his head popped up above the nightgown with one foot in the air while André removed a shoe. "You do have a healthy, well-formed pecker, don't you? Has it grown in all right?"

All André could say was, "*Oui, monsieur.*"

Voltaire sat down on his bed and said matter-of-factly, "Well, let's see it, then. We must see if it has grown into a good shape. You know your King's pecker was misshapen and for seven years the Queen could not have a child. When he was a *dauphin*, he was a sullen young man, taciturn and withdrawn, and now as king, he is aloof and unresponsive, all because of a misshapen prepuce! It is strange when you think of it: one sees incalculable political, social and historical repercussions, all due to a minor sexual anomaly. Come on, then, put the candle down and let's see it, my boy."

How could André refuse a world-renowned sage whose knowledge of medicine, it was told, was encyclopedic? He looked to see if anyone was around and then lowered his britches until his genitals were exposed. Voltaire bent over his subject for a closer inspection, moving his spectacles this way and that. "*Hé hé*! ha ha! What a beauty! They do grow them big and healthy in the country! Where is it that you're from?"

"From Normandy, *monsieur.*"

"Aha, it's all that Calvados! Hey, that's what I need for my bedtime. Run to the kitchen, my dear boy, and get me a half-glass of that rot-gut. A lot of good it'll do my innards, they're gurgling and lurching already. Ha ha! That's it now, and run along, and see if Sylvie can't warm it up a mite."

---

29   Rousseau was actually in town, staying at the home of a friend on the rue des Plâtrières, a comfortable promenade away. Like everyone else in the universe, he had of Voltaire's triumphal return to Paris heard, but Rousseau never forgot nor forgave Voltaire's frequent quips about his own philosophical writings. It was just as well: Rousseau was as agoraphobic as Voltaire was gregarious, so the only solitary *philosophe* stayed away.

André had run into the kitchen where Sylvie prepared their guest's strange nocturnal caprice. By the time he came back into the bedroom, Voltaire had eased himself under the sheets. He had on a nightcap with a pompon on the end that moved erratically about his face with every flick of his head.

"Ah, come in, my boy. What is it that they call you?"

"Corday. André de Corday."

"Ah, yes, Corday. Corday. From the countryside near Caen, I think the *marquise* said. Yes, yes, aren't your family relations of the Corneille family?"

"Yes, I believe we are, *monsieur.*"

"But if this is so, your family possesses a name of distinction, of nobility."

"We are poor, *monsieur.*"

"Ah, what a pity. To have a noble name, but a pittance for it. Still, you have a famous ancestor. You have read his plays, haven't you?"[30]

"Yes, *monsieur*, a few of them."

"A genius, he was. A genius. Up to a point. I reworked some of his plays, you know. Great tragedies! Wonderful comedies! Some superfluousness, a few errors in judgment, but inspiring, nonetheless. Well, then, thank you for the Calvados, *monsieur* de Corday. Thank you, thank you. Oh, it is nice and warm. This will make me warmer than my nightcap! It will certainly soothe my tripes. Ah, delicious."

In a few quick sips Voltaire finished off his liquor and let out a satisfied guttural "Aah!" and said goodnight.

"Goodnight, *monsieur.* Sleep well."

"Goodnight, my dear boy. *Écrasez l'Infâme!*"

While he was falling asleep that night, André wondered about Voltaire's strange request to see his privates. But now that they were here, in public, the celebrated geezer was entertaining a *salon*-full of the *crème de la crème* with impetuous irreverent commentary.

"The sole reason why I have come back to Paris at this time is because the *Comédie française* has been begging me to put on a new play of mine."

"Ah, you have written a new play, *monsieur* de Voltaire?" somebody asked.

"Indeed I have. It is called *Irène.*"

"Oh, what a pretty name. We've never seen a play or read a book by that name, have we?" said a refined lady.

"Of course you haven't. Who else would have used such a terrifying subject?"

"What is the subject, *monsieur* de Voltaire?" someone asked.

"It is a beautiful and magnificent story. At the same time it is absolutely horrifying. It is about the Empress of Constantinople, you know, the one who had her son's eyes put out."

"Oh, how horrible!" exclaimed one of the ladies.

"But that's a terrible subject, *monsieur* de Voltaire!" said a gentleman.

"Why should that be so?" replied the old man. "There is a certain beauty to all the passions. There is love, but there's also lust. There is charity, but there's also envy. There is motherly love, but there's also parental castigation. How often have you, *monsieur le*

---

30   Pierre Corneille (1606-1684), dramatist, author of *Le Cid, Horace, Cinna, Polyeucte.* Voltaire had an acclaimed treatise on him in 1764 published and with the extensive profits had been able to provide a dowry for a descendant of the playwright, a penniless granddaughter *mademoiselle* Marie-Françoise Corneille, whom he had in Ferney adopted. He later discovered that in reality she was a first cousin twice removed.

vicomte, wished that your progeny were banished forever from your house? And you, my dear *duchesse*, how often have you quarreled with your sons?"

"But those are mere trifles," answered the *vicomte* in his defense. "Children are wont to do mischievous things, and my anger doesn't last long..."

"Not my sons," answered the *duchesse*. "They are stain-free. It's my daughters-in-law. It is because of their reckless behavior that my sons..."

"Ah, there you see!" said Voltaire. "Your children become independent of you. They go off in their own direction. They are influenced by others. And then they take stands against you. They become Protestants and then you want to kill them!"

Everybody laughed at this allusion to the Calas and Sirven cases. Wagnière laughed the hardest. He enjoyed knowing that no one there suspected that he was a Protestant. A Calvinist, even.

"And don't neglect to take a look at my musical friend here," continued Voltaire, motioning to Jean-Joseph Rameau. "Your brother was the most famous musician in Europe, and your own melodies are very contagious. How do you see your scions?"

"They are all of them bandits. They come sniffing around when their money is running low. They don't care a whit about improving their intellect. All they care about is what opera singer *du jour* they can seduce..."

"All they care about is exhibiting their loins to the first pretty thing they see," cried Voltaire, pretending to undo his breeches.

Several of the ladies present screeched at this and pretended to look away.

"I wonder what the late *marquis* de Villette thought of his eldest son," said Voltaire in a hoarse whisper when the younger *marquis* de Villette was busy away in the vestibule. He threw *Belle et bonne* a wicked little glance. She had to laugh. She didn't know much about her husband's previous life as a bachelor. There were twitters throughout the room. *Madame* Denis, always slow to react, slapped her kneecap with one hand and with the other stifled a yelp of delight.

"I wonder how the staid banker felt," continued Voltaire, "when his son refused to follow his footsteps into the grand profession of finances but instead took up the pen to write poetic trifles about loves and passions and torments of the soul."

"But you yourself have also taken up the same pen, *monsieur* de Voltaire," said his old friend the mathematician Jean Le Rond d'Alembert with a sarcastic twinkle in his eye.[31] "And perhaps the *marquis* de Villette is taking after his father, after all, his true father."[32]

"Would that it be so," retorted Voltaire deliciously. "At least, when it comes to your own case, we don't have to worry about the reaction of your own beloved father when you started doodling and scratching with numbers and figures!"

Everyone laughed, including d'Alembert. D'Alembert was probably the most famous bastard of his time. His mother, *madame* de Tencin, possessor of a fine philosophical mind in her own right, had helped her son and his friend Diderot with the editing of their banned *Encyclopédie*. His supposed father, the *chevalier* Destouches, had been too busy to marry his mother, but she had been too busy as well. "He

---

31   D'Alembert, essential encyclopedist, brilliant mathematician, skeptical philosopher and perpetual secretary of the *Académie française*, had also made a mark in a social way: his lover, *mademoiselle* Julie de Lespinasse had held the most famous Parisian salon until her tragic untimely death at the age of 44 two years before.

32   Please remember, kind reader, that gossip, which sometimes holds a kernel of truth, had it that Voltaire was the *marquis* de Villette's father, having had an amorous relationship with his mother, *madame la marquise*.

fled as soon as he had touched," said Voltaire to amused smiles. (Voltaire used the word *touché*, with its *double entendre* in fencing; at the same time he thrust his bony pelvis toward the crowd.)

But Voltaire didn't let up now that he had his prey cornered. "What was it that your mother wrote in her younger days? *Les malheurs de l'Amour*?[33] How's that, ladies and gentlemen, for an intellectual lady who was proud of what her son had become?" Voltaire wrapped his arms around himself and swayed. "Ah, maternal love. That is what my play is all about."

"But that mother had her son's eyes put out!" exclaimed the Queen's favorite *madame* de Polignac whose own eyes were the envy of all, being a luminous violet and which she used to great effect.

"Yes, but it was for his own good! I am writing about maternal love in all its manifestations. In the absence of an emperor, the empress looks to her son to take her husband's place."

"What will he say next?" asked *madame* Denis, if anything to let Voltaire know that he was treading on dangerous ground. Nobody in that room knew, or even suspected, with the exception of Wagnière, that Voltaire and his niece had enjoyed an incestuous relationship since 1749.

Voltaire shot a glance at his niece to let her know that she need not fear anything.

"All I am saying is... is... is that Nature in all her glory imbued by her Creator, hatches diverse and powerful manifestations that humans cannot predict or even fathom. We are all exemplifications of the cornucopia of Nature. She has compounded everything into each and every one of us. All we have to do is lend our ear to what She is whispering to us."

"But sometimes what She whispers to us is construed as abomination," said Diderot who was sitting in a corner.[34]

"If Nature advances it, God willed it," said Voltaire sternly.

"*That* statement is an abomination, my friend," answered Diderot with a broad smile.

Several of the Christians in the group crossed themselves. Diderot was the most famous atheist of the time.

Denis Diderot looked pensive. "What was it that Montaigne said? 'Man cannot create a worm, and yet he creates gods by the dozens'?"[35]

Voltaire turned to Diderot and said, "Oh, my dear encyclopedic colleague, 'if God didn't exist, it would be necessary to invent Him'."[36]

---

33   *The Misfortunes of Love*. It was not a well-known fact that *madame* de Tencin had left her infant son on a church doorstep.

34   Denis Diderot, a quintessential *philosophe*, a pantophile with a quill in every pie: materialistic philosopher, prolific novelist and short-story writer, playwright, social critic, art critic, encyclopedist (editor of the first French encyclopedia ever published), denouncer of hypocrisy, liberator of sexuality, humanist, atheist, moralist, historian, critic of acting methods, musicologist, correspondent, political writer, aesthete, satirist, attacker of organized religion, academist of the Academy of Arts in Saint-Petersburg, friend of Catherine, Empress of Russia, political prisoner (in royal retribution to his writings), apologist for divorce, liberator of sequestered nuns, indefatigable advocate of social progress...

35   «*L'homme est bien insensé: il ne saurait forger un ciron et forge des dieux à la douzaine.*» Michel de Montaigne (1533-1592) *Essais*, 2.12.

36   «*Si Dieu n'existait pas, il faudrait l'inventer.*» Voltaire had said in 1770 of his own famous quote, "I am rarely content with my own verses, but I avow that I have a paternal tenderness for this one."

"Granted," said Diderot, "but according to the *marquis* de Sade, 'the idea of God is the only wrong for which he cannot pardon man.'"[37]

"And look at what abomination he turned out to be," said d'Argental who heretofore had remained silent.

With that, all minds turned to the Bastille where the infamous *marquis* was spending his days of late.

The *marquise* de Villette looked at the floor. No one but her husband knew that *madame* Renée-Pélagie *marquise* de Sade, her cousin by marriage, had just turned down her invitation to come stay at the *hôtel* de Villette while her husband was in prison. Fearing her husband's jealousy (Sade had called *madame* de Villette a "little Sappho"), *madame* de Sade had instead decided to go live in a convent.

The *marquis* de Villette had just come into the *salon* and upon hearing the name of that gentleman also looked at the floor. He believed it was the *marquis* de Sade who had bestowed a nickname on a new type of carriage that recently had become popular. Sade called this new carriage "*voiture* à la Villette", considering that one entered it from the back. It was just as well that the *marquise* de Sade had not taken up the *marquise* de Villette's offer of hospitality. Everyone in that room despised the *marquis* de Sade, but some more than others. Everyone despised the Bastille even more, especially Voltaire who before his exile had endured two involuntary stints within its walls. (Diderot had been a tenant of the prison at Vincennes.)

Madame de Sade would nevertheless have made Voltaire's sojourn at the *hôtel* de Villette even more interesting.

For the rest of the evening André continued opening and closing the door. Later that whole night in bed he dreamt of opening and closing a door. A door to what he could not tell.

---

37   *«L'idée de Dieu est, je l'avoue, le seul tort que je ne puisse pardonner à l'homme.»*

February 12, 1778

Finding a Propitious Moment

Zénobe was bitterly disappointed by his failure to see Voltaire. He realized he might have to go back home to Savoy or at least to Dijon where he had last found work. Would he still be welcome there, considering he had left brusquely four days before? What a quandary to be in, unable to move forward, unable to go back. His desperation was so great to see Voltaire that he decided to make a third attempt. He would have accepted seeing Rousseau, but that particular man of influence was receiving no one at all. Besides, it was Voltaire who offered the best solution to his problem, to his country's problem, for Voltaire of all the *philosophes* had the political capital and the penchant for *causes célèbres* that Savoy desperately needed.

After two days in Paris, Zénobe's money was running low. Bread cost four times as much in Paris as it did in Annecy. He could not afford much else. If it weren't for the goat herders who sold him milk and cheese in the morning he would be starving. Herds of animals were not allowed to come up as far as the Seine. He had to go to the Faubourg Saint-Jacques on foot. This morning he had already had his breakfast of bread, goat's milk and goat-cheese, and was back at the quai des Théâtins by 10 o'clock. The lines of pedestrians and carriages were already in full vigor.

But today the young blond man who had been greeting people the previous day was not posted at the front door. It was a jovial-looking middle-aged man with an affable voice who had replaced him. Just one glance that he received from the new doorman was all Zénobe needed to goad him into approaching the front entrance. This glance which had been flashed his way, one of curiosity and interest, was one which invited self-motivation and impetus, so Zénobe moved forward quickly.

"*Monsieur,*" he said. "If you please. I have no calling card. But I would like to have a word with *monsieur* de Voltaire."

The *maître d'hôtel* read Zénobe's face and person with a Mesmer-like electric perusal that left no detail untouched. The doorman's vigilant attention made Zénobe glad that he had not neglected to tend to his clothes: he would not have dared to approach the *hôtel* with dust on his sleeves or scuffs on his shoes. In spite of his discomfort at being examined so closely by the *maître d'hôtel*, Zénobe continued to speak.

"It is a matter of utmost importance, *monsieur.*"

Maurel had to drag his ogling eyes away from this handsome boy with his stunning pair of celestial eyes and attend to a coachman who was handing over a visiting card and had already coughed in impatience. While that transaction was going on, Zénobe tried to look over the *maître d'hôtel*'s shoulder into the recesses of the *hôtel*. He could make nothing out.

Maurel took the coachman's card, told him to be patient for a moment, then disappeared into the vestibule after having shut the door, but not before hitting Zénobe with another discomfiting bolt of eyes.

The coachman turned to Zénobe and said, "Everybody is chomping at the bit to see this man. He's more famous than Jesus!"

Zénobe smiled in acquiescence. "*Monsieur* de Voltaire is just as fantastic. He performs modern miracles. That is why I am here."

The coachman glanced quickly behind them towards the Quai. "Everybody wants a piece of him. My mistress seeks him out for 'philosophical nourishment' as she tells it. She has an entire set of the 'cyclopedias hidden in her boudoir, she has. They will have to burn down her whole house if they want to burn those books, she said. Very heavy they are, too. She let me look at the pictures of the saddles and the horses. Gave me great ideas. My mistress–"

The *maître d'hôtel* popped out the front door and to the coachman said, "*Monsieur* de Voltaire will have the honor of seeing *madame* Suzanne Curchod at this time," and to Zénobe he said, "Who are you, *monsieur*?"

"That is not important, *monsieur*. I am an unknown and a foreigner. But what I have to say to *monsieur* de Voltaire is of life and death to a whole country of people."

"You seem very young to have the destiny of an entire country in your hands."

"I am old enough to know injustice when I have seen and experienced it, and I am old enough to have read everything that *monsieur* de Voltaire ever wrote. I have memorized his *Treatise on Intolerance*."

Maurel looked on this passionate youth with a bemused smile.

"Well, I can tell you are sincere. But listen, my son, *monsieur* de Voltaire is much too busy today. Why don't you come back in a few days when the furor has died down a little?"

Zénobe looked crestfallen. He could not blurt out to the *maître d'hôtel* that he had no more money left to remain in Paris. He also could not tell him that he did not believe the furor at Voltaire's arrival would die out any time soon.

Maurel for his part could not tell this young man that he ardently wished him to come inside so that the *marquis* de Villette could behold him. It was unfortunate that he had no time now for leisurely seductions or finesse. Still, the handsome young man seemed civilized enough. There was perhaps a *soupçon* of the dangerous about him. But if he had really read the *philosophe*'s writings he must be intellectual enough for his master. Just what the *marquis* liked. Looks and books.

When Maurel noticed that the young man had sunk into despair he asked for his name.

"Marie-Jean Zénobe Bosquet, your servant, *monsieur*," came the immediate response, with a slight military bow and a click of his heels. It was too much for Maurel.

"Please come back in a few days. I would very much want you to see your *philosophe*. He will still be here next week."

Zénobe smiled at the *maître d'hôtel*'s kindness. "Thank you, *monsieur*."

Then the man's attention was diverted to the next visitor, *madame* Curchod who had gained easy entrance because of her efforts on Voltaire's behalf a few years before to commission a bust to be made by the sculptor Pigalle. Seventeen *philosophes* had come together to pay for this bust.[38]

Zénobe dejectedly made his way back to the Seine, but instead of going back to his dilapidated inn in the *Quartier latin*, he directed himself south on the *rue* de Beaune. His idea was to go find work in the wealthier but more bourgeois Faubourg Saint-Germain where perhaps he could be engaged as some family's preceptor. He really had no idea what he could do in Paris. But he could not go back home. That was impossible. Going back to Savoy meant certain death for him. He had been branded a proscript, a criminal, a rebel, a threat to society. Voltaire was the only man who could bring some sort of justice to a bleak situation.

As Zénobe made his way through the throng, he walked past the gates on the side of the *hôtel* de Villette. He thought he saw one of them open and shut quickly. He glanced more carefully out of curiosity, and saw that the young blond man, the one who had been in control of the front door yesterday, had slipped out with a basket in his hand. Zénobe immediately lengthened his stride and modified his direction to initiate a meeting. As soon as he was close enough, he said to André, *"Bonjour."*

André shot back a glance and immediately recognized the young man whom he had seen milling about the front street all day long on the previous day. *"Bonjour,"* he replied while continuing to walk, perhaps quickening his own stride.

"My name is Bosquet. Zénobe Bosquet. I am from Savoy. Do you mind if I walk with you?"

"Why would I mind?"

"I thought it polite to ask. What is your name?"

"André."

"Do you mind, then, if I walk with you?"

"Walk with me if you want. I'm just going to the market. Our cook is too ill to go, and I need to get sage for *monsieur* de Voltaire."

"Oh, then, please don't mind if I walk with you. It would be a pleasure and an honor to assist you in this most important errand."

"It's just sage."

"Yes, I know, but it is terribly important that *monsieur* de Voltaire have the stamina to stomach so many visitors. I know I would have been exhausted by now."

André's Normand distrust of strangers started to soften. "I know what you mean. I started to get dizzy with fatigue yesterday afternoon. I had to drink a half-glass of port. None of us had dinner or supper yesterday, not even *monsieur* de Voltaire. I don't know how he did it."

"I do," said Zénobe, matching his stride with that of André's. "He was going on pure excited energy. Like a perpetual machine that looks to itself to renovate its power. That's how he was in Ferney, where the intellectuals of Europe made their pilgrimage to the seat of Humanism and Tolerance, to bask in the brilliance of the King of Philosophy."

"You sound an awful lot like the people who have been visiting him."

"What, you don't recognize *monsieur* de Voltaire as the King of Philosophy, the Monarch of Wisdom, the Apostle of Reason?"

---

38   Even Rousseau had pitched in. This bust is now in the Louvre.

"I didn't know anything about Voltaire except from what my sister told me, and she prefers Rousseau. Jean-Jacques, as she calls him. I don't even know Voltaire's given names."

"François Marie Arouet."

"François Marie Arouet?"

"That's right."

"That doesn't sound very royal, does it? Perhaps if it had been François Capet, or François Bourbon, instead of Arouet."

"No, indeed not. There is nothing royal about that name. He is a man of the people."

"Why do you call him king, then?"

"Because he sways more people with a stroke of his pen than does any king alive today with a stroke of his scepter. Voltaire's opinions have more clout than George III's navies or Frédéric II's cavalries or Maria Theresa's swordsmen or Catherine II's hussars or Louis XVI's dragoons or Marie Antoinette's lovers."

"Voltaire is more important than all those?"

"Yes, and you're sleeping under the same roof as he."

"Well, not really. I'm sleeping in the servant's quarters behind the house. But they're very nice quarters, to be sure. I have a very nice view of the garden."

A clever idea crept into Zénobe's mind. "Do you think there's enough space there for me?"

"What?" André's Normand distrust came immediately to the fore. "Why would you want space there?"

Zénobe realized he had spoken too soon. "It's just that I… I've run out of money, and I must stay in Paris to see Voltaire. I wouldn't be any trouble, really."

André began walking faster. "Well, you'll have to take that up with *Monsieur* Maurel–"

"Is he the *maître d'hôtel*?" interrupted Zénobe.

"Yes, and he runs the house like a Swiss clock. You'll have to take it up with him."

"He told me to come back next week. And I have no place to stay until then."

Zénobe said this with a beginning hint of desperation, and this awoke within André a certain feeling of compassion. Even in Normandy one tried to help those who were destitute and deserving of Christian hospitality.

"Why do you want to see Voltaire?" ventured André, more to continue the conversation and assess Zénobe's sincerity than to find out the answer. If he felt that Zénobe was not telling lies, perhaps he would decide to help him.

Zénobe slowed his gait and took André's arm to force him to slow down as well. His clear blue eyes looked up to the heavens and he said, "I wouldn't know where to start."

André replied, "Well, we're walking to the *Halles*, so you have plenty of time to figure out where your story begins."

"It's true. I just don't know what part of the story will interest you. It has to do with politics, and social injustice, and the fact that my father was murdered for having wanted to take his family to a better place, across the border, to France."

"You think France is a better place? You mean, there are places worse than France?" André could not help asking this question with incredulity. His own father could only speak of the imbecilities that the French population had to put up with because of the way the aristocrats were running the country. Thoughts of his father made him understand the full meaning of what Zénobe had just told him. "Your father was killed because he wanted to leave his country?"

Zénobe remained silent.

"I offer you my condolences," André told him.

"Savoy is still a bastion of feudal terror," said Zénobe. "The nobles hold us like the Americans hold their slaves. We can do nothing if our *seigneur* does not allow it, including marrying, or building a house, or moving away, or even planting different crops. My father gave me a surreptitious education. I found out what it was to want to live free. I found out that in France and in Switzerland liberty was not a chimera—"

"A what?"

"An illusion. At least here, you have more freedom than where I come from."

"This is true. My family will be moving soon to a bigger town, to Caen. And I was allowed to come live in Paris. We had to ask for no one's permission."

"The only freedom we have in Savoy is to die when we want to. That is what happened to my father."

"But what do you think Voltaire can do for you?"

"He can announce to the civilized world the plight of all Savoyards. What he has done for the Protestants he can do for us. He can bring to light this great injustice under which we have to toil and suffer and die. There is no other hope for us. Our sovereign rules with an oppression that is only equaled by the Church, and between the State and the Church, my people are being crushed to death."[39]

By this time, André and Zénobe were crossing the Pont Neuf, with the Place Dauphin coming up on their right. Guards were posted at the entrance, a potent reminder that only members of a certain class were allowed in. The two boys turned right along the quai de l'École and then made their way up on the rue Saint Denis. Already the whores were plying their trade to morning passersby. The sight of two well-bred, healthy and handsome young men, one blond with brown eyes, the other dark with blue eyes, made more than one of the women call out to them.

"Come here, my lads. I'll take care of both of you for half the price."

"Ah, looky whass comin' up 'ere! Over 'ere, *messieurs*, bring yourselves over ta 'ere. You wanna share? Two o' you for two o' these?"

Both boys tried not to look at any of the women, but they could not help but be amazed at the sight of naked breasts so early in the morning. Of course, neither one of them could tell that the other one was a virgin as well. They both had been brought up in country naïveté, and both had been taught to respect women. They held the belief that carnal knowledge of women before marriage would doom them to hell. Both were completely unaware that their dormant proclivities made it easier and simpler for them to eschew traffic of this sort.

They turned off the rue Saint Denis as quickly as they could, and when they were safe, relatively speaking, on the Rue Quinquempoix, they both burst out in laughter. Zénobe flashed such hilarity in his eyes that André thought that perhaps they could be friends. This would be something new for him considering the paucity of other children his own age in his tiny village. In Zénobe's case, it would be novel to have a friend as well. Back home, it had been mistrust of the other Savoyard families that had made his father keep him away from other children. It was true that Zénobe was trying to get to Voltaire through André, yet he liked this simple boy who was not from Paris and perhaps would not yet have learned to be sophisticated and dissipated. In a situation

---

39   Victor-Amédée III succeeded to the throne of the duchy of Savoy in 1773. Presiding from Turin, he rescinded the land reforms begun by his predecessor Charles-Emmanuel III, throwing all of his realm back into a retrenched feudal system. Countless peasants died due to the resulting clashes with the gentry.

that was bewildering to him, in a city that frightened him, it was agreeable to happen upon a fraternal association.

Of course, neither one of them could know that this incipient friendship of theirs might have certain consequences in the home of the *marquis* de Villette which was run by his *maître d'hôtel monsieur* Maurel.

After having procured sage and other necessities at *les Halles*, André and Zénobe returned to the *hôtel* de Villette by way of the Pont Royal back across the Seine. As they walked past the eastern boundary of the Tuileries Gardens, they could not possibly have known of events that had happened some years past in those very grounds. In 1766 a domestic of Villette's was arrested one evening along with three young men who were caught entertaining a certain *monsieur* de Léomont in the shrubbery. According to the report filed by the lieutenant of police, the *marquis* de Villette, who happened to be in the vicinity, spoke on behalf of his servant, stipulating that this domestic was no longer in his employ, having dismissed him some months previously, more for stupidity than for misconduct. The valet was let go. In 1769 police interrogated Villette about a different occurrence at the Tuileries Gardens involving his then secretary Carrier. Apparently Carrier was caught drunk, also in the evening, fraternizing with the son of the *marquis* de Fleury on May 15 behind the thick trunk of a linden tree. Someone who looked like the *marquis* de Villette had shown up and touched the young Fleury in his privates, who became angry and pushed the offending aristocrat into a fountain. Carrier stabbed Fleury. The man who looked like the *marquis* took flight. Both Carrier and Fleury were arrested. Fleury was released in view of his social standing. Carrier was also released, but only after having been coerced into a secret deal to inform the police on Villette's visitors. For three years the police thus had reports of several young men who were "antiphysical" visiting the *marquis*.[40] What was unknown to the police, the *marquis* de Villette's *maître d'hôtel monsieur* Maurel, forbade–forbade!–his master from any more nocturnal visits to the Tuileries Gardens. He stated that there were too many matters out of his control there. It was also Maurel who discovered the secretary's espionage, and had Villette send him off to a distant relative in Marseille where the secretary was promptly murdered during a secret nocturnal foray to one of the quays.

André and Zénobe were going back to a tightly-run house, where the able, affable, personable, courteous *maître d'hôtel* kept controls on all, including the master. The *marquis* de Villette did not mind. On the contrary, he welcomed such assiduity in his *maître d'hôtel*. He had what he wanted. A handsome town house with a prestigious address, a presentable marriage to a beautiful and educated woman, handsome boys who were now brought to him, and–crowning glory–the envy of all of Europe: Voltaire in his house. They had to go through the *marquis* to see the *philosophe*.[41] How more complete could life be?

As André and Zénobe walked back to the *hôtel* de Villette, André did not know how in the world he was going to introduce his newfound friend into the household. He was dreading Maurel's reaction.

---

40   *Antiphysique* was the preferred word to denote homosexuality in the Eighteenth century, demonstrating the erroneous belief that the condition was "against nature."

41   He said, "*Pour voir Voltaire, il faut passer par moi. Vous en voulez du Voltaire: en voici. Mais faites courbette devant Villette.*" "In order to see Voltaire, you have to go through me. You want Voltaire? Here he is. But first take a bow to Villette."

They slipped into the side gates and André took Zénobe immediately into the servants' quarters, knowing that there would be nobody there at that hour of the morning. André told Zénobe to be quiet and invisible, and that he would be bringing him food and drink later. Then he entered the kitchen door to hand the eagerly-awaited sage to le Parnaud, Voltaire's cook. Voltaire was in the *salon* with visitors, but was planning to take a break for dinner and would need sage tea to soothe his irritated bowels.

André tried to look as if nothing untoward had happened. He thought, I haven't just let in a complete stranger onto the premises, have I? He took his place by the front door, replacing *monsieur* Maurel. The *maître d'hôtel* couldn't help noticing André's attempts at nonchalance, but he had much to do in the kitchen and couldn't dwell on it.

André could hear that someone was playing the harpsichord in the *salon*. *Madame* de Villette came out a quarter of an hour later with a resplendent expression on her face.

"Gluck is playing our harpsichord! The divine Gluck is here!"

Madame de Villette was having a moment of supreme pleasure. She caught sight of a beautiful *bergère* in the vestibule and would have liked nothing better than to sit in it and review her incredible luck, but she had no time for that. Just think, she thought to herself: ten years ago she was an orphan girl with nothing to look forward to. And now here she was, in a beautiful house with a proper *salon,* which welcomed world-renowned celebrities to come hobnob with each other, and with her. She had been educated by Voltaire, not like a woman, but like any human being should, and she was thankful for it. She had a wealthy and famous husband who was, it is true, a bit distant and strange, but she suspected that all French husbands were like that, according to her aristocratic women friends. She disappeared into the dining room where a congregation of men were awaiting her instructions for entry into the *salon*. The *marquis* de Villette came out of the *salon* in turn, also with a beaming smile. "The delegation from the *Académie française* is here! The Immortals have sent their representatives to our house!"[42]

He ran off to the dining room as well, and before long the *marquis* and *marquise* returned solemnly to the *salon* where Voltaire and Gluck were entertaining the crowd. Following the host and hostess the delegation of gentlemen from the *Académie* paraded in and offered the *philosophe* a tirade of laudatory remarks worthy of all Immortals and seldom heard in these environs. Whenever André approached the entrance to the *salon* he saw the seated Voltaire frequently consorting with both of his secretaries, whispering into their ears. The Immortals thought that Wagnière and Bigex were furiously writing down their wordy laurels. In effect, as André found out later, Voltaire was dictating lines to his play *Irène* which was slated to be presented to the public at the end of March and which he had yet to finish. Only Voltaire could write rhyming alexandrine couplets on a Byzantine empress in the midst of a fancy peroration pronounced in his honor.

Before dinner all guests were eased out and the masters ate in the dining room followed by the servants' meal in the kitchen, including both secretaries who continued correcting each other's copies of Voltaire's dictated text. André slipped out with a bit of bread and

---

42   The *Académie française*, founded by the *duc* de Richelieu in 1635, was an institution run by forty "Immortals" whose purpose was the purification and standardization of the French language. It was their *Dictionnaire* that had the final say on definitions, grammar and usage. Voltaire had been elected member in 1746 but because of his exile had to write his opinions in. Not all forty members came to see Voltaire on February 12, 1778; the Academicians who were ecclesiastics stayed away.

rillettes, an apple and half a bottle of wine to take to Zénobe in the servant's quarters. Only Maurel with his Scandinavian mountain hawk's eyes noticed it. He arched an eyebrow and wondered what was cooking. But seeing that André came back almost immediately, he said nothing, especially after noticing a lightning-fast glance of guilt coming from the young man's eyes. Maurel liked the idea of plots hatching in his household.

But the afternoon and evening seances had to be taken care of. It was again after 10 o'clock that evening when the front door closed for the last time. Everyone was worn out. Voltaire especially looked pale. His arms trembled a bit as André helped him to bed, and the *philosophe* was unnaturally taciturn. He did call for his niece and instructed her to call for *docteur* Tronchin for the following day. *Madame* Denis suggested that this errand be done on the spot. André was instructed to run to the Palais-Royal to alert the world-famous Genevan doctor that one of his patients would need assistance the following day. André did not welcome this inopportune task that would take him at least half an hour round trip at a running pace (it was not worth hitching up the horses for an errand-boy), for he was impatient to get back to the servants' quarters before the rest of the servants started ambling in. His impatience was not lost on Maurel who was observing him at a distance. He was surprised when André returned after only twenty minutes, much out of breath. After the boy was dismissed for the night, Maurel followed him after a couple of minutes.

He caught André trying to hide Zénobe in bed under the blankets.

"What have we here? A secret?" he asked excitedly.

André started. Zénobe stopped breathing.

"I absolutely love secrets. You were planning on telling me, weren't you, André?"

"Yes, *monsieur,* why yes. I was planning to, but I didn't have a chance all day, what with all the people and all…"

Maurel approached the bed and drew back the blankets. He recognized the blue eyes immediately.

"Aha, look who we have here! The gentleman from this morning who ardently wished to see *monsieur* de Voltaire! For a matter of life or death for his entire country, I believe."

Zénobe slowly came out of hiding.

"Well, you won't find Voltaire in there," continued Maurel, in a non-threatening voice that invited both boys to confess to their extravagant sleeping accommodations.

"I was going to tell you, *monsieur,* I swear to you I was, and I'll explain–" André started to say.

"Shush, shush," interrupted Maurel. "We're all too tired to explain anything tonight. You and *monsieur* Bosquet, did I get your name right?[43]–you need to rest after an arduous day. We will all see the light tomorrow morning. You can do your explaining then, understood?"

And with a paternal pat on each of their heads, he helped André into bed, pulled the covers to their shoulders, and bid both of them a splendid slumber.

He snuffed the candle out with his fingers and left the servants' quarters. Had anybody been in the garden as he walked back to the main house, he would have seen Maurel smile to himself and heard him murmur, "Well, that was easier than I thought it would be! Perhaps Providence does exist after all!"

His exit from consciousness that night was eased by the image of both boys' beautiful heads on the same pillow, telling him in unison "Good night, *monsieur.*" He dreamed of angels and of the highest levels of Dante's *Paradise* that night.

---

43   Zénobe's surname would not be easily forgotten. *Bosquet* means Little Forest.

The Moribund Philosophe

In spite of his extreme fatigue, André barely slept during the night. Sleeping with Zénobe was not at all like sleeping with his sister Charlotte. Being so close to his new friend gave him a fidgety energy and a few times in the dark he threw off the covers to see the outlines of Zénobe's sleeping form. A couple of times Zénobe murmured, "It's cold," without really waking up. André brought the blankets back up and gingerly placed a hand on his bedmate's arm for only a second or two. There were too many blankets on the bed and André felt warm.

Zénobe, however, enjoyed a full night's deep sleep, André's fidgeting notwithstanding; with André hovering around him, he didn't have to worry about thieves skulking in to relieve him of what little he had, mostly his precious clandestine books that he had brought over from the inn.

When Zénobe woke up, the light of the dawn was just starting to diffuse on the tallest pear trees in the garden. As soon as he opened his eyes he saw André sitting in bed next to him.

"Have you slept at all?" he asked, whispering so as not to wake the others in the next room.

"Yes, of course. But soon *monsieur* Maurel will come to get us."

"Nice fellow of yours, this Maurel. It's your good luck to have happened upon him." Zénobe yawned. "More often than not, they're slave-drivers."

"*Monsieur* Maurel is very sympathetic. From the very beginning, when he saw me up on a ladder pruning the apple trees."

"You were pruning apple trees? Where was that?"

"At my family's farm near Caen."

"The farm belongs to your family?" Zénobe sat up in bed too.

"Yes."

"You are lucky. In Savoy we're not allowed to own our land. It's the land my family has been tilling for generations. The land, along with everything on it, belongs to the *seigneur.* Even we belong to him."

"Oh," said André, then cleared his throat. "I think you slept well, didn't you?"

"Oh, yes," answered Zénobe letting himself fall back onto the pillow with his hands behind his head. His thick hair draped over the top of the pillow. "It was heaven to sleep so well. After two days on the street… It's tough to be on the street, especially here in Paris. And the people at the inn treat one like a thief. Perhaps because there are so many of them there. I wouldn't have wanted to sleep there another night."

He flashed a look at André. In the weak light, Zénobe's eyes looked almost colorless, like water in a blue glass.

"Thanks to you, I didn't have to," he continued.

"Thanks to *monsieur* Maurel," countered André.

"Yes, indeed."

Zénobe's expression turned dark.

"I wouldn't wish anybody to be on the streets of Paris. What an unforgiving city! I've seen more horrific things here in two days than I saw in all my life in Savoy. The bleakest of poverty, the vilest of stenches, the most repugnant of sights, people drowned in the Seine–"

"People drowned in the Seine?" interrupted André.

"Sh!" warned Zénobe, pointing to the other rooms. "Well, one woman drowned in the Seine. It was horrible. Some people who had been witnesses to her jumping into the water ran away rather than help me look for her."

"That's terrible!"

"Apparently there's a reward for bringing back drowned people, but none for saving them."

"Oh, that's evil!"

"But that's nothing. Yesterday I visited the Place Louis XV to see the grand statue.[44] Juxtaposed to this obscenely magnificent, ostentatious square, I saw some children off to the side playing in the muck by the entrance to the gardens.[45] The *guet* was trying to get them to run off. It was the same *guet* who had told me I had no business there, either. I wasn't allowed into the gardens. I suppose the riffraff isn't to be let in. So, the filthy children were playing in the mud and the *guet* started beating them off with his stick. The children's mother came running out of nowhere and started a violent ruckus. The *guet* called out to the guards and they carted off the family beggars. Someone next to me told me that most probably she'd end up in the Petit Châtelet prison and her children taken to the orphanage. Her crime was that she had taken her brood too close to the wealthy people who go strolling in the Tuileries."

Zénobe looked towards the growing light coming in from the window and sighed.

"And that's not all," he continued. "While I was looking at the statue of your previous monarch, an old man struck up a conversation with me. He looked sad and dejected and when he spoke was full of vituperation–"

"Full of what?" asked André.

"Vindictive anger, he was full of anger," answered Zénobe. "His name was Ponthieu. He told me that he hated the kings, that previous one, and the present one, too. For when the present king was a *dauphin*, on the day of his marriage to the Austrian harlot Marie Antoinette, there was a public feast given on the Rue Royale.[46] The old man said that thousands of people turned out, including himself, his son and his daughter.

---

44   In the middle of the grandest square in Paris stood a huge statue of Louis XV seated upon a monstrous horse. It was pulled down and destroyed by the mob during the Revolution in 1789. The revolutionaries gave the square a new name: the Place de la Révolution. It has since been named the Place de la Concorde.

45   The Tuileries Gardens, beginning on the east side of the Place Louis XV. On the west side of the Place Louis XV the Avenue des Champs-Élysées did not yet exist.

46   This celebration took place on May 30, 1770. A total of 132 people were trampled to death by the crowd or drowned in the river when they fell over the banks.

His daughter, he said, was only fifteen years old. There was such a crush of people that everyone started to panic. In the ensuing stampede, his daughter Marie Catherine Ponthieu died. He said her little bones were protruding from her flesh. He picked up her body and he knew that she was gone. On a day that was supposed to be a great celebration he had found tragedy. I told him that Marie Antoinette was also fifteen on the day of her marriage to the *dauphin.* Perhaps I shouldn't have told him that. I told him that I would remember his daughter's name and tell everyone I knew about her. That seemed to make him feel a little better. I didn't want to leave him."

From the little room at the end of the servants' quarters André and Zénobe began to hear faint stirrings coming from the other rooms. A female voice boomed, "Little André must be talking in his sleep!"

André called out, "Sorry, *madame.* I hope I didn't wake you."

The voice came back, "Wake me, no. I was awakened by the melodious voice of Voltaire in my sleep. He was talking about the clergy again, priests and bishops and monks and how they liked a little thingumbob every now and then, 'like the rest of us.'"

Another female voice in the same room started to giggle. "A little whatchamacallit? What's that, pray tell?"

"You know what I mean," said the first voice, laughing as well. "Voltaire was saying that everybody from the Pope down to the *curés* of the tiniest villages—"

"Oh, the Pope! He's as handsome as he is holy!" exclaimed the second voice.[47]

A masculine voice from the farthest room then spoke. "You mean a little *fornication,* don't you? For-ni-ca-tion, repeat after me, for-ni—"

Zénobe and André started to laugh too. Even out of their presence Voltaire was still making them laugh.

Suddenly, Zénobe sat up in bed again and whispered to André, "When do you think I can talk with *monsieur* Maurel?"

André walked over to the window. "He'll be here any moment now. He comes with the light of the dawn."

The servants in the other rooms started to stir. One of the women from the adjoining room popped her head into André's room out of curiosity and announced to the rest of them, "Eh, André has a handsome friend in his bed."

Said one of the manserverants, "Well, I hope he'll help with the flood of visitors. We could use more hands."

When Maurel walked into the servants' quarters, he was surprised to see everyone already in movement.

"Well, everybody is already up and about?"

"Yes, *monsieur,* we were awakened by André talking in his sleep and Voltaire talking in mine," said Suzanne who was the one who had dreamt of Voltaire speaking of the clergy's sexual needs.

Maurel gave a perplexed look and said, "Well, there's a complication today, but in the end I think it'll be a blessing in disguise for the rest of us. Voltaire is feeling ill and will be taking fewer visitors."

"That is indeed a blessing. It's a good thing I was speaking well of the Pope," said Marianne, Suzanne's roommate. "I am exhausted. All the constant curtsying and grinding of the coffee and taking the tray out and then back. We're going through pounds and pounds of coffee, tea, chocolate and sugar. My legs are killing me!"

---

47   Pope Pius VI, known in his youth as much for his good looks as for his good works.

"And me too, along with my back," added Suzanne. "We are not used to this sort of commotion. *Monsieur* de Villette is very calm, compared to *monsieur* de Voltaire. *Monsieur* de Villette barely entertains. He prefers to go out all the time. Look at me, the muscles in my hand are trembling from fatigue. The Ferney clan are fresh as morning roses; they've had years of this sort of experience. But we're not used to this, *monsieur*."

"I know, Suzanne, I know," said Maurel who was getting ready to walk into André's room. "But this won't last forever. *Monsieur* de Voltaire is an old and feeble man, and see? His composition cannot take the battering he has had to confront with all the constant visitors. Today, *madame* Denis has given express orders that only *monsieur* de Voltaire's *philosophe* friends be let in. This will reduce the visitors tenfold. Voltaire will be entertaining in his bedroom."[48]

"*Merci, monsieur* Maurel," said Marianne. "We're not used to this pace like the Ferney servants are."

"Yes, I know, but all in all, I think our household has done very, very well, considering the pandemonium of the last two days, and I am very proud of all of you."

"*Merci, monsieur* Maurel," said a chorus of voices.

Maurel finally went into André's room. Zénobe was still in bed, but André, shirtless, was splashing water on his face from a big metal cauldron.

"I see that you are also awake," said Maurel. "*Bonjour, bonjour.* Did you sleep well, master Zénobe?"

"Yes, very well, thank you, *monsieur*. But I'm concerned... You said Voltaire was not well..."

"*Monsieur* de Voltaire is fatigued and has been having stomach cramps all night. He should do well to rest." Maurel turned to face André.

"André, you'll still be required to stand by your post at the front door today. I'm afraid that you won't get much rest. You'll just have to send most everybody away, giving *monsieur* de Voltaire's excuses that he is feeling ill. Perhaps master Zénobe can assist you with this task. André, where do you keep your butler's uniform? Ah, there it is. I think Zénobe will be able to fit into it. Aren't you about the same height as André? Let's see. Why don't you come over here by the light and let's see how close you are to André's size. I think this might work out, don't you?"

Maurel was enjoying putting pieces of André's butler uniform next to Zénobe's body. First he tried out the vest and the coat, then the breeches. He caressed the clothes where they were pressed against Zénobe's body, ostensibly to smooth out the creases.

"I think the coat will fit marvelously well. But the breeches will need taking down a bit. Come over here, André, let me compare the two of you."

Maurel placed Zénobe and André back to back, and admired their profiles.

"Aha, just as I thought. Zénobe is a little bit taller than you, André. And it's not in the torso. It's in the legs. See, Zénobe's buttocks are placed a little higher, and they're a bit rounder as well. I wonder if I'll have to let the trousers out there, too? What do you think, Zénobe? Here, why don't you try them on and we'll see if they need to be let out. That's a good lad."

---

48   [From the author] Lest the modern reader think it strange for Voltaire to entertain guests in bed or for André to sleep with Zénobe, the Eighteenth-century bedroom was not considered as private as it is today. All the aristocrats enjoyed the company of their friends while still in bed, having not just coffee but whole meals together. And sharing accommodations with someone did not necessarily connote carnal relations. It was quite innocent, really.

Maurel stood there marveling as Zénobe did as he was told, first removing the undergarment in which he had slept. Maurel gave little guttural sounds of approval and encouragement. When Zénobe stood there shirtless as well, wearing the butler's black trousers, Maurel's face beamed.

"Oh, yes, you see? They're a bit too short. But Suzanne will take care of that in a flash. She used to be a seamstress, you know, and before that, a nun. It was *monsieur* Diderot who helped her to get this position after a priest helped her to escape from the convent. Oh, Suzanne? Are you there? Oh, good. Please take down these seams, won't you? Just a couple of inches, no more. Do you see? Very well, Zénobe, we'll have you taken care of in no time. I still have to speak to the *marquis* on your behalf. But I don't see any complications on that front. Have you ever served, master Zénobe?"

"No, *monsieur*. Well, just with my father. Oh, and lately, at an inn in Dijon."

"Were you a good son?"

"I tried to be, *monsieur*. He was the best father anyone could ever have. He had me receive an education, with the village *curé*. At great sacrifice to himself. He believed what Voltaire said all along about the importance of education for young men. Even in the countryside. Books were very expensive to get. We had to get them from Geneva."

"Oh, that was very good. The *marquis* de Villette has had several of his books published in Geneva. No Paris house would take them." Maurel was quite sure that the *marquis'* salacious books would not have been among those that Zénobe's father had acquired for his son.

Maurel went to the doorway. "Well, let's get ready. It's going to be another long day, I'm sure."

"*Monsieur?*" said Zénobe.

"Yes, master Zénobe?" asked Maurel.

"Do you think I'll be able to meet Voltaire today?"

"Absolutely, my boy. But please refer to *monsieur* de Voltaire as *monsieur* de Voltaire. The *marquis* is *monsieur le marquis*, and the *marquise* is *madame la marquise*. I will let you know how to address the visitors. And of course, I am your humble servant, *monsieur* Maurel."

Zénobe smiled. "Thank you, *monsieur* Maurel, thank you so very, very much."

"At your service," said Maurel, and popped out of the room.

"Ah," said Voltaire as Zénobe followed Maurel into the *philosophe*'s boudoir. "You must be *monsieur* de Corday's new preceptor. Maurel, is this the young man of whom you spoke?"

Voltaire was sitting up on a mountain of pillows in his bed. The bed curtains were all pulled back, attached to the posts by flame-colored ribbons. Gauze had been strung up on the backboard to make sure Voltaire's bony body did not hit the naked wood. There was somebody already seated in a chair in the shadows of the *petite ruelle*,[49] but Zénobe could not make out who it was.

---

49   The *petite ruelle* was the "private" side of the bed, the space between the bed and the wall, as opposed to the *grande ruelle* which was the more public side where most of the company sat.

"Excuse me, *monsieur* de Voltaire?" asked Zénobe dumbfounded, for he had heard nothing about being a new preceptor. He was trembling a bit in his hands and knees.

"Maurel tells me you are a young man of distinction, who in the recesses of the *Haute Savoie* managed to get himself an education."

"Thanks to my father, *monsieur*. It was he who was adamant that I receive a good education."

Voltaire turned to Maurel. "'Adamant'," he said. "Not too many young men would use the word 'adamant'."

"And what, pray tell, did your father think constituted a good education?" asked the *philosophe*, this time with a stern expression on his face.

"Well, *monsieur*, when I was still a child, he had the *curé*[50] teach me Latin and Greek so I could read Plutarch's *Parallel Lives*, also his *Moral* writings, then the complete works of Xenophon, Thucydides, Herodotes and Homer, and of course Demosthenes–"

"What about more modern works?" interrupted Voltaire.

"Well, *monsieur*, I read *Don Quichotte*, Rabelais, all of the *Essays* of Montaigne, the *Décameron*, the *Heptaméron,* the fables of La Fontaine, the letters of *madame* de Sévigné–"

"No, more modern than that."

"*Gil Blas de Santillane, The Plurality of the Worlds*, the plays of Marivaux, *The Persian Letters, The Spirit of Laws*, the maxims of Vauvernagues, *l'Emile, La Nouvelle Héloïse...*"[51]

Voltaire chuckled at the mention of the publications of his rival Jean-Jacques Rousseau.

"*...Philosophical Thoughts, Letter on the Blind...*"

The figure in the shadows of the *petite ruelle* leaned forward and said "Aah..." Voltaire turned to his friend Diderot and smiled.

"*... Letter on the Deaf and Dumb*, many articles of the *Encyclopédie...*"[52]

Voltaire remarked to Diderot, "His *curé* must have been quite the rebel!"

Diderot answered, "Just my type of ecclesiastic, the one who works from within."

"*...Les lettres philosophiques, Zaïre, Mahomet...*"

"Aah," said Voltaire deliciously. "Here we go..."

"*... Traité sur la tolérence, Le dictionnaire philosophique portatif, Les Questions de Zapata, Candide...*"

"This *curé* was extraordinary!" exclaimed Voltaire.

"*...Poème sur le désastre de Lisbonne, Histoire de Charles XII, The Henriade, Essay on Morals–*"[53]

"Enough, my lad," interrupted Voltaire, with a broad smile. "That's quite enough. But tell us, if you please, because I am sure that my colleague–" Voltaire looked at Diderot, "is as intensely curious as I, to find out what this village *curé* must have been like, that he allowed you to read writings that have been burned in Paris, put on the *Index* by the Pope, and in general been very hard to come by?"

Zénobe was beside himself in excitement and nervousness. Of course he had recognized *monsieur* Diderot and he could not believe his luck to be in the presence of *two* of his philosophical gods.

---

50   The village priest.

51   *Gil Blas* by Lesage; *La pluralité des mondes* by Fontenelle; *Les Lettres persanes* and *L'Esprit des lois* by Montesquieu; *L'Emile* and *La Nouvelle Héloïse* by Rousseau.

52   *Les pensées philosophiques, Lettre sur les aveugles, Lettre sur les sourds et muets,* were by Denis Diderot.

53   All these last were, of course, written by François Marie Arouet, better known by his *nom de guerre,* Voltaire.

"Father Anselme is, *monsieur*, a spectacular teacher. He used the *Index* as a guide to his readings."

Voltaire and Diderot burst out in laughter.

"As a matter of fact, he used the list of books in the *Index Librorum Prohibitorum* for me, and the *Index Expurgatorius* for himself.

This brought out another peal of mirth from both *philosophes*. They were having a great time with Zénobe.

"But, but, what was the man like?" asked Voltaire.

"He never wanted to be a priest. He was forced into an ecclesiasic life by his family. He would have rather wanted to be a world traveler, like Cook or Bougainville, or—"

"Ah," said Diderot in disgust at the tyrannical system that forced unwilling individuals to give up their lives for the Church. "Another of those wasted lives!"

"But his life was not an entire waste, *monsieur* Diderot," said Zénobe, looking directly into the *philosophe*'s eyes. "He taught me well and he taught a slew of other country children, and he taught those of us whom he deemed worthy of it and who were trustworthy as well, in secret, so as not to get any of us in trouble. I think teaching us what was prohibited was his way of thumbing his nose at the whole system that had taken his dreams from him. Well, Father Anselme still lives in Annecy, and he teaches still. He is an admirable man. He is a man worthy of the title of teacher. It was at his prompting that I left Annecy after my father was killed and my own life was in danger."

"What was it that happened, my child?" asked Voltaire.

"My father always wanted to be independent. He resented Victor-Amédée's abrogation of the rescindment of feudal laws established by his predecessor Charles-Emmanuel, so he flouted the rights of hunting and fishing—"[54]

"Oh, that was stupid—" began Diderot.

"…because he believed that the aristocrats were the last to need to eat from the land. They could afford to buy their food in Lyon and Dijon and in Geneva."

"But that was not an intelligent way to fight back against the nobles," reiterated Diderot.

"If your children are starving you wait for no one's permission to kill a passing deer or to go fishing in the middle of the night," said Zénobe. "The land should belong to everbody."

"Unfortunately, the efforts of Charles-Emmanuel to push back the onerous laws of feudalism never took effect as law in Savoy," observed Voltaire. "His peasantry had the misfortune of seeing their king die too soon."

"That is true, *monsieur*, but at least His Majesty was on his way to pulling back the cobwebs of archaic injustice."

"His degenerate and ungovernable vassals made sure that his attempts at reform were assailed at every turn," remarked Voltaire. "Every time that I looked into the matter I could tell he was losing the battle. And then when he died and his son mounted the throne, I knew all was lost. Victor-Amédée undid all the progress and prosperity of his reform-minded father by giving the wealthy what they clamored for. Of course, what the rich do best is run up the country's debt. The peasants began to starve. That was back in 17–, 1771, was it not?"

---

54   In many areas where the vestiges of feudal overlordship still existed, the *droit de chasse* and the *droit de pêche* forbade the peasants from hunting or fishing in the *seigneur*'s lands.

"Victor-Amédée took the throne in 1773," Zénobe answered, "and he immediately threw himself into the spirit of politics in the traditional feudal repressive sort of way. He made sure just last year to put all of Charles-Emmanuel's edicts to sleep. The *cens* and the *corvée* are back, and the *dîme* never left.[55] As anachronistic as that sounds, Savoy has taken a big leap backward."

"He never answered any of my letters," Voltaire sighed.

"What, *monsieur*, you wrote to Victor-Amédée?" asked Zénobe with great surprise.

"Indeed I did, at the same time I wrote His Majesty the King of Sweden; His Majesty the King of Denmark; Her Royal Highness, Catherine, the Empress of Russia; His Royal Highness Frédéric II; and Her Royal Empress Marie-Thérèse. What a big difference in their behavior! At least those other five monarchs had the decency to respond to me and to put up at least a pretense that they were enlightened despots. This other little tyrant, the king of a molehill—no insult to the inhabitants of Savoy and Sardinia, my lad..."

"No insult perceived, *monsieur*."

"This king of a tiny realm had the audacity not even to acknowledge my letters."

"His vassals keep him eclipsed in Turin, *monsieur*."

"Sounds like another king of our acquaintance," said Voltaire, with a contemptuous tilt of his head in the general direction of Versailles. "These leaders who think they are governing satisfactorily but who surround themselves only with sycophants. How I abhor those people who say yes to anything their king fancies because they are afraid of losing whatever power and prestige they enjoy for the moment. They lose a whole nation for their own selfish reasons. Those are not patriots. And yet they call their rivals unpatriotic who look at the circumstances in a more general and disinterested fashion and try to right the wrongs. It is a tragedy, really."

"Nevertheless," threw in Diderot, "in His Majesty's defense we must add that he is kept in an eclipsed fashion by his beautiful Queen."

"That Austrian bitch?" exclaimed Zénobe so suddenly that every one in the room started. "She can choke on all her jewels, I'd ram them down her throat!"

Voltaire and Diderot were taken aback by Zénobe's vehemence. Maurel took a step towards Zénobe with a hand outstretched.

"Hush," remonstrated Voltaire in a serious tone. "It is a good thing that there are just the four of us in my bedroom, but very soon there'll be others here. And Her Majesty has many, many people who report back to Versailles, at least in terms of gossip. You do not want to make enemies in Paris. It dawns on me now that the passion that runs in your veins is what got your father into trouble."

"But, *monsieur*, the troubles of my country—"

"The troubles of your country are one thing, but the way we go about trying to rectify these troubles here is another matter entirely different."

"Listen to your elders," added Diderot. "We have considerable experience in these matters. We have the scars to prove it." All there took pause to remember the physical punishment suffered by Voltaire at the hands of the *chevalier* de Rohan's servants.[56]

Zénobe was mortified. He bowed down low and said, "Forgive me, *messieurs*, I regret my imprudence. You are indeed my masters, and I respect you and adore you and will defend you to my dying day."

---

55   The *cens* and the *corvée* were two taxes levied on the peasants by the lord of the domain. The *dîme* was levied by the Church.

56   The *chevalier* de Rohan sent his valets to beat the young Voltaire with sticks in order to put him in his place.

Maurel was in awe of his little protégé.

Voltaire chuckled. "You are intelligent and knowledgeable, and I see you are malleable. Not bad for *monsieur* de Corday's preceptor."

Zénobe looked at Maurel with an inquisitive glance.

Maurel whispered to him, "Master André."

Voltaire continued: "I shall personally guide you in our young friend's tutelage. I'm afraid you'll find that his education was sorely neglected in Normandy. I should say, landowner farmers in Normandy shouldn't be in a worse-off state than landless serfs in Savoy, don't you think, *monsieur* Diderot?

Diderot showed a malicious twinkle in his eye that was his trademark. "People have a tendency to get fat and comfortable and uncomplaining when thrown a few bones for possessions. Once we ourselves are content, who cares about the rest of the world? Aren't we all self-satisfied materialists at heart?"

"Ah, my friend, I love your delicious *double-entendres.*" (Afterwards Maurel asked Zénobe to explain this last to him; Zénobe taught him the two meanings of 'materialist', the doctrine of physical matter and the adjective meaning 'desirous of possessions'. "Ah," said *monsieur* Maurel, not quite sure how one could get a pun out of that information.)[57]

"*Monsieur,*" said Zénobe to Voltaire.

"Yes, my boy?"

"*Monsieur,*" ventured Zénobe, looking a bit sheepish. "Don't you think I might entreat you to write about the injustices happening in Savoy and the predicament in which her people–"

"Oh, no, my boy. I'm no longer in the business of getting other people out of trouble. There is not enough of me left to continue being the *don Quichotte* of all those broken on the rack or strung up. From the four corners of the Earth I can see the most barbarous injustices. People believe that our century is but ridiculous; it is horrible. Sometimes Lally and Sirven, Calas and Martin, the *chevalier* de la Barre, come to me in my dreams.[58] Perhaps that is why I don't get any sleep any more. My lad, do not gaze upon me like that. Do not weep. Rather, weep for me. I am more on my way out of this life than in it. I have given away my health to the world, my life to people I never even met–"

"But, *monsieur*, you are the most famous person in the world. Everybody recognizes your name. People are saying that you are more famous than Jesus."

Diderot let out a guffaw at this last. Maurel thought that he would have more on his hands than just another handsome boy in his household.

"Everybody pays attention to you," continued Zénobe. "Your every word is in all the newspapers since you came to Paris. I know for I've been reading them, in order to find out what has been going on inside the *hôtel* de Villette. People are starving for your every utterance. When your name is mentioned, people put down what they are doing. They–"

"Oh, come now, you are surely exaggerating," said Voltaire with his crooked smile, enjoying every word.

"Oh no, *monsieur*, I exaggerate not a word. To me you have always been the genius of our century, the guiding hand who will fix the problems of all the iniquities that

---

57   What perhaps Maurel was unfamiliar with was the philosophical theory that nothing in the universe exists outside of matter. Everything on earth, including humans, are composed of physical substances, and the rest, the soul, the spirit, the ghost, invisible gods, are not part of reality.

58   All of these were victims of intolerance and injustice whom Voltaire helped.

oppress us. And you as well, *monsieur* Diderot, to be sure. Both of your writings have sought to take us out of the shadows of the feudal system and of the Inquisition. The oppression of the Crown and of the Church is great, against the poor, the peasants, the low-wage earners, but also against the bourgeois who have no voice in the government, in the way things are run. It is your writings and those of le *baron* de Secondat that have been influencing the Americans in their united effort to throw off the English yoke.[59] Benjamin Franklin is now here among us to get the French to help in their cause. You must certainly realize it, *messieurs,* that your life's work has brought very pragmatic and positive consequences."

"What are you, my little friend," asked Voltaire with feigned mistrust, "a lawyer? Or are you what I thought you were, a fair and enlightened individual?"

Even Maurel had to laugh out loud at that quip.

"But, *monsieur,*" insisted Zénobe. Who else would there be to help me undermine the only remaining feudal servitude in all of Europe?"

Diderot was quick to add, "If you don't count Russia, of course!"[60]

Voltaire turned to Diderot and said, "I see through his flattery but I care to believe it anyway. Why not? More important people than this young lad have been saying those very things these past three days."

At that moment the two secretaries Wagnière and Bigex came into the bedroom with paper, plumes and bottles of ink in their hands. They exchanged greetings with the two *philosophes.*

"Ah, saved by the secretaries, as is the usual case", said Voltaire. "This impertinent young man," said he to them, motioning towards Zénobe, "would have me save the world from tyranny and absolute despots."

"But you have already done that in many parts of the world, *monsieur,*" said Zénobe.

"Oh, I think you are a young man who adores me, and who also adores my friend Diderot," Voltaire said, bowing to Diderot. "And that is why I like you, and shall keep you. This afternoon you will start giving *monsieur* de Corday his first lessons. We can save the world on another day. By the way, are you good in mathematics?"

"Passably, *monsieur.*"

"Well then, you shall start with ancient history and then mathematics. I don't think you can get into much trouble with that. We'll have to alert d'Alembert to bring some books on mathematics..."

The secretaries started jotting down notes.

"...and later on for French history we must find a copy of my *Life of Louis XIV* some-place. And you, my gentle friend Diderot, can you bring by some books on general history, the Greeks and the Romans—"

"Oh, I have those with me, *monsieur,*" said Zénobe.

"So much the better. And then we'll need something for pleasure reading. Let's see, let's see, what can you think of, *monsieur?*" Voltaire asked Diderot.

---

59   Charles Louis de Secondat, *baron* de La Brède et de Montesquieu, author of the book *On the Spirit of Laws* which the founding fathers of the United States will take to heart when drafting the laws of their new country. Incidentally, Thomas Jefferson corresponded regularly with the *philosophes.*

60   Diderot spent four months of his life in Saint Petersburg trying to convince Catherine II to soften her feudal stance, to no avail.

"Oh, I know!" cried Diderot with a sprightly malevolent look in his eyes. I have the perfect book for these young lads. It is a book that will both instruct and edify them. *Les Bijoux indiscrets!*[61]

All the older men laughed in the warm tones of conspiratorial fellowship.

"I really enjoyed that book, *monsieur,* said Zénobe. I think André will get much enjoyment out of it too."

Diderot stopped laughing and looked at Voltaire with amazement. "That *curé* left no stone unturned."

"Well, run along now," said Voltaire, suddenly impatient. "Maurel I'm sure will look to your needs. Work imposes its duties. I need to continue dictating my tragedy to *messieurs* Wagnière and Bigex. It won't get written by itself and the actors will be wanting the text soon in order to start memorizing it."

"You are writing another tragedy, *monsieur?*" asked Zénobe excitedly.

"Yes, and the *Comédie française* is anxiously awaiting it. As a matter of fact, this is the prime reason why I have returned to Paris in the middle of winter—and this sojourn is killing me. All I do is for the muse, my boy, the muse."[62]

"*Monsieur?*"

"Yes, my son?"

"Could you possibly read a tragedy that I have written?"

Everybody in the room laughed again, this time embarrassing Zénobe.

"Oh, you dabble in the arts, too?"

"Yes, *monsieur,* I call it *Ibycus.*"

Voltaire scratched his cheek. "Ibycus, Ibycus, who the hell was Ibycus?" Voltaire looked at Diderot. Diderot shrugged, also pulling a blank. The secretaries and Maurel shrugged.

"Ibycus, *messieurs,*" answered Zénobe like a schoolboy who is terribly proud that he knows the answer to a very difficult question. "Ibycus was a young man, a poet, blessed by Apollo who bestowed upon him a mellifluous voice and a talent for composing beautiful songs. One day he was making his way to the chariot races and musical competition of the Isthmus of Corinth, convinced that he would win there, the musical competition, that is, not the chariot races. For he had neglected his learning of the martial arts and feats of physical prowess in order to give all his time and energy to the thing he loved best: the writing of beautiful poetry."

Zénobe observed that he had the two greatest philosopher-novelist-playwrights on earth eating out of his hand. They both had their eyes intently set upon his face, and he could detect a formidable intelligence in the brilliance of their eyes. They were already working out all the angles of this little-known Greek myth.

Zénobe continued the tale, slowing down a bit for greater effect. "On the day he was walking to Corinth, a bright and cool autumn day where his only companions were the beasts and birds of nature, he heard a flock of cranes flying overhead on their migration south. As they flew in formation they called out to each other in noisy companionship. Ibycus bade his fellow travelers a good strong flight, and told them that he too was in

---

61   *The Indiscreet Jewels,* one of Diderot's first published books, a rather pornographic novel that as a youngster he wrote for easy money. It is the story of a magic ring that makes its wearer invisible and able to listen to women's real thoughts, as spoken through their, shall we say, lower lips.

62   Voltaire is doubtlessly invoking the muse of Tragedy, Melpomène, who, along with her eight sisters, inspire men in the creation of all the arts.

search of warmth and hospitality. He thanked them for their presence, for cranes were considered a good omen.

"Suddenly, Ibycus was accosted by two brigands. They told him to hand over all his possessions, including his precious lyre, and that he would have to stand and fight or suffer the consequences. Ibycus knew that it was impossible to fight two thieves who were as acquainted with brute force as he was with melodies and odes. The two ruffians beat him and broke his body, took all he had, and left him in the dirt to die. But as Ibycus took his dying breath, he looked overhead to the cranes and said, 'Take pity on your friend, ye cranes who gladdened me on my voyage, and avenge my death, for no other voices but yours have heeded my cries.' Then he closed his eyes to open them no more."

Voltaire turned to Diderot and said, "It's a pity the hero dies in the first act."

Zénobe continued: "When the competitions had begun and the friends of Ibycus were worried that he had not arrived, they went out looking for him and discovered his mangled body. They were distraught. The whole of Corinth was saddened, for they had heard of the poet's talent. When all were in the amphitheater, everybody demanded that the culprits be brought to justice, but it was impossible to find the guilty. Perhaps these criminals were in the crowd now, enjoying the fruits of their atrocity. The laments among the people grew stronger, and the Chorus took up their plaints. Stronger and stronger became the wails of the Chorus, and their hair danced upon their heads like the serpents of the Medusa. Their lamentations sounded like the roar of the sea, and entranced all who heard them. They were dressed in black, and everybody present said that they had transformed themselves into the Furies. 'We will seek them out wherever they run and we will not give them a moment's peace. They will never again know the tranquility that a guiltless conscience brings. They think they can escape? We will pursue them to the edge of Hades and beyond. We will bind their legs with our serpents and throw them to Cerberus.'

"Just then, overhead, a flock of cranes flew over the theater and joined their cries with those of the Furies. Over and over they flew in a circle above the crowd, swooping low and calling forth in thunderous voices. Then a voice, then another, started to yell out a new cry: 'There they are, there they are, they have betrayed themselves!' Indeed, the two thieves were pale with terror and racked by guilt. They were taken before the judge and they confessed their crime. They received the punishment they deserved on the very stage where Ibycus was to have sung his poetry."

Zénobe took a deep breath when he had reached the end of the story. Voltaire and Diderot kept their gaze on the young man.

"Very, very interesting," said Voltaire. I'm very curious to see how you treat the scene at the theater. A play within a play. Not bad. And how will you get cranes flying over the stage? Hmm, very, very interesting."

"Does this mean you are willing to read my play?" asked Zénobe enthusiastically.

Voltaire sat back on his pillows. "A wily one, this one is, heh heh! He'll have me reading his play in no time. And he'll have you (denoting Diderot) reading his philosophical treatises on how the brain cogitates. But not now! Not now, my boy! I'm feeling ill and tired, and there is much work to be done. Off with you now, there'll be time for saving the world and reading Greek tragedies afterwards. Go, go. Maurel. Take care of this young whippersnapper. But wait. Maurel. Someone is scratching at my door."[63]

---

63   People scratched, not knocked, on doors. It was considered more discreet.

It was the *marquise* de Villette. She looked rather worried, and embarrassed at the same time.

"My father..." she began, addressing herself to Voltaire.

"Yes, *Belle et bonne*? What has you so flabbergasted?"

"*Madame* de Polignac has returned, and she wishes to speak with you."[64]

"Oh, *merde*! Will I not be allowed to write today?"

"I am sorry, *monsieur*," said the *marquise*. "I just didn't feel it was possible to send her away."

"Of course not, my dear," answered Voltaire. "*Madame* de Polignac sits at the right hand of Her Majesty the Queen. But I suppose she can't come to my boudoir to see me here?"

Maurel knew the answer to this one. "Oh, no, *monsieur*, that would be construed as very bad form."

"Oh, I suppose you are right. Oh, *merde, merde, merdeuh*," said Voltaire, accentuating the schwa of the third '*merde*'. Voltaire sprang up from his bed and commanded Maurel and Zénobe to help him dress. At the same time he spoke to the secretaries. "Wagnière, Bigex, you come with me. I'll get you some lines in edgewise. These court women are long-winded. What takes me an alexandrine couplet to say it often takes these ladies reams of pulp."

Voltaire was dressed in a flash, including his wig that was *de rigueur* during the reign of Louis XV, when Louis XV was young, and escorted out the door by everyone except Diderot. The author of *Les Bijoux indiscrets* considered the courtly lot a royal bore. He took leave of his friend.

Voltaire told him while they headed towards the front of the house, "You are lucky, my friend, that nobody but the Russian court takes a fond interest in you. Catherine has a real head on her shoulders, and a real brain in her head.[65] These French ladies are halfwits whose brains have been squished to mush by their heavy wigs. Too much powder has gone into their ears. I agree with you, my friend. I hate these *cronophages* as much as you do.[66] But what can I do if she has been sent here by the Queen?"

Madame de Polignac was seated in the company of two other ladies-in-waiting. They were being chatted at by *madame* Denis who was enthralled to be speaking with the Queen's favorite for a second time that week. She could not tell these ladies of the court, of course, that it was Voltaire's secret, very secret desire, (not even his secretary Wagnière knew), to one day be received by Louis XVI. After all, Voltaire had been received in all of Europe's other courts. Frederic II of Prussia had had him for two years as his right-hand *philosophe*, although sometimes he treated him like his pet *philosophe*. In addition, Voltaire had written Louis XIV's life-story, and Louis XV's as well. As a matter of fact, Voltaire retained to that very day his title of royal historiographer. Louis XV had never recalled it. If Louis XVI wished, Voltaire could write His Own

---

64   *Madame* Yolande Martine Gabrielle de Polastron, *marquise* de Polignac was Queen Marie Antoinette's favorite lady-in-waiting. So great was the Queen's love for this pretty noblewoman that half of the treasury was being spent on her attire and jewels. The Queen would send her as royal ambassadress on the most delicate of errands.

65   Catherine, empress of Russia, had her husband murdered so she could sit on the throne; aggressive, intelligent, demanding, sexual, she briefly toyed with the *philosophes'* ideas of the "enlightened despot," invited Diderot to Saint-Petersbourg, bought his library, but longrun, disappointed him.

66   Voltaire's neologism, meaning "devourers of time."

Majesty's biography. Youth certainly did not exclude wondrous deeds worthy of being immortalized. *Madame* Denis was trying to shove the conversation in that general direction when Voltaire and his coterie arrived. Zénobe of course was in rapture to be receiving alongside Voltaire (though the truth be told, he was posted by the door), in spite of the fact that he had heard terrible stories of this Polignac woman. This minor aristocrat, who pleased the Queen in a physical way, was apparently a succubus on Marie Antoinette's breast, literally and figuratively, simultaneously sucking at her breast and sucking the royal treasury dry.

General salutations and social niceties ensued which took fifteen or twenty minutes. Coffee and tea were served. The little cakes that Sylvie usually prepared were not present because of the cook's indisposition, but *madame* Denis thought that those that le Parnaud had made in their stead were just as delicious. Voltaire did not try the cakes but had enough time while the three court ladies were munching on theirs to mentally compose and discreetly whisper into his secretaries' ears a page or two more of *Irène*.

Madame de Polignac finally got to the nitty-gritty when she modulated her voice to a secretive stage whisper and said, "*Monsieur* de Voltaire, we are so honored to be in your presence and to breathe the same air you do. *Tout Paris* is agog with excitement. You manage to fill us all with such enrapture that we will be talking of your visit to Paris for years. Imagine! Finally to be receiving the wisdom, in person, from the Sage of Ferney! You couldn't possibly have continued to bury your light in the countryside, even though after so many years living there, Ferney must be the warm hearth where you prefer to be cozy and snug." She smiled at her ladies-in-waiting and they tittered and nodded their heads in the affirmative. "I have also heard from numerous sources, that now that you have left Ferney, temporary as that may be, the tourists on the Grand Tour will no longer have any place to visit between Milan and Lyon. They will probably be forced to visit Geneva! Can you imagine that, going to a place where you are every-where surrounded by Protestants?" Her ladies sympathized with such a predicament. Wagnière glanced at Voltaire, whose eyes were already on him as if to communicate, "These are silly women with empty heads and not worth our trouble."

"The lion has left his lair," the Polignac woman was saying, "and the Grand Tour is missing one of its best destinations."

Voltaire answered, "It is easier, I think, for people to come see me here in Paris, along with the other monuments, rather than in one of the farthest reaches of the realm."

Madame de Polignac laughingly agreed: "Indeed I should say so!" Then she retook her stage whisper, imbuing it with a sense of urgency. "I bring to you an important message from Her Majesty. She has instructed me to tell you that while you are in Paris, she will see to it personally that no mishap, no adversity shall befall you."

Neither *madame* de Polignac nor her Queen were old enough to remember how the younger Voltaire had to suffer being accosted in the street and struck with walking sticks by the valets of the *chevalier* de Rohan before being carted off to the Bastille; somebody must have told them about those 'mishaps'.

"We wish you to know that Paris is a welcoming city to all its children, especially those who are coming back after years of absence, an absence in which you were sorely missed."

Did nobody tell that woman about Louis XV's oral banishment of Voltaire from Paris? It is true that there was no written proof of it.

Zénobe became so angry in Voltaire's defense that he could have speared the Polignac bitch in the eye with one of the fireplace pokers that glowed red in the flames. But one glance at Voltaire's face was all it took for him to regain his calm and composure. He could see Voltaire's jaw muscles working, but the man was all smiles and intermittent thank-yous. His expression said, "I am exercising my smiling muscles, to be polite, but it is nothing but pretense."

"*Monsieur* de Voltaire's arrival to Paris has been even more spectacular than *monsieur* Franklin's," continued *la* Polignac.[67] We assure you both that you have nothing to fear while you are in our fair city."[68]

"Thank you, thank you, *madame*, for your kind words. I humbly acknowledge and express my appreciation for Her Majesty's most generous protection. We in this household are much obliged to enjoy the Court's benignity and safeguard. Indeed, it would surpass our utmost joy to be able to express to Her Majesty personally how beholden we are to such royal kindness."

Madame Denis looked expectantly at the Queen's favorite, who had a few more smiles and said a few more kind words, a sort of palaver that even she could see was drivel. Then the court lady and her pair of ladies-in-waiting took their gracious leave, but not before Voltaire and Wagnière and Bigex had played a bit as a trio of secret ballet and poetic composition-dictation, the two secretaries traipsing behind Voltaire at some secret sign of the *philosophe*'s that only they could discern. *Madame* de Polignac saw flatteringly that the secretaries were taking down her words for posterity. Zénobe saw that their papers were filling up amazingly fast with more verses for Voltaire's play.

What Zénobe could not see was that Voltaire's intimate friend Condorcet, who had read *Irène* the day after Voltaire had arrived, had alerted him to more than a few weaknesses in its composition. Voltaire took his friend's counsel to heart, and it was those defective parts that he was busy rewriting. Condorcet was the youngest of Voltaire's *philosophe* friends and as such was in tune with the latest of literary fashions. He rightfully identified that Voltaire's style as a playwright owed more to Racine of the Seventeenth century than to Beaumarchais of the Eighteenth. Rhyming alexandrine couplets were showing their age, but who was Condorcet to tell his friend Voltaire that his play needed an entire overhaul? This was the man who had held entire Parisian audiences in a trance for weeks on end in 1732 and 1738 with his *Zaïre* and his *Mahomet*. But Condorcet knew that with a few changes here and there to this latest play, the Paris crowd of 1778 would be satisfied, Voltaire would be extolled as the returning King of the stage, and after the curtain fell everyone would go home.

Something else that Zénobe did not see during this conversation with the Polignac woman was that this dainty, porcelain-complexioned doll with delicate features and violet eyes had noticed him. As he stood by the doorway of the *salon*, his image was admirably reflected by a rococo mirror whose coincidental strategic placement afforded *madame* de Polignac ample time to realize that the young man was a counterfeit. He did not stand still, as true domestics were trained to do. If she had a servant this fidgety

---

67   Benjamin Franklin arrived in Paris with two of his grandsons, sixteen-year-old Temple and seven-year-old Benjamin, known as Benny, on December 21, 1776. Parisians lined the streets in the hope of catching a glimpse of this simple "Quaker," discoverer of electricity and a thousand other inventions. He was staying in Passy in one of the estates owned by Jacques-Donatien Le Ray de Chaumont, midway between the *salons* of Paris and the court of Versailles.

68   This was patently untrue, although in her defense *madame* de Polignac possibly never learned of it. A suspicious man barged into Ben Franklin's apartments in early July of 1777 and would most likely have killed him had it not been for the quick-thinking and bravery of his porter and of one of Franklin's friends who seized the intruder and threw him out of the house.

she would dismiss him forthwith. This handsome young man with the tall stature and muscular build was certainly dressed in the uniform of a butler, but he had no wig; his fingers, his hands and his arms were in constant motion; he threw his weight first on one leg, then on the other, his buttock muscles flexing and relaxing accordingly. His shoulders were delightfully broad and strong, his stomach flat, his biceps solid. She could admire his lips that were voluptuous enough although he apparently had a habit of chewing on the lower one. Still, those teeth were white and even. Once or twice his tongue flicked out to moisten those lips. He held his head cocked a little to one side, and his cool blue eyes scanned everybody in the room with what seemed to be a scowl. Drinking her tea and chatting contentedly, *madame* de Polignac had time enough to daydream about kissing those well-delineated lips and sucking on that tongue. She imagined being embraced by those strong arms and feeling the weight of that torso on her breasts. She would know how to remove that scowl and replace it with expressions that would best display his masculine features.

Voltaire was wrong: courtly women were not empty heads; they could think of two different things at once.

André closed the front door fast on the heels of the Petit Trianon triumvirate. After the ambassadress sent by Marie Antoinette was safely out of earshot, Voltaire let loose with a thundering concatenation of vulgar epithets. It truly was a litany of the best cursing Zénobe had ever heard. Voltaire felt much better after the anger and hatred had left his body. *Madame* Denis was disappointed to know that they would never be received in Versailles.

Voltaire started to cough from the departing ire in his throat and said to all present, "Get me back to my room. Their visit has killed me."

As he pulled his wig off and fanned himself with it, he asked Wagnière and Bigex to read back what he had dictated to them. As they read out verses they all walked back to Voltaire's room, including *madame* Denis who was admonishing her uncle for getting upset. All that did, she asseverated, was attack his own spleen and make his blood boil. She suspected that he would have to be bled and that would put an end to all the visits.

That reminded Voltaire of his doctor's visit. "And where the hell is Tronchin? Is the famed doctor to the aristocrats coming, for God's sake? Or is he a country doctor who takes hours to arrive by his patient's bed? He shall find a dead patient by the time he gets here."

Madame Denis rolled her eyes to the heavens.

"He's gotten too famous for his own good," continued Voltaire. "He cures all the *belles dames* of their vapors and their hysteria. It's a good thing he's a Protestant or he'd bed them as well! Bigex, what was the last verse after Alexis says, «*Et j'aurais dû m'attendre à cette atrocité!*»?

«*Il se flattait qu'en maître il condamnait Comnène. Il m'a donné la peine,*» answered Bigex.

Voltaire instructed, "Well, change that to «*Il a signé ma mort.*»[69] That's stronger."

"You'll be signing your own death warrant," said *madame* Denis, "if you don't rest, *mon maître.*" (*Madame* Denis had always called her uncle "my master.")

"With you as my nurse how could it be otherwise? You're the one to make me get out of bed in the first place to meet with people who will finally kill me."

"Yes, my master."

---

69   "And I should have expected such an atrocity. He flattered himself that as master he condemned Comnène. He made me suffer." This last sentence was changed to: "He signed my death warrant."

The *marquise* said, "I'm afraid that was my fault, my father."

"Yes, *Belle et bonne*, but my adored niece could have made that bitch go back with a bone to gnaw on."

"My father!" said the *marquise* in shock.

"Imagine the gall to tell me that I have nothing to fear. Of course I have nothing to fear! I am Voltaire! Who would dare attack me now?"

"They would have to go through me first, my father, my master!" said Zénobe in valiant style.

"Ah, my son, are you still here? I'm glad you are. I have renewed vigor to fight these noble aristocruds[70] and I shall fight the scoundrels to my dying day, which may be sooner than anybody thinks."

Madame Denis rolled her eyes again and said to nobody in particular, "He has been dying since 1756!"

Voltaire was by now in his bed and wearing his nightcap. The pompom danced drunkenly upon his brow. "I am perhaps more moribund than ever, maybe even more!"

Madame Denis retorted, "Yes, that's how you have arrived at the ripe old age of 83 years!"

"84 years. Don't remove the attributes that I deserve."

"Ah, you take care of my uncle, Maurel," said *madame* Denis. "I'm going upstairs to rest. I'll send le Pernaud with his sage tea and his poultices."

She and the *marquise* abandoned Voltaire's room to the men. Voltaire told his secretaries to take a new letter. It was to be an open letter to be published in the *Journal de Paris*. He motioned to Zénobe to come and sit beside him on the bed. "Address the letter to His Majesty Victor-Amédée III, King of Sardinia, Duke of Savoy.[71] Are those his correct titles, my boy?"

"Yes, *monsieur*."

"Let's see. How shall I begin it? Let's try this," he told Wagnière and Bigex. He held out a bony hand as if he were reading the headline of the *Journal*. "*J'accuse*... Oh, I do like the sound of that. But perhaps it's a little too peremptory."

"Oh, no, *monsieur*," said Zénobe. "It sounds just like something that Mahomet would say."

Voltaire chuckled. It's true that he had infused a lot of fire and audacity into that character of his.

Just then the door flew open, and *docteur* Tronchin tore in.

"I advised you to stay put in Ferney. What do you do? In the middle of winter you undertake a long journey and once in Paris you begin to see thousands of people. My God! When you disregard your doctor's orders you disregard them to the highest degree. Not a single one of my other patients is as recalcitrant and as imprudent as you. You want to kill yourself? Well, I'll have none of it. I wash my hands clean of your death!"

"*Bonjour, docteur*," said Voltaire, genuinely glad to see his doctor.

"*Bonjour*, my friend, you old rascal." Tronchin immediately went over to the *petite ruelle* and took Voltaire's hands. "You'll be my bane to your dying day—"

"Which might be very soon," interrupted Voltaire.

"You seem to be in a hurry to get there."

---

70   A*ristocrottes*, in the original French, has a stronger meaning: aristoshits, or perhaps aristocraps.

71   The duchy of Savoy, along with Piedmont and Genoa, was under the jurisdiction of the Kingdom of Sardinia. Not until the Revolution would Savoy become part of the French nation.

"There are things to get done, important people to see, letters to write. We must do our utmost to *écraser l'Infâme!*"

"You and your *Infâme.*" Dr. Tronchin started to remove Voltaire's nightshirt to begin his auscultations. "I have a friend who is convinced that what you have been saying all these years is *'Écrasez la Femme'!*" He pressed on his patient's bladder. "How is your urine?"

"Piddling slowly."

"And your blood?"

"It circulates lethargically. I haven't been bled since you did it in Ferney."

"Oh, that has been way too long. I must bleed you immediately. That will settle your kidneys. *Madame* Denis told me that your strangury was keeping you awake and that your gout was acting up."

"Among other things."

"Well, who will hold the basin?" The doctor was holding a Voltairean foot in his hand.

Zénobe was the closest. "I will, *monsieur le docteur.*"

The doctor's sweeping movement was expert and done in a trice. Drops of Voltaire's blood started to fall from his foot into the basin and then became a leak, and Zénobe held the basin as if he held Jesus Christ's heart itself. As he looked at the bright red liquid whose color seemed to gladden the doctor, Zénobe started to feel something strange that started in his temples and quickly descended into the nape of his neck.

"Quickly!" yelled the doctor. "Catch him!"

Maurel was over Zénobe in a flash and caught him before he could land on the bed and spill the *philosophe*'s blood.

"Poor tyke," said Voltaire. "He's never seen my blood."

"I doubt he's ever seen anybody's blood, from the looks of him," said Tronchin.

Voltaire responded, "I think he saw his father's blood the day he was murdered." He shook his head in compassion. He was already feeling paternal about Zénobe.

"Poor chap," said Tronchin, and as Voltaire told the doctor of Zénobe's tragedy, Maurel half-dragged the boy to the nearest armchair and started giving him some gentle slaps on his cheeks and putting Zénobe's hands on his own cheeks. Zénobe came to and became embarrassed.

"I'm sorry," he said. "Did I faint?"

"Indeed you did, my boy," said Voltaire. "But I have something that will perk you up. My eyes are too weak and my health is too bad for reading your play. But you can read it to me, if you wish, as I lie here on my sickbed. I can do two things at the same time, dictate *Irène* and have *Ibycus* read to me."

Zénobe's joy knew no bounds. He was more awake than at any other time of his life. He had known all along that his god, his... his... *ami philosophe*, would not let him down.

Tronchin continued to probe and prod his patient who continued to feed Wagnière and Bigex more lines. Maurel took Zénobe and André to their afternoon dinner after which Zénobe began André's first lesson: the history of the French monarchs, including all the dullards, drunks, lunatics, imbeciles, liars, cheats, idiots and deviants that had spent their time on the throne of the Franks.

But before he left them, Maurel told Zénobe that he was very surprised that *monsieur* de Voltaire had decided to undertake Zénobe's cases, both as an enemy of feudalism and as a budding young writer. The last literary protégé Voltaire had fostered, a young man by the name of Jean-François de La Harpe, had betrayed Voltaire's trust, forced his affection on *madame* Denis (who had returned it), and then stole manuscripts from the *philosophe* which later showed up published, in La Harpe's name, in different parts of Europe. Zénobe promised himself that he would show his gratitude to Voltaire at every turn and never betray him. Betray Voltaire? The thought itself was not possible.

André proved to be a very good student. His attention to his preceptor was razor sharp. André looked into the cerulean depths of his teacher's eyes, noticed how his beard hairs were already showing on his white skin, and how white and strong his teeth looked. He saw how Zénobe's nostrils flared a little whenever he pronounced an m or an n. He also noticed how passionate he became as he told stories of the injustices done to the people by past kings. His raven blue-black hair danced dramatically around the nape of his neck.

Maurel left the two boys in the kitchen and felt as if he were walking on air. He prepared a tray of coffee, cream, sugar and brioche and placed it on the dumbwaiter. Then he directed himself upstairs to the *marquis* de Villette's bedroom where his master would be just about ready to wake up. (The *marquis* never went to bed before the sun rose.) Maurel gently scratched on the door and heard a rustling from inside the boudoir. He knew to give enough time for the *marquis'* companion to vanish into the secret staircase and return to his own room upstairs. After twenty seconds, Maurel opened the door and sent a melodic "*Bonjour*" into the depths of the *marquis'* curtain-clad bed.

"Hmmmm," came out in return.

After reversing the pulley which brought up the dumbwaiter into the room, Maurel took the occasion of Villette's sleepy stupor to introduce the subject of the new preceptor that *monsieur* de Voltaire had hired for the education of André.

The *marquis* threw the sheets and blankets from off his head and yelled, "Maurel!"

Maurel drew back one of the bed curtains.

"Yes, *monsieur?*"

"What is it that you just said?"

"A certain young man by the name of *monsieur* Zénobe Bosquet has been hired by your guest *monsieur* de Voltaire as a preceptor for our young master André de Corday. I think it will be a good fit."

"Who will be paying this *monsieur* Bosquet's salary?"

Maurel minced no words. "In all honesty, you shall probably do so, *maître.*"

"Oh, this man infuriates me!" grumbled Villette, speaking of Voltaire. "It astounds me that this old man wants the whole world to be educated, especially at my expense! Doesn't he realize that some people need to remain *un*-educated so that they can function in the roles that life dictated to them? When will he rein in this profligacy of liberal policies towards the universe's downtrodden, or at least pay for it out of his own pocket?"

"Need I remind you, *monsieur le marquis…*" said Maurel cautiously, knowing full well that he was close to trespassing on grounds that could have him labeled as impudent to his master. "…that Voltaire undertook your own wife's education? You can certainly agree with all of Paris that *madame la marquise* has been the perfect culmination of *monsieur* de Voltaire's largesse, and that they all think her a worthy companion to the *marquis* de Villette and a *salonnière* with a brilliant future."

"Hmmmff," came the gruff reply, acquiescent to Maurel's statement.

"Moreover," continued the *maître d'hôtel* who was also the *marquis'* right-hand abettor, enabler and facilitator, "you have not yet seen the young Bosquet's countenance."

"Ah, that's the same thing you told me about Corday! And he has yet to show me any affection."

"Patience, *monsieur*, patience. One cannot just take what one admires. Some things are delicate and need preparation. Some things cannot be rushed. Seduction is an art. Besides, now that the two of them are together, I presage an easing of the proceedings. I do believe that they like each other rather well."

"What do you mean, like each other?"

"Let me put it to you this way: when they look at each other, it is with a certain curiosity and…" Maurel paused to choose his word carefully, "tenderness. There is a three-year difference in their ages, so sixteen-year-old André looks up to Zénobe as the big brother he never had. Zénobe is already a man of the world, or so he imagines, seeing the way that he carries himself. It is true that he has lived. And he has had to fend for himself for the past year. And now he has been presented with a little *mignon* of a pupil. Zénobe takes his responsibilities seriously, and he will be devoted to André. He will teach him about history and writing and arithmetic, but I believe there will be lessons that Zénobe himself does not surmise he has in him and that he cannot predict. They will come. I believe these lessons will be those that he himself will learn at the same time as his charge. I will be there, of course, to direct and instruct, push when needed, restrain at times, proselytize when asked."

"Proselytize?" asked a perplexed *marquis*.

"Why, yes. You don't expect 16 and 19 years of tyrannical Catholic upbringing to be washed away in a flash? You don't think human nature to be that unbesmirched by the Church that two boys would be allowed to think that their budding tenderness is an acceptable part of nature? You don't think that guilt will neglect to raise its ugly head and perturb, nay, terrorize two inexperienced young men until it overrides their love? Guilt is the Church's way of subjecting the human race under the dictatorship of a misguided and ignorant fraternity of irrational patriarchs, all under the guise of 'morality'. What did these patriarchs do to earn their authority? They grew old and stooped and grew white beards. That is all. They did not grow wiser. They took the system of morality that they themselves had received and they just passed it on. Perhaps they just elaborated upon it, adding more rules and more superstitions. The only thing that these unquestioning asses can do is replicate the same misery for each generation. That is, until the power of Reason checks their path of destruction. And Reason, thank God, has excellent defenders during our time. You don't think that *monsieur* de Voltaire has a paternal friendship with you for the sake of your intelligence alone? (Did Maurel's tone betray a light touch of irony here?) Do you think that your inclination has dampened for a minute his affection for you and acceptance of you? Do you think that he ever looked upon you with disgust or the contempt of superiority? How many times did I catch you and him depilating each other's beards? How many times did I witness your endearing conversations about your heart's wanderlust and his loving admonitions that you clean up your public image? *Monsieur* de Voltaire is a wise man, who along with *messieurs* Diderot and d'Alembert and Condorcet, accepts us for what we are: manifestations of an impersonal Nature where morality, guilt and remorse play no part. It is men who afterwards create the moral rules to fit their own stubborn misconceptions. And then they blindly defend these rules under the hallowed name of Tradition. Well, we know who wins the war between Tradition and Reason. I say we should have only one moral guide: 'Do unto others as we would have done unto us.' We are what we are, no more and no less, and we sin upon no one. And as God is my witness, I will not allow André and Zénobe to be subjected to anachronistic, dangerous, erroneous and evil ideologies. No catechism will be repeated in this household as long as I have a breath. *Écrasez l'Infâme!*"

For a full minute silence reigned in the *marquis* de Villette's boudoir. Maurel busied himself strenuously with the preparations for the *marquis'* ablutions. Then, in a small voice, the master asked, "Do you think I could have a cup of coffee now?"

The rest of the afternoon was calm. Voltaire rested and had poultices applied to his body. He continued to keep his two secretaries busy. Maurel taught Zénobe his new duties and lovingly took measurements for a new uniform. *Madame* Denis took a nap for most of the afternoon. The *marquis* went out with his guest, leaving through the secret subterranean gallery that exited out by the stables. The servants who felt overworked were much better by the evening. The only visitor who was invited in before supper was Piccinni who regaled the whole household with arias from his latest comic opera. The *marquise* was beside herself: this on the day after Gluck had played scenes from an opera that he was working on, *Écho et Narcisse*. She had indeed arrived, thought the *marquise* to herself, she had indeed arrived.

The Muse Awaits

Unlike most nouveau-riche aristocrats, the *marquis* de Villette was not very ostentatious. The *hôtel* he had built for himself was a masterpiece of subdued, elegant, neo-classic design. To the trained eye it of course still bespoke of great wealth. The fortune he inherited from his father the banker was everywhere, down to the last gold-plated eagle-claw of the last candelabrum foot. Like most aristocrats the *marquis* did not work, but lived off his *rentes*, thus he had an abundance of time to squander on planning the finest architectural and decorative splendors. In view of his special lifestyle, he gave much personal attention to his favorite part of the structural plan: by the *petite ruelle* side of his bed, hidden by painted *trompe l'œil* oak panels which were screened behind the voluminous silk bed-curtains the color of cream, ran a secret staircase. It took one up to the attic or down to the guest bedroom next to *monsieur* Maurel's own rooms on the ground floor. In addition, there was a subterranean exit from the guest bedroom to a secret door in a tiny vestibule built next to the stables. The architect, Charles de Wailly, did not think it unusual for a husband to ask for a secret passageway within the walls of his town house; he had two of them himself.

Monsieur Maurel's living arrangements, as befitting his essential role of overseer and troubleshooter in a very busy household, did not bear the marks of any skimping or sacrifice on the part of the *marquis*. On the contrary, Maurel's two rooms, antechamber and boudoir, bore the marks of a very generous master who had as much appreciation of his *maître d'hôtel's* discretion as for his *sang-froid*. Only Maurel knew of the master's house guest, *monsieur* de Thibouville, who had been coming and going since before the *marquis* had traveled to Ferney, that is to say, before he married. Sylvie the cook knew that a person was staying in a room on the third floor, but she had yet to gaze on that person's countenance. She assumed it was a young woman. The person didn't eat that much. As for the rest of the household, nobody else knew. Of course, the *marquise* could not even entertain a suspicion. A wife was never told directly what her husband's past history had been like, and the wilder the history, the less likely she was to find out. Nobody knew and it was in nobody's interest to know. Maurel kept a tidy and contained *ménage* with no loose strings and no loose lips. For this reason he had had *madame* Denis placed on the second floor even farther away from the *marquis'* boudoir than the *marquise's*. In a back-corner bedroom, she was far from her dear uncle's room as well since that was on the ground floor. The less this rotund little busybody could observe, the better it was for all the inhabitants of this grand *hôtel*.[72] [73]

Also on the third floor, without ever having seen *monsieur* de Thibouville entering or leaving his room, were staying *monsieur* de Voltaire's two secretaries *messieurs* Jean-Louis Wagnière and Simon Bigex. Also up there was his cook Ménalque le Parnaud, without whom all cultural activity in the house would cease, for on the state of Voltaire's bowels hung in the balance all of the wondrous affairs of state played out on the premises and perhaps in the country itself: the whole capital had come to a halt while everyone came to the *hôtel* de Villette to pay his respects to the old sage.

Even the Minister of Foreign Affairs Charles Gravier *comte* de Vergennes had interrupted his important activities during the first four tumultuous days of Voltaire's arrival. By one of those strange coincidences of history, this statesman had just been to the same quai des Théâtins a few steps from the *hôtel* de Villette. In the offices of the foreign ministry on the previous Friday February 6th, he had met with the representative of the government of the Thirteen Colonies of America, Benjamin Franklin, to sign the accords to the first Franco-American alliance in which each country pledged trade and military aid to the other. He didn't know then that on the following Tuesday another luminary would arrive at the same *quai*. In this particular case, it was the luminary Voltaire who had done the most to set into motion the rallying cry of freedom among the revolutionaries of the world's newest nation.

André knew nothing of all this as he approached Voltaire's bedroom on the morning of the philosopher's fifth day in Paris. *Monsieur* Maurel and *madame* Denis were already present, along with *messieurs* Wagnière and Bigex. As André brought a kettle of hot water into the room he could see both the secretaries' plumes dancing over their sheets of paper as Voltaire spoke. He understood not a rhyming word of it.

André had slept much better that night, but he still felt tired. He attributed his fatigue to the perpetual commotion and frenzy that circulated around Voltaire. In bed, the small old man seemed the last thing on earth capable of engendering so much movement. At home in Normandy nobody paid much attention to André's old grandfather who prattled all day long. But here, this old man's prattle was memorialized by two secretaries, and every day the newspapers published for all to see witnesses' accounts of what Voltaire had pronounced on the previous day. André was perplexed. He was puzzled all the more because that morning he had awakened with his face in Zénobe's hair, and that had made his heart gallop faster than if he had been running. He could not fathom why, and his train of thought escaped from his brain as soon as he came into the philosopher's very busy room.

"The actors are coming, *monsieur*," Maurel said to Voltaire. As soon as he saw André with the kettle he motioned to him to place it on a table by the window. Maurel went to it and started pouring the steaming-hot water into a bone china basin. *Madame* Denis started to dip some funny-smelling cloths into the water. They smelled of bread and clay.

---

72   The *hôtel particulier* de Villette still stands, at no. 27, quai Voltaire. On its front wall there is a plaque denoting its importance as a historical site. It states: «Voltaire / born in Paris / 21 November 1694 / died / in this house / 30 May 1778»

73   [From the author] I really must complain. *Herr* Ralph is giving away all my secrets and spoiling the surprises! Nobody need know here the date of Voltaire's death.

"It is such a shame that Lekain won't be among them," moaned Voltaire.[74] To the secretaries he dictated, "*Ne pouvant repousser de sa sombre pensée / le douloureux fardeau qui la tient oppressée.*"[75] Voltaire scrunched up his face into a mournful expression. One of the calamities of old age was seeing one's friends die, but it was especially difficult to take the death of one of his much younger friends. "What a talent he had! He could make me weep at the drop of his intonation."

Madame Denis approached her uncle with the poultices and as she applied them to his lower abdomen she said woefully, "We shall not see the likes of him any time soon." And then she said to her uncle, "Here, drink the rest of your sage tea."

"Thank you, my nurse," said Voltaire meekly like a child. And to the secretaries: "That's it for Act 5 scene 2. What is it we need to do for Act 5 scene 3?"

Wagnière responded, "Irène's rapprochement with her family."

"Ah, yes," remembered Voltaire. '*Allez trouver mon père, allez trouver mon père.*' I don't really like '*Implorez sa pitié,*' so change that to '*Implorez son pardon*' and then follow it with, with, '*Amenez-le ici*' or maybe '*Revenez avec lui...*'" Voltaire interrupted himself to say to nobody in particular, "It is about time that I prepare myself for the hereafter."

"What do you mean, my dear uncle?" asked *madame* Denis in surprise.

"It is time that I made peace with the Church. I have been battling against her for more than fifty years."

The two secretaries' pens stopped in midair.

"You are not proposing a truce, are you?" asked *madame* Denis incredulously.

"Of course not. I just don't want to end up in the garbage heap like poor old Lekain.[76] [77]

"Oh, not you, *mon maître,* that would not be possible," countered his niece. "You will be in a grand mausoleum covered in Italian marble, in a grand cathedral, with statues of all nine Muses smiling down upon you."

Voltaire looked at his niece with such an expression of disbelief for her statement and pity for her naïveté that André could not refrain from emitting a laugh. Maurel

---

74   Henri-Louis Lekain had Voltaire's favorite actor in the *Comédie française* been. He had the day before the *philosophe's* arrival died, at a tragically young age (at least, from Voltaire's perspective; the actor had only 49 years old been). Voltaire had last his actor friend seen when he had for a visit to Ferney in 1776 come. While there, he had in one of the plays which Voltaire presented periodically to the Genevan community acted.

75   From *Irène*: "Not able to push away from her somber thoughts / the painful burden which keeps her oppressed."

76   It is a fact that the Church denied final absolution and burial in a Christian cemetery to actors. Also denied a sacrosanct tomb were prostitutes, regicides, *philosophes,* Jansenists, desecrators of crucifixes and any other individuals who by their actions or beliefs turned away from the teachings of Jesus Christ. But here I am afraid I have again the author in an error caught. Henri Louis Lekain made peace with the Church right before his death and denounced his profession, and was consequently under holy ground buried.

77   [From the author] I wish mightily that the editor had chosen another fact-checker, one who knew about the exigencies of writing historical fiction, including the exigency of brevity which I must defend. I know that Lekain received the full sacrament of Last Rites and was buried on holy ground. For Pete's sake, you can go see his tomb in the nave of the Church of Saint-Sulpice. What I did here, for the sake of brevity, so that I wouldn't have to add another character and another footnote, I blended two historical figures into one. This is called consolidation. It was Adrienne Lecouvreur, Voltaire's favorite actress, who was thrown into the city dump and covered with lime. Voltaire, not being in Paris at the time of her death, was not able to do anything about it. Forever more, Voltaire expressed his shock at the insensitivity, the inhumanity of the Church, and had nightmares about the same thing being done to him.

turned a lightning-fast gaze onto his protégé and André instantly became serious again. He took the empty kettle and made a quick bow before exiting the room.

He was in haste to go see Zénobe. His friend was posted at the door with the instructions to admit only the actors of the *Comédie française*, and no one else. '*Monsieur* de Voltaire is feeling unwell,' he was to say to all callers, 'and cannot receive today.' Only Voltaire's bosom *philosophe* friend, Condorcet, would be allowed to keep him company.[78] Oh, and if the ever-popular *docteur* Tronchin deigned to arrive, he should be let in as well.

It was to be an easier day, and André was feeling, for some inexplicable reason, happy. He waited by the vestibule until Zénobe came back inside and shut the door. Zénobe was already wearing his very own butler's uniform tailored to his dimensions. André thought he looked dashing. His breeches followed closely the outline of his anatomy. *Monsieur* Maurel had added at the last minute little red and blue epaulettes with gold tassels which lent Zénobe a military air, and André told him that they suited him.

"Ah, thank you, André. What is happening with *monsieur* de Voltaire?"

"He's speaking of his death."

"What do you mean?"

"He said he doesn't want to be thrown into the city dump, which is apparently where an actor friend of his ended up."

"Well, he won't end up there if I have a breath left in me."

André watched with fascination his friend's nostrils flare in anger. His eyes spit blue fire. He realized that he wanted nothing more than to continue watching his firebrand friend, but he knew he would be needed in the kitchen.

Zénobe apparently caught a look in André's eyes, because he approached him and asked, "What is it?"

André was caught off guard. "Nothing," he said, "nothing."

The door-knocker filled the vestibule with its metallic echo, and Zénobe backed away from André.

"I have to go to the kitchen now," André said quickly, and spun on his heels.

Zénobe went back to his task. "No, *monsieur* de Voltaire regrets to inform you that he is not receiving today for he is feeling ill... No, it's nothing serious, just a case of indigestion... Yes, yes, I shall tell him, goat's milk sounds wonderful, but I believe he's imbibing that already... The doctor is expected to see *monsieur* de Voltaire sometime today... It is *docteur* Tronchin... Yes, the one from Geneva... Yes, he is a very good doctor, indeed..."

All morning long everybody gave medical advice to Zénobe, mentioning camphor leaves and basil compresses and bloodletting from Voltaire's earlobe. Unfortunately, neither he nor anybody else, not even *docteur* Tronchin, knew the real identity of Voltaire's ailment.

---

78   Marie Jean Antoine Nicolas Caritat *marquis* de Condorcet, forty-nine years Voltaire's junior, was, of all the *philosophes*, Voltaire's favorite. The reason for this can only be surmised. Was it Condorcet's vehemence in his own fight against the Church that made him the elder philosopher's brother-in-arms? Was it his skepticism of all things religious balanced by his ardent belief in a humanistic moral code? Was it his personal overwhelming compassion for the victims of injustice caused by the intolerant Church? What is not in question was that Condorcet was adored by Voltaire as if he were a member of the family.

"Then I shan't go out today," said the *marquis* de Villette to *monsieur* Maurel as soon as his *maître d'hôtel* had told him that the actors of the *Comédie française* were coming that afternoon. "And I'm glad you woke me up early. I'll need more care with my *toilette* today."

"But what shall you do with *monsieur* de Thibouville?" asked Maurel with a look of nervousness about his eyes.

"Oh, yes, yes, yes… What shall I do with *monsieur* de Thibouville. Well, he can just stay in his room."

"He will not like that, *monsieur*," answered Maurel who knew that if the *marquis'* gentleman friend were told to stay in his room he would be like a caged hungry lion. "May I remind the *marquis* that *monsieur* de Thibouville's rooms are right next door to *madame* Denis' boudoir?"

"You are right, of course. That won't do. He'll come out as soon as he hears the hubbub from downstairs. He'll recognize *madame* Vestris' voice. It always rises to the rafters. Well, he can stay in my room. That's what we'll do. We'll bolt the door."

"*Monsieur*! Please be reasonable. You know very well that the *marquis* de Thibouville cannot be contained. He will make a scene. People will know that he frequents this house, that he *lives* in this house. Why, if *madame* Denis…"

"I know, I know, you don't need to remind me of all that. No, no, you're right. I shall see to it that he's out of the house. I'll send him on an errand. Don't worry, Maurel, I'll take care of it. Leave it all to me."

Maurel answered, "I was going to, *monsieur le marquis.*"

As soon as Zénobe let the troupe of actors in, madness ensued. Who would have thought that a group of eight human beings could make such a splendid racket. Zénobe was taken aback: a bunch of wild children suckled by a she-wolf would have been more circumspect. Spontaneous and free-spirited, the actors, led by *madame* Vestris, gamboled and joked all the way to Voltaire's boudoir. It was after dinner, when around two in the afternoon,[79] André relieved Zénobe at his post by the front door, but Zénobe forewent his own meal in order to witness this marvelous human spectacle.

The stentorian cackling in Voltaire's room turned into a roar of laughter after the *philosophe*'s welcoming statement to *madame* Vestris: "*Madame*," said the old man with a peevish smirk, "I worked for you last night like a young buck of twenty."

"I am sorry, then, that I wasn't here to guide your indulgent hand!" came the response. *Madame* Vestris was not a candle, but a torch burning resplendently. Her lack of daintiness was obvious even in her voluminous hair, her own real hair, dark wavy brown thrown negligently all to one side of her face and neck. Her smile was larger than life, and her laughter voluble and authentic.

Zénobe stood transfixed upon the scene. *Madame* Vestris had come to *monsieur* de Voltaire's bed and flung herself full-length on him, her body over his body. Voltaire was in rapture. *Madame* Denis grunted in horrified disgust and ran out of the room. But neither Vestris nor Voltaire saw her leave. They were giving each other kisses on both cheeks.

---

79   Meals in the Eighteenth century were breakfast, dinner and supper.

"*Monsieur* de Voltaire, *monsieur* de Voltaire, how I adore you, how I've missed you. If only our jailer would let us out every once in a while I would have come to see you in Ferney.[80] All of Europe goes to the shrine of the sage of Ferney but us, and we have more reason than others to go adore you. Without you, we would be starving to a horrible death."

Voltaire knew that she did not mean starving from lack of food. "Ah, my beautiful, talented, splendid, voluptuous coquette. Every once in a while, less now than when I was younger, the Muse throws me a morsel of sustenance that I gladly share with you."

"But what a morsel! It feeds us all and invigorates our soul and gives us the courage to go on!"

All of the actors acclaimed this last in unison. From his bedroom the *marquis* de Villette heard this last uproar and knew the troupe was in the house. He hurried down the stairs to be among their party.

The two secretaries had laid down their pens and paper and started merrily to greet everybody in turn. At the *marquis'* appearance, the five actors and three actresses all planted two kisses alternatively on each of his cheeks, that is to say, four for each one, or thirty-two in total. *Monsieur* de Villette was happy that his wife was not in the room to see Vestris infuse her kisses to him with extra abandon.

"And here is this improbable scion of a philosopher's loins! What have you got to say for yourself, you scoundrel? You know you left *madame* Métis high and dry after your last escapade. The duke himself had to intervene, and you know how he hates to get involved! Poor *madame* Métis was sent to the provinces!"

"That is indeed a shame," said the *marquis* with a half grin. "She will be sorely missed."

"I'm sure the feeling is not mutual," said Vestris. "But life must go on!" She turned her attention to Voltaire once again and went to sit in bed by his side. She beckoned to the *marquis* patting the space beside her and he squirreled himself into the bed as well. Zénobe marveled at this strange *ménage à trois*: an outrageously unceremonious *actrice* lounging on the sheets between an aristocratic fop and a celebrated *philosophe*. Everybody else draped themselves on sundry chairs, stools and a *chaise longue* in the room. As soon as the *marquis* took his position on the bed he noticed for the first time the new butler-valet who was standing by the door. He was off the bed again before the young man could react.

"Ah, you must be..." said the *marquis* as he leaned in to greet Zénobe.

Monsieur Maurel was faster than the *marquis*. "...*Monsieur* Zénobe Bosquet, of Annecy, *monsieur le marquis*," he announced before the *marquis* could say anything that would wound the young man's honor or pride.

"Yes, yes, *monsieur* Zénobe Bosquet. Maurel here was telling me excellent things about your person and character. Is it true, then, that you are a victim of your *seigneur*'s feudal rule? It is difficult to have to bear this sort of news that in our Europe of today these horrible things still exist."

"What, *monsieur le marquis*?" called out Voltaire's bed companion. "In today's Europe? Where have you been living? Under a bush at the Jardins des Tuileries? The *duc* de

---

80   The jailer in question was the *duc* de Richelieu himself. As the duty supervisor of the *Comédie française* he ran it like he ran everything else, as if it were his own little kingdom where he was the unquestioned despot. Lekain had hated the duke all his acting life at the *Comédie* and could not hide his antipathy for his patron. It was widely suspected that the actor's death was not entirely natural, and that the duke was not entirely innocent.

Richelieu manages his actors as if we were his personal serfs. We don't have the liberty to relieve ourselves in the cloak room during rehearsals if he doesn't see fit!"

Poor *marquis* de Villette. He was visibly torn between going back to bed with Vestris or continuing to chat up his new butler-valet-preceptor. Zénobe won the battle.

"But you must come and tell me about your troubles, young man. In this house you will not suffer any insults or prejudices from any of its inhabitants."

Nobody heard Maurel's groan because it was inaudible to anyone but him. He bodily came between the *marquis* and Zénobe as if he were shielding the boy from a marauding bear and the *marquis* thought it best to go back to his position in bed.

When the *marquise* de Villette came into the room a few minutes later and saw her husband sharing the bed with Voltaire and *madame* Vestris, she laughed and exclaimed, "Why, my husband is in bed with another woman in my very own house. What is this world coming to?" (She did not know that her husband was in bed with another man just about every night.) Then she greeted the actors with delight since she had known them all of her life. Her youth as Voltaire's adopted daughter had been quite different from the norm, and she did not share the common belief that actors were intrinsically immoral. Refreshingly sincere, yes. Ebullient and transparent as well. In spite of their assumed professions they did not cloak their real feelings.

Zénobe was very well entertained that afternoon. *Madame* Vestris kept asking Voltaire what she should feel in certain scenes from *Irène*, and she tried on several moods and countenances for size and Voltaire asserted that they all fit her very well. The secretaries would look for the appropriate scenes among their papers and the actors would take part in the impromptu bedroom production. Voltaire put a stop to it by exclaiming that they should all come back on the following day for a real rehearsal. They all agreed enthusiastically. Of course *madame* Denis was livid when she found this out later: "How are you going to get better with all this fracas going on," she shouted at Voltaire and stormed upstairs letting her room door slam behind her.[81] [82]

In addition to the amusement he felt at that afternoon's diversion, Zénobe was also intrigued by the *marquis'* keen interest in him. True, *monsieur* Maurel as well had been very obliging and sympathetic towards him since the very beginning. He wondered if the *marquis* remembered that their eyes had met five days ago? Zénobe had never had a master of an aristocratic house be so fawning towards him. His lord in Savoy had always ignored him. This new attention made him feel important. It also made him feel appreciated that *monsieur* Maurel never let his eyes wander when Zénobe was deep in conversation with the *marquis*. The *marquis*, however, would wander back and forth between the actress and his valet. After a while, Zénobe thought that the *marquis* was perhaps being obsequious with him, pestering him too much with worries about his past troubles in Savoy. He was relieved when the actors left and he was free to give André his afternoon lesson. He had already planned his lesson in his mind beforehand and was rather looking forward to spending this quiet time with André. André was as

---

81 I must an omission at this junction identify. The major theme of the conversation between Voltaire and the actors on February 14th was the death of their fellow actor Lekain. Voltaire, who had fainted when he first the news heard on the day of his arrival to Paris, shed copious tears and commiserated with *madame* Vestris and the other actors. Lekain had a true and longtime friend been.

82   [From the author] Dear Lord, I have a back-page driver here. Yes, Lekain had been a famous actor and Voltaire sorely missed him, but the reader doesn't know the actor, and the actor's life and death do not add significantly to my story. If *Herr* Ralph only knew how many other details I had to cut from my story, in the effort to keep the book under 500 pages. Because of these extraneous footnotes, this effort might fail.

compliant as the *marquis* was overbearing, and he much preferred his role of preceptor to a servant boy than as the target of a sycophantic *marquis*.

Part of his lesson for that day was on the orthographic change of words ending in '-ois' but that were pronounced '-ais', so that '*françois*' should be spelled '*français*'. Voltaire had already proposed this change years before to the *Académie française* but the intransigent old fools of that august organization had minimized the problem and waved aside the recommended solution. The simplicity and logic of Voltaire's spelling reform had not seduced the majority of the Immortals. All by himself, Zénobe had already changed his own writing to reflect the philosopher's dictum, as had thousands if not millions of other francophones throughout Europe, including Catherine II Empress of Russia. That afternoon, Zénobe taught André that Voltaire was more influential than the whole *Académie françoise* put together.

Rehearsing

In order to avoid the previous morning's consternation of waking up with his face in Zénobe's silky hair, André had decided the previous evening to sleep with his head at the foot of the bed. This did not help the situation any because when he woke up in the morning his eyesight was on a level to see Zénobe's feet, and the sight of the short black hairs growing on his friend's very white toes along with the pattern of veins along the side of one foot caused André as much anxiety as the feel and smell of his friend's hair had the previous morning. His pulse quickened. He stared at the beautiful patterns that the hair follicles made on the middle joints of his friend's toes, and gazed at his strong calves where the hair on his legs started abruptly at his ankles, almost as if it were a carefully sown hem.

André had an overwhelming impulse to lift the bed sheets over Zénobe's legs and continue a close inspection of his sleeping form. Did the hair on Zénobe's legs get thicker? André untangled his own legs from the blankets and saw they were practically hairless compared with Zénobe's. He pretended to lift the sheets for just a moment to enable himself to shift his weight on the bed, and he caught a quick glimpse of Zénobe lower body, a hairy thigh, a bulge straining against his woolen undergarment. This made André's mouth turn dry and his heart gallop faster. As he lay there looking up at the gathering light at the window, he realized that he wanted to take another look. What compelled him to want to do this and how he would achieve it, he didn't know. His chest felt constricted, his face flushed. He decided to get out of bed in order to have another excuse to take a peek at Zénobe. This he did, with the slowest of motions, holding his breath and taking a little longer this time, and with the utmost of care, since he didn't want to wake his sleeping friend. He held the sheets up while he slowly slipped off the bed. Zénobe's body was fascinating to watch, and on top of that fascination, André felt the titillation of one who can see but whose presence is unknown. André had time enough to make out the outline of Zénobe's penis. Part of Zénobe's nightshirt was drawn up and in the darkness under the blankets André could discern a profusion of hair on Zénobe's stomach. Zénobe stirred, but André kept the sheets up as he pretended to get off the bed. Finally Zénobe murmured, "It's cold." André dropped the sheets and got out of bed. Only then did he realize it really was very cold.

"Time to get up?" asked Zénobe with his eyes still closed.

André's first attempt to speak caused his throat to seize up since his saliva had all dried up. He cleared his throat. "Yes," he managed to say. "It's time. *Monsieur* Maurel will be coming in soon."

Monsieur Maurel came in as if on cue. Of course as soon as he took in his two boys with an all-embracing glance, he detected that André was flustered. The boy quickly turned towards his basin of water. Zénobe was half-asleep.

"Wake up and from your eyes shake the cobwebs away," said Maurel with a musical intonation. "We have a busy day today."

"Yes, *monsieur* Maurel," answered Zénobe while André continued splashing cold water on his face.

"I trust you both slept well?" asked Maurel as he sat on the edge of the bed.

"I did, very well, thank you, *monsieur,*" answered Zénobe who then turned to André and asked, "How about you, André?"

André could not turn around because he realized his arousal would be visible to the two of them, so he looked over his shoulder and said, "Yes, very well, I slept like a, like a, like a baby." He quickly went to a corner chair on which his breeches were draped and quickly put them on. Maurel missed none of his discomfiture.

We must let nature take her course, Maurel thought to himself. I love nature. She will come out no matter what one tries to do. She is untameable. Rousseau is right. We must all try to go back to our primitive natural selves. We must identify within us the good part of ourselves before civilization stifled us and made us artificial, callous, and unnatural. To find our true '*anima*' we must put our trust in nature.

Maurel, who had received a good education, had always loved the Latin word for soul. It allowed one to appreciate the life force that animates human beings. This most intellectual of *maîtres d'hôtel* entertained the happy thought of André and Zénobe living in a hut in a forest, dressed like savages, that is, barely dressed at all, clambering up trees to gather eggs from birds' nests, and running after boars on the prairie, then after a feast dozing deeply by a pellucid mountain stream. He had never really lived anywhere but in the city. But his imagination painted jungles in the liveliest of colors, and river banks on an American prairie were decorated with wild bird calls and blood-red sunsets. Zénobe getting out of bed broke his reverie.

Maurel wasn't ready to get out of their room until both boys' ablutions were over. Only when both of them were fully dressed did he turn to leave, but Zénobe stopped him with a timid voice.

"*Monsieur* Maurel?" he ventured.

"Yes, *monsieur* Bosquet?" Maurel suddenly realized how à propos Zénobe's family name was. *Monsieur* Little Forest.

"I wish to thank you for everything you have done for me. You saved me from a terrible danger. The streets of Paris are hard—"

Maurel interrupted him. "Shush," he said. "I recognized your talents immediately. You would have gotten along very well without my help, I'm sure. You can offer this household much service and the *marquis* de Villette and I certainly appreciate your presence during this time of agitation and excitement."

Zénobe looked so sublime in his butler's uniform that Maurel couldn't help pressing the young man's lapels down onto his chest and fluffing up his epaulettes. Then he took him by the shoulders and planted two strong kisses on either cheek. He then offered André the same treatment to offset any jealousy. "Thank you," he told both of them. "Thank you for your good service, wonderful service."

They looked at each other and beamed.

"Come on, then, let's go," he told them. "Look bright, it's going to be another full day."

The *Comédie française* actors brought a nervous animation that flared up the whole *hôtel. Madame* Vestris was so electric and fidgety that she would have given Mesmer a short circuit.[83] She kept torturing a lace handkerchief and pacing up and down the *salon* as if she were already on stage. Voltaire had been placed on a *chaise longue* in a corner of the grand room. Unnecessary chairs and the harpsichord had been moved into adjoining rooms. The actors thus had ample space to act out their play, although Vestris kept crowding the other actors out.

The rehearsal was going stupendously well with Voltaire yelling enthusiastic comments. Condorcet, d'Alembert, Diderot and Grimm[84] were there to offer both moral support and necessary suggestions, although Voltaire was going to make damn sure that *Irène* remained a classic tragedy and did not become one of Diderot's teary *bourgeois* melodramas. The *marquis* and *marquise* de Villette along with *madame* Denis and Voltaire's two secretaries were playing the role of the audience. They were joined by the *marquis'* own secretary, Ursus Requain, in case the pace of dictation for changes and additions became too fast. Ursus was a small monkey of a man, hairy and bowlegged; Maurel never knew why the *marquis* had this secretary in his employ, but he suspected that the man's gracious handwriting was not the least, nor the biggest, of his talents.

André's task was to support the cast and spectators by bringing or removing props and refilling their wine glasses, which was quite often. Zénobe, stationed at the door, had strict orders not to let anyone in. Maurel was busy in the kitchen overseeing the preparations for dinner, since everybody had been invited to both the afternoon meal and later on that evening for supper as well. It was to be a day dedicated to rehearsal. And the rehearsal would have continued going very well had it not been for the unfortunate arrival of the composers.

Maurel's absence was the reason why Zénobe allowed the two musicians to enter. Christoph Willilbald von Gluck had come to visit Voltaire on February 12, and Niccolò Piccinni had come the day after. Gluck had at first delayed a trip to Vienna and then canceled it outright, in view of Voltaire's momentous return to Paris. Piccinni also was beside himself with elation to have the *philosophe* among them. Since both musicians' previous visits had filled the *hôtel* de Villette with such irrepressible gaiety and wondrous music, Zénobe naïvely felt that their visit today would also be considered opportune. Indeed it would have, had the two musicians come at separate hours. Without consulting a soul, the inexperienced butler invited the composers in, explaining that *monsieur* de Voltaire was rehearsing his actors.

Zénobe was a sensible young man who had received a commendable education in the provinces, but nobody had thought to teach him about music. If someone had, perhaps Zénobe would have been aware that Gluck's arrival fifteen minutes after Piccinni's

---

83   Friedrich (Franz) Anton Mesmer, in Paris in 1778, came to see Voltaire at the *hôtel* de Villette but was turned away; Voltaire did not fraternize with pseudo-*philosophes*.

84   *Baron* Friedrich Melchior von Grimm, a good friend of Denis Diderot, was another of the *philosophes* and helped them to spread liberal ideas throughout Europe with his prolific letter-writing.

would turn out to be a combustible event.[85] Adding the actors' kinetic sparks as they played the tragedy of *Irène* would be the *pièce de résistance.*

The Neapolitan composer took his place with the audience, sitting beside *madame* Denis. The Austrian composer, upon espying his rival homologue in the salon, preferred to sit with Voltaire and the four other *philosophes.* Recognizing his good friend d'Alembert, he sat down next to him. Piccinni followed Gluck's every move with his peripheral vision. Gluck tried very hard to pretend that Piccinni was not there.

It was the first scene of the second act that the actors were playing. When the brave Alexis hesitates before seeking audience with his caesar, he explains that it is remorse which slows his pace. The audience murmured its agreement that it was indeed remorse and not cowardice, *madame* Denis rolling the word *"remords"* deliciously in the back of her throat. Piccinni remarked to no one in particular that some people were born coldly incapable of remorse. A few verses later when Alexis feels the pangs of guilt for loving the wife of his caesar (*J'ose être son rival; je crains le nom de traître;* I dare to be his rival; I fear the name of traitor), Gluck mentioned in passing that some people in society were always meant to be traitors. When Alexis hints that the caesar Nicéphore is the usurper of the throne that by all rights should be his, Piccinni said, a little louder this time, that usurpers always took over by force what they could not get by the rights of reason. When Alexis tells Nicéphore to his face that he will not yield to his despotic ways, Gluck said even louder that he would never yield to Machiavellian and other Italian methods. When Alexis promises with dashing courage that he will never be Nicéphore's prisoner, Piccinni cried out that his fate would never be circumscribed by any tyrant. When Alexis asserts his valor in the face of despotic oppression (*Ce tyran ténébreux, ce despote aveuglé!* That gloomy tyrant, that blinded despot!), Gluck yelled out that he would never give in to heavy-handed cowardly attempts to curtail his art. When Alexis finds out that his beloved Irène, Nicéphore's spouse, has been arrested by this most despotic of rivals, and then with his face to the heavens cries out for liberation (*Ce palais funeste a produit l'habitude et de la barbarie et de la servitude!* This deadly palace has produced the habit of both barbarity and servitude!), Piccinni rose from his chair and proclaimed an end to all *barbarie* and *servitude.* Gluck rose from his own chair and demanded an end to the affliction of slavery. When Alexis excoriates the caesars who sit on their frightful thrones and think that they can reign without laws and speak like sultans (*nos césars pensent régner sans lois et parler en sultans!*), Piccinni and Gluck were at each other's throats.

Luckily harpsichordists never attempt to hit hard since they don't want to break their fingers. Still, it took several of the actors, the *marquis* and André to separate them. It was at this particular moment that Zénobe let *docteur* Tronchin into the house. The doctor, who expected to find a docile Voltaire being treated in the tranquility of his boudoir, found him instead yelling at the top of his lungs, running around the *salon* trying to regain peace among his guests. Tronchin, recognizing Gluck and Piccinni immediately, realized that his moribund patient was trying hard to reduce the resentment that both musicians apparently harbored for each other. The *philosophe* kept yelling

---

85   Gluck and Piccinni were at opposite ends of the *Querelle des Bouffons,* a musical quarrel that pitted all European musicians, including Jean-Jacques Rousseau, into two camps: pro-French versus pro-Italian music. Vituperative and vindictive, the conflict made even the King and Queen take sides. After the dust settled, the quarrel resulted in the eclipse of French lyrical opera behind light Italian opera buffa, to which Mozart and Beaumarchais would join their own forces.

that this *salon* was no place for the Quarrel of the *Bouffons* to have a battlefield. He was seconded by his fellow thinkers. This *salon* was meant for intellectual pursuits, pointed out Condorcet, not martial ones. This *salon* is for cogitating and conversing, not fighting, yelled d'Alembert. Why do artists have to be so pugilistic, asked Grimm. Diderot was the only one who had remained in his seat, but he did call out for "Peace, my brothers, peace!" Meantime, the "audience" had dispersed among the actors and let their own opinions be known. Maurel and the kitchen servants came to take a look at what was happening. From the front vestibule Zénobe heard the clamor and abandoned his post. He could not believe his eyes and ears. At first, he thought it was all part of the play. "But in what kind of play does the audience join the actors and vie with them?" he asked himself. He thought that *madame* Denis was overacting.

The doctor's Protestant voice put a stop to all others. "What in all the gods' names are you doing?" he yelled at Voltaire. "You are supposed to be dying in your room and here you are recreating the Battle of Saratoga in your *salon*?"[86] Tronchin was so angry he sputtered. "Of, of, of, of all people you should know better! Where is your precious reasoning here, I ask! Where is the rational thinking of which you all speak so highly here? I have seen more rational discussions at *les Halles*!"

Voltaire was so abashed that the only thing he could think of doing was to faint. His frail little body started to crumple and sink, but luckily Zénobe was on hand and in a blink of an eye had caught his *philosophe*.

"Ah, there, you see, you see?" Tronchin continued berating the crowd. "Is this what you wanted? Are you all satisfied now? Are you all happy that *monsieur* Voltaire is going to meet his demise here and now?"

Zénobe really thought that Voltaire was dying and started to weep. "*Monsieur* de Voltaire, *monsieur* de Voltaire! Don't leave, please don't leave!" His tears were copious and warm as they fell on Voltaire's face.

"Give him room, give him room!" yelled *madame* Denis whose face registered authentic emotions of fear and hysteria. "Let him breathe, let him breathe!"

Vestris started to wail like only an actress could, using her diaphragm.

André forgot who and where he was and sank into a chair, his fist at his throat.

Zénobe laid Voltaire's limp form on the *chaise longue* and other hands placed cushions up and down his body to keep him from falling.

Maurel had gone into the kitchen and back in a flash, carrying a bowl of water and some pieces of cloth. *Madame* Denis tore the cloth away from Maurel's hands and plunged it into the cold water. In a second she was applying it to her uncle's forehead and neck.

Vestris shrieked. "He is dead! He is dead! His face is white! Someone bring a mirror!" Her intention was to place it under Voltaire's nose to see if his breath condensed on it. "What are we going to do?" she moaned, wringing her hands. "Opening night is in a month!"

Zénobe was sobbing over his hero. *Docteur* Tronchin unceremoniously pried the young man from Voltaire's body and released him to the closest person, who happened to be the *marquis* de Villette. Maurel tried to edge in closer to his master but it was too late. Zénobe buried his face in the *marquis'* shoulder and sobbed and the aristocrat, envisioning himself as a virile Alexis come to life, tried to console him.

---

86   The recent Battle of Saratoga was on everybody's mind. October 17, 1777 was the turning point of the war for independence of the Thirteen American Colonies and helped turn the tides of opinion in Europe. The news did not hit European shores until December 4.

Vestris flung herself at Voltaire's feet, wailing sonorously, while *madame* Denis, the color drained from her face, stood at attention. The four *philosophes*, with Diderot front and center, struck poses of disheartened fatality. The two musicians tried to make themselves small, for they knew that the newspapers the next day would say that it was they who had killed Voltaire. For a few seconds nobody moved. All were frozen in a tableau of overwhelming disbelief. Finally, Tronchin waved a vial under Voltaire's nose. The patient inhaled rapidly and opened his eyes. "What happened?"

There was a loud sound of relief which came from everyone but Tronchin. "Is this what you want?" he asked the old man. "Between your strangury and your gout and your capricious intestines one would think you would be a sensible man. But, no. You are exposing your health to serious calamity."

Zénobe wanted to pull away from the *marquis* to see his hero but the *marquis* held on.

"Oh, my master, we thought you had left us," said Vestris with tears sparkling in her eyes.

Madame Denis' relief was overpowering, and touching. She started to tremble all over. If her uncle were gone, she really would not know how to keep on living.

Maurel walked to André, swept him out of his chair, walked to where the *marquis* was still clutching Zénobe, and encircling both young men with his arms walked them both out of the room and delivered them into the kitchen, which was empty now since all the servants were gathered at the entrance of the *salon* to see what tragedy had befallen Voltaire. Maurel went back to gather his flock of servants so they could get *monsieur* de Voltaire's sage tea started, the bleeding cup readied, the camphor oil and the quinine poured, in sum, all the things that needed to be done to bring an old man back to life.

While Maurel was gone from the kitchen, André took one look at Zénobe, saw that he was still very affected with turmoil and emotion, and took him into his arms and whispered in his ear, "He'll be all right. The doctor will revive him. You'll see." They stood there embracing for what seemed to be a long time. Then André pulled away to go into the pantry and poured out a glass of the *marquis'* favorite cognac. "Drink this."

Zénobe emptied the glass in one backwards flick of his head. "More," he instructed.

André filled the glass and again the contents were gone in a flash.

This time it was Zénobe who gathered André into his arms. He felt consoled and energized by his friend's touch. The incoming servants gave them nary a glance since they were too distraught from the events in the *salon*, but Maurel gave them a deep draught of an ogle, taking them both in with his eyes.

"I refuse to believe that a man of your experience, cerebral talents and encyclopedic knowledge would neglect that which reason so completely dictates to one in your situation." Tronchin was giving his patient an earful. Voltaire was still stretched out on the *chaise longue*, sunken in a sea of cushions. The actress was still at his feet, cradling them in her arms. *Madame* Denis was in a chair holding one of her uncle's hands in hers. His other hand was providing a pulse for the doctor to feel. Tronchin continued, "I am of a mind to write a letter to the *Journal de Paris* to let all of Paris know that you must be left alone. *Tout Paris* is killing you and you are letting them do it."

Vestris looked up at the doctor and spoke for *le tout Paris*. "It is just that we love him, *monsieur le docteur*. We don't have him here with us all the time, and we can't stay in our own homes knowing that he is here. We love him so very much!"

Voltaire smiled at his favorite actress. *Madame* Denis was still so relieved about her uncle not being dead that jealousy had no room to breathe within her expanded bosom.

"Yes, you are all loving him to death!" exclaimed Tronchin.

"But what a glorious death it will be," said Voltaire, with a flourish of panache in the movement of his eyebrows (since all his other extremities were in use). He was thinking metaphorically, like in literature, not literally. Voltaire had always been such a busy man that death had never seemed to be too real to him, despite what Montaigne had said about philosophy, that to philosophize was to learn how to die. To Voltaire, preparing for his death was a lot like rehearsing for one of his plays. He continued to believe that he would always be on hand to bow before his adoring public on opening night.

Docteur Tronchin left the *hôtel* de Villette that afternoon and went directly to the printing presses of the *Journal de Paris*. There he dictated an open letter to the City of Paris to be published the following morning, saying that the philosopher Voltaire was an aged invalid who could not possibly continue to tolerate the onerous agitation of the interminable visits to which he was being subjected. Inexplicably, for he usually was more circumspect and discreet than this, in an unpardonable breach of the code of confidence of medical ethics, he placed the responsibility of Voltaire's life, and possible death, squarely on the *marquis* de Villette and his entire household. "If the situation continues unabated," ended Tronchin's letter, "his strength must soon be exhausted, and we shall all be witnesses, if not accomplices, of the death of *monsieur* de Voltaire." Tronchin was Genevan, and in spite of his having moved to Paris five years previously, he still did not know Parisians. All his letter did was exacerbate the visitations, for now truly *le tout Paris* wanted to pay their respects before Voltaire actually died. The following day, February the 16th—a Monday for goodness' sake!—saw more than a thousand visitors trying to come in.

There was to be no afternoon lesson for André this Sunday. The household was swarming around its most precious inhabitant with frantic and nervous energy. The old man needed much attention. Still, Voltaire felt much better as soon as Tronchin departed, along with the two contrite composers who had grown so meek and affable that they practically walked away arm in arm. The recuperating patient pleaded with *madame* Denis and the actors to resume their rehearsal of *Irène*, and he promised them that he would sit still and say nothing. He said he would leave the editing process to his four stalwart philosopher companions. They proceeded cautiously.

In the meantime, while his *maître d'hôtel* was busy elsewhere, the *marquis* de Villette came into the kitchen looking for his butler. Having been hugging the bereft boy the way he had in the *salon*, he was wondering if he couldn't use his prerogative as master of his house to promote Zénobe to chamberlain, but wanted to tell the servant boy himself before he approached Maurel gingerly with his decision. The *marquis* may have been the master, but Maurel ruled behind the throne, and the whole household knew it.

The *marquis* found the two boys before the pantry doors. Zénobe was still a bit unstable, so the *marquis* instructed André to pour him out a cognac. "As a matter of fact, pour us both a glass of cognac. And you have one, too, Corday," he said to André, feeling generous and consoling.

André did as he was told, and Zénobe sipped his third glass daintily. The first two were already warming his veins.

"You had a big scare, didn't you, my boy?" asked the *marquis*. Without waiting for an answer, he asked, "What is it about Voltaire's fainting spell that made you panic? You very well realize that he won't last forever."

"We, uhm, he still has many things to do. His tragedy, for one."

"Oh, that play is already written. Besides he has his four friends to help him out, and myself as well, I might add."

The *marquis* had tried several times, and failed every time, to have himself elected member of the *Académie française*, and almost died of jealous apoplexy when La Harpe *père*, was elected in 1776. Villette had had several volumes of his own fiction published in luxurious tomes of marbled calf leather, gilt tooled spines, and bordered by gilt embossing inside and out. He fancied himself an indispensable author. "Many an author has achieved greater success posthumously," he told Zénobe in order to make him feel better, speaking of Voltaire, as if it were possible for that author to be even more famous.

"I admire *monsieur* de Voltaire a great deal, *monsieur le marquis*, and his death would be such a blow to all the world."

"Yes, indeed it would. And it would take place in my house. Be that as it may, I would like to find out," and here the *marquis* put his hand around Zénobe's shoulders and walked with him away from André, "I would like to find out, and you will tell me if you are in complete agreement, of course, since I would never want you to do something that is against your wishes, and those of Maurel's, I would like to find out, and mind you, you can take your time to decide, all the time you want, there is absolutely no pressure, my boy, I was saying, I would like to find out if you would mind being promoted to the position of chamberlain."

Zénobe repeated, "Chamberlain, sir?"

"Yes," insisted the *marquis*. "Chamberlain. You do know what the duties of a chamberlain are?"[87]

"Yes, I most certainly do, *monsieur le marquis*. Most of the communication, what little there was, between His Majesty Victor-Amédée and my family was conducted by his chamberlain Lovera di Maria of the House of Savoy."

Nineteen-year-old Zénobe, his loathing for aristocratic appurtenances notwithstanding, knew he needed a diplomatic response to the *marquis'* invitation. He did not want to leave Voltaire, and he did not want to leave André, either. Besides, the streets of Paris scared him to death.

"Thank you, sir, for your most generous offer," he told the *marquis*. "You do me such an honor as I don't deserve—"

---

87   At that time, of course, everybody knew what the duties of a chamberlain were. Usually, however, such a position was reserved for the highest echelons of the aristocracy, the chamberlains of the King, the Princes, the Ministers, for those who, in addition to being important members of their society, also were in possession of essential governmental posts and who therefore needed assistance in the successful acquittance of their duties. The *marquis* de Villette, although far wealthier by far than most aristocrats, could not, in his wildest dreams, be justified in purporting to be of such lofty stature.

"Oh, be quiet, you deserve it and more!"

"–that I am at a loss as to what to say."

"Well, say yes, then. It would give me great pleasure to see you getting on in the world."

The *marquis* realized that something was troubling Zénobe. "What is it, my boy?" he asked impatiently.

"What about André? He has been here a while longer than I have, and I would be saddened if he felt unappre–"

"Oh, don't be silly, boy! André is a very serious, very responsible boy and he carries out all tasks before him quite satisfactorily. But André, as good a worker as he may be, has not your education and your bearing. He is only sixteen years old. He perhaps has the family credentials, but the Corday family hasn't had money in years. Your family perhaps doesn't have the crest and the escutcheon that all could wish for, but your person certainly has the outside appearance and the intelligence to become a successful chamberlain. Now, I need to return to the *salon* and I don't want to hear about any more obstructions. I need to attend to our house *philosophe* and Maurel needs to be apprised of the situation. I will tell him of our decision." Then he added a quick "*n'est-ce pas?*"

"Yes, *monsieur le marquis*," said Zénobe respectfully. He wasn't quite sure that all was legitimate and proper, but he was certain that he did not want to leave the *marquis'* household. If he were to refuse the *marquis'* offer, perhaps he would succeed in wounding the aristocrat's dignity, and then be dismissed from the premises. He could never willingly separate from Voltaire at this stage of the philosopher's life. Besides, he still wanted the *don Quichotte* of the downtrodden to help him in his political quest to make things right in his country.

The *marquis* de Villette left his quarry and André immediately came to ask Zénobe what the *marquis* had said to him. Zénobe told him everything. André said he understood, although he really couldn't grasp but a tiny part of what was happening. He understood enough to tell Zénobe while shaking his head, "You know, last fall, before any of this was happening, we did have a chamberlain. It happened before the *marquis* went off to marry. *Monsieur* de Voltaire had wanted to help a young man in Ferney but couldn't use him there, so he sent him to the *marquis* de Villette here in Paris. I remember that part of the story very well because this person's presence caused such havoc in the house. He was such a snob, wouldn't talk to anybody in the household unless it was to command or scold. Two other boys who had been here before I came on left because they couldn't stand that *énergumène*[88] being here. *Monsieur le marquis* and *monsieur* Maurel bickered often about what the chamberlain's exact duties were. They never did arrive at a conclusion. Let me think, what was his name, what was his name?[89] Oh, I don't remember, but he had already been at his post for a while before I arrived. In any case, the *marquis* dismissed him in a big row that upset the whole house. There was yelling and screaming, from both the *marquis* and his chamberlain. It was terrible, and very

---

88   This word has no proper translation. It is said of someone who rants as if possessed by the devil.

89   His name was Michel Alexandre de La Harpe, son of Jean François de La Harpe, and as much of a weasel as his father. La Harpe *père* had enjoyed the patronage of Voltaire and lived for free with his wife in the château in Ferney. He repaid his host, first by stealing some of the philosopher's manuscripts and having them published, and pocketing the profits, and second, by toying with *madame* Denis's affections. *Madame* Denis fell under La Harpe's power, and left Ferney from February 1768 until October 1769. La Harpe *fils* learned just as well the paternal lessons of using friends, dropping names, and defrauding confidences.

embarrassing. Ah, I remember. His name was the name of a musical instrument. *Monsieur* du Violon? *Monsieur* de la Trompette? *Monsieur* de la Flûte? *Monsieur* du Hautbois?"

Maurel returned to the kitchen at that moment and stopped André's recitation. Maurel said curtly, "There's no time for a lesson this afternoon. I thought I had made that clear. *Monsieur* Bosquet, go to the front door. No one else is to be granted admittance, absolutely no one else. I don't care if it's Jesus Christ himself. André, go to *monsieur* de Voltaire's bedroom and help get it ready. As soon as the rehearsal is done he will go back to bed. He will be having supper in bed." He turned towards the stoves to find out what was happening to the preparation of the meal. Zénobe stopped him.

"*Monsieur* Maurel?"

"Yes, *monsieur* Bosquet?"

"The *marquis* de Villette has asked me to become his chamberlain."

"What?"

"The *marquis* has asked me if I would agree to become his chamberlain."

Maurel gave a look of dire supplication up to the heavens and extended his hands out to the side, half as if he were pleading, half as if he were already nailed to the cross. It was acting that was equal if not superior to what was going on in the *salon*.

Maurel returned to himself. "We shall see about that, *monsieur* Bosquet. *Monsieur le marquis* is sometimes, how shall I say it, too enthusiastic for his own good. He does not believe in letting the pace be natural and slow. He is a failed *philosophe*, you see. He has the intelligence, certainly, to be one, but he was never one to wait for the results of an experiment, or for the conclusion of careful deliberation, or even for a caterpillar to become a butterfly. He would like to rush nature and all of her creation and catapult himself into a future of his own making, but in the end, it is that very future that is going to unmake him. The course of events cannot be rushed, should not be rushed. 'To everything there is a season, a time for every purpose under heav'n; a time to be born, and a time to die; a time to plant, and a time to reap.' "

Zénobe continued the verses. " 'A time to kill, and a time to heal; a time to break down, and a time to build up.' "

André began to chant as well. " 'A time to weep, and a time to laugh; a time to mourn, and a time to dance.' "

The other members of the kitchen heard what was happening and felt moved by the recitation. Everybody was on edge after the frightening and realistic scene of Voltaire's rehearsal for his untimely demise. They could not help but join in as well.

" 'A time to keep silence, and a time to speak; a time to love, and a time to hate; a time of war, and a time of peace.' "

After this momentary impromptu communion, everybody went back to work feeling teary-eyed and strangely buoyed. They were the inner clockwork that made the household perform. They were the springs and cogs that enabled this stage to produce its theater. They were the "*machina*" that would be there for the "*deus ex*", whenever that came. They all felt deeply the responsibility of what their house was providing for Paris, for France, for Europe, for the rest of the world. They were providing the stage for Voltaire's last days on earth.

Voltaire himself provided the ending for this hectic day's events. There was trouble with the second and third scenes of the fifth act. The actors were uncomfortable with the timing, and the *philosophes*, for once speaking of a voice, criticized the justification of certain actions of the characters. Voltaire in disgust tore those scenes to bits of paper. "Rewrite," he announced. "We must rewrite."

His energy had returned, the Muse burned in his veins and in the brilliance of his eyes. He began to compose at such a pace that Diderot turned to d'Alembert in awe and said, "Now I can see how he wrote *Olympie* in six days."

D'Alembert retorted without removing his admiring eyes from Voltaire, "And on the seventh day he rested."

The three secretaries could hardly manage to keep up. They would each write alternating rhyming couplets, but Voltaire was too fast for them.

"Get me *monsieur* Bosquet," said the old playwright. "Go get me *monsieur* Bosquet!"

The *marquise* de Villette rushed to the front door and unceremoniously pulled the butler-valet into the house by the arm. "Come, quickly," she said, out of breath, her tall coiffure swaying. "*Monsieur* de Voltaire needs you!"

"*Monsieur* de Voltaire needs me?" asked Zénobe in utter incomprehension and delight.

As soon as he was in the *salon,* Wagnière gave him some paper on a wooden board and Bigex gave him a pen and Requain plopped the ink well closer to him, and the four of them dipped their pens alternatively and took furious dictation for the world's most famous dramaturge.

In spite of the frenetic pace of the dictation, Wagnière, Bigex and Requain were able to notice between ink dips that Bosquet was managing to keep up with them. But it was Wagnière who noticed first, and then the other two realized, something truly bizarre. They could not refrain from being surprised, perhaps a bit shocked, when they saw that *monsieur* Bosquet was holding the board with his right hand, and that the quill which danced in the air stupefyingly fast was dancing above his left hand, and that left hand was writing from right to left. They could not give too much time to this observation, and the queasy feeling it brought them was gone in a Voltairian *hémistiche.* In a flash, all were giving their full attention to Voltaire's definitive version of the momentous and thrilling act V of *Irène,* the last act of the last play that he was to put on the stage.

February 14, 15 or 16, 1778

Initiation into Courtly Comportment

During one of Zénobe's sorties to les Halles, or perhaps when he was sent to summon *docteur* Tronchin, an unknown and elegant *berline* sidled up to him and reduced its pace in order to remain beside him. Zénobe stepped closer to the walls of the building he was passing in order to give the *berline* more leeway, but the vehicle stuck to his walking pace. Curious, he looked towards it, but the glass of the windows was opaque, black, and the only image it afforded him was his own puzzled countenance staring back at him. Looking up at the coachman, he saw a mound of a figure draped in black robes among which he could not see any face.

Zénobe stopped. The horses were reined in and the *berline* came to a halt a few paces in front of him. The door opened, and a woman's gloved hand emerged, beckoning him to approach. The glove was shiny as satin, and brilliant rings adorned three of the five fingers. Zénobe thought he recognized the hand, but just as quickly he discarded such an inane idea.

What would she want with me, he wondered.

The dainty little hand disappeared within the darkness of the interior.

Out of curiosity he approached the door which remained ajar. When he was next to it, the door swung all the way and a female voice cheerily called out to him, "Enter, young man! Be at your ease, I promise I won't bite. Well, not at first, anyway."

Zénobe's surprise knew no bounds. It was indeed she! What would *madame* de Polignac, the Queen's favorite lady-in-waiting, want with him, a mere butler at the *hôtel* de Villette?

Sweet perfume wafted out of the vehicle. The elegant hand reappeared with a big brown button on its palm.

---

90   [From the author] The reason for the puzzling aspect of these chapters entitled «Mystery Chapter Specimens» is two-fold. First, even though it is fairly certain that the actions—and activities—described therein did take place, or rather, must have taken place, the time in which they transpired is indeterminate and speculative. "Must have taken place," of course means that eventual actions during later events must necessarily derive from these initial contacts between individuals. Second, these Ur-occurrences are not corroborated by any written conveyance from the contemporary participants of the period covered by this chronicle, not even in the journal of André Corday, whose proximity to Zénobe Bosquet must have rendered him an eyewitness to these events, or at least privy to them. In order to remain an omniscient author, I have tried to reconstruct the timeline of these events to the best of my ability. When the participants of certain scenes remain tight-lipped, it is frustratingly difficult to recount their association with any degree of accuracy.

"Look what I have for you, young man. I wager you've never had one of these!"

Too curious for words, Zénobe stepped into the *berline* and sat opposite the lady whose voluminous skirts took up all the space on her seat.

Finally remembering his lessons on courtesy, he bowed in his seating position and said, "It is a pleasure to see you again, *ma chère dame.*"

Obviously, caught by surprise like this, Zénobe had forgotten that only a few days ago he had thought of skewering this refined courtly lady through the eye with a fireplace poker. But here she was now, Marie Antoinette's meddling lady-in-waiting, now patiently waiting for him, a graceful hand held aloft in front of her, palm down. After a few seconds, Zénobe finally figured out what to do. He gently took the lady's hand and brought his head down towards it. He knew enough not to actually kiss the back of her hand; his lips just hovered over it for an instant before he released it.

"The pleasure is all mine, I assure you," said *madame* de Polignac in the breathless carefree way that was her fashion. Another of her distinctive characteristics became conspicuous: she blushed scarlet, which set off her violet eyes to great effect. She had kept this dramatic feature from her youth and had learned to apply it in all sorts of social encounters for it brought her beneficial reactions from others. In the same way, she had learned that strategically allowing her beautiful eyes to tear up at poignant moments yielded profitable results as well.

She flipped her hand onto one of his own and the button landed in his palm. Zénobe looked at it. It was no button. It was thick and round but had no holes in it. It was also softer than he had thought.

"You eat it," she said helpfully. "Try it. You'll see. You'll like it. I wager you will adore it!"

Zénobe took the button and smelled it. Then he nibbled it on one side, tasting for the bitterness of a dangerous substance. It did taste bitter, but there was a concomitant sweetness that thrilled him. He popped the whole thing into his mouth, and the button seemed to melt in anticipation of his delight. It was like the host of the Eucharist, only this was thicker, and dark brown, and way more delicious. It was gone in an instant, and he barely had to chew.

"Don't worry, there's more!" said *madame* de Polignac, who proffered a transparent silk bag full of the heavenly buttons. "It's chocolate!"[91] [92]

While Zénobe was engaged in untying the knot of the silk bag, the noblewoman quickly closed the door and with a baton wrapped in ribbons thumped twice on the roof of the *berline*. The vehicle lurched forward.

As Zénobe stuffed more chocolate discs into his mouth, *madame* de Polignac laughed melodically and swept up her skirts to allow the young man to sit beside her. He took the invitation and changed seats. Still giggling, she closed her eyes, opened her mouth and stuck out her little pink tongue, as if to receive Holy Communion. Zénobe placed a disc on it and she closed her lips tight around his finger. This unexpected movement startled Zénobe and he removed his finger as if it had been burned. Her eyes opened and she leaned her head towards his and kissed him. He could smell her perfume, and

---

91   Chocolate (*Theobroma cacao*) had to France in the 17th Century traveled, but it even into the 18th a food only of the gentry remained. Seeing as it came from France's tropical colonies, it was expensive to import and expensive to process.

92   [From the author] I wish mightily that *Herr* Ralph, even though he means well, would not interrupt my most dramatic scenes.

before he knew it her soft lips parted and he could taste the chocolate. It was heady, the aroma, the savor, and when he brought his hand to her face, the touch of her smooth skin.

His provincial distrust, his qualms about Parisian aristocrats, his enmity against the ruling class, they all melted away as easily as the chocolate in his mouth. In spite of his prodigious book-learning, his youth and bucolic upbringing had imbued him mostly with candid naïveté and ingenuous gullibility. He was so far gone into this experience of luxury and sensuality that he could not even identify the danger he was in. No snare could have been so invisible. No spider's web could have been this silken. The closest his imagination could come to the true actualities of what was happening to him was that he was a Roman patrician come to the boudoir of Jezebel, or was it Salome? Perhaps Delilah, but Zénobe all of a sudden was intoxicated by the bravado of masculine pride as he began to lift layers of tulle and silk brocade, Indian muslin and Florentine taffeta trimmed in gold braid, satin and, way down, Flanders lace and stiff baleen (in the corset). No scratchy wools here, nor dingy linen nor fleece nor flannel. Everything that touched *madame* de Polignac was velvety and soft, and Zénobe plunged his senses into a lavish world of indulgence.

Wherever the *berline* started its journey, whether it was close to les Halles, or close to the Palais-Royal where *docteur* Tronchin lived, or even if it was initially someplace else, it began a lethargic amble in circuitous routes around what would later be called the First Arrondissement. Once on the quays it would pick up speed. It crossed the Seine several times, going into residential areas, going as far as the Marais where the dilapidated aristocratic homes of the preceding century lay in an attitude of ruined splendor. It is doubtful if the occupants of the vehicle had the wherewithal to admire the passing scenery, but a more comprehensive tour of the old parts of Paris could not have been possible. It is certain where the *berline* ended its excursion. It was at the Bois de Boulogne, uninhabited as it is today, and deserted in the daylight. Only nocturnal forays by brigands or sexual adventurers were *de rigueur.*

The *berline* came to a stop. The door opened, and out tumbled a young man, disheveled and discomfited, unsteady on his feet and uneasy in his comportment. He seemed not to know where he was. He started to climb back into the *berline*, but the door slammed shut and the vehicle took off at high speed. The young man looked after the trail of dust climbing higher and higher into the air. Closer in, one of the horses had left a pile of round brown turds that was still steaming in the cold.

Thank his peasant upbringing, for the lad looked towards the sun, which was difficult to pinpoint through the dark branches of gnarly trees and the February clouds, but as near as he could find it, he regained his bearings and started walking towards the east, eventually traipsing through Passy and into Paris. He was easily able to get back to his interrupted task, no worse for wear, perhaps a bit more worldly, definitely a lover of chocolate. [93] [94]

---

93   I have kept quiet until now, but in the name of the Truth and of Disclosure, I must the reader alert to the specter of the P word, anathema to any author. Has *monsieur* Luna not learned the laws governing literature, has he not realized that one cannot "borrow" whole scenes from previous works of literature and incorporate them into one's own? Emulation is one thing, but wholesale appropriation is another.

94   [From the author] Hapless *Herr* Ralph, how I pity you! From your comments I gather that you have never had even the remotest experience similar to the one that Zénobe underwent with *madame* de Polignac. Truly, you have never made love in a vehicle while driving around Paris? You never had an amorous bent, I'm sure, or otherwise you would know that this sort of thing goes on all the time in the City of Love. Why I myself, in that same Bois de Boulogne, in a taxi… Well, perhaps I should not disclose such details. I feel sorry for you, *Herr* Ralph, that you should raise the accusation of Plagiarism simply because you have never enjoyed such an experience. Even that stick-in-the-mud Flaubert had that notch in his belt, at George Sand's insistence, of course, although they limited it to kissing, heavy petting and fumbling while fully clothed. I do suggest you try it, Herr Ralph. You are still not too old. It is an exhilarating adventure: the speed, the turns, the squeak of the springs, the bumpy potholes, the sudden decelerations, the honk of the klaxon, and, above all, the activity, the hubbub, life as it goes on around you a mere few feet beyond the confines of the vehicle, it all serves to excite you to a fever pitch, like the frenetic pistons on the motor engine. Of course, in the Eighteenth century it would have been the clackety-clack of the horses' hooves. I will, however, accept the charge of emulation: I have always loved Emma, admired her passion, and felt compassion for her misfortunes, even though she brought them onto herself.

A Plethora of Visitors

During the night André had not bothered to sleep with his head at Zénobe's feet. He was too tired after that day's scare and commotion to predict trouble with the sleeping arrangements. It wasn't until he woke up at dawn that he realized he should be nervous about being next to Zénobe. The crux of the matter was that André was much too aware and sensitive about his friend's corporeal presence in bed next to him. Why this should be so, why discomfort would be the overwhelming feeling that he could identify, he could not know. Why did he not feel indifference to his friend's being there in bed with him? Even as he slowly came to consciousness, he realized with anxiety he had been dreaming of a feeling on his left arm. Perhaps that was what had awakened him. He could feel a soft grazing and warmth, and realized it was the hairs on Zénobe's arm that were barely touching him. Without a thought, André pressed his arm squarely against his friend's, and felt the warmth increase. Like an automaton, he brought his other hand over and with his fingertips he felt along Zénobe's arm, feeling the soft skin, feeling the hair thickening towards the wrist. He listened for Zénobe's breathing and heard it was regular; he was still asleep. André felt anger welling up inside of him. Why couldn't Zénobe ever wake up before him and be out of bed before he was? Why was it always up to him to wake up first? Before, when he slept alone, waking up had not been fraught with such complications.

Still, André couldn't keep himself from doing what he did next: he brought that left arm of his down and reaching with the back of his hand, he felt for Zénobe's body. His hand made contact with Zénobe's undergarment. André took his hand farther down and made contact again, this time with bare skin. The back of his hand was touching Zénobe's thigh. If his bed companion woke up now, André could pretend he was still asleep. Asleep? His heart was pounding against his chest. He could hear his pulse in his ears. Something else was throbbing, too. The penis that Voltaire had commended for its size and health was straining against his linen drawers. This was too dangerous. He drew back both of his wandering hands and moved to the edge of the bed, as far away from Zénobe's body as he could. Zénobe stirred and sighed with a moan. Then, under the sheets, much to André's surprise, Zénobe felt around for his bed companion's hand and in a flash found it and brought it back to his thigh. André felt his head go woozy and his pulse double its already frantic pace, but could not bring himself to any more action.

Dawn slowly rose about them, and lying still all André could do was follow its light as it materialized the shadowy contents of the room: his clothes draped on a chair, Zénobe's butler suit hanging from a peg by the doorway, a print of a smirking Voltaire that Zénobe had propped up on the table, candles of varying heights rising from mismatched candlesticks, Zénobe's books, the white ceramic bowl and glass pitcher filled with water standing next to it. As the light grew, André's heart rate lessened and he felt frightened no longer. The room was still the same; he enjoyed seeing his friend's possessions mingled among his own. He tried hard not to think of Zénobe holding his hand against his thigh. He could hear his friend breathing rhythmically.

They heard the others starting to stir, and then they heard some of them greeting *monsieur* Maurel. André moved quickly and Zénobe let go of his hand. By the time Maurel entered their room, André was like in a daze in front of the bowl, pouring water out of the pitcher.

"*Bonjour*," sang Maurel, "rise and shine, the sun is shining to the east and all must scurry awake!"

"*Bonjour, monsieur* Maurel," said the boys in unison.

Zénobe asked with a look of concern, "*Monsieur* Maurel, how is *monsieur* de Voltaire this morning?"

"Absolutely fine, more than fine. One could not tell that he fainted yesterday. He still has trouble urinating and the small of his back is wreaking havoc with him, but other than those two perennial symptoms, he is feeling just fine. *Madame* Denis was already in his room by the time I got there. She's a very capable nurse to him."

"I am glad," answered Zénobe as he got out of bed.

It was his turn to splash water on his face and neck and as he did so Maurel admired from behind that the freezing water did not take Zénobe's breath away. The *marquis* de Villette always needed to have his water heated. Thibouville had to have his scalding. These two country boys, however, were used to the vigors of winter and the simple ways of a rural milieu. One day, Maurel thought, he would buy a farm in Normandy and live where the air was clean and pure. He would invite his boys to live with him. Everybody would be so happy. They would live in harmony with nature, cultivate a *potager*, cook together, and eat as a family.

But Maurel could not linger and daydream when the day was just starting. There were many things to do. When his two boys were ready, he escorted them into the main house and the three dispersed to go about their duties.

Benjamin Franklin came calling on this day. He had not been able to come the previous week because he had been very busy, together with his French counterpart, the Minister of Foreign Affairs, Charles Gravier, *comte* de Vergennes, hammering out the wording to the new treaty uniting their two countries in military defense and commerce. They came to the *hôtel* de Villette together, the two elderly statesmen, basking in the glow of heartfelt congratulations from the people already in the *salon*. These included many of Franklin's friends whom he had known for years, either from his political connections, from his social affairs, or from his scientific endeavors. Condorcet, probably Franklin's closest French friend, who was enamored of the scientist as well as of the person, was already at the *salon*. Condorcet had said of Franklin that he was "a man who believed in the power of reason and the reality of virtue." The mathematician had yet to miss a single day since Voltaire's arrival, and today, being the only one to know of Franklin's surprise visit, had come early. The Minister of Finance, Anne-Robert-Jacques Turgot, another friend of Franklin's, was also present. Antoine-Laurent Lavoisier, the chemist, the discoverer of oxygen, the Farmer General (tax collector) and, most recently, the Manager of Explosives, greeted his old friend with pride and warmth. Another scientist, *docteur* Ignace Guillotin, with whom Franklin had had many a pleasurable conversation on the building of a modern utopia, was on hand, one more man of science who would be on hand to give testament to today's momentous occasion of the first meeting ever of two peerless minds.

Many ladies were present at the *salon* that day as well. These included the already famous and the famous-to-be: *madame* du Barry, the countess who had replaced *madame* de Pompadour in the arms of Louis XV, today unwelcome at the court of the priggish Louis XVI and his holier-than-thou Austrian-born Queen Marie Antoinette; *madame* du Deffand, *salonnière* whose *salon* remained the most eminent in all of Europe, though now elderly, blind and feeble, her imposing intellect and acid tongue could still in seconds shred reputations or emasculate men not worthy of her mordant, cynical wit; and *mademoiselle* Necker, daughter of the man who would replace Turgot as Minister of Finance and who, after she was to marry the Swedish minister to Paris, would become an author to be reckoned with under the name of *madame la baronne* de Staël. Of course, *madame* de Polignac could not be pried away. Her entry into the Villette *salon* could hardly be denied in view of her preferred status at Versailles. Such beauty, such grace, so many jewels hanging from her ears and wig! Her vainglorious ways were not surprising in view of her meteoric rise in the court of the Queen from a peripheral aristocratic family scionette to principal Lady-in-Waiting to Her Majesty Herself.[95] It was Zénobe, stationed at the door, who announced her, and she walked regally by him as if he did not exist. But before he could form a thought excoriating her fickle morals and her feigned indifference, at the last second before stepping into the *salon*, she brusquely thrust into the bewildered butler's hands her gloves and her fan, without even looking at him. She sailed away from him in winsome poise and criminal sang-froid.

The *philosophes* had their perennial quorum as well and were well represented: aside from Condorcet, also present were Diderot, d'Alembert, Grimm, and a newcomer, *l'abbé* Étienne Bonnot Condillac, author of *The Essay on the Origin of Human Knowledge* and *Treaty on Sensation*, which espoused the idea that thought is not innate but is derived from sensations and experience.[96]

It must not be forgotten either that another class of persons was present on the day Benjamin Franklin came to call on Voltaire: the servants. Except for André de Corday who came from aristocratic but impoverished stock, the rest of

---

95   All of *madame* de Polignac's family and relatives received lucrative posts at Court, at great cost to the Royal Treasury and at great animosity from the other aristocrats. Marie Antoinette endeared herself to no one in France, except perhaps to the jewelers, the perfumers, and the dress- and wigmakers.

96   *Essai sur l'origine des connaissances humaines* and *Traité des sensations*, published in 1746 and 1754.

the staff all originated from a solid bourgeois or even *hoi polloi* milieu. Though not as fortunate to have been born to a better name or to have a Voltaire to help them rise from their station, as was the case of their mistress, the rest of the staff had not done too badly either. Zénobe Bosquet, for instance, had in a few days banished the vestiges of rusticity from his bearing just by existing in the Villette residence while demonstrating great promise for higher learning. The two cooks, Voltaire's le Parnaud and the Villette's Sylvie, together, were the envy of the surrounding environs. Suzanne, Philippe, Henri and *madame* Denis' Hélène were all proper, dignified, discreet individuals who were proud of their service to both the Voltaire and the Villette retinues. Their presence in the *salon*, though intermittent as they went about their duties, was as substantial as it was important.

Also present at the *hôtel* de Villette on this day were Jacques-Donatien Le Ray de Chaumont, at whose estate in Passy Franklin was sojourning, along with his beautiful and gracious neighbor, Anne-Louise Boivin d'Hardancourt Brillon de Jouy, with whom the flirtatious Franklin had fallen "furiously" in love, throwing to the winds of desire with abundant *innocent* flirtation the commandment about coveting the wife of one's neighbor. Yes, Franklin flirted innocently, lightheartedly and frivolously, and never bedded the ladies he wooed. In the American's defense, he had not concealed his attentions from her husband, although the truth was that *madame* Brillon de Jouy limited her American suitor to kisses, embraces, and sitting on his lap, calling him "*mon cher Papa.*" *Monsieur* Brillon de Jouy, along with *le tout Paris*, had noticed Franklin's amorous attentions towards his wife. One day, having returned home unexpectedly the husband wandered into his *salon* to find his wife and the First Electrician standing next to each other but facing opposite walls, noticed their amusingly guilty countenances, and said sternly to Franklin, "I am certain that you have just been kissing my wife." And, as he rushed towards him, he added, "My dear doctor, allow me to kiss you back in return!"[97]

Benjamin Franklin and Voltaire had never met before today, so this was an electrifying moment for all the witnesses present at the *salon* de Villette. The American came to visit Voltaire with his grandson in tow. Temple Franklin was 18 years old and served as his grandfather's private secretary. In the year that Temple had been in France, he had learned to speak the language fluently, much better than his grandfather, and had conquered half the hearts of all Parisian *demoiselles*, a lot fewer than had his grandfather. He was a younger, taller, leaner and longer-lashed version of his proud grandfather. The *marquis* de Villette looked the boy up and down as he tried to find a reason to borrow him from Franklin for a day or two.[98] *Messieurs* Franklin were accompanied by the older man's fellow diplomats—a veritable

---

97   Of course, no one yet knew that *monsieur* Brillon de Jouy was being unfaithful to his wife with their children's' governess, whom one of Franklin's American colleagues, John Adams, had described as a "plain and clumzy woman," in contrast to *madame* Brillon who was considered by all to be a true rare beauty. Even Adams, ordinarily a stick-in-the-mud, was so struck by her beauty that years later it loosened a superlative from his pen: "*Madame* Brillon was one of the most beautiful women in France."

98   A second grandson, Benny, 9 years old, who had also accompanied the old man to France, was preparing to go to boarding school in Geneva.

American delegation in *madame* de Villette's *salon*–John Adams[99] and Arthur Lee (both of whom had served as commissioners in the lengthy, and touchy, negotiations of the Franco-American alliance),[100] the dashing naval captain John Paul Jones, and Franklin's extremely handsome secretary Edward Bancroft.[101]

The *marquis* de Villette's eyes flitted from Temple Franklin to Bancroft and back, but Bancroft eventually won the aristocrat's undivided attention. The sage from Philadelphia made an image only on the periphery of his retina.

The rebellious colonists came in, then, in tandem with the Minister of Foreign Affairs, *le comte* de Vergennes, all were introduced and seated, and immediately the talk turned to *mister*[102] Franklin's scientific discoveries, marvelous theories, pragmatic witticisms, and playful *bagatelles*.[103]

Voltaire and Franklin, of course, had recognized each other immediately. Their images were being sold as prints and medallions on every street corner and both were identifiable just by their garb. Franklin joked that he was more visible than the man

---

99   I must my abhorrence at this junction of the story declare. When I first read this scene, no letter, not even an electronic mail transmission, was adequate to my sense of indignation, and I threw economy to the side for I needed a transatlantic call to the author to make. Mind you, I am not even supposed a note at this juncture of the text to write, but I must caution the reader that a liberty has been here taken, due to the fact that on 16 February, 1778, John Adams could not have by the side of Franklin been, for the exact reason that he was across the Atlantic, on his ship, the *Boston*, buffeted by high seas and ferocious freezing winds, waiting for a break in the inclement weather, about to set sail for France. The ship had barely left Boston, had gotten only as far as Marblehead, where for two days the roaring seas kept it at anchor. Not until 17 February were they able Cape Cod to clear and their voyage to resume.
When I was able finally *monsieur* Luna to reach, I in no uncertain terms my umbrage communicated, and he stammered–I believe that he very nervous was–that all this he knew. But that as a writer of fiction he felt he was allowed "to slide" or "glisser," he in French said–some historical events into others. That interaction between Adams and the other characters did in fact take place, but at a later date. *Monsieur* Luna also said that *madame* du Deffand, as well, had not been present on 16 February, 1778, but only a couple of weeks later, a statement which miffed me because I had not that particular anachronism caught. He said that this was to heighten the dramatic effect, and to shorten the length of the novel. Curtail, synthesize and abridge, such are the exigencies of fiction. *You should try it*, he told me. Moreover, according to *monsieur* Luna, his literary agent (who, by the way, has an angel by heaven to me sent been), has many forceful reminders for expediency made, because people no longer purchase thick books.
Our transatlantic conversation then to a halt came because professor Luna had to go teach class. I see, dear reader, that my role as blurber must now to other functions expanded be: I gladly take on the role of historical policeman, and I promise to inform whenever the author has from verifiable paths strayed. "Historical truths are but probabilities." [Voltaire: *Philosophical Dictionary*, article «Truth»] Voltaire never said anything about historical truths being possibilities.

100   Franklin always viewed his two aides as being more of a hindrance than a help. Adams was vain and paranoid, Lee was bilious and a rigid perfectionist. Neither was given to compromise. Sadly, such temperaments, which are not very useful to diplomats, boiled over in jealousy and resentment of Franklin, who was the minister plenipotentiary. Historians concur that Franklin the French and the Americans together single-handedly brought, and the treaty was in spite of his two commissioners signed. But this success would be marred by the character assassination that Adams and Lee were surreptitiously for their leader back home planning.

101   Bancroft served as Franklin's secretary for official business; Temple took care of his grandfather's personal correspondence.

102   Pronounced as a homonym of "*mystère*."

103   The gay and frivolous, devil-may-care attitude of the Parisian aristocrats inspired Franklin to pen some of his best texts: clever and amusing word pirouettes which show off best his witty, playful, but still humanist, side. They are a joy to read.

in the moon.[104] In these popular images the American wore more often than not his signature coonskin cap. This Canadian fur-cap was emulated by many in Europe. Even Jean-Jacques Rousseau took to wearing one, but not at the rakish angle that Franklin sported his. Tonight, however, Franklin wore no head covering, not even a wig.[105] Voltaire wore garb that had been stylish during the reign of the preceding monarch, including an oversized wig that cascaded down to his shoulders. The *dernier cri* in wigs was lighter, smaller, less undulating, but that would not have suited Voltaire's personality. Franklin came in wearing his Philadelphia-made drab-brown suit of velvet, which was far from new. He expected to outdo the brilliant silks, taffetas and crinolines of the other visitors with the brilliance and colorfulness of his mind.

As soon as Benjamin Franklin and his coterie were presented to the august Voltaire, the wise old *philosophe* stood up and in grandiloquent fashion announced, "On behalf of all our friends and guests, indeed of all France, allow me to say to you that we are all electrified by your presence, galvanized by your science, and voltified by your erudition. Fancy that my name, Volt-air, would receive such an etymological jolt of an electrody-namic charge![106] And you, of course, are the "frank" benefactor, the new Prometheus, the clever conductor of God's ideas to those on earth, the thunderbolt, the spark from the heavens whom nobody can resist!"

Voltaire let out a chuckle at his own puns and bowed his head.

Franklin bowed lower. "*Monsieur* de Voltaire. You leave me breathless, and shocked into humility, with your kind words. You make me feel like the *Christophe Colomb* of elec-tricity.[107] I received less of a jolt when I flew my kite during that electric thunderstorm!"

Franklin pretended to be holding on to the string of his kite and then being electrocuted.

"Oh, *mister* Franklin," gushed the blind *madame* du Deffand, pointing her eyes at the general vicinity of where Franklin stood. "You amuse us so, and inspire us to educate ourselves to a higher degree, even though I myself find this newfangled science to be such incomprehensible rigmarole that it all might as well be magic and alchemy. My cranium cannot hold it all. But is it true," and here the acerbic old lady took on an expression of wicked glee, "is it true that you tried to marry your grandson to one of *Madame* Brillon's daughters?"

Temple looked down at his shoes. *Madame* Brillon de Jouy would have preferred not to have this subject aired out in public for she adored Franklin. But the American's family was not of noble birth—far from it!; besides, they were not even Catholics (what were they?). Temple could not marry her daughter.

"Ah," continued *madame* du Deffand, "your silence gives you away. Nevertheless, you should take solace in the fact that *mademoiselle* Brillon was betrothed to a certain

---

104   Even Louis XVI had Sèvres produce a portrait of the American savant, which he instructed be put at the bottom of some chamber-pots. He presented a particularly beautiful one with gold leaf on the rim to the Polignac woman. The whole court found it very amusing.

105   According to a Parisian peruke-maker who tried to fit his eminent American client with a wig, Frank-lin's head was too big. This criticism did not displease Franklin. He took to visiting society, including the King and Queen, with head uncovered.

106   Luigi Galvani: Italian physicist, father of galvanism; Alessandro Volta, Italian Count, inventor of electrical machines.

107   A subtle pun on the name of Charles Augustin Coulomb, French physicist who did research on elec-tricity and magnetism. Christophe Colomb is Christopher Columbus' name in French.

monsieur de Tonnerre.[108] So you see, she was not able to escape being struck by a *coup de foudre!*"[109]

"I would never defend myself against the truth, *madame*," said Franklin as he bowed in her direction.[110] "Moreover, I am sure that in your time you have been known to create your own sparks."

The old lady seemed pleased enough with his response.

"Speaking of which," chimed in *monsieur* Lavoisier, "*monsieur* Franklin counseled the Royal Academy of Science on the subject of the protection of the Arsenal by installing lightning rods."

"But it is he who creates violent explosions in the halls of science with his wild imaginings," said Condorcet expansively.

"Oh, *docteur* Franklin," said *madame* Brillon, "your visions are inflammatory! You are like a God who calms even the waves upon the sea!"

"Ah, that was nothing," said Franklin self-effacingly. "That was just a trick of mine which relieves the water's surface tension, and it was only a small body of water."[111]

"Yet you incite us with exhilarating new concepts," erupted the *baron* von Grimm. "The whole world awaits your every move."

"Oh, it is very kind of you to say that. But it is true that my imagination runs wild sometimes. Sometimes I see in my inner vision wonderful, fascinating things: vehicles that don't need horses to pull them, automata that do tasks around the house, perpetual machines that work with sparks of electricity, building materials which won't burn and which will make house fires a thing of the past, hospitals that will open free of charge to the poor, stoves and ovens which will cook food quickly without human supervision, transportation to the heavenly bodies, universal access to all books ever written, including your *Encyclopédie*, universal education in the art of good society so that all may know how to function and be confident in genteel company, such as this one (this made the servants look up), universal money which will unite the European States like it has united the American Colonies, spectacles that are not just bifocal[112] but whose lenses will darken automatically to protect the eyes from too much sunlight, machines that will take dictation—not that I don't highly appreciate my secretaries' invaluable efforts on my behalf," he interrupted himself while turning to Temple and Bancroft. "But the world is a thrilling place, and one's mind can't help but be swept up by the excitement of trying to think of better ideas to improve the lot of mankind."

"Ah, spoken like a true humanist," said Voltaire who had by this time taken his seat again. Franklin, Vergennes and their group all took seats, as André, Suzanne and Marianne passed refreshments around.

---

108   *Tonnerre* means thunder.

109   *Coup de foudre* means both "a bolt of lightning" and "love at first sight."

110   Another pun in French: "*De la vérité, jamais je ne m'en défends, madame* [du Deffand]."

111   Franklin had startled observers when he had calmed the waves of a pond by secretly pouring oil into it out of his walking cane. Because of the surface tension between the oil and the water, the oil spread into a thin film and made "an instant calm, as smooth as a Looking Glass."

112   Bifocal spectacles, which Benjamin Franklin invented. The Franklin stove, by the way, was another of his multifarious inventions, and, as was his wont, whose plans of construction and operation he gave away freely.

"We have heard," said *madame* de Villette, "that you recommend killing fowl with an electric shock; it makes the meat unusually tender."

"That is my understanding, *madame*. The electricity apparently loosens the muscle fibers."

"Can such a method be used to dispatch larger animals, like cows and horses?" asked *docteur* Guillotin, ever the pragmatist.

"Oh, no," laughed Franklin, "the electrical charge necessary to kill larger beasts would be so high that it might instead kill the hapless cook!"

"Ah, *monsieur*," said the *comte* de Vergennes who had just spent a week holed up with his American homologue. "You are so marvelous you have half the girls in France in love with you, and half the boys wanting to follow you to America."

"I am not sure about the first half of your gracious statement," Franklin responded as he cast a sidelong glance at *madame* Brillon de Jouy, "but the second half is true enough. You should see the bedlam in our offices with so many men clamoring to be transported overseas. Men want to fight for us, yet it is diplomatically sensitive to have to tell them that they all can't have a brigade over which to captain. I'm afraid that I must say to all those who wish to go to America having no trade or art by which to make a living and who expect to be valued by their birth or quality, that these things bear no price in our markets."

Madame du Deffand was the first aristocrat to take offense. The servants of the *hôtel* de Villette, however, could not be pried away from the *salon*, even though new refreshments needed to be brought out from the kitchen.

"Pray tell, *docteur* Franklin, what qualities do serve in your country as being of higher value?" asked the imperious *marquise* with the self-assurance of one who knows that the idea of noble birth is sacrosanct, untouchable, and irreversible.

Franklin knew he was on dangerous ground. Yet he felt fearless and comfortable, for the old sage sitting directly in front of him, the most famous man in France, and he himself, Benjamin Franklin, son of a candlestick maker, the most famous American in France, had not been able to call upon noble rank for their meteoric rise in public esteem.

"My most dear *madame*," said Franklin in such a low voice that nobody dared rattle a teacup. The servants, including André, stood frozen in place, holding their trays to their sides. (Zénobe, unfortunately, was at his post by the front door.) "My most dear *madame*, what Americans value most are not what we are not responsible for. Our birth into a wealthy noble family or into a desperately impoverished one is an accident, ruled over by constellations or the fates or by a Supreme Power over which we have no say. Where we do have a modicum (Franklin had to whisper the word in English to his secretary and Bancroft whispered the French translation back, "*un tout petit peu*"), a tiny little bit of power and influence is in our own selves. Here I speak of character, for in the pursuit of our livelihood, there where we wish to garner success, our most valuable allies are industriousness, perseverance, financial prudence, frugality, honesty, stoicism, public service and modesty."

Voltaire had smiled during the enunciation of each of these words except for the last.

"What is modesty doing in this otherwise wonderful list?" asked Voltaire. "Why not flaunt what you have? You've earned it, be proud of it."

"Because that, *monsieur* de Voltaire, will attract the envy of those around you, those who lack what you have, be it money or intelligence; it will bring you enemies and open you up to thievery, slander, flattery, blackmail and hatred. Be humble instead, minimize your qualities, and people will leave you alone."

"Yes, I think I know what you mean," answered Voltaire rubbing the wig on his head. "Too bad I didn't have this thick peruke to protect me from the beatings I received when I was younger."

"Running after superfluities will expose one to dangers that are also superfluous. Don't go running to America to seek fame and fortune; your future is here, and with your God-given talents you can be successful enough for yourself, your family, and your nation. And this last may be of consolation to everyone, from the most successful to the least successful. The satisfaction, the restitution for what you have received, the knowledge of helping one's society—according to one's abilities—are a wonderful boon to the soul, a moral compensation for the heart, a munificence which gives returns to your generosity."

"Hear, hear," said Diderot. "I couldn't have said it better myself!" Usually a bit more reticent and circumspect, Diderot was known to have his flashes of enthusiasm. "Isn't this what we are all trying to do here, those of us who dabble in the printing of words? It's in the service of our society that we travail. However, society is oftentimes not yet ready for what our efforts have produced on her behalf. Most of us have spent enough days and nights in the Bastille or at Vincennes to give us pause and reflect on this injustice. We seek to serve, but we are chastised for it."

Zénobe had come in on the middle of this commentary and took longer than usual to whisper into the ear of the *marquis* de Villette about the latest newcomer. The *marquis'* answer was not to let the visitor in, but Zénobe, out of curiosity of the American visitor, waited around for Franklin's response to Diderot's comment.

Benjamin Franklin's chin sank to his chest. "Yes, my dear gentleman, so are the ways of the world. But, then, we have to seek the good that is intertwined with the bad. Nobody here can say that an *embastillement* has been bad for his career. We need to be pragmatists. The longer we stay in the Bastille, the more our readership goes up. A little bit of persecution goes a long way to make us more famous in the eyes of society."

Vergennes, the King's main minister, laughed the hardest. He had been on the wrong side of royal favor often enough to realize that the wheel of fortune never stops turning.

"Ever the sober-minded American," said Diderot.

"Not always!" ventured *madame* Brillon de Jouy who had seen Papa in a different light.

"All humor aside," offered the mathematician d'Alembert, not wanting to throw cold water on the festive mood but doing so anyway, "society often abhors us because she doesn't see us as being friends of society (he winked at Franklin to emphasize the pun on "Society of Friends"),[113] but rather as the Devil's helpers who steer society onto a path away from God. I for one see us as providing another, different path towards God. For in mathematics and science, we essay to uncover God's veil, his innermost workings, his methods of creation. Why do people accuse us of being godless, *docteur*? What would you say? The rainbow is no less beautiful for having been demystified as Nature's prism. The thunderbolt is no less powerful for having been construed as an atmospheric discharge. Newton's astral bodies are no less glorious for having been explained in their gravitational forces. Perhaps it will be found that Fontenelle's worlds are no less astounding for harboring other civilizations, even though that, too, will

---

113   Most Europeans still thought of Franklin as being a Quaker, a reputation that the American statesman was negligent in refuting.

have no Biblical reference.[114] Our discoveries, of the past, the present and the future, are another path to God, however you may construe Him. We seek the wonders of His creation and need not fear diminishing Him by our scientific discoveries. Indeed, by any definition of God, God cannot be diminished. And it was God who gave us this magnificent brain of ours. Are we to waste this divine gift by inhibiting its impulses and putting it to disuse?"

"Indeed not," answered Franklin, revolted at the very suggestion. "You are advancing on territory that is juxtaposed between science and religion, and this is why in the Constitution of our United Colonies I shall seek to establish a clear demarcation between the provinces of State and of Religion. We want no religious Sect, including our own personal one, to interfere with the workings of the State, which must be run according to the dictates of Reason."

"But Reason sometimes doesn't explain the difficulties, or the complexities, of Life," said *madame* du Deffand, hoping secretly to trip up the American doctor.

"Quite so, quite so, and that is why we scientists and philosophers must work energetically and sincerely to bring our Arts into fruition. That is why we must decry the false scientists and the false philosophers from wresting power away from us. Look at this Mesmer fellow who has just come into Paris. Numerous times has he sought an audience with me, with *docteur* Guillotin, and I believe with *monsieur* de Voltaire."

"That is correct," said the old sage. "But we did not allow him entry, did we?" he asked *monsieur* de Villette.

"No, I don't believe we did," he said as he looked to his wife and Maurel and then to Zénobe. They all shook their heads.

Franklin continued. "It's as if he were trying to gain acceptance, and legitimacy, for his ideas–which I have perused!–but which smack of pseudo-science, false philosophy, which incorporates a huge dose of religious jargon and fervor that serves only to confuse people and serves not for their edification."

"It does serve to part certain fools from their money!" said Voltaire. "I hear Mesmer is making fistfuls of lucre, and none of it on credit, take notice!"

"Ah, *monsieur*, you do *le Bonhomme Richard* an honor.[115] 'A fool and his money are soon parted'!" he said in English. "But if truth be told, that saying was around ages before Richard Saunders set it down to paper."

"We all make use of what preceded us," said Voltaire. "But it is worse to be an opportunist like Mesmer who invents Science which does not really exist and uses it to his own advantage."

Condorcet responded, "We fight against these charlatans as strongly as we fight against entrenched superstition."

Benjamin Franklin waxed philosophical for Condorcet had touched his soft spot.

"Ah, my brother Condorcet, and my brothers the *philosophes*." Benjamin Franklin had stood up in order to sweep both his arms expansively across the room. "The reason why I consider you my brethren, intellectually, spiritually, and morally as well, I want it to be known, is not just because I share your penchant for irreverence, but also, and especially, because we share this commitment of constructive criticism. A humanist

---

114   Bernard de Fontenelle, author of the popular *Conversations on the Plurality of Worlds*, in which he mused about the existence of Extraterrestrials.

115   The French version of *Poor Richard's Almanach* (in French, the title became *The Science of Good Richard*) was by now a raging bestseller, and went through numerous printings.

cannot help but want for his fellow man, and woman," he said, bowing in the direction of the ladies, "to improve their lot in life."

The ladies smiled in gratitude for having been included.

"The humanist does not want to destroy society or tear down institutions. Not completely, in any case. The humanist wants to relieve the oppressed, to bring the disenfranchised to a higher level so that they may participate fully in their society in an equal fashion. Perhaps utopia is an impossibility, but that doesn't mean that one should not strive to raise society to a higher level of beneficence for all its citizens."

At these last words the *salon* burst into applause.

Edward Bancroft had whispered a few corrections into Franklin's ear, but after one of those instances Franklin insisted that he was correct. "'A humanist cannot help but want...' is correct French, I believe," he said. Diderot corroborated that *monsieur* Franklin was indeed correct. *Madame* de Villette declared *monsieur* Franklin's French charming. *Madame* Brillon voiced that she found his little errors to be "*mignonnes comme tout!*" *Madame* du Deffand said that his every word was electric and that she could feel the sparks in her very soul. *Mademoiselle* Necker remained silent, but enjoyed a frisson up and down her spine that was tingling and very satisfying. *Madame* de Polignac was trying her best to memorize exactly what the American had said in order to report back word for word to her mistress in Versailles. *Mister* Bancroft sat down and said nothing further, but could not help shutting his eyes hard every time *monsieur* Franklin made one of his cute little errors. He said '*bénéficence*' instead of '*bienfaisance*'; but his gist was clear and all understood. The language of reason found no linguistic barriers.

Zénobe was enjoying the warm glow of camaraderie and philosophy in the *salon*, but suddenly he remembered he had to go back to his post. André watched his friend walking back to the front door and wished he knew the science behind certain of his physical reactions at watching Zénobe in his official butler's uniform with the blue, red and gold epaulettes that made his back look broader, and the black breeches which delineated his buttocks. He was going to have to ask Maurel what the physiological connections were between his heart and his penis, between his pulse and his scrotum, which tightened in a strange and alarming way he had never felt before. Wresting secrets from Nature is very difficult for a lad of sixteen to do. Yet, he knew as he watched Zénobe walk away that Science might help him explain what he was feeling, this foreign force that felt electrical, or magnetic, which was affecting his nerves, making them twitch, making his penis engorge with blood. What was it? He was going to have to ask *monsieur Maurel* about it.

Behind him Zénobe heard that the conversation had turned to the enumeration of differences between real science that brings concomitant progress to society, and illuminism, which holds progress back. But then he had to turn his attention to the front door as he offered his regrets to the footman in front of him that *monsieur* de Voltaire would not be able to see his mistress, oh, my apologies, his master, at this time. The next person in line was the carriage driver of a certain *chevalière* d'Éon, and Zénobe misheard, repeating the name as the *chevalier* d'Éon, but the coachman repeated "*la chevalière* d'Éon" and then expounded, "Charles Geneviève Louis Auguste André Thimothée d'Éon de Beaumont." He then added, "Accompanied by *madame* Rose Bertin."

Zénobe was used to long names, and was used to given names being both masculine and feminine. But he wasn't used to the fact that this obvious man's name was being preceded by a feminine title, and a title that he had never before realized even had a feminine form. As far as he knew, there never had been a feminized form for 'knight'. 'Knightess'?

He whispered to himself the caller's full name as he walked back into the salon, in order not to forget it. As soon as he whispered the name into the *marquis* de Villette's ear, the *marquis* grinned and repeated in astonishment, "Charles Geneviève Louis Auguste André Thimothée d'Éon de Beaumont? The *chevalier* d'Éon is here?" This brought the conversation in the *salon* to complete silence.

"Ah," said Benjamin Franklin in utter pleasure, "*madame* d'Éon is here!"

Voltaire asked, "*monsieur le chevalier* is here?"

Now, Zénobe was utterly confused. He whispered to the *marquis* that the coachman had insisted the title was *la chevalière* d'Éon. And that she was accompanied by a *madame* Rose Bertin.

Madame de Polignac burst out, "Ah, *madame* Bertin is here! The Queen's dressmaker! I wonder what she will be wearing!"

There was a generalized buzz, and after conferring with Voltaire for a few seconds, the *marquis* de Villette instructed Zénobe to let *la chevalière* and *madame* Bertin in. Before he left for the front door, Zénobe noticed the expression on the *marquise* de Villette's face and realized that she was as confused as he was.

At the door, he told the coachman that *monsieur* de Voltaire would have the pleasure of having *la chevalière*'s and *madame* Bertin's company.

Back in the *salon*, Voltaire was explaining that he had been following the *chevalier* d'Éon's career for years, but had not heretofore had the occasion to meet him.

"I have been wanting to meet him for years, especially after he came back from Russia."

Diderot explained, "The *chevalier* was Louis XV's ambassador to the court of Catherine and was quite successful there."[116]

Voltaire continued, "I'm afraid that once I called her an 'amphibious creature" but I have since recanted this unfortunate description. Now, I cannot help but marvel at how a woman was able to pull off the feats that she did."

Several voices around the room inquired as to what those feats could be.

"They are so numerous!" exclaimed Voltaire. "As captain of the Dragoons he won single-handedly many battles during the Seven Years' War.[117] He showed so much courage in spite of being wounded several times that he was awarded, at a very young age—"

"She was only 35 years of age!" offered Franklin.

"—the Cross of Saint-Louis. He helped negotiate the peace treaty of 1763. He served as Louis XV's plenipotentiary minister to King George, and was a spy at the same time, looking for ways for France to invade England."

"She is now looking for ways to be reinstated as Captain of her beloved Dragoons and be sent to America to fight for our cause," gushed Franklin. "I have told her, '*Madame*, it is time to rest on your laurels and let younger hands take care of this,' but she insists on somehow being useful to us. She is a charming, an endearing person. And she has been a Freemason at the Lodge *de l'Immortalité* since 1768 and is now a Junior Warden."

---

116   Of course, nobody knew that the *chevalier* d'Éon was sent as a spy into the Russian court and was instrumental in the formation of a secret correspondence between the Russian empress and the French monarch. Its purpose was to establish diplomatic relations and to divvy up the rest of Eastern Europe between the two superpowers. In Russia the *chevalier* was the power behind the French throne.

117   Better known on the other side of the Atlantic as the French and Indian War, 1756 to 1763.

Many of the occupants of the *salon* were agog with excitement about meeting this curious person.

Madame du Deffand gave her opinion, "She is a hermaphrodite, I believe."

Franklin responded, "I assure you she is not, dear *madame*. She is a full-blooded French woman, coincidentally born in Tonnerre (which doesn't surprise me: her thunderous, electrical personality is suffused with many ethereal qualities), in Burgundy. Her brother-in-law, Thomas O'Gorman, has been keeping me supplied with Burgundy wine since my arrival in Paris. Wonderful wine! Marie Antoinette herself asked her dressmaker to furnish *la chevalière* with a complete wardrobe, now that *mademoiselle* d'Éon is retired from military service. All this in keeping with His Majesty's order that *la chevalière* abandon all ideas about returning to military service and instead begin a new life as a respectable matron."

Madame de Polignac could not refrain from saying, "Yes, perhaps, but she will never have the bearing to be a Lady-in-Waiting."

"You are absolutely correct in this, dear *madame*," answered Franklin, with a roar of a laugh. "She is too muscular for that! She is too energetic, too impatient, too much of a man, to be satisfied with a cushy and tranquil position at Court. She still wants to lead attacks at the head of her dragoons! She still wants to ply her martial trade and be bellicose to her heart's content! She doesn't want the *marquis* de Lafayette to get away with all the glory!"

Back at the front door, the figure that presented herself to Zénobe was astounding. He bowed to her and to her companion, *madame* Bertin, and ushered them into the *salon*.

At their entrance a murmur arose. *Mademoiselle la chevalière* d'Éon was dressed in a pale blue-gray velvet dress, with matching muff, a blue and red satin sash from right shoulder to the left part of her waist, low shoes, and the Cross of Saint-Louis pinned prominently over her heart. She was not tall for a man, but for a woman she manifested quite a presence. Her arms could not hide their musculature, and her neck was too thick to be called feminine. Her hands she kept hidden deep in her muff. Her composure was feminine enough, and she walked into the middle of the *salon* with dainty timidity. When she saw her friend Benjamin Franklin she curtsied. When she recognized Voltaire she curtsied even lower.

She and *madame* Bertin were both wigless. They wore their own hair without additions or extensions in tight little curls around the face. Both the *marquise* de Villette and *madame* Denis asked themselves if this were an *haute-couture* vision of the future. The *marquise* was proud of her own luxurious hair, long and black, although it was very straight. How ever would she make it curl like that? As for *madame* Denis, she was ashamed of her thin stringy mouse-brown and gray hair (Thibouville had called it the color of fatty meat). But her lifelong proximity to the *philosophes*' optimistic mode of thinking made her jump to a conclusion: perhaps there was a way to dye hair like we dye cloth!

The *chevalière* and the *haute-couturière* sat down next to Voltaire while the old patriarch expounded on why he had been wanting to meet d'Éon for such a long time.

"I have been following your career since you made a name for yourself publishing learned treatises on law and economics."

La chevalière looked down at her muffled hands and smiled with a mixture of self-consciousness and pride. She had been a lawyer in her youth, and had dabbled in the young science of economics, and she could not deny having had success in both fields.

Voltaire went on, "And when you were in Russia giving Catherine a run for her rubles, I would read the reports with much curiosity. Tell us, was it true that the Great Empress gave balls in which the men dressed as women and the women as men?"[118]

"Oh, yes," responded the *chevalière* with warm enthusiasm and a glint of nostalgia in her eye. "Oh, yes, every Tuesday night all courtiers were coerced into wearing the opposite sex's clothing and we all had so much diversion. We wore masks, too, so at the beginning of the *soirée* it was difficult to tell who was who. We wore shoes of different heights to make identification even more difficult. Her Majesty the Empress enjoyed herself enormously, and she would kiss those dressed as women and those dressed as men with equal fervor, so when she was seen kissing a man we all knew she was doing something very naughty."

The *salon* burst into laughter, including Zénobe who could not have been dragged away from this visitor. He had not known that Paris could harbor individuals like her, *euh*, like him. Like her.

Madame de Polignac saw Zénobe laughing and could not help thinking that he was a terrible butler. He should remain aloof and discreet and not interact with the guests in the *salon*. That young man had a lot to learn, she thought as she rolled her vivacious violet eyes away from him in disillusionment. He had a lot to learn, both about society and about matters of a more intimate nature.

"Oh, how droll!" cried Benjamin Franklin. "Something very naughty indeed!"

"How disgusting," said John Adams, who was sitting next to him, very much under his breath. Up to now, he had been half-listening to the conversation, which so long as it had been centered on his colleague Benjamin Franklin, interested him but little. His interior monologue had carried him from his wife Abigail back home (and how horrified she would have been of these Parisian aristocrats) to pending matters at the office.

"Oh, tush, tush," Franklin responded to Adams, not under his breath, reacting like a father who is correcting his child's malfeasance. "In the dark, who can tell if the skin next to yours is male or female, who can tell if the lips you are kissing belong to a female friend or to a male friend *(à une amie ou à un ami)?*"

"Unless, of course," added the *chevalière*, "there are long whiskers over the upper lip!"

Adams made a grimace of disgust but Franklin laughed wholeheartedly.

"Oh, *madame*," he said with forthright glee, "you are so droll, so droll."

"*Mademoiselle*," she corrected. "I have never been married, *monsieur* Franklin."

"Well for that I am truly sorry," replied the practical *mister* Franklin, alias le *Bonhomme Richard*. "You could have made a fortunate man very happy. But why do I use the past tense? This is still viable, and if you look around you, many a man would feel lucky, and honored, to call you his wife."

D'Éon looked demurely down at her muff while John Adams' eyes got as big as saucers.

Voltaire weighed in with his own opinion. "*Ah oui, ah oui, mademoiselle.* You will make a man happy to the extreme, and proud to the extreme. Such a man would need no bodyguard, either. Think of the benefits of such a match!"

Diderot had one of his tart, or wench, thoughts, and shared it with the *salon*. "Oh, our friend Jean-Jacques should have made such a match! He who is always extolling

---

118   [From the author] *Incroyable!* I can't believe *Herr* Ralph left no footnote here! It wasn't Catherine who gave these ambiguous-sex balls. It was her predecessor Elizabeth. But I think that *Herr* Ralph has finally understood that I need to contract history, consolidate events, compress characters.

self-sufficiency. He who is paranoid to the extreme. He thinks everyone is out to get him. He could certainly use such a bodyguard. *Mademoiselle* d'Éon's household would be self-sufficient in all matters, for in one lovable person she has collected wit, intelligence, grace, eloquence, perseverance, loyalty, and superior body strength. To think, Rousseau would have had this valiant wife to protect him from all his enemies, instead of that immaterial laundress of his. Think of it, a maternal, tender, luscious friend to help him through the night, and a strong, strategic warrioress to protect him during the day!"

Adams looked as though he were going to gag.

La *chevalière* d'Éon seemed grateful for all this support. It is true that Louis XVI had given her a direct command to appear in public dressed only in feminine garb, but she still insisted on pinning the Cross of Saint-Louis on her dress, directly over her heart. Foregoing her breeches did not mean foregoing her pride or her memories of uncommon bravery in battle.

"I would not mind having such a beautiful protectress," said Franklin.

"On that note," asked Voltaire, "would *mademoiselle la chevalière* care to give us a demonstration of her prowess with the foil? I am sure that the *marquis* de Villette would not mind lending you his?"

The foil was produced in a few seconds, as was a suitable contestant. The young nephew of *monsieur* d'Argental, Voltaire's very good friend, was unanimously and unceremoniously pushed into the center of the room. The *chevalière* d'Éon handed her muff and gloves to *madame* Bertin. Everybody marveled at the Amazon's big powerful bear-paws. The *chaise longue*, the harpsichord, the harp, and sundry poufs were dragged to the sides of the room. All the guests hurried to take their position to witness this extraordinary martial exercise. The flurry of movement and ensuing rustle brought out the rest of the household staff to the doorway of the *salon*, and all eyes had but one target, save for *madame* du Deffand's blind ones, which she had closed, now that she was biting her lower lip in jealousy. This was a spectacle that was certain to make the other Parisian *salonnières* green with envy. It was sure to be in all the papers the following day.

D'Argental's nephew was twenty-two years old; *mademoiselle* d'Éon was fifty.

They bowed to each other. At first the lad held back in deference to his rival's age and sex. But this lasted for all of five seconds. The *chevalière* made her foil cleave the air with whooshing sounds that seemed to come from all directions and the young man had to bring the whole of his education and experience to the fore, and he still had difficulties staving off his fencing partner. As for the *chevalière*, she was in her element, like a blue-gray frog in a pond, jumping from lily pad to lily pad. On tiptoes, with her left hand hitching up her skirts, legs bent, she thrust, parried, twirled in semicircles, the clackety-clack of the foils mingling with the oohs and ahs of the crowd. Her chest heaved within her bodice; young d'Argental's perspiration started to run down his forehead. She was breathing heavily. He grunted as he thrust. They both jerked to one side and back as they tried to subdue each other. When the younger combatant's foil came close to one of d'Éon's arms, they heard the rip of a sleeve and the crowd gasped.

"Ah, my dress!" yelled the *chevalière* in falsetto, out of breath. "You fiend, you'll pay for that!"

The boy's cravat, or half of it, went flying in one direction, and a piece of his lapel in another. D'Argental's nephew wore an expression of extreme concentration, his tongue off to one side between his teeth. *Mademoiselle* d'Éon's face was a study in tranquility, as if she were doing a *contredanse noble*. The tempo, though, was a bit faster. In a flash it was over: the tip of *mademoiselle*'s foil was on the young man's chest while he held both of his arms helplessly to either side. His own foil had gone clattering down the floor into the hallway. André brought it back and with a bow presented it to its owner. The *comte* d'Argental's nephew, ever the gentleman, bowed in turn to his victorious rival and said, "It has been an honor, *mademoiselle*, to have had you as my *escrimeuse*." It was rare to hear the word *escrimeur* in the feminine.

The crowd let out its excitement in an uproar of yells, whistles and applause. Voltaire and Franklin were swept away in awe. When the noise died down a bit, *monsieur* Franklin spoke.

"In such a way have you pierced my heart, *mademoiselle* d'Éon. Take it, it is yours! (*Prenez-le, il est à vous!*)"

The crowd redoubled its roar and the *chevalière* sat down heavily into a *bergère*, still terribly out of breath, but smiling at the crowd's approval. Even the *hôtel* de Villette's servants were jumping up and down and applauding in the hallway. *Madame* Bertin handed *la chevalière* a fan that she took with a smile and fluttered it in front of her face with zeal, bringing her other hand to her heart, right over her military award. In a second, she had two other ladies fanning her as well (ladies know how hot one can become underneath all those layers of voluminous skirts).

"That was superb!" cheered Voltaire. "I too am breathless!"

Mademoiselle d'Éon cried out in mock horror, "Oh, I must look very disheveled! Allow me to use one of your boudoirs to rearrange myself. Perhaps *madame* Bertin can stitch me up in a jiffy. Look at what that handsome young devil has done to my dress!"

La chevalière and *madame* Bertin were whisked off to another room by the *marquise* de Villette and *madame* Denis, followed by a bevy of ladies who were not only admirative of their fellow lady but also curious to see how much bosom they would be able to see.

During d'Éon's absence Voltaire expressed how sorry he was that he had ever thought the *chevalier* a monster of nature, an amphibian who could transform itself at will from one form to another and then back again. Now that he had seen her in person for the first time, he realized that she was a magnificent creature, able to reconnoiter in two differing worlds, with talent, and adroitness even. "I have a new perception of her," he said, "and it is clear to me that her mind, and her heart, are clear, rational, and good."

John Adams, who seemed horrified of the creature, shared his thoughts with the *salon*: "But that person is not natural. Nothing in nature exists which could begin to approximate this individual. I don't believe there is anything rational about, about…"

Benjamin Franklin retorted, "About *her*? Get your pronouns out, man! I could not disagree more. One may speak to *her* of womanly things, and one may speak to *her* of manly things, and she converses knowledgeably on both. She crosses over our socially arbitrary dividing line between the two sexes like you or I cross over our threshold, or go from the land into a refreshing swim in the water."[119]

Diderot analyzed the metaphor more scientifically: "Perhaps she is not an amphibian who is born a water creature and then inexorably becomes a terrestrial creature. One might better view *la chevalière* d'Éon as a chameleon, changing her appearance, if not her form, from one manifestation to the other, at will, with her volition ever the mistress of her transformation. Imagine! How clever! A caterpillar which becomes a butterfly, and then becomes a caterpillar again! It is still the same species, it has not changed intrinsically."

---

119   Franklin was among the first proponents of swimming as an enjoyable past-time, beneficial as an exercise and excellent as a diversion. He also invented the swimming fins.

Benjamin Franklin addressed the crowd, *"Eh bien, messieurs et dames,* in the same manner one can say that the soul is without sex. Our soul has been infused into a body that is of one or the other sex (to say nothing at all about androgynous individuals). After all, is it not the soul which most interests our Platonicists, this soul without sex?"

The American scientist, and eternal flirt, winked to his neighbor *Madame* Brillon de Jouy.

Adams sputtered to Diderot, "I assume by caterpillar you mean a man. This is a most distasteful metaphor." Adams had never believed that the *Encyclopédie* was good for anything but looking good on a shelf. Its editors were really just good-for-nothing immoral atheists.

Diderot gave a Gallic shrug. (No shoulders, just a raising of the eyebrows and a lowering of the corners of the mouth.)

Franklin took over where Diderot had left off. *"Madame* d'Éon might be a man on the exterior, with all the appurtenances thereof as Nature might have supplied. But in the interior of her person, she feels like a woman. This is the side for which she has an affinity and which she has decided to expose to the society of her equals. This is the part of her inner nature to which she wishes us to give importance during this part of her life. The Cross of Saint-Louis which she proudly wears on her bosom is testimony enough that in a previous part of her life she was a man who did manly things, and did them better than most men, I should add. With undeniable courage, strategy and fortitude. With great qualities of leadership. His dragoons loved him and would have followed him to the gates of Hades itself. But now, that war has been over for years. Now *la chevalière* d'Éon has put her manly belligerence away—none the less proud of her past accomplishments, mind you. Now, she listens to that part of her soul that leads her to believe that she is a woman. How can we, as civilized, sensible and sensitive people deny her that right which she finds honest and forthright? Indeed, how can we be the first to cast stones?"

Here there was a pause, as Franklin searched for words in French—but then as Franklin gazed on his colleague's smirk, he realized that Adams was a tough nut to crack, a joyless killjoy who liked to have a plan and then follow it uncompromisingly to the last letter, no matter what changes had occurred since he had formulated it. Inflexible to the last degree. Adams would never be convinced about anything that was already decided in his head, no matter what new light was thrown on the subject.

Franklin threw his hands up in the air, laughed, and blurted out, "But then, what do I care? I see a charming lady in front of me, with two adorable dimples on either cheek, a bit shy, blushing at my every utterance. Ah, I cannot help but be charming in return and try to kiss those dimples whenever she gives me leave to do so. Ah, she is returned. Allow me, *Mademoiselle,* to kiss those playful dimples on your cheeks which give you such an air of *enfant fôlatre* (a frolicsome child)."

"Oh, *non, monsieur* Franklin, what will the *habitués* of this *salon* say?"

"The *habitués* of this *salon* will say that *monsieur* Franklin is in love with your beautiful and talented person, that he has been caught by your bounteous charms as a fly ensnared by a spider, and that he goes to his doom with the sweet fatalism that this is his destiny, to be thy heart's plaything, for you to do with it what thou willst, and to be thine forever."

Mr. Franklin's switch to the *"tu"* form in French brought out gracious laughter and admiration from the members of the *salon.*

Franklin continued, "And I hope that the love affair of the century will be bruited about so that *madame* de Brillon and *madame* Helvétius will both be head over heels in jealousy.[120] Furthermore, what better mate could I possibly hope to have to help protect me if there ever is a prowler in the house?"

As Mr. Franklin stood on his toes to give *la chevalière* d'Éon a kiss on either dimple, he saw over the *chevalière*'s broad shoulder that John Adams' mouth was agape, his countenance frozen in amazement. Edward Bancroft beside him was grinning from ear to ear, enjoying the kissing scene less than Adams' stunned figure.

Benjamin Franklin's love of women did not shock the French. To them it was wholesomely normal for a man to flirt and to court women, their marital status notwithstanding, either his or theirs. "I love to make them laugh and to amuse them with little 'trifles' about quotidian enjoyments, and ills," Franklin was fond of saying.

Adams truly was a jealous spoilsport, even though it was laughable that a 43-year-old could begrudge a 72-year-old his joyful moments of flirtatious and innocent escapades with French women.

Voltaire stood up. "Let me emulate my American colleague and fellow *philosophe* and welcome *mademoiselle* d'Éon to my host and hostess' abode. My visit to Paris has been enriched by your gracious presence," he said to the *chevalière*. He kissed her, too, although chastely, on the hand. *Mademoiselle* d'Éon curtsied in return.

Franklin turned to Voltaire and said, "You have graced all of Paris by your presence, *monsieur* de Voltaire, and by ending your exile you give us all hope that a better world will ensue."

There was much applause and shouting and several of the *philosophes*, and even Zénobe, joining in, cried out, "Hear, hear!"

Franklin continued, "My young grandson has joined me in our endeavors here in France. I would be appreciative to my dying day, *mon très cher monsieur* de Voltaire, if you were to give him your blessing."

Franklin bade Temple to come to his side. He directed the youth to stand in front of Voltaire. Once again in the *salon*, there was a hush of respect and expectation.

Voltaire raised a hand to beckon the young man to approach, but Temple was so tall that the old *philosophe* would never be able to reach his head. He took Temple's hand and directed him to kneel in front of him. Temple did so, and instinctively bowed his head in reverence and awe.

Voltaire took his bony right hand and placed it on Temple's wavy dark-brown locks. The *marquis* de Villette was so overcome to see his old mentor blessing this healthy, handsome, American boy that he had to stifle a sob with an embroidered lace handkerchief.

Voltaire slowly and solemnly pronounced three simple English words over the lad's head, "God and Liberty." After this, there wasn't a dry eye in the house, save for *madame* du Deffand's, for she had seen much in her long life.

---

120   *Madame* Helvétius, widow of the *philosophe* Claude Adrien Helvétius, was another lady whom Franklin had wooed. He had even asked her to marry him, but she had politely declined.

That night, both André and Zénobe went to bed in a dreamy, introspective mood. Unbeknownst to them, they were both thinking about the same thing, but they dared not speak to one another about it. Neither one had experience enough to even identify it.

Zénobe felt exactly how he had felt years ago in *Haute Savoie* when as a child he had met *madame* Jourdan, the old matriarch of Annecy. She had been 104 at the time, and to a child of ten or eleven this had made a deep impression. A walking skeleton is what he remembered, bony protuberances everywhere, including her temples. A raging mane of snow white hair, deep wrinkles furrowing her face, and fingers that grasped his hands in an ossified embrace. And how she loved to tell jokes! She had certainly defied the Reaper countless times, and she probably did it by telling him a joke or two in order to dissemble and have him be distracted from the serious matter at hand. After this encounter, Zénobe walked away a meditative person, and went to the kitchen garden to weed and cogitate. This, too, is what awaited him, if he were lucky to make it to 104. And was it luck to reach the age of 104, even if you still liked telling jokes and being witty and liking to wear your white hair long and loose?

André was also taciturn and meditative, with the same eyes that looked inwardly and could not focus on the outside. He knew Zénobe was in the room, and by the light of a single candle could tell that he was getting ready for bed, as he himself was. But in his mind and body, an energy had left him. What he could not understand, of course, was that this energy was his young libido, a natural energy electrified by overbearing hormones, and that this energy had been affected, and interrupted, by the sight of the *chevalière* d'Éon earlier that day. This is exactly what was entertaining Zénobe's mind. They were both thinking that they could very easily end up like that strange apparition, a man, but also a woman. Especially André, who although younger, had his hormone levels higher than Zénobe's. Zénobe's testosterone had gone into the production of much body hair and a bigger Adam's apple and thus a deeper voice. André's was wandering around his arteries, seeking an outlet, not finding an appropriate one. In short, both were afraid that their attraction for each other would make them end up like the *chevalière*, a woman in disguise. In spite of what the *philosophes* had said about her, she frightened the two young boys; they were too inexperienced to realize that homosexuality had nothing to do with transvestitism or transsexuality. Indeed, those subjects were too rare even to be taboo; they were just unheard of. In their profound ignorance, the two young men closed up tight into themselves and slept quite apart from each other. A bigger bed could not have been big enough. They had never felt lonelier.

Initiation into Clandestine Assignations

Before the evening was over, Zénobe, who had placed *madame* de Polignac's gloves and fan on a little table in the foyer, espied a folded-up piece of paper stuck in-between the folds of the fan. Notwithstanding his principal responsibility as butler, he managed to extricate the piece of paper in the interval separating the arrival of some guests and the departure of others. He managed to read the elegantly written words without anyone noticing because the material was scant. In florid script there were transcribed a place and a time, which he quickly memorized, not necessarily because he ardently wished to pursue this romantic entanglement, but rather because he had a quick mind that systematically and involuntarily arranged pieces of information in his memory. It is not known what he did with the piece of paper but it is evident that he could not have responded to the note since he had access neither to a quill nor to ink.

Once again, the details are vague, and since the participants of the arranged rendezvous never related their accounts of such an event, either through speech or by recording it in a journal, little may be construed with satisfying veracity, and much could be destroyed with wanton speculation. Therefore, in the service of verisimilitude, let us not conjecture unproven proceedings or propose wild imaginings. It is plausible that *madame* de Polignac and *monsieur* Bosquet did manage to meet sometime during the next few days, but the details must be left to the musings of the reader. The omniscient author surmises that the alleged affair took place at the Convent of the Perpetual Adoration on the rue du Temple where *madame* de Polignac had a certain credit with the Benedictine nuns and, through her charitable works, was able to benefit every now and then with the discretion of the sisters who would entrust her with the use of one of the cells in the outer cloister. The nuns were secluded and spoke to no one outside the convent's walls, and during the Terror in 1793 they were murdered and could therefore reveal no secrets subsequently.

Zénobe inside a convent is an occurrence of such sufficient importance that, one feels, he must have told someone about it. But if one deduces certain possible confidants, one must conclude that each in turn is a possibility with no viable prospects. *Monsieur* Maurel? Zénobe would have had to confess that he had not asked for the *maître d'hôtel*'s permission to leave the premises at such a busy time and go engage in an illicit tryst with an aristocratic woman. Perhaps Maurel would have been willing to grant such permission, especially if it was for just one hour or two, but no permission was forthcoming, and no such confession materialized. *Monsieur* de Corday? Would Zénobe ever have confided in his bedmate André that he was furtively absconding from the *hôtel* de Villette, and momentarily leaving both him and Voltaire in order to seek an adventure, or solace, perhaps a diversion, or a quick peccadillo, or, more seriously, a bout of sexual discovery, or some sort of epicurean experience or educational undertaking, with an older, affluent and influential patrician who would later, much later, when Zénobe himself had become a revolutionary, grant him access to the palace of Versailles? All of this conjecture certainly has its place in the exacting minutiae of constructing a feasible narrative, but, alas, it must cease under the vexatious paucity of credible evidence.

Being Philosophes

S ometime during the night, both André and Zénobe must have forgotten about the astonishing amphibious apparition of the *chevalière* d'Éon in the Villette's *salon*, and about the notion of sleeping as far away from each other as their bed would allow. They shuddered at the thought of becoming a manly woman, or a womanly man, but the night was long and cold and André ended up being the outer spoon to Zénobe's inner spoon. Neither one of them woke up during this nocturnal shuffle. Throughout, while they slept, it was a very busy night. After all of the preceding days' events, they needed to dream to sort things out. One of the manifestations of all this sorting out was that each of them realized he needed a friend. So for André, the fear of turning into the *chevalière* d'Éon dissipated under the reality under the sheets. While he changed positions during his sleep, he realized during one of his dreams that there in front of him lay his friend, and it was a friend who was not in the least bit effeminate. On the contrary, Zénobe was strong, muscular, rugged. During this time of stress and agitation, it was easy for him to press his chest against Zénobe's back and to bring his arm over Zénobe's torso and place his open palm next to Zénobe's beating heart. As far as Zénobe was concerned, when he felt André's warmth behind him, it was very natural for him to press his own hands over André's hand once he had placed it over his heart. He jutted out his buttocks as well to make better contact with André. In this way, unbeknownst to either of them, they slept most of the night comforting one another from the fears of the dark unknown. Of course, their biggest fears were of each other and of this desire erupting within them that remained aloof and ineffable. Yet at the same time, their physical presence represented their biggest comfort and consolation. In a word, if being together was the illness, then being together was the panacea. They slept soundly, safe from the tremors of conscience brought on by their young lifetimes steeped in theology, prejudice, hearsay, faith, ignorance and superstition. In the warmth of each other's body heat, they also felt safe from the impressive image of *mademoiselle* d'Éon on the preceding day. Still, her presence remained manifesting itself in their dreams. In one of Zénobe's dreams he was wounded in a great battlefield that stretched to the horizon and *mademoiselle* d'Éon played the role of nursemaid to him. André dreamt that he was in a carriage with the *chevalière* and that he was busy explaining to her that he needed to be a true, faithful friend to Zénobe. In the midst of such fitful dreaming, being together like two spoons in a drawer felt so good, so comforting, so warm.

They were still sleeping soundly when the dawn brought the sounds of stirrings from the other rooms. When Maurel walked into their room he felt like a man who has walked into a forest glen and falls upon a unicorn. He stood transfixed. He had never seen a more beautiful sight: blond and black hair intertwined, the two boys' forms symmetrical under the blankets in double zigzag–heads, shoulders, hips, knees, feet–sleeping like angels. When finally he had to wake them, Maurel sat on the edge of their bed and pressed his hands lightly on their heads. They woke up slowly, and when they realized what was happening and where and how, they both tried to spring out of bed. A little increased pressure on their heads by Maurel assured that they would stay put. Without saying a word, he brought his hands down to their shoulders and pressed their bodies together, as if to show them that they belonged together. André and Zénobe looked sheepish at first, as if they had been caught drinking wine in the cellar, but then they realized Maurel was their friend. They would be able to talk to him and ask him questions. For now, nothing was said, and the boys snuggled together even closer, André burying his face in Zénobe's hair.

The servants in the next room were up and around, and before anybody could take a look into his boys' room, Maurel stood up and gave both of them a slap to the rump.

"Rise and shine," he said with an emotional intonation, as if he were an actor in one of Voltaire's plays. "Rise and shine. The sun is to the east and all must break the sweet embrace of Morpheus."

Zénobe knew what Maurel was talking about, but André scrunched up his sleepy eyebrows.

"Morpheus," explained Zénobe. "The god of slumber."

Zénobe jumped out of bed first, removed his nightshirt and began to splash water on his face.

Maurel had news. "Today will be lighter on all of us. *Monsieur* de Voltaire will curtail most of the visits. We have already called for *docteur* Tronchin."

Zénobe turned around in a flash, water dripping down his face onto his chest. The image took Maurel's breath away: the water formed rivulets trying to find the path of least resistance among the growth patterns of Zénobe's chest hair. In a sweep of his eyes, Maurel traced those alluring patterns: on his chest, a semicircular pattern running symmetrically towards his nipples and almost obscuring them, but with the hair closest to his neck growing straight up, as if rebelling from the uniformity of the rest. The pattern narrowed down to a thin band along the middle of his abdomen, then flared out again to cover a good part of his belly, disappearing down his undergarment. Taking in the image, Maurel decided right then and there that he, the *maître d'hôtel* of the Villette household, would work hard to keep his master's paws off of his boys. Offers of fictional posts or no, these two angels were special. They were too good, too innocent, and the *marquis* de Villette was not going to have them. Some things on earth were meant not to be manhandled.

"Is Voltaire ill?" Zénobe asked, a look of worry on his face.

"*Monsieur* de Voltaire," corrected Maurel, then quickly added, "–is quite well, just fatigued. And after *docteur* Tronchin's remonstrations of the other day, *madame* Denis thought it best to have a more restful day today. So, *monsieur* Bosquet, you are to offer *monsieur* de Voltaire's regrets to everybody but his colleagues. Just say that he is feeling indisposed. After dinner I'll post Philippe or Henri at the door, so you and André can have your afternoon lesson. You haven't been able to have it these past two days. Progress must continue. André must pursue his education and become a learned young man. What is the lesson to be today, *monsieur* Bosquet?"

Zénobe, relieved about Voltaire's state of health, stated his lesson plans with enthusiasm, "We shall continue with Herodotus for history, then a bit of Montesquieu for political systems, and since André didn't know who Morpheus was, I shall begin to present all of the gods and myths of antiquity, including the Norse gods, not neglecting the Hindu gods, all the way up to our own trinity of gods, ghosts and virgins, and sundry saints, angels and demons."

Maurel was duly impressed. "Well, well, that will be a mighty lesson. I shall see to it that you won't be disturbed. You shall use my apartments and I'll light a fire. You shall be cozy and warm."

It was André's turn in front of the ceramic bowl. "You, André," continued Maurel, "I need to send to market this morning. We are short on all sorts of herbs, and we also need some ipecac for *monsieur* de Voltaire. You can get it all at the apothecary's. I'll give you the money for it as soon as you're both in the kitchen for your breakfast. Understood?" he asked as he prepared to leave their room.

"Understood," they both said in unison, mimicking Maurel's musical intonation.

And then he was gone.

They didn't dare say anything to each other, because of the people in the other room, but they looked at each other with a new vision. The night had changed things. It was a frightening new situation, but also exhilarating. For the time being, they were happy for the restrictions which kept them from talking to each other, yet—without it making any sense to them—they felt a concomitant desire to exchange words, not just glances. André's glances bordered on sly embarrassment. Zénobe's were more direct, happier, like Archimedes when he cried out 'Eureka!' in his bathtub. A new discovery was in the process of being made, but this time it touched him, Zénobe, directly. Of course he had encountered this form of Greek behavior in his readings of ancient texts (so long as they hadn't been expurgated by modern French editors), but it was different, and vertiginous, to experience it for oneself.

While they were dressing, Zénobe smiled and raised his eyebrows at André, as if to say, "I'm feeling happy. How about you?" André did smile in return, but then quickly looked down in order to direct his leg down his pants' leg. It went into the wrong leg anyway, and as he hopped around in order not to fall over, he laughed, and Zénobe laughed with him.

"Hey, something's amusing this early in the morning," said Suzanne from next door.

"Who's jumping? Somebody must be reenacting la *chevalière*'s fencing demonstration from yesterday," offered Sylvie.

"What sleight of hand!" exclaimed Marianne. "Did you see those arm muscles?"

"And did you see that crouching position?" asked Suzanne. "She was like this," she demonstrated, "for more than fifteen minutes. *Aïe*, it hurts!"

André and Zénobe heard strikes of wood and shuffling of shoes. They peered into the girls' room and saw Suzanne and Marianne giving their own demonstration of their fencing agility with a broom handle and a candle snuffer. Sylvie, still in bed, could not stop laughing.

André and Zénobe laughed as well. Zénobe brought one arm over André's shoulders and watched the mock contention in the servant's quarters. They couldn't have been happier.

Maurel was not a man to procrastinate, and he wasted no time in preparing his master for an eventual disillusionment on the subject of ever physically enjoying his two household boys. As soon as the *marquis* de Villette was sufficiently awake and drinking his coffee in bed, Maurel gave him the bad news.

"I don't think these boys will come around, *monsieur le marquis.* They are being recalcitrant, obtuse, and thoroughly obstreperous, as only country bumpkins can be. I do not think they are made of the right material and will never be suitable."

"You're not thinking of dismissing them, Maurel?" asked the *marquis* in authentic alarm.

"Oh, no, *monsieur,* we cannot do that. They are badly needed for the household. Especially now that *monsieur* de Voltaire is here. And I dare say that they are both working out satisfactorily in their duties. But insofar as the…" and here Maurel lowered his voice and raised his eyebrows, "…the surplus, is concerned, I think they have no knowledge, no imagination, no experience, and no inkling as to what the 'unnameable' could be."

"Oh, give them to me for an evening and I'll teach them what that is," was the response from the aristocrat who was as petulant as he was imprudent.

Maurel thought to himself, yes, that would certainly scare them off right away, wouldn't it. But to his master, he respectfully remonstrated that he had been trying day and night to get the two boys to understand between the lines what would be expected of them between the sheets. "I think we would be wasting our time to pursue this any further with these two boys particularly. Remember what happened with Philippe and Henri? They were never receptive to cajoling, to bribes, to any ways known to bring them over. Look how useful they are to us now, but it never worked out for the… surplus."

"Yes, and now they're too old, and Henri is too fat." The *marquis* put his coffee cup down. "But André and Bosquet are still young enough. They are but young saplings, and can be made to grow into any direction we wish. They can be convinced, whittled down, bent! They will yield, I think." He thought for a moment about what he was going to say next, and then shrugged. "You know that I offered Bosquet the post of chamberlain."

"Ah, really?" asked Maurel, all naiveté and surprise.

"Yes, and he seemed to be rather interested. I feel that if he were under my direct supervision, we would have some success in bringing him around, and with him in the fold, André couldn't be far off."

"I wouldn't be too sure," was Maurel's answer, as he tidied up around the boudoir.

"Ah," reminisced the *marquis.* "I still prefer the days when we just went out on sorties and took our walks in the Tuileries Gardens, or at the Père Lachaise Cemetery. Near the tombs of La Fontaine and Molière, there would always be some merriment awaiting, some frolic to raise our flagging spirits and dissipate our boredom. I remember well! It was invigorating, it was inspiring, a bit dangerous, to trawl among the shadows of the tombs, until one found something worthy of an escapade. Oh, it brings back such pleasurable shudders." He twisted his spine back and forth while sitting in bed.

Maurel looked at him askance. "You must be forgetting the troubles you had with brigands who took your valuables and nearly your life, to say nothing of the detectives who also did their own trawling."

"Oh, those devils! They do in the name of the law what they would have liked to do were it not for the shame they feel. Many of them let themselves be caressed, among other favors, for more time than was necessary. Ha ha! I remember a fellow inside a mausoleum who had removed his britches down to his ankles, and only when he heard his partner rooting about outside—a full five minutes later!—did he cry foul murder. How to explain that?"

"What you say certainly has an element of truth, but it still doesn't deny the fact that you had to be rescued from the prefecture because of your indiscretions."

"But that was so minor considering that many times we did manage to hit the jackpot. All those beautiful men, pushed to these acts of baseness, of moral decrepitude, because they were poor, threatened by debtor's prison or being thrown out on the street. And I was there to lend them a helping hand. For me, it was a charitable transaction. You see, it was a two-way street (*un va et vient*), and afterwards each participant of the covenant walked away happier, lighter, less preoccupied, and ready to face another day." Maurel could only say "*Oui, monsieur,*" in agreement.

"The way things are now," continued the *marquis* de Villette, "we have to bring the boys in, *engage* them and all that tralala, and then wait an *eternity* before they can be brought to fruition. My God, my beard will grow longer waiting for them."

Maurel was preparing the *marquis'* shaving equipment and said, "But you sport no beard."

"You know what I mean."

The *marquis* got out of bed and came to sit on the divan in front of the mirror. Villette was short and stocky, of a feisty temperament, but his beard was sparse. As a matter of fact, in the château in Ferney, Maurel had witnessed a couple of times his master and Voltaire plucking out each other's beard hairs with tweezers. Shaving the *marquis* was purely a ceremonial affair. Maurel took a steaming towel and wrapped it around his master's face.

"It's too difficult the way we're doing it now," came the muffled voice from the towel. "I'd rather go back to the previous system we had."

"But, *monsieur le marquis*, you are married now, and as a *paterfamilias* you have to worry more about your reputation, you need to be a pillar of society, and need I remind you, you have to work at getting a little *marquis* de Villette started. The next generation must arrive promptly."

"Well, you certainly have ruined my morning, Maurel."

Maurel removed the towel and spread some *mousse de savon* on the *marquis'* face.

"You did use the right word, however: work. It'll be work to get this little *marquis* going. That's why I need some activity that will get me inspired, excited, and therefore functional, for when I'm ready to take the plunge. Something will have to keep me going in this endeavor, and memories of Bosquet, or André, preferably both, will be sufficient to arouse my continued commitment to procreate. I shall be a veritable piston!"

Maurel started to shave his *marquis*, who continued speaking, making Maurel's task more difficult. "Ah, the things we do for the genealogical tree. Why should I care if there is no other *marquis* de Villette to replace me? Look at Voltaire. He's not leaving any progeny behind him."

"*Monsieur* de Voltaire is irreplaceable," replied Maurel drily, concentrating on not cutting his master's throat by accident.

"Besides, the *marquise* just doesn't inspire me, like Bosquet or André does."

"She is a woman, *monsieur.*"

"True, true. But she is beautiful. What a diminutive waist she has."

Maurel thought it best not to comment on the figure of his master's wife.

"Still, don't you think I could have Bosquet as my chamberlain? He could perform serious tasks. We could teach him about economy, about the Bourse,[121] he could manage the accounts—"

"You would entrust this boy with your accounts, a boy whom you have known for less than a week?"

"Well, why not? He seems trustworthy enough."

"I won't disagree with you on that point, but I think he is still too young for such responsibilities."

"Well, then, damn it! We'll have him acquit himself of duties to which he is commensurate. Use your head, man, you've always had much more imagination than I!"

Maurel couldn't agree more. Still, he told the *marquis*, "You know that master Zénobe came into this household because of the presence of *monsieur* de Voltaire. He wishes to be in the presence of the *philosophe*—"

"Well, confound it, man! Everybody wants to be in the presence of the *philosophe*. So what?"

"In addition, master Zénobe has his duty to teach master André, and this was at *monsieur* de Voltaire's bidding."

"I could crack your head open sometimes, Maurel. Next thing I know, you'll be having me put Sylvie at the Sorbonne and Marianne and Suzanne with preceptors and, and, and with masters of dance and English as well!"

"Master André comes from an aristocratic family that calls Corneille one of their own."

"And my descendants will have *me* to call as their own as well, one day."

The *marquis* was getting irritated, so Maurel threw the towel down into the hot water, wrung it with refined but barely controlled violence, and then wrapped the *marquis'* face with it again, this time massaging his newly shaved face so he couldn't say anything for a while.

Maurel took advantage of this to say, "*Monsieur*, you have to be reasonable. I am working diligently to get masters Zénobe and André to come to certain conclusions. Most would already have arrived at them. But these two, coming from the sticks as they do, are too naïve. Apart from watching goats and sheep fornicate, they have not been exposed to anything remotely resembling sexuality, to say nothing of the... unnamable. I imagine that in the deep recesses of Savoy, master Zénobe did not have access to *monsieur* Diderot's exposition about sexual mores in Tahiti.[122] What could he have possibly read that could have announced the existence of the unnamable?"

There was a muffled sound from under the towel. Maurel removed it and asked, "I beg your pardon, *monsieur*?"

The *marquis* repeated, "The Greeks."

Maurel bit his lip. He had just lost major ground. "This may be true, but only if he had intact texts. Most editions remove whole sections—"

---

121   The French Stock Market. Stemming from a house of exchange of merchandise established in Bruges by a Belgian bourgeois, a certain *monsieur* van der Buerse, the Bourse was in Toulouse and Lyon installed before it was by royal decree in Paris in 1724 founded. The Revolution will not hinder its development, save for temporary emergency closings.

122   Not too many people had access to Diderot's *Supplément au Voyage de Bougainville* which trafficked as a manuscript and was not published until after all of the *philosophes* were dead, such was the danger of what the text postulated: why should sex, a purely physiological activity, be constrained by arbitrary moral values?

"Not the older editions. I suppose Zénobe did not have the wherewithal to purchase brand new books. In any case, I should ask him, what books he has read that speak of–"

"I must counsel patience, *monsieur*. You know with these Italian types one must advance with great caution. Their idea of masculinity is so caught up with Biblical references and entreaties to 'go forth and multiply,' that to them, finding where to stick their pricks becomes a holy mandate. Look at your friend Casanova. Would you ever try to bring him into the fold?"

"Ha!" laughed the *marquis*. "He is so proud of his escapades and accomplishments with women, he'd rather have me impaled with great pomp on the Place Louis XV than risk having his escutcheon besmirched."

Maurel sighed with relief inside himself. Yet, he continued the campaign, for he was fighting for the innocence of his two angels. "If you had ever tried anything louche with that Venetian *don Juan*, I guarantee you he would have exposed you and calumniated you among the courts of Europe." Then, while removing the shaving equipment, he offered a parting word, "Let me take care of this, *monsieur le marquis*. You know I have the magic touch, and the patience to work wonders. Remember La Harpe, *fils*? You have forgotten how supple he became in our hands?"

"Well, yes, but then he showed his true colors when he became overly ambitious. He was far too expensive."

"He was bitter, and this was partly out of envy, since his father didn't have your fortune. It was his insolence to try to get back at you. But it was also partly out of fear because, if you will allow me to say it, you came on too strong, *monsieur*."

"Oh, I think that's silly."

"*Monsieur*, with all the respect that I owe you and that you deserve, I must tell you that at times people see you as a predator, a lion in the forest who pounces on indefensible prey, on baby deer and hatchlings. You must learn to have a lighter touch, and a more delicate demeanor. Either that, or go after hardier prey worthy of your ferocity."

The *marquis* de Villette did not abhor the image of himself as a lion. When Maurel saw that his master was appeased, for the moment, he bowed and prepared to take his leave, saying, "I must look in on *monsieur* de Voltaire, *monsieur*. Would you like me to stay and help you dress?"

"No, no, Maurel, go look after Voltaire. I am in no hurry. I want to read the *Journal*. I want to see what was written about me. You may come back later."

And Maurel was off to his next task, this time with *Madame* Denis.

He found her in *monsieur* de Voltaire's boudoir, where the *philosophe* was still in bed. She was holding on to her uncle's hand, beseeching him to end the overwhelming visits. "You heard what *docteur* Tronchin said. This constant commotion is doing you no good. It is draining your health. And it is keeping you from working on your play."

"Oh, my dear, you are no good at debate based on good, solid reasoning. *Docteur* Tronchin is a charlatan, my visitors adore me and fill my vanity (*mon amour-propre*) with glory, my physical condition is nothing that a good night's rest won't relieve, and *Irène* is nearly finished. The plot has been laid to rest, just a tweak of rhyme here and a stage-instruction there, and it's done. Have you any other ammunition to fire at me?"

"*Mon oncle*, I say this for your own good. You make it seem as though I were attacking you, criticizing you for the sake of criticizing. I see you turn pale, go through paroxysms of pain, faint dead away, and I suffer so every time you are bled. All I want is your good health, your happiness, and your glory on stage."

"Ah, *ma chère nièce*, my beloved nurse, my succulent piece of ass, I know you want my every comfort and my complete happiness. You need to know that I am completely comfortable and happy with you by my side. Never again do I want to go through the anguish of your absence. Ask Wagnière how I suffered, not knowing if you were well, not knowing if you were in want of anything, not knowing if you were happy. That ungrateful jackass La Harpe almost stole from me that which I need to be a complete man."

Voltaire knew that these details of *madame* Denis' past indiscretions made her more pliable during arguments.

"This commotion," he continued, "these visitors vying to see me, it is all just temporary. You'll see. Soon, the novelty of my presence here will die down, and we'll be left in peace and solitude. Once *Irène* is on stage and I have received my acclamations, we shall go back to Ferney and live the sweet life of retirement and meditation. We shall collect a few *philosophes* with us, and finally those who think shall live together."

Madame Denis, who wasn't born yesterday, who had indeed asked Voltaire's secretary for the details of Voltaire's reaction to her absence from Ferney, and had found out that her uncle had truly gone through a period of depression, was not so easily disengaged. She gave him tea, while Maurel discreetly kept to the background, doing a few odds and ends, then picked up the breakfast tray and was about to leave. He took advantage of the momentary lull in their conversation, and asked, "Will there be anything else, *monsieur -dame*?"

"No, thank you, Maurel," came the reply from *madame* Denis.

"I have sent André to the apothecary for *monsieur* de Voltaire's powdered basil and ipecac. They should be here promptly before dinner."

"Very well, Maurel."

"Also, *monsieur* d'Alembert has sent word that he would be pleased to join you for dinner, if *monsieur* de Voltaire is not too fatigued."

Voltaire replied, "Never. I will never be too fatigued for my esteemed and lovable Plato!"

Then Maurel made eye contact with *madame* Denis and said in as nonchalant a manner as he could, "Master Zénobe has voiced interest in being placed under your tutelage, if there is no inconvenience."

"That young hellion," reacted Voltaire. "There's one who is full of energy and irreverence! He reminds me of me, a younger me, when I was still chomping at the bit!"

Madame Denis shrugged. She wouldn't mind having another pair of helping hands in the care of her uncle. "That would be fine," she responded.

Maurel said, "He demonstrates keen gratitude of serving in this household during *monsieur* de Voltaire's sojourn here, as, indeed, do we all." Maurel made a little bow. "On this historical occasion, all of the staff recognize the supreme importance of your continued success in Paris, and if there is anything you need, please do not hesitate to ask."

"Thank you, Maurel," said *madame* Denis. "You have taken care of our every need, and indeed, you have even anticipated some. We would be delighted to wrest you away from the *marquis* for when we return to Ferney."

Maurel smiled and bowed deeply, and then left the room. He was still smiling as he entered the kitchen. His next stop: back to the *marquis'* bedroom to announce the unhappy news that *monsieur* de Voltaire had expressly given the instructions to have master Zénobe present for *monsieur* d'Alembert's visit at dinner, and probably at supper as well. Something having to do with matters of state in Savoy and sundry other feudal concerns. By the time Maurel had climbed up the stairs, he also had a few kernels of appeasement planned to help undo the *marquis'* disappointment: the fact that young Zénobe needed Voltaire's expertise and connections to help bring Savoy to a more modern political state; Frédéric II[123] had written to *monsieur* de Voltaire to offer his condolences on the loss of the actor Lekain; the *marquis* de Villette could help bring about Frédéric's influence as a beneficial and enlightened monarch to create pressure on his fellow king Victor-Amédée III; the chains of feudal tyranny would be loosened in Savoy; such an act of aid to *monsieur* de Voltaire's perennial war against the injustices of the world would serve to raise the *marquis* de Villette's star among the leaders of Europe's gentry; the *marquis* de Villette's name would be in all the papers, not just the *Journal de Paris*, but the *Gazette de France* as well, all the widely read publications of the Continent. The newspapers would publish the names of Voltaire and Villette in the same sentence, names of quality and of valor, names to be glorified and set to immortality for their efforts in the search for Justice and Liberty! *Ecrasez l'Infâme!*

By the time Maurel left the *marquis'* boudoir, the *marquis* was dressed and raring to go, requesting the presence of his secretary Ursus Requain. They would then go to the offices of the *Journal de Paris* and the *Gazette de France*, to see about the publication of the *marquis'* letters, which meant that the *marquis* would not be among the dinner party that afternoon. Maurel raised his eyes heavenward. Praise the god of Vanity! Adore the deities of Self-Interest! Bow down low before human *amour-propre!*

Maurel could then breathe a sigh of relief: Zénobe was now out of the grasp of Villette's possessive hands, and in the hands of Voltaire. Now all Maurel had to do was prepare Zénobe for this new set of circumstances. It was his turn to become Zénobe's preceptor. It was he who was going to initiate his young charge into the arts of diplomacy, of dissimulation, and of flattery; and also into the sciences of social morality and of the code of hypocritical conventions. He would have Zénobe read La Rochefoucauld, La Bruyère and *madame* de Lafayette,[124] and they would discuss the differences between Being and Seeming (*l'Être et le Paraître*). Maurel planned for the young man nothing other than the complete demystification of human nature. He couldn't wait to begin the rest of Zénobe's education.

It turned out that the *marquis* de Condorcet also came to dinner early that afternoon. This provided a boon for Maurel who gaily abandoned Zénobe to the dining room where the young man would assist in the duties of the kitchen staff, although he would not be going into the kitchen itself. With Philippe posted at the front door of the *hôtel* to keep

---

123   The King of Prussia, at whose court Voltaire spent three years of his life, trying to coax a glimmer of enlightenment out of his despotism.

124   Authors of 17th-Century works on moralism and social interplay.

out all visitors, Zénobe would now be in close proximity to his beloved Voltaire. He would be privy to free thinking, rational viewpoints, and philosophical conversation.

In addition to the three *philosophes*, the two ladies *Belle et bonne* and *madame* Denis were also present. It was an intimate gathering, far from a theatrical viewing of Voltaire who was noticeably subdued by his not being on display.

The soup was being served while Zénobe poured the wine, a piquant full-bodied Bordeaux that went well with the sort of *ragoût mêlé* that le Parnaud had prepared with the addition of two brand new ingredients: pumpkin from North America and chile pepper from South America.

Voltaire tasted the ragoût of chicken, chicken livers, nonlaid eggs,[125] mushrooms and hearts of artichoke and exclaimed, "Delicious, and spicy! I hope my intestines can take it. My mouth certainly can!" Then he squinted into his bowl and asked, "What is this orange food?"

La marquise de Villette answered, "It is *potiron, mon cher Papa.*" Apparently she had liked what *madame* de Brillon called *monsieur* Franklin.

"What is that?"

"It is a type of gourd that comes from America."

"Ah, from America! So, what is it called in American?"

"You mean in English," corrected *madame* Denis.

"No, I mean in American," came the stern reply. "The version of English as it is spoken in the United Colonies is already quite sufficiently different to warrant a different nomenclature."

"Oh," said *madame* Denis. "I was unaware of this."

"Language doesn't sit still for anyone," laughed the sage who had done more than his part to transform, improve, and burnish the French language. "So what is this called in the nation whence it hails?"

"It is called *pumpkin*," answered the *marquise*. A funny name, isn't it? It grows on a vine that is allowed to trail on the ground."

"On the ground? It is not trained to grow on trellises?" asked the *marquis* de Condorcet who was thinking of grape vines.

"No," continued the *marquise* de Villette. And apparently it dies after just one season. You have to plant it all over again in the spring."

"Quite interesting, quite interesting," expressed Condorcet, who took another bite. "I much like its flesh. It is grainier than the *pomme de terre* (potato), closer in color to the *pomme d'or* (tomato), but has a distinct taste all its own. Delicious," was his final conclusion.

"You are indeed lucky to have le Parnaud," said the *marquise* with nostalgia. "Where does he come up with these culinary ideas?"

Voltaire answered this question. "The man is a *philosophe* of the kitchen. He is not afraid to try new things, he instinctively knows how these novel comestibles will taste along with traditional cuisine, and he puts his trust in the learned opinions of men of science!"

With a flourish, he stuck another spoonful into his mouth. As soon as he had swallowed and emitted an "aah" of satisfaction, he asked, "Are you aware that many Europeans think that the tomato is dangerous to eat, even fatal? Of course, it didn't help that Sir John Hill, the English botanist, who had the misfortune of dying three years ago, named this new plant *lycopersicon*: wolf peach. Still, the natives of America have been eating this fruit for centuries. It is even called the *pomme d'amour*, believed

---

125   The shell-less eggs found inside a laying hen.

to be beneficial for sexual prowess and stamina. Blame the fruit for being a lustrous, unapologetic red. Give a common European this juicy, Devil-red fruit the color of blood, and he will quake in his boots. Le Parnaud has for years been cooking our eggs with onions, garlic, peppers and *pomme d'or*—from a recipe brought back by a Spaniard from the Guatemalas—and, even though I can't vouch for its aphrodisiac qualities, we from Ferney can certainly attest to its aroma, taste and other nonpoisonous virtues."

"Oh, yes," said the *marquise*. "Le Parnaud used to make us stuffed tomatoes as well. Stuffed with crab meat and crowned with shrimp."

"Yes, which the Jews won't eat for reasons I have yet to fathom," added Voltaire.

"Even our food is burdened with false ideas and fraught with concepts of moral values." This was said by d'Alembert whose brow felt the weight of culinary prejudices. "On the other hand, you have the example of the Orientals who vie with each other to eat the flesh of a certain fish which also is thought to possess aphrodisiac qualities. However, if the fish is not well prepared, it can, and does, prove to be fatal. The fish's natural defenses are an array of spines which become longer and harder when it puffs itself out to look more ferocious and therefore be too big to be swallowed up by a predator."

"Well, what a choice to be faced with!" exclaimed Voltaire. "A hard prick or pricked hard (*une pine dure ou une dure épine*, closer to 'a hard prick or a thorny spine')!"

"Almost," explained d'Alembert. "Apparently it is something in its digestive tract that proves to be poisonous."

"Ah, sounds like my own digestive tract. Louis XV was never able to swallow me, was he?" Then Voltaire looked around his body with an air of innocence. "Nonetheless, I have no natural defenses."

"Oh, yes you do!" came the voluble cry from around the table with simultaneous laughter.

Madame Denis voiced the unanimous verdict: "It is your tongue, *mon cher maître*. Your tongue is barbed. You have an acid tongue. When you have finished licking your enemies, what is left has to be picked off the ground."

Voltaire laughed good-naturedly. "Yes, but at least it is not forked, is it?"

"Never, my dear uncle!"

"Another glass of wine?" asked Voltaire of Zénobe. Zénobe dutifully approached with the carafe. The young man was greatly enjoying the conversation and had a big smile, something about which Maurel had purposely neglected to tell the young valet: one doesn't react to the conversation around the table. Voltaire looked up at Zénobe and said, "And you, too, my dear *monsieur* Bosquet, the volatile young man of the little forest, you too have a glass of wine to drink to my health and my unswallowability!"

None at this table was surprised by Voltaire's request. Voltaire had always treated the household staff with such amicable and sympathetic terms. Only the *marquis* de Villette, today absent from the meal, stood out for his haughtiness and air of superiority.

Zénobe poured himself a glass of wine and offered a toast, "To *monsieur* de Voltaire's tongue, to his digestive tract, to his whole body. To *monsieur* de Voltaire's unswallow-ability! Long may his tongue lick and rule!"

"Hear, hear," said Condorcet and d'Alembert. And everybody took a swallow.

Maurel stood discreetly behind the open doorway, unseen by anyone in the dining room. He was slightly stooped, and held his hands together in the gesture of a prayer of thanks to the deity of dining room chitchat. He had been following every word. When his angel showed himself to be quick and nimble, Maurel's smile could not have been more beatific.

After dinner, Maurel sent André to beckon *docteur* Tronchin once again (he had already been summoned that morning, but to no avail; he still hadn't come). André returned without *docteur* Tronchin, who had turned out to be in Saint-Germain-en-Laye taking care of a patient. In keeping with his plan, Maurel set André up in his rooms with Zénobe for their lesson. When Maurel returned downstairs, he was told by Philippe that there was a visitor at the front door who wanted to see *monsieur* de Voltaire and who would not take no for an answer. This person was insisting that he had to come in, that it was a matter of imminent danger concerning Voltaire's very safety, salvation or permanent death. Maurel had had experience with crazy people demanding to see Voltaire, but from what he could gather about this new visitor, and from the possibility of real danger coming to the *hôtel* de Villette's famous guest, he realized that it would be best to attend to the front door and see for himself what was afoot. As he made his way to the front of the house, he felt like a soldier, the first line of defense in the protection of *monsieur* de Voltaire. He even puffed out his chest a little, all the better to show his fortitude and courage. He was sure that he would be able to take care of anything. He didn't notice this, but from some place deep within himself, *la chevalière* d'Éon was giving him encouragement as well.

The man waiting patiently outside the door was small, and meek; wearing a black frock so long it touched the ground. Holding his hands together as if in prayer, he bowed and rapidly introduced himself. "I am *l'abbé* Marthe and I have been sent to speak with the *philosophe monsieur* de Voltaire for a matter of urgent importance."

"You have no doubt been told of *monsieur* de Voltaire's indisposition today?" was Maurel's answer.

"Precisely so. This is the reason why I must speak with him immediately. We don't have a moment to lose. We have heard that *monsieur* de Voltaire is ill, that he might be dying. I would carry this burden on my conscience until my dying day if I didn't come and speak with him."

"Perhaps you can tell me what it is and I will be most happy to tell him in your stead, when he is feeling better." Maurel wanted to be polite yet firm about sending this nervous little man away. The *maître d'hôtel* noticed that *l'abbé* Marthe's pate was tonsured.

"No, no, no, no," said *l'abbé* Marthe earnestly and pleadingly. "No, no, I must see him myself. It cannot be done any other way. I have to speak to him directly, for no one else can be a mediator. You see, I *am* the go-between, and I myself cannot have a go-between. Please, for the love of Christ, I beseech you, I must see *monsieur* de Voltaire right away!"

Maurel realized why Philippe was not able to get rid of this man. "Please wait right here," he said finally. "I shall go speak with *monsieur* de Voltaire and ask if he is up to receiving a visitor. I shall be right back."

The abbot nodded his head and said "Yes, yes, thank you, thank you," and kept nodding his head. Maurel had to repeat, "I shall be right back," and "Please, please", a couple of times more until Marthe realized he had to step back a little to enable the *maître d'hôtel* to close the door.

What an insistent little bugger, Maurel thought to himself as he walked towards Voltaire's boudoir. He found him back in bed, conversing with Condorcet who was spread out at the foot of the bed and d'Alembert seated in the *petite ruelle.*

When he was inside the room he apologized for the intrusion, but there was a man outside who insisted that it was a matter of danger, perhaps physical danger for *monsieur* de Voltaire, and that this is why he had been sent to warn him.

"Well, what's his name and who has sent him?"

Maurel answered, "A certain *abbé* Marthe," and I ignore who has sent him, but I surmise it was his ecclesiastic superiors."

"*L'abbé* Marthe, *l'abbé* Marthe?" wondered Voltaire. "Do you know of an *abbé* Marthe? I don't know anyone by that name."

Condorcet and d'Alembert didn't recognize the name either.

"He is being very insistent, and I fear he might have knowledge of something that might prove harmful to you, *monsieur* de Voltaire. I didn't dare take it upon myself to send him away."

"Quite right, quite right, Maurel. You might as well send him in because now curiosity has gotten the better of me. And once curiosity has gained a toehold in me, it will not let go until it has been assuaged."

As Maurel quickly returned to the front door, he asked Philippe to accompany him and the strange little visitor back to Voltaire's room in case it was the abbot himself who would prove to be the danger. One couldn't be too careful these days, he told himself. He knew that even if *l'abbé* Marthe were hiding a weapon inside his cassock he would be no match for the combined forces of Philippe and himself. He now recognized that *la chevalière* was there within him. If a woman can show no fear in defending what she knows is right, well then certainly I cannot show any fear, he thought. Nobody would ever be able to say that I wasn't brave.

But everything turned out to be safe. As soon as Maurel announced him at the doorway of the boudoir, *l'abbé* Marthe threw his little body into the middle of the room and sank to his knees.

"Oh, thank God that I have been able to see you, *monsieur* de Voltaire!"

"Good day, sir," said Voltaire, "I am most happy to see you here among us," and he proceeded to introduce his two *philosophe* companions to the *abbé*, who recognized their names immediately. When Marthe realized in whose presence he was, he rolled his eyes hesitantly to the heavens in silent prayer as if to ask for added courage. The abbot realized that what he had to say to Voltaire, he must now say in front of a total of three *philosophes*: a deist, an atheist, and a *libertin.*[126] One could see his little heart sink and his hands flutter to their position of prayer.

"My *maître d'hôtel* didn't catch the name of those who have sent you…" continued Voltaire.

"No man has sent me," said the startled *abbé*. "I have been sent directly by God!"

Something made d'Alembert chortle a quickly-stifled laugh: was it the *abbé*'s spunk, was it his avowed personal relationship with the deity, was it the drab-brown cassock or the tonsured hair?

---

126   *Libertin* was the catchall phrase for 17th- and 18th-Century freethinkers and skeptics who proclaimed personal freedom of conscience and religious belief. Consequently, they eschewed organized religion. In turn, they were vilified as atheists and immoralists bent on the ruination of everything sacred.

Voltaire rolled his eyes in impatience. "On whose behalf have you come, Father? Some ecclesiastic superior must have sent you."

"Why, no, that is not the case," responded the *abbé*, feeling hurt. "It is the Lord himself who has sent me."

Voltaire looked the *abbé* up and down and said, "Well, then, kindly show me your credentials."

D'Alembert and Condorcet couldn't keep themselves from exhaling a quick laugh which they then pretended had been a cough.

"*Monsieur*," pleaded the *abbé*. "Please don't make fun of a poor servant of God who has come here to do His bidding."

"I wish I knew so easily what is God's bidding," said Voltaire.

"You can very easily find out, *monsieur*, for it is in your own heart."

"Oh, *mon père*, there are so many things that are found in my heart. A bountiful, magnificent, conflictive, mutually exclusive collection of things that are found in my heart. How do you propose that I identify that part which shows God's will?"

"Meditation and patience, prayer and solitude and abnegation–"

Voltaire was an old man and he had heard all this before and was in no mood to hear it again.

"Tell us, *cher abbé* Marthe, what you see as God's will here, with me, now."

"You must confess, my son, you must confess your sins, and your soul will receive eternal salvation."

Condorcet and d'Alembert were kind and polite men, but they seethed with anger and vituperation and inclemency when aroused by such words. Even if Voltaire was going to play with this *abbé* like the cat plays with a mouse, they still realized that it was words like these that had led, and were still leading, to the demise–the torture and the killing–of otherwise noble and intelligent human beings. The purifying flames of autos-da-fé were always accompanied by such language.

"You must confess, you must confess, or you will die without receiving absolution and your soul will dwell in the eternal fires of hell. I can help you, my son, I can help you here, today, right now." Marthe started fumbling at his neck inside his cassock looking for something. Maurel and Philippe were startled and took a step closer in case the *abbé* took out some sort of weapon, but all he produced was a crucifix on a chain.

Voltaire spoke to no one in particular: "I have been waiting impatiently for the doctor who will cure me of my physical ills, and now God sends me someone who will cure me of my spiritual maladies. Perhaps I should learn to be better at prayer."

"See? It is a sign of God that thou hast been waiting for succor, and now I am come unto thee, my son. All God wants is a simple act of faith, thy confession, and he will grant thee salvation, and recompense will be thine: paradise forevermore."

Condorcet sat up in bed and made ready to get up. Voltaire put out his hand in a gesture of patience. "Wait, this will only take a moment." Voltaire again turned his attention to the priest. "I really must thank thee, my blessed Father, for having undertaken the effort to save my undeserving soul from eternal damnation. But as thou knowest, thy Church and I have not seen eye-to-eye on a number of things for many, many years now. However, I do know her rather well, and I would bet my everlasting soul with the Devil (Marthe crossed his chest several times at this) that she understands my confession to be a recanting of the things I have been saying these last, oh, seventy years. How sayest thee?"

The *abbé* got up from his knees and approached the bed. He was hardly taller than d'Alembert who was seated. "I have read thy works, my son, and feel great compassion for thee. I understand that thou hast been wronged, repeatedly, but by men not of the Church. Nobody from within the Church has ever laid a finger on thee."

"Not on me, yes, thou art quite correct there, my friend. But she has certainly laid many fingers on my works, which are an extension of me. They are part of me, they are my corpus, and the Church has constantly denied the dissemination of said works, has condemned them, put them on the Index, has had public burnings of them on the steps of Saint Bartholomew. And certainly the Church has never lifted a finger to defend me from the vilest accusations and even physical attacks on me, nor has it ever sought to protect my friends from their attackers."

"But thou must understand, that what you philosophers and freethinkers write, these words that you publish, everything you say, lead people astray, make them deviate from the path of salvation."

Condorcet got up from the bed.

"My dear Condor," said Voltaire. "Please do not go." And then to the *abbé* he said, "As thou canst see, Father, now is not a good time to speak of this. Perhaps thou canst return in a few days, when I'm feeling better, and we shall have a go at it, yes?"

"Perhaps thou art right, *monsieur le philosophe* de Voltaire. I shall come back. I shall come back. It will be a pleasure to come back and speak with thee. It will be a pleasure."

Maurel and Philippe escorted the abbot out of the room and forthwith out the front door.

Condorcet laughed and asked his friend, "What was *that* all about?"

"Ah, you young whippersnapper. You are not old, as I am. Your days are numerous ahead of you. Mine, however, are counted and counting down. The fact that my end is nigh makes me look at things a little differently. Ask me if when the end comes I want to be dragged to the nearest garbage dump. This would destroy *madame* Denis and upset my friends. I am thinking of a tomb, any little old tomb will do, a nice marble slab with a cover to keep me dry from the elements and safe from packs of marauding dogs. What harm can there be if I can satisfy the ecclesiastics in order to get a tomb for myself?"

"But they're going to insist on a complete recantation," observed d'Alembert.

"They're not going to get that, you might as well know now," responded Voltaire.

"And they're going to sprinkle that benighted holy water on you," mentioned Condorcet.

"I'll be dead already, so what's the harm?"

"I don't know," said Condorcet. "One cannot deal with the Church."

"Listen, perhaps God did send me this little fellow of an *abbé*. I think it's just the person I need to get a decent burial for myself."

Both d'Alembert and Condorcet gave him looks of incredulity.

"No, no, you'll see. I'll take care of the kindly *abbé*. And in the end, he'll take care of me."

Voltaire gave them his wicked little grin, and both of his friends realized that this little old man, their friend, a spindly bony man with a wise and beautiful brain, had, in the end, always gotten what he wanted.

Condorcet couldn't stay for supper, but d'Alembert was available and spent some time alone with Voltaire. There was still no word of *docteur* Tronchin, so the two old encyclopedic friends had the luxury of conversation together, which was such welcome pleasure for both of them. *Philosophes* never feel jealous of each other, with the exception of Jean-Jacques Rousseau, who preferred to think with his heart more than with his brain and thus spent his life feeling envious, paranoid, and excluded. It was a relaxing afternoon that d'Alembert and Voltaire spent with one another. The mathematician got to voice some of his worries about Voltaire's state of mind, as well as his health. Voltaire soothed his preoccupation with entreaties that he had never felt more in control. Yes, he knew that *Irène* was not going to be the best play he'd ever written, even though it was certainly going to be his last. But he suspected that he was not going to be remembered for his plays, anyway. It was his political, philosophical and social works that were going to be remembered, judging by the rage with which his contemporaries had greeted them. They then played a game of chess, and as they moved the pieces without much offensive strategy, they reminisced about the past they had shared and about the loves of their lives who had died young, too young; Julie de l'Espinasse for d'Alembert, and Gabrielle-Émilie Le Tonnelier de Breteuil, *marquise* du Châtelet, for Voltaire, who had died in childbirth 30 years ago.

Meantime, upstairs on the third floor, Zénobe and André were assiduously doing their lessons at a small desk in Maurel's bed chamber. Both boys were hard at work, Zénobe giving the lesson and André listening and writing down the names he heard. Smack in the middle of a history lesson, as Zénobe wrote down the name of the exiled king of Poland, Stanislas Leczinski, André noticed Zénobe's left-handedness and asked him about it, for he had heard terrible things about the sinister, or gauche, side. Zénobe very patiently discussed the differences between "received ideas" and "reasoned ideas" and between "false thinking" and "Cartesian thinking." He explained that ignorance made parents of "lefties" tie their children's left hands behind their backs to force them to use their right hands. He said that studies had been done with monkeys and a similar percentage of monkey groups as in humans, about 10%, had a marked preference for using their left hand. Zénobe decried ascribing moral values to a simple physiological difference. "After all," said he, "most of us have our hearts to the left of the sternum, and none of us thinks of calling that inferior or evil or even odd. So for the very few humans who have their heart to the right of their sternum, what should we say, that they are better, holier, morally superior?"

André looked at Zénobe's sternum and asked, "Do you have your heart on the left or on the right?"

"Don't you remember from last night? It's on my left. Just like yours."

"How do you know where my heart is?"

"Because the pulse in your neck is stronger on the left than it is on the right."

"The pulse in my neck?"

"Yes." And he proceeded to show André by taking his friend's hand and feeling for the pulse points in his own body. "Here at the base of the neck where, if you watch closely, it is visible. Here at the temples. Here on the wrists."

Touching Zénobe was very difficult for André to do. His head started spinning as his pulse quickened and he had to bring his hands back to himself.

"You don't have to be afraid, André."

"I'm not." Then he thought better of it and confessed, "Well, maybe a little."

"What we're feeling, it's part of nature, too. And in some cultures it not only has been tolerated, but it has been encouraged. In ancient Greece, a boy always had a mentor, usually a man much older than he, somebody who would teach him, who would counsel him. In Thebes, the army was made up of male couples, and they proved to be ferocious soldiers because they were not only fighting for their fatherland, they were also fighting for their lovers."

André imagined a battle in which he was fighting side by side with Zénobe. Of course he would attack an enemy who made any sort of move on Zénobe. He would shred the assailant into little pieces.

"So, why haven't I heard about this, these… feelings, that I have, when, when, I, when I look at you?"

"Because our society wants to hide certain things and forget about them. Sexual matters remind humanity about their proximity to animals, and man doesn't feel comfortable considering himself an animal. The *Précieux* of Molière's age banned words that contained smaller words dealing with certain parts of the anatomy. You couldn't say any word that had '*cul*' (ass) or '*con*' (cunt) in it. You had to avoid anything with '*bite*' (dick) in it, or '*pine*' (prick), or anything like that. Certain books were not read, like Rabelais, or Chaucer. In our own century, Diderot's *Les bijoux indiscrets* has been banned for being too sexual and perverted."

"What's it about?"

"It's about women who lie with their mouths but tell the truth with their cunts. Diderot is playing with the etymological root of lips (*lèvres*), *labia*, and playing with anatomy and speech. It's wonderful. And funny."

"Are we going to read that?"

"Oh, I suppose, especially if Diderot keeps coming over to visit. But we have many more serious things to read first. The first novel you're going to read is *Don Quichotte*, by a Spaniard named Cervantes. It is a masterpiece."

"Are there any naughty parts in it?"

"Well, I suppose there are. For one, *don* Quichotte is in love with a whore named Dulcinea."

"Oh, what a pretty name."

"In Spanish, *dulce* means *douce* (sweet)."

"Do you speak Spanish?"

"A little."

"What other languages do you speak?"

"Piedmontese, of course, and Latin and Greek, and a bit of English."

"Incredible. And I speak only one. I'm a dullard, aren't I?"

"Of course you're not. You are very bright, I think. You just weren't exposed to education the way I was."

"But you lived in the sticks just like I did."

"Yes, but my father, in spite of his own ignorance, knew the value of education. He had always wanted to learn to read, but at that time, it just wasn't done. Our social class never learned to read. My father bothered and bothered Father Anselme until the village *curé* thought it easier to give him the lessons than to keep pushing him away. By the time I came along, my father made sure that I was to be educated. But it had to be done in secret, so the *seigneur* would never know about it."

"What was your father like?"

"He was a good man, and fair." Zénobe's eyes took a faraway look, as an expression of tenderness came over his face. "He was a good husband to our mother, and provided for all of us. There were eight of us. The three sons were all educated at the hands of Father Anselme."

"Is your mother still alive?"

"No, she died giving birth to my youngest sister."

"And your two brothers?"

"Dispersed. After Father was killed, his sons had to escape, or the Seigneur would have had us killed as well."

"What awful power is that, that a lord can kill whomever he wants."

"It's the power of feudal tyranny. It's the same power your own king has."

"Louis can't just come out and have any of his subjects killed, can he?"

"This Louis is still young, and he's very stupid, as is his harlot of a wife, Marie Antoinette, who whores her cunt to the ambassador who gives her the most jewels. But his grandfather and great-grandfather, Louis XV and XIV, certainly had their fill of torture and killing. They had absolute power over life and death, or over secret imprisonment for life, on any subject of their choosing, for any reason, verifiable or imagined. Just because Louis XVI hasn't yet awakened to the possibilities of his limitless powers doesn't mean that he won't, one day."

They returned to the subject of the Polish king, and then went on to a lesson in grammar, when Maurel came in.

"The household is in order, *madame* Denis and the *marquise* de Villette are taking their naps, *monsieur* de Voltaire is playing chess with *monsieur* d'Alembert, the *marquis* de Villette is chasing rainbows at the *Journal de Paris* and the *Gazette de France*, and my two angels are having their lesson."

The boys seemed pleased with Maurel's new word for them. Angels? They supposed so. Neither one of them thought of himself as a naughty boy.

With André in the room, *monsieur* Maurel started his own lessons and reading assignments with Zénobe. It turned out that this humble Savoyard had already read the moralists of 17th-Century France. Still, he hadn't read them according to Maurel's perspective and interpretation. Zénobe found out that one could pattern one's life choices on the acerbic teachings of these authors. They were books not just on the identification of characters and analysis of the diverse types of humans that there are, but they were also a primer on, or a methodology of, living in society. They could be used both for recognition and for imitation. It was difficult to view society in the harsh terms used by the moralists, but Maurel was giving a novel twist to the readings: one's *amour-propre* and foibles took a grander scope the higher one was in the social hierarchy. A regular person's *amour-propre* was simply a way of defending oneself against somebody else's manipulations, and would make others pay as dearly as possible for any slights. But the King's *amour-propre* was so immense it had to be defended by the whole nation. In other words, if George III insulted Louis XVI, whole armies would have to pay for the snub.

Monsieur Maurel found Zénobe to be a dedicated and malleable student, and discovered from the young man's comments and responses that he had a natural penchant for diplomacy. He also had natural discretion. Two things that the *marquis* de Villette had never had.

In the evening, André was sent one final time to the Palais-Royal. Though it was too late for *docteur* Tronchin to come visit Voltaire, perhaps arrangements could be made for him to come to the *hôtel* de Villette the following morning. Unfortunately, the doctor was still out. *Madame* Denis went to bed worried. Voltaire merely insulted the doctor's Protestant mother.

Zénobe was already undressed and in bed when André came into their bedroom. His eyes followed André's every move as he undressed and draped his clothes on a chair. He reached under the bed to retrieve the chamber pot and urinated in it, taking care to turn away from Zénobe. Zénobe thought André's modesty touching. André then snuffed out the candle and got into bed.

That night, they were to have a different kind of lesson, one in which they were both students. No questions were allowed, and the experience ran like a science experiment, full of observation and analysis. There were effects and causes to be studied, stimuli and impeti to be deduced, and all was duly noted and committed to memory. All this experimentation took place, of course, in a laboratory little used for scientific pursuits, and it all happened without the light of a single candle, in complete darkness and silence. Zénobe felt that he was Condillac's living statue,[127] comprehending the world through the senses of touch, smell and taste, but not vision or hearing. It was easy for Zénobe to feel like the statue, for he was imbued with novel feelings never experienced before. Now he knew what skin was for, and the thousand combined pinpricks of soft caresses were almost too much to bear.

Even though Zénobe had already been taught a few tutorials in the school of sex, no less by a woman of greater social stature than he, he quickly realized that what he was experiencing now with André was decidedly distinct. It had nothing to do with the awkward groping, the grotesque humping, the rough thrashing, of his sweaty jostles with the Polignac woman. Here with André, finally, was the slow, sweet Epicurean pleasures that he had been promised would come with a loving relationship. There, the egoism of the aristobitch made the rutting feel like a rapid combat, with animalistic mechanics devoid of sensuality or depth. But with André, lovemaking was precious, unhurried, sublime, and he could feel both with his skin and with his, his...; his interior. He did not even know what to call it. His soul, perhaps, which is what poets always wrote about, with lyrical excess and unbelievable palaver, but Zénobe did not believe in the existence of the soul. Then it could be his heart, maybe, although what he felt was not in his chest, it was lower, perhaps in his diaphragm, or lower still. His stomach was at the center of it all because he could feel it tensed, contracted, and it was releasing such warmth into the rest of his body that even his skin tingled with it. This intense feeling was also at his spine, close to the base, for he felt a peculiar vibrancy there which made his legs go weak and his pulse quicken. It was all an outstanding experiment.

André thought that he was going to die and then go to heaven, his chest was heaving so. He had to bite his lip to keep silent. The rhythmic pulses he felt when he was released from his ordeal felt like a musical resolution after a series of strident chords, or like, like—as he imagined during his spasms—like the electricity which Benjamin Franklin had discovered and which had somehow penetrated deep into his body. He remembered a science lesson Zénobe had told him about, on Newton's energy, and

---

127   Étienne Bonnot de Condillac's *Treatise on the Sensations* speaks of a statue who learns of the world successively through each of the five senses; in all five cases, his idea of the real world is necessarily different.

as his body calmed down, he realized that helping to dissipate excess thermal energy was wonderful.

In the end, the cool truth of science won the day, or in this case, the night, because at the end of it all, there were no broken illusions, no remorse or guilt or dejection. André and Zénobe had shared in a behavior which was new and enticing and which excluded the rest of the world. The two young men were still friends, still comfortable with one another, and still very much in love with each other.

Hemistich: The Author Takes Stock

A week had passed since Voltaire's triumphal return to Paris. It is time now to take stock, not of the multitudes who clamored to come and pay their respects, or to reconnoiter the territory, but of those who, for some reason or another, did not come.[128] True, the vast majority of those who had tried to see the old *philosophe* had unfortunately been turned away. Most understood. The old man was feeble and sickly, and one did not have the credentials, the name, the renown, the notoriety, or lacking these, the social connections, to have the honor to be shown into the interior of the *hôtel* de Villette. A certain group of people did have the wherewithal, such as Friedrich (Franz) Anton Mesmer, but Voltaire and his other fellow men of science would never have given them the legitimacy that these pseudo-scientists craved. How could Voltaire or Condorcet be seen hobnobbing with those they called the followers of fallacy? Benjamin Franklin was also turning these people away in droves from his own residence in Passy. The Followers of Reason found it very hard to sweep their temple clean of the intellectual riffraff that the winds of popularity blew in. But clean they must keep it. Necromancers, phrenologists, magnetists, alchemists, astrologists, and quicksilver quacks sought funding and sponsorship from the true experts who fortunately had skepticism on their side. The divide between the two groups remained wide.

Many different kinds of persons did not even attempt to come and see the great Voltaire. It would be beneficial to enumerate them in order to understand why certain factions of society were antipathetic, or at least indifferent, to Voltaire. Jean-Jacques, for instance. Rousseau was living but a half-league away. Yet, as self-righteous and vainglorious as he was, he did not even want to accept Voltaire traversing their own divide to come and see *him*: Rousseau's paranoia, resentment and pride saw to it that he remained defiantly and constantly alone, as if in the solitary confinement of the pariah who knows that he has always been right. The inventor of the concept of the noble savage continued to nurse his own old age in agoraphobic seclusion, away from the offending crowds, at the center of concentric rings of impenetrable obstacles.

Johannes Chrysosotomus Wolfgangus Theophilus (Amadeus or Amadée) Mozart had also recently come into town, with his mother Anna Maria, *née* Pertl, as chaperone. The young Mozart had insisted on traveling to Paris, more in defiance of his father Leopold's tyranny than for the pleasures of being in a city always hungry for new talent and new spectacles. Leopold had always told his son to establish himself in a city like

---

128   [From the author] It is important to note, however, that even for these people who did not wish to pay their respects to Voltaire, it was Voltaire who would ultimately empower them and enable them to find their future voice.

Paris, for there he would find the appreciation of artists, the esteem for genius, and the deference for talent, which his son so evidently deserved. The young composer carried with him letters of introduction to Diderot, d'Alembert and Grimm, although Grimm, being German-born, was the only one he and his mother ever came to see.[129] The Austrians wound up sojourning in the *hôtel* d'Épinay, the elegant home of *madame* d'Épinay, famous in her own right for her own enlightened intellect and for her own literary *salon* which attracted all of the *Encyclopédistes* of the time and competed with the *salon* of *madame* du Deffand. *Madame* d'Épinay was also Grimm's mistress. Still, in spite of being surrounded by thinkers of all kinds, Mozart could not shake his father's image of what a philosopher was: a surly, cynical, misanthrope who lives in his ivory tower and never deigns to come down to street level. Mozart and his mother never went to see Voltaire. Truth be told, the news that Voltaire was in town made hardly a ripple in Mozart's imagination, not even a semiquaver. His head was too full of music. Besides, this son of a social-climbing bourgeois sycophant could hardly be jealous, envious, or even solicitous of Voltaire, whom old Leopold Mozart discredited as being godless and overreaching. No wonder his son would write home a few months later to announce the old *philosophe*'s death: "The arch-scoundrel has kicked the bucket like a mongrel, like a beast; that is his reward." He also composed at this time the "Paris" Symphony that was performed to great applause and mentioned with great critical acclaim in the *Courier d'Europe*.[130] [131]

Giovanni Jacopo Casanova de Seingalt was also residing in the City of Light. He did not come to see Voltaire, either, not because he felt he was better than the *philosophe*– on the contrary, he had always admired all the *philosophes* for their constancy in their pursuit of intellectual, rather than sensual, pleasures–but because he was very busy. He had started to write his memoirs, as soon as his last conquest was but a memory. The name of the target of his last seduction was, coincidentally, *Irène*. By this time, his physical attributes had begun to wane as well. Gravity was pulling on his body and on his conscience, thus, à la Rousseau,[132] he wanted to justify his life. Was it a bad conscience? Was it out of pride? It is true that Casanova wished to call attention to his exploits, which were sure to garner some grudging admiration from his contemporaries. In any event, he was much too busy being the narcissist on reams of fine-grained

---

129   Frédéric Melchior, *baron* de Grimm, ancient friend of Rousseau and Diderot, who had broken intellectual and amicable ties with Rousseau as resoundingly as Diderot and Voltaire had, was a man of letters famed for his literary criticism and his incisive portraits of contemporaries. He also corresponded with Catherine II of Russia and Frederick II of Prussia, and surprisingly, defended the Italian side against the German side in the musicological *Querelle des Bouffons*. Mozart came to Paris in the midst of the fight between the Gluckists and the Piccinnists.

130   [From the author] History sometimes gets back posthumously at people with the great equalizing effects of irony: Voltaire finally did get to have a tomb, and then years later a superb mausoleum in the heart of the Pantheon in Paris; Mozart's body was thrown into a common dump with other beggars.

131   [From the fact-checker] I without a question object to the word "beggar" used in conjunction with Mozart. I do the author accuse of prejudice against the German race, and hold the reader as witness, and as fellow denunciator, of such bias.

132   [From the author] Of all the *philosophes*, none left thoughtfully to posterity as many autobiographical traces as Jean-Jacques Rousseau: in addition to his *Confessions*, he also left us his *Rêveries du promeneur solitaire*, his *Dialogues* on *Rousseau juge de Jean-Jacques*, and his self-*Portrait*. No one else had to do so much self-explaining. Will Benjamin Disraeli be thinking of Rousseau's copious justifications and self-revelations when he will state famously and pithily, "Never complain and never explain"?

vellum paper, working as if in a trance, as if Mesmer had given him lessons. Casanova wrote like a man magnetized by his own egocentric mind that, now that he had come to the end of his libido, could only meditate endlessly and nostalgically on the sexual exploits that had ever given his existence its only meaning. Not even Diderot would have given so much time and thought to sex.

The future miscreants of the Revolution were already in Paris as well. They were magnetically attracted to the city from all corners of France and they were arriving in throngs. Only a city like Paris could contain their ambitions for wealth and fame. None, however, ventured to see Voltaire. These men, and women, much preferred Rousseau. It was Jean-Jacques who was the hero of the dispossessed, the marginalized, the zealous and the resentful, the ones who tried to make it according to the Old Ways of the *ancien régime*, failed, and then moved on to think of New Ways to make their mark. The future Revolutionaries had a soft spot for Voltaire's main adversary, his arch-nemesis, the man who counseled man to get back to nature and therefore back to his inner feelings. These young and restless upstarts, who came from all levels of society, were certainly in touch with their consciences, and it was Jean-Jacques who had taught them how to do it and they loved him for it. Ironically, Rousseau would not allow any of these young admirers the honor of paying him their respects.

Maximilien François Marie Isidore de Robespierre, for example, who was 20 at the time Voltaire returned to Paris, was fresh out of law school and about to defend a man who had erected a Benjamin Franklin lightning rod on his house. His neighbors feared that it would attract lightning bolts and cause their own houses to burn down. One woman voiced her worries that the rod would bring about the miscarriage of the infant she was carrying. The neighbors petitioned that the lightning rod be taken down. Robespierre was well in place as the lawyer who would argue brilliantly in favor of this newfangled invention and thereby win the day. He would be sure to forward his speeches to Franklin who, of course, was to receive them with much interest and pleasure.

Jean-Paul Marat, 35 years old, had already written to Benjamin Franklin the year before, anxiously trying to interest him with an essay on the properties of fire, and would indeed manage to coax him, and several other Parisian scientists, to visit his laboratory for a demonstration of his discovery of "igneous fluid," and would somehow manage to shine his beam of light through a microscope onto Franklin's bald pate. Afterwards, one of the academicians present would describe the effect of a halo around the American's head, like the aureole of a saint in a painting. The year before that, Marat had tried to interest the philosophical world with a monograph entitled *On Man, or On the Principles and Laws of the Influence of the Soul on the Body, and of the Body on the Soul,* to which replied a critical Voltaire in the *Gazette littéraire* since the main tenet of the work was that the constitution of the body must needs shelter a similar intelligence; only herculean bodies could produce geniuses. Now, Voltaire's body was small and frail, but his genius was not. Needless to say, Marat would make no money or reputation off of his discoveries in science or his treatises in metaphysics, and would instead turn to politics as a way to make a name for himself.

Marie-Jeanne Manon Phlipon, the future *madame* Roland, was in 1778 a young, fresh, bright, 24-year-old Parisian *bourgeoise* who grew up in front of the Pont-Neuf and who only now had an inkling as to what love and politics were all about. Eternally surprised by the impudence and ostentation of the aristocratic class, she is being affected by the works of Diderot, d'Alembert, Helvétius, d'Holbach, Voltaire and Rousseau.

Especially Rousseau. She discovers his *Julie ou la Nouvelle Héloïse*[133] in 1775 and begins a cult of worship for the Swiss writer that will last her whole life. She will write in her memoirs, "Rousseau was the nourishment which was the proper interpretation of the feelings I had, but that he alone knew how to explain to me." Like Rousseau, she goes into a rage when she witnesses the spectacle of the Ministry of Finance and the devil-may-care profligacy of the Court. In 1772, her ire knows no bounds when she is invited, through some cousins, to a dinner given at the opulent home of the farmer-general Hadry de Soucy, and learns that she is to dine, not at the host and hostesses' table, but in the scullery, along with the household staff. She has already evolved an affinity for those whose indignation has been growing and festering, and who have been turning to ideals of republicanism, including her future husband, Jean-Marie Roland de la Platière. They have already met, in January of 1776, but in February of 1778, *monsieur* Roland has not yet decided whether he will marry the beautiful and cerebral *mademoiselle* Phlipon, whom most of his friends and family view as being beneath him in social stature. But in the end, love and compatibility will win out, and the couple will go on to have power and influence in political circles. But for now, the young Marie-Jeanne cannot even imagine that one day she will have a *salon* to rival those held by her elders, *madame* d'Épinay, *madame* du Deffand, and *madame* de Villette.

Honoré Gabriel Victor Riqueti, *comte* de Mirabeau, 29 years old, would probably have liked to come visit Voltaire. A soul-in-arms, he had already dared to criticize the powers-that-be, and had to his credit the publication of an *Essay on Despotism*, and had already enjoyed exile, by way of Holland, and the hospitality of a couple of prisons for having done so. As a matter of fact, in February of 1778, he was safely ensconced in the dungeon of Vincennes, where in order to escape boredom he has been reading voraciously and writing profligately, dissipating his febrile intellect on short stories, tragedies, translations of Tacitus and Boccaccio, a study on inoculations and another one on grammar, his opinions on music, on Islamism and the Koran, and a history of Holland.

Georges Jacques Danton, 19 years old, hasn't even yet become a clerk at an attorney's office, which he will do in 1780. Still in Arcis-sur-Aube, east of Paris, a tiny town of 2,000 souls, two separate incidents with cows' horns have left the robust farmer's son with a part missing from his upper lip and a crushed nose, and a bout with smallpox has left his face pitted for life. Ugly as evil, he is nonetheless honing his skills at seduction with the village girls. Courage he already had: when he was sixteen he ran away from his boarding school in order to witness the anointing and coronation of Louis XVI at the great cathedral of Reims on the 11th of June, 1775. There on that day, he witnessed all the pomp and circumstance that the Nobility and Church could in sacrosanct unity muster.

Jacques-Louis David, at 30 no longer a youngster, isn't even in the country at all. He is off in Rome, learning under the tutelage of the French Academy there, discovering the aesthetics of proportionality and classic ideal beauty, grace, unity, and harmony; in short, he is incorporating ideas into his head about the beauty of noble simplicity and sedate grandeur which he will shortly bring back with him to France in order to become the Revolution's portraitist and principal public relations man.

---

133   This bestseller by Rousseau, first published in 1761, has by 1778 already gone through 38 prodigious printings and will have 44 more before the turn of the century. It will affect generations to come, like no other tome in history, for well over a century.

Claude Joseph Rouget de Lisle is 18 years old and living with his family in Lons-le-Saunier, in the Jura Mountains. Already a precocious poet, he could still not even begin to anticipate that in 1792 he is to compose the best known of all patriotic hymns, the *Hymne des Marseillais*, which will become almost immediately known as *La Marseillaise*.

Charlotte Corday is still only 12 years old, still reading voraciously, still admiring the writings of Jean-Jacques Rousseau. Her family has moved from Saint-Saturnin-des-Ligneries to Caen, the closest town, and she has just written a letter to her brother André, who is in Paris, informing him of the move. Her brother has been serving in the household of the *hôtel* de Villette during Voltaire's stay in Paris. But Charlotte could not be bothered about that particular detail. In her letter to her brother, she has included another letter to be forwarded to Rousseau. It is a letter of gratitude to the old Swiss anti-*philosophe*. Perhaps a bit puerile in style, her letter speaks of her undying love for Jean-Jacques, and it betokens of a vast, inexhaustible devotion that only a young girl's heart could contain.

Not in Paris but close enough, Louis XVI and Marie Antoinette, at 24 and 23 years of age, are, unbeknownst to themselves, their own worst enemies. They cannot, of course, leave Versailles in order to see a mere mortal *philosophe*, even one who had become wealthier, by dint of much toil, energy and personal perseverance, than most other European sovereigns. The young royal couple had already invited Benjamin Franklin to their palace and made sure the son of a candle-maker was put in his place. He was invited to stand behind the Queen and look on while the Royal Family supped. But Voltaire, the bane of Louis XV, could not even remotely be welcomed, to say nothing of being accepted, into their presence. That particular divide, between king and *philosophe*, was especially insurmountable. Moreover, in their quotidian efforts to be left in peace, the King and Queen of France could only hide behind their favorite pastimes: he, hunting and tinkering in his workshop, she, pretending to be a shepherdess in her make-believe Little Hamlet, or putting the finishing touches, at great expense, to her Little Trianon, or having new fashions created by *madame* Bertin, or play-acting in her little rococo theater where she presented the popular plays of the day, including Beaumarchais' seditious *The Marriage of Figaro*, which had been banned by Louis, but put on by Marie Antoinette anyway to please her favorite lady-in-waiting *madame* de Polignac. The Queen herself had already played the role of Rosine in another of Beaumarchais' plays, *The Barber of Seville*, the comical and lively story of a beautiful young girl who will use ruse, lies, scheming and insolent deviousness, in order to escape the oppressive tyranny of Bartholo who wants to keep her forever under his brutal subjugation. The Queen of France could not see that art could function as the slippery funnel that was hastening them all—King, Queen, ministers, subjects, lawyers, *salonnières*, writers, *philosophes, bourgeois*, servants, peasants—into an inalterable, fatalistic, and inevitable doom.

Pierre-Augustin Caron de Beaumarchais had not yet come to see Voltaire. He was around but divided into many directions, overseeing as he was the collecting and the sending of illegal arms to America, a highly dangerous maneuver which he had to hide from Lord Viscount David Murray Stormont, Earl of Mansfield, the British ambassador to Versailles, a Scot, and the thorn in the sides of both the *comte* de Vergennes, the French minister of Foreign Affairs and of Benjamin Franklin, the American minister plenipotentiary. Beaumarchais was also busy seeing to it that his friend the *chevalière* d'Éon was behaving in her new role as a woman, and trying to keep her from running off to America to fight the British, for whom d'Éon harbored a deep-seated grudge ever since, as French minister plenipotentiary in London, she had witnessed how the Brits amused themselves by taking bets on her real sex. What she didn't know, although she suspected it, was that Beaumarchais himself was the one who had fanned the winds of curiosity, thereby making himself an easy £100,000 on the wagering after the British government officially declared d'Éon a woman and therefore was to be sent home. Still, Beaumarchais really did like the *chevalière*, admiring the fact that she could drink, smoke and swear like the best of men. She was a good friend to have, and an appreciative audience as Beaumarchais wrote and edited his plays, which was another of his occupations which kept him from coming to see Voltaire immediately. What Voltaire had not dared do openly for most of his life, publishing seditious texts within France and under his own name, Beaumarchais did, unapologetically, and under the very noses of the government. True, he was standing on Voltaire's shoulders, and under the influence of the ever-affable, lovable, and kindred spirit that was Benjamin Franklin.

The Trouble with Letters

Only a week after his return to Paris, Voltaire was exhausted after a whirlwind of visitations and social hubbub. His digestion, out of sorts from its customary habits, was at a standstill. His strangury was ornery. But this particular day was going to be tranquil and quiet, entirely devoted to putting the final touches on *Irène*. The actors of the *Comédie française* were waiting for the finished product in order to start memorizing their lines. The *duc* de Richelieu had approved the play, and the opening night had been decided upon, March 16th, less than a month away. But the Muse was absent today, and Voltaire kept picking at his play the way he picked at his breakfast, absent-mindedly and without appetite. His only secretary present at the time was Zénobe, who had a manuscript of the play in front of him and was reading parts of it out loud to the playwright. It was ten o'clock in the morning and Voltaire was in bed, still wearing his pompom nightcap.

Alone with Voltaire, Zénobe was within the stratosphere of heaven. He was thinking that if he were ordered to choose between a tête-à-tête with Voltaire or one with André, he would be hard-pressed to employ his volition.

Voltaire suggested a slight change to a verse, and they mulled over the possibilities of a new bi-syllabic word that rhymed with *-eur*. *Cette heure*? No, it has a final mute 'e'. The old-fashioned *cet heur'*? *Non pas*, Voltaire was against obsolete orthography. How about *d'humeur*? Better. *Crève-cœur*? That's three syllables. All of a sudden, Voltaire sat up in bed rigid as a lightning rod and stared at Zénobe's hand. His left hand. The one that was writing across the page.

"Great thundering gods!" resounded Voltaire's voice in his boudoir. "What is this that I see? *Monsieur* Zénobe, what hand are you using to write with?"

Zénobe was used to this reaction. "My left hand, *monsieur*."

"You mean to tell me that your father, or your priest preceptor, never did anything to dissuade you from writing with your left hand?"

"No, *monsieur*, nor from eating with my fork in it or from tilling with it."

"How can one till with one's left hand?"

"The way one can till with one's right hand."

"You don't say," said Voltaire, who, despite his enlightened mind never really thought about leaving a child free to choose whatever hand he saw fit to use. "I surely must consult the experts on this."

"Don't give yourself the trouble, *monsieur* de Voltaire. All the usual experts universally condemn the use of the left hand and go through great lengths to describe and illustrate sundry methods to constrain the child from using the left hand. By binding the hand behind the small of the back, or putting it in a sling, or leaving the whole left arm under the shirt, the child has no choice but to use his right arm. My father never subscribed to this cruelty, and Father Anselme apparently agreed. Nobody ever mentioned it to me, and it wasn't until I left Savoy that I saw how people were surprised, and offended, by the use of my left hand. *Monsieur*, it feels natural to me. My right hand is almost useless to me since it is much less coordinated than my left hand. With my left hand, in order not to smudge the ink, I have to write backwards, in other words, from right to left, and inverted."

Voltaire asked to see a demonstration of this. Zénobe showed to Voltaire the verse they had just been working on, and when Voltaire saw what was written on the page, he asked Zénobe to bring him a mirror. Zénobe complied, and Voltaire chuckled when he saw that the verse was indeed written in a perfect mirror image. "How delightful!" he cried. "I haven't seen this since I studied da Vinci's texts on anatomy." He looked up and asked, "I wonder if *he* was left-handed?" Then he looked down at the image of the page in the mirror and said, "Yes, this is fine, let's keep the *terreur*; it goes well with *empire* and *mon cœur*, and in the previous act we already have *trompeurs* rhyming with *malheurs*, so we have an evocative '*heur*' throughout. But tell me, *mon cher enfant*, weren't you warned about the sinister side, the devil's side?"

"Not until it was too late. By that time, I was already old enough to know that the stories that tell of the sinistral side being the inauspicious or evil side, were, well, old-wives' tales, like the one that states that eating from the pot in which you cook your food will turn you into a stutterer."

"Oh, I've never heard that one."

"Besides, studies of mollusks, and many other animals, clearly point out that sinistrality exists everywhere in nature. There is nothing to fear from the left side of the body. Don't all men everywhere have their left testicle hanging lower than their right one?"

"Oh, by Jove," laughed Voltaire, "I have never heard about that one, either! I have never had the occasion to observe it! This is proof that one is never too old to learn new knowledge. But is this true? Are you certain, *monsieur* Zénobe? Let me see."

Voltaire got himself out of bed and unceremoniously brought the hem of his flannel nightshirt to above his navel. "That's an affirmative with me. Now, let's see you. And we'll have to send for André and all the rest of the men in this house."

As Zénobe was showing Voltaire the distribution, size and disposition of his own genitals, André was opening the door to the postman who brought the mail over several times a day. When he took the package to Maurel, the *maître d'hôtel* handed one of the letters back to him and said, "This one is for you." André was surprised, but not as surprised as when Zénobe came looking for him, and also for Maurel, to tell them that *monsieur* de Voltaire was beckoning them to come to his boudoir. They complied immediately, and when Voltaire instructed them to take their pants down in the name of science they complied just as easily. One couldn't deny Voltaire anything. For André, this was not the first time he was showing off his healthy Normand penis to the sage of Ferney, although this time it was his testicles that seemed to interest him. Maurel thought he was going to have a fainting spell when he saw Voltaire take close inspection of André's twin swinging brothers and then ask to see Zénobe's again–again?–for comparison. And then Voltaire was requesting to see Maurel's own private parts. The realization that it was his turn next to display himself to the *philosophe* brought on the mortification of having to show a raging erection to all present. He took as long as he could, thinking of the least sexual things he could evoke in his mind: a dead woodpecker he had seen by the chestnut tree earlier that morning; skimming off the scum from the potatoes boiling in the kitchen; removing the lint from Zénobe's uniform. He even pretended that one of his buttons had gotten caught in its hook. But when André brought his face down towards his fly to see where the button was caught, Maurel realized the feint would do no good. He finally released his genitals and felt the cool air come upon them. All were duly impressed, especially Voltaire who cried out, "Aha! Your left one is definitely hanging lower than the rest of all our left ones, and the degree of difference seems to be greater in yours than in ours. Here, take your prick out of the way." Maurel duly obeyed. "Well, *monsieur* Zénobe, I don't know where you are getting your information, but in this experiment, in four out of four men, the left testicle is definitely hanging lower than the right testicle. I will certainly have to confer with Diderot about this. There is no reason for this to be so, but Nature has posed many a conundrum for us, and this one is no different."

Maurel and André were dismissed, and Zénobe continued to work on the editing of *Irène* with Voltaire.

As soon as André got to the kitchen, he unsealed the letter addressed to him and recognized instantly the handwriting of his parents and of his sister. They informed him of their move to Caen, of their new address, and asked about his health and happiness. They asked him to write more often. His sister's message was rather laconic, and she asked André to take a second letter, enclosed in the first, to Jean-Jacques Rousseau, whom she knew to be residing in Paris, but she didn't know the name of the street. As André went looking for Maurel to ask for permission to go deliver this letter to Rousseau, he crossed paths with the *marquis* de Villette, who was just coming down from his bedroom on the first floor. The *marquis* was already dressed and ready to leave the house on his daily rounds of visits to newspapers and appearances of social importance.

"Ah, André," said the *marquis*. "I'm glad you're here. Listen, I need you to give this to *monsieur* Bosquet. Maurel told me he is with Voltaire this morning working on *Irène*, and I don't wish to disturb their work."

In his hand he held a letter, with the name *Zénobe Bosquet* written on it in a very florid hand.

"Yes, *monsieur*," replied André. "I shall be very happy to give it to him."

The *marquis* squeezed one of André's earlobes and smiled at him and then he was off. But after a couple of steps, he turned on his heel and called out to André who was already headed towards the kitchen. "André, don't mention this letter to anybody, agreed?"

"Agreed, *monsieur*," said André with a slight bow.

When Maurel had heard André's request for permission to go deliver his sister's letter to Rousseau, he said, "You better go tomorrow. It will take you an hour just to walk there and back. *Monsieur* Rousseau is staying on the rue des Plâtrières, just above a fish shop, on the fifth floor, I believe. The rue des Plâtrières is just beyond Saint-Eustache and then away from the rising sun.[134] He's there with his wife, *madame* Thérèse Rousseau. You can leave right after everybody has had breakfast, so you can be back in time for dinner. *Monsieur* de Voltaire will not be receiving tomorrow, either, so your absence for a while shouldn't be an inconvenience. We're still waiting for *docteur* Tronchin. If you have time, maybe you can pass by the Palais-Royal to see about his coming to see us. We hope he'll be coming soon, in view of *monsieur* de Voltaire's discomfort with

---

134   The rue des Plâtrières is today called the rue Jean-Jacques Rousseau.

his digestion and urination." Maurel peered out the kitchen window. "It's been raining, so I'll give you some solid boots with which to tramp through the city's streets. Some become rivers, you know. You will be careful, won't you?"

"*Oui, monsieur*," said André. "Thank you very much."

It wasn't until André met Zénobe for their afternoon lesson that he was able to give him the letter from the *marquis* de Villette. Curious, Zénobe tore through the seal and his ethereal blue eyes ran through the text in a few seconds. He looked at André and scrunched up his nose as if smelling some malodorous thing.

"What does he say?" asked André.

"Here, listen." Zénobe took the letter up again and started to read: 'My much esteemed and obliging *monsieur* Zénobe, You have been employed at the *hôtel* de Villette now for almost a week, and in that short time I have become aware of your polyfacetic talents—'

André interrupted. "What does that mean?"

Zénobe explained, "It's a made-up word, from the Latin words *poly*, which means *many*, and *facet*, which means *surface*. He's saying I am multitalented."

André nodded and Zénobe continued to read. '—your polyfacetic talents which cause me no small amount of wonderment and admiration. Indeed, the knowledge that you can hold your own against Voltaire and our other philosopher colleagues, that you can feel at ease in their conversations and expostulations, and that you even manage to influence said conversations with your own erudite commentary, makes me proud and confident in the knowledge that you are already in my employ.

'Nevertheless, insofar as your tasks and responsibilities are concerned, I must insist that your talents could be, and would be, better implemented in more sophisticated and adventurous ways. The offer of chamberlain still stands, and I am assured that you would acquit yourself of said responsibility in an indisputably efficient and commendable manner. Think of it! You would see more important people, not just artists and philosophers, but also essential personages of noble quality in the higher echelons of government. Imagine, being in the presence of the King, or being presented to the Queen! You would be serving me in a higher capacity, with more responsibilities. You could be an envoy who would represent me and thus you would travel to other countries. You would move in high financial and diplomatic circles. In short, you would see barriers only where your imagination would not be able to take you. Be convinced that I am decided in this. It would certainly be advantageous on my behalf were you to be my right-hand man.'

André tittered. "The poor sap, doesn't he know you're a lefty?"

"Worse than that," said Zénobe. "Doesn't he know I would murder Marie Antoinette were I to be in her presence?"

Zénobe continued reading the letter: '*Monsieur* de Voltaire is planning to return to Ferney after his play *Irène* has had its run at the *Comédie française*. At that time, it is my hope that you will stay on at the *hôtel* de Villette and that you consider my proposition which, of course, comes with a financially rewarding remuneration of 500 *livres* a year. (André cried out in admiration.) It is also my hope that you may turn your efforts to aiding me in my own multifarious interests. Your sweetness of character, your utmost politeness and docility, your modest conduct and your utter lack of guile and affectation, render you admirable and dutiful to my eyes, and I would much appreciate your able and enterprising assistance. I most sincerely beseech you, dear Zénobe, to accept my continued offer of employment, and to be persuaded of the esteem, of the friendship and of the distinguished sentiments that I feel for you. Signed: Charles-Michel de Villette. Post-Scriptum: Please do not mention any of this to Maurel. I am convinced that he does not appreciate what is in your best interests. Be aware of the danger of confidences with a *maître d'hôtel* who does not know the larger world as I do. Keep this just between the two of us.'

"So," asked André, "now what are you going to do?"

"I don't really know, but from what I know of the *marquis* de Villette, I don't really want to work for him. He likes to make a lot of noise to call attention to himself, but in the end there is not much to all that bustle. Rabelais used to speak of the *substantifique moëlle*, that when you give a dog a bone he guards it jealously and keeps it for a long time in order to chew on it and chew on it and finally get to what's inside: the marrow. Well, where Villette is concerned one can chew and chew but there will never be any marrow. That man is hiding nothing of substance or value. I imagine it's the money that makes him think he offers the world something essential, but it's all empty fortune. Sort of like your King and Queen. They have all the money of the realm, and what do they use it for? For nothing that serves their subjects. They fritter it away on their clothing and jewelry and bibelots and their precious entertainment. They require entertainment night and day. Neither one of them can stand to be alone for ten seconds and try to have real thoughts. It's like Pascal said: idiots plunge themselves into activities that are amusing and fun, because it takes them away from important thoughts on life, love, faith and death. They don't want to have to think about the things that matter the most, the things that have real meaning. After a while, these people cannot have any real thoughts, for lack of practice. They become automatons looking only for fun. Their whole life through becomes a long, pitiable search for amusement, and they try to hold death away as long as possible, but in the end, it is death that shows up their lives as empty and wasted. They did nothing to help anybody else but themselves. They took up space and corrupted all those with whom they came into contact. Of course, if it's the king and queen doing this, it then becomes a crime *and* a sin, offensive to both state *and* God.

"Villette ruffles his feathers—excuse me, *monsieur le marquis de* Villette, ruffles his feathers and clucks as if he were always busy concocting ideas and courses of action. But in the end, he lays no egg. I've seen his type before. La Bruyère has as one of his *Caractères* a false *philosophe*, named Clitiphon. This creature moves papers from one end of his desk to another and gives an act of utmost frenetic activity. His days are consumed in a flurry of copying and signing and shuffling of documents, reading newspapers and writing articles, sending out for books, then sending out for more books. When the sun goes down, he writes bibliographies in order to say that he uses up fifty candles a night. He calls it his profession. When a visitor comes to see him, Clitiphon gives word that he is much too busy, but to please come back on another day, but when that day comes, it is to see him busier than ever. The reason why he leads such a precipitous existence is that he really has nothing original or interesting to say. He feels that he cannot allow you to pin him down and find him out.

"The real *philosophe*, however, is always accessible, and always makes a point to see and be seen, to be sociable, to be needed, and to be necessary to society."

Their afternoon lesson continued in such a haphazard way, going back and forth from Rabelais to Pascal to La Bruyère, then to the more modern La Mettrie and d'Holbach. André was a sponge of a student. He loved the way his preceptor taught, and it took all his effort not to reach across the desk and kiss his teacher's lips. Zénobe probably wouldn't stop talking, anyway, André thought to himself. He had so much to say. But, great gods, did he love Zénobe's brilliant blue eyes and those long lashes that curved way up. Over his lip and on his chin was already visible the stubborn stubble of his Italianate beard. His straight hair danced around his ears as he taught his lesson. Suddenly, André realized Zénobe had just asked him a question on the recompense that the true philosopher asked of society.

"If it isn't praise, and not monetary rewards, what is it?" asked Zénobe with impatience.

When André hesitated, Zénobe answered for him: "It is the satisfaction of making men better!"

Maurel walked into their lesson just at this moment. They were in his bedroom again, just for the afternoon, and Maurel wanted to know if they wanted some refreshments. Maurel espied the *marquis*' letter on the desk and asked about it.

Zénobe, who had already decided to confide in Maurel, told him about it and even had him read it.

During his perusal of the letter, Maurel alternatively chuckled and frowned. At the end, he put the letter down on the desk hard.

"This man will be my bane to my dying day!" he cried out. "If I didn't know him better than he knows himself, it would be a hard life for me."

Then he looked at the two boys and stood a while in thought. "This is what we are going to do. Zénobe, are you willing to take dictation from me and pass off a letter as your own?"

"A letter in response to this one?" asked Zénobe, picking up the *marquis*' letter and holding it aloft.

"That's it."

Zénobe smiled.

"*Oui, monsieur*, I'd be willing."

"Let's get to it, then. Voltaire and *madame* Denis are taking their naps, and the *marquise* is playing piquet in the salon with *mesdames* Suard and de Saint-Julien and *la comtesse* d'Argental. *Voilà*. Here's a clean sheet of paper. You have your quill. Are you ready?"

"*Oui, monsieur.*"

"Here goes. '*Monsieur le marquis* de Villette, it is with utmost respect and humble gratitude that I acknowledge your support and thank you most kindly for your protection. In exchange for your assiduity as my Mentor, I offer you my most tender and respectful attachment.' New paragraph. 'It is not every man, indeed not every *marquis*, who could manage to harbor in his home *monsieur* de Voltaire, the greatest mind of our time. Figure that I came to see the *philosophe* and wound up being invited, as he was, into the home of the *marquis*. My joy in this knows no bounds, and I recognize that you, that you…' that you are writing with your left hand. Master Zénobe, you are writing with your left hand!"

"*Oui, monsieur.*"

"How is that possible?"

"As possible as this!" He flourished his quill in his left hand as if he were writing *Le Traité sur l'intolérance* itself.

Maurel was quite taken aback. "I can see that. Still, or rather, *euh*... Well, I must confess, that... *Eh bien!* I suppose you're a unique individual in many ways. I don't know why I would have thought that you would use your right hand to write. If to write you used that appendage that you showed *monsieur* de Voltaire this afternoon I wouldn't be surprised, either!

Both André and Zénobe laughed. So did Maurel. They were his boys, under his tutelage, and he realized that he had a paternal side, after all, and it was telling him to protect them. And protect them he would, from the big bad wolf, the wolf de Villette who staked so much on the façade—the façade!—his own and others', without caring about what was inside the hearts of people. All of a sudden, he thought of Candide,[135] and he understood that he had two Candides to take care of: two young innocents who were as good-natured and profoundly benevolent as Villette was egocentric, grasping, and ambitious.

They finished writing the letter. The *marquis* was going to receive from Zénobe a response that was vague, noncommittal, and respectfully uncompliant to his desires that Zénobe become his chamberlain. The future holds much promise, wrote Zénobe, with Maurel's help, and after *monsieur* de Voltaire was gone back to Ferney, who could tell what would happen?

Maurel told Zénobe that it would be best if Zénobe handed the letter over to the *marquis* on the following day. There should be no intermediary for such a delicate operation. Maurel also suggested to Zénobe that he have an immediate task on hand so that the *marquis* would not be able to have the time to molest him.

Zénobe thought he understood and nodded. Then Maurel went off to the kitchen and brought back for them a tray of tea and sweet biscuits to accompany their lessons. In their whole lives they had never had anyone who treated them so sweetly.

The servants were all dismissed early that night for dinner was a simple affair with no visitors. André and Zénobe were both looking forward to going to bed, yet they still lingered out in the garden after everybody else had gone into the servants' quarters. It had rained all day, and the wispy gray clouds scurrying overhead had lost all their moisture and from time to time uncovered patches of stars here and there. The leaves of the ivy growing on the back wall of the house and the twigs of the deciduous trees glistened with tremulous drops. It was still quite cold, but neither one of them felt miserable because of it. Youth is resilient and stoic, seeks adventure and sensual extremes, almost as if they knew that the warmth of the bed they were to share would be pleasurable in inverse proportion to how cold they could get. After walking up and down the plantless rows of the *potager* garden, then visiting the standard dwarf fruit trees, they spoke of what all new young lovers of all the ages and lands speak of: how

---

135   *Candide*, published in 1759 to tremendous success, was, and is, Voltaire's greatest claim to fame. A slim book, it packs a wallop, for in it, Voltaire's enemy *l'Infâme* becomes a multitude. *Écrasez l'Infâme!* becomes: Squelch all fanaticism, intolerance, ignorance, provincialism, superstition and corruption.

beautiful the stars looked, how wonderful it'd be if they saw a shooting star, how nice it'd be if the moon showed her face. That is to say, they spoke of everything except for the feelings they had for each other. They looked for the moon all over, but she remained out of sight. Finally, when their breath became more visible and their teeth started to chatter, they went inside. They traversed the boys' room and then the girls', where all was quiet and dark; then at the end of the building they found theirs. Without lighting a candle, they undressed, although this time they undressed each other. In the dark again, and in absolute silence, they felt for each other's body, searching for buttons, taking off layers of clothing, and in-between the removal of articles, as flesh started to be liberated, they would kiss each other on these patches of bare skin, first the arms, then the neck, the chest, the belly. Yet, one couldn't call it kissing, really, for kissing makes a sound. This was more like the laying of the lips on the skin, first with the lips closed, then naturally opening up to allow the tongue to come into play, and from this, licking followed in swirls of gentle caressing.

Neither one of them knew what he was doing. It was the voice of Nature telling them what to do. Voltaire the scientist would have had his breath taken away from witnessing this scene, which aptly betrayed the untamable power of Nature in all Her glory. Nothing ingenious or inordinately sophisticated came to the two boys' minds. Just gentle caressing, the pressing of their bodies as they stood by the bed in their small bedroom, one or the other twirling the other around to touch and kiss him on his back. In the dark they explored each other's bodies, letting their pleasure be their guide. They lay on their bed, embracing in a joy that did not know guilt or shame. They felt that their love was good, and that their tenderness was benevolent.

As young and inexperienced as they were, it was not long before their activity reached fruition. They both reached resolution simultaneously, still without making any noise, experiencing their orgasm not in a bubbling up of a volcanic explosion, but rather retaining it like a long implosion, with deep intakes of breath that felt as if they were inverted sighs.

Ending a Dangerous Liaison

It is perhaps to be supposed that *madame la marquise* de Polignac, who because of her favored status in the halls of Versailles was used to having her way, put up a fuss when master Zénobe, a mere butler at the *hôtel* de Villette, told her in an impolitic and abrupt way that he no longer wished to see her. But one cannot underestimate the power of a guileless blue-eyed gaze and a tall, healthy stature, not to mention any other parts that the lady was privy to and to which we were not. Still, what a churlish young man, she thought to herself, right after he had said that their liaison was dangerous to him and that therefore he wished to put an end to it.

He had just stepped into her luxurious *berline* and she hadn't even had the time yet to present him with her silk sack of enticing chocolates.

"Dangerous, you say?" she asked while she flashed a derisive smile conveying the message that this adjective was grossly hyperbolic. "You think I'm dangerous?"

"I do not think for a moment that you yourself are dangerous, *madame*. It is the liaison we have devised that is dangerous. I feel that I am abased because your attentions toward me are based solely on the physical attraction that you have for me."

"You must be jesting, young man. I do not speak of your belief that you feel debased because of the way I have put you to use, for that is your conclusion and I have nothing to do with your mode of thinking. I mean that you jest for entertaining the possibility that there could ever have been anything else but physical attraction between us, from the beginning of our little liaison to its ending at any time in the future or in the present."

Her diamond pendant earrings danced around her neck to mirror her querulous mood. She even let out a snort of pique, as if to say that this situation was not to be believed.

"I believe you are mistaken, *madame*," answered Zénobe, "for I have never seen with you anything in the future but what we started out with, and I am not implying that our relationship could have ever developed into something emotional or even amorous. And that is precisely why I do not wish to continue to prolong it."

"Is it because I began to put *louis d'or* into your chocolates?"[136] [137]

"That only served to emphasize the dramatic imbalance of our milieux, *madame*, although I suppose that in order not to be an ingrate I must thank you for your generosity. But here is the crux of the matter: I can only try to please you with the satisfaction of your desire, whereas you have so many options at your disposal to try to please me, and yet, and yet I feel that I can get no satisfaction, that the more I see you the lower my degradation sinks, and the more my self-esteem (*mon amour-propre*) is undermined. I am demeaned at a time when the rest of my existence is elevating me to higher dignity and to propitious circumstances. You have no idea what my life was like before I met you; you were never curious enough to ask. But my life ensuing promises me much hope, and I wish to embrace my future with as much integrity as I can muster. I hope you will forgive me for putting an end to our association, and I hope you will remember me kindly."

Madame la marquise de Polignac reacted in one of the two following ways, but it is difficult to know which. She was 29 years old when she had her fling with Zénobe, still as beautiful and dainty as a porcelain doll. It is necessary to know that she was the one who dropped her lovers, not the other way around. Her aristocratic ego was enormous, and yet, to her merit, her empathy for the poor, it was said, was just as prodigious, and it is possible that on this day a battle waged in her heart between admiration for Zénobe's sincerity and contempt for his peremptory dismissal of her. Throw in the lust she held for the boy's beauty and we might have a clearer image of her conflicted feelings, but, alas, no palpable way to discern her true reaction.

A: Zénobe: "… I hope you will forgive me for putting an end to our association, and I hope you will remember me kindly."

Madame de Polignac: "Indeed I will, *petit*. I didn't know boys from the nether reaches of the provinces could speak like that. You are cerebral as well as articulate. But never you mind, dear, I think I understand what you mean. I can see what has happened here. For once, the roles are reversed, and I am the one who has been chasing you, directing the programme. I am the don Juan, and you are the damsel fallen into debauchery. I shall miss you. Boys like you are not often found in such good, healthy shape: young enough for vigor, and innocent enough for malleability. Let me kiss you one last time, and you take the chocolates for being so honest."

---

136   The *louis d'or* was a coin of the realm whose value was at 24 livres fixed. In spite of its name, it was of copper, not gold, made. A provincial female servant received between 24 to 33 livres per year; a stable-boy between 60 to 66 livres; their foreman between 84 to 90 livres. Their food and lodging, and clothes, were by their employers paid. Paris wages were a little better, but journeymen could not find work every day. A skilled labourer could up to two livres for a day's work earn, but a female weaver or spinner made less than half of that. Those same city workers were 100 livres for leaving an employer without the employer's written consent fined. On the other side of the social hierarchy, the Polignac family were almost 500,000 livres in annual pensions from the Treasury receiving. This does not count the gifts that the Queen showered on her friend Gabrielle: dresses costing several thousand livres apiece, jewels and perfumes and furniture.

137   *Gott im Himmel, Herr* Ralph! You must be relying too heavily on weak online pseudo-resources that more often than not get their facts wrong, absolutely wrong. The "wisdom of the masses" is an oxymoron, for the masses are witless, unscrupulous, bigoted and downright mendacious; they lie for the pleasure of it. The *louis d'or* was *d'or, d'or, d'or*! During Louis XVI's realm, the coin's circumference was 23 mm, and it had a weight of 7.65 g of .917 fine gold; on the obverse was the profile of Louis XVI, and on the reverse the motto «*Le Christ règne, vainc et commande*» (Christ reigns, vanquishes and commands). I agree with the rest of your footnote, but do you really have to interrupt my best scenes like this?

B: Zénobe: "… I hope you will forgive me for putting an end to our association, and I hope you will remember me kindly."

Madame de Polignac: "I doubt I shall remember you at all, *mon petit*. For once that the tables are turned, the roles are reversed, and I'm the don Juan to your helpless damsel fallen into debauchery. You're a boy. Why are you being so fastidious? It was only physical, what passed between the two of us. You make it sound like some cheap sordid calamity. Just dust yourself off and carry on. You're only a butler, and it was I the one who had to descend quite a number of rungs in the social ladder, *petit*. You should be thankful that a lady of the stature of the *marquise* de Polignac deigned to accept your kisses. But you've overstayed your welcome. Away with you. Be gone!"

She thumped on the roof with her baton and the carriage came to a stop. La Polignac opened the door without a word, and remained silent even after Zénobe said, "*Excusez-moi, madame*," as he stepped out.

It wasn't until he had started walking back to the quai des Théâtins that he noticed that by some means she had managed to slip the silk sack of chocolates and *louis d'or* into his coat pocket.

Meeting Another Giant

It had started to rain again during the night, and it was still raining in the morning, so André was very glad Maurel had given him a pair of galoshes to wear. The streets that were not cobble stoned, and even some that were, had a propensity to turn to mud. Every street had a rivulet of viscous malodorous mire running inexorably down towards the Seine. André tried to stay on the higher ground, but carriage-drivers had the same idea, and pedestrians were wise to yield to horses' hooves and fast-turning wheels.

Shortly before André left the *hôtel* de Villette, Maurel had told him to go change his clothes. He initially had chosen his best outfit, the one he used to wear to go to church, that is, when he used to go to church back in Normandy: a somber charcoal-gray wool coat with silver threads running vertically about an inch apart, with a matching waistcoat and pants. The coat had big cuffs with five big brass buttons on each side. The culottes ended right above the knees and had a leather string to pull the ends closed tight around his leg. White socks which went all the way to his thighs, disappeared at the knees under his culottes. He had on his best pair of shoes that had big silver-plated buckles on top. To finish his ensemble, André had included a scarf around his neck and an oversized hat of black velvet with a big ostrich plume sticking out the back. Maurel told him to take it all off. He suggested no socks and no hat at all. He told him to wear instead that dingy coat of worn velvet that he had, without a waistcoat, and definitely not this long woolen scarf that Maurel had given him, the one that he could turn around his neck three times. No, he had to wear a skimpy little scarf whose ends were frayed and which had a few moth holes in it. André thought it was because Maurel didn't want his clothes to get mucky during his walk to go see *monsieur* Jean-Jacques Rousseau. In truth, Maurel wanted to make sure that by the time André got to the rue des Platrières, his teeth would be chattering audibly and perhaps the philosopher or his wife would take pity on this waif and invite him in.

Which is exactly what happened. Especially after André prematurely turned north on the rue des Croix des Petits Champs instead of turning northeast on the rue Grenelle which turns into the rue des Platrières after the rue Coquillère. By the time he walked all the way to the Place des Victoires and turned right onto the rue du Reposoir and another right onto the farthermost side of the rue des Platrières, his teeth were definitely chattering. Even after he had walked up the five flights of stairs, his limbs were still trembling in the feeble attempt to bring warmth to his numb fingers and toes. When Thérèse Rousseau opened the door for André, the sixteen-year-old boy looked bedraggled and homeless, but had lost none of his angelic appeal. With his eyes teary from the cold, his cheeks flushed red, and his blond hair to his shoulders, he reminded Thérèse of the fresh-faced *putti* in northern Italian paintings which she had seen in the churches of Valle d'Aosta during one of the numerous times that she had become involuntarily separated from her husband. The innocents' painted expressions matched André's exactly: dolorous, forlorn, but with a radiant inner joy of spiritual hope. André seemed to Thérèse like a young, Viking-looking Jesus Christ. Then she had another thought: her oldest child would have been about the same age as this beautiful boy standing in front of her door with his teeth chattering and his limbs trembling. Her heart went out with motherly warmth to this indigent child, and she took him by the shoulders and dragged him in.[138]

"Poor boy," she told him. "What are you doing out on a day like today? It's drizzly and cold. Why, you don't even have a hat! Come here and let me dry your hair. You need something hot in your stomach. Your nose and cheeks are a bright red. Here, come with me, child."

Indeed, André's white skin was as red as Normand apples. He was thankful for *madame* Rousseau's hospitality, and realized Maurel's wisdom once again.

"*Merci, merci beaucoup, madame*," he repeated several times to *madame* Rousseau. "Thank you, *madame*, I was lost."

"Lost?" she asked, as she led him into a dark part of the apartment that served as her larder, pantry and cellar combined. "If you were lost, that must mean you were going someplace with some purpose in mind."

On a little charcoal stove she had a pot of water boiling. She told him to get closer to the fire to warm his hands. He held his hands against the small fire and felt his fingers tingle as they came back to life. In the meantime, she emptied some of the water into a pewter cup into which she had placed some crushed tea and mint leaves.

"I am come to see your husband, *madame* Rousseau. You are *madame* Rousseau, aren't you?"

She peered at his face, fearing to recognize a sign of an ulterior motive or an indecent proposal, but she saw only innocence and benevolence. "Ah, you are come to see *monsieur* Rousseau? And you became lost?" She dumped a spoonful of dark sugar into his cup and without stirring the tea she offered it to André.

"Thank you, *madame*, you are very kind." He drank some of the tea immediately, hoping it would calm his chills. The tea was very dilute, compared to the tea served at the *hôtel* de Villette. He also had to pick tea leaves off his lips. Still, he was glad that it was piping hot.

"Whence did you begin your journey?" asked *madame* Rousseau. Her face showed lines of anguish which had become permanent, and which gave her a look as if she were constantly on the verge of bursting into tears. She took off her shawl and used it to gently dry André's hair.

---

138   Jean-Jacques had only married his lifelong companion, Thérèse Levasseur, a laundress, in 1767, after 22 hectic years of discontinuous cohabitation, if it can be called a marriage when the groom invites the mayor over to dinner, speaks lachrymosely of the sweet bonds of marriage, and then exchanges impromptu vows with the blushing bride, who is blushing not out of virginal modesty, but out of shame for the strangeness of the peremptory ceremony. Moreover, as a Protestant, Jean-Jacques could never have married a Catholic legally. Furthermore, there was the problem of the five abandoned children—no, not *abandoned*, but rather, *given up* to the orphanage, according to the Swiss philosopher's *Confessions*. Thérèse's life with her mate can best be described as being filled with much *Sturm und Drang* (of which he was the originator). The cross Thérèse had to bear throughout her life was Jean-Jacques. Still, it was he who provided her with the wisps of consolation for the monumental grief that he caused her.

"Thank you, *madame*. I am come from the *hôtel* de Villette, across the Seine, in the Faubourg Saint-Germain."

"Oh, you don't have the aspect of one who comes from the Faubourg Saint-Germain."

"I belong to the servant's staff of the *marquis* de Villette, the host of *monsieur* de Voltaire, *madame*."

Madame Rousseau drew back. "*Monsieur* de Voltaire has sent you? You would do well to go back home after you have finished drinking your tea and warming up your hands. My husband will not see you. He will never forgive, nor forget, the great Voltaire for the unkind things he wrote about him."

"No, *madame*, you misunderstand. I serve in the house that is hosting *monsieur* de Voltaire, but I have not been sent by *monsieur* de Voltaire. It is rather a personal service about which I've come to see *monsieur* Rousseau."

"Oh, my child, you and a thousand others wish to see my husband about a thousand personal services. Everybody wants to make of my husband a facilitator of a thousand movements, an agent of a thousand ideologies, and they come here in droves and present us with a thousand ploys, just to see him, just to touch the hem of his coat. They prostrate themselves in a thousand postures and tell us a thousand lies. My husband wants no part of humanity's duplicitousness. He wants to be left in solitude and continue learning from the book of Nature. He is now old and tired. He has well paid for society's follies and now deserves to be at peace."

"But, I just wish to give him a letter," said André as he reached into his inside coat pocket and produced the letter from his sister Charlotte.

"A letter? A thousand letters come every day," responded the tired woman as she pointed to a pile of letters on a *chaise longue* of the little *salle de séjour*. "See? My husband couldn't possibly go through all of those." She walked over to the pile and lifted up a handful of the letters as if to gauge how much they weighed. She took a few and fed them to her little fire.

"Lately," she continued, "things have taken a turn for the worse. Many of these epistles you see here are from the strangest creature you've ever laid eyes upon. A woman who doesn't wear a trace of femininity, who, although she is dressed as a woman, moves like a man, and an impatient one at that, and she has been pestering and pestering us for these past few weeks trying to get my husband to see her."

"Is his—her—name the *chevalière* d'Éon, and does she have the Cross of Saint-Louis pinned to her dress right over her heart?" asked André.

Madame Rousseau made a little jump of surprise. "Why, yes, how did you know that?" She approached André with a look of curiosity.

"She came to visit *monsieur* de Voltaire a few days ago. She made quite an impression on the *salon*, and she even showed us a bout of fencing, of which she is a master, *euh*..., a mistress. A master. (*dont il est maître, euh..., maîtresse. Maître.*)"

"Yes, she did impress me as being aggressive and even bellicose. She pretends that my husband is the patron saint of the marginalized, the countless nameless that have never had a protector or sponsor. She has said that Jean-Jacques must become the political representative of the inconsolable masses, those shoved aside with no hopes of legitimization. She would make of my husband the solution to all that ails society. Whereas he has time and time again laid out what the problems are and what the solutions to those problems are. He has no more to say about any of all that. His only remaining yearn is to justify himself in the eyes of his critics. That, and to study the plants of God's creation. His writing is still important to him, and he picks his thoughts like he picks the flowers of the meadows, and both pursuits make him happy. Those are the only things that make him happy. Visitors, I'm afraid, have an opposite effect."

André understood quite well what Thérèse Rousseau was telling him. Still, his sister would be disappointed. He made one final attempt.

"What is one more letter, *madame*, one more letter from my twelve-year-old sister who lives in Normandy and who has found in *monsieur* Rousseau an *âme-sœur* (a kindred spirit), who loves him and appreciates him for all that he has done in favor of a society that has repaid him dishonestly, sometimes with malevolence, and always with ingratitude."

André didn't know what he was doing. He had never had to play the role of advocate, and he found himself doing it on behalf of his sister when he didn't even really believe in what he was saying. He just remembered what their father had told them, and was repeating it like a dictation from memory.

Thérèse capitulated, not from anything that André said, but because his young brow was furrowed somberly in what seemed like unaccustomed seriousness, and because her maternal instincts, still healthy after the years of attempted amputation of them, told her that Jean-Jacques might just like the company of this boy who would remind her husband of himself when he was young and free from the wicked influence of civilization and the icy pangs of guilt.

"Come with me," she said as she took the pewter cup from his hands. "I shall take you to see my husband. You will be able to talk to him, and you can give him your sister's letter yourself."

They approached the apartment's *salon* where two big closed windows provided the sole light. André could see a lone silhouette sitting in an armchair, doubled over in an attitude of concentrated study.

Maurel was not worried about André traversing the short distance to Jean-Jacques Rousseau's house. But like any being with a maternal instinct, he now fretted that perhaps he should have sent him accompanied by Zénobe. Still, he realized that André would take longer than an hour to get back to the *hôtel* de Villette since he would have to take a detour through the Palais-Royal. But that would not be hard to do, just take the rue des Plâtrières all the way back to the rue Saint-Honoré and directly to the Palais-Royal. But after an hour and a half had gone by, Maurel kept going to the windows of the first and second floors facing the quai des Théâtins. He would lean out to look towards the Pont Royal, which he figured would be the direction from which André would come. Then preparations for the household's dinner took him away, and when dinner was finished, he heard the big clock chime the one hour in the salon's anteroom, and he realized with dismay that André had been gone for three hours. What could have happened to him? Had *monsieur* Rousseau detained him? That didn't seem possible. The old philosopher was known for his antisocial sentiments and oral reticence. Was he writing a letter of response to André's sister? That didn't seem likely, either. Rousseau only bothered to write back to persons of high social standing for those would be letters that would be made public. Had André gotten lost? Was *docteur* Tronchin at home and was it he who was detaining his angel boy? A brooding cloud of thought hazed over Maurel's mind as the minutes ticked away and still André did not come home. Was the boy run over by a wayward carriage, mangled under horses' hooves, in the sort of accident that happened several times a week in Paris? Had he been captured by brigands who would turn him into a pickpocket? Had he been taken in by a prostitute who would have her way with him? Had he been stolen by someone who fancied a beautiful youth and would place him in a cage in his dungeon or manacle him in thick, heavy chains? Maurel's imagination would not leave him alone, and the tasks at hand were not enough to pry him from a thousand calamities.

When Zénobe came to the kitchen to see *monsieur* Maurel and to find out where André was so they could have their afternoon lesson, Maurel took him by the arm and went into the pantry with him. Zénobe could see the worry on Maurel's face, and when he heard that André had not yet returned from the Jean-Jacques Rousseau residence, he, too, became concerned. He quickly volunteered to go look for him, and Maurel acquiesced.

"Yes, yes, but you'll reverse the order in which André was supposed to have walked. Go first to *docteur* Tronchin's at the Palais-Royal. Ask there if André has already stopped by. You might as well find out if the *docteur* is returned and if so, when he can be expected to come see his patient *monsieur* de Voltaire. If André has already been there, scour the streets from there back to the quai des Théâtins. If not, then take the rue Saint-Honoré directly east to the rue des Plâtrières, which you take from the rue Grenelle, proceeding north, to the house over the fish shop. *Monsieur* and *madame* Rousseau live on the fifth floor. You can't miss it. An odor of fish permeates the air."

Zénobe started to turn away but Maurel grabbed his arm. "Do you want to take Henri or Philippe with you?"

"No, *monsieur* Maurel, I'll be fine, thank you. I'll be back with André in an hour." He started to turn away but then made a half-turn. "By the way, *monsieur* Maurel, I have just given the *marquis* de Villette the response we wrote to him yesterday."

Maurel nodded and gave a half-smile. Zénobe could see that he wasn't in the least bit interested in responses to the *marquis* de Villette.

"Thank you, *monsieur* Bosquet. I know I can rely on you."

In a flash, Zénobe was out the door making his way through the streets at a quick trot. He was still in his butler's uniform. The buttons on his jacket and on his sleeves and the golden-yellow tassels of his epaulettes shone against the blue-black of the cloth. He had removed his wig and the breeze and his speed swept his hair back from his forehead and made it dance around his shoulders every time he took a step. His eyes had the color of blue smoke this afternoon, refracting the gray of the clouds from which a soft "*pisse de vache*" was falling. The fine droplets evaporated as soon as they hit his body. Zénobe smiled at the Normand expression he had learned from André. *Cow piss.* It was quite à propos.

He crossed the Seine at the Pont Royal in less than five minutes, and thought it also quite à propos that Rousseau would be staying on the opposite bank as Voltaire. Of course, he thought to himself, this had to be. Rousseau absolutely had to sojourn on the opposite bank. Zénobe also instinctively knew that the rue des Plâtrières was going to be as dingy and dark as the rue de Beaune was light and spectacular. If he knew his philosophers, and he thought he did, he knew that Jean-Jacques could not be in a neighborhood he would enjoy, which he could possibly enjoy. As he walked into the brilliance and opulence of the Palais-Royal,[139] he knew that the rue des Plâtrières was going to be lackluster, perhaps dull, and depressing, a sort of *melancholia* to counter the *cornucopia* of the area he was traversing now.

He knocked at the door of *docteur* Tronchin's town house and the doorman informed him that the doctor was not in, that he was still in the countryside and that he was not expected to return until the following day or possibly the day after that. He also told Zénobe that nobody else from the *hôtel* de Villette had been by that afternoon, and that he was sure of this since he had been attending to the door all day. Zénobe thanked him and was off to the rue des Plâtrières. The closer he got to the street, the truer his intuitive supposition became that Rousseau's neighborhood was not going to be very gay.

André was having a second cup of weak tea. *Madame* Rousseau wanted the lad to accompany the Swiss thinker who was enjoying one of her infusions. She had always relied on herbs and other botanicals to cure her husband's ailments, of which he had a profusion. André wished that the tea were stronger, for he needed fortitude in being able to provide the philosopher with adequate company. Meditative perorations filtered out of Rousseau's mouth at such a dismal, sparing rate, that André feared falling asleep. Rousseau spoke very slowly, very deliberately, and very quietly, and sometimes halted in the middle of a sentence, and then, after a sharp intake of breath—or was it a sigh?—he would begin on a new thought. He spoke about the plants he was discovering thanks to Linnaeus' book[140] that he was studying of late, on the pleasures of solitude and solitary pleasures (André thought he might be talking about masturbation), and on the waste of living life amidst city noise, bad air, and evil distractions.

Rousseau had placed the book of botany on his lap, using André's sister's letter as a bookmark. He had barely glanced at the letter, and André feared he would never read it. André thought he caught sight of three or four other letters ensconced in the pages of the thick tome, like the prayers one places in a missal.

Madame Rousseau had been right. Rousseau took to this lad in his tiny *salon* as if André were the perfect visitor to his brand of philosophizing, which was pedantic, judgmental, and proselytizing. André hardly said anything, and would only nod in agreement at crucial times. André certainly could put up no objections, but did instead offer comments that seemed to communicate acceptance of Rousseau's themes. For his part, André recognized that his father and sister shared Rousseau's outlook on many

---

139   The Palais-Royal was the center of leisure and pleasure for the wealthy classes. A pedestrian zone, it contained boutiques, restaurants, theaters, galleries and gardens, and two Swiss guards at every entry to keep out the riffraff. The Palace itself was the residence of the dukes d'Orléans, cousins to the king. Apartments for lease were available to the affluent.

140   The *Philosophia botanica*, published in 1751 and purchased by Rousseau in 1765. Along with his *Systema naturae*, Carl von Linné provided Rousseau with years of contented study. In a letter to him, Rousseau called himself a disciple who wished to render homage to the Swedish botanist, thanking him for the tranquility of meditation that he had tasted amidst the cruel persecution and hatred of the world. He beseeched him to continue the interpretation of the book of nature. He closed his letter with the sentence: *«je vous lis, je vous étudie, je vous médite, je vous honore et je vous aime de tout mon cœur.»* ("I read you, I study you, I meditate on you, I honor you and I love you with all of my heart.")

things. He knew his father would never have moved to Caen from the countryside if farming had provided a more lucrative business. Giving up the hills of Normandy to go into the narrow dismal streets of Caen was not *monsieur* Corday's first choice for the Corday family. And here was Rousseau espousing the same ideas. He wondered if there was a connection. For as long as he could remember, Rousseau's books had always been on their tables and on his father's bedside stand. And his sister Charlotte had taken to Jean-Jacques at a very early age. Come to think of it, he had never seen one of Voltaire's books at home. He concluded that he had grown up in a one-philosopher household.

All of a sudden, he realized that the quiet philosopher had asked him a direct question, and André had to hear the echoes in his ears of the last words spoken, and caught the name Arouet. How was *monsieur* Arouet's health these days? Thank God Zénobe had told André Voltaire's birth name, and he was able to respond, "*Monsieur* Arouet? *Monsieur* Arouet has been having severe health problems, and we have been trying to have *docteur* Tronchin come and take a look at him.

"*Docteur* Tronchin from Geneva?"

André was reminded that he still had to stop by the Palais-Royal, and he began to worry about all the time he had already spent in the presence of Rousseau.

"I believe so, *monsieur.*"

"That Tronchin family! They are everywhere!"[141] I wonder why they're not content to stay in Geneva."[142]

Without thinking, André observed, "But you, *monsieur*, you didn't stay in Geneva, either."

Rousseau turned to André with a flash of impatience, but he saw no guile and no wicked recriminations in the lad's eyes.[143] He saw just an innocent from the countryside who looked as freshly picked as a, as a, as an apple.

"You say you are from Normandy?"

"*Oui, monsieur.*"

"Ah, I wish I had one of your apples now."

"My family's apples were the best in the province, *monsieur*, big and red and sweet and luscious."

"Stop! You are making my mouth water just from the thought." And the great Rousseau smiled upon the boy.

"But tell me," said Jean-Jacques when the smile had waned from his lips. Why have you left such a beautiful country to come to this Godforsaken soulless place?"

"Paris, *monsieur*? Well, I wanted to visit famous places, see important things, meet celebrated people."

---

141   The Tronchin family from Geneva had scions in many lucrative fields: Jean-Robert Tronchin was Voltaire's main banker and financial adviser in Lyon; François Tronchin, was a leading oligarch in Geneva; Jean-Robert Tronchin, a cousin, was the Genevan attorney-general; Louis-François Tronchin, son of Théodore, was secretary of the English ambassador in Berlin; and, of course, Théodore Tronchin himself, doctor to the highest spheres of European society. Perhaps his greatness was due to the fact that he killed fewer patients than other doctors.

142   Confederatio Helveticus did not yet exist. Geneva was a republic at this time.

143   What André did not know was that Rousseau was ordered out of Geneva by the town patriarchs who, after burning his books and stripping him of his citizenship, changed their mind and ordered his arrest. Meantime, Rousseau had fled to the canton of Berne from where he was also expulsed. He finally had to seek refuge in the Prussian principality of Neuchâtel. All this, which happened in 1762, was still fresh in Jean-Jacques' memory.

"And you really think that all those things are worth being in a place of such wickedness?"

"Well, *monsieur*, I try to close my eyes when I see it."

"Oh, closing your eyes is enough, is it? Well, wickedness certainly enters the spirit mostly through the eyes. But what about the ears, when someone whispers malevolent suggestions into them? How do you stop that? And sometimes, evil enters through the skin. How will you put a stop to the evil that enters through a caress, through a light kiss, through a wanton touch?"

André's eyes grew big. Did Rousseau see the signs of wickedness on his skin? Could he see the marks of Zénobe's caresses and kisses? Could the philosopher detect something in the expression of his face? Could Rousseau judge that he, André, was becoming wicked?

The old man sank back in his chair. "Oh, yes, yes, many dangers lurk in Paris. You should have stayed in Normandy, for here in Paris your soul will stray on a thousand paths, and most of them will lead you to your perdition, and perdition is eternal. You best go back to your family. Go back to your apples. Apples are not evil of themselves, it's what they represent. They are a symbol of carnal knowledge, evil doings, diabolical temptations."

"But, but, *monsieur*... There is no evil in the country?"

"But yes, but yes! It is the evil that people take back from the city. But you are as yet untouched, unsullied by the tempting flowers of evil. Turn your attention away from them! They will entice you and with their lovely scent and appearance will lead you onto a path which you will take for happiness, but which in the long run will end up in wickedness and disease, and which will shrivel up your soul like the sun shrivels up the cyclamen."

Rousseau opened up his book which he handed to André and had him read out loud the paragraph on the cyclamen which, apparently, preferred shadier alpine retreats. André also saw Charlotte's letter to Jean-Jacques. He saw her fine, flowery penmanship, and wondered what she saw in her philosopher.

"My sister admires you so, *monsieur*. I hope you read her letter."

"Let me read it now," he said. André handed it over and Rousseau unsealed and unfolded it. It took him but a minute to read it.

"Very sweet, very sweet. Your sister sounds like a gentle maiden. She writes that she has enjoyed my epistolary novel *Julie, ou la Nouvelle Héloïse*, and that for her, Julie will always live on in her heart. She says that she went through a period of mourning for her. So did I, you know. In the end, it is gratifying to know that I have touched souls out there. Nevertheless, it is a burden to think that I might also have muddied your sister's pure heart with impure thoughts of adultery and fornication. One treads a fine line between moral concerns and unintended corruption. I want to teach the soul to remain good, while holding up the sins to be avoided at all costs. How old is your sister?"

"She is twelve this year, *monsieur*."

"Ah, what a relief. She is certainly precocious, but much too young to entertain thoughts of immoral love. Even you, I imagine, my young friend, are too inexperienced to know of what I speak."

"I think I may know, *monsieur*. But I'm not quite sure."

"Well, do not worry your young head with such unworthy subjects," laughed Rousseau. "We should speak only of the plants of God's creation. They alone are worthy of our attention and our research."

The conversation continued along the lines of the bounty of botany. Rousseau the botanist expounded: "Nature covered the nudity of the earth with such rich variety that it charms the eyes and surprises the imagination; it is the study of that profusion of riches that the botanist, among all the other men of science, can admire with the most ecstasy. He alone can appreciate the divine art and the exquisite taste of the Creator who made the dress of our communal mother."

Madame Rousseau came to interrupt them with an announcement of another young visitor from the *hôtel* de Villette.

"It's Zénobe!" cried André and he ran out to the front door. He was not mistaken, and as soon as he saw his friend he rushed into his arms. "I'm glad you are come for me!" he whispered into his ear.

"We were worried about you, *monsieur* Maurel and I," answered Zénobe.

Madame Rousseau had followed André to the front door. "Come in quickly, before anyone else shows up," she told Zénobe. She went out onto the landing and glanced down the staircase. She herded the boys into the apartment and closed the door.

Clearly, she had been impressed by Zénobe's presence and by his epaulettes. He held himself like a soldier: straight posture, shoulders back, buttocks up, unearthly eyes politely gazing straight into hers. Boys like that did not show up on her doorstep very often. A couple of lads like André and Zénobe did not show up together ever. She beckoned to Zénobe. "Come have some hot tea. You must be chilled to the bone."

She herself joined the two boys in the presence of her husband. She was glad for the company, for sometimes she thought that Jean-Jacques was too often alone. Their one regular visitor was Bernardin de Saint-Pierre, and he could only come when he was not under the pressure of his responsibilities.[144]

Rousseau greeted the newcomer with gracious nonchalance. But when he found out that Zénobe came from Annecy in the Haute Savoie, tears came into the old philosopher's eyes and fell down his face.

"Come here, my boy, and embrace me."

Zénobe did as he was told. The philosopher smelled musty, like an attic full of cobwebs.

"Ah, Annecy, Annecy!" exclaimed Rousseau. "It was there that I met *Maman*, my beautiful, charming, kindhearted *Maman*. She was my first love, my first wonderment, my introduction to God's gift to man, she who was taken from Adam's rib and rendered unto him to be his lifelong companion. *Madame* de Warens, *madame* de Warens!" he said to Zénobe with a wobbly voice. "You have brought her back to me, if only for a little while. You have brought back to me that time of innocence, when my heart was new, when my heart was at its freshest, most sensitive state. By your simple presence, my dear young friend, you have brought back a profusion of sweet and sad memories. If I had but known that this afternoon would hold such a pleasant retreat into the world of the past! I search for serenity, and thanks to you, I have found it in the voluptuousness of remembrance, and I breathe in the pure air of the ethereal regions of nostalgia. Tell

---

144   These responsibilities included the publication of his extensive *Études de la Nature*, the product of a lifetime of voyages to exotic places. He also traveled around Europe in an effort to promote his ideology to regenerate corrupt occidental society. Volume four of his corpus includes the novel *Paul et Virginie*, which is to sweep Europe off its feet in 1784.

me, dear friend, do you know the street where I used to live, the rue Saint-François in Annecy?"[145]

"Of course, *monsieur.* That's where my father and I would set up our vegetable stall on market days."

"Oh, yes, yes! The market! The market! I would so enjoy going down to street level and join in the profusion of produce and flowers. The Reblochon was exquisite, on *pain à lardons!*[146] Oh, my friends! Twice today you have made my mouth water! First with the thought of crisp, succulent apples from Normandy, and now with Reblochon and *pain à lardons* from Savoy. What a bounteous mixture we have with us today, *hein,* Thérèse? Normandy and Savoy. Savoy and Normandy. And what a nice pair of handsome boys. I can see their wholesomeness, their benevolence, in their eyes. Oh, Thérèse, what say you if we regale ourselves in the company of these two wonderful boys! Why don't we have some hot chocolate!"

Thérèse looked up in surprise. Her husband was indeed going through a paroxysm of pleasure. She got up and went to her tiny kitchen to prepare what her husband had asked for. But she also had in mind breaking into the box of biscuits that the *chevalière* d'Éon had brought on a previous day.

With cups of steaming black cocoa, bitter and sweet, the four of them sat and began munching on the biscuits, which were complex concoctions of twice-baked triangles of sugary, buttery pastries with a layer of smooth marzipan inside. *Madame* Rousseau remembered that d'Éon had said she had procured them at the Procope,[147] but she dared not say anything to her husband for fear of upsetting him. At the first mention of d'Éon, Jean-Jacques would begin to grumble. She was already in a fretful state, since d'Éon always came by around this time, and she certainly didn't want her philosopher husband to—

Almost as if on cue, like a play at the theater, a loud impatient rapping on the door interrupted her interior monologue. Zénobe, ever the gentleman, got out of his chair and announced, "Seeing as how I'm still in my butler's suit, permit me to go and see who is at the door, *monsieur* and *madame.*"

Madame Rousseau giggled. *Monsieur* Rousseau had a biscuit in his mouth and nodded as he chewed pensively and methodically.

Zénobe went to the front door, opened it, and before he could bow and say "Good afternoon," he froze in recognition of a figure he had just seen at the *hôtel* de Villette a mere three days ago. *Mademoiselle la chevalière* d'Éon was alone, dressed in full *salon* regalia, wearing a huge boat on her headdress that, prow to stern, must have measured a foot and a half.[148]

"*Mademoiselle la chevalière* d'Éon!" said Zénobe in surprise.

---

145   Today this street in the oldest part of Annecy is known as the rue Jean-Jacques Rousseau. During the Revolution, in 1794, all street nomenclature with saints' names was de-baptized and given the names of the Revolution's heroes. Behind the *hôtel* de Warens, which is now a music school and a police station, the city has built a *"Balustre d'Or"* to commemorate the place where the young boy Jean-Jacques and his patroness, later to be his lover, Françoise Louise, *baronne* de Warens, first met.

146   Local Savoy cheese and bread with pieces of bacon baked in.

147   The Procope is the oldest restaurant in Paris, on the rue de l'Ancienne Comédie. It had been a favorite haunt of Voltaire, and to this day his desk and bust are in prominent view.

148   This wig was very much of the moment. It commemorated the triumph of Liberty, and was named *"Coiffure à l'Indépendance"* in honor of the United Colonies of America.

"*Oui, mon cher,*" said she. "It is I. I didn't know *madame* Rousseau had engaged a majordomo."

"She hasn't, *mademoiselle*," Zénobe responded as he made a belated bow. "I am a butler at the *hôtel* de Villette, where your presence a few days ago became the talk of the town."

"Oh, how amusing. Voltaire's majordomo at the residence of Jean-Jacques Rousseau. How very amusing. And how very fortuitous," she said as she barged in. "Please allow me to enter before *madame* Rousseau asks me to take my leave."

She had to bend at the knees in order to leave room under the doorway for her naval wig to make its ingress at the same time she did. Zénobe could not help noticing that she did this without having to steady her coiffure with her hands, and while she took a couple of steps into the apartment with her knees bent all the while. He wondered if he would be able to do the same while balancing a basket of fruit on his head.

"Do I know you, then, young man?" she asked Zénobe.

"Oh, I don't think so, *mademoiselle*," I'm just a butler under the direction of *monsieur* Maurel, the *marquis* de Villette's majordomo.

"Ah, I see. But don't sell yourself short, young man. You are not *just* a butler. You have the bearing and the countenance of a military man. I could use a young man like you in my Dragoons."

"Thank you, *mademoiselle*," said Zénobe as he took another bow. "Please follow me. *Monsieur* and *madame* Rousseau are in their *salon*."

"*Enfin!*" said the *chevalière*. "At last I get to speak with *monsieur le philosophe* Jean-Jacques Rousseau!"

Zénobe led the way and the *chevalière* followed, curtailing her soldier's swagger the better to pace behind the butler's more subdued stride.

When *monsieur* and *madame* Rousseau saw this apparition in their tiny *salon*, their eyes got huge and *madame* Rousseau dropped her biscuit on her lap, yet she continued bringing her hand to her mouth and she took a bite of air.

Zénobe was announcing the visitor: *mademoiselle* Charles Geneviève Louis Auguste André Timothée, *chevalière* d'Éon de Beaumont."

The *chevalière* was impressed by Zénobe's prodigious feat of memory. She curtsied low, very low, and Zénobe was prepared to help her back up, but d'Éon managed to right herself without any outward sign of strain. Her legs must be solid muscle, thought Zénobe.

Both Rousseaus had risen from their seats, not out of courtesy, but out of sheer panic. What were they to do now? This strange specter of a creature had managed to intrude on their tranquil solitude and now how would they get rid of her? For the moment, they could do nothing. Rousseau stared at the *chevalière* d'Éon's boat atop her head with trepidation that it would topple off at any moment or that it would sail off into the sunset. It had seven sails, three banners on top of the three masts, and teardrop pearls hanging from the cannon ports.

"*Madame*, you have a boat on your head!" exclaimed Rousseau.

"No, it's a galleon," explained the *chevalière* with coyness and pride. With a shy smile she continued, "*Monsieur et madame Rousseau, quel plaisir, quel délectable plaisir de vous voir, enfin!* You know, *madame*, that I have had for your husband through all these years, an unadulterated, an unalloyed admiration bordering on adoration. He struck me years ago with his unremitting attacks on the corruption of society and seduced me with his poetic pages on love undying. Between his works on politics and society and those on the human heart, I am strung up, unable, and unwilling, to disassociate myself from the tender but terrible ideals of this most noble of all thinkers."

Zénobe thought to himself: Spoken like a true woman.

D'Éon then turned her attention to *monsieur* Rousseau. He was standing in front of his armchair like a timid schoolboy, with his book tucked under his arm.

"*Oui, monsieur, oui, vous!*" continued the *chevalière*. "It is indeed you whom I am come to cherish and before whom I lay down my life."

Rousseau said nothing. *Madame* Rousseau said nothing. Therefore, the *chevalière* d'Éon continued speaking.

"You have *le tout Paris* agog with excitement. The newspapers write about you on a daily basis. Hundreds of admirers wish to see you. And yet you visit no one and allow no one to visit you."

Rousseau had regained some of his composure. "It is because, *monsieur–*"

"*Mademoiselle*," said d'Éon with a smile.

"*–monsieur*, Paris for me is a gutter. It is a city full of noise, smoke and mud, where women no longer believe in virtue or men in honor."

D'Éon stood up for her rights. "I beg you, my dear *philosophe*, to believe that there are still women in Paris who share your love of honor, and one can still find men for whom virtue is an unassailable treasure to be kept close to the heart." Her right hand went up to her Cross of Saint-Louis.

"Ah, *monsieur–*"

"*Mademoiselle.*"

"*–monsieur*, you speak only of the young." Here, Jean-Jacques motioned to Zénobe and André. André smiled at the *chevalière* and took a bow. Between Rousseau and d'Éon, André would prefer to seek solace in d'Éon's friendship. *Mademoiselle* d'Éon smiled at André and gave a small curtsy in return. Rousseau continued, "Only the young, freshly come from the desert, are untainted. But I fear for them, and my heart goes out to them. If they remain in Paris, their souls will degenerate to the point that all ideas of honor and virtue will flee from them. It is not to be helped. It is inevitable."

D'Éon had not been asked to sit down, but she did so anyway, on the chair that Zénobe had vacated. André sat down, and both Rousseaus had no choice but to sit down as well. Only Zénobe remained standing, as he was playing the role of butler.

"Look at the ruses that people have been using to get me to open up my doors for them," continued the philosopher. "*Madame la comtesse* de Saint-*** sent me some music to copy,[149] but later confessed that it was but a pretext to come see me. She avowed it herself! *Monsieur le comte* Duprat has been needling me to come and stay in his house, in Lyon, but I would die first rather than suffer the presence of men of society who despise me."

Zénobe thought to himself: And suffer the intolerable weight of gratitude for a friend who offers you asylum!

Rousseau continued, "All I want, *monsieur–*"

"*Mademoiselle.*" The *chevalière*'s voice had gone up a notch in volume and emphasis.

---

149 Rousseau never does give the *comtesse*'s full name in his writings. Throughout his life, people often gave him commissions in music; he was a musician of note and a popular composer, too. He was also the main proponent of Italian *opera buffa* in the *Querelle des Bouffons*, asseverating that French was too overbearing and not sonorous enough to communicate the subtleties of human emotions.

"–*monsieur*, is to forget the hatred of men and to live my life in solitary tranquility. I need to forget the hatred, for that oblivion is what I need to live and die in peace. I thought that here in Paris I would find refuge in anonymity, that I would be able to hide in plain sight, but I see that, once again, I was wrong in assigning certain signs of respect to my fellow man. People continue to pester me all day long."

Zénobe felt compassion for *mademoiselle* d'Éon. He felt Rousseau was unfairly attacking her self-respect. He broke the first rule of Maurel's list of the sacrosanct laws of butlering: he spoke up and joined in the conversation.

"But, *monsieur* Rousseau, *mademoiselle* is come only to pay her respects to you."

"I need no one to pay his respects to me."

"Her respects," offered the *chevalière*, with a quick glance of comradeship to Zénobe. "Indeed, *mon cher monsieur* Rousseau, my visit here is innocent. You have often spoken of how you have been betrayed by your fellow man. Well, I am come to trade melancholy stories of the same type of betrayal. I, who was the minister plenipotentiary in London, and a spy in the Russian court before that, and captain of the Dragoons during the Seven Years' War before that, and now I have been relegated to the stature of a lowly, helpless woman who–"

"Precisely so, *monsieur*, precisely so!" This time, Rousseau's pronouncement of the title of *monsieur* made it impossible for anybody to correct the Swiss philosopher. "You are the type of person from whom I am most trying to hide. I cannot abide by your previous stature and your current one. There is something grievously amiss in their juxtaposition. How could you have been captain of the Dragoons, ferocious to the degree that you were given the Cross of Saint-Louis which you now wear pinned to your breast? And how are you then metamorphosed into a woman, an elegant modern woman at that, with a headdress that is not to be believed, with an air of dignity and conceit to match, when heretofore you were someone else, and someone else of a different sex? No, *monsieur*, not in my house, not in my presence. You are an abomination, an abomination of which the Israelite patriarchs have spoken and warned us about. You are situated somewhere in between two states of being, neither man nor woman, therefore neither subject pronoun can be employed to describe you: you are neither a *he* nor a *she*. You are an *it*. You don't even have a soul, a soul that could be called corrupt or degenerate. As an object, an object of scorn and ridicule, you are an *it*, and as such, you are without a soul!"

The *chevalière* d'Éon's eyes erupted in tears and her lower lip started to tremble. She had swept up her skirts in preparation for getting up out of her chair, but a voice behind her halted her movement.

It was Zénobe. André could tell that his friend was trying to control and to conceal his ire. His nostrils were flaring, and his eyes had narrowed, throwing off an icy light that André had never seen. His voice trembled.

"*Monsieur* Rousseau, you of all people who have belabored for years the desertion of many of your friends and the outright accusations of your enemies, even lapidation from the rabble,[150] you of all people should understand, if not identify with, individuals such as *mademoiselle* d'Éon."

Rousseau said with venom, "I now have a butler judging me?"

---

150   Zénobe is referring to the frightening episode in 1765 in Môtiers, Switzerland, when rocks were thrown at Rousseau's house by a crowd of locals. Some of the rocks broke through the windows, and one landed near to where he has just been.

"By the same token, *monsieur*," riposted Zénobe, whose ironic pronouncement of the title of respect left no room to maneuver, "you who hurl out judgments like a volcano vomits forth rocks of fire, answer me this: Who made you God that you should condemn, nay, pronounce people's sins, and then condemn them? You are no *philosophe* to me, for you have battled injudicious prejudice only to replace it with your own. Your whole life through—and your works show it—you have mistaken *your* needs, *your* predilections, *your* sentiments, *your* beliefs, customs, superstitions and prejudices, and foisted them *in toto* onto man's society at large. You have confused your own nature with culture, without assigning an iota of importance to the individual, and to the myriads of idiosyncrasies that differentiate us. You want to treat us as if we were all little examples of the paradigm called Jean-Jacques Rousseau. Well, *monsieur*, you are no paragon of virtue yourself. 'Why dost thou behold the splinter in thy brother's eye, yet not consider the plank in thine own eye? Thou hypocrite!' People have thrown stones at you because you threw them first! The reason why you want us all to abandon the cities and hide out in the primitive confines of forest and jungle is because you are a primitive yourself! Primitive in thought, primitive in action—"

At this stage, d'Éon swept up her skirts again in order to stand up. André stood up with her.

"—primitive in your very soul. You, Jean-Jacques Rousseau, you are worse off than not having a soul. For your soul is an unforgiving, intransigent and recalcitrant thing. Your soul is nothing. You are the one who should be walking on all fours!"[151]

"Get out, get out, all of you!" yelled Rousseau. *Madame* Rousseau thought her husband was going to have an attack of apoplexy. She was close to having the vapors.

She shooed the visitors towards the door as if they were a gaggle of geese. But they were already on the way to the door of their own accord. Zénobe opened the door with fury. The *chevalière* took a couple of steps with bent knees to pass under the door, André followed and then Zénobe hesitated in order to garner all of his physical forces. He threw the door shut with all of his might. The noise was satisfyingly explosive, shaking the rafters above him, breaking one of the hinges. He thought of breaking the door down to annihilate the last frangible vestige of Rousseau's separation from the rest of the world, but, upon second thought, he followed d'Éon and André who were by now descending the flights of stairs.

When they were all on the rue des Plâtrières, *mademoiselle* d'Éon took them both into her expansive embrace, holding them both tightly against her bosom. André's cheek was pressed painfully on her Cross of Saint-Louis.

"My heroes," she cried out. "Yes, yes, I want you both to be in my Dragoon regiment."

"You, *monsieur*," she said to Zénobe, "I knew it from the very moment I laid eyes on you. You are strong, you are feisty, you are a credit to mankind, and you've read your Jean-Jacques Rousseau!"

The *chevalière*'s carriage driver had come to them.

"*Vite*, Robert! Quickly! Bring the carriage 'round because we must depart these premises immediately. The rue des Plâtrières no longer means anything to me. There

---

151   Zénobe is quoting from Voltaire's public letter of criticism of Rousseau's idea of «*le bon sauvage*», the good savage, or the primitive man who lives a moral life in the very heart of nature. "*Il prend envie de marcher à quatre pattes quand on lit votre ouvrage. Cependant, comme il y a plus de soixante ans que j'en ai perdu l'habitude, je sens malheureusement qu'il m'est impossible de la reprendre.*" "One feels a desire to walk on all fours when one reads your work. However, since I lost that habit more than sixty years ago, I feel, unfortunately, that it is impossible for me to take it up again."

is nothing here for me, nothing here for anyone." She looked around the street with a look of contempt tinged with sadness and then twirled around and mounted the vehicle.

The *chevalière*'s magnificent and elegant *berline*, pulled by four black stallions, swept them away in a roar of horses' hooves and a clatter of wooden wheels on cobblestones.[152]

As they set out, Zénobe heard d'Éon give instructions to her driver to head for the *hôtel* de Villette. Zénobe was still in a very altered state. He noticed that André had taken hold of one of his hands and was not letting go. He sat back on the seat finely upholstered in a thick royal-blue velour embroidered with little fleurs-de-lys in golden thread.

Zénobe could not believe what he had just done. He couldn't understand it. He had, of course, read Jean-Jacques' works, even though by all rights his Catholic priest preceptor, Father Anselme, should have added them to the region's prolific bonfires. Zénobe had never been attracted to Rousseau's texts, yet he would not have harbored any ill will against the man. So what had just happened in Rousseau's *salon*? Why had Zénobe stood up for this woman sitting in front of him, who, after all, did indeed present a strange figure? He harbored no loyalty towards her. As a matter of fact, he would be hard-pressed to defend her out of personal conviction. Nevertheless, he had defended her. And he had just insulted Jean-Jacques Rousseau's soul in doing so. Why had he done that? Was it perhaps because he was instinctively following voltairean principles? Had not Voltaire, along with Benjamin Franklin, welcomed the *chevalière* d'Éon into the *hôtel* de Villette? Had they not only treated her with the respect she deserved, but with the accompanying corollary that here indeed was a paradigm worthy of emulation? Would not Voltaire and Franklin have defended her as well? And was Zénobe not supposed to act on their behalf, in their stead? He felt better after this last thought, and he let out a long sigh of relief. The *chevalière* took Zénobe's other hand and patted it. She was smiling in gratitude, admiration and bliss, as if Zénobe were the great Alexander himself, victorious on the battlefield. He smiled back at her. He thought to himself: no wonder d'Éon's dragoons always loved her, *euh*, him. Her.

"I must thank you a thousand times, my brave knight (*mon preux chevalier*)," she told Zénobe as the carriage wended its way past pedestrians who flattened themselves against the walls of the houses. It wasn't the first time Zénobe had been in a carriage, but it was the first time he had been in a carriage traveling this fast, so he felt like his stomach had been left back on the rue des Plâtrières. "You were a marvel back there and I need to thank you profusely for your courage and sense of justice. I am of a mind to write to the *Journal de Paris* and narrate the whole of my visit to the Swiss philosopher Jean-Jacques Rousseau!"

"Oh, please, don't do that," beseeched Zénobe. "It would do no one any good to know that I spoke harshly to *monsieur* Rousseau, and it would perhaps embarrass him."

"Ah, you need not be worried for the man. I believe nothing embarrasses him. And everything that falls on him, criticism, chiding, harsh words, insults, sticks and stones, serve only to strengthen his position: that he is a man beleaguered from all sides, all alone, without the least defense, hated by all. The more attacks he receives, the more righteous he feels. He's Jesus all alone on the mount. Well, if he is alone, he has chosen it for himself. The least he could do is to stop complaining about it."

Zénobe offered *mademoiselle* d'Éon his observation on Rousseau: "He offends people, and then calls their reaction persecution."

---

152   This carriage had been a gift from Louis XVI, in recognition of the *chevalier* d'Éon's loyal services to his grandfather Louis XV.

"Well said, young man, well said. What is your name?"

"My name is Marie-Jean Zénobe Bosquet, *mademoiselle*, from the Haute Savoie."

"And you are...?" said the *chevalière* as she turned to André.

"*Oui, mademoiselle*, my name is André Armand Cyrille Corday, and I am from Normandy."

"And you both live at the *hôtel* de Villette?"

"*Oui, mademoiselle*," they answered in unison.

Zénobe said, "And night has started to fall. Our *maître d'hôtel* is going to be sick with worry."

"And we didn't go to the Palais-Royal to summon *docteur* Tronchin!" said André, suddenly remembering.

"Don't worry, I've already gone," Zénobe told him. Then to d'Éon he asked, "*Mademoiselle*, what is it that you would have wanted from Rousseau?"

She couldn't withhold a guffaw. "Oh, the irony," she said, laughing, but with tears in her eyes. "I am so sad and dejected. I, who thought that Jean-Jacques Rousseau was going to be the solution to all of my problems. I, who have lionized the man, who have been greatly influenced by his writings and sentiments. I, who thought that those sentiments were sincere and benevolent. I am doubly wounded by his reaction today. First, he has disappointed me in his philosophy, and second, he has rejected me personally."

"Where do you find the irony?" asked Zénobe.

"The irony is in that Rousseau rejected me, and Voltaire did not. Rousseau is supposed to be the savior of the dispossessed. I knew that Voltaire helps those who are the victims of religious intolerance and political persecution. But it is Rousseau, or so I used to believe, who is supposed to stand up for those poor souls who cannot find their way in society, those who are victims of *social* intolerance, who, because of one reason or another, do not fit in and are thus ejected and damned to be eternal outsiders."

"But you are not an outsider, *mademoiselle*," said André as he put his hand on top of hers.

"Ah, *le mignon* (what a sweetheart)," said the *chevalière*.

"André is right," added Zénobe. "You are not an outsider. An outsider does not get awarded the Cross of Saint-Louis. An outsider is not in the thick of things politically and socially. I think perhaps you have been a victim of the change of monarchs. Louis XV was aware of your worth, sent you abroad as his representative, gave you power and status, and now Louis XVI orders you home to serve as a curious ornament."

"Yes, my young friend, you are right, and you do not know the full extent of your verity. The monarch who is sitting now on the throne of France recommended that I go into a nunnery. Imagine that! I, in a nunnery. You will realize the full extent of my faithfulness to the Capets[153] when I tell you that I did go visit quite a few convents. The one at Saint-Cyr was beautiful, and very calm, very tranquil. I would be able to write my memoirs there."

Zénobe asked, "But are you a believer, *mademoiselle*?"

"Oh, yes, there has always been a deeply spiritual side to me. I may not be a complete papist, but I like the passionate side of Catholicism. I am privy to the sufferings of the Christ our Savior. *Sainte* Thérèse and *Saint* Jean de la Croix have always attracted me."

Zénobe was mystified. "But how does *mademoiselle* reconcile the two parts of her existence: philosophy and commitment (*philosophie et engagement*) on the one side—I speak

---

153   The family name of the monarchs named Louis, going back to Hugues Capet, King of the Franks, in 987.

of commitment to the social convictions of human rights and justice for women, and concomitant energetic action towards those goals—and Catholicism on the other side, that is, faithful acceptance of Church doctrine and a reactionary attitude to anything that seeks to change the *status quo*?"

The *chevalière* d'Éon seemed momentarily disoriented by Zénobe's question. She finally answered: "One doesn't truly change anything unless it is from the inside. One must be a member of the institution, of the society, of the organism, and so forth, if one wants to make changes. By being part of the Church, I can help transform it the better to see it respond to changing perspectives. You have not yet seen to what extent I am willing to fight for social progress."

Zénobe seemed disappointed. "The Church speaks only of universalities and it speaks of them with great authoritarianism. The Church is not interested in change, for anybody or anything."

"Ah, I see you are a true follower of our friend *monsieur* de Voltaire. *'Écrasez l'Infâme', n'est-ce pas?* Oh, yes, I can see you will go far, my young and handsome new friend, *monsieur* Marie-Jean Zénobe Bosquet. And you as well, *monsieur* André Armand Cyrille Corday.

The carriage was crossing the Seine at the Pont Neuf. The prostitutes had already emerged from the shadows of the rue Saint-Denis, now gathering on the bridges and quays. The last glimmers of the sunset were turning the surface of the rippling waters a dark rufous, and the houses across the river, including the *hôtel* de Villette, reflected the dying light with soft tones of gold and mauve.

By the time the carriage stopped in front of the *hôtel*, night had completely fallen. Maurel, who had been stuck to one of the street-level windows, miscreantly and wantonly disregarding the preparations for supper, flew to the front door and flung it open. He certainly was not expecting his two boys to come out of the carriage of the *chevalière* d'Éon.

As André and Zénobe jumped off the *berline*, Maurel said, "Why, *mademoiselle* d'Éon, I don't understand… André and Zénobe were with you?"

Mademoiselle remained in her carriage. "*Oui, oui, monsieur.* I see you are nervous about your precious eaglets being away from their nest so late, but you need not be concerned with their safety when they are with me. I was there to protect them, you can be sure of that. And they in turn will tell you all that they did to protect me. Your young man there," she said, pointing to Zénobe, "will make a marvelous *chevalier*, and you must let me borrow him to give him instruction in the martial arts. He does not need any more book learning. *That* he has completely dominated. But once I have finished with him, he will be able to be in my Dragoons for when we go fight the English in America. We shall fight for Liberty and for the insuperable pleasure of forming our own destiny. *N'est-ce pas, mon mignon?*" she asked Zénobe.

"*Oui, mademoiselle,*" said the young man, with a bow.

"*Au revoir, messieurs,*" said the *chevalière*, and Robert whistled loudly to goad his horses into action and the *berline* went careering off into the night.

One would have thought that Maurel was a father welcoming his two sons back after a long absence. He actually hugged them and kissed each of them several times on their cheeks.

"I don't know whether to embrace you or punish you," he said to them. "I was so worried, I was sure you had been spirited away by a gang of bandits."

"No, no, *monsieur* Maurel," said Zénobe. "We were both detained by Jean-Jacques Rousseau and then by the chance visit of the *chevalière* d'Éon."

As they made their way to the kitchen, Zénobe gave Maurel an abridged version of the afternoon's occurrences, with a promise to tell him the whole story later on that evening.

When they entered the kitchen, everybody made a comment. "Ah, there they are!" "Are they in one piece?" "The wayward boys are back!" "They were not lured away by Trappist monks after all!" There was much relief and laughter.

Both young men, especially Zénobe, felt warmed by their reactions. He smiled with pleasure, knowing that he and André belonged to a household where their presence was desired, and where their absence was a cause for worry. He told no one, except for Maurel later on that night, that he had berated Jean-Jacques Rousseau. He didn't want to get the reputation of being a presumptuous interloper, especially among the staff. He'd rather feel like one of them.

Still, as the evening came to a close and he and André were getting ready for bed, Zénobe came to the conclusion that Paris was a wonderful city. It was big enough for both Voltaire and Rousseau. Two giants of philosophical thought, one holding court on the Rive Gauche, the other refusing to hold court at all on the Rive Droite. Two spheres of influence, separated by a mere league, that remained isolated by insurmountable obstacles.

Maurel came to tuck them into bed and Zénobe recounted the whole story of the animated afternoon. Maurel was a bit taken aback by Zénobe's effrontery, but acceded to the necessity of protecting *mademoiselle* d'Éon's virtue. She was a good and honest person, and nobody had a right to vilify her, not even Jean-Jacques Rousseau.

Maurel asked Zénobe if he would be interested in the *chevalière*'s offer to form him in the martial arts.

"As if I were a gentleman?" asked Zénobe.

"Remember what the *chevalière* said. These days we need to fight to shape our own destiny. If the *chevalier* captain of the Dragoons was able to become a woman, you certainly have all the right, and the wherewithal, to become a gentleman. *Monsieur* de Voltaire was born into a simple family with no known connections to aristocracy, but look at him now: confidant to Kings and Emperors, a thorn in the side of Governments, a shaper of public opinion, and the Voice of Social Conscience against the Infamy of authoritarian powers. Benjamin Franklin was supposed to have lived a small, quiet, and obedient life in a Society of Quakers,[154] but look at him now: an honorary member of our own Academy of Sciences, celebrated throughout the civilized world. He unveils the secrets of nature to the rest of us. What is more, take Antoine Laurent Lavoisier who comes from a family of humble origins. But he is now Royal Commissioner of the Arsenal, Farmer General, and discoverer of the very air we breathe: he was the one who isolated the component of the air that keeps us alive, the very combustible, but respirable, *oxygène*, and that has made Lavoisier's name known even to the beggars on the street. "'Don't use up my oxygen,' they now say in the streets of Paris when they want someone to keep away. The musician Gluck, whom you met in this house, could have been a forester like his father, but now he tutors the queen and composes wonderful operas to great acclaim. Look at Pierre-Auguste Caron, who didn't even get the particule *de* Beaumarchais until he married and took it from his wife; the son of a clock maker, what is he now? He is an eminent playwright who transforms public opinions through

---

154   The idea that Franklin's forefathers were the pacifist Quakers was a fallacious belief, to be sure, but one which Franklin never actively sought to rectify.

his art, and who moves thousands of *livres* worth of ammunition past English ships. And look at me, who was supposed to become a notary in a small town in Normandy, sort of like what you could have expected in your own life, André. And you, Zénobe, what were you supposed to be in Savoy, a peasant farmer? It doesn't matter, because now we are in Paris, at the *hôtel* de Villette, in the very lion's den, as it were. We are surrounded by people who took destiny into their own hands and by the dint of their effort made their own way in the world."

Maurel paused, as if to gauge the impact his words were having on his two boys, and continued: "Birth and lineage as basis of rank and character? How incredibly outmoded. The subordination to a hierarchy, which does not mirror the reality of personal worth, of an individual's merit? Passé! These people have shown us that the old static ways can be budged, perhaps eventually even overthrown. Set your sights higher, my boys! But throughout, remain honest and forthright. Above all, never remain stagnant. Hold your personal virtues up to those who run society, and show them what an individual can do—the only limit is what your own imaginations won't provide.

"Why do I say that you must never lose sight of honesty and virtue? Because you'll never be able to attack the powers that be on moral grounds; they might be the most shameful, deceitful and despicable of characters, but they are too well protected. However, never give *them* any reason to attack *you* on moral grounds, and in order to do that you will have to be virtue incarnate. Which means, then, that you will have to hide certain natural propensities that are viewed by the majority as being a blemish on virtue. Of course, the two of you and I know that this is not so, but unfortunately, the ignorance of the general population is such that they'd rather throw you into the Bastille as drown you in the Seine."

Maurel looked deep into their eyes to see that they had understood his counsel. Then shaking off his seriousness smiled at them.

"Ah, look at us! Look at me! Here I am, a father of two very dutiful sons, about whom I have grown to care deeply, and whose absence worries my heart and distresses my nerves. I hope never to know such a worrisome afternoon such as the one I had today. I thought the two of you were lost, gone forever and, perhaps— *oh, quelle horreur!*"

"We'll never give you another scare like that," said Zénobe, and André agreed as well.

"Ah, my beautiful sons, all is well that ends with the two of you in your bed where you belong." And giving them each a couple of kisses goodnight, one on either cheek, he blew out their candle, and with his own candelabra shining the way out for him, he left their room. He was quick to leave them, for he didn't want them to see the tears in his eyes.

Social Climbing

The *marquis* de Villette gave his servant, Zénobe Bosquet, the whole of his yearly stipend in one fell swoop. Being a chamberlain carried weight, and the red velvet purse the *marquis* thrust into Zénobe's palm was full of coin and its heft pushed down heavily on his hand.

"*Voilà*, take that," said the *marquis* early in the morning on his way to his bedroom. Zénobe observed that his master looked rumpled and his eyes were bloodshot.

Where does he go at night? He was about to object to this money being given to him, but he had no time to formulate a delicate phrase of refusal as the *marquis* took the stairs two at a time. When Zénobe looked into the sack, he saw the gleam of *louis d'or. It must be the full sum of five hundred* livres. He had never seen such a huge amount of money in his life, let alone held it in his hand. He had of course seen *louis d'or* before, but only three or four at a time, surrounded by a lot of chocolate. The richest workers in Savoy were the master masons and they only made 40 *sous*, or two *livres* per diem. Even for those who were the most successful and managed to find substantial jobs, these would frequently be followed by a long hiatus of unemployment. At the most, such a mason could make 300 or 400 *livres* per annum. And here he was, 19 years old, receiving more money than a master mason made in a year.

André came up to Zénobe and asked what was wrong. In answer, Zénobe held up the sack and shook it to hear the metallic clinks. André whistled.

"What am I supposed to do with this?" asked Zénobe rhetorically. "This money is supposed to be for services of which I have not acquitted myself, indeed, of which I am altogether ignorant. How can I feel that I deserve it?"

"I'll relieve you of it, if you wish. I wouldn't want it to weigh heavily on your conscience."

"Thank you, André," answered Zénobe with a wry smile. "You are indeed a true friend."

Zénobe tossed the bag in the air and caught it again, and said, "You are right, of course, to mention my conscience. I wouldn't have the slightest glimmer of knowledge or experience, or for that matter, imagination, to say what a chamberlain is expected to do."

"Ask your friend *monsieur* de Voltaire," answered André pragmatically. "There's nothing he doesn't know. Although…"

"Although what?"

"Although I'll wager you that these wages are for services that are yet to come and that have nothing to do with the duties of a chamberlain."

"What do you mean?" asked Zénobe. "I am to be the *marquis* de Villette's chamberlain, in addition to being *monsieur* de Voltaire's secretary."

André, whose love for Zénobe was giving him powers of analysis beyond his years, replied, "You don't understand. You are to be the *marquis* de Villette's *chamber*lain, you are to be his chamber boy."

André's smile was so wide, Zénobe didn't know whether to smack him or kiss him. But he was beginning to comprehend André's insinuations. Carnal knowledge has a way of maturing minds and developing a more sophisticated perspective. "I do believe *monsieur* de Voltaire will be able to advise us more on the subject. But I think I'll ask *monsieur* Maurel first, just the same."

A few minutes later in the kitchen, over their coffee and eggs with beef followed by oatmeal with cinnamon and honey, Zénobe perused Maurel's copy of the *Journal de Paris,* which the *maître d'hôtel* had given him permission to read. The Villette household subscribed to four copies of the daily *Journal,* four of the weekly *Mercure de France,* and one of Simon Linguet's *Annales politiques, civiles et littéraires,* published in London and smuggled into France, and secretly brought into the *hôtel* de Villette by a special courier disguised as an itinerant cutler, although he really did sharpen the household's knives once a week as well.

Zénobe was scanning the newspaper for the publication of Voltaire's open letter to Victor-Amédée and when he found it, he seemed satisfied.

"This will put pressure on my lord," observed Zénobe.

André was about to take a mouthful of gruel. "You mean the *marquis* de Villette?"

"No, no. I mean that now we'll get somewhere with that criminal lord whose subjugation of, and whose cruelty for, his people makes him Europe's most despicable despot. I am speaking of Victor-Amédée III, son of Charles-Emmanuel III. Now the Lord of Reason will wipe him out, along with all the Lords Whose Time Has Passed. They will have no more reason to exist."

Looking at him, André found it hard to believe that someone as sweet and as kind as Zénobe could take on such a hard look of hatred when speaking of royalty.

Continuing to glance through the rest of the *Journal,* Zénobe's eye caught on an article: it was a short column on a young woman who had given birth to an illegitimate child. In her desperation, she had stifled the child and then drowned herself in the Seine. The article went on to explain that the girl committed infanticide and suicide in spite of the fact that she had received the sympathy and the support of her community. According to the *Journal,* the unfortunate unmarried mother was a maid at the *hôtel* de Valmont where she had been getting advice and economic aid from her fellow servants and female domestic neighbors who took it upon themselves to minimize the religious importance of her situation, calling it neither a sin nor a crime. Alas, they were not able to dissipate her melancholy. She was terrorized by the punishment God would mete out for her. It was strongly suspected that the master of the house, the infamous *vicomte* de Valmont, was the one who had fathered her child, but lacking sufficient proof, the prefect could not lodge a complaint against the gentleman in question. The *vicomte* expressed his heartfelt condolences to the girl's family and friends. Zénobe wondered if this was the woman who had committed suicide the morning of his arrival into Paris. He admired the woman's neighbors for their attempts to console and encourage her. At the same time, his ire at the thought of the malevolent master rose to redden his face and set his icy blue eyes on fire.

From his position across the table from him, André felt that he was reading the paper along with Zénobe, just from the play of successive emotions that he could read on his friend's face.

A bell rang in the kitchen and both boys saw on the row of bells above them that the summons was coming from the master's apartments. Zénobe made a gesture of impatience. "All lords are the same," he said to André. "They're always bidding and ruling and dictating. They think that their merest utterances should be taken as law and that their commands be followed instantaneously, no questions asked." Then, observing André unperturbed and having his breakfast, Zénobe softened his stance. "With the exception, of course, of *monsieur* de Voltaire. He is different to all other lords. *He* has always known how to treat his household servants and his village peasants, making sure they are gainfully employed and warmly clothed. Under his lordship, no one starves to death. You know, he initiated the manufacture of watches in Ferney, stealing away master watchmakers from Geneva by offering them better salaries and better housing. In a few years, he was selling watches to the crowned heads of Europe. Catherine the Great of Russia is his best customer."

Just then, *monsieur* Maurel walked in, a dark foreboding on his face.

"The *marquis* went to bed barely twenty minutes ago but cannot fall asleep. He has asked for both his coffee and his chamberlain, immediately. You're to take a dictated letter to *monsieur le duc* de Richelieu about those blasted actors."

Zénobe stood up as a soldier might, to await his orders.

"But wait, my son, as I dispatch master André on his daily quest." Maurel instructed André to return to the Palais-Royal, once again, to look for *docteur* Tronchin. This was to be the last attempt to have the doctor come minister to his philosopher patient.

As for Zénobe, Maurel put an arm across his shoulders and they marched upstairs. As they approached the *marquis'* boudoir, Maurel counseled him on how to handle the master. "Always acquiesce, but use your reasoning power as leverage to get what you want."

Zénobe did not react.

Maurel asked him impatiently, "What is it that you want?"

Zénobe looked exasperated. "I have no idea! Perhaps you should instead be asking me, *monsieur*, what it is that I don't want. I certainly don't want to be the *marquis* de Villette's chamberlain. It would be fraudulent. I have no idea what is to be expected of me! Moreover, I wish to serve *monsieur* de Voltaire."

Maurel responded, "You are a quick learner, and I an adequate teacher. But you need to realize that you must first and foremost look after your own desires. Your master's comes second. Of course, you can never ever let him know this. To his face you say that his every wish is your command."

There was no more time. Maurel scratched at the door whereupon their master let out a gruff, "Come in!" The *maître d'hôtel* opened his master's door with one hand and thrust Zénobe inside with the other. He knew better than to follow him in. As the boy walked in slowly, the *marquis* de Villette called out, "And my coffee?"

"It will be coming right up, *monsieur le marquis*," Maurel said from the threshold. "Master Zénobe will pick it up in the dumbwaiter."

Then Maurel closed the heavy door with a thud. He slowly descended the stairs with his hand on his heart, like Persephone descending into the Underworld.

In the kitchen, André was putting on his galoshes in preparation to go outside. His young face wore a furrowed brow and an absent look in the eyes. Maurel walked back into the kitchen, went to the stove and took the coffee kettle and emptied it into a porcelain coffee pitcher. He waited while Sylvie took out a tray of brioches from the brick oven and placed two of the steaming buns along with butter and marmalade onto a Gien platter. Maurel put the components of the *marquis'* breakfast onto a silver salver, which then went into the dumbwaiter, and as soon as he had moved a lever back, the system of pulleys took everything upstairs. Maurel stuck his head into the shaft, even though he had always been afraid of the dumbwaiter accidentally falling and cutting off his head. He yearned to hear something from the *marquis'* room. He could detect nothing but the gentle clinking of porcelain as the *marquis'* breakfast slowly ascended.

Before leaving for the Palais-Royal, André followed *monsieur* Maurel's instructions and delivered Voltaire's copy of the *Journal de Paris* to the philosopher's room. At the same time, he delivered *monsieur* Voltaire's morning mail, which he noticed was as prolific as *monsieur* Rousseau's, if not more so.

Voltaire was sitting up in bed having his morning tea in a huge cup that could have supplied an entire family. Hovering over him were *madame* Denis and the *marquise* de Villette, both in *negligée* and *peignoir.*

"Ah, here's the *Journal,* and my correspondence. Surely one of them will have news of my letter to Victor-Amédée."

"Page six, *monsieur,*" said André with a smile.

"Wonderful!" admired Voltaire. "Even *monsieur* de Corday is in the know. That's what I like. The whole household must be aware of what is happening within these walls and without, for activities in here will have worldwide repercussions." As he spoke, *madame* Denis was opening the newspaper to the desired page and when her uncle saw his letter, he took his cup, drank from it and then let out a satisfying *ahh* and André didn't know if it was for the letter or for the tea.

"Now we'll get some sort of response from this picayune prince. How could he have dared to overturn his father's good works! If things were left to him and those of his ilk, we'd have a new Middle Ages settle upon us, and the wisdom of the ancients would again be lost to the vast majority of humanity. You know, *monsieur* de Corday, democracy used to exist. It was a political system whereby the citizens had a say in the matters of their republic. Has *monsieur* Bosquet covered this part of history in your lessons?"

"*Oui, monsieur.* Among the Greeks. Although according to *monsieur* Bosquet, one could participate in the democratic system only if one were a man, and only if one were a landowner."

"What, *monsieur* Bosquet would have women and peasants have a voice in a democracy?" Voltaire exclaimed with a chortle. "That young rapscallion! He will be a revolutionary, that one!"

Voltaire had his published letter in view and read it silently. "Wonderful," he finally said. "This should set off some fireworks." Then, in order for André to understand, he added, "This was *monsieur* Zénobe's doing, you know. I never would have written this letter but for him."

Smiling, André took a quick bow and left the room. He wrapped his scarf three times around his neck and decided to leave the *hôtel* through the front door. His would be the first watch of the day as doorman as soon as he returned from his errand. A draft of cold air rushed in and twenty persons threw themselves at him. It wasn't even 8 o'clock yet. "*Monsieur* de Voltaire has just awakened and is still having his breakfast," he announced, as he extricated himself as deftly as possible and ran towards the Seine.

Zénobe approached the *marquis* de Villette who was wigless and had been writing a letter at his desk. He had put his quill in its holder.

"*Monsieur le marquis*," began Zénobe, forgetting the sacrosanct rule to let the master speak first.

But Villette was also too much in a rush. "I have here a letter..."

"*Excusez-moi, monsieur...*" Zénobe started to apologize for his impertinence in speaking first.

"...a letter..."

"*Oui, monsieur?*"

"a letter... which I want you to rewrite and correct and embellish, *et cetera*, addressed to the *duc* de Richelieu."

"It will be my pleasure, *monsieur mon seigneur...*"

"You should continue to address me as *monsieur le marquis.*"

"*Oui, monsieur le marquis...* But, I... *euh...* I..."

"*Oui, monsieur* Bosquet? What is it you would like to say?"

"I, *euh*, with your permission... I'd like to say that, *euh...* that..."

Zénobe did not know how to act or what to say so that *monsieur le marquis* would annul his position as chamberlain. With a gesture of impatience, he took out of his pocket the purse that the *marquis* had given him earlier that morning and placed it on the desk, although the heavy gold made more noise on the boiserie than he would have wanted. "Excuse me please, *monsieur le marquis*, but your lordship does me too much honor, and this remarkable indulgence, while generous to a fault, is perhaps misdirected when his lordship grants such responsibility to me, who am only recently arrived—"

"What, you don't want this position of chamberlain?" asked the *marquis* curtly, picking up the sack of money.

"It is not that I do not want it, *monsieur*, but I am indeed not certain that I merit it."

"Ah, Bosquet, you really need to do something about your lack of confidence. It might lead people to think that it is instead a lack of enthusiasm."

"Oh, but, *monsieur*, it is not enthusiasm which I lack, it is, *euh...* it is..."

"Well, what is it, then?"

"It is a lack of *savoir-faire*, of that attitude which to your lordship comes so naturally, so innately, which shows to the world that you are indeed a sophisticated, cultured man, worthy of the title of *marquis* and, and..."

The *marquis* did not interrupt Zénobe for he was curious about what was to follow, but Zénobe needed to hesitate to collect his thoughts, since diplomacy and dissimulation were two arts that he had never had to worry about. Up to this point, everything he had said about the *marquis* was true, although bordering on sycophancy, and he had one final thought to express about what he thought his relationship to his master should be. Still, this was the *marquis*' house, his boudoir, his roof over his own measly subordinate's head, and yet it wasn't about his own self-esteem that he was worried. Zénobe was more worried about the self-esteem of the gentleman in front of him seated at his Louis XV writing desk of rich mahogany and ornate ormolu with an albino peacock's tail feather two feet tall towering over a pair of gold clam inkwells encrusted in the rococo double tails of a sea monster. What would the *marquis* say, what would he do, were he to find out that Zénobe was far from being interested in his offers of employment?

"And, and, even if I find your offer most generous and flattering, I find that in all justice and frank divulgation, it would be dishonest on my part to accept a position whose duties would be beyond my experience and even my aptitude."

"Ah," said the *marquis* with comprehension and resolve. "Ah. I do believe I understand. Well, then," he said while opening up the sack of money and removing a solitary gold coin which he placed on the inlaid marquetry of his desk. Zénobe noticed that the scene was of a ship on a storm-tossed sea. The *marquis* closed the purse again, took his valet's right hand, stuck the purse in it and then wound his fingers tightly around both. With his other hand, Villette made a tight grip around Zénobe's fist, and pulled him forward a step.

"Then you shan't be my chamberlain, if that is your concern. You shall be my librarian. Even that empty-headed Marie Antoinette has her own librarian, that unbearable *monsieur* de Campan, so why shouldn't I have my own?"

The boy realized that he could make no attempt to extricate his hand from his employer's grasp and when the *marquis* pulled him in even closer he had a sinking feeling that this was only the beginning of a difficult situation. His imprisoned fist was very close to the *marquis'* mouth and Zénobe believed that his employer was about to kiss the back of his hand.

A creaking noise of pulleys and a final bell announcing the arrival of the dumbwaiter was a godsend.

"*Monsieur le marquis'* breakfast is here!" exclaimed Zénobe tearing himself away too abruptly to be courteous.

In a flash, he was opening the dumbwaiter doors. Since he needed both hands to grab the tray, he placed the blighted purse in a corner behind the basket of brioches, hoping that the *marquis* wouldn't see it.

When he turned around he saw that the *marquis* was on his feet.

"Where shall I put *monsieur le marquis'* tray?"

"Throw it into the fireplace and come here!"

Zénobe placed the tray onto the marble top of a *bahut* and, arms to his side, head held high, like a grenadier ordered to face his enemy, he strode to his superior.

Villette met him half way and embraced him. Zénobe found no other way but to allow himself to be embraced. The top of the *marquis'* head was below his chin.

"My dear *monsieur* Bosquet. I understand now your reticence. But don't let that be a burden to you. You shall be my librarian. Surely your knowledge of books will allow your conscience to be at ease and to enable you to be of my assistance."

Zénobe could smell the flour of the *marquis'* hair powder and the humid fragrance of the *eau de fleur d'oranger* for which the *marquis* had a preference.

"*Oui, monsieur,*" said Zénobe with as much deference and as much enthusiasm as he could muster.

Villette's arms were over his own, but when the *marquis* repositioned his arms to be under his and wrapped them around his waist, the young man felt even more awkward. What would he do with his own arms now? What a position to be in, to have your superior wound tight around you with his ear on your heart. He brought his hands up to the *marquis'* shoulders, partly to convey his acquiescence and partly to be in an advantageous position to push him away should he try to kiss him. With his palms, he tapped him on his shoulders a couple of times, as if comforting him.

"Oh, embrace me, *monsieur* Bosquet. You need not fear me. I shall be a very generous patron and under my auspices, you shall go very far."

Zénobe decided that it couldn't be helped. He enveloped the *marquis* in a bear hug, and tightened his embrace even more, just to show Villette that he'd be able to break his back if he needed to. The *marquis* made little falsetto squeaking noises as if he were in heaven. Zénobe felt like a tropical serpent he had read about in Buffon's treatise on rare and exotic animals, a serpent that kills its prey by tightening its coils every time its victim exhales until the unfortunate creature asphyxiates. In one of his ever-tightening squeezes, the valet knocked the breath out of the *marquis*, who started to laugh in wondrous glee at his marvelous good luck.

Villette had just decided that *monsieur* Maurel deserved an increase to his salary.

For Zénobe it was strange to be embracing his benefactor, especially in view of the fact that the older gentleman was much smaller than the man Zénobe was now used to embracing. André was much taller than the *marquis*, as tall as Zénobe was. And André's back was much broader. The impression Zénobe had now was of holding someone delicate, a coquet who didn't come up to the standards of the one he loved. This thought made him marvel. He realized that he loved André, and it was André only whom he wished to embrace.

"*Monsieur*," he said to the *marquis*. "*Monsieur?*"

"Yes?" answered Villette as if he were waking up.

"Where in the *hôtel* de Villette shall we install your library?"

Voltaire was unloading his hostility towards feudal lords on his niece and adopted daughter, who clearly wished to speak to him of something else.

"Don't these tyrants know that they cannot enslave others and use and abuse them at their will? These despots take their victims' possessions, nay, their very selves, into their own personal domain! The serfs' bodies are but a possession to them. They are an expendable commodity, and when war comes, they are fodder for the cannons. A citizen in Amsterdam is a man, but an unfortunate creature living but a few degrees longitude south from there is a beast of burden."

"*Mon oncle...*"

"Nature doesn't create a despotic state. There is no country or nation which has ever told a man: 'Sire, we give your gracious majesty the power to take our women, our children, our goods and our lives, and to have us impaled according to your good pleasure and your adorable caprice!'"

"*Mon père...*"

"These unnatural kings take possession of their subjects' bodies and do with them what they will, without their consent, and send them to fight their useless wars, use them as chattel, as miserable pawns, as–" Voltaire was spluttering.

"*Mon oncle*, don't get yourself so upset. The cream will curdle inside of you."

"Why is it that there are monsters who wish to enslave others? Why can't they live, and let others live? Why do they always want more, why do they have this cruel desire to lord it over others? There is always somebody more voracious, more vigorous than the others, who then takes everything for himself and only leaves the crumbs for the rest."

"Please let us speak to you about something that is close to our hearts," said *madame* Denis.

"Oh, look," exclaimed the philosopher excitedly. "There is a letter here with the seal of the bishopric of Paris. You don't suppose..."

"We've been meaning to speak to you about something important," said the *marquise*.

"Oh, and what is that?" Voltaire suddenly had a look of suspicion as he realized both women in concert wished his solicitude.

"Well," began *madame* Denis as she sat down on the bed beside him and put a hand on his bony knee. "You know how I love Paris. And *Belle et bonne*, who has come to appreciate the culture and the—"

"And the shops of the Palais-Royal," interrupted Voltaire.

"No, no, the proximity of a high level of social connections—"

"And the proximity of the shops on the rue de la Paix."

"Well, those are not that close to us here on the rue de Beaune. But *Belle et bonne* does miss us so, and she, and I, were wondering if we, meaning you and I, could possibly acquire a little pied-à-terre somewhere—"

Voltaire had swallowed a bullet which exploded somewhere in the middle of his esophagus. "A pied-à-terre? A pied-à-terre! I'll give you a *pied au cul* which will take you all the way down to the *terre*!"

The *marquise* threw herself on Voltaire's neck and cried, "*Oh, non, mon père*, please don't get upset. It's just that I do feel lonely here without you and I do wish so very much you could live here in Paris."

"Well, we'll come visit you, anytime we can get away, just as we are doing now. There is absolutely no need for us to get a pied-à-terre! What, *monsieur le marquis* your husband won't allow us to stay here in the future? This is a lovely home, and huge, with plenty of rooms to spare. I wouldn't deign to deflate the pleasure that *monsieur le marquis* so obviously experiences while we are in his house. He's like the rooster of the hen-house and I'm his favorite hen, the one with the golden eggs."

"Of course he will have you stay at the *hôtel* de Villette whenever it please you," replied the *marquise* with a glance to *madame* Denis. "You can stay here at any time, at your convenience."

Madame Denis bit her lip and squared her shoulders. "You know, my dear uncle, that there is another reason why I should wish to live in Paris."

Voltaire continued to pick at letters and began to separate them into different piles. "Well, I have heard enough. I need to return to Ferney. That is my home, that is where I have my library, and all my papers and manuscripts are there. Besides, I have my responsibilities with my villagers and I have established a way of life there. The country agrees with me and the air is pure and I don't have to contend with congestion in the streets and malodorous vapors wafting up from the Seine."

"But, *mon oncle*—"

"I know you were once tempted to stay in Paris. This is an old chapter in our lives that we don't need to reread. Nevertheless, it is true that you don't share my love for the countryside, for the pleasures of cultivation and eating the fruits of one's labors. You're more attracted to the expensive excitements of the capital than to helping the peasant population of Ferney become independent and self-sufficient. I was never able to see you in the role of Cérès or Flore, but as for myself, I see that every poet has rightly sung the praises of the pastoral life, that happiness attached to rural concerns is not a chimera, and I find even more pleasure in plowing, sowing, planting, and harvesting, than in making tragedies, and having them played."

"But think of your admirers, *mon oncle*," said *madame* Denis. "They throw flowers at your feet and place laurels on your head."

"That's because I'm part of the news," he retorted, picking up the *Journal de Paris* that had been running a daily commentary on Voltaire's every utterance and publishing the list of happy people who were granted a Voltairean audience. "When I'm no longer news then the only people left who will throw anything at me will be the religious fanatics who'll hurl stones through the windows. No, no, leave me in Ferney, *ma nièce*, leave me in Ferney. The end of my life is very close, I can feel it."

"*Non, mon oncle, mais non!*"

"I knew I should have married a girl who was an apothecary's daughter, who knew how to give a clyster, or how to fatten poultry and read aloud."

"Now you are being cruel and unfair!"

"Moreover, and this shall be my final word on the matter, my tomb is in Ferney. I had it made specially for me, half of it inside my church, and half of it in the cemetery, so that the miscreants will say that I am neither completely out nor completely in. Were I to die in Paris..."

Voltaire interrupted himself as he reached for the letter sealed at the ecclesiastical seat of Paris. "Let me see if the Bishop of Paris will deign to give me a Christian burial."

He swiftly unsealed the letter and his eyes darted across the page. "Oh, it's not from the Monsignor himself, it's from some subordinate, a certain *abbé* Gaultier. Oh, Lord. Dear God. He wants to see me. My God. Dear Jesus. I am sure to be thrown onto the city dump!"

Maurel continued to preside over the preparations of breakfast for the *marquise*, *madame* Denis, and the secret one, the one for *monsieur* de Thibouville, which he always delivered himself to the room that was joined to the *marquis'* boudoir through a secret passageway. Henri Lambert *sieur* d'Herbigny, *marquis* de Thibouville, of a long line of Norman aristocrats, was a very private person, and had been a friend of Voltaire's for years but had never chosen to cast his name to the four winds. He wanted no more than to go unnoticed by society at large because when he was younger and more carefree, certain secrets of his had been found out and bruited around town. By now, he and Villette had ceased altercations based on their differences of comportment. Villette wanted to see his name mentioned in the contemporary chronicles of the time, no matter what was discussed; Thibouville wished to set off not a ripple.

Maurel had the same thought every time he used the back staircase to the third floor: society had done Thibouville such an injustice when he was just beginning his literary pursuits. His first play, a tragedy called *Thélamire*, which he had presented anonymously, had only had four representations at the Théâtre Français. The criticism was so stinging ("This play announces neither genius nor talent...") that when pressed, Thibouville gave the pseudonym of Denise Lebrun as the playwright. His authorship was found out anyway, with the added sin of travesty thrown in for good measure. His second, and final, attempt at theater was another tragedy, *Namir*, whose presentation ended in the middle of the fourth act, attended by hisses and catcalls. The actor playing the title role, Lekain, broke character, came to center stage and asked the public if they wished to see the play concluded. The answer was resounding, and the troupe substituted with a shorter play on reserve. Thibouville melted into the shadows. Maurel had read his two plays, and a novel he had published years before, *The Force of Friendship*, and felt that they were fair works of literature. Perhaps not what audiences clamored for. He felt they were very true-to-life, very plausible, as opposed to heroes and heroines being thrown into unrealistic situations where gods punished them for passions and vices out of their control. In any case, Voltaire was Thibouville's friend and pardoned him his attempts to pay homage to the Muse. Voltaire called him *mon ange.*

Maurel scratched at the door twice followed by a knock, and after a few seconds, heard the occupant unlatch the door. As soon as the door opened, Maurel proceeded with the tray to a small table by Thibouville's bed.

The aristocrat asked, "At what time did Villette come in this morning?"

Maurel bade him, "*Bonjour, monsieur* de Thibouville." He put the tray down and turned to face Thibouville. "*Monsieur le marquis* de Villette arrived about three quarters of an hour ago, *monsieur le marquis.*"

Thibouville was dressed in an Oriental silk *robe de chambre*, a huge scarf about his neck, bright blue velvet slippers on his feet.

Maurel handed him the fourth copy of the *Journal de Paris.*

"Will Voltaire be receiving today?" asked the *marquis.*

"I believe he will, *monsieur*, but not from among the general public. Perhaps just *messieurs les philosophes.* We are still waiting for *docteur* Tronchin."

"What are the *marquis'* plans?"

"*Monsieur le marquis* de Villette has started the day with a letter to *monsieur le duc* de Richelieu inviting him to accompany his troupe of actors for another rehearsal of *Irène* tomorrow, and also to stay for supper."

"Another boring day, I see."

Maurel smiled. "*Oui, monsieur.*"

"Can you please ask Requain to come up once he's finished with the letter?"

"*Monsieur* Requain is not taking that dictation, *monsieur.*"

"Oh, who is?"

"*Monsieur* de Voltaire's secretary, *monsieur* Bosquet is, *monsieur.*"

Thibouville rolled his eyes, then thanked Maurel and told him that would be all.

After a bow, Maurel left and was relieved not to have had to go through lengthy explanations of why Zénobe Bosquet was spending so much time in the service of the *marquis* de Villette. The *maître d'hôtel* wondered why the *marquis* de Thibouville insisted on his relationship with his master. Even though Thibouville was past his prime, he was still a rakish-looking older man, perhaps on the thin side, but with a virile stride and a solid abdomen. He still had all his own teeth. That, and with his fortune, he could have any man he wanted.

On the second floor landing Maurel was tempted to listen at the *marquis* de Villette's door, but he couldn't be caught in such an act lacking in decorum. He decided to go to Voltaire's bedroom to see if his services were required there.

While the *marquis* de Villette was having his breakfast, Zénobe was at the *marquis'* writing desk rewriting, correcting and embellishing the letter to the *duc* de Richelieu, who was the major patron and director of the *Comédie française.* Such a noble and grand lord had to be cultivated and honored. A grandnephew of Louis XIII's chief minister, and a distinguished diplomat himself, having been made *maréchal* of France in 1748, Louis

François Armand de Vignerot du Plessis, *duc* de Richelieu, was a man, Zénobe rightly surmised, who was accustomed to being addressed in a certain manner, and Zénobe's knowledge of Imperial Roman turns of speech was more that adequate for such a fop.

The *marquis* had seen the sack of gold on the breakfast tray and had told Zénobe, "I want you to keep this stipend, my boy, as a token of my esteem for you."

Zénobe answered respectfully, "It is I, *monsieur*, who feel much esteem and gratitude for you."

Villette continued, "And for whatever you will be, in whatever capacity, and with whatever title, and however you shall serve me, as my valet, my librarian, my secretary (you can share, for the love of God, the secretarial duties of Requain), all I want is for you to accompany me in my endeavors, in my desire to, to, to spread the influence of philosophy, to continue the rigorous task which Voltaire has embraced all his long life, and which he must now, sadly, relinquish and bequeath to younger minds. I suspect that he always knew that I should be the man who would take over for him, and that is one of the reasons why he was always interested in cultivating our relationship. That, and of course, his close relationship with my mother right before my birth. It would be quite natural for me to continue his endeavors."

Zénobe, in spite of his serious doubts about what Villette had implied, dutifully and respectfully did the *marquis'* bidding. The following day he was to visit the booksellers and make his first big purchases for the *marquis'* library. He would meet with Charles de Wailly, architect of distinction, who had refurbished the *hôtel* de Villette five years previously, and, more importantly, had created the library at the *hôtel* d'Argenson, known as the finest library in Christendom.[155] One of the bedrooms on the northern side of the house overlooking the Seine would be chosen as the library. *Madame* Denis might have to be chased out!

Maurel did not wait as long as he usually did to retrieve the *marquis* de Villette's breakfast tray. He also came with instructions from *monsieur* de Voltaire for Zénobe's service in taking dictation of a letter to be addressed to the Paris bishopric.

"Why can't Wagnière take that dictation?" asked the *marquis* with a shrill tone to his voice.

"*Monsieur* Wagnière has been sent by *madame* Denis to see about a house for sale on the rue de Richelieu and is consequently unavailable."

"What about Bigex?"

"He has a cold, *monsieur le marquis*, and *monsieur* de Voltaire fears being contaminated by him."

The *marquis* de Villette seemed on the verge of throwing a tantrum.

"Where's Requain?"

---

155   Today the library of the *hôtel* d'Argenson is known as the Bibliothèque de l'Arsenal, located at 1 rue de Sully. Antoine René de Voyer d'Argenson, *marquis* de Paulmy would give access to his collection of books, manuscripts, maps and engravings to men of letters and researchers. Two years before his death in 1787, the *marquis* will sell his library to the king's brother, the *comte* d'Artois, in order to avoid dispersion of the library's holdings. After the Revolution, in 1797, the library, enriched by the revolutionary confiscations of ecclesiastic and personal aristocratic libraries, becomes a public library.

"You sent him on an errand to the Hôtel de Ville with your plans for a new theater."

"Oh, that's right."

In the end, Villette could do nothing but allow his *maître d'hôtel* to walk out of his bedroom with his newly appointed librarian.

On the way to Voltaire's boudoir Zénobe gave Maurel a quick report on his interview with *monsieur le marquis*. Maurel gave a sigh of relief when he found out that the *marquis* had not foisted his untoward attentions on the lad. An interminable and uncomfortable hug did not seem too perilous. Still, Maurel was aware of his master's irrepressible and sudden urges, and knew it wouldn't be long before the *marquis* attempted to do something more drastic.

When Zénobe entered Voltaire's bedroom he perceived immediately that the old philosopher was in a foul mood. He was alone at this time, *mesdames* de Villette and Denis having gone to enjoy their breakfast elsewhere. Voltaire had left his bed and was sitting, or rather, sagging, on a *bergère*, holding a letter in one hand, his legs thrown over one of the chair's arms. He looked like nothing more than an empty nightgown thrown forlornly over a piece of furniture. Except that the letter in his hand kept moving, and the eyes peering at him looked brighter than usual.

The old *philosophe* began this session with his interminable profession of fatigue, moribundity and hopelessness.

"I can't tell you, *monsieur* Zénobe, how tired I am of the constant morigeration the Church obliges us to show her. I am tired to the very center of my soul, and I believe that it is finally killing me. Have I lost the will to continue? Have I lost all hope?"

Zénobe could not think of anything to say that would alleviate Voltaire's suffering. He had always agreed with the philosopher's published animosity towards the Church's obdurate dogmas and to its entrenched influence in social and political affairs. All he could do was come closer to him and hear the rest of the lamentation that the old man evidently wished to air.

"I've spent a lifetime fighting the enemy, in the name of philosophy, in the name of humanity; but every time we turn around, every time we discover a new land, or turn a page in a book, or decipher a new facet of Nature, there the Church is again, this indefatigable and ruthless foe. She is born anew every time we let our guard down. She is prolific, rushing into our every strategy with the imbecility to overturn what our reasoning has attempted to erect: a system of beliefs and moral values imposed not by fanatical prejudice and intolerance, but by a universal code where rationality gives meaning to our lives, and based not on mythological texts written by ignorant men but on a science which has as its center the study of man.

"But I am tired of fighting. It is time for new soldiers to take our places on the line of attack. It's time for people such as you to fight the proliferation of religions, the discord between peoples, the self-righteous murder of humans.

"Remember, Zénobe, in order to smash the Infamy, you have to make others see that religions are founded on systems of fiction, and that these systems become received ideas which engender ever more fiction. At the same time, you must show reason as a tenable alternative, one where even a society of atheists would be successful in forming a civic organization replete with moral values and a sense of justice. It is my dream to live no longer in a world where we can have a case like that of the *chevalier* de La Barre, the young man—only 17 years old!—whose tongue was torn out, his right hand cut off and his body hacked to pieces and fed to the fire, all for having committed the terrible crime of not doffing his hat during a passing procession. My soul is wrenched from its moorings. And when one hears of what is happening in other lands, one realizes that we Christians are certainly not alone in monumental lapses of rationality. In India, I've heard, a widow must fling herself onto her husband's funeral pyre. If she is reluctant to do so, her brethren will do it for her. Also in the East, if a girl is raped, she must be killed. Imagine that! An innocent must pay the ultimate price for the crime of her aggressor. In Africa, every woman must pass under the blade, carrying the Jews' practice of circumcision to its irrational extreme: she must lose everything that could ever give her sexual pleasure. In the Americas, the gods of the savages demand still-beating hearts ripped out of chests. Closer to us, we coerce boys into sacrificing their genitals in the name of sacred music. Music! How divine can a god be who visits such malevolent acts on his believers? How good can dogmas be which demand the immolation of precious human life and the sacrifice of our god-given gifts? How beneficial to humanity can religion be if it names heretics at will and instructs that they be tortured and killed? This separation of "us" and "them" into the holy and the pagan, into the believers and the heretics, is madness and only leads to destruction and despair."

Voltaire lapsed into silence. Zénobe took over for him.

"It is my opinion that man is born with a profound mistrust of others, in increasing strength, of his neighbors, of his society, of the people who live in the next village, in the next province, in the next country, of people who speak other languages, of people who profess other religions, of anyone in which they cannot see themselves. By the time he gets to those who speak other languages *and* profess other religions, these foreigners are so far removed from his everyday experience that they become an easy enemy. Particularly if they look different, although this last is not necessarily a paltry reason when choosing one's enemies. Catholics and Protestants look the same, and yet they exterminate each other with relish. In the long run, religion becomes just one more component in the justification for belligerence. Religion is a reason to kill those who are different, those who are not a part of us."

Voltaire seemed to be energized by Zénobe's observations.

"This is indeed a pessimistic surmise of humanity," he said with commiseration. "Well, we must then take each of those reasons which enable men to slit each other's throats and denounce them as fallacies. We must take each of these reasons, one by one, and show in the name of humanity how they are far from being rational, to say nothing of being reasonable. It is irrationality that is killing us. In the name of religion, yes, in the name of arbitrary and outdated superstition, in the name of what can only rationally be seen as the weakest, most inane of justifications. But tell the dead and the murdered that they died for a lie. Tell the parents of a child dead from smallpox that their son or daughter could have been saved by inoculation. Their parish priest forbade it, out of fear and ignorance and superstition. Tell the family whose father died in a battlefield far away in another country, in another continent, that he died for his king's folly, for his leader's deficiency. The family will not believe you, for the king is their leader, and their leader certainly has God on his side and therefore must have made the right decision in going to war. Their dead give credence to the lunacy that they died for a reason, for the bereaved use false logic in order not to admit that their beloved died in vain."

Voltaire sat up in his *bergère*. "We shall start with this son of a dog (what is his name?), this idiot *abbé* Gaultier. He says that he wishes to see me. I know what he wants. To the exterior world he wishes to save my soul from its inexorable march to hell. What he really wants is to see me recant all my criticisms of his unholy Church. Well, let's see how far he gets. Meantime, let's attract the bastard. Let's have him come here, tomorrow, and we'll have it out with him. He's an envoy of the archbishop of Paris who doesn't have the courage to encounter Voltaire on his own. Look at what Gaultier writes. 'Many persons, *monsieur*, admire you and sing your praises in beautiful verse and the most elegant prose. I wish from the bottom of my heart to be among the number of your admirers. I will have this advantage, if you wish, it depends on you, I am sure, there is enough time.' "

Voltaire interrupted his reading to ask, "Time enough for what, I wonder? And who taught this man to write?"

He continued reading from the letter: " 'But since I do not dare to flatter myself that you would procure for me such a great happiness, I will not for that forget you in the Saint-Sacrifice of the mass, and I will pray with the most fervor that it will be possible to just and merciful God for the salvation of your immortal soul which should be judged on its actions.' "

Voltaire looked up at Zénobe. "The grammar is all wrong there, isn't it? You'd think a just and merciful God would have told him where to put his commas and how to manage his subordinate clauses."

" 'Pardon me, *monsieur*,' " Voltaire continued to read, " 'if I took the liberty to write to you, my intention is not to offend you but to render to you the biggest of all services; I can do this with the help of he who chooses that which is the weakest in order to confound that which is the strongest.' "

"What do you think he meant by that, *monsieur* Zénobe?"

Zénobe shrugged.

Voltaire continued, " 'I will believe myself happy if the response with which you will honor me would perhaps be analogous to my sentiments.' "

"Ha, ha," laughed Voltaire. "Has he heard the reports around the city that I am the Messiah newly arrived to tear the skies asunder and offer the ultimate sacrifice in order to regenerate humanity?"

Zénobe laughed with him. "No, *monsieur* de Voltaire, I don't believe he has. Had that been the case, he'd have sent the Holy Inquisition to the *hôtel* de Villette."

"Oh, my dear *monsieur*, don't make me laugh so. I'll split my side."

Handing the *abbé* Gaultier's letter to Zénobe, Voltaire said, "Well, let's work on a response to this dear ecclesiastic who has taken the onerous task of saving my soul. We shall make his efforts easier, shall we not, *monsieur* Zénobe?"

"Indeed we shall, *monsieur* de Voltaire," was Zénobe's enthusiastic reply.

"Well, here, then: 'To Louis-Laurent Gaultier,'—we'll leave the title *abbé* out, that should goad him; in any case, I didn't see him addressing me as '*monsieur* de Voltaire, *philosophe*'—'Your letter, *monsieur*, appears to be as one coming from an honest man, and that is sufficient to determine me to receive the honor of your visit, on the day and moment which it please you so to do. I will tell you the same thing I said when I gave my benediction to the grandson of the illustrious and sage *monsieur* Franklin, the most respectable man in America, and perhaps in Europe, who asked me for such an immediate benediction. I only pronounced these words: God and Liberty. All present shed tears of emotion. I flatter myself that you are of the same assumption. I am 84 years old and soon shall appear in front of that God creator of all the worlds. If you have something in particular to communicate to me, and which be worth the trouble, I will make it a duty and an honor to receive your visit, in spite of the sufferings which burden me. I have the honor of being, *monsieur*, your very humble and very obedient servant, signed Voltaire, *gentilhomme ordinaire de la chambre du Roi*.' "

"*Pardon, monsieur?*" asked Zénobe.

"That's right. '*Gentilhomme ordinaire de la chambre du Roi.*' That's my correct title, given me by his Majesty Louis XV. I was also 'royal historiographer', but I don't think we need to put that down. No sense in exhaustively implementing all our titles."

The letter to the *abbé* Gaultier went out with the afternoon mail, along with the *marquis* de Villette's letter to the *duc* de Richelieu. Incoming mail brought another load of correspondence to the *philosophe* of the house, and a letter addressed to Maurel as *Monsieur le maître d'hôtel, hôtel de Villette, Quay des Théâtins.* Maurel tore it open and read a note written in bold strokes of thick ink, from the *chevalière* d'Éon. She had set up an appointment for fencing lessons, at her expense, for Villette's ward, *monsieur* Zénobe Bosquet, at the fencing academy of La Boëssière, on the rue Saint-Honoré. Maurel was in awe. Look at what little Zénobe's heroism had done to merit the magnanimous patronage of a benefactress! That fencing school was the best in Paris, run by *monsieur* de La Boëssière who was one of the few fencing masters to have won the braid of master at arms. It was also widely known that he had escaped the provinces after his family had decided he would become a priest. His academy received the scions of the best aristocratic families.

Maurel realized that this gift was very generous. He also realized that, beyond the funds for the school to be provided by the *chevalière*, he was going to have to come up with some serious money to have Zénobe play his part in this scheme, the scheme of learning the martial arts, and—who knows?—learning to become more of a gentleman. How to keep this knowledge from the *marquis* de Villette? Not the least of his worries was that there might be penalties in passing off a Savoyard peasant as an aristocratic gentleman. Indeed, Maurel's talents would all be required here, his inventiveness, his diplomacy, his thoroughness, his daring. He couldn't help tittering, however, at the challenge: *Is it possible,* he thought, *that I could quite possibly succeed in this enterprise?*

Without a moment to lose, he walked briskly to the front door, whisked André away and instructed him to go find either Philippe or Henri and have one of them replace him at the front door. André was then to go meet him in the kitchen. By the time he got there, Maurel would have a list for him. "There will be a list of shops, and a list of material to be purchased. Do not talk to anyone when you come back, and for heaven's sake do not show this material to anyone. There is so much to acquire, you might have to return home and then go back out again. I wish I could give you either Henri or Philippe to help you, but you must go alone. Go. I'll be waiting for you in the pantry."

In the meantime, Maurel went to speak to Suzanne. Her services were to be needed that evening, after all her other responsibilities were concluded. She was to meet him and Zénobe in his bedroom tonight after supper, and she was to take Zénobe's measurements for a completely new outfit, according to Maurel's instructions. She would be relieved of her responsibilities in the morning to enable her to complete this task as soon as possible. The clothes would be needed before 3 o'clock in the afternoon the next day. He also swore her to secrecy.

"Will this outfit include a coat?" asked Suzanne.

"Not the usual kind of coat. I shall provide you with the patterns. In all, we shall need breeches, a shirt, a coat, a waistcoat, a jabot, a cravat, a cloak, and a tunic. Oh, and the shirt will have cuffs, long, lacy cuffs."

"*Aïe, aïe, monsieur*! I won't get any sleep tonight!"

"Perhaps Marianne can help you in the morning. Just don't tell her for whom the clothes are intended."

"*Oui, monsieur.* But she'll know they're not for *monsieur le marqui*s. They'll be too long for him."

"I know I can count on your circumspection, Suzanne. It's for the good of the household, you can trust me on that."

"*Oui, monsieur*," she answered and curtsied. "Mum's the word."

Well, then, Maurel thought. *That's that.*

His next act was to go borrow one of *madame* Denis' *magazines de mode*. He knew just what he was looking for.

After a two-hour nap, Zénobe was awakened for the third time that night, for his final fitting. Suzanne was working miracles with her needle and thread, and Maurel could not cease praising her.

The three were in Maurel's bedchamber, late at night, or rather early in the morning, with André sprawled asleep on Maurel's sofa. Zénobe would stretch out on Maurel's chaise longue when he wasn't needed.

As she cut and sewed, Suzanne told them the story of her escape from the convent the previous winter. That was the last time she had had a *nuit blanche* (a sleepless night). A cleric who wanted to escape from his monastery as badly as she wanted to escape from her convent had come for her and helped her to scale the tall perimeter wall. It was a night she would never forget, the night of her escape. It was due to *monsieur* Diderot that she was able to do so; it was he who had secured her a position at the *hôtel* de Villette.

Suzanne handed the breeches to Zénobe and he put them on: a pair of bright chartreuse, made of chamois, that clung to his skin.

"I believe they're a bit tight," said Zénobe.

"No, no," answered Maurel. "That is the way they are meant to fit."

Indeed, thought Maurel to himself, they show every muscle and sinew beneath. No one will have to take the trouble of imagining anything. With every thrust and parry, every contraction of muscle or elongation of tendon will be visible.

"Your outfit is a copy of the *comte* Axel von Fersen's Swedish dragoon uniform.[156] Gustavus III himself designed it. Green, blue and white are the colors. Suzanne, place the blue material for the cloak under master Zénobe's eyes. Aha! It is just as I thought. His eyes glow with an even stronger intensity. What do you think, Suzanne?"

"Ah, yes, *monsieur* Maurel. Zénobe will look mighty dashing in the colors of the Swedish dragoons."

---

156   Axel von Fersen was a frequent guest of the Queen's. As a fellow foreigner, and a handsome and charming young military man, he quickly became one of Marie Antoinette's favorites.

"Try on the shirt as well," said Maurel, although he would have preferred him to go shirtless all night long.

"Ah, dashing is the word, Suzanne," observed Maurel. To Zénobe he said, "You will be the most dashing young man in the best fencing school of Paris."

Zénobe, laughing, modeled the clothes for Maurel and Suzanne. He unfurled the blue material for the cloak and pretended to be on a mission, looking for the enemy, and then pouncing with force to run the foe through with his imaginary foil.

Yes, thought Maurel, you certainly are meant to conquer, my dear young Zénobe. That is precisely what you are meant to do.

Then he gestured to Zénobe, indicating that he follow him into his vestibule. They left Suzanne busy at work and André sleeping soundly and slipped into the small room where Maurel kept his *garderobe* and a little writing desk underneath a window. Maurel closed the door behind them.

"I have a couple of presents for you," said Maurel as he took out two packages from a chest.

"Open this one first."

Zénobe took the smaller package and undid the ribbon. When he opened the box he found in it a new wig, a small one, with the silver-white hair worn close to the skull and a medium length pony tail with ruby-red velvet ribbons attached at the middle and at the end.

"Ah, it's beautiful," said Zénobe.

"Let me put it on you," offered Maurel.

Maurel swept up Zénobe's hair towards the back of his head and affixed the wig over it. Then he stepped back and admired. Zénobe didn't need to ask him if it suited him. Maurel's expression said it all.

"Open this one now," said Maurel as he presented Zénobe with a long rectangular package.

Zénobe tore through the ribbon, dropping the cover onto the floor. He took out an épée that shone brightly in the candlelight of the vestibule. The handle and the guard were engraved with intricate rococo patterns, and the triangular blade tapered out to a fine point, onto which was affixed the blunt stop.

"The handle is of silver," said Maurel.

Zénobe admired the épée from end to end, and tears came to his eyes.

"*Monsieur* Maurel," he started and stopped. He began anew. "*Monsieur* Maurel, I lack the proper words to thank you for these presents, and for all you have done for me. Just a week and a half ago I was on the streets with a future in front of me too frightening to behold. Now look at me, dressed in these resplendent clothes, brandishing this wondrous épée…"

Maurel did look at Zénobe. The young man's eyes gleamed brightly behind their sheen of tears and Maurel felt weak at the knees. But then Zénobe did something unexpected. He thrust the épée's handle into Maurel's hand, and bowed down in front of him on one knee.

Maurel had read of such events in stories, and he thought he knew what he was supposed to do: He gently brought down the blade of the épée first on one of Zénobe's shoulders, then on the other, saying, "Kind and gentle *chevalier*, he of the eyes filled with the sky and of the mind filled with bright ideas, I dub thee *monsieur le chevalier* Zénobe Bosquet… Zénobe Bosquet *de* Maurel, my son and heir, orphan no more."

Zénobe looked up at Maurel with a gaze full of devotion, and Maurel was overtaken by such a wave of emotion that he teetered on the brink of a fainting spell. Before this emotion manifested its full force, Zénobe sprang to his feet and threw his arms around him. Maurel could not faint now. What, and be unconscious during the happiest moment of his life? Maurel regained control of himself, throwing his arms tightly around Zénobe, bringing their bodies so close that Maurel could feel Zénobe's stomach constricting jerkily with each silent sob.

"My son," Maurel repeated into Zénobe's ear. "You are an orphan no more."

En garde!

Zénobe had been told by *monsieur* Maurel that it was not a form of deception to withhold information from one's master. Even so, Zénobe could still not help but experience pangs of conscience that threatened at any time to break forth into his conversation this morning with the *marquis* de Villette. Zénobe felt that in spite of his trust in *monsieur* Maurel, he would have to avow all to his master. He was inexperienced with these feelings of guilt. Fortunately, the aristocrat was so occupied with the sparkling creation of extemporaneous rhetoric and the gracious delivery of his own lofty sentiments to his valet/librarian that he misidentified Zénobe's reticence and hesitancy, attributing it to the nervousness of having to accompany him on their first errand together. Zénobe pondered different ways of informing the *marquis* that he had an afternoon rendezvous at the La Boëssière fencing academy. According to what Maurel had told him previously, the *marquis* himself had studied there and had been a fairly decent student, although liable to get carried away in an overly exuberant execution of rococo ripostes. His swordplay must have been just like his wordplay. Zénobe could not find entry into the *marquis'* steady chatter that was as untiring in its length and strength as it was inane in its composition and performance. In spite of the dictates of his conscience, Zénobe was not allowed the relief of easing his feelings of guilt. Besides, he was seeing for the first time a part of the *hôtel* de Villette which he hadn't even suspected was there: the *marquis* was taking him down the secret staircase which led to the subterranean passage into the stables.

The carriage had been brought round and the horses harnessed, for the *marquis* had other errands to run after he delivered his librarian to the bookseller's. Zénobe found himself thus in the second carriage ride of his life (not counting the directionless ambles of the *marquise* de Polignac's *berline*), this time in the *marquis'* small phaeton which seated only two and could more easily maneuver around the congestion in the streets.

"*Monsieur* d'Argenson has certainly had a head-start," the *marquis* was saying, "but he only began his library three years ago so I cannot see any hindrance in my being able to collect as many books as he.[157] The dullest people become poetical and expansive when they praise his library to the skies, but d'Argenson doesn't have Voltaire in

---

157 Antoine René de Voyer d'Argenson, *marquis* de Paulmy, founded his library in the former Arsenal of Paris in 1757. The *marquis* de Villette is here referring to the refurbishment and expansion of d'Argenson's library by the architect Charles de Wailly, starting in 1775. Note of Special Interest: d'Argenson was a member of the *Académie française*, and thus a colleague of Voltaire's, as well as a member of *l'Académie des Sciences*, and thus a colleague of Franklin's.

his house, does he? Ha, ha, he may have all of Voltaire's publications, including those merely attributed to the old scoundrel,[158] but I have the dried-up old *philosophe* himself! We shall see who gets the upper hand when my library is as grand as d'Argenson's. They say he also has a collection of medieval manuscripts. Well, he probably was alive back then! I wonder where we could get our hands on some of those? Well, I'll leave all of that heavy burden on your shoulders, my boy. You have very nice, very broad, very strong shoulders. Ah, I also want to see about procuring you permission to visit d'Argenson's library so you can take a look at it for yourself. How about this very afternoon?"

The color rose into Zénobe's cheeks and he felt the adrenaline rush into the pit of his stomach. *He had the fencing lesson this afternoon!* The god of the fates was with him, however, because the *marquis* continued his monologue without even a glance at his young helper's face; he was too busy looking at his body. "Oh, no," continued the *marquis*, "I could not possibly pass by the Arsenal today. I'm going to the *hammam* and once there I won't want to feel rushed. We'll leave it for tomorrow morning. And we'll leave Wailly for later on this week.[159] I want him to get started on the disposition of the bookcases as soon as possible. I have let this stupendous idea of my own library unattended for too long. I, too, wish to be known for my kindness and generosity when I open its doors to other philosophers, students and researchers, people like you, my boy, who lack the funds to have proper access to books.[160] You see, it took your intervention to help me progress in this direction, and I can foresee a time when the library of the *hôtel* de Villette will give that of the *hôtel* d'Argenson some competition. Have you given some thought to the first books you shall choose?"

This was a question which Zénobe could answer with ease. "I have, *monsieur le marquis*, and I find it exciting, and a great honor, to be able to aid you in this endeavor. Today I shall start with a two-pronged attack: the Ancients are of course of utmost use to any library worthy of the name, but at the same time the Contemporaries are not to be neglected. You have no objection, *monsieur*, to the complete set of the *Encyclopédie*?"

"Why, absolutely none that I can think of," said the *marquis*, bringing his face closer to Zénobe's. "But, tell me. Why would anyone have an objection to having the complete set of the *Encyclopédie*?"

"It is illegal to possess it, *monsieur.*"

"Oh, that," chortled Villette. "Oh no, my boy, Zénobe—ah, the poor little thing!—I have never been squeamish, nor have I ever had any qualms whatsoever about delving into the illicit or the illegal or the immoral. On the contrary, the underbelly of the law fills me with a certain *je ne sais quoi* about committing certain prohibited acts. And the more prohibited, the greater the *je ne sais quoi!*"

"The *Encyclopédie* is also very expensive. 700 *livres*, to be sure."

"Ah, my boy, whom do you take me for? You still don't understand, do you?" Villette goaded his horses to go faster. "Zénobe: you do not have to consider such a vulgar idea as cost when you build me my library. No concern, whatsoever, do you hear me? You will have *carte blanche*, complete *carte blanche*. Do not even ask the bookseller. I prefer

---

158   Since many books were published anonymously, any work which was deemed to be brazen, insolent or irreverent was naturally assumed to have been authored by Voltaire. Of course, the book would also have to be well-written, witty, and very entertaining.

159   Reminder: Charles de Wailly had also been the *marquis* de Villette's architect in the refurbishment of the old *hôtel* de Bernières which became the *hôtel* de Villette.

160   Benjamin Franklin's idea of lending libraries had not yet crossed the Atlantic.

that you not ask at all about the price of books. I do not want any representative of mine to even suggest the remotest, most minuscule, possibility that his master would ever, could ever, experience economic pusillanimity. You provide me with what is necessary, without notice about the status of the books on the Index, or worry about their cost. Understood?"

"*Oui, monsieur*, understood," said Zénobe with a huge smile, such a smile that it took the *marquis* de Villette's breath away, and made him want to be, for a very brief moment, his valet's servant.

By this time, the phaeton was stopped in front of 18, rue des Poitevins, at the old *hôtel* de Thou. There was a huge sign over the front door announcing Panckoucke, the biggest bookseller of Paris.[161]

"Have the books delivered to the quai des Théâtins," instructed the *marquis* before the phaeton was off to his *hammam.*

Zénobe walked into the shop like a pious believer walking for the first time into the cathedral of Notre Dame de Paris: slowly, reverently, and with mouth agape in tremulous anticipation.

Floor to ceiling and wall to wall, books arranged on shelves, and the surface of many tables invisible because of the amount of books organized in ordered piles on them. Zénobe approached the first table and read the titles on the spines, and recognized many dear old friends, but now wearing fancy new clothes. Many of these had recently been spoken about by Zénobe himself at the *hôtel* de Villette. Some of them, true, a minority, were not familiar to him. He ran his fingers along the red, black, brown and cream-colored calf leather covers, turned to the frontispiece of one, and was amazed by its title: *Hypnerotomachia Poliphili.* It was the first book he had touched at this bookstore, and he had never read it. Indeed, he had never even heard of it. With quite an amount of pique, he realized that his education was not quite done.

One of the many Panckoucke progeny who worked in the store approached Zénobe.

"May I be of service to *monsieur*?" asked he.

Zénobe flinched. He was being called *monsieur* by a total stranger. He quickly regained composure and replied, "Thank you most kindly, yes. I would like this book, and its other volumes.

"There is only one more."

"*Ah, merci bien.* I'll take both volumes, please. And this one as well, the Fontenelle, and the Buffon. This set of Corneille..."

"All of them?"

"All of them, please. Also, this Molière (is it complete?), and have you all of Racine? Thank you, all those as well. Before I forget, I'll take everything you have of Voltaire, Diderot, d'Alembert, Condorcet, Grimm, Helvétius, Condillac, and the *Encyclopédie* as well, along with all the *Planches* available."[162]

---

161   Charles-Joseph Panckoucke made his reputation, and his fortune, by publishing the works of the *phi-losophes.* He had 27 printing presses on the premises, and they worked twenty-four hours every day trying to keep up with the demand for books, new books, and new editions of old books. Of course, it was a well-kept secret that this publisher could also provide the book-lover with certain titles that had been proscribed; those sold all the faster.

162   The Panckoucke edition of the *Encyclopédie* had 17 volumes, and by 1778 he had only published three of the volumes of the *Receuil de Planches* (the illustrations to accompany the previously published articles), so for those book buyers wishing to purchase the *Planches* in their entirety, Panckoucke would sell them the complete 1772-1776 Geneva edition in 11 volumes.

The young Panckoucke's eyes got bigger and bigger as Zénobe continued with his order. It was not every day that a book buyer came in and with such authority ordered so many books. Perhaps he was a spy sent by Lenoir, the police lieutenant. The young bookseller asked, "Who may I ask will be responsible for this purchase?"

"All these books are to be delivered to the *hôtel* de Villette."

"On the quai des Théâtins?"

"Yes, please."

Panckoucke the son looked at Zénobe as if he were an angel come to announce the Messiah.

"Pray tell, are they for *monsieur* de Voltaire or for the *marquis* de Villette?"

"They are… they are for me."

"Oui, *monsieur*, it is indeed a pleasure to make your acquaintance. I was unaware that the *marquis* had a son."

"Oh, he doesn't. I am not a son of the *marquis* de Villette. He doesn't have any children, at least, not yet. I am rather a child of… of Voltaire, engendered by him not too far from Ferney, on one of his trips to the hinterlands of Savoy."[163]

"I had no idea…" said the child of Panckoucke who had to steady himself on a double column of thick Littré dictionaries.

"Why, yes. Not too many people realize that Voltaire has raised an army of orphans, bastards and lost children in Ferney."

"I reiterate, therefore, with amplification, my pleasure at making your acquaintance," said the Panckoucke, and bowed.

"The pleasure is all mine, I assure you," said Zénobe as he passed on to the second table. There, Zénobe almost began to salivate: in marbled Havana calf leather, gold-leaf lettering on the spine, folded maps within, were the continuing voyages of Captain Cook. In citron Moroccan leather, he found Catherine the Great's instructions on a new Code of Laws, published by the Imperial Press in Moscow. In a small octavo publication in eight volumes he found the anonymous memoirs of a traveler to the Middle East. He held a heavy quarto volume of an epistolary novel written in English. Tears came to Zénobe's eyes.

No table remained unscathed, and the bookshelves would look like toothless smiles after the young librarian was through with them.

"*Eh, bien, voilà!*" exclaimed Zénobe breathlessly as if he were already at his fencing class. "Not bad after just…" Zénobe made as if to look for his watch. "Oh, dear, I forgot my watch."

"Please allow me, *monsieur*. It is half past ten."

"Not bad after just an hour's perusal. I believe I shall return sometime next week."

"I already anticipate the pleasure, *monsieur*."

"Don't forget to deliver the tomes of the *Encyclopédie*," said Zénobe.

"That is not to be a cause of worry, my dear *monsieur*, you have my personal affirmation that all will be delivered just as you have stipulated."

"Thank you from the bottom of my heart," said Zénobe graciously.

"And mine," returned the Panckoucke progeny with a bow.

---

163   From Ferney one could veritably walk into Savoy, or at least you could, if you were Rousseau. Lest we forget, Rousseau's five children were among the orphans abandoned in the vicinity. For all we know, Voltaire could have ended up taking care of Rousseau's lost children.

Upon leaving, Zénobe was sorry not to have the phaeton to whisk him away. Nevertheless, his gait was light and swift. Several hundred books were to be delivered to the *hôtel* de Villette that very afternoon. They would probably already be there upon his return from the fencing lesson. Ah, what joy, what pure unalloyed joy!

After the half-hour's walk from the Quartier Latin, Zénobe returned to the quai des Théâtins and reported to *monsieur* Maurel. His next task was to be with *monsieur* de Voltaire during the interview with the *abbé* Gaultier, which could be at any minute.

The *marquis* de Villette walked from out of the cold winter sunlight on the quai d'Orsay into the warm and obscure interiors of the *hammam*.[164] He walked in slowly and hesitatingly, but not from any uncertainty. His were the calibrated movements of the effete hedonist who anticipates with fervor the delights that he is to savor. Like the gastronome who chews lingeringly, or the don Juan who exquisitely delays orgasm, the *marquis* tiptoed in. His imagination ran rampant: what images of exposed flesh would today be seared into his lascivious retinas? What alluring tactile pleasures was he to experience at the strong hands of his dark and alien masseur? What odors would waft up to his nostrils, what manly voices, what virile laughter would charm his ears? And what about taste? What could he soon be tasting, ensconced in one of the individual sauna rooms, enthralled in a *vis-à-vis* with some smart young lad, in a *vis-à-vit* embrace?[165] His resolve, and his anticipated figments, stiffened.

The barge on which the *hammam* was located moved slightly to remind the visitor that he was not on *terra firma*. As the *marquis* ambled slowly to the massage rooms, he tried to give the appearance that he wasn't ogling the other customers as he passed by their booths. His expectations were thwarted, however, when he didn't see much of interest. He was even more crestfallen when one of the disappointing clients identified him and enthusiastically called him out by name. Discretion and anonymity were now dashed, *nom de Dieu*!

"Ah, *monsieur le marquis* de Villette," said the resounding voice which had a definite English accent to it, or as Voltaire would have put it, an *American* accent.

The *marquis* wheeled around. Who could so inopportunely be calling out to him in such a conspicuous and vociferous a manner? "Who is it?" he asked, rather curtly. "Where are you?"

"*C'est moi, ici,*" called out the American, *the* American, for it was, indeed, the voice of Benjamin Franklin who had called out to the *marquis* de Villette. The minister plenipotentiary was laid out on his corpulent stomach, naked atop a table with only a square of material to hide his buttocks. "You seem so surprised to see me here!"

---

164   Turkish baths, along with other exotic imports, were the rage in pre-Revolutionary France. Known as *turqueries* and *chinoiseries*, these alien fashions influenced everything from furniture-making to dress styles, from cuisine to personal hygiene. This particular *hammam*, located on a floating barge next to the quai d'Orsay (the part of which today is called the quai Anatole France), was named Bakchich, *Pot-de-vin* in Turkish, in its meaning of "bribe", and constituted rooms for bathing and for massage, saunas, and compartments for individual meditation. The name was misconstrued as "Poitevin."

165   *Vis-à-vis* = face to face; *vis-à-vit* = face to prick.

"Indeed, *mister,* I am." (Again, the pronunciation of the English word was homonymic with the French word "*mystère.*")

"Well, I can stand the pleasures of work, protocol and diplomacy for only so long before I yearn to either play chess, play at science, or play here in the role of a slab of meat in the huge hands of my incomparable Nebuchadnezzar." Indeed, the burly masseur gave the American's torso such a tremolo of slaps that Franklin's sides jiggled. "Ah, delightful," said Franklin in English. To Villette he said in French, "Thank you very much for your kind attentions the other evening. You had such a motley gathering (but in French he said, 'You had such variegated company') that it was such a treat to be a part of it."

"Ah, it was nothing, *mister,*" answered Villette in English. "My wife has such variegated company all the time. Sometimes I feel like the only sane person there!"

"Ah, ha," laughed Franklin with his diplomatic laughter that was second nature to him. "Your wife is so very lovely, admired by all, simply and absolutely captivating. *Monsieur* Bancroft was telling me so just yesterday, wasn't it so, Edward? Wasn't it yesterday you told me this?"

In the gloom Villette could now see that there was another cot on the far side of the room. A rich, melodious, virile voice rose up from the depths of the darkness.

"I certainly did," answered Franklin's British secretary.[166] Bancroft could never learn to appreciate his colleague's penchant for putting him on the spot, in this case, to extol the qualities of another man's wife, in the husband's presence. But he was used to Franklin's bantering and playfulness in melding and confusing the cultural differences of the English and the French. A Frenchman would not have had compunctions about praising the wife of another Frenchman to his face. But Bancroft was a rather timid fellow, in spite of his youth and handsomeness. He lacked the wealth that made some ugly men act like kings.

Villette didn't care if Bancroft were a pauper naked on the streets. In his zeal to get a better look he tiptoed into the room, but Franklin's cot was in the way. The *marquis* could tell that Bancroft was also wearing only a flimsy fragment of a sheer tissue over his buttocks. Bancroft's masseur was working on his calves, and Villette was hoping that the movement would make the tissue fall off.

"Thank you, indeed, kind *mister,*" said the *marquis,* addressing Bancroft in English. "It is as you wish, to come visit my wife whenever you have the caprice so to do," he offered. "It would be my pleasure to see you at the *hôtel* de Villette. Come to supper, if it suits your fancy."

"Is that an invitation for the both of us?" asked Franklin. "After all, I am the first one who spoke admiringly about your wife."

"Yes, *mister* Franklin. Your face in my salon will always be welcome."

"I hope my stomach in your dining room will, too!"

"But of the course, of the course," said Villette as he tried a different vantage point to spy on Bancroft's body.

As Franklin's lightning fast mind fastened on a pun between Villette's 'of the course' and the courses he would enjoy in Villette's dining room, he heard a yelp and saw a blur

---

166   Edward Bancroft was indeed born in England but he was as English as Thomas Paine. Both had lived in the colonies and both thought of themselves as American. In Franklin's mind, there were no objections to using a man born in the enemy country as his official secretary whose eyes saw everything the American diplomats' eyes saw.

to his side. Then came a couple of thuds as the *marquis* de Villette came to rest on the planks of the floor, the first thud for his posterior, the second for his head.

"Oh, *monsieur*, you are fallen!" yelled Franklin.

Bancroft was faster on his feet. He came to the *marquis'* rescue, explaining that Villette had fallen because of the massage oil on the floor that had first been slathered upon the American philosopher.

But it was of no use. When Bancroft had rushed off his cot, the tissue of covering had fallen off his buttocks. When the hapless Villette opened his eyes as he tried to get up, he saw a beautiful man kneeling at his side, a man whose glistening skin and taut muscles were inches away from his face, and whose penis was dangling tantalizingly back and forth. He caught a waft of coconut and olive oil and promptly fainted away.

There was a moment of embarrassed confusion in the early afternoon as André allowed entry to the *abbé* Louis-Laurent Gaultier while at the same time the *duc* de Richelieu was taking his leave. André forgot who had right of way in the vestibule. The *duc* realized that he had it, but the confrontational *abbé* thought that his black cassock would open the path to both paradise and to the *hôtel* de Villette and insisted on coming in as the *duc* tried to get out. He wasn't going to let the scarlet-and-gold uniformed *maréchal de France* think that those gaudy colors held sway over his somber black. There was a skewed dance à trois until finally the *duc* grabbed a hold of one of the *abbé's* sleeves and pulled him into the vestibule. He then took his ostrich-plumed hat, which he held pinned under his arm and snapped it upon his head, looking all the while at the uppish *abbé* as if he, the *duc*, were the Gorgon ready to turn the lowly clergyman into stone. But the *abbé* met Richelieu's stare in a peaceful manner until the colorful aristocrat left in a cocky huff.

André was mortified, but for the life of him he couldn't remember who had first dibs, the envoy of the archbishop of Paris, or the grandnephew of Cardinal Richelieu, who was also the patron of the *Comédie française* and thus the cultural éminence-rouge of France.

Richelieu had just left Voltaire. The two had had a conversation about the actors of the *Comédie* and the progress of the rehearsals. Since time was of the essence to get the production of *Irène* ready for performance, Voltaire would have to stop rewriting. As soon as Richelieu got to the *Comédie française* to give them the command, he would send the troupe over. It was imperative for Voltaire to rehearse them.

And now here was the *abbé* Gaultier come to ready another type of performance: that of Voltaire's last curtain call on earth before he appeared before his final, and most difficult to please, audience. The *abbé* was here to intercede between Voltaire and God and save the philosopher's immortal soul.

"I am the *abbé* Gaultier here to seek an audience with the *philosophe*."

André noticed that the word *philosophe* was not pronounced with the same awed tones of respect that most visitors to the *hôtel* exhibited.

"We have been expecting you," said André in as gracious a manner as he could muster after his doorman's nightmare of a blunder. "Please follow me."

The *abbé* seemed to be floating along in his cassock as if he were André's shadow.

"Permit me," he told the *abbé* with a smile and then he scratched at the door to Voltaire's boudoir.

"*Entrez,*" said the desiccated voice of the resident philosopher.

André went in and announced, "The *abbé* Gaultier to see you, *monsieur.*"

The old man was in bed wearing his pompom nightcap, the covers lifted up to his chest. Sitting at the foot of the bed was Zénobe, who immediately stood up and smiled at André. André flashed a smile back, and gave a half bow to the *abbé,* which was the sign for him to enter into Voltaire's private chamber. As André left, shutting the door behind him, Voltaire signaled Zénobe to approach, and he whispered quickly into his ear, "Be alert. One must always be *en garde* against these ecclesiastics."

To the ecclesiastic who was now approaching his bed, he said out loud, "Oh, how good of you to come, most kind *abbé.* I am without doubt cognizant of your busy schedule under the instruction of the most venerable primate of Paris, the saintly archbishop Christophe de Beaumont, who has a thousand things to do, and better things than to bid one of his best soldiers come to give succor to a moribund old man."

The *abbé* began, "May God grant us..."

But Voltaire wasn't quite finished. "...a moribund old man already caught in the jaws of death and who turns to you, not for physical salvation (there is no more hope of *that*), but for spiritual enlightenment."

This time the *abbé* waited to see if Voltaire had finished, and where no more was forthcoming from the old goat in front of him, he said, "May God grant us a peaceful life, and a happy end." Then he bowed towards the feeble old man who did look as if he were in dire need of last rites. Gaultier was prepared for any such contingency.

Zénobe could not help but admire his Cartesian lord, realizing that he was giving a performance. Voltaire's chin had sunk to his bony chest, his arms draped heavily on the cushions propping him up, and his expression was a dour one. Zénobe looked closely at Voltaire's mouth. Was that dribble coming out of one corner? And his face, his face seemed to have taken on a pallor that wasn't there a few minutes ago when Voltaire was having a cup of hot chocolate and energetically debating with the *duc* de Richelieu. It couldn't be a coincidence, could it, that Voltaire had taken a turn for the worse just as this representative of the Church had ambled in? With a look of worry, Zénobe took one of Voltaire's wrinkled old hands and the picture was complete. The *abbé* approached the bed, convinced more than ever that he had to write that letter for *monsieur* de Voltaire to sign before it was too late. He had gotten here in the nick of time.

He realized, nonetheless, that he could not treat this intelligent mind, no matter how moribund, the way he treated most of the souls in his safekeeping. He could not cry out, "Repent, repent, cast out your evil ways and embrace your Lord and Savior Jesus Christ! Repent or be cast down yourself into the fire and brimstone of Hell everlasting!" No, he had to take a significantly different route in order to effect the salvation of the soul of the *philosophe* Voltaire, he of the keen mind and devastating cynicism, he of the wisdom of Minerva and the incredulity of Montaigne.

"My son," he began slowly. "The Holy Scripture should impregnate life, but, but by so doing, we should not take this as a passive assimilation."

"I beg your pardon?" asked Voltaire, sincerely perplexed.

"If it is true," continued the *abbé*, picking up more momentum and self-confidence as he unfurled his reasoning to get to his point, or as close as he could get to it. "If it is true that certain passages in the Holy Scripture are difficult to understand, we cannot for that reason eliminate them or consider them as being out-of-date or without value.

On the contrary, we must impress ourselves to find this treasure in the field, to pry out this precious pearl, which demands an effort in order to be discovered and savored."

"Ah," said Voltaire in his best moribund voice that nevertheless could not help but emit a tone of recognition. "You speak of the bone that Rabelais' dog rabidly defends and cracks open to get at the nutritious marrow inside."

The *abbé* did not know what Voltaire was talking about. In any case, the *abbé* was not thinking of that Renaissance author whose anticlericalism would lead his readers to clobber an ecclesiastic on the head as soon as have him hear their confession.

"No, no, my son," he responded. "No, therefore, it is not the individual who interprets Holy Scripture, but rather Holy Scripture which becomes active in the individual's life and interprets the life of the individual and so on and so forth and the life of his confraternity, all together, in a harmonious Christian community."

Voltaire said nothing but looked as if he didn't understand, so the *abbé* continued bravely forward. "Holy Scripture, with the full weight of wisdom and of tradition, becomes the concrete reality of the individual and of the community, which in conclusion–I know how much you philosophical types love syllogisms!–opens us up to unknown perspectives and leads us to a path of liberty."

"Ah," said Voltaire with a hint of contempt creeping into his voice. "You speak of the same path of liberty which leads so many brothers and sisters into becoming prisoners of their monasteries and convents, condemned never to see the outside world again."

"No, no," explained the *abbé* who remained nonplussed. "They are prisoners of the state of their souls, because the soul has its maladies just like the body has its own, and these spiritual maladies end up by making us arid and dry, and give us death, the same as the corporeal maladies which give us death. What are these maladies of the soul? Vanity, pride, greed, lust, disobedience…"

"Disobedience?" asked Voltaire so loudly that the abbé started. "Disobedience? *Monsieur l'abbé*, it is the opposite, blind and idiotic obedience which has lead more men to their death than all the corporeal maladies in all of history put together!" Then Voltaire remembered that he was moribund and put his chin back on his chest.

"My son, my son, do not harden your heart, do not stray from the path of the light (*de la lumière*)!"

"But it is towards the light that I have ever journeyed."

"But you have risked erring from the right path by not adopting the humility of he who fears the Lord."

"I however have never wanted to fear the Lord but prefer to adore Him."

"But yes, my son, yes, that is it! Let us adore our Lord Who loves us so and Who so wants us to be good and kind and moral. Let us adore Him Who dictates to us that we should listen to Him. We should write down His dictation the way your secretary writes down what you dictate to him. Let us listen to the Lord, let us hear Him, and let us take down His dictation. For following the will of the Lord frees us completely from all the terrible errors that we could make. Strict obedience produces resolute faith, which results in godly people."

Voltaire looked at Zénobe and pointed to the writing implements. "*Monsieur* Bosquet, take down this dictation please." He waited while Zénobe went to the portable scriptorium and picked up the quill. The *philosophe* dictated and the secretary wrote it all down.

"Let us awake. Let us adore the Lord and sing a *Te Deum*. Let us break fast with our brethren. Let us go out and spread the word unto the world. But before we leave our neighborhood, let us lapidate our neighbor's wife to death for having forgotten her place and the sanctity of marriage when she fornicated with another man. Let us leave for the market. At the market, let us burn alive all those who do not demonstrate a saintly life. Let us also buy fruits and vegetables. Let us make our way back home. On the way, let us flay alive those who do not follow the path of the virtuous. Let us return home. Let us partake of our supper. Let us write letters to our Christian brothers indicating to them the justness of our behavior and beseech them to exercise the same actions we have committed. Let us adore God, let us sing another *Te Deum laudamus.* Let us go to bed, and let us sleep. The sleep of angels on earth."

Voltaire was silent and Zénobe put his quill down, but then he took it back up again when the *abbé* resumed his comments. This conversation was worth saving for the ages to come.

"The biggest obstacle to listening to the voice of God is that of the hardened heart. The heart that is hardened, proud, and obstinate, removes all possibility of hearing His calling. Only he of the humble heart may listen to Him."

Voltaire sighed. "I can have the most humble heart in the world, yet it has no power to move the Triumvirate: the Parliament, the Crown, and the Church. All three are in cahoots. Are you aware that in Dijon there are many ecclesiastic members in Parliament? You will not be surprised, then, to know that the Church was in perfect harmony with the State in their decision that people not go to the cabaret. You see, *monsieur l'abbé*, the magistrates are involved with all sorts of activities in which they have no expertise. They forbid people from having a little amusement. They have their tentacles all over the arts and sciences. In manufacturing, they have rules and regulations for weaving silk, spinning flax, blowing glass, riveting bolts. The vaccine against smallpox, it convinces them of nothing, especially of its benefits to mankind, because of their monumental stupidity. They call it that 'hydra of inoculation' and condemn it outright! The experimentation and research that have gone into it are suspended by their religious laws based on nothing but ignorance; science is interrupted, or halted outright, and all of mankind becomes the victim of this loss. The English are derided and their therapy is outlawed, and thousands of people continue to die uselessly.[167] There, my friends, are your Parliaments!

"I suppose I should feel honored to be included in your Church's denunciations, along with my fellow *philosophes.* I have an inclination for my fellow 'perturbers of the public peace', as we are called. Our books are censured, and then they are burned, at the foot of the Saint Bartholomew staircase, might I add, no small irony here considering his saint's day, August 24th, is the day of commemoration of the most repulsive massacre of Protestants by Catholics there ever was. I never fail to light votives on that day, and I spend the day convulsing under the weight of such cruelty. Our books, too, are stabbed and sliced, cleaved and lacerated, and they go into the fire as the unrepentant apostates, impious heretics and blaspheming schismatics who came before them.

"Well, nowadays practicality wins over, for the magistrates burn our books in effigy; they keep for themselves the volumes which their very condemnation has made rare and valuable. I wonder how much I am worth on the black market?"

---

167   The English had noted that milkmaids who fell ill with cowpox were inoculated against smallpox, a much more serious disease. From that observation to the practice of intentionally vaccinating people (from the Latin word for cow, *vacca*) was but an obvious rational step. The French, however, criticized the English as being, according to a satirical Voltaire, «*des fous et des enragés*» (crazy and raving maniacs), for giving their children cowpox.

The *abbé* Gaultier was not sure if this last were a rhetorical question, besides, he would not have known the answer. His tongue was stilled, and Voltaire's debate had gone too far afield of his prepared statements for him to be able to get back on track. All he could do was ask Voltaire in a feeble voice, "What is your point, then?"

Voltaire looked surprised at this seemingly honest question, and responded, "I speak of the necessity of tolerance and the absolute primacy of a single and universal morality over dogmas and rites."

The door to the bedroom had opened and then quickly closed, as Condorcet quietly slipped in, but after hearing the last two statements from the two adversarial interlocutors he proclaimed, "Ah, I see I am come at a most propitious moment!"

Voltaire introduced the mathematician to the cleric, and their discussion resumed.

"*Monsieur de* Voltaire," said Gaultier, "You were speaking of a single and universal morality, and I am most happy to inform you that the Church agrees with you! We have only always espoused a single and universal morality, but in the case of the Church, it is our dogmas and our rites that take us along that sacred path. How could you desire us to forego our beliefs, our sacred rites based on centuries of tradition, stemming from Jesus Christ himself?"

With his next response Voltaire tried to raise himself up higher on his pillow and Zénobe helped him.

"I desire that you keep whatever beliefs and rites you wish, so long as your rabid fanaticism does not impede others from doing the same. The crimes of which I am accusing the Roman Catholic Apostolic Church of establishing in the name of God are intimidation of the reasonable, rational and enlightened activity of free inquiry, prohibition of the pursuit of scientific truth, and espousal of irrational doctrines."

"What you call rabid fanaticism," answered the *abbé*, "I call enthusiasm, and protection of the faithful, and encouragement of joyous belief."

"It is not very joyous for your victims. How joyous was it for Hypatia to be hacked into little pieces with shards of pottery and then thrown into the fire? And the person responsible for that, the archbishop of Alexandria, is today considered a saint! Saint Cyril must indeed be enjoying the pleasures of heaven. He set his pack of wild monks on an intelligent, compassionate Greek woman who was as beautiful as she was kind, and who held knowledge and teaching as her sacred trust to society. What was her sin? She had dared to protect, defend, and propagate ancient Greek mathematics."

Condorcet the mathematician, who had not yet taken a seat out of politeness as the *abbé* was also not seated, said, "Your Church anathematized mathematics in the Fourth Century after Christ. Mathematics was deemed evil by your predecessors. If memory serves, the council of Laodicea forbade priests from being mathematicians and studying the sciences of Euclid and Ptolemy. A female such as Hypatia, heathen that she was, was allowed to indulge herself in such a science, until the archbishop considered her a danger to the rest of society. With her died the study of mathematics in our society and the advance of science. Numbers were considered to be Satanic! Which is why Christians were forbidden to work with numbers and percentages, and which is why the Jews, then, became the moneylenders."

Gaultier had an explanation for that, and said in his best imitation of a theologist at the Sorbonne, "It was astrology and divination which were outlawed, the sciences of Satan. And Christians weren't allowed to work with money to create more money. Only human procreation was permitted." Turning to Voltaire he continued, "The Church has always to take a stance against devilish enterprises. Surely, *monsieur*, you agree that you must deny the Devil."

Voltaire laughed. "At my age, *monsieur l'abbé*? Is this a time to make enemies? But to continue with our theme of happiness, the only people who are happy under the yoke of your dogmas are either those who profit from them, or those who live in the comfort of ignorance and the tranquility of sheep, and they do so only because you have indoctrinated them."

"We instruct them in the saintly traditions that have existed for a thousand years!"

"What you call 'saintly traditions', *monsieur l'abbé*, I call a thousand years of erring! You deceive people into accepting and believing so-called sacrosanct doctrine as coming directly from God, but in reality it is a set of arbitrary rules invented by yourselves, the better to govern your faithful—and unquestioning—flocks."

"The better to sweeten their lives and to live harmoniously one with the other. You, on the other hand, make people unhappy by turning them into apostates. You lead them astray, you make them yearn for something that cannot make them happy! You give them an illusion without substance, for how can non-belief make people happy to be alive in God's creation and make them accept inevitable death with tranquility?"

"You imprison people in the traditions of a faith that does not produce happiness, only bovine subjugation where people feel comfortable in the repetition of useless rituals as if they were mechanical automata!"

The *abbé*'s voice rose. "And your ideas of free inquiry fall short of the reality of things. People have to be told what to do."

Here was the crux of the *abbé*'s illogical thinking, and Voltaire charged into it like a Crusader charging into Jerusalem.

"Here, my dear *abbé*, we are in complete harmony. People do have to be told what to do. For eons they have been taught to accept your doctrines without resistance. They know not what Reason is. They have never gained the power nor seen the lights that Reason alone can bring. The vast majority of men have been deceived into accepting irrational, arbitrary, and subjugating dogma as truth; well, those men have to be told what to do. They must let go of falsehoods and illusions, they must deny the deception and the illusory, in order to become enlightened. Superstition must be dispelled before people can become enlightened. Courage is necessary in order to let go of old ways of thinking and replace them with the new, which are based on facts. Once enlightened, people need never be told what to do. They can think for themselves, and they can behave the way that philosophers have done so for centuries: live and let live."

Condorcet joined the discussion. "And how do we propose to elevate the masses to an enlightened, humanistic state? By educating them, all of them, both men and women, in a secular fashion—far from the claws of the Jesuits who only perpetuate superstition.[168] Only then will a society be able to produce, and maintain, an enlightened population."

The *abbé* brought himself up to his full stature. "I am afraid that what you call enlightenment is throwing the faithful out into the cruel world without the sweet succor of Jesus Christ. Without the sweet balm of belief, people will encounter fear in their lives, and like frightened animals, will go on a rampage. Chaos and anarchy will ensue."

Voltaire shot back, "There is fear and chaos already, caused by your Inquisition which tortures men, women and children, hacks them to pieces and makes bonfires out of them."

---

168   The Jesuits were responsible for education in the *Ancien régime*.

"Alas," whined the priest, "God be praised, some must be held up as examples to the multitudes. The souls of the nonbelievers and the heretics must be purified by the flames if they are to cross over to the Kingdom of God. You use Reason like a sword to hack away at what you perceive to be superstition, and leave people with nothing, not even traditions which give them resolve in times of uncertainty. And it is you, you who bring this uncertainty into our world and endanger our yearning for peaceful existence."

As Zénobe continued recording their conversation, he realized all of a sudden that Voltaire and Gaultier were sparring, fencing. One finds one's adversary's weakness, and plunges the foil all the way in. Zénobe's heart was beating fast.

The hem of the *abbé*'s black robe danced on the parquet floor. "Your habit of free inquiry will always lead you up blind alleys (*huis clos*) since the mysteries of God are unknowable. You take pride in your intellect; your intellect will be foiled and disappointed at every turn. Your precious Reason destroys everything: tradition, customs, time-honored practices, respect for authority, dependence on God..."

Zénobe could not contain himself any longer. "Just a second. You accuse us of destroying God and putting Reason in His place; to hear you and those of your ilk talk, we might as well be worshipping at the altar of Notre Dame de la Méthode!"

The *abbé* Gaultier looked at Zénobe more out of surprise that a mere secretary were joining the conversation than at what the secretary had actually said, although that too was surprising.

"I have been thinking about these problems of religion, for a long time now," continued Zénobe, a vein at his neck bulging at the excitement of adrenaline flowing in his blood. "I therefore suggest the complete obliteration of Jerusalem. Have the inhabitants leave empty-handed, taking no reliquaries with them, no talismans, no tokens of symbolic value having the physical power to remind people of what Jerusalem represented: the holy of holies for three conflicting religions. Burn the city until nothing remains, not a wood lintel, not a stone column, not the tiniest splinter of a church left. No charms, no objects of spiritual magic, no relics, no body parts of people long dead. Only empty space will remain of what used to be Jerusalem, so that when people go back to it, if they can even tell where it was, there will be nothing to remember it by."

Voltaire and Condorcet both realized that Zénobe was rabidly irreverent, and, since he was so young, fearlessly so. They needed to step into the conversation before the lad said something that the Inquisition would be interested in. But it was too late, Zénobe had gone on to his next point, and both Voltaire and Condorcet were too curious to hear it to stop him.

"Please answer me this, *monsieur l'abbé*."

"If God grants me the ability to do so."

"Man is supposed to have been made in the image of God, is this not so?"

"Quite so, young man."

"I mean, in Genesis, the Scripture stipulates that God said, 'Let Us make man in Our image, according to Our likeness.' "

"Yes, indeed, that is the Word of God."

"Then that must mean that God has a penis. Now, I don't know about you, but I cannot fathom why God would have the need for a penis. But Reason tells me it must be for the possibility of procreating."

Gaultier was disconcerted, but managed to spurt out, "God created *us*!"

"But he didn't make us by using his penis. He made Adam out of a lump of clay, and Eve out of a rib of Adam's. No, God has a penis and I don't know why He should have a penis. If

He does have a penis, is He circumcised? And if He is circumcised, who circumcised Him? Did he circumcise Himself? In any case, my God-given talent of reasoning leads me into strange territory: God's penis would imply that there is another Being who would have the female organ. A female God. And what would they procreate? Little infant Gods? But this doesn't make sense to me, especially when you say that there is only one God, complete unto Himself, although you manage to divide Him into three components, anyway. It therefore makes more sense to say that God's penis is, in this case, a useless appendage. But does God create useless things, or worse, is a part of God useless? Therefore, I prefer to fall on something even more revolutionary: The person or persons who wrote the Bible must have been mistaken, and God didn't create man in his image, or perhaps not completely in his image. In order not to continue creating Men, subsequent Men, from lumps of clay, God created, along with Man and Woman, a mechanism, the ability for them to continue creating themselves, just like the rest of the animals. Mind you, you must accept the fact that Adam and Eve's children, when they weren't being fratricides, were incestuous, in order to get the third generation going. But quite conveniently, God set them up with the ability to procreate, so that he could absent himself from further work."

Voltaire and Condorcet were silent in meditation; Gaultier was aghast. Never could he have found the right words to counterattack Zénobe's heresies. He let out a couple of half-strangled sounds, and Zénobe continued speaking.

"But I'm not finished yet. My final conclusion must be, if the writers of the Sacred Texts made a mistake in this detail, then the door is opened to the possibility that they made other mistakes elsewhere in their Bible. Thus, those of us who give credence to our gift from God, the use of Reason, must examine the Bible for further distortions, errors and perhaps, downright deceptions."

Gaultier must have wished the Inquisition present here and now to take over this conversation with this young apostate, no matter how angelic he looked. The *abbé* figured that the Devil was as good-looking as this young man, all the better to seduce his victims. But he wasn't going to be seduced by Zénobe, in spite of those beautiful blue eyes and that white, flawless skin and those long eyelashes and that tall stature. Gaultier slowly dropped to his knees, took his eyes off Zénobe and raised them to the heavens and started to pray.

Zénobe looked disappointed that no riposte would be forthcoming from the *abbé*, and looked to Voltaire with raised eyebrows, as if to say, 'That was an easy *touché*, or perhaps it was the final *tué*.'

Voltaire was suppressing laughter. He didn't want to show the contempt he felt for Gaultier because he needed the *abbé* to ensure sepulture of his mortal remains. The arm of the ecclesiastical law was long and could reach all the way to Ferney. If the archbishop of Paris wished to seize Voltaire's dead body, he would be able to do so with impunity.

"Come now, *monsieur l'abbé*, don't let this young firebrand puncture your joyous mysticism which rises to the heavens along with your prayers. I am sure that God's penis has under canonical law a reason to exist. But if I may draw your attention to an insignificant and more mundane matter, by your leave please allow me to…"

But Voltaire's voice trailed off. The *abbé* was in no condition to hear what he was saying. A soft yelping came from the religious man's vocal chords, like a dog chanting. The *abbé* was reciting litany.

Voltaire sighed a very deep sigh, so deep it inflated his skinny chest to its maximum. He let it escape slowly from his thin lips in a shibilant exhale. He turned to Zénobe with a look that Sisyphus must have given before he rolled his boulder up the hill for the thousandth time. The tired old philosopher whispered, "The actors will be coming soon."

Zénobe realized that Voltaire needed his help. He needed Zénobe to be just hypocritical enough to have the *abbé* accede to the philosopher's wishes of being allowed to be buried on hallowed ground, and not be thrown into the city dump like so much detritus.

"*Mon cher père,*" said Zénobe to the cleric who was still kneeling on the floor. "*Mon très cher bon père. Monsieur* de Voltaire is tired and throws himself at your feet."

The *abbé* looked up at Zénobe.

Zénobe's expression had changed to one of extreme piety. "In spite of what you today have heard here, and in spite of what *monsieur le philosophe* has exclaimed and published all his life, it is time now for him to make peace with you and the Saintly Institution which you so diligently and respectfully represent. The time has come to prepare his soul for all eternity, and the man who lies on his deathbed in front of you has chosen you over all the other servants of the Church for so important a task. So please forget all that has come between him and the Church, for all of that is like water under the bridge. The philosopher is now a babe in your arms, his soul just as precious and just as fragile. For did not Jesus Christ say, 'Let the truly penitent come unto me and have their sins washed away'? The destiny of François Marie Arouet, *sieur de* Ferney, *dit* Voltaire, is in you hands, as are his salvation and his presence among God and His angels."

Zénobe saw Voltaire smile. "The boy is right. My destiny is in your hands," he repeated.

L'abbé Gaultier reacted favorably to Zénobe's exhortations. His stance softened visibly, his shoulders relaxed, and he understood better the matter at hand. He stood up and asked Zénobe if he could take a dictation.

"*Avec plaisir, mon très bon, mon très cher père.* My quill is at your disposal."

When the *marquis* de Villette came to, he realized that he was on one of the massage tables and that Benjamin Franklin and Edward Bancroft each had a hold of one of his hands. Franklin was slapping the hand he was holding, saying, "*Monsieur le marquis, monsieur le marquis,* are you with us?"

The monster Nebuchadnezzar ran up to the cot with a bucket of sloshing water. Franklin took a cloth and immersed it in the water. He then wiped Villette's face with it. Bancroft meanwhile was unbuttoning some of Villette's heavy wool clothing.

"He needs air, he needs air," Bancroft was saying.

Villette put his head back, enjoying the attention. But the back of his head hurt. "Am I bleeding?" he asked.

"No, you are not, sir," answered Franklin. "You have just received a slight bump to the head, and it will certainly hurt you for a few days. But we are in the dark about why you fainted. The concussion could not have been too great."

Villette knew why he had fainted. But to his attendants, he explained, "The blood must have rushed too quickly to my head. I'll probably have to be bled."

"You will do nothing of the kind, sir," said Franklin. "We will instead remove your attire so you can be plunged into a bath of steaming water. That is what the body needs after a shock."

Villette was dying of curiosity about Bancroft's nakedness and he raised his head to catch a glimpse, but unfortunately both men had draped towels toga-like around their bodies.

"Only if you join me," said the recalcitrant patient whose sense and imagination had not been diminished by the bump on the head. "And we'll order a bottle of champagne to calm my nerves."

"Ah, dear me," said Franklin. "What a splendid idea! To soak in a hot tub sipping on ice-cold champagne. Make haste! To the tub!"

In a few minutes, they were immersed up to their necks in hot water, surrounded by swirling vapor and the scent of fragrant perfume. The steam inhaled was chased by the champagne imbibed, and Villette forgot all about his accident. He felt so much better that he thought of playing footsies with Bancroft, but he decided against it. Some of those feet might be Benjamin Franklin's.

It was an unhappy Gaultier who took leave of Voltaire. After having dictated to Zénobe a complete retraction of Voltaire's anti-religious philosophy, a renunciation he hoped Voltaire would sign, Voltaire had refused. The *abbé* was crestfallen, "but I'm not defeated," he said. "I shall soon be back."

It was at this very moment that the troop of actors from *la Comédie française* arrived, and even though they bowed respectfully and enunciated theatrically good, solid sentiments to the man in the cassock, he in turn gave himself a wide margin of safety, backing away from them, as if they could give him the pox, or the clap, with pustules on his penis or with hair on his palms and soles. He who had never seen and heard *madame* Vetris in her reprisal of the role of Zaïre could not imagine her talent, her sensitivity, her extreme connectivity with her character, a child survivor of Muslim massacres of Christians who was brought up Muslim herself. The sultan Orosman, son of Saladin, falls in love with her and wishes to marry her, but she discovers she has a brother, and also a father, who still crawl as captives in the recesses of Orosman's dungeon. She realizes that she herself was born into a Christian family, and wishes to be baptized as such. But when she asks the sultan to postpone the wedding, Orosman, played to perfection by Lekain, suspects his betrothed of foul schemes, becomes jealous, and, when Zaïre meets secretly with her brother Nérestan, Orosman, waiting in the wings, storms out and stabs her to death. She dies a glorious martyr's death on stage, and the sultan, quickly and tearfully disabused by Nérestan, horrified by his awful mistake, kills himself in turn. If only the *abbé* had realized the extent to which *madame* Vetris had pushed the agenda of Christendom, he would not have considered her quite so pestilential. On the contrary, he would have flung himself at her feet to thank her, over and over again, and tell her how wonderful her portrayal of a virginal young Christian girl had been. But he had never entered a theater in his life. Making signs of the cross before him, not to bless the actors but to ward off malignant contagions, he receded into the hallway and dashed into the front vestibule and out the front door as soon as André could open it for him.

Maurel joined the crowd in *monsieur* de Voltaire's boudoir, and after having left them in the midst of their rehearsals for *Irène*, retrieved his valet and took him up quickly to his own bedroom.

"You must not show that you have an épée when you are on the streets," he told Zénobe. "It is illegal for a *roturier* to wear a sword, and if you are caught, goodness knows where you will be sent.[169] We would have to reach Lenoir, the police lieutenant, and it might be up to a week before we got you back. If you thought life on the streets was bad, you surely do not want to find out about life in the prisons. I shall hang the épée from your neck behind you, and your cloak shall conceal it."

Zénobe could not contain his excitement nor conceal his nervousness. As Maurel dressed him and transformed him into a quite passable simulacrum of a gentleman, the young man's agitation grew.

Maurel saw Zénobe's hand tremble as he buttoned up his breeches. He realized he had to give him some courage. "If the *chevalière* d'Éon is there, she will welcome you to the school. Remember, if a woman can fence, so can you. If she is not there, remember to mention that you have been sent there as her guest, and as such, you must convince yourself that you have a right to be there. From the looks of you, my dear Zénobe, you might already belong at Versailles."

The *maître d'hôtel*'s hands were all over his valet, pulling, patting, preening, buttoning, caressing. Zénobe looked delicious, in his chartreuse-colored breeches and his royal-blue cape. He gave Zénobe two quick pecks on either cheek and said, "I know that as a *roturier* you are not allowed to learn the aristocratic art of fencing, but times have changed, and you have been given this chance, by a woman, no less, who by all rights should not be fencing, and yet, she is. Go then, most charming boy, and give those aristocrats a taste of their own medicine, for you go representing me, and André, and the rest of us little folk at the *hôtel* de Villette, and we are with you and a part of you, and your experience will be our experience, your adventures our adventures. So carry your head high and be proud of yourself and of us. Suzanne made your uniform, she who only a year ago was a prisoner in a convent, and only through *monsieur* Diderot's help was she able to get out, and now you wear what she made for you, and it is the uniform of freedom. Go, then, and carry us in your heart, and then come back to us in triumph."

George Washington himself was standing in front of Zénobe, and the young man was in Saratoga carrying high the banner of liberty. With a surge of confidence, he flung himself into Maurel's arms, then dashed off to the front door where he flung himself into André's arms.

"I shall protect you always," he told the much surprised young Norman. "I shall defend you to the death!"

Then he was off into the cold and dreary landscape, and the Seine was the Delaware, and the quays of Paris were the harbor of Boston where the Tea Party had rebelled to cast off the yoke of oppression.

Maurel had followed Zénobe to the front door, and now he and André followed him with their eyes until he was lost among the pedestrians and the vehicles, their hearts aching for him.

La chevalière d'Éon was unfortunately not at La Boëssière's establishment, but La Boëssière, *fils*, was present and he knew of Zénobe's coming.

"My father told me to expect you. Welcome to our fencing academy. Have you any previous experience?"

---

169   A *roturier* was a member of a lower class of society, a plebeian, a commoner.

But before Zénobe could answer, the young La Boëssière asked a second question. "Tell me, *monsieur*. What is it like to live in the same house as the famous Voltaire?"

They were standing to one side of the main exercise area. A dozen pairs of students were clanging away in clamorous mock combat.

"It is a bit like, like…" answered Zénobe, searching for the right metaphor. "It is a lot like seeing what paradise will be. To be sitting at the right hand of Voltaire, who is wisdom personified. He knows everything. And nothing–absolutely nothing–surprises him. He is omniscient, not just about our own times, but about all times past. The human heart is also completely known to him. I never have to explain anything. My mind is transparent to him, and he sees better than I what I hold in my thoughts. He sums up in a few words what I say, and teaches me to be pithy and direct. He calls me his firebrand."

The young La Boëssière was not sure what pithy meant, but he understood enough to correlate Voltaire's teachings with fencing.

"Well, I sure hope you can be pithy and direct where fencing is concerned. Let me take you to the beginner's group."

Zénobe followed La Boëssière, *fils*, to a smaller area adjoining the hall.

"My father always takes the beginners. He says that the beginning is the most important time in learning how to fence. Someone might be ruined for life if they don't have the beginning right. Says something about learning the wrong things, when that happens it's hell to throw 'em out and install the right ones in their place. Nobody touches the beginners but him."

Zénobe's heart sank when they reached the group of beginners. They were all boys of twelve and thirteen. *Monsieur* La Boëssière interrupted the class to go greet Zénobe.

"Ah, this must be *la chevalière* d'Éon's protégé. Welcome, welcome, my son, to the La Boëssière academy of fencing, where we form not just young bodies but also young minds. Your sword, please."

Zénobe had not taken his épée out before entering into the premises, and now he awkwardly reached behind him under his cloak to reach for it. No sooner did he have a fingerhold on the handle that it would slip back down. Some of the young fencers started to laugh. The young La Boëssière had to help the red-faced young man extricate it.

"Oh, beautiful épée, beautiful épée," said the elder La Boëssière. "Let's remove these…"

Between the two fencing masters, Zénobe was helped out of his cloak, his tunic, his coat, his jabot, and his waistcoat, and was left only in his shirtsleeves and cravat.

"No need for a mask today. We are just practicing our lunging movements." And then to the rest of his little group he cried out, "*En garde*, gentlemen, attack mode!"

La Boëssière with an assuring tilt of his head invited Zénobe to imitate his movements, and Zénobe joined the class as best he could. In fifteen minutes his leg muscles were on fire, but he had forgotten that he was much older than the other pupils.

During one of the exercises, La Boëssière told Zénobe that he had a friend who wanted to meet *monsieur* de Voltaire, and wondered if an introduction would be possible. Zénobe, out of breath and with his hair clinging to his perspiring face, answered that it would be his pleasure to arrange a meeting.

La Boëssière was surprised that such a young gentleman could have in his power the ability to arrange an audience with the greatest mind of the age. He decided to make this student one of his favorites. After all, the young man had a natural grace that most others didn't. And master Zénobe ended his lunges with an energetic flourish of the hand that held the épée. And it was the left hand that held the épée. Oh my, oh my! He thought all that a strange coincidence, for the only other person he had witnessed having a similar flourish and preferring his left hand was precisely his friend who wanted to be presented to Voltaire, the *chevalier* de Saint-George.[170]

Zénobe was useless for the rest of the evening. When Maurel saw that he was hobbling around because of muscular distress, he sent him early to bed. Maurel also realized that Zénobe was dying to get into the crates of books newly arrived from the Panckoucke bookstore. When the *marquis* de Villette asked for the whereabouts of his librarian, Maurel told him that master Zénobe was organizing the first five hundred and fifteen books for *monsieur le marquis'* library. The *marquis* was upset: he realized that he was going to have to send Zénobe back to the bookstore for lots more. The *marquis* d'Argenson's library had thousands of volumes.

That night, André was denied the enjoyment of Zénobe's attention. Nor was he able to find pleasure in his intimacy with him. When André finally dozed off sometime after one o'clock in the morning, Zénobe was still reading in bed by candlelight. André fell asleep to the sound of Zénobe turning pages of the huge first volume of the *Encyclopédie*. The young Norman didn't know that one could read the *Encyclopédie* the way one read a novel. That night André dreamt that he and Zénobe lived in a book, a huge book with several chapters for stories. They lived at one end of it, and Voltaire lived at the other, holding court with all the other *philosophes* who would point to a part of the book and said, "I wrote that part" the way an architect would say, "I built that part." André could see that it was a very sturdy bookhouse, rock solid, and that nothing from the outside would endanger its inhabitants safely ensconced inside.

---

170   Joseph Bologne, *chevalier* de Saint-George, son of a wealthy colonial landowner who made his fortune as a sugar grower, made a name for himself with two talents: fencing and music. Considered to be the best fencer in France, he was also a wonderful violinist and composer, and became Marie Antoinette's musical adviser and teacher until the arrival of the Austrian Gluck.

Following and Being Followed

Zénobe received so much attention at La Boëssière's fencing school where he universally became known as Voltaire's orphan that it gave birth to his vanity. It proved to be such heady enjoyment answering questions about the sage of Ferney who, according to the young fencers, was come to Paris to foment social and political trouble. "He is not come for that," answered Zénobe with a smile. Furthermore, he explained, since he was Voltaire's newest secretary, he could tell them without a doubt that he himself had taken dictation of the play which was to be performed in less than a month's time; and it was this play that had prompted *monsieur le philosophe* to leave the provincial wilderness since only something literary like that could have ever tempted him to return to the cultural capital of the world. And yes, *monsieur* de Voltaire, old as he was, was enjoying himself tremendously in Paris. And no, the *philosophe* was not confessing his guts out to a succession of priests. Those priests were less interested in listening to an old man's litany of sins than in a full and unprecedented recantation of all the philosophical anti-religious views he had ever held. And Voltaire, he reassured them, was recanting nothing. Zénobe's fellow fencers had also heard reports that Voltaire was offering up to the altar a myriad of unpublished manuscripts that even Voltaire himself had viewed as too dangerous to be published. Zénobe laughed at such rumors.

"Voltaire brought no manuscripts with him. He left all his papers back in Ferney, to where he is planning to return after the opening of his play at the theater of the *Comédie française*."

"Then why were *madame* Denis and *la marquise* de Villette seen, and heard, visiting *hôtels* on the rue de Richelieu, announcing to the world that the patriarch wished to appropriate for himself a *pied-à-terre* in Paris?"

This was news, even to Zénobe, which he could neither corroborate nor deny, but knowing *madame* Denis, he surmised it to be possible, probable even, that she should be looking for a home in Paris without the knowledge of her uncle, so he suggested plausibly to the reporter of this tidbit that if Voltaire wished to purchase another home, after Les Délices in Geneva and the *château* in Ferney, then that was his prerogative as a man of ease. After all, he had more money than many European monarchs. After *Irène* there would be other plays, Zénobe theorized out loud, and it would make the playwright's life that much easier to have his own place in town where he could come and go as he pleased. Being a man of such importance, he was used to doing what he wanted.

But the rumor which Zénobe found utterly ridiculous, yet which still managed to get his bile up, was the report that Voltaire's fatal illness, which according to these careless flapping tongues had him flat on his back on his deathbed, was also bringing to him spasms of remorse and contortions of regret as he prepared to meet his maker in a writhing of agony.

Zénobe looked at the announcer of this gossip with a mixture of incredulity, contempt and mirth. His nostrils flared.

"What are people doing? Inventing stories to fit their longings? Voltaire has no fatal illness, nor is he on his deathbed, and I assure you most vociferously, that Voltaire has neither regrets nor spiritual sorrows of any kind. Were he to die tomorrow, he would go in peace, content in the knowledge that his lifelong ambition to end tyranny and prejudice was both justifiable and necessary."

In the midst of fencing exercises, Zénobe would have to fend off all sorts of questions and comments about his hero. He realized he had become Voltaire's representative, and as such, put much effort into being as worthy and faithful a servant as he possibly could, answering all questions the way the philosopher himself would, with honesty, but also with irreverence.

Had the Archbishop of Paris sent an emissary to *monsieur* de Voltaire?

"Well," answered Zénobe thoughtfully. "Wouldn't you? That primate *monsieur* de Beaumont must be shaking in his ecclesiastical robes, having in such close proximity the Prince of Reason. If I were he, I would find that frightening. He must not be getting any sleep, that is, if such an unearthly, spiritual fellow even deigns to sleep. Frankly, I don't think there's room enough for the two of them in this city, as big as it might be. Still, since the province of the Archbishop is all that is spiritual and invisible, I'm sure that he will become as vaporous as the morning dew with the coming of the rays of the sun. Ethereal and insubstantial, that's what the Archbishop shall become, in his realm of the incorporeal."

His listeners laughed. One of them said of Zénobe, "It's evident he has never felt the sting of Christophe de Beaumont's parries. If he had, he wouldn't be saying it was insubstantial. *Aïe, aïe!*" cried the man, holding his buttock as if it had just been stung by an épée.

Zénobe noticed that a few of the others were looking at him as if they expected him to fall on his sword at any minute.

Monsieur de La Boëssière came in to scatter the students back into their respective groups. "Come, come, my boys. There are better things to do than stand around chattering like a group of market women."

Monsieur de La Boëssière was revered by his students, and everybody returned to the business at hand.

But the damage was done. Zénobe, a good student to be sure, thrust his foil with a brio that had been absent on the previous day, and his attacks were so ferocious that the master fencer knew he would soon have to remove this pupil from the group of twelve-year-olds and place him with those closer to his own age and strength. What nerve! What vivacity! What would prompt a novice at fencing to throw out so vehemently his innate caution, to ignore so completely nature's attempts at self-preservation? He was sparring with three children at the same time; it was time to show him his limits. La Boëssière stepped in and in two seconds the épée flew out of Zénobe's hand, but the young man smiled, then laughed—with glee!—instead of cringing or snorting in frustration or letting out a *nom de Dieu*! La Boëssière

had to smile back, enchanted at his new pupil who understood the amusement of
fencing, the intrinsically thrilling aspect of the sport which had nothing to do with
self-defense. On second thought, La Boëssière decided, he would take over this
young man's martial education himself. Then he thought of the *chevalier* de Saint-
George, whom he had molded himself, and like a teacher who senses the arrival of
a new star pupil and all the concomitant pleasure that goes with that prospect, he
dedicated an hour, épée-à-épée, with *monsieur* Bosquet. He left the twelve-year-olds
in the care of his son.

The thrill of being at the center of attention, and the energy imbued by his blood
from the exertion of fencing with the master, made Zénobe at his departure from
the school on the rue de Saint-Honoré walk towards the east as if he were pursuing
a dragon, or a coterie of thieves, or Marie Antoinette on a steed. Not only had he
forgotten to hang his épée from his neck behind his back underneath his cloak,
he was holding it in his left hand, scaring passersby with it as he sliced through
the air. What kind of devilish creature was this, thought they, a foreigner cleaving
and whooshing his foil in the air, and using his left hand to do it! But Zénobe was
ensconced in his own mind, and after Marie Antoinette his next important enemy
was his *seigneur* back in Savoy, and his expression took on a serious (to the passersby,
a half-crazed) look, as he realized that a preciously thin blade was all that stopped
him from wreaking vengeance for his father's murder. By the time he happened
onto the Jardins des Tuileries, nothing could have held him back. He remembered
how the Gardens had been barred to him when he first arrived in Paris, wearing
his provincial clothes. But now he was on a Scandinavian dragoon's reconnoiter.
With rapier in hand he approached the northern entrance gate, glowered at the
two Swiss guards flanking the wrought iron doors, and, when neither guard made
a move towards him to impede his progress, he kicked open one of the doors and
marched right in.

The *hôtel* de Villette had been relatively quiet for a couple of days. Since the
rehearsals on Saturday last, Voltaire was seeing no one, even refusing to see the *abbé*
Gaultier. That tiresome priest kept insisting on exchanging letters with Voltaire: for
a letter from him expostulating a clean bill of spiritual health for the old man, the
abbé wished to receive one in which Voltaire recanted the means, the methods, the
results, and the processes of his irreligious philosophical way of life. Gaultier wanted
Voltaire to realize that his whole life had fruitlessly been given up to an effort not
rewarded by God, in fact, eschewed by God Who prized only humility, obedience
and chastity. Let Voltaire become like a child again, a child who dutifully obeys
the eternal Father, and he, too, could have everlasting life.

But Voltaire would have none of it. It was a doctor he needed, a new one since that
recalcitrant Genevan *docteur* Tronchin refused to come. A new physician had been dug
up, a certain *docteur* Anne-Charles Lorry, of whom the *marquis* de Villette had heard
from his friend the *marquis* de Thibouville. Dr. Lorry had been called upon to exsan-
guinate Louis XV when that monarch was dying of smallpox. Furthermore, he was an

expert on skin illnesses, nutrition, and nervous conditions.[171] André had already been instructed to go fetch him, and he was readying himself for that task.

Not that he was in any mood for any tasks. He was ready to spit fire. For the past three nights Zénobe had been in muscular distress and fatigue, too tired and in pain to embrace him, but not too tired to have his nose buried in the huge tomes of the *Encyclopédie*, half of which were now littering their little room. André's temper, as well as his testicles, were ready to burst. From one day to the next, Zénobe had become a different person. No caress, no cajolery, no seductive glance could entice him from his books. Sunday afternoon, when André had brought tea for the philosophical master, he had found the door ajar and heard Zénobe and Voltaire speaking in Latin, having a bloody conversation in Latin, like when the priest back in Normandy would give mass, except here they were talking to each other, and they laughed as if something had been a joke, perhaps what they call a witticism, and what made them laugh had been in Latin. What a pestiferous tongue, this Latin was. And Zénobe spoke other languages as well, Savoyan or whatever it was they spoke where Zénobe was from, and he knew English as well, although how can one pick up English in the mountains of Savoy? He, André, should be able to speak English. Wasn't William the Conqueror a Normand? Those English should speak Normand, not the other way around. And where does this *docteur* Lorry live, anyway. He wasn't sure where the Place Royale was,[172] and he certainly wasn't in the mood to go out into the cold looking for some new charlatan to come take care of the old man. Besides, why didn't Maurel let Zénobe go looking for this doctor? No, he was out being diverted by his fencing lessons. He was too good and too important to be sent out on mere errands. And because of Zénobe's fencing lessons, his own lessons had been suspended. So while Zénobe was out learning new things, he, André, was going to get stupider and stupider. He was jealous of the *Encyclopédie*. If somebody had cared to ask him if he would have liked to know what was in those books, André would have answered yes. But every time that he opened one to take a look, when Zénobe was away, that is, he could barely manage to understand the basic theme of the articles. Why did these people write like that, so thickly, so murkily? Same thing with Voltaire, who even spoke that way. Oh, why didn't they just let the old man die in peace, he's so old. Let peace and tranquility come back to the *hôtel* de Villette. That way, Zénobe would have time for his books and for his fencing and also for him. André found it difficult to understand: how could Zénobe prefer a cold nonliving object to his warmth, to his life? What's so great about a book!

André had just let himself out from the kitchen door dreaming of the return of peace and tranquility to the *hôtel* de Villette and how Zénobe would come back to him, when he saw something very curious and very irregular. Quickly he hid behind a trellis. A well-dressed man had just come out of a door in the stable where no door had ever been observed by André. This man walked with the confidence of one who had used this secret door countless times before, but who still had the presence of mind to look behind his shoulder before he traversed the driveway and slipped out into the street by the carriage gate. André was taken aback, and in his present mood of wishing for calm in the household, he was not pleased that a strange man had been on the premises. And

---

171   Dr. Anne-Charles Lorry published in 1765 a treatise titled *De melancholia et morbis melancholicis*. His *Essay on Food* established his reputation as much for its elegance as for its scientific rigor.

172   Today's Place des Vosges. Its old name is to be eliminated by the rebellious anti-monarchists during the Revolution.

a strange man who acted as if he belonged there. André ran to the gate and poked his head out to see what direction the man had taken. He was on his way to the quai des Théâtins. But he did something queer. At the intersection of the rue de Beaune and the *quai*, the man flattened himself to the corner house and stopped and looked around the corner ahead of him, as if he, too, were following someone. When the man deemed it safe, he made a left turn and quickly traversed the *quai* laterally to the northwest and then stopped behind a lamppost before deciding to cross the Pont Royal.

Now, André had not received instructions about following any man leaving the *hôtel* de Villette, especially if following such a man meant going in a direction away from the Place Royale. Well, it's still on the Right Bank so I would still have to cross the river someplace, was André's justification for continuing to follow this strange man.

What André didn't know was that this strange man was the *marquis* de Thibouville, and that the man whom Thibouville was following was no other than André's master the *marquis* de Villette. Villette was up to something, Thibouville knew, and he was damned sure going to find out. For the past three evenings, Villette had had an excuse about not allowing him to spend the night in his boudoir and from numerous times past, Thibouville knew that Villette had someone stuck in his mind. Villette would take passing fancies to someone, and in the meantime, Thibouville would become *persona non grata*. He who had done his utmost to have Voltaire and Villette become the best of friends, who had frequently helped Villette write the poetry, nay, written the damned stuff himself, to seduce Voltaire into accepting Villette as a man of letters, and indeed, the philosopher called Villette the new Tibulle.[173] Well, so much was due to him, Thibouville, and you'd think there would be some tiny little crumbs of gratitude coming his way, but no. No, no, Villette used him, abused him, just to get what he wanted, then discarded him like Frédéric II discarded Voltaire after he had used him up and sucked him dry like an old desiccated orange. But this time Thibouville was going to get to the bottom of things. He suspected that Villette had developed a keen interest in Franklin's grandson, and he found out from Maurel that he had gone to Passy to visit the American but the American had not been at home. Maurel had also delivered the detail that Villette was planning to take a walk in the Tuileries because there was a rumor that the Queen would be there before she went to the theater, and he wanted to see and be seen. If Marie Antoinette were to speak to him, Villette had told Maurel, he would like to mention the enthusiasm with which *monsieur* de Voltaire hoped for a meeting with their royal Highnesses. Maurel shared Thibouville's misgivings about Villette being in the Gardens, unsupervised, but the reason for his being there seemed reasonable enough. Voltaire *had* wanted to meet the King and Queen. He corresponded with Kings and Queens like one corresponds with one's friends, counting them among his friends. Only his own King and Queen gave him the royal cold shoulder. Why, oh why, couldn't the French monarchs come around and give even a pretense at being enlightened rulers, instead of the blind, diffident and unreasonable despots that they were? They were too young, too inexperienced, too stupid to be clement and tolerant. Here was *tout* Paris clamoring to see Voltaire, and here their Majesties were pretending that nothing was happening. What fools! They needed someone like Voltaire by their side to help them with the business of ruling. They, who never even dreamed of

---

173   The old Tibulle (Albius Tibullus) was a Roman poet writer of elegies, many of which sing the praises of love and lust, of enchanting, bedazzling shepherd boys. Perhaps the scarcity of his poems (there were only two books of his verse extant) was a further reason for Voltaire to call Villette by that name.

becoming the King and Queen of France, never planned for such an eventuality. Louis XVI's father and older brother both died of smallpox, leaving him, third in line for the throne, at the front of the queue. Why, he was never even taught Latin, for heaven's sake. And some blot on the face of pedagogy had allowed him to learn about locks. Well, he could tinker to his heart's content, and he could lock himself up at Versailles for all he cared, for Thibouville was on the side of the *philosophes*, and would have been at the forefront with them if it hadn't been for his agoraphobia. Thibouville couldn't stand the glittery hypocrisy, the elegant backstabbing, the "don't live and don't let live" of the *beau monde*. His days of trying to hold on to a niche in high society were over. He had given up his boxes at the theaters, and preferred to stand anonymously in the *parterre* with minor aristocracy and wealthy *bourgeois* rather than have to demean himself with the contemptuous, fawning, craven, cruel-hearted *aristocrottes*, to use the word Voltaire had christened them with.

Thibouville saw that Villette was headed for the southern entrance gate to the Jardins des Tuileries. So he had been right to follow him. He felt even stronger about it when he saw Villette head not towards the northeast where the Queen was known to take her walks, but to the northwest, zigzagging along the pathways that only somebody like Villette could know so well. Daylight was faltering, and even though the sky was overcast, the blue-gray light of the blue hour, dusk, which was Thibouville's favorite part of the day, was just starting to play among the tops of the leafless linden trees. He looked forward to that hour, this *heure bleue*, since it would take the lamplighters that long to illuminate the interior of the Gardens. *Heure chérie, chérie heure*, said he to himself, citing a long-ago poem he had written for a long-lost lover whose face he couldn't see any more in his mind but the poetry he had inspired was still strong in his memory. Actually, he could also remember the man's body. The poetry and the body, that was all that remained. The name and the face were gone.

Suddenly he realized that Villette had stopped in his tracks and hidden himself behind the trunk of a huge sycamore. He'd seen somebody. Villette stepped gingerly out onto the pathway, only to take a few steps and then hide behind another tree trunk. So they continued, Thibouville following Villette who was following someone else. Who was it? Thibouville couldn't see, but whoever it was must have been ambling very slowly. Perhaps it was someone who liked *l'heure bleue* as much as he? Then they weren't on the path any more. Villette had gone into a tangent, into a part of the Gardens thick with shrubbery, a little unkempt if one asked Thibouville. Now he had to make sure that he didn't make any noise stepping onto a dead branch. He felt like a savage in the New World, reconnoitering through a thicket hunting for prey. But what kind of game was he after, or rather, was Villette after? It was man prey, to be sure. Thibouville was determined to find out why Villette was on the prowl.

The ease of his entry into the Jardins des Tuileries made Zénobe look back at the two Swiss guards, but neither one of them had budged. He wondered why he had been allowed to go in. Was it Maurel's confection of a Swedish military uniform? Was it his look of ferocity as he rushed past the gate? Was it that he was acting as if he belonged there? Only aristocrats were allowed into the Tuileries. So what was he? Was he the gallant scion of a noble lineage stretching back to Charlemagne? Did his pedigree show on his face, his escutcheon in his manner? No, no, that was not it at all. His confidence, Voltaire's confidence, was what granted him entry into the aristocratic park. Between the rows of flowers and topiary, on the walkways of gravel, in the waning light of the afternoon, his head held high, he wound his way among the ladies and gentlemen out for a stroll in spite of the cold weather. Because of Voltaire, he had a right to be there among them, and he thanked Maurel in his heart for having made it so. They made climbing the echelons in the social hierarchy a thing of ease. Zénobe was as good as any aristocrat. He was definitely more intelligent than any aristocrat, certainly better educated. Soon, he would be able to skewer most aristocrats, if they deserved it. In a whim-wham of ebullience he wanted to brandish his foil again, but he dared not press his luck here in aristoland.

But Zénobe had never been inside the Tuileries Gardens and when he zigzagged towards the south and east, intending to come out of the southeastern gate that was the closest to the Pont Royal, he took a wrong turn and he wended his way down a minor allée which turned out to be a dead end. Instead of doubling back he proceeded courageously into a thicket, for he never doubled back. Had Descartes not written in his *Discourse on the Method* that the thinker should proceed forward so as to avoid mindless wandering? Once the direction of the path had been chosen, based on sound rational thinking, the way was clear. Any impediments to progress had to be cleared, traversed or destroyed and were he to—

A huge impediment loomed in his way. It was a mighty *Quercus*, and this, he knew, he would have to go around. As he did so, he felt rather than perceived the presence of a person who a split second later was startled by Zénobe barging into his space. That person let out a vituperative utterance in a foreign tongue (ah! it was English: *blood of Christ!*), and then Zénobe heard a bottle hit the ground and roll among the tree roots.

In the shadows he saw a man dodge for the bottle, but before Zénobe could even apologize for the accident, before he could even help the man regain his bottle that was probably spewing out its contents, before he could even switch his épée from his left hand to his right in preparation to do so, Zénobe himself was startled when he heard the voice of a second man, beyond the tree, who exclaimed in surprise, "What the devil are *you* doing here?"

The man with the bottle was also startled by the voice, for just as he was getting up from his crouching position he twisted his body around in the direction of the voice, caught his foot on a tree root and fell on his behind, letting the bottle drop from his hands again. He ended up in a sitting position nestled between thick gnarled roots. But Zénobe had no time to observe the fallen man for he had recognized the voice of the second man. It was his master the *marquis* de Villette.

"What the devil are you doing here?" the *marquis* repeated. "And what are you doing in these clothes? And what were you doing in the shrubbery with *mister* Bancroft?"

Villette had walked over to take Zénobe by the arm and then he saw the glint of his épée. "And what in God's name are you doing with this épée? It is drawn! What are you about, scoundrel? Speak!"

Just to make sure, Villette drew his own foil and stood there in stupefaction while waiting to see if there was indeed any danger to fend off. But would he really have to defend Bancroft against Zénobe, his valet? His valet? His valet had an épée?

Zénobe didn't know which question to answer first. But certainly the third question was as much a surprise to him as it was to the *marquis* de Villette. He certainly didn't know what he was doing there in the middle of the Jardins des Tuileries at dusk in the shrubbery with the secretary of *monsieur* Benjamin Franklin.

The *marquis* de Villette looked aghast at the foil still clutched in the boy's left hand. Zénobe's discomfiture was such and the *marquis'* outrage was such, that neither one of them saw Edward Bancroft slip his bottle within the confines of his cloak.[174]

All Zénobe could do was extend a hand to the fallen English-American gentleman secretary and help him to get on his feet.

The *marquis* de Thibouville, and André thirty paces behind him, saw this whole episode acted out before their very stunned eyes. André immediately took ten paces closer on a diagonal to get a better look, and he was as surprised as anyone when he realized that the *marquis* de Villette had caught Zénobe alone with the American secretary behind the trunk of a huge tree. He could hear Villette splutter up a storm of invective. Then he heard Villette offer up some extremely flowery apologies to Bancroft, asking him if he was hurt, if his valet had molested him, if he could offer his services in any way. "After all, you have most generously given me succor during my hour of need after a brutal fall, please allow me to return the favor."

Bancroft was dusting himself off. "Please, don't be concerned. I am quite all right, really. But, please, I must be… Thank you, thank you much, anyway. However, I must take my leave, my presence is required, uhm, elsewhere. But thank you most kindly."

Villette had taken Bancroft by the arm, to steady him or perhaps to prevent his leaving. The American secretary had to take Villette's hand in the guise of shaking it furiously and proceeded to put some distance between them.

"Thank you, *monsieur le marquis*, most kindly. Perhaps we shall have the pleasure of seeing you soon, in Passy. Well, *au revoir.*"

Bancroft turned on his heels and slipped into the shadows.

Villette turned his attention to Zénobe.

"A naked blade, you have a naked blade out in the open? What am I allowed to think, catching you like this with your épée drawn?"

Zénobe realized much too late his blunder and began to hide his blade behind his back, but he couldn't slip it under his cloak.

"What are you doing?" asked his master. "Have you no scabbard?"

"*Si, monsieur le marquis,* I do, but we decided it would be safer to leave the épée hanging behind my back underneath my cloak."

"*We* decided?"

"*Non, monsieur le marquis, I* decided to wear the épée hanging behind my back."

André could tell by Zénobe's quivering voice that he was in distress. He saw Zénobe offer the foil to Villette by the handle.

"*Non,*" said the *marquis* gruffly. "You keep it. With me by your side, nobody will dare say anything. Let's go home. On the way, you explain everything to me."

Only the *marquis* de Villette could see Zénobe's lower lip trembling. He suspected his valet was swallowing back tears. His eyes looked glossy. The boy had never seemed so handsome to him, dressed as he was in the colors of Gustave III. He saw Maurel's

---

174   How would History have been altered had the *marquis* de Villette or Zénobe realized that Bancroft's bottle held state secrets from Franklin's office and which were to fall into British hands? Every Tuesday a courtier would arrive after nightfall to retrieve the messages in the bottle placed in the hollow of a dead branch. Such are the vagaries and the coincidences of history, and indeed of all stories, including this one. Perhaps the War of Independence would have been of shorter duration, fewer people on both sides would have died, Lord Stormont the British ambassador in Paris would have died of apoplexy brought on by frustration, George III's army and navy would not have known which ships to attack and where. In short, things would have come out a lot differently.

paw prints all over this. With a gesture, he instructed Zénobe to come closer to him. Zénobe complied.

From his vantage point, the *marquis* de Thibouville could not see the *marquis* de Villette kissing Zénobe. All he knew was that they had stopped speaking, and strain his eyes as he might, he could not discern a thing in the darkening twilight. Then he heard a twig break behind him to his left, and he quickly backed away from the scene. He had seen enough, enough to accuse Villette of nocturnal rambles and secret *rendez-vous*.

André, however, still hadn't seen enough. From his vantage point he could clearly see the two, master and servant, bring their faces together, and he could guess that they were kissing. He made a movement closer to them, but he stepped on a twig and decided to stand absolutely still.

The *marquis* de Villette also heard the twig and said, "Let's get out of here. There is much danger about. The police lieutenant enjoys sending out his scouts to look for loiterers. Come, let's go."

André waited to make sure the pair had left. He guessed that the mysterious gentleman he had been following had already taken his leave. He slowly made his way to the Gardens' exit, not knowing what he felt. It was anger and despondency and rage and melancholy. Then he ran all the way to the Place Royale to make up for lost time.

Jacques-Henri Maurel, the *maître d'hôtel* to the *hôtel* de Villette, who had been in the employ of his master since the *marquis* was twenty-eight and had struck out on his own after having been gently nudged out of the parental nest by the late *marquise* de Villette, his mother, beautiful lady, intelligent mind, and friend to Voltaire; and after having given the best years of his life to his master, was instantaneously aware of the necessity of his magic touch to effectuate damage control, as soon as he saw his master return to the *hôtel* with his visibly disturbed valet-librarian by his side, and, forty-five minutes later, out of breath and equally disturbed, a second male servant of the household.

Since the *marquis* had taken Zénobe directly upstairs to his boudoir and both were thus inaccessible, Maurel took André by the arm and led him to his own room. As they climbed the stairs, André thought that Maurel's sense of urgency had to do with the tardiness of his arrival from the errand to the Place Royale, and said, "Dr. Lorry was not in, so I left word with his staff to please call on *monsieur* de Voltaire at the *hôtel* de Villette as soon as possible."

"I am pleased to hear it, André," said Maurel as he shut the door to his room. "But that's not what I want to question you about."

André looked at Maurel whose expression of deep concern and agitation was such that he knew he could tell him everything. He threw himself into Maurel's arms and burst into sobs.

"Oh, *monsieur* Maurel, Zénobe has been deceiving us. He has not been going to his fencing lessons. Instead, he has been loitering around the shrubbery at the Jardins des Tuileries with *mister* Edward Bancroft, Benjamin Franklin's secretary."

Maurel, who was widely read and had gathered from fiction, and also from barely veiled *mémoires*, his favorite genre, a myriad of the multitudinous possible, probable, improbable and highly impossible plot lines of stories, therefore possessed a good sense of what could happen and what couldn't, in real life. After hearing André's plot line, he realized he had never heard of one so impossible. He pried André off him to look into his face.

"You jest, master André."

"*Non, non, monsieur* Maurel. How could I be jesting at a moment like this, about something so serious, so cruel, so diabolical. Zénobe has sinned against us, for instead of attending to his duties and responsibilities, he has been doing terrible things in the shrubbery with a man he met in this house."

Maurel's mind ran in different directions, scattering his thoughts into an incoherent, disorderly riot. To quell his mind, he thought of Voltaire. To quell André's dishevelment, he told him, "You must be mistaken. Zénobe is not the type of person who would do something that dastardly. Who could have debauched him?"

André said between sobs, "I… I… I have."

Maurel could not suppress a smile.

"It's true, *monsieur* Maurel. Zénobe and I have been… have been doing things, at night, and I sup-suppose he wanted to try it out on somebody else."

"Oh, *mon cher petit* André. I know of your sweet nocturnal activities. It's all imprinted on your faces as you catch sight of each other during your daily activities. And a few kisses stolen beneath the covers doesn't lead you to go prowling at night at the Jardins des Tuileries."

"It hasn't just been kisses, *monsieur* Maurel. It's been other things as well."

As much as Maurel would have liked to continue with this subject of interrogation, he had other ground to cover.

"In the first place, André, what were *you* doing in the Jardins des Tuileries?"

"I was following a man."

Here was another tidbit that sounded highly improbable.

"You were following a man? But how did you get into the Gardens dressed in your valet's uniform?"

"I followed him into the Gardens. In order to get into the Gardens, I placed myself close behind a group of *aristos* as if they had taken their servant with them. I've done that many times before in order to take a shortcut across the Tuileries. There's no harm in that, is there, *monsieur* Maurel?"

"No, there is not, not in the least," answered the *maître d'hôtel* who, in spite of his surprise at not knowing this detail about a servant under his guidance, could not help but admire this bit of spunk.

"But tell me, André, what possessed you to follow this man into the Gardens?"

André had forgotten this interesting part of the story. "He… he… he came out of the stables, here at the *hôtel* de Villette!"

Maurel was astonished, then curiously relieved. The story was beginning to make sense.

"This man left from a secret door in the stables?"

"Yes!"

"And what was he doing, this man, as he left the *hôtel* de Villette?"

"He was following someone, but I couldn't see then who it was. All I know was that he was acting suspiciously, the man I followed, I mean. He crossed the quai des Théâtins, then the Pont Royal and went into the Gardens. It wasn't until fifteen or twenty minutes after that I realized that the man he had been following was the *marquis* de Villette, because I heard his voice when he became upset at witnessing Zénobe and *mister* Bancroft going at it in the bushes."

"Did you see Zénobe and Bancroft 'going at it' in the bushes?"

"*Non, monsieur,* it was too dark by that time, and I didn't want to get any closer because I still had that strange man between me and the *marquis* and Zénobe and Bancroft. As it was, I stepped on a stick which snapped and made everyone scatter."

"Did you see if Zénobe was in a state of undress?"

"*Non, monsieur.* As a matter of fact, *monsieur le marquis* made a big deal about Zénobe brandishing his épée in the air. Zénobe answered something about carrying it under his cloak. So, you see, he had his cloak on."

André was feeling much better about things. But as soon as Maurel asked him the next question, he looked crestfallen again.

"Did you see anything else which looked suspicious?"

"Well, yes, *monsieur,* it was after Edward Bancroft left. *Monsieur le marquis* ordered Zénobe to come closer, and then he kissed him."

It was Maurel's turn to look crestfallen. Now he knew what *monsieur* de Villette was doing with Zénobe in his boudoir upstairs. He had the servant boy inside his big bed, under the brocaded curtains, propping him up on pillows this way and that, now on his back semi-reclining, now flat on his stomach with his hands clinging to the bedposts, now hanging half-off the bed with his mouth yawning open. Maurel had to close his imagination's eyes for fear of going insane. Besides, he had to take the report of Dr. Lorry to *madame* Denis and André had to report to his duties.

"Not a word of this to anybody, you understand?" was Maurel's parting instructions to André. "We shall talk of all this later."

"*Oui, monsieur,*" answered André before heading downstairs.

Maurel was quite mistaken. He did not know what was going on in *monsieur le marquis* de Villette's big bed. By the time his master and Zénobe had ambled back to the rue de Beaune, the *marquis* de Thibouville had run back and taken the secret passageway up to Villette's boudoir with plenty of time to catch his breath and compose his expression to one of serenity and nonchalance. He even had the presence of mind to be surprised when the *marquis* de Villette barged in with his valet-librarian. The illusion was complete: Villette thought that he had caught Thibouville by surprise. Thibouville made as if to escape through the secret door but it was too late. So he sat back down on the chair by the writing desk.

"Oh, *monsieur,* I didn't know that you were here," said Villette.

"Pardon the intrusion, *monsieur,* but I was waiting for you to see if you had been able to see the Queen."

"The Queen?" asked Villette. "Oh, yes, the Queen! Oh, no, dash it all, it was nothing but a false rumor. The Queen apparently did not take a promenade at the Tuileries before going on to the theater."

While Villette was speaking, Thibouville took a leisurely look at the librarian who had frozen by the door, too timid to walk into Villette's bedroom by himself. But he saw enough to make his soul heave in anguish and make his testicles tauten. What a bleeding tasty morsel this librarian was! He realized he was a librarian in name only for someone this handsome could not be bright as well. Besides, he looked so dopey hanging out by the threshold like that. For the life of him, however, he couldn't guess as to why he was wearing the colors of a foreign military person.

Villette saw Thibouville giving his librarian the once-over, so he turned to Zénobe and said in a loud voice, "That will be all for today, my boy. Remember that you have an appointment at the library of the *marquis* de Paulmy d'Argenson tomorrow at half past noon. And be sure to let me know this week when the architect gets here. I wish to have a word with Wailly myself. The wood for the bookshelves should arrive by the end of the week. That's it. Off with you. Good-bye."

Zénobe didn't have to be told twice to make his escape. He darted off to his little servant's room to undress and to give thought to the unnerving occurrences of the evening. Later, after he had confessed everything to *monsieur* Maurel, the *maître d'hôtel* would shed light on the contretemps in the Tuileries gardens.

The *marquis* de Villette wasn't quite so lucky. He closed his door and turned to face the *marquis* de Thibouville who seemed all happiness and ease, but who, as times past had taught Villette before, harbored a full set of his own teeth as steely as knives and a tongue that darted deep into his heart.

The following day, a chastened and sedate *marquis* de Villette instructed his *maître d'hôtel* that subsequently his librarian was to wear his épée sheathed in a scabbard hung from his belt. If any trouble should come from this, he would answer for it. There was a multitude of foreign military types in Paris, so no one would suspect that Zénobe was not one of them.

"Have him speak in a foreign tongue when he's out in public. Let's just hope that he won't meet up with any Swedish dragoons. They'll be sure to ask him questions, and I have no jurisdiction over them. Why don't we just change the color of Zénobe's breeches? Vanilla cream would go better with the blue of the coat and waistcoat, anyway."[175]

"*Non, monsieur le marquis*, those are the colors of the Russian hussars. And knowing the Russians, they'd have him arrested and taken immediately to St. Petersburg. Then we'd have to call on Diderot to go ask his friend Catherine the Great to release our Zénobe and send him back to us. Would he get back to Paris in one piece?"

"No, no, that wouldn't do at all," responded the *marquis*. Just, just change the color to something that hasn't been taken!"

"Oui, *monsieur le marquis*. I shall take care of it."

Inwardly the *maître d'hôtel* was thinking of doing nothing of the kind. The chartreuse of Zénobe's breeches was perfect. Besides, how many Swedish dragoons were running around Paris? In order to stave off his master, however, he decided that the color of Zénobe's breeches for indoor wear would have to change. It would be a pristine color, a hue unsullied by mud, untarnished by rust, a color so immaculate, so stain-free it would remind one of heaven. He wondered why he hadn't thought of it before. It would be a color that would set off Zénobe's eyes like nothing up to then. The color of his breeches would be: cerulean.

Later on that afternoon, Zénobe, still wearing his chartreuse-colored breeches, but his épée in a scabbard hanging from the side of his belt, presented himself for his appointment at the *hôtel* d'Argenson on the rue de Sully. From the street, it didn't look grander than the *hôtel* de Villette. But once inside, the comparison failed, to the detriment

---

175   Vanilla had been to the French known since the days of Louis XIV, but it was still very expensive. Because efforts to introduce it into the Île Bourbon (La Réunion of today) failed, its only source was still Mexico, since the plant was pollinated by a bee endemic to the region. In the 18th century, only the very wealthy could afford it.

of the *hôtel* de Villette. For one, the doorman was dressed in a most admirable fashion: velvet and silk from top to bottom, but in subdued colors, so as not to outshine the master. The doorman was older, too, much older than Zénobe, André or Henri. He moved with grave grace and dignity. Zénobe thought that he would have to emulate him when the duties of the front door once again befell him. The doorman asked Zénobe to follow him into the library, informing him that his grace the *marquis* de Paulmy d'Argenson would be joining *monsieur* in the library in a few minutes. As their steps echoed in the great halls, Zénobe thought of another difference between the two *hôtels*, but this one fell in favor of the *hôtel* de Villette. Here, silence reigned. Solitude. He thought he heard whispers, but they were mere echoes, as if the male speaker were far away, or as if the echo was still reverberating in the vast spaces from some time in the past.

After a series of arches, double Corinthian columns and huge empty niches in the walls, the valet opened a pair of enormous double doors and asked Zénobe to step into the library. Zénobe's jaw dropped. The room was long and narrow, with the sides alternating between bookshelves and windows. The books went all the way up and touched the coffered ceilings, twenty-five feet over their heads. Tall ladders on wheels could be manipulated in order to climb up to the heavens.

"Please take a seat, *monsieur*, and *monsieur le marquis* will be with you shortly."

With that, the valet shut the doors and Zénobe was left alone in the silent solitude of this book cathedral. During the days he had been wandering alone in Paris, he had entered into Notre Dame de Paris and had dismissed it as a waste of space. But here, here someone had realized what a vast space should be used for. D'Argenson had taken over the buildings of the previous military arsenal, and had filled them up with something even more explosive than bullets and cannon shot.[176]

Zénobe could not keep his seat. He had to walk among the books. With his gaze directed upwards, Zénobe admired the physical beauty of the volumes: they were splendorous. There were more books here than twenty Panckoucke bookstores laid end to end and stacked up on each other.

He heard footsteps, and it took a half-minute for the *marquis* to walk over to Zénobe from the far end of his library.

Monsieur Marc-René de Voyer de Paulmy, *marquis* d'Argenson, was an uncommon aristocrat. In his youth he had gone through the regular paces, aided by his father and his uncle, the *marquis* and the *comte* d'Argenson, to obtain coveted positions in the service of Louis XV. With stints as director general of His Majesty's stud-farms, Governor of the *château*–and prison–of Vincennes, ambassador to the Swiss states, Poland and Venice, he succeeded his uncle as Secretary of War in 1757, but the advent of the Seven Years' War brought on too much responsibility and stress, and he resigned, retiring from government service at the young age of 48 in order to pursue activities of a more intellectual kind. His library had more than a hundred thousand volumes, the catalog of which he insisted on composing and organizing himself. By 1778 he had initiated, edited and published over 40 volumes in his *Bibliothèque universelle des romans*, and was

---

176   Having been the *Grand Maître de l'artillerie de France,* the *marquis* de Paulmy d'Argenson had lived in the Arsenal since 1755 and started almost immediately transforming it into a library to house his growing collection of books.

already far advanced in his next project: a synthesis based on the different aspects of the political, military and literary history of France.[177]

As Zénobe observed the *marquis* walk towards him, he recognized him as one of the representatives of the *Académie française* who had showed up to the *hôtel* de Villette to pay respects and to honor Voltaire.

The *marquis* d'Argenson was pleased to see wonderment and respect on his young visitor's face.

"It's not every day that I have the pleasure of receiving the visit of a fellow librarian, and a novice one at that."

"*Monsieur le marquis*," responded Zénobe with a bow.

"It is a wonderful library, is it not?" asked the *marquis*. "Every time I come in here I cannot but be filled with awe. I sense the power, the magnificence, of this collection of books. The world is at our fingertips, young man, right here, and the universe itself comes that much closer to us, in the midst of this one library. I have approved of each book myself, you know. No entry has been allowed to books that are on the margins of science. Mesmer has been pestering me, offering me his books for free, so he can say that the *marquis* de Paulmy d'Argenson has accepted them into his library. But I send them back to him half read. We at the Academy of Sciences cannot accept such books. Books of real science, yes, books of poetry which teach us about the veracities of the human heart, novels inspired by real life and improved upon by the art of the human imagination, all that, yes, but not charlatanism based on pseudo-science. Tell me, young man, how do you like *monsieur* Arouet?

Zénobe answered this first question easily. He had had much practice with it at the fencing academy, and it was pleasurable to give words to his admiration, his love, his opinion that Voltaire was the greatest man alive. While he spoke, d'Argenson felt jealous that Voltaire had such an acolyte, and a beautiful one at that, and one so faithful and so loving. Seeing his eyes that were a piercing blue, the *marquis* wondered what color hair he had. His eyebrows were jet black, and rose and fell with emotion as Voltaire was extolled to the skies.

"So, then," said the *marquis*, "you think that *monsieur* de Voltaire is greater than Louis XVI?"

Zénobe was taken aback by the question. Was this a trap? He thought he must use diplomacy in answering the *marquis*, but his hesitation, in and of itself, would have meant his undoing in any other social context with aristocrats. D'Argenson was too old and wily to be fooled.

"Young man, you must be careful if you wish to enter the world of the ruling class. I have heard that you are receiving instruction in the martial arts from the *chevalier* d'Éon. You have now gained entry into my library with a letter of recommendation from Voltaire himself. Well, know that your patron and benefactor was a young man like you once. The physical bruises he received as he learned his way into the world of the gentry may be gone, but the memories of them, I am sure, lurk somewhere in his mind. As a matter of fact, I know the perfect first book you'll read in this library. Come with me."

D'Argenson took Zénobe into a different part of the cavernous room. There were books everywhere. Zénobe was too enthralled to worry much about the question of who was greater, Voltaire or Louis.

---

177   This project, the great work of his life, will take 65 volumes and will be published in Paris as the *Mélanges tirés d'une grande bibliothèque*, from 1779 to 1788.

D'Argenson climbed halfway up a ladder to retrieve a certain book. *"Les Chroniques de l'Œil-de-bœuf,* volume two, 1697, 1698, 1700, 1702, 1704, 1705, 1706… Let's see, let's see… Ah, here it is. This is the first thing you'll read, quite à propos, and I'm sure you'll find it of interest. Let me find the page… Install yourself here, put your feet up on this pouf. *Voilà!* I'll have coffee brought up to you. If you need anything, pull on that cord there."

D'Argenson left Zénobe seated in a deep *bergère* whose back towered over the young man's head. As the *marquis'* footsteps died down, Zénobe admired the artistry of the binding, the heft of the volume. Then, he dutifully began to read.

> The dirty laundry of news which our amiable members of the court unfurl each day to l'Œil-de-Bœuf has recently been enlarged by certain, quite singular details: I cannot pass this novel innovation by in silence; still, I am altogether quite embarrassed to speak of it without some modicum of reserve… Let us attempt to convey the event, nonetheless.
>
> During the course of the summer, *monsieur le duc* de Vendôme, upon taking leave of the king in Marly, informed him that he had to retire to his country estate to have himself treated thoroughly for a certain malady, one which certainly was not among the most pure of the conquests of Christopher Columbus,[178] and that this medical retreat would at the same time give him the leisure of putting some order into his finances.
>
> His Majesty smiled and responded, "Good-bye, then, my dear duke. I wish that upon your return we may embrace with more pleasure than today, and that you will no longer be the dupe of either your health or your finances."
>
> The following day, while the king was making an inspection of his troops, His Majesty expressed surprise at seeing *monsieur le prince* Emmanuel de Lorraine on foot among the ranks.
>
> "Your brother, *le duc* d'Elbeuf," said His Majesty to him, "gives you not the wherewithal to buy a horse?"
>
> "Sire," answered the embarrassed young officer. "It is not a horse which I'm lacking."
>
> "Still, an officer of the cavalry is hardly ever on foot for that reason."
>
> "I beg His Majesty's pardon, but that which I lack is the possibility of keeping myself on a saddle."
>
> "Most extraordinary! Did you not spend your youth in riding schools?"
>
> "Yes, no doubt, Sire, but all my moments were not consecrated to riding… and my health…"
>
> "So then, *monsieur,* your health…"
>
> "Is quite impaired… *Monsieur* de Vendôme…"
>
> "Procured for you a glorious military exploit in Spain," interrupted the king, "and such a regimen is always salutary to young *seigneurs* such as yourself."

---

178   It was a widely held belief that Christopher Columbus inadvertently brought back venereal disease from the New World. The fact is that it was the other way around.

"I must humbly supplicate Your Majesty to be persuaded that I do not complain of the dangers of war."

"Ah, that! Of what do you complain, then?"

"Of victory, Sire, some of whose fruits are just as bitter for me as they are for *monsieur* de Vendôme, and this is what makes a horse..."

"Enough, I can guess the rest. Address yourself therefore to my surgeon Félix, and may that be the end of it. You shall see," added His Majesty as he moved away from the duke, "that I should be the medical consultant for my entire court."

The king's personal medical consultation was not at hand to alleviate the condition of another worthwhile *courtisan*, in this case, a *courtisane*. *Mademoiselle* de Lanclos, so long famous for her beauty, her gallantry and her wit, died on 17 October, at five in the evening, in her house on the rue des Tournelles; she was within touching distance of her 90th year.

Feeling unwell at the moment the sunset was shooting forth its last ray of light, Ninon entreated her chamber woman to keep open the window that she was about to shut.

"I wish," said she, "to see that pale gleam which is extinguished at the same time as I. Isn't the glimmer of that last sunray sweet! I regret that it doesn't take my life away along with it."

She was still speaking when the arrival of the parish priest was announced, guided to the house, no doubt, by some zealously pious soul, and who was come to that old sinner to try to save hers, just one more soul.

"I thank you kindly," said *mademoiselle* de Lanclos to him, "for your actions on my behalf; I believe in the excellence of your mission; I believe in the efficacy of penitence. I would even be quite disposed to give you my confession... but," she added with an imperceptible smile, "not enough time is allotted to me for such an endeavor. Bless me, and may God forgive me."

An instant later, Ninon was no longer of this earth.

We could make a very amusing book based on the archives of Ninon: there are all kinds of wit and sentiment to be had there. In her house were found all sorts of declarations of love, madrigals, love sonnets, love letters, romances, stuck away in all the furniture. From passions contemporary with Louis XIII, to rhymes of more recent vintage. The latest, and most novel, discovered in a drawer perfumed most sweetly, were the quatrains of a boy named *Arouet*. Ninon had predicted that the author would be a man of genius, and this modern Laïs, after having met and entertained this child, after having been charmed by his conversation, amazed by the sparks emanating from his eyes, declared that he seemed called to a brilliant destiny. Since she judged that his father's fortune was limited, she bequeathed to him the sum of two thousand francs with which to buy books. This legacy was faithfully fulfilled.

Zénobe put the book down on his lap. Voltaire's first amorous adventure, and his first remuneration! And that preceding episode about the *duc* de Vendôme and the *prince* de Lorraine. What was that all about? What conquest had Christopher Columbus made that was impure, and what connection did it have with a shared ailment? And why couldn't the *prince* de Lorraine ride a horse? The young librarian had a lot to learn, for he had never seen a book like this one. Even the title was enigmatic.[179] A book which told not of exploits and grand discoveries but of personal illnesses and amorous innuendo, and yet he couldn't put the book down. Were these episodes really eyewitness accounts? Leafing through the book, he caught sight of the name of Charles II, one of the Spanish monarchs whom he loved to despise since he and Louis XIV had uselessly waged war against one another. He was soon to find out something he didn't know about that king.

A month before his death, Charles II had the somber fantasy of visiting the remains of his father, his mother, and of his first wife Marie-Louise d'Orléans. In vain his doctors tried to convince him that the weakness of his constitution would not permit him such a lugubrious spectacle, and that the emotions produced by such an event could in him produce a deathly result. Nothing was able to change the king's determination. The tombs of the three illustrious personages, entombed in the subterranean sepulchers of El Escorial, were uncovered. Charles, supported between the arms of the cardinal Portocarrero and the *conde* de Monterrey and followed by his confessor, slowly made his way towards that place of death. Charles followed the path that by an almost imperceptible incline leads under a long succession of vaults to the tombs of the princes of the house of Spain. His legs rendered weak by an illness of four years trembled under the thin body that they could barely support. A secret terror took hold of the king as he approached the fearsome place he had wanted to visit. Finally they arrived. Twenty bright lamps shone over the spectacle of the mausoleums and lit up the marble figures recumbent among the tombs, making the deceived imagination believe by their trembling light that those cold effigies were alive and moving. A nauseating odor rose up from the three opened coffins, the remains of putrefaction which art may disguise but not prevent.

"Sire," said the confessor. "You wished to see your father Philippe IV. Here he is."

The priest pointed to a tomb next to which Charles had halted. The king bent over the desiccated cadaver and cried out, "Hello, Father, may your soul be enjoying the repose whose expression I notice on your features. Perhaps I have disappointed you in the way I have reigned over the States you bequeathed to me. Say, Father, are you satisfied with me?"

---

179   *Œil-de-bœuf:* a large convex mirror that supposedly hung in Louis XV's antechamber, and that let the observer see more that just what was in front of it; one could also catch glimpses of what was around the corner, off to the sides, on the edges of what was happening.

"Cease, Charles," cried out the confessor, "to interrogate the tomb whose realm is in silence. Its only eloquence is to the eyes, for it is the spectacle of annihilation which it offers to the vanities."

After having kissed the remains of his father, Charles turned to his mother.

"Oh, God," he shouted with a fear which distorted his features. "So much anger still remains on her face! Those empty orbits still seem armed with the rage that you showed when I was about to lose Spain to her enemies. But I didn't lose her. Rest in peace, Mother."

And the unhappy prince made the vaults echo with a smack that he planted on the fleshless cheek of the skeleton.

"There you are, then," continued the king after he turned to face the sarcophagus of Marie-Louise d'Orléans, his long-departed wife. "There's what destruction has left of those charms which used to inebriate my senses…"

"Then, turning around with a convulsive movement, Charles cried out, "Who has spoken of poison?""

The cardinal Portocarrero answered, "Nobody, assuredly," trying to calm the king's agitation. "Sire, in the name of God," he added, "let's leave this place, let's return to the palace."

"No, no," insisted Charles who grew more and more troubled. "I know what I heard… A terrible reproach came out of my wife's coffin. She is right. I should have punished her assassins… I knew them…"

"I beg of you, my king," cried the cardinal, "follow me… Let's get out of here."

"Leave me, leave me," replied the prince whose hair was bristling. "I want to tell Marie-Louise that I adored her, that I wept for her. I am weeping now for her, my tears shall moisten her bones, and…"

At this point, the father confessor took Charles by the arm in readiness to drag him away. "Enough of these mundane memories. King of Spain and of the Indies, remove yourself. The thoughts of sin should not sully this domain."

The king cried out one more time, "Marie Louise… hatred… poison… ah, close my mother's tomb!" before he fell unconscious, exhausted by his sickness and the heart-rending emotions, into a tomb which had made him stumble.

"It's his own," said the merciless confessor coldly. "I know not if in truth he has that much life in him to warrant us removing him from it. Dying in the middle of this saintly place of pilgrimage, his soul would fly away all the purer."

The king was removed, still unconscious, to the palace. Four weeks after this event, Charles II was laid out for all eternity in the tomb that he appeared to have tried out the month before.

Zénobe pried his eyes away from the book in anguish and was surprised to be sitting in a library. He had momentarily become deranged, for he had felt he had been in the mausoleums of El Escorial in Spain.

"What power is this?" he asked out loud. His own voice echoed around the great room. He had only been reading for a few minutes, but already he had learned more about recent history than he had in his whole lifetime. And he had learned of things that were usually not written about. He looked up at the stacks of books overhead climbing up to the ceiling, and suddenly he felt overpowered. How long was it going to take him to assimilate what was in these books? It would never get done. He had read only a few pages of the book he held in his hand. It would take him the rest of the week to read the rest, and then a couple more weeks to read the other volumes of these *Chroniques de l'Œil-de-bœuf.* And then there was the *Encyclopédie.* And the rest of the library at the *hôtel* de Villette that under the direction of the *marquis* was to grow by the week. But the time of his fencing lesson was fast approaching.

He plunged into the book again, coffee arrived, and when the *marquis* d'Argenson returned and offered to take Zénobe to the scroll rooms, the young man had to decline politely because of his fencing lessons.

"Ah, yes," said the old man, "we must not neglect that. In spite of all the wisdom held between these walls, we still need the fencing lessons. Remember, *monsieur* Bosquet, that beneath this library, as beautiful as she may be, remains her previous incarnation, that of the Arsenal, and we must imitate her in that. On the surface, be a gentleman who is erudite, debonaire, gracious, but on the inside be a ruthless primitive who has the power and the stamina and the courage to stand up for his convictions."

Zénobe thought about this lesson all the way to his fencing class.

There, he finally met *monsieur le chevalier* de Saint-George who was come precisely to make his acquaintance, and through him obtain an audience with Voltaire. Not that the *chevalier* needed Zénobe to be introduced to the sage. He would have gained entry into the *hôtel* de Villette on his own merits. Nobody could have denigrated him by saying he lacked the credentials necessary for such an introduction.

"I was Marie Antoinette's harpsichord tutor," he said to Zénobe after *monsieur* de La Boëssière had introduced them. "Until her precious Gluck arrived. That unhappy homesick girl was so tearfully happy to see her old musician friend, I knew... I knew my tutorial days were at an end. Not that I minded. The Queen is such a mediocre pupil. And I was tired, tired, dead tired, of the intrigue and the machinations of the court. Moreover, I had the directorship of the *Concert des Amateurs* to run, and I did not want to see its reputation fall. Since 1775 it has been considered the best orchestra in Europe. And that makes me very proud, you understand?"

What Zénobe could not have known, was that Saint-George was also an *habitué* of other *salons*, notably those of *madame* de Montalembert, of the *marquise* de Chambonas, and of *madame* L'Épine, who had a delightful coloratura voice. *Madame* Elizabeth Vigée-Lebrun, the Queen's portraitist, was also opening her own *salon*, and Saint-George was welcome there. But it was thanks to the influence and patronage of *madame* Charlotte-Jeanne de Montesson, wife of the *duc* d'Orléans, that Saint-George's star rose further: she made him director of her theater and orchestra, the *Concert des Amateurs*, which soon rivaled those of the *Comédie française.* In addition, Saint-George was a mason at the *Loge des Neuf Sœurs* and two other lodges. Sadly, when the King offered Saint-George the directorship of the *Académie royale de Musique*, known as the *Opéra de Paris*, three of the divas there wrote a letter of complaint that they would never work under him. Louis

XVI kept the *Académie* without any director for a year.[180] What Saint-George did not tell Zénobe was that he, Joseph Bologne, *chevalier* de Saint-George, was also known as the Black Voltaire, for the humiliations and the physical beatings he had had to endure, and as the Black Mozart, since the Austrian composer attended a few of Saint-George's concerts in Paris and managed to filch a few melodies and incorporate them into his own compositions.

"Ordinarily, a man of my social standing would not be snubbed by a new *salon*, even one offering the world's most celebrated philosopher," said Saint-George to Zénobe. "However, my life has taught me to build reinforcing columns of support before I try anything new. With this in view, you as the orphan and secretary of Voltaire would most graciously provide such a column, in order to have a personal audience with Voltaire, which I most strongly desire."

For Zénobe it was a shock to meet the *chevalier* de Saint-George. He had already seen, and met, a few Negroes and Mulattoes, but they functioned as servants. When *madame* du Barry, Louis XV's last mistress, came calling on Voltaire a week ago at the *hôtel* de Villette, she brought with her the black servant that her royal lover had given her.[181] On the streets one would often espy dark-skinned postillions and even valets, but Zénobe had never met one dressed as a *chevalier*. Impeccably so. What is more, he treated Zénobe like an equal. Of course, Zénobe remembered, he himself was not dressed as a valet, but as some sort of foreign gentleman.

When the *chevalier* broached the subject of meeting Voltaire, Zénobe most generously answered that he would speak with the philosopher to see if he would be willing to meet Saint-George on the following day.

"*Monsieur* de Voltaire has been feeling tired of late, what with rehearsals of his actors for his play and correspondence with kings. But the visit of one person should do no harm, I think."

"Ah, I thank you indeed, *monsieur* de Bosquet," answered the *chevalier* warmly. "I never had a chance to meet *monsieur* de Voltaire in Ferney, and now this wonderful occurrence has us enthralled: he is in our midst, he is here, and this will be the beginning of a new revolution."

Zénobe was about to correct the *chevalier* de Saint-George's presumption that he was of aristocratic descent—he had no *particule* «de» in front of his family name, but this last word was so shocking that he forgot and let the error stand.

"Revolution?" asked Zénobe.

"Absolutely," came the quick enthusiastic reply. "The French cannot continue in the old way. The rest of the world has moved on, has continued in its mad dash towards the future. But in France, everything is at a standstill, an uneasy standstill. Elsewhere, liberties are granted to or simply grabbed by those who up to now had nothing to grab. Look at England, look at your own country (he meant Sweden), where the people are coming into their own. The aristocrats here have nothing left to infringe upon. Even their time is running out. Liberty is a word that the Americans are teaching to us, and

---

180   Even John Adams knew of Saint-George, and gave an account of him in his diary: "a Mulatto Man, Son of a former Governor of Guadeloupe, by a Negro Woman. He is the most accomplished Man in Europe in Riding, Running, Shooting, Fencing, Dancing, Musick. He will hit the Button, any Button on the Coat or Waistcoat of the greatest Masters."

181   Zamor was from India, and du Barry insisted on dressing him up in outlandish Oriental costumes, with tall bejeweled plumed hats and dangling earrings.

they are teaching us how to take it by force, if need be. They are no longer open to the rapacity of the English king and the English lords: they want to keep their bounty for themselves. Well, the people in France want to keep their meager possessions for themselves. The era of the victim is at a close. You understand? They realize that it is not part of God's divine plan to have to give up a huge percentage of what little they have and share it with the bloated aristocracy and with that parasite on humanity called the Church. Strung out between taxes and tithes, the people have had it. Patience? What's that? Fatalism? A thing of the past."

Zénobe was, for the second time this day, jolted by what he was learning. First by reading, and now by listening. Thank God they were alone, Zénobe thought, because his instincts told him that such a conversation would be dangerous around the scions of noble houses. He noted that Saint-George was not in the least worried if anyone overheard.

"And you think Voltaire had something to do with this changing world," observed Zénobe.

"Absolutely, my dear *monsieur.* He and Montesquieu and Diderot and even that lunatic Rousseau, they have all had a lot to do with these transformations. You think I would have stood a chance to be musical director of a world-famous orchestra twenty years ago? Absolutely not. It is our generation that is going to see real change, and sparks will fly, I assure you. We are going to be witnesses to the eclipse of the old order, and these French *ducs*, *marquis*, and *barons*, they don't have a clue. The ground on which they stand is no longer solid; it has been undermined by Voltaire and his philosophical brothers. Siblings, I should say, for women are finding their voice as well."

Such went Saint-George's conversation with Zénobe. By the time the young imitation gentleman returned to the rue de Beaune, he was filled with ideas about how he would undermine the ground under his hated prince Victor-Amédée III. The respect for the institution that his monarch, that all monarchs, had enjoyed, was eroding. Only fear of their military might was left. Well, military might could be checked, met with an opposing force and eventually overturned. Zénobe was looking at his philosopher hero in a new light: the overturner of the old order. The destroyer of kings. The annihilator of despotism.

But when he spoke to Voltaire about this, the *philosophe* looked at him as if he had gone mad.

"I, squelch the power of the monarchy? I have never said anything of the kind," said Voltaire, his pompom dancing over his head. "You do me a disfavor, *monsieur* Bosquet, to suggest that I have. Tell me, whence come these interpretations?"

Zénobe told Voltaire about his encounter with the *chevalier* de Saint-George at the fencing academy.

"Hmm. I've heard of this young man, son of his father's slave whom he of course could not marry, but whom he brought back to Paris dressed like a queen. His father bought the *hôtel* du Bac whose previous owners were indebted to me. Isn't this *chevalier* de Saint-George involved in music in some way?"

Zénobe gave Voltaire a full report of all he had learned about the *chevalier*, and added that Saint-George wished ardently to meet him.

"I, too, wish to meet this young man who is interpreting my life's work in such a peremptory and revolutionary a manner."

With the interview planned for the following day—the *chevalier* de Saint-George was to follow Zénobe to the *hôtel* de Villette after the fencing lessons—Zénobe set about taking dictation for the sage's correspondence, including a long letter addressed to the *Académie française* about the importance of publishing a new edition of the official *Dictionnaire*, the last one having been published in 1762. The dictionary had to keep up with an evolving language, and the *Académie* had to demonstrate its modernity and justify its existence. Besides, previous editions adhered to the policy of defining only the most elegant, the most exclusive of words, in the knowledge and pride that French was the most rarefied of languages. Voltaire argued that the continued purification of our already precious language would eventually render French useless. He wanted all words defined, all the ugly words, the bastard words of dubious foreign origin, the misbegotten words, the ill-sounding words, to reunite the whole lexicon once again. At the end of his letter, Voltaire generously suggested that he himself was willing to write the definitions of all the words beginning with the letter A.

Zénobe looked at Voltaire to see if he was serious, and discovered that he was. When would they find the time to define all the words starting with the letter A?

At some moment during the composition of this letter, André entered the room with *monsieur* de Voltaire's evening tea. Zénobe looked up quickly from his page and smiled, but André averted his eyes to look at the old man propped up on his mountain of pillows. Zénobe could detect something was amiss, but Voltaire's continued dictation meant that Zénobe could not pause.

By the time Zénobe finally went to bed that night, André, who had preceded him by over an hour, was already asleep. This evening, Zénobe did not keep a candle lit to shed light on more articles of the *Encyclopédie*—he was up to the D's—but blew it out and went immediately to sleep.

Zénobe was witness the following day to a fencing match between Saint-George and the *chevalier*'s friend and former fencing master La Boëssière. It was an exhilarating confrontation, and all the young men of the academy were spellbound. "Hurrahs" sounded out when one of the adversaries seemed to get the upper hand, but it always proved to be momentary, and cries of fright went up when something unexpected happened, and only a deft movement of parry or dodge saved one of the combatants from defeat. The two were evenly matched, although none could know what La Boëssière suspected, that Saint-George would never defeat his master in front of his pupils. Zénobe was quivering in his excitement, impassioned by such talent, such boldness, such manliness. Saint-George was much younger than La Boëssière, and he looked crisp and undaunted in the contest, although his shirt was just as damp as the master's. He was a tall man, and his broad shoulders tapered down to a thin waist, and his buttocks and thighs bulged with the muscles necessary to perform brilliant sequences of lunges, *glissades* and *flèches*. The percussion of the two blades was swift and dynamic, almost as if Saint-George were keeping time to a composition in his mind. After a half-hour of invigorating flurry, as if to an unheard command, both opponents stopped at the same time, breathing heavily and grabbing on to the nearest pupils for support. Loud whoops and applause broke out from the marveling boys. They had enough inspiration to last them through weeks of practice.

Zénobe was the pupil whom Saint-George grabbed for support. Zénobe felt the weight of the *chevalier*'s physicality and felt the heat emanating from his body. The proximity of such tangible primitive power engulfed Zénobe and he stopped applauding to bring both of his arms around Saint-George's torso, as if to bolster him. Zénobe could feel the muscles in the *chevalier*'s abdomen contract hard with laughter.

Several of the younger children were supporting La Boëssière, and a circle of them gathered around their master to cheer him. La Boëssière could not have been happier.

Zénobe followed Saint-George to the washroom. The *chevalier* removed his shirt and undergarments, and hot water, sponges and soap were brought to him, but in order not to get his breeches wet, he removed those as well, and stood there only in his underpants. Zénobe's exhilaration turned to a different kind of energy, and the glistening dark skin of the *chevalier* gave Zénobe's exuberance a broodier character, and he grew silent, as those about him darted around in useful employment tending to the *chevalier*'s ablutions.

A quarter of an hour later, Saint-George, dressed against the cold once again, was walking beside Zénobe towards the quai des Théâtins. The *chevalier*'s unrestrained physical power was not superior to his vivacity in conversation, thought Zénobe, for Saint-George's effusive comments deftly flitted from musical performances to royal authority to the inane administration of the country's economy.

"Aristocrats make the world's worst audiences. They don't listen to us the way the people do. When noblemen and noble ladies are in their boxes, they act as if we were providing them with music as background for their frivolity. The people in the *parterre*, however, know how to listen to musicians. They come to hear us, to enjoy our performance.

"The king is losing his hold on society. No one believes the absurd thought that his touch can cure the sick. It would be comical if it weren't so tragic. Our king is a joke and even his cousin makes sport of him.[182]

"The king is no longer running the country. Cunning individuals use his ignorance and stupidity to operate the day-to-day proceedings, and as they fill their pockets and impoverish the nation, Louis just sells more and more titles which invites more and more people to be parasites on society. Everybody is just selfishly taking and taking without regard for the good of the country as a whole. France has become a public whore to be used and abused. Absolutely! France hides her face in shame."

So ran the conversation until they arrived at the *hôtel* de Villette. It was André who opened the front door for them, but Zénobe observed that his friend showed neither pleasure at seeing him nor surprise at seeing the guest who had accompanied him home. The cold reception was unmistakable. Zénobe had no time to speak with André, for he had to escort the *chevalier* de Saint-George into *monsieur* de Voltaire's boudoir.

The old philosopher was sitting in his *chaise longue* with a book in his hand. He looked up as Zénobe walked in with his new friend and smiled his mischievous smile, full of the sarcasm and impudence that had been his life, but in this day's case softened by a friendliness of the eyes.

"Ah, *voilà mon cher chevalier* de Saint-George. Please permit me to remain on this *chaise*. My doctors have said I must remain supine."

---

182   Louis Philippe Joseph, *duc* de Chartres (and upon his father's death, *duc* d'Orléans), was not Louis' best friend. He thought the king stupid, boorish, and lacking in that imagination, artistry and symbolism so necessary in majestically dressing up the royal façade. He was convinced that he would make a much better king, or at least, not botch the job up as much as Louis was doing.

He stretched out a skinny wrinkled hand that the *chevalier* took as if it were a fragile and saintly relic and brought it up to his lips as he came down on bended knee.

"The doctors' orders are sound, and your continued health is on everyone's lips these days," the *chevalier* said.

Voltaire snorted. "Oh, I would hardly say 'on everyone's lips'. There are plenty of people who would have me dead. Dead long ago and no longer a thorn in their side."

"Those people," responded Saint-George, "do not merit your presence in Paris. The Academicians who affronted you by their absence, those empty-headed ecclesiastics who have shown the least Christian hospitality and charity towards you, do not deserve even an afterthought from their own Savior Jesus Christ. Everything their religion teaches them, they desecrate and insult on a daily basis by their very thoughts and actions. They do not deserve you at all."

Voltaire looked at Zénobe as if to say: Why hadn't you brought the *chevalier* de Saint-George over before today?

"You are most gracious, my kind *chevalier*. Please sit down and watch over an old man in his last days. You, too, Zénobe. Sit."

"Last days? But, *monsieur*, these are the first days. Your inspiring entrance into Paris is your ultimate triumph, it is an initiation into the future, and we are now living through the first days of glorious revolution."

"So my young friend *monsieur* Bosquet has told me. Pray, how is this revolution unfolding?"

The *chevalier* sat bolt upright in his chair to expound on what was apparently a theme close to his heart.

"Up to now, it has been your books, your representatives, which have trickled in to us. Secret tomes, covert pamphlets, carried into Paris in concealed spaces of carriages, under the false bottoms of trunks, wrapped around abdomens under voluminous clothing, to keep out the cold? Perhaps. But more so, to keep out the enemy."

"Oh, I like that metaphor," said the *philosophe*.

"But now you are come unto us, body and soul, to take command, to achieve the usurpation which has been a long time brewing, to bring humanity ineluctably into an improved society wherein men will be judged by who they are and not by what they are."

Voltaire looked kindly at the *chevalier*, and said, "You would have me be the general of your brave new society and I thank you for your generosity and confidence in me. However, look at what I am become. *Anima est forta atqui corpus est debilis.*[183] The way of the future belongs to rapscallions such as you and *monsieur* de Bosquet. It is up to you to continue the battle against *l'Infâme*. All that injustice, all that egotism, all that prejudice, looms between you and that noble future towards which you wish to guide society. But you young people must take over the reins. I can hardly sustain myself over the production of an inconsequential little play, let alone continue to fight the giants who rise up like mountains. I have only ever been but a little mountain stream, which wends its way through pinnacles and valleys, cutting a path for itself, sometimes disappearing under boulders but reappearing here and there to remind people of the way to truth."

"*Monsieur* de Voltaire, you have been a torrent loosening great boulders, causing them to crash down from mighty heights and into the precipices below and break into a thousand pieces."

"Pity those who lived below."

---

183   The soul is strong, but the body weak.

"You dwarf..."

There was a scratch at the door, and upon Voltaire's impatient command, André appeared and said, "*Monsieur l'abbé* Gaultier wishes for permission to see *monsieur* de Voltaire."

The philosopher said in a tone of exasperation, "This *abbé* doesn't choose his moments well. Tell him that I am indisposed. No, wait! Tell him... tell him that I am teaching a lesson on how to annihilate mountains."

André's expression could not have been more quizzical, but all he said was, "*Oui, monsieur* de Voltaire," and left.

"You were saying...?" said Voltaire to Saint-George.

"I've forgotten."

Voltaire looked at Zénobe, but Zénobe had forgotten as well.

André definitely had looked depressed, or indifferent. A suspicion arose in Zénobe that he was the cause of his friend's ill feeling. But he couldn't go to him now. He needed to be involved in this conversation. He searched his memory and remembered what Saint-George was about to tell Voltaire."

"You said, 'You dwarf'."

"Oh, yes. You, *monsieur* de Voltaire, dwarf all those around you. There is no other thinker alive in Europe today who has your combination of perseverance, courage and prestige."

The *chevalier* de Saint-George continued his panegyric in a similar vein, and although Voltaire seemed to enjoy the adulation, he nevertheless was wise enough to be troubled by the furor in this mulatto's voice. History has shown us time and time again that revolution is never an answer. Change, slow and arduous, in fits and starts, with many a false step, now advancing and sometimes reversing, was better than bold revolt. Rebellion always destroyed more than necessary, to the detriment of all adversaries. How many times had revolutionaries harvested only death and chaos, because starting anew was all but impossible. Voltaire thought of all of this, but he was 84 years old, and he was tired, and he did not bring any of this up to Saint-George.

That evening Zénobe made sure that he went to bed at the same time as André. André was indeed upset at him, and Zénobe asked for André's pardon for his neglect and his indifference. He explained that so many things were happening that he barely had time for much. He promised not to read in bed any more. The fencing he would continue since it was an opportunity that he could not pass up. After that, all it took was a short lunge, a parry and a couple of feints, and André was in Zénobe's arms. The *glissade* was sweet, and the two blades clashed with electric discharges, though in Zénobe's imagination the naked muscular body of Saint-George made a few thrusts of appearance, as did the sweet handsome face of the embarrassed Edward Bancroft.

The Wrath of God

In spite of the sweet night André had spent with Zénobe, ensconced in his arms that seemed more muscular since he had taken up fencing, he nevertheless harbored a misgiving upon waking up at dawn. The more he learned about Zénobe's body, the less he knew about his mind. The more he explored him in a physical way, the less he knew him in a spiritual way. The enjoyment he felt when feeling, when caressing his friend's physicality, was counterbalanced by the feeling of sadness, yes, sadness he felt about his ignorance of Zénobe's inner feelings. This feeling of sadness permeated him even as he woke up. The happiness he should have been feeling about having Zénobe at his side and about his promise not to read anymore in bed late at night and consecrate more time to him, was replaced by sadness. It was as if Zénobe were gone on a long voyage that would last for weeks and André was feeling the loneliness of separation, of being left behind. But Zénobe was right there in bed with him. All he had to do was extend his arm and feel the solidity of his body. Why he should feel this melancholy nostalgia with Zénobe present, André could not say. How could he miss Zénobe, and have Zénobe right there? Zénobe really wasn't traversing latitudes and longitudes. André thought that his friend was gone into distant spheres of knowledge, inside his head, and there he could not follow. André wished he could think like a *philosophe*, put thoughts into words, accurate words, and organize those words into a coherent whole. Then he'd understand. He would understand the mysteries of the heart, as explained by the mind. He also wished he had paid more attention in school. The only thing he recalled that could help him this morning was a disembodied snippet from Pascal: "The heart has its reasons which Reason itself knows nothing about." He couldn't glean enough understanding from it to shed light on his current dilemma.

But Zénobe stirred, and André's heart leapt at the realization that his companion was not an automaton. He liked this word he had picked up from the house philosopher. The old man denoted by that a person who goes around living life, going through the motions of everyday existence, without questioning anything. A person who doesn't observe, doesn't think, doesn't try to differentiate between what's a habit and what's a prejudice. Or something like that. In other words, somebody who just accepts everything that society has chosen for him, as opposed to somebody who is more in control and questions everything, and might even refuse to do something or other because he sees the inanity behind it. Zénobe was far from being an automaton. He thought for himself. He was independent. André realized with a jolt that it was this independence, this almost haughty behavior in Zénobe, that made him love him all the more. Then how in God's name could he suppress that independence by making him not read in bed anymore, or order him instead to spend the time with him? There was something unreasonable here. He was going to have to think this through. Moreover, André thought, if there's a vast distance between them, then it's up to him, not to Zénobe, to close this distance. There was a three-year difference in age, after all. He needn't feel inadequate when Zénobe had had a three-year head start. He could start reading the *Encyclopédie* as well. He would read it with the Academy's dictionary beside it, ready to look up any word he didn't know. It would be slow reading, but progression may still lead to progress.

This decision made André feel a lot better, and he nuzzled under the covers between Zénobe's shoulder blades. Zénobe turned around and whispered, "Good morning."

"'Tis a wonderful morning," André whispered back. "Yesterday, you were laughing with Voltaire. The two of you were in stitches. What were you laughing about?"

Zénobe laughed. "That's a strange topic of conversation with which to begin the day."

"Well, I've been thinking about it, and I forgot to ask you last night."

"All right, let's see... Well, Voltaire and I are always laughing about all sorts of things while we converse. What do you remember?"

"I remember nothing. It was all in that gibberish which you call Latin."

"Voltaire and I share many jokes, and frankly, I don't remember in what language they are spoken."

"Well, I know that the *marquis* de Villette must have been part of it because I heard Voltaire call the *marquis* the new Tibulle, taking it for granted that we all knew who the old Tibulle was."

"Ah, that," said Zénobe, and started to laugh anew at the pleasantry from the day before. He then remembered the people sleeping in the other rooms and put his hand on his mouth. André could feel Zénobe's sides shaking.

"That's not very polite, to be enjoying such an amusing story and not share it with me."

Zénobe managed to control himself and explained, "Albius Tibullus was a Latin poet. He was the court poet of the proconsul Marcus Messala, who was a great patron of the arts. Tibulle enjoyed Messala's personal attention, and was dedicated body and soul to him. The poet even accompanied the statesman on military exploits, including dangerous ones to quell disturbances in the Empire, notably one in Aquitaine, which Messala subjugated ruthlessly. Tibulle was there every step of the way. What we don't know exactly is, did Tibulle go along on these expeditions because of his love and gratitude for his master, or, as Voltaire suggested to me yesterday, was he merely a camp follower?"

Zénobe burst out in stifled laughter.

André said incredulously, "That's it, then? That's what is supposed to be that funny?"

Zénobe asked him, "Do you know what a camp follower is?"

"Well, let's see. Someone who follows military camps from battle to battle."

"It's a bit more than that. Yes, following from camp to camp is part of it, but it's usually used to describe nonmilitary people who intend to derive personal gain at the expense of the soldiers, and it's mostly used to identify the prostitutes that move along with the army."

André thought about it for a while. Then he said in disbelief, "You mean to say that Voltaire was calling the *marquis* de Villette a prostitute?"

"Well, in a way, yes."

"But that is shocking!"

"As are all of Voltaire's *bons mots*. But like all of Voltaire's witticisms, this one was also brilliant. 'Camp' in Latin is *castra*. 'To follow' is *comitari*, in the sense of 'to accompany'. Voltaire took the word *comito*, 'I accompany', and changed it to *committo*, 'I commit', and then changed *castra*, 'camp', to *castrare*, 'to castrate'. From camp follower, Villette became a castrator, for his known preferred vice is 'emasculating' his victims, that is, taking them from the rear."

André was completely mystified. "You mean, in a military way? Taking the army from the rear by surprise?"

"It might be by surprise, but it means taking one victim at a time from the rear."

André still couldn't understand.

Zénobe, the patient teacher, explained, "It's when one takes this…" Zénobe guided André's hand to his penis, "and shoves it up here," he said as he patted André on the behind.

André put so much distance between them that he fell off the bed with a thud.

Zénobe, still laughing, pulled himself to the edge of the bed. "André, you have nothing to fear from me! I'm not an emasculator!"

André looked up at his friend and believed him. But he still didn't believe the *marquis* de Villette did things like that. He remembered him lurking in the dark at the Jardins des Tuileries, and his predatory nature became clearer.

From the edge of the bed Zénobe continued his lesson.

"Tibulle has a beautiful elegy on the love for boys. When we resume our lessons, I'll start teaching you Latin with his text. It tells us all about what we do for love."

Maurel caught those last few words as he walked in to wake the boys up, and was not surprised to see them up with the dawn. What did surprise him was André who was not in bed.

"André," he asked, "What are you doing on the cold floor?"

"'Twas Zénobe who pushed me off!"

"I did no such thing!" Zénobe exclaimed, pushing himself off to land on André. "And I will extricate a full apology to keep my honor and veracity intact."

"Oh, no you won't," said André as he laughed.

Maurel's heart gladdened to see his two young wards in the midst of a wrestling match so early in the morning.

A sleepy voice called from the other room, "What's going on over there? It sounds like the Americans giving it to the English!"

Maurel was of a mind not to stop the happy pugilists, but work and responsibility called. "Boys, boys, my sons. We must get ready. *Monsieur* de Voltaire…"

Zénobe's attention instantly focused on Maurel. "*Monsieur* de Voltaire?"

"*Monsieur* de Voltaire will have a tranquil day with no guests, save for whatever philosophical friends show up. André will be posted at the front door, as usual. You, master Zénobe, will take dictation from the *philosophe* until the afternoon meal, and *monsieur* Wagnière will take over when you must leave for your library visit and fencing class. Oh, and master André? There will be a new person coming in today, and every Wednesday hereafter. *Madame la marquise* de Villette and *madame* Denis have hired the services of a hairdresser, a *madame* Lafontaine, who will be arriving at eleven. *Entendu, mes enfants?*"

"*Oui, monsieur* Maurel," answered the boys in unison.

Maurel stayed in their room until the boys' ablutions were over, after which the *maître d'hôtel* felt sufficiently energized to commence his duties. *Madame* Denis had decided that he had best deliver the news to the *marquis* de Villette, along with his morning coffee, that the *marquise* his wife had hired a hairdresser to make weekly visits. He had instructions to emphasize that it was to be only once a week, and not to fail to tell the *marquis* that *mesdemoiselles la chevalière* d'Éon and Bertin received *their* hairdresser twice a week.

All was quiet today, and Voltaire's dictations were calm and subdued. A few personal letters were followed by more definitions from the letter A, and then the *philosophe* had Zénobe read to him a recently mailed *mémoire* on Voltaire's favorite actor, Lekain, who had died just before Voltaire's arrival to Paris. Voltaire was touched and shed a few tears.

When the reading was over, Voltaire told Zénobe, "You know that Lekain had to recant all that he ever said and all that he ever did. His whole life was examined and repudiated by his father confessor. The greatest actor of all time, but to the Church he was an obdurate sinner whose whole life did not amount to a pile of rosary beads. But I know how Lekain felt. And I know that he lied to his confessor. Just to be able to acquire a few square feet of dirt in which to deposit his last remains. How sad. How sad. But let us write to this, what's his name? Théophile Imarigeon Duvernet, to thank him for his *mémoire*. It is small, but it is a work necessary for literature."

Voltaire dictated:

"This old man, who has arrived in Paris excessively sick, is consoled by the letter which *monsieur l'abbé* Duvernet has done him the honor of writing to him. He will be even more consoled if *monsieur l'abbé* were to do him the honor of coming over for a visit. All days are good, as are all times. We can console each other by speaking of Lekain..."

When Zénobe put his quill down, he noticed that Voltaire was still feeling sad. He wished he could change Voltaire's mood by talking about the *marquis* de Villette as Tibulle, but he wished to show no disrespect for Lekain. Zénobe had Voltaire sign the letter, sealed it, and asked him if there would be anything else.

"No, my son, thank you. Go to the Arsenal. I think I'll close my eyes for a moment before I call for Wagnière."

"'Till this afternoon, then, *monsieur. Au revoir.*"

He went upstairs to Maurel's room to change to his Swedish gentleman's attire, and stopped for a bit of dinner at the kitchen before he left for his afternoon tasks. He didn't even see Maurel before he left. Exiting the *hôtel* de Villette by the front door, he gave a quick good-bye kiss to André. He noticed that there weren't any people milling about on the *quai*. How disheartening, he thought, that even a momentous occurrence such as Voltaire's arrival in Paris must in the end peter out.

An hour later at the Arsenal Library in the tranquil solitude of his reading, faraway insistent thuds echoing from some cavernous distance made him sick to his stomach. He knew they were for him. By the time the *marquis* d'Argenson's doorman had come to him, he had already put away the book he had been reading high up on a shelf.

"Your presence, *monsieur,* is required at the front door. A master André is here bidding you follow him to the *hôtel* de Villette."

"*Merci, monsieur.*"

As Zénobe followed the valet along the stately halls to the faraway front door, walking not running, his mind was already racing over the possibilities: all centered on Voltaire. The philosopher had fainted, he had fallen, he had not woken up from his nap. Zénobe should have never left him. Voltaire had been feeling so low. He had shed tears. Zénobe decided right then and there that Voltaire would have a sepulcher. Zénobe would fight the Church, he would enjoin the other philosophers to fight with him, and they would give Voltaire a proper burial so his body would be protected from the snow and rain and the wild dogs. *Please, let him be still alive so I can tell him that his remains, so dear to all of us, will have a proper burial.*

One look at André's face and Zénobe knew his worst fears had become reality. They spoke at a trot.

"What happened, André?"

"*Monsieur* de Voltaire is bleeding from the nose and mouth."

"Is he alive?"

"Yes, but he's very frightened. He's called for *docteur* Tronchin. He's also called for *l'abbé* Gaultier. Philippe was sent for Tronchin. Henri was sent for Lorry. I was sent for you."

"Who's with him now?"

"Everybody. *Madame* Denis. *Madame la marquise. Monsieur* Maurel. Wagnière has been with him all the time. A gentleman who has been living in the *hôtel* unbeknownst to us is also in his room. *Monsieur le marquis* is the only one who has not been at home. He took the phaeton to go pay a visit to *monsieur* Franklin in Passy."

"How is Voltaire feeling?"

"Not well. Frightened. The bleeding won't stop. It's like a spigot. If he reclines, he starts to asphyxiate. He is bent over with a mountain of sheets beneath him. The household is running out of linen."

By the time they arrived at the quai des Théâtins there was already a crowd forming. Tronchin's carriage was in front of the side entrance, but they found the gate locked. They were forced to run back and ram their way through the crowd to the front door where they had to announce themselves before the door opened. It was Philippe posted there, looking very nervous. The boys slipped in and had to help Philippe force the door shut against the crowd who was yelling for news of Voltaire.

The door to Voltaire's bedroom was open and Sylvie, Suzanne, Marianne, and even *madame* Denis' *femme de chambre*, Hélène, were scurrying in and out with sheets and towels drenched in red. Zénobe looked down on the parquet floor and followed drops and streaks of blood all the way to Voltaire's bed. André was close behind him.

Voltaire was on his stomach, his faced pressed against the linen. One of his feet was raised over a basin, and Tronchin had just finished bleeding him. The pool of red glistened as the doctor handed it out to no one in particular for somebody to take it away. Zénobe was closest and he took it. Behind the bed, huddled in the *petite ruelle*, were *madame* Denis, *la marquise* de Villette, Wagnière, and the man who had been in the *marquis* de Villette's bedroom the other day, whom Zénobe took to be their fellow resident. They were all silent and pale as ghosts. The only voice heard was Tronchin's.

"My warnings could not have been clearer. Two weeks ago I said that this whole trip was a great error. Traveling from Ferney to Paris in the middle of winter. A schoolboy could have expressed the folly in that. What possessed…"

Tronchin cut off his sentence in a strangle of vexation.

Voltaire raised his face from the linen. Zénobe flinched. The whole bottom half of his face, from below his eyes to his chin and under his neck was a mask of red. "We've had no visitors this past half-week," he started to say in a voice so hoarse and so plaintive it broke Zénobe's heart.

"Silence," ordered Tronchin. "You must not speak. In order for the blood to coagulate and staunch the flow, you must not even move. Consider it a miracle that I don't have to perform a tracheotomy. You are such a recalcitrant patient, have always been, but now your very life hinges on your ability to keep silent and immobile, although I imagine that for you such a thing is a physical impossibility!"

Zénobe did not like the way Tronchin was speaking to his patient. The least he could do was come to his defense.

"We had a very quiet morning, *monsieur le docteur.* A few dictations, no visitors, no commotion at all."

He didn't mention the tears Voltaire had shed for his friend Lekain.

The doctor didn't seem to have heard him. But Voltaire raised his head again to look at Zénobe and with his eyes told him that he was happy he was there. There was another look as well, saying *Look at what's happening to me.*

Wagnière came to Voltaire's defense as well. "Same thing this afternoon. It was very quiet. We were in the middle of a dictated letter, when I heard silence, then a cough, and when I looked up from the page I saw the blood pour forth from *monsieur* de Voltaire's nose and mouth. 'Look, I'm bleeding,' was all he managed to say."

At this moment, a gentleman walked into the room, strode decisively to Voltaire's bed, observed the scene for a few moments, and took the basin from Zénobe's hands. He swirled the blood in it and brought it to his nose and sniffed.

"It's not an esophageal hematemesis," he announced.

Tronchin looked around and greeted the stranger. "Ah, welcome to the bedside of our celebrated patient. You must be *docteur* Lorry."

"And you must be *docteur* Tronchin. I have been following your work since your move from Geneva two years ago."

"And I yours, for a lot longer than that, I must say. Your research has traveled far and wide."

"What have we got here? Hemoptysis?"

"Right you are, as I believe as well. It's not of the pharynx or the esophagus. Without doubt it's a bronchial tumor that has produced a pulmonary hemorrhage. Blood flow has been quite copious, as you can see."

"We'll need to rule out a fistula. But whatever the case, these phthisics usually run themselves out all by themselves. We can, however, palliate the symptoms with an emollient fumigation, don't you think?"

"Yes, yes, either that or a linctus."

"And if the patient is deprived of sleep, an opiate julep is in the offing."

Docteur Lorry walked over to the head of the bed, ignoring the small group clustered in the *petite ruelle.*

"*Monsieur* de Voltaire. Do not speak or make unnecessary movements. You are to sleep on your stomach tonight. We will place boards around your sides so you don't move. Someone will stand watch over you during the night to make sure you remain motionless and prone."

To the people behind the bed he said, "Have you someone who can remain vigilant throughout the night?"

Zénobe took a step forward to volunteer, but so did André behind him, and Suzanne and Hélène who happened to be in the room when this was said, also came forward.

"*Oui, docteur* Lorry," ventured *madame* Denis, tears in her eyes. "We have a whole household of people who will do as you bid."

"Good," responded Lorry. And for the first time, he touched his patient. Resting a hand on Voltaire's shoulder, he said, "See, *monsieur* de Voltaire? You have many people who care for you and will nurse you back to good health. As for your salvation, another person is come to see you about that, but under no circumstance are you to whisper a word or make the slightest gesture."

To make sure everybody understood this last command, he turned to the whole room and repeated, "Under no circumstance. Understood?"

Everybody nodded.

The newcomer was an *abbé*, dressed in black, but not tonsured. He, like all, had to wait until the two doctors were finished with their patient and had left precise instructions as to the number, type and length of medications to be given to their august patient. But august or not, he was primarily a patient now, and these instructions had to be carried out to the letter.

When the doctors were finally gone, the *abbé* started to speak.

"My name is Tersac. I am come at the express wishes of his Most Illustrious and Most Reverend Lord the archbishop de Beaumont. I am the curate of Saint Sulpice, the parish church to which the *hôtel* de Villette belongs, although you could not guess it from the visits we have *not* received from the residents of said *hôtel* at the said church. As a matter of fact, none of the residents here has ever set foot inside any of the surrounding churches, not even the Église des Théâtins, whose territory borders on your garden and whose bells announcing the hours of prayer could certainly not pass by unnoticed. If it weren't for the wall, some of you could roll right out of bed on Sunday and land more or less at the altar. *D'hôtel en autel.*"

He laughed at his own wit ("from *hôtel* to altar"), but nobody else made a sound.

"I have heard," continued Tersac, "from trustworthy sources, that in this house, nobody, absolutely nobody, not the masters, not the servants, not the simplest little scullery maid, not the humblest postillion, makes the sign of the cross."

He paused as if waiting for an answer, but when none came he continued to speak with mounting zeal.

"But let me turn from the godless inhabitants of this place to what brings me here today. It is this man in front of us who on this day and in our presence is laid low and bows down in front of the Holy of Holies. But I say unto you, brothers, I say, live under the influence of the Spirit of God, only then will you not be subject to obey the egotistical penchants of the flesh. For the penchants of the flesh are opposed to those of the Spirit, and the penchants of the Spirit are opposed to those of the flesh."

He moved throughout the room, looking at each person in the eyes as he spoke, finally coming to a halt in front of Voltaire.

"One knows very well to which actions the flesh leads: debauchery, impurity, obscenity, idolatry, witchery, hatred, quarrels, jealousy, wrath, envy, divisions, sectarianism, rivalries, drunkenness, gluttony, and other things of the same kind. I warn you, as I have warned countless others, those who act in this manner will not inherit the kingdom of God. But hearken to what the Spirit produces: love, joy, peace, patience, goodness, kindness, faith, humility and self-control. Those who are in Jesus Christ have crucified within them the flesh, with its passions and egotistical penchants. Since it is the Spirit that makes us live, let us be lead by the Spirit.

"You, *monsieur*, who lie low and are bent down by your sins, who dare not show your face to the Holy of Holies, who must in effect hide your face which is the color of shame, for shame is come out of you spouting forth as from a fountain to color this boudoir, nay, this whole dwelling with the color of shame—red, red like the color of the apple, the fruit of all evil, of the fall from grace, of the ousting from Eden, you, *monsieur*, who have not, and have never had, shame, today you are covered in it. Have you no brains, *monsieur* de Voltaire, you whose very name is accompanied by reverential cries of genius, who throughout the civilized lands have been named the very paradigm of reason and intelligence, tell us please, where those intellectual talents have brought you today. Are you to tell us, with your usual sarcasm and mockery, that you do not have the brains, *monsieur*, to comprehend that it is the wrath of God which has you locked up in its jaws, which will chew you up, which will crush you, unless you wake up and realize that you must recant? You must take back all you have ever said and written, all those words you have ever spoken and written which have wounded the Church. But hearken! All is not lost. All does not have to be lost irretrievably and forever. The proof of the immeasurable power of pardon of the Church is that She loves you, in the same way that Jesus Christ loves you. Your sins against your mother Church and against God the Father and the Son and the Holy Spirit are like mere raindrops in the vastness of the sea, and you are forgiven, my son, if only you recognize your errant ways. Please wake up, wake up before it is too late, for even the power to pardon must yield to the Father of Time. Please, do not quit this life for an eternity of hellfire. A few words from you now, in which you humbly show us that you are remorseful, will save you from eternal damnation. Trade a few moments of your life now to allow yourself an eternity at the right hand of God. Surely, *monsieur*, you must wake up!"

Tersac was looking towards the heavens, his voice trembling, his hands beseeching the Lord.

Voltaire's face rose from the towels heavy and sour. He was tired of tasting blood in his mouth and of hearing these words from the curate.

"I want to speak with the *abbé* Gaultier. It was he who initiated the efforts of my salvation, and it is he who is going to receive the credit of its completion, not some interloper who is ignorant of the situation of my soul."

Wagnière bent down to stop Voltaire from talking. "Please remember what the doctors said: 'No talking!'"

But to Zénobe, Voltaire's words were instructions enough to escort the priest out of the bedroom and all the way out the front door. He was still in full gentleman's costume, and his foil proudly peeked from under his coat. The *marquis* de Thibouville apparently had the same thought, for he moved around from the *petite ruelle* and walked over to Tersac's side. Zénobe was already flanking the priest on the other side. Each took an elbow and pressed. But Tersac was not going to go quietly.

"Will you be responsible for Voltaire's soul? Are you willing to have his spirit plunged into eternal damnation, never to receive the soothing balm of forgiveness of God the Father?"

Thibouville answered, "You heard the man. He wishes for *l'abbé* Gaultier to be sent."

"Who is this *abbé* Gaultier? I am the curate of Saint Sulpice. I have been sent by His Excellency the archbishop..."

Thibouville retorted, "Well, the *abbé* has been sent by a higher authority than that."

Tersac was astonished. "His Holiness the Pope?"

Thibouville smiled. "No, higher. God himself."

The parish priest let out an explosive puff of air. "You jest with me, and I am being as serious as death."

Thibouville and Zénobe pressed a little harder, and they managed to budge the recalcitrant priest towards the door.

"Please," said Thibouville smiling all the time, but with a smile that hardly concealed the gritting of his teeth.

"*Monsieur*," added Zénobe, mimicking the older man's smile. "This way. The patient needs repose and silence."

"He will never have repose nor silence. Hell is full of a thousand demons who fill the flames with the screams of torment. And the proper way to address me, young man, is *mon père*, not *monsieur*..."

Tersac's voice trailed out of the bedroom and soon was heard no more. *Madame* Denis collapsed on Voltaire's buttocks and started to sob. Voltaire could not turn around to see her, but sent one of his hands to try to console her, but his hand couldn't find her. It was the *marquise* de Villette who grasped her benefactor's hand and held it tightly.

By the time d'Alembert, Diderot and Condorcet arrived Voltaire was sleeping, wedged between the two halves of a door that had been sawn in half for this purpose. They sat around, speaking in soft voices, finding solace in stories from the past. Zénobe was going to watch over him at night, with André sleeping in the room as well, and they both listened with intent interest to the *philosophes*' stories of when Voltaire was young. There were several glimpses of *madame* du Châtelet, Émilie, who had been the love of Voltaire's life.

After the three *philosophes* had left, later that evening, *mademoiselle* d'Éon dropped by the *hôtel* de Villette, wishing to speak with Zénobe. Maurel allowed her in, for she was Zénobe's benefactress. He brought tea for them in the empty *salon*. D'Éon told them that the news around Paris was of Voltaire's illness, and that wild rumors were flying about. They told her the true version of events, and she seemed relieved.

"I once had one of my dragoons in such dire shape. He had been shot in the lung. You would have thought he would have bled completely out, after seeing him bleed so much and for so long. But he made a complete recovery. Ah, the powers of nature, *messieurs*, are breathtaking."

And she took a deep breath of astonishment, raising her outstretched hands in front of her, then gave a giggle.

"I stopped by *monsieur* La Boëssière's to see if master Zénobe were enjoying his fencing lessons and finding them profitable. But *monsieur* La Boëssière was astonished that his star pupil had not come today, telling me that up until now you had not missed a single day, including Sunday. But then we found out about Voltaire's indisposition and we understood why you did not go. But do not worry. *Monsieur* La Boëssière will still be there when you get back. He speaks quite highly of you. You will go far, he says, in fencing. But I wish to add my own thoughts on this: you *will* go far, in everything."

Maurel was beaming more than Zénobe was. Zénobe felt more relief in his worries than pride in his fencing skills after hearing the story of the *chevalière*'s wounded dragoon and hearing Voltaire's condition referred to as an "indisposition".

That's all it was, an indisposition. He had to go back to Voltaire, and he took leave of the *chevalière*. In Voltaire's bedroom, André's expression told him that the status of the patient was unchanged.

It was Maurel who escorted *mademoiselle* back to the front door, thanking her for her visit and for the fencing lessons for master Zénobe.

"Well, I'm still getting over Rousseau's affront, and I shall always remember your young man's kindness and the alacrity with which he came to my rescue. He really put up quite a confrontation and put Rousseau in his place. That Swiss person might be a great thinker and a great writer, but master Zénobe cut him down to size. And now, and now I have a new appreciation for *monsieur* de Voltaire's works. I find that I am turning completely around. Good evening, *monsieur* Maurel."

Maurel handed her over to her coachman who was to escort her through the crowd. After the door was closed, he heard the *chevalière*'s booming masculine voice beseeching the crowd to disperse. No need to be milling about so late in the evening. *Monsieur* de Voltaire was in a guarded state, but was definitely not moribund. She told them of Voltaire's hemorrhage and of her wounded dragoon in the Seven Years' War, making them laugh about bullets reaching their intended addresses but not necessarily dispatching the victim to a different state of being.

Maurel was impressed by d'Éon's ease in crowd control.

By the time the *marquis* de Villette came back home, the crowd in front of his *hôtel* had already dispersed. Having heard nothing out in Passy about the earlier state of emergency, he spoke at length to his *maître d'hôtel* about his disappointment in not finding Edward Bancroft at the *hôtel* de Valentinois where Franklin was residing. The *marquis* complained that the elder statesman had held him for over an hour in order to speak of Voltaire. Franklin thanked Villette profusely for the case of champagne he had brought with him, but he nevertheless thought that neither he nor Mr. Bancroft would need any more wine, considering that they had a source of fine wines from Tonnerre, thanks to a brother-in-law of the *chevalière* d'Éon.

Since he saw none of the agitation in the house, the *marquis* was not alarmed by the news of Voltaire's hemorrhage. He was peeved, however, by the fact that two doctors had been called in. He was still bothered by his wife having a hairdresser come in every week. But all this paled in comparison to what Maurel told him next. He became very alarmed by the news that the *marquis* de Thibouville had come down from his bedroom.

"Why did he have to do that?" asked the *marquis* de Villette as Maurel helped him out of his clothes.

"It was a matter of some urgency, *monsieur le marquis*. The whole house was in an uproar."

"Now what am I to do? *Madame la marquise* doesn't even know Thibouville. How am I going to explain him, and the fact that he sleeps under this roof? I don't want her suspecting anything, nor do I want that niece of Voltaire's, who has most definitely inherited some of the inquisitiveness of his family, to stick her nose into places where she shouldn't. She always wants to know everything, even if it has nothing to do with her uncle. I certainly don't want *her* to come to any conclusions!"

"*Madame* Denis was too fraught with worry to have even acknowledged the *marquis* de Thibouville's existence, *monsieur*." Maurel didn't tell his master that Denis and Thibouville were standing elbow to elbow by Voltaire's bedside for most of the afternoon and evening.

"You may recall," continued Maurel, "that the *marquis* de Thibouville and *monsieur* de Voltaire have been friends ever since *monsieur le marquis*' youth. Say that the *marquis* de Thibouville is staying at the *hôtel* de Villette on account of *monsieur* de Voltaire."

"Ah, brilliant. Yes, that's it, that's it, Maurel. You're a genius."

"*Merci beaucoup, monsieur*," said Maurel, who couldn't have agreed more.

The next day, since they came to the *hôtel* de Villette at precisely the same time, there was in the front vestibule a repeat dance à deux between the red *duc* de Richelieu and the black *abbé* Gaultier. This time, however, André was ready, and proceeded to give preference to the *duc*'s entry first, although the grandee took matters into his own hands and said in his noble baritone, "I'll only be a minute with Voltaire," and was gone in a scarlet flash unescorted to the philosopher's bedroom. André, walking slowly, escorted the *abbé* who followed patiently in his flowing black robe. By the time they were in Voltaire's bedroom, the *duc* was on his way out.

"See," he said. "I needed but a moment. I'll show myself out."

Madame Denis was in the room with Voltaire, along with an old friend of her family, the *marquis* de Villevieille, and her brother *l'abbé* Mignot, who had been called in from his parish in the abbey of Scellières, in Champagne near Troyes. *Madame* Denis beckoned to André who walked over to her, and she slipped a vial into his hands.

"Tell Zénobe to keep this with him at all times," she whispered. "It is from the *duc* de Richelieu who has instructed that it be used only at night, to make my uncle sleep better. And go get Wagnière."

André went upstairs to call Wagnière, then went to the servants quarters behind the *hôtel* to wake Zénobe up, who also had wanted to be present when the *abbé* Gaultier arrived. He also gave the vial and the instructions to Zénobe. His friend looked so befuddled and agitated at the same time that André wanted to fling his arms around him and comfort him. But there was no time. He helped Zénobe get into his butler's uniform and they ran across the garden to the house.

In Voltaire's bedroom, they found Gaultier already warmed up with tremulous fervor and holding forth on the reckoning of time. Time was running out. God was granting Voltaire a little more time to make his peace with Him before having to face Him on the Day of Judgment.

"And why have you not signed the letter of repentance that I drafted for you? In it I do not ask you to relinquish your erroneous ideas. In it I do not ask you to take back your disrespectful tone against God and the Realm. God realizes that you had a playful nature, and you wished to embellish your writing with comedy and amusement. Why, even Molière asked the artist to join the agreeable to the useful. Your wit made people laugh, it added merriment to your diverting texts. You didn't want your readers to fall asleep. God realizes what you were after, since even a king has his fool. But more than for your humor, God is wont to forgive you even for your errors. *Errare humanum est.* Isn't that what we say? To err is human. How is it possible to know the truth of the universe and of the Maker who brought it, and us, forth from the darkness? Why, even you philosophers mention the futility of ever knowing all that is, and you yourselves fall into disarray and disagreement about the interpretations of the unknowable. Why don't you please sign the letter and be done with it?"

Voltaire, looking haggard and pale, instructed Wagnière with a gesture to produce the *abbé*'s letter, and then to read it out loud.

While Wagnière read, the *abbé*'s lips moved in unison with those of Voltaire's secretary.

> I, François Marie Arouet, dit Voltaire, having come to the end of my life,
> and having the proper volition and disposition of spirit, do solemnly repent
> of my irreligiosity and my disrespect for the Catholic Church, and, in the
> spirit of reconciliation and penitence, regret all opinions and judgments
> which I have held throughout my life and which are contrary to the teach-
> ings of Jesus Christ our Lord and Savior, and abhorrent to His representa-
> tives on earth. I recognize and confess my sins, and renounce them until
> death.

After the reading was over, the *abbé* Gaultier was so excited that he sang out, " 'If thy eye causes you to sin, tear it out. It is better to enter into the kingdom of God with one eye, than to remain with two eyes and be cast into hell fire.' Will you take confession, my son?"

Voltaire beckoned Wagnière to come closer, and whispered into his ear. Wagnière stood up and said, "*Monsieur* de Voltaire does not feel it is proper to mix his own blood with that of Christ's."

Gaultier was abashed.

Voltaire again beckoned Wagnière. "*Monsieur* de Voltaire has a question for you. Who exactly are you?"

Gaultier responded breathlessly, "I am a chaplain at the Hospital of the Incurables, rue de Sèvres.[184]"

Voltaire transmitted another question. "Have you been sent by the archbishop Christophe de Beaumont?"

Gaultier answered, "No, I have not."

Voltaire, again through Wagnière, asked for a piece of paper and a quill, and asked everybody to leave the room.

Everyone followed his order. Only the *abbé* remained in the room with the *philosophe*.

But Wagnière did not close the door behind them completely. His reasons became clear when he kneeled to eavesdrop on the conversation inside. *Madame* Denis and *l'abbé* Mignot also lent an ear.

In a few minutes, the *abbé* called for the group to come back inside, saying, "*Monsieur* de Voltaire has given me a little declaration here which doesn't signify much, but I would be pleased nonetheless if you were to sign it as witnesses."

He showed the page written in a shaky scrawl. Wagnière took it and read out loud, *I die adoring God, loving my friends, not hating my enemies, hating superstition. 1778 Fev.*

Monsieur le marquis de Villevieille and *monsieur l'abbé* Mignot signed it without hesitation.

Gaultier, understanding that Voltaire was not going to sign the letter he had prepared for him, left with the fifteen-word statement that the philosopher had written in his own hand and signed, but asked Wagnière to keep the first, in case Voltaire should change his mind later.

After that, the *hôtel* de Villette entered into a period of mournful quiescence. That evening, Zénobe gave Voltaire his first few drops of the opium that the *duc* de Richelieu had left for him. It did have the desired effect, for the philosopher slept in such a motionless state that frequently Zénobe would have to get close to him and verify that he was still breathing.

---

184   This hospital still exists: *l'hôpital* Laennec.

André returned to the servants' quarters at night, while Zénobe stayed up to watch over Voltaire. They would trade places at dawn. Zénobe would get up at noon, have his first meal of the day, then go to the Arsenal library and to his fencing lessons. The only time he and André would have together was late at night in Voltaire's bedroom, after the rest of the house had fallen asleep. They would barely talk. Keeping watch on a dying philosopher was a somber business, but sometimes they would sit together in the same armchair and be at peace in quiet solitude.

As for Voltaire, his voice was silenced, but not his pen. In aphonic whispers he continued dictating letters to correspondents, letters of gratitude to those who inquired after his health, letters to his publisher Panckoucke, and, for his dream dictionary, to which the *Académie française* had not yet given its official approval, more entries of words beginning with the letter A.

The Show Must Go On

Zénobe woke up in the dark. He couldn't remember where he was, and when he glanced to where the window was supposed to be, he saw only darkness. Then he remembered he was in Voltaire's room where the curtains were shut up tight. He didn't remember if André were there as well, or if he had gone back to the servants' quarters. It was very quiet, and he could hear only his own breathing. But his breathing seemed inordinately loud. Rhythmic and loud. It was peaceful as well, and he could have gone back to sleep. But he realized that he was holding a book in his hands, and both his hands were pressed over his breast. That's odd, he thought. He had not been reading that evening when he blew out the last candle. He brought the book up as if he were going to attempt to read its title, but he realized that the darkness would render that action completely useless. His book hit something like wood and made a thump, and then Zénobe realized what was happening. It was André who had put the book in his hands at the last minute, wanting Zénobe to hold on to something after he was gone. Zénobe remembered that he had died and that he had been placed in a coffin. Everybody had thought that Voltaire was going to die first, but Zénobe had preceded him, and since he was just a butler-librarian, the Church had allowed him a coffin and a burial on hallowed ground, but now there was a problem. He wasn't dead. He dropped the book and felt around him, and he could feel the box wherever he placed his hands. It was dark and silent, save for his breathing which came faster now, but he tried to slow it down so as not to use up all the oxygen at once. His mind raced. But what if oxygen is getting in, and I won't suffocate to death? I'll starve to death, all alone in this box. No, I'll die first from lack of water, a slow agonizing death that might take days. If I don't die of lunacy first. His heart thumped hard in his chest. He had the thought that maybe there were still people around who could hear him if he cried out. He opened his mouth to speak, but no sound would come out. He tried to scream, but could not. He tried to pound his feet on the coffin, but his limbs were strangely paralyzed. He could do nothing to let anyone outside his coffin know that he continued to live, entombed in darkness and in silence.

His attempts to scream resulted in a hoarse moan and it was that, his own squeaky moaning that woke him up. He realized with a start that he was in Voltaire's room, on the *chaise longue,* and the candle had gone out. He sat up, his heart pounding, and tried to remember where the candle was. He stood up heavily and went to the table where he lit it, then a second, and a third.

He glanced over at Voltaire ensconced between the two halves of a door, but could make nothing out. He walked closer to him and could see the philosopher's rhythmic breathing.

Zénobe felt horrified, and guilty. He was not supposed to fall asleep while he was standing guard over Voltaire. He needed to be vigilant. Were anything to happen, he was supposed to run upstairs to wake up *mesdames* Denis and Villette and *monsieur* Maurel.

He sat down in a *bergère* and tried to quell his nerves by thinking of the articles he had last read in the *Encyclopédie*. What he really needed was André, but he dared not traverse the whole first floor of the house, then the garden and the row of servants' bedrooms. He might wake somebody. Besides, he wouldn't be able to stay long with André. And what if something happened to Voltaire while he was gone? He got up and went to Voltaire's bed again. He carefully removed the half-door behind the *philosophe* and placed himself there instead, on top of the covers. Slowly and carefully he encircled Voltaire's torso with his free arm. Voltaire did not wake up. His rhythmic breathing calmed Zénobe and dispelled his thoughts of death. While the old man was still alive, Zénobe knew he had something to do. He vowed to protect and defend Voltaire from all his enemies, and they were legion. While Voltaire was alive, Zénobe had a definitive purpose and responsibility: to take care of him. Zénobe realized that it was Voltaire, through Maurel, who was taking care of him here in Paris, and as one of his secretaries, he would be no ingrate. The *hôtel* de Villette was a little pocket of air, and everybody inside breathed the oxygen of Reason. Voltaire was providing them this oxygen. After a few minutes, Zénobe felt much better, the last remaining images of fright having been chased out of his mind. He carefully got out of bed, replaced the half-door, and for the rest of the night, paced around the bedroom.

Irène was on schedule to have its first performance on the 15th of March. Until then, the household would be quiet and serene. No noise was allowed in and around Voltaire's boudoir. The philosopher's visitors were curtailed to the bone: only *messieurs* d'Alembert, Condorcet, and Diderot, *le duc* de Richelieu, and *docteurs* Tronchin and Lorry were allowed in, and then stayed only for a minimum of time. Tronchin had stipulated, under pain of abandoning his patient, that nobody speak to the old philosopher on the topics of literature, politics, and above all, religion. For this reason, no ecclesiastic personage was allowed entry, leading to the dolorous disillusionment of the *abbé* Gaultier, who would come by every day in the ardent hope that God would have given somebody in that household the light by which to see the blinding truth. But everybody at the *hôtel* de Villette remained perfectly blind.

Le marquis de Thibouville, now that his secret was out, and because there were no longer masses of visitors to aggravate his agoraphobia, also came into the philosopher's room from time to time for quiet chats and to read to Voltaire from the plays and novels that were currently being performed and published. Voltaire did not take well to most of them, considering them too mired in the business of the rabble, and not representative enough of the classical world of grand mythology and sublime history. He would wave his hand in a certain way in order to have Thibouville skip to the next act or to the next chapter, and if the hand wave was dismissive enough, to the next book. Beaumarchais' plays seemed to interest Voltaire, for with these works he asked not to skip a single page, and during the readings would raise his eyebrows and cluck his tongue on his palate, although it was difficult to say if it were out of sensing a delicious new taste in literature or of harboring misgivings about this new playwright who fearlessly baited the aristocracy.

Zénobe, then, had more time during the day and went back to his own readings, visits to the Arsenal library (where the *marquis* d'Argenson came by for a daily report on Voltaire's state of health), and to his fencing lessons at La Boëssière's academy (where he continued to consort with future *marquis* and *ducs*, and where he crossed paths with *le chevalier* de Saint-George from time to time). Zénobe and André even had time to get back to André's lessons, and they also started to practice fencing at home, thanks to *monsieur* Maurel who purchased a foil for André. They would practice in the garden where they had much space and could make as much noise as they wished. *Monsieur le marquis* de Villette would look down longingly at them. Above his bedroom window, unbeknownst to him, *monsieur le marquis* de Thibouville would also observe the bouts of fencing.

It was during this time that erroneous reports of Voltaire's full confession to either Gaultier or Tersac were being bruited about Paris. A few reached the *hôtel* de Villette, Zénobe having heard one of them by way of the *chevalier* de Saint-George. Saint-George believed him when he asseverated that nothing could be further from the truth. But the damage was being done, and gossip was as difficult to extirpate from within society as superstition. Voltaire's supposed confession and disavowal of his philosophy went something along the following lines:

> This 26th of February (or 2nd of March, etc.), I the undersigned, François Marie Arouet de Voltaire, residing in Paris at the house of *monsieur le marquis* de Villette, Écuyer, *Seigneur* de Ferney, Semaise and other places, *Gentilhomme ordinare de la chambre du Roi*, royal historiographer, one of the forty of the *Académie française*, etc., declare that, finding myself attacked, for four days (or a week, etc.), by the vomiting of blood, at the age of eight-four years (eighty-three years, eighty-five years), and not having been able to render myself to church, *monsieur le curé* of Saint-Sulpice, in whose parish I find myself, having had the charity of adding to his good works[185] that of sending to me *monsieur l'abbé* Gaultier, I have confessed to him; and if God disposeth of me, I die within the communion of the Holy, Catholic, Apostolic and Roman Church, into which I had the joy of being born, hoping for divine forgiveness which She might deign to pardon my sins; and I declare that if I ever scandalized the Church, I humbly beg God's pardon and Hers. In faith of which, I have signed in the presence of *monsieur* l'abbé Mignot, my nephew, and *monsieur le marquis* de Villevieille, my friend, on the same day and year as above. Signed, Voltaire.

---

185   Sic: The charity belonged to the *curé*, not to Voltaire; this rhetorical meandering, and other errors, certainly prove that Voltaire could never have written lines such as these. Even moribund, Voltaire could never have committed the sin of bad writing.

Supposedly, according to the rumors, Voltaire's philosopher friends, d'Alembert, Condorcet, Diderot, and Grimm were all outraged by this confession, and they rushed to Voltaire's sickbed to reproach his weakness. The word 'coward' was overheard, but it was not known which of the four said it. Voltaire ordered them all out, crying out that his father in 1683 had been one of the carriers of Saint Geneviève's bier, and that the patron saint of Paris would forgive the calumny and false impiety that had been heaped on him for all his life. The philosophers were consternated. As they left, they agreed that a sad day had indeed arrived which saw them in disarray and without a leader.

These reports, and others of their ilk, made Zénobe sick to his stomach. They also made him last longer and fight harder during fencing practice.

None of this was ever told to Voltaire.

Every night, as Zénobe prepared to stay in Voltaire's room, he would dutifully give the philosopher his regular dose of opium. The *duc* de Richelieu had counseled two drops in whatever drink Voltaire chose, which was usually goat's milk. Voltaire slept like a baby. Zénobe was on watch all night long and never again fell asleep. He took to the habit of bringing books with him and would read whole volumes during the night.

All in Thrall

T
he Queen was there! She was in the theater! Not even the Queen Succubus could stay away from the opening night of Voltaire's play. Zénobe heard murmuring around him and he turned in the direction of the glances and he saw that indeed she had deigned to come. She was with *madame la marquise* de Polignac—who did not seem to have caught sight of Zénobe—and a couple of her other ladies-in-waiting who had previously been to the *hôtel* de Villette. But tonight there was no spite in Zénobe's heart. It was too full of nervous energy, and all he could manage was a deprecating look at the Austrian bitch and, since all her box companions were women, a final dismissive thought that she probably was guilty of the German vice after all.[186] He never thought to give those noble ladies a second glance for the rest of the evening.

The box of the *marquis* de Villette was opposite that of the Queen's, three levels higher, but also very close to the stage. His household was well represented, with Zénobe and André representing the servant staff. Since there was no more room, they had to stand in the back of the box. Squeezed behind the *marquis* and *marquise* were the three secretaries whom a royal decree could not have kept away since they had the text memorized. Besides Wagnière and Bigex sat Requain, who, even though he was really the *marquis'* secretary, had taken enough dictations to be interested in the project as if it were his own. The *marquis* de Thibouville sat in the front beside the *marquis* and *marquise* de Villette. He had braved the crowds for this, a most rare and joyous occasion: a new play by Voltaire, probably his last.

Paris was trying to fit into the *Théâtre français* but was having a difficult time. Ten minutes before curtain time, the *parterre* was already filled over capacity with people standing shoulder to shoulder. The boxes were overfilled as well. Thibouville eyed the crush below him with fear, and thought that if there were a fire tonight, he'd prefer to perish in the flames up at the rafters than to brave the ensuing stampede below. He held out his hand over the balcony, and he could detect waves of heat rising from the

---

186   I must vociferously a statement here interpose, for in spite of the fact that this phrase in Eighteenth-century France was used to denote lesbianism, it should nevertheless to the vocabulary trash heap relegated be, to join its lexicon cousins "french letter", "french leave", the "English disease", "a dutch bargain", "Dutch treat", "Spanish fly", and other distasteful phrases based on spurious characterizations of nationality. It is to me surprising that Zénobe of all people would beholden be to irrationalities and prejudices of this nature. In his defense, and for him in the story being sympathetic to continue, we surmise that he, like countless others before the Revolution, was greatly affected by anti-Austrian propaganda. This is indeed an example of how difficult it is free of prejudice to remain.

collected bodies below. Amazing, he thought. The energy, heat, the vector of the rising warmth of the crowd, he'd have to look into that.

Voltaire's philosopher friends were two levels below them. The *duc* de Lauzun had invited them into his box, more out of the intellectual cachet they would give him than out of generosity. D'Alembert, Diderot, Condorcet, Grimm, and several liberal members of the *Académie française* were practically sitting on each other's knees, and were all wearing the smile of happy expectation.

Zénobe, who had never ever been to a theater, was overwhelmed with joy and sadness at the same time. All of Paris was here, but Voltaire was too feeble to come and enjoy the spectacle himself. How he would love this. Zénobe turned to André and had to practically yell in his ear, "Don't forget to mention the audience's reaction." André nodded. Then he pointed out the *duc* de Richelieu to André. His box was two removed from the Queen's, and the blot of red was unmistakable. But even his box was bursting.

The *marquis* de Villette beckoned Zénobe over. "You will have to start moving before the end of the act. If you wait until it's finished, you will never get back in time. Five minutes before it's finished, you start to move downstairs. You have the *duc*'s letter?"

Zénobe patted his pocket and nodded. It was his pass to be able to get back into the theater later. André had one, too.

There was a sudden hush. They all looked towards the stage and saw a deep purple velvet curtain moving up, and then a golden one behind it part from the center out. There was a communal gasp of awe: there was a Byzantine palace on the stage. Richelieu had thrown open the theater's coffers for his friend Voltaire. The Corinthian columns looked massive, the stones were real, the sky beyond an open window announced a beautiful sunlit morning and it was no longer night, no longer 1778. The community was transported to Constantinople, anno Domini 803, to the events in the life of the Empress Irène.

Zénobe could barely recognize *madame* Vetris. She had transformed herself into the female ruler of Byzantium whose regality was superior to that of Marie Antoinette's. After her first husband died, she had been loath to relinquish power to such an extent that when her son came of age, she preferred to have him blinded rather than turn the reins over to him. In Voltaire's hands, a different woman became visible. Here was a woman in the jaws of passion, and a woman who was prey to her indecisiveness. Her new husband Nicéphore was a despot, even over her, even while she loved another, Alexis, who promised to set her free. Her presence on the stage filled the theater and her husky voice caressed Voltaire's alexandrine verses. Zénobe himself became so enthralled that he had to shake himself and glance at the *parterre*. He was here to observe, after all. Everyone was motionless in the boxes as well. Voltaire could still tame the masses.

Eventually, Wagnière turned around and touched Zénobe in the arm, signaling to him that he should start to go. The halls and staircases behind the boxes were clear, so Zénobe had no trouble descending to the ground floor. Once there, however, he had to use his broad shoulders to thread himself through the crowd. No one seemed to mind much, no one seemed to realize that he was even passing through. Act I gave way to Act II, and Zénobe took flight.

The way had been chosen days before and rehearsed. From the rue de Richelieu, through the Tuileries Carousel, where the guards were alerted and ordered to let Zénobe and André pass, across the Seine on the Pont Royal, to the quai des Théâtins. Seventeen minutes later, Zénobe had three minutes to relate what had gone on during the first act. Even though he was terribly out of breath, it took him two minutes, since there wasn't much to tell. Complete silence had greeted the presentation of the theme and no one was so much as budging. Nobody seemed surprised that Irène's tyrannical husband had pushed her to seek solace in the arms of another. Adulterous love was not a thing to raise eyebrows. But that other man, Alexis, was the rightful heir to the throne. Perhaps he did deserve the love of an empress.

Then Zénobe was off again. He ran into André in the Carousel where they threw themselves into each other's arms and danced in a complete circle before they separated and continued running in their opposite directions. André reached the *hôtel* de Villette where he proceeded to communicate in halting breath that the audience had gasped when Alexis refuses to obey Nicéphore the usurper, and they had moaned when a trembling Irène comes to the frightening realization that either her husband or her lover is going to perish in the conflict. Then André ran back out into the night. He met Zénobe again in the Carousel and they clung to each other for a second before they ran off. Zénobe hurriedly told his report on Act III at the *hôtel* de Villette: the audience had cried out to learn that it was Alexis who won over his adversary and managed to kill Irène's husband in the battle on the Bosphorus. But they reacted in shock when the assassin comes to the palace looking for the woman he loves. Irène is aghast and pulls back in horror. He is still covered with the blood of her husband. She calls him a murderer. Does the assassin think that she is his accomplice? Alexis calls her an ingrate. He has saved her from a tyrant who would eventually have killed her. She vows to flee from both her love for Alexis and from their horrible crime. The audience was on the verge of rapture. But forty minutes had to elapse before the next segment of the report came. André came back with the shocking news that the audience had gone wild when Alexis calls his beloved Irène a willing victim of religious fanaticism: how can she not see that freed of her oppressor Nicéphore, she still remains the prisoner of ancient rules which dictate that she cannot marry him, Alexis, who by great courage and through constant danger to himself, brought freedom to her. He sadly realizes that one can bring freedom to the religious, but one cannot make them embrace that freedom. The last report, on Act V, took an eternity to come. The mob was so great, and the joy and wonderment that the end of the play brought to all was so overwhelming, that Zénobe encountered great trouble in extricating himself from the theater. That, coupled with the fact that this was his fifth league that he was running that night and he was just about at the end of his physical strength. It was pure emotion and enthusiasm that was propelling him forward. As soon as he ran into the *hôtel* de Villette and into Voltaire's bedroom, he collapsed on the *bergère* in front of the old *philosophe* who was in bed with his niece. *Monsieur* Maurel stood at attention beside them.

"*Alors, mon fils?*" asked Voltaire with great expectation.

"The audience… the audience was crazed with anger, with fear, with anguish."

Voltaire threw his arms in the air and asked, "Were they weeping, were they weeping?"

Zénobe thought about it and answered, "No, I didn't see tears. I saw… I saw rage. I saw awareness of loss, of stupid senseless loss. Yes, they were horrified that Irène prefers to stab herself than to face the possibility that she will be placed on the throne next to the assassin of her husband. When she unsheathes the dagger, the audience shouted out in unison, "*Non, non, non!* Don't do it!" When she has plunged the dagger deep into her heart and she says, 'Here is my heart; it is there where Alexis is. I betrayed marriage, nature and you. Alexis was my god, and now I must sacrifice him to you,' people went wild. Then when Irène cried out, 'I adored Alexis, and I punished myself for it,' the public yelled out, 'how horrible, how horrible!'

"They thought the play was horrible?"

"*Non, non, monsieur de* Voltaire! They thought the play was sublime, sublime, sublime. They were angered by the terrible waste of a life, of a love, of the possibility of happiness, free from oppression, free from tyranny. But the victim wouldn't have it. She was still too wrapped up in the antique way of looking at things, in which you have to follow outmoded laws where reason has no place. Why couldn't she love her liberator freely? Because she was not ready for freedom. Even though she was unhappy when she was under the rule of a despot, when she is freed, she does not have the capacity to escape the despotic rules of religion. It is her religion that shackled her; it is a prison that she cannot escape."

Voltaire was smiling when he turned to *madame* Denis and said, "But they weren't weeping. I wept for Irène. Irène, who had been a woman who always knew what she wanted, but eventually became this creature who could not anticipate the terror of irresolution. Her quandary, between the passions of her heart and the faith she owed to her religion, became her undoing. How could you not weep for someone like that?"

Zénobe answered Voltaire's rhetorical question. "I think the audience would have killed her had she not died by her own hand."

Monsieur Maurel suggested hot cocoa for everyone to celebrate. He ran off to the kitchen to oversee the preparations and by the time he came back, the theatergoers were returning. They all rushed into Voltaire's room and offered their congratulations to him. Voltaire's bedroom became festive. It was eleven o'clock at night but the mood was one of jubilation and delirium. The philosophers, surprised, to be sure, by the phenomenal success of Voltaire's play, were trying to analyze why it had succeeded. The *marquis* de Villette kept shouting out the lines of the play that had been greeted with strong reactions from the audience, and here, the reaction was even stronger. The *marquise* de Villette climbed into bed with Voltaire and his niece followed in quick succession by the two *marquis* de Villette and de Thibouville. Champagne was produced and the popping of corks joined the gaiety and laughter of the moment.

The *marquis* offered a toast and the room quieted down.

"To *monsieur* de Voltaire, to *monsieur* de Voltaire, who fell into Paris like a comet plunging into tranquil waters; the waves billow and undulate in widening concentric circles, touching everybody and everything. Voltaire back in Paris is the beginning of a revolution, and nothing that he touches will ever be the same. His waves will ripple throughout and stir all that needs to be stirred, churn all that needs to be churned." Villette raised his glass of champagne high. "To Voltaire, the *philosophe* of the century!"

"To Voltaire," the whole room erupted. "The *philosophe* of the century!" Zénobe's voice was the loudest.

Monsieur de Voltaire was dwarfed and subdued by all the noise of the celebration. He was not able to voice his opinion that all this talk of revolution was disconcerting and pretentious. He looked at his three philosopher friends, and they all wore smiles as they brought the champagne to their lips. Perhaps they thought that this mention of revolution was but a metaphor. According to the old thinker, the revolution he had brought forth was already quite old: *Think for yourself, and never let anybody else do the thinking for you.* How simple, yet how revolutionary. Well, perhaps he would also drink to that. He raised his own glass of champagne and drank, and then he drank to his own health and to the health of *madame la Raison*, and then he drank to the auspices of Notre Dame de la Méthode, at whose altar he had travailed all those many, many years.

Buying a House in Which to Die

Madame Denis had settled upon a house she wished her uncle to buy. *Monsieur* Barthélemy Louis Rolland de Villarceaux, proprietor of 102 rue de Richelieu, however, needed prompting to make up his mind to sell it, nay, to finish constructing it first, then to sell it, and the niece, seconded by *madame* de Villette, was hard pressed to coerce Voltaire into providing convincing financial stimulation.

"Think of it, *mon bon oncle, monsieur* Diderot will be your neighbor. He lives only a few houses down!"

"But he comes to visit me here. I have no need even to displace myself."

"You'll be able to walk to the theater."

"I'm not going to do much walking henceforth."

"We'll be steps away from the Palais-Royal."

"It is you who wants to be steps away from the Palais-Royal, not I."

"Well, from the Louvre, then."[187]

"Oh, my droll little niece. Stop trying to convince me. There is no money to buy an *hôtel* in Paris. I have been reduced to philosophy."

"Your *bon mots* won't work with me, uncle. We have to stay in Paris. Were you to leave, you know you would never be allowed to return to Paris."[188]

"And if I didn't wish to return to Paris?"

"Ah, *mon oncle*, that is your affair. I, for one, don't wish to leave Paris."

"You mean, you will not go back to Ferney with me?"

"*Non, mon oncle.* Once again to bury myself in the country…?"

Madame Denis took on a strange expression of forlornness and distaste. She brought a pudgy hand to her temple as if she had a headache.

"*Non, mon oncle, non.* I cannot go back to Ferney. You will have to go back without me."

It was Voltaire's turn to look forlorn. He brought up his hands as if to show the world they were empty.

---

187   *Madame* Denis was referring to the fact that in 1778 *l'Académie française* was housed in the Louvre.

188   It had been bruited about town that the archbishop Beaumont had pronounced a sermon in Versailles in which he called attention to the fact that Voltaire and his fellow *philosophes* held "a hatchet and a hammer" with which they were awaiting a favorable moment to "overthrow the throne and the altar". It would be a simple matter to convince the pious Louis XVI to impede Voltaire's return to Paris, forever.

"What can I do, my dear? I'll send Wagnière to go get my things."

"To get your things for the trip back to Ferney?"

"No, to go retrieve my papers and my books from Ferney."

"Oh, thank you, *mon oncle*, thank you from the very center of my heart."

Madame Denis rushed off accompanied by *madame la marquise* de Villette to write a note to *madame* Bertin that she would be needing dresses and wigs now that she was definitely staying in Paris.

It was Zénobe, sitting discreetly in a corner of the room, who alone heard the philosopher say, "I probably won't live long enough to regret it."

When Wagnière heard about this, he exploded in a rage that proved that Protestants are not all that different from Catholics.

"That blasted woman is going to be the death of you! Tronchin said it, and I repeat, you cannot remain here in Paris. It is the countryside that keeps you alive. It is the healthy air, the salubrious mountain water, the simplicity, the quiet. Here it is the commotion, the perturbations, the odoriferous exhalations of the sewers, the pressing crowds, the inquisitive guests, the meddlesome priests that will see to your prompt demise. And all because of a woman! It is women who invented finery and jewelry and fashion and etiquette and a thousand puerile and conventional niceties and you will die over these superfluous inanities? She wants wigs and you are willing to die over it?"

Voltaire said in an aside to Zénobe, "The angrier he gets, the better his vocabulary becomes."

To his first secretary he said, "I know that you speak to me like this because of your love for me. But in my old age, my beloved Wagnière, I must not leave the last woman I've loved. How could I start over again, at my age? And you, aren't you missing *madame* Wagnière? You will go to Ferney for a couple of weeks, get me the things I need, and as soon as the weather begins to warm up, I will allow you to take me back to my vassals and my clock-makers. They love me, too. I will spend the summer months there, and then I'll come back to Paris. I shall write to the Polignac woman and figure out a way to come back."

Wagnière left in three days. After a tearful farewell to his master in which both of them said many beautiful and loving things, he picked up a sack full of letters dictated in those three days by Voltaire to all the people in Ferney who would be happy to receive them. There were about a hundred epistles. One, in particular, pleaded with *madame* Wagnière not to hold her husband for too long, for he would be coming back soon thereafter, with Voltaire in tow.

Ever since he had helped Zénobe escort the *abbé* Tersac out of Voltaire's boudoir, the *marquis* de Thibouville could not chase out of his mind thoughts about the *philosophe*'s young protégé, the *marquis* de Villette's peasant librarian. Zénobe Bosquet was his name, and he hailed from Savoy. But Zeus! The lad was not at all like other Savoyards. He was not meek and servile. He was proud and independent. Thibouville's mind kept going back to the first moment he ever laid eyes on him, when he was standing at the threshold to Villette's bedroom after they had all come back from the Tuileries Gardens. The lad looked chastened, embarrassed, although not in the least defeated, and oh so handsome with his eyes cast down. Thibouville's mind kept turning him around and around, from all sorts of angles and in all sorts of light. That straight black hair, which when free fell to his shoulders, those piercing blue eyes which looked as if you were peering into the soul of some Olympian god, that well-delineated mouth with its full, sensuous lips, that white skin with its rosebud shade of pink under the cheekbones, that hair peeking out from the unbuttoned top of the young man's shirt. Oh, saints of the heavens, how he yearned to unbutton the rest! Spying on him as the lad fenced in his shirtsleeves with André out in the garden, Thibouville admired the way the boy carried himself as he manipulated his blade. The small of his back, which curved into his buttocks, had powers of magnetic attraction even from three floors away. Thibouville had not fenced in over thirty years, but the young servant boys underneath his window lit a fire beneath him. He went to his armoire to check on his foils, unsheathed one—it had not seen the light of day in years—and when he saw stains and patches of rust, decided to have the whole lot cleaned and rubbed. Alone in his antechamber, he tried out some steps in front of the mirror. He gazed at himself from different angles. He might not be very swashbuckling, but he had no paunch, and he was proud of his teeth, which had managed to hang on more than his hair. But his wigs were all quite modern and fit his skull closely around the front and sides, ending with thrice-tied bows at the tail. He stopped swishing his blade after he noticed he was out of breath. Ah, this won't do. Perhaps some exercises *chez monsieur* La Boëssière could improve one's stamina. And he could coincide his visits there along with master Zénobe's, and *monsieur* de Villette would be nowhere near the premises. Let that recalcitrant second-generation aristocrat be sniffing around the *hôtel* Valentinois all the way over in Passy wasting his time with Franklin's secretary, or is it the grandson now? There is much better prey to catch here. It shall be seen who has the most success.

The following afternoon Thibouville was entering the doors of La Boëssière's fencing academy, something he hadn't done since he was twenty years old. Even though the fencing master had forgotten who Thibouville was, the experience was nonetheless bracing, for there were youngsters of all sizes and ages there. Youths with strong bodies and happy faces. As Thibouville gazed upon them, his whole life passed before him, and he realized that there was a new generation poised to replace him and those his age. La Boëssière had his son who would eventually stand in for him directly. But who would replace him, Thibouville? Oh, he was easily replaceable, thought he, somebody with money could step into his shoes. Mediocre talent and irregular ambition were optional. And who would take over Voltaire? What about Voltaire? Who could ever replace Voltaire? Impossible. Even the thought was sacrilegious.

The fencing master was not surprised by Thibouville's desire to refresh his fencing skills. Many a time an older gentleman would come back in for practice before a duel was called. The thought crossed La Boëssière's mind that the *marquis* de Thibouville would best be served with pistols for his duel, in view of his age, but it was none of his affair what an aristocrat had in mind. Besides, it was established that the *marquis* would pay after every session. La Boëssière assigned his son to take Thibouville into a private room and work with him individually.

It was when he was leaving the establishment that Thibouville saw young master Zénobe. The exquisitely dressed boy, who was quite successfully passing for a foreign-born gentleman, was receiving a grueling regimen from La Boëssière, *père*, and the energetic young fencer was so concentrated in his game that he did not see the *marquis* spying behind a column. Thibouville lingered for a few minutes in order to regale his eyes. Zénobe was the most beautiful man he'd ever seen, and the *marquis* de Villette was the most stupid idiot in Paris. Had he been Zénobe's master, he would already have found a way to seduce the servant boy. After all, the lad was from the provinces. Literature was littered with stories about young creatures come from the provinces who fell into the able hands of wily masters, and mistresses, of the Sodom and Gomorrah of the West. To be sure, there was a substantial difference here between Zénobe and the rest of the provincials. This boy was intelligent, well read, and a follower of Voltaire. The voice of Reason was strong within him. All the more so, Thibouville set a challenge for himself that he would be able to seduce Zénobe within a week. And just in case it worked, he would keep a journal about it, and perhaps a published story could be the end result. Thibouville left the fencing academy with a jaunty lilt to his step.

It was widely known that Rousseau was working on his autobiography. Casanova, as well. Thibouville would follow their example. He would call it: *Thibouville en ville.* Then again, perhaps such a story would best be kept unanimous. *Euh...* anonymous. Thibouville laughed at his slip of tongue, although he hadn't been speaking out loud at all. Slip of mind, then. He was so far inside his head that he didn't hear a *cabriolet* approaching from the rear on the rue Saint Honoré.[189] He failed to yield away from the center of the street and one of the horse's harnesses swiped him at arm level and turned him cleanly around. His feet twisted beneath him, and he fell, thank God, away from the carriage's wheels, into a pothole filled with muddy filth. A lady on the street screamed in alarm. Three or four *décrotteurs*[190] materialized in seconds, and a small crowd started to gather to see the sight. It was unusual to see an aristo mired in the street, and this one seemed to be lacking a *berline.* Shopkeepers came out of their shops. The report that reached the academy was that a man had been run over in the street, so all the young fencers piled out of their building and into the rue Saint Honoré. Zénobe followed out of curiosity. He had seen many terrible things on the streets of Paris before he was taken into the *hôtel* de Villette, but a man struck down by a vehicle had not been one of them. All he saw, however, since he was one of the tallest in the crowd, was a man standing with his head, or rather, half his head, from crown to chin, covered in mud. He recognized the face. It was *monsieur le marquis* de Thibouville.

Zénobe shouldered his way into the mass of people and was at the center of the maelstrom in seconds.

"*Monsieur le marquis* de Thibouville," he said, "Are you in need of assistance?"

Monsieur le marquis de Thibouville was sorry that all of humanity now knew his name and social standing, but seeing this apparition of solicitous beauty, he managed graciously to say, "Ah, Jupiter in heaven, my boy, you're here. Indeed I do. Please get me out of here, in the name of all the saints."

Thibouville's breathing was shallow and fast. It wasn't his close call with the carriage that was making him feel dizzy and clammy. It was the *décrotteurs* whose busy little fingers were feeling him up and down, it was the multitude of people pressing in on him, it was the lack of air and space which was bringing on a feeling of malaise and

---

189   *Cabriolets* were smaller than the aristocratic *berlines*, pulled by only two or four horses, and were therefore quieter, and were prone to surprise pedestrians who did not hear their approach. Metz had already prohibited them, and Parisians were demanding that their city do the same thing.

190   Street urchins who for a few *sous* wiped the mud off of shoes and apparel.

nervousness, of panic, yes, that's it, panic, like Pan and his forest-dwellers during an electric storm with high winds, falling branches and twittering birds flying all about scattering feathers in the gale. The last image he remembered was the face of an angel with cerulean eyes gazing at him with beatitude and concern.

On the rue Saint Honoré Zénobe held Thibouville's crumpled body in his arms. "Quickly, get me a *chaise!*" he yelled.[191]

A *chaise* was produced in a minute and the crowd parted to let it into its midst. Zénobe dumped the body within, and directed the bearers towards the *hôtel* de Villette on the quai des Théâtins. He would walk alongside it. But he had left his foil and the rest of his clothes back at the academy, so he directed the bearers to continue and he would catch up with them in a few minutes. He dashed back inside, said a quick word to La Boëssière, then ran back out, leading the master fencer to believe that more was happening at the *hôtel* de Villette than most people knew.

Monsieur Maurel could not believe his eyes when a *chaise à porteurs* dropped off a filthy and shaken *marquis* de Thibouville, accompanied by Zénobe. For a few extra *sous* the bearers transported the inert *marquis* to his bedroom on the third floor. The *maître d'hôtel* could not figure out, however, after Zénobe had given him the details of what had occurred on the rue Saint Honoré, why Thibouville remained under his fainting spell. Yes, a *coup d'agoraphobie* could make a man faint dead away—with him it was spiders—but once the danger was passed, the man should again come back to life. As he and Zénobe removed Thibouville's soiled boots and clothes, wiping off the mud from his face and hands with moistened towels, Maurel thought that something was amiss, for the *marquis* was moaning like a woman with the vapors. Maurel bit his lip and chided himself for his slowness when Thibouville thanked and dismissed him but asked for Zénobe to remain behind.

"*Monsieur* de Voltaire is in need of master Zénobe's services," he informed the *marquis* as matter-of-factly as possible.

"Nonsense," said Thibouville. "*Monsieur* de Voltaire doesn't yet know that master Zénobe is returned from his fencing. I shall release him at the time he would have come back."

"*Oui, monsieur le marquis. Monsieur le marquis* de Villette should be back home soon."

Thibouville's moan took a different tone, as if to say that he wasn't as gullible as the *marquis* de Villette. "*Monsieur le marquis* de Villette is in Passy. He'll try to extract a supper invitation out of the American in the hopes of seeing either his son or his secretary. I hope it's the *chevalière* d'Éon who shall be there instead."

Maurel suggested that Zénobe would better go downstairs to give André his afternoon class early since they had a lot of catching up to do.

Thibouville moaned again as he fluttered his eyelashes with impatience. "Master Zénobe will be down in a moment." He had been about to say, "I just wish to thank him properly for his aid and succor," but he realized that he owed no explanation to the *maître d'hôtel.*

Maurel realized he had run out of objections and said a curt, "Very well, *monsieur.* Will you be needing some refreshment?"

Thibouville waved him away.

---

191   *Chaise à porteurs*: a sedan chair, used to transport a single person, borne on poles by two bearers.

Maurel gave a half-bow and moved quickly to the door where he found a new idea and turned around but before he could even speak, Thibouville said, "No, thank you, Maurel, that will be all."

As soon as the door closed, Thibouville said, "Come here, my boy," and designated a space on his *chaise longue* where he wished Zénobe to sit.

Zénobe sat. Thibouville put a hot hand on the boy's thigh and said, "You know, I had heard of the assistance you brought to the *chevalière* d'Éon when she was treated with disdain by that most insolent Swiss scribbler. I thought then what a sense of gentlemanly charity you showed to an unfortunate, if not an entirely defenseless, lady. Today, however, my image of you has gone up several notches, for today you showed the same kindness, the same empathy, for a gentleman. By Jove, I find that extremely comforting."

"Thank you, *monsieur.* You are a member of this household, and this household has treated me very kindly, generously–"

Thibouville interrupted. "That may very well be true, but many young people in the employ of an aristocrat would not have volunteered their help to the lengths that you have. You, master Zénobe, go farther than the simple call of duty. You have a conscience, you show kindness, and kindness is in such short supply these days."

Zénobe, not knowing what to say, simply said, "*Oui, monsieur.*"

Thibouville's hand on Zénobe's thigh gave a squeeze.

"My boy," said the *marquis* mustering a little more energy. "I want you to walk towards that *secrétaire* and open up the first drawer on the left."

"*Monsieur?*"

"Please do it. It's all right. I am giving you my permission. It is going to be, I think, something rather pleasant for you."

Another squeeze of Thibouville's hand, farther up Zénobe's thigh, prompted Zénobe to get up and walk to the *secrétaire.* Opening up the drawer, what should greet his eyes but a bound manuscript, with a beautifully scripted title on the cover. *Ibycus*, it read, *par monsieur Zénobe Bosquet, de Haute Savoie.*

Zénobe took it in his hand. It felt hefty. He had never seen, or felt, his manuscript in such a formal condition. He turned around to face the *marquis.*

"But I don't understand. How...?"

"Ah, you see, my boy. I know what goes on in this house. I knew you had told Voltaire of your play, but because of the constant commotion and never-ending throngs in this household nobody had given your play any more thought. But I hadn't forgotten. A quick word into master André's ear and he dug up from within your affairs what I asked him for, and here is the fruit of your, and my, our, labors. It is ready for the printers! Panckoucke, Voltaire's own publisher, has accepted the consignment. All it awaits is your final approval. Apart from a few orthographic inconsistencies, your manuscript was quite perfect. Don't you think Requain did a fine job? He's a hairy little beast of a man, but his calligraphy is faultless. Look at the second page."

Dumbfounded, Zénobe turned the first page of the manuscript, and there discovered the royal censor's seal, approving the text for publication.

"We will have a run of two hundred," continued the *marquis* de Thibouville, "to start off with. We'll see where that takes us."

Zénobe walked slowly back to Thibouville's *chaise longue.* "*Monsieur,* I..."

Thibouville guffawed. "Oh, my boy, you can thank me later. We still have to see about getting the two hundred copies sold, before ordering another print run. We'll have to foment a flurry of reports, and broadcast them to the different journals, send copies of the book to those influential individuals who will talk about it, circulate the information that the author is a protégé of Voltaire, living in the *hôtel* de Villette, that he is a man of distinction, a gentleman of repute, a writer of note."

Zénobe's eyes got wider and wider as he was pelted with these exciting words. He could not believe it. He tried to open his mouth to speak but couldn't. He remembered his readings on the wheel of fortune and how the wheel would grab somebody, anybody, a complete unknown, and shove him skyward with boons, but up to now it had been but a theory. His previous adversity had been exchanged for a life of ease, of success, of upward mobility, and it all had appeared, what, providentially? No, he did not believe in that. Neither did Voltaire. Voltaire had made his fortune by the dint of hard work. That first financial contribution he had ever received, from old *mademoiselle* Ninon de Lanclos, was due to the fact that he had made an impression on her. That lottery which Voltaire had won when he was young was because he and d'Alembert had computed mathematically all the chances of winning and had cornered the necessary number of tickets in order to win it. *Candide* had sold in the thousands in 1759, and was selling in the tens of thousands twenty years later. Voltaire still touted his watches manufactured in Ferney as if he were a fruit seller at les Halles. He tooted his own horn. He was energy and intellect combined. Perhaps he, Zénobe, had intellect and energy, but all this marvelous fortune was coming too fast, too soon, and too, well, undeserved. His peasant nostrils flared and sniffed a rat. Or rather, the trap to catch a rat. He was the rat.

Monsieur de Thibouville, who had been enjoying the display of the sequence of emotions on the beautiful young man's face, all of a sudden recognized one which didn't bode well for him: distrust.

Jehovah in heaven, these provincials were not as naïve as people thought them to be. Perhaps it was the chicanery that they needed to develop when they had feudal lords who ruled over them with indifference and even cruelty. He needed to take a step back.

"It's up to you, master Zénobe. Take the manuscript with you, examine it for errors, and we'll send it off to Panckoucke at your earliest convenience."

"*Merci beaucoup*," said Zénobe with a reverential bow. "There are no words..."

"And I don't want to hear those words, or any other words to that effect, any more. One doesn't express one's gratitude, one shows it, through one's actions," said Thibouville petulantly, getting off his *chaise longue* and going to his *secrétaire*. "Send Requain up immediately, won't you?"

"*Oui, monsieur*," answered Zénobe.

Since the young servant didn't move, Thibouville said, "That will be all, master Zénobe, go back to Maurel, or to André, or to Voltaire, wherever you need to go. We'll talk about your manuscript at a later date. But bring it with you to Voltaire's room. Perhaps that will be the play I shall read to him this evening. He certainly enjoys being read to, and I'm sure he'll enjoy your play tremendously. I know I did."

"*Oui, monsieur*, with great pleasure."

Zénobe left the *marquis'* bedroom and wended his way down to the kitchen, still thinking of the wheel of fortune and its slippery slopes going up, and then back down. But perhaps he could allow his writer's vanity a chance to hope. If he managed to keep it to a minimum, perhaps there would be no harm to anyone, least of all to himself. Besides, the *marquis* de Thibouville certainly did not look dangerous. What harm could there be in proceeding with the publication of his manuscript? Two hundred copies didn't sound like much. As to the gratitude that he would later have to show the *marquis*, he was sure he would be able to come up with something. Well, maybe Maurel would be able to come up with something.

There was an epigram going around town about Voltaire's confession. It was the *chevalière* d'Éon who brought it to the attention of the residents of the *hôtel* de Villette and to its main guest. It ran thusly: people in general approved of the choice of the *abbé* Gaultier as the one to have lent his ecclesiastical services to Voltaire, who may have been known as the world's most famous living philosopher but who in churchly circles was known simply as that old recalcitrant curmudgeon and infamous sinner. Crack that nut and you would have a place in heaven. In fact, Gaultier seems to have been very well chosen; the honor of such a cure had been reserved by good right to the chaplain of the Incurables.

The *chevalière* cackled and Voltaire drew merriment from both the pleasantry and the *chevalière*'s falsetto laughter.

Zénobe could see that his master was feeling better. Voltaire was speaking of other events and other people, and was enjoying more speaking of himself.

"I'm having a medal struck," he reported to d'Éon. "On the obverse there is to be a portrait of *monsieur* George Washington, in regal profile, with the inscription, 'George Washington, Esquire, Commander of the Continental Army in America.' On the reverse is a couplet I wrote in his honor: 'Washington *réunit, par un rare assemblage, / Des talents du guerrier et des vertus du sage.*'"[192]

"Ah, that is so impressive," said the enchanted *chevalière* in English. She had lived in London for many years, serving as Louis XV's minister plenipotentiary and privy to the King's Secret, a covert offensive against Great Britain which, while never having borne fruit, was nonetheless instrumental in improving the *chevalière*'s handling of the English language.

But returning to French, she said, "You know that *monsieur* de Beaumarchais, who is a watchmaker and a playwright such as yourself, has been wanting to come pay his respects to you, but his responsibilities with the American army are such that he has not been able to break away from the coast."[193]

"What is he doing on the coast?"

"He is outfitting ship after ship with arms and uniforms for the Americans. Then trying to outrun the English ships."

"In tandem with *mister* Franklin, then?"

---

192   "Washington unites, by a rare combination, / the talents of the warrior and the virtues of the sage." The General's likeness on this medal is not accurate since it relied on Franklin's and Adam's memory of it.

193   Pierre Augustin Caron de Beaumarchais, watchmaker to Louis XV who married into landed, and moneyed nobility, had in 1775 a play written, *Le Barbier de Séville*, whose main character Figaro, will in 1784 reappear in the greatest anti-aristocracy piece of writing up to that time, *Le Mariage de Figaro*. Beaumarchais and the *chevalière* d'Éon had been friends when they were both living in London, until d'Éon discovered that Beaumarchais was taking wagers on d'Éon's dubious sexuality. He claimed to English newspapers to have kissed her. He reaped 10,000 pounds. By 1778, after d'Éon had come out to society as a woman, they had become friends again.

"Oh, yes. But the reports are coming back that his arms are not of the best quality. His uniforms, however, are beautiful and hard-wearing."

Voltaire commiserated. "Ever since Louis XIV's last victories it has been the French armies' lot to look wonderful even as they are routed."

"Oh, but we do have a few exciting victories of which we are very proud," said the *chevalière*, caressing the Croix de Saint Louis next to her décolletage. Her pearl and ruby earrings, a gift from Louis XVI, danced around her head.

"Speaking of which," said Voltaire, "the *marquis* de Villette was also at the battle of Minden. Did you happen to see him there?"

"We must have been on opposite sides of the battlefield."

Voltaire chuckled. "It's hard to imagine our *marquis* de Villette in the thick of war. But apparently he acquitted himself with valor and dignity."

"Until he got his horse shot from underneath him. Then it was such a din."

"You heard him from the opposite end of the battlefield?"

"No, no. We heard about it later. He demanded a litter even though it was only an arm that was injured when he fell off his horse."

The *chevalière* held an impossibly big hand in front of her mouth as she laughed.

"And furthermore," she continued, "he dismissed the first two litter bearers and demanded to choose a new pair himself."

Voltaire laughed with nostalgia. "Ah, that chap was always such a ne'er-do-well. Always trying to find an advantage, even during a hectic moment. That is why I dubbed him Tibulle; he's always thinking of aesthetics. Even in the midst of battle."

"I am so glad he finally turned his life around," said the *chevalière*, looking around her as if the *hôtel* de Villette harbored the happiest of couples in the best of all possible households.

The worldly *philosophe* looked astounded. "You think he's turned his life around? He leaves his wife all day and goes cavorting to the *hôtel* de Valentinois to uncover goodness knows what. He should remain here and try to fabricate a new *marquis* de Villette."

"Ah," said the *chevalière* who, because of her history of espionage and state secrets, felt that she was privy to whatever it was the *marquis* was trying to uncover. "He is up to no good, mark my words. *Monsieur* Franklin has told me that Villette is molesting his secretary, *monsieur* Bancroft. He takes up his time, he won't let him write out the necessary correspondence, he is constantly bringing him sweets and champagne, he follows him to the Turkish baths. In a word, he tails him like an English bulldog."

Voltaire laughed at the image of Villette as a bulldog. A rabid bulldog, he thought.

"Oh, my," continued the *chevalière* out of breath. "I do so enjoy your company, *monsieur* de Voltaire. And to think that the king told me that you would have a corrupting influence on me. Nothing could be further from the truth!"

This gave Voltaire momentary pause, but the thought of the asexual locksmith monarch warning the hermaphrodite *chevalier* of the *philosophe*'s supposedly evil effect on people was too deliciously ironic not to enjoy with authentic mirth.

Zénobe, who understood the joke, too, laughed out loud, louder than a true valet should. In any other circumstance, this would have been enough for *monsieur* Maurel to have rebuked his servant. But around Voltaire, Zénobe was not quiet and discreet, nor did he hide strategically behind the furniture, pretending he wasn't there. He wasn't even just a secretary when he was around Voltaire, but rather more like a companion. Only Villette treated him like a servant, giving him long barrages of orders, which he read from notes that sometimes took up two full pages.

Except for his visits to the Arsenal Library and la Boëssière's fencing academy, and for his tutorials to André, Zénobe was constantly in Voltaire's bedroom. The last thing he would do for Voltaire at night was to administer the *duc* de Richelieu's medicinal potion of opium, which made the *philosophe* drowsy and assured his uninterrupted sleep. At night, Zénobe kept watch over the old patient. Sometimes, when he himself became too sleepy, he would crawl into bed with the old man and drape a hand over Voltaire's side, to be alerted as to any irregularities in his breathing. He watched over the world's most famous mind, and it took his breath away that he had been given this responsibility. To him, that was tantamount to being on top of the wheel of fortune.

Zénobe's little book did rather well. It didn't take two weeks to sell out, and then a second run of five hundred was ordered. What the young playwright never knew was that the *marquis* de Thibouville purchased forty copies himself, to send to influential friends in the countryside and abroad.

The critics' interest centered around the writer as opposed to the work, since there was an element of curiosity about Voltaire's young protégé. It was said that he was the scion of one of Victor-Amédée's bastards, or perhaps the bastard himself, for the king of Sardinia and of Savoy was still an actively sexual monarch. This rumor drew the attention of two of Victor-Amédée's daughters who lived in Versailles, the princess Marie-Josèphe de Savoie, married to the *comte* de Provence, Louis XVI's younger brother, and the princess Marie-Thérèse de Sardaigne, her sister, married to the King's youngest brother, the *comte* d'Artois. The two princesses were asked about this rumor. Neither one of them gave credence to the existence of any possible half-brother living under the same roof as Voltaire, and it was Marie-Josèphe who responded, "We have no writers in our family," with a particularly contemptuous accent placed on the word *writers*.

Zénobe, too, seemed none too happy to be placed on the same familial plane as the two daughters of Victor-Amédée III, although *his* objections were not made public. They went only as far as Maurel.

"Those two bitches? They can jump into the Seine along with Marie Antoinette d'Autriche. Their jewels will make sure they sink all the way to the bottom!"

Maurel was by now used to Zénobe's anti-monarchical stance, and he gave him a hard look as if to say, we must only think about these things and not say them out loud.

Zénobe responded, "Well, it's true! What do those princesses do for anybody? What does that queen do for anybody? All they do is take and use, take and abuse. They produce not a thing. They are like leeches on the side of society. Marie-Josèphe de Savoie is not even liked by her fellow Versaillais. They shun her and call her *la reine velue*.[194] Just because she's the great-granddaughter of Louis XIV, that's only one eighth of the royal blood line, and for that she has the right to sit and eat all day and look like a sow."

Maurel said nothing but just looked at his errant adopted son and smiled proudly. Zénobe smiled back, knowing that Maurel agreed with him, but would never admit it.

---

194   The hairy queen. Her sister, Marie-Thérèse de Sardaigne was none too well liked by the residents of Versailles, either. The foreign triumvirate of conjugal queens would always remain outsiders at the French court.

Le marquis de Thibouville had been diligent in his responsibilities towards Zénobe's little publication, and even though the reports coming back to him all agreed that the play was unplayable (how could one get cranes to fly around the stage?), he was nevertheless determined to make it a small critical success as a play of imagination, even if it could not be a financial success. He figured he would be out about a thousand *livres*, costs, which included thoughtful little *pots-de-vin* sent to tepid critics to make them a bit more enthusiastic. Diderot, without any prompting whatsoever, wrote a little blurb in the *Correspondance littéraire*, a publication founded by Grimm sent to subscribers all over Europe, including Russia. The philosopher and playwright thought the play imaginative and amusing, and furthermore, symbolic of the hardships artists face in indifferent societies. He was also grateful that the writer was waiting on Voltaire hand and foot. Thibouville made sure that copies of the play were shipped to those markets that the *Correspondance* served.

When it came time to ask for a modicum of gratitude from his literary protégé, Thibouville thought he was well within his rights to do so. One morning when Maurel had brought him his breakfast and newspaper, Thibouville asked him to send Zénobe up that afternoon before he left for the Arsenal library. Maurel could do nothing but comply.

Zénobe came promptly at the appointed time and at the threshold stood at attention in an attempt to show respect but succeeded only in displaying a certain submissiveness to inevitability. The *marquis* de Thibouville rolled his eyes as he walked away from Zénobe.

"Please come in and shut the door. Take a seat."

"I, uhm..."

"Master Zénobe, when you are in my boudoir you are not my servant. You are my colleague. We are equals. And as my equal you are permitted to sit in my presence. If it makes you feel better, I will sit at the same time as you."

"Thank you, *monsieur*," said Zénobe as he slowly took a seat so as not to complete the action before *monsieur le marquis* had.

"So," said the *marquis* as he settled back into his *bergère*. "Your play is selling well and it is now time to ask you to write another."

"*Monsieur?*"

"Well, yes, Zénobe, we must act while people are beginning to know your name. We must keep your name in front of the public. Once your first play is out of print, they will buy your second. This second play is to have a run of a thousand copies."

"A thousand? Really, *monsieur?*"

"Absolutely. Indubitably. I know my public."

Thibouville leaned over with an air of conspiracy and whispered, "There is only one little thing, however, that I'm going to need to ask of you."

Ah, thought Zénobe, here it comes. The gratitude that Jean-Jacques Rousseau was always loath to display to his mentors and backers. What will the *marquis* de Thibouville have me do?

Thibouville raised a finger to the middle of his chin, as if about to choose among attractive forms of payment which Zénobe's debt of gratitude could take.

"I want you to write a play which will be playable on stage. In other words, you must take care that all the actions will be physically possible for a production in front of an audience."

That was it?

"You want to produce a play, a play of mine?"

"Well, not necessarily me. Someone might wish to produce a play of yours. It all remains to be seen. You know, Zénobe, I used to dabble in the art of Melpomene.[195] I've had a couple of plays of my own presented to audiences. The first one was entitled *Thélamire*, which I wrote at a time when I lacked confidence so I presented it under an assumed name, *mademoiselle* Denise Lebrun. Later, I wrote another under my true name, called *Namir*, about a camp master in the Queen's Regiment, our previous queen, that is. Unfortunately they were not very well received, but they did open at the *Théâtre français*."

Of course, the *marquis* de Thibouville did not avow to Zénobe that *Thélamire* had only four representations before it closed for ever, and that *Namir* lasted hardly an hour, before the audience began to clamor for another play. Thibouville had been at the back of the theater when he witnessed that the actors dared not disobey, rather than have a riot on their hands.

Zénobe was surprised that the *marquis* de Thibouville knew his way around a stage, and thrilled that he wanted him to write another play. He didn't have to think about it too long.

"I've been wanting to write another play."

"Ah?" said Thibouville intrigued.

"I have an idea for a marvelous one."

"What is it about?"

"About *monsieur* de Voltaire."

"*Monsieur* de Voltaire?"

"Yes. When the *philosophe*'s health takes a turn for the worse, a priest is sent to extract a confession from him. But what this priest doesn't know is that Voltaire has exchanged places with his secretary in the sick bed, and it is the secretary who confesses to the unwary ecclesiastic. I am thinking of rendering the portrait of the priest by taking the gullibility of *l'abbé* Gaultier and combining it with the zealousness of *l'abbé* Tersac. That should make for a wonderful idiot, the ideal foil to the voice of Reason."[196] [197]

"Is this play to be a tragedy, then?"

"Oh, no, on the contrary. It's to be a comedy."

"A comedy? How can you make all this out to be a comedy? Voltaire has come to Paris to die!"

---

195   Melpomene is the Muse of Tragedy.

196   This play of Zénobe's sounds suspiciously like the one written by the future Revolutionary Jean-Baptiste Cloots, today better known under his *nom de guerre* Anacharsis Cloots. He was in Paris in 1778 living and claims to have Voltaire at the *hôtel* de Villette visited, although no corroboration of this has ever been discovered. The name of his play was *Voltaire triomphant, ou les Prêtres déçus* (*Voltaire Triumphant, or The Disappointed Priests*).

197   [From the author] Oh, how ironic that I must defend myself from the person who was hired to explain things for the benefit of the modern reader. Jean-Baptiste Cloots, originally Clootz, was indeed living in Paris in February, 1778. He never claims he saw Voltaire, only that he came to the *hôtel* de Villette several times but was not allowed in. (He did manage, however, to have an audience with Rousseau on the rue des Plâtrières.) While I reserve the right to maintain secrecy about certain facts of this novelization of a slice of history, I will, however, disclose to the reader that Cloots was born a Prussian but his family was of Dutch descent. Marie-Jean-Baptiste Zénobe Bosquet was a Savoyard of Piedmontais descent or, in modern terminology, French of Italian descent. I will further add that aristocrats of that time, or rather intellectual aristocrats, thought of themselves as citizens of a higher order, and viewed their philosophical class as brethren, no matter their place of birth or station in life. When Robespierre will have Cloots arrested during the Revolution, Cloots' cellmate will be Thomas Paine, an American of (recent) English descent.

Zénobe flinched as if he had been struck. The *marquis* de Thibouville immediately regretted having spoken so bluntly.

"My son," the *marquis* continued with a softened tone. "You cannot expect him to live forever, and he is tired and sick. He is eighty-three years old."

"Eighty-four," said Zénobe. "Please don't diminish his victories."

"I, too, will miss him greatly. But he cannot be of this world for much longer."

"Yes, he will. He will endure, he will be immortal. His ideas will live forever, and his laughter as well. Any play based on his life must be a comedy. That is how he lived his life, and that is how he will always be remembered. He always laughed in the face of danger, and laughed the hardest when the danger came from despotic types who wielded their arbitrary authority over him like some idiot trying to contain the winds. Voltaire laughed, in rebellion against the hypocrisy and the servile conventions of the aristocracy. He laughed, against the irrationality of religion. He laughed, against the stupidity of men, who cling to fallacies rather than face the truth with courage. He laughed especially hard at those who would have him silenced, and who thought that by so doing they would silence the voice of Reason within him. No, *monsieur le marquis* de Thibouville, that voice will never be silenced. And his laughter will forever resound in each new era, in faraway lands, wherever despotism and orthodoxy oppress freedom, our freedom to speak our minds, our freedom to view God as we see fit, our freedom to choose our way in life so long as it doesn't impinge on anybody else's freedom. No, his enemies could never silence his voice! Time and time again Voltaire exposed their folly by revealing their utter stupidity and their hypocrisy. And ridicule provokes laughter. What would Voltaire be without his laughter? When he reminds us of what the Gospels say of Jesus, he tells us that these tales are worthy not only of the Old Testament but also of Bedlam, never for a moment forgetting that the original name of that insane asylum is Bethlehem. He tells us that Jesus's miracle of changing water into wine happened during a meal when the guests were drunk. Jesus dried up a fig tree for not giving him any figs, during the season when fig trees do not bear fruit. In the temple, Jesus whips up a storm of protest, overturning the merchants' tables and flinging their money to the floor, and those thirty or forty men allow him to beat them and chase away their chickens, their pigeons, lambs, and even their cows. Voltaire tells us that nothing in *Don Quichotte* even remotely approaches this extravagance. And where does all of this take us, he asks. To Jesus' punishment and death. He was executed publicly, but resuscitated in secret. Why was no one allowed to witness him ascending to the heavens? This would certainly have made quite a bit of news in the world."

The *marquis* was smiling. "Voltaire's irreverence was always shocking."

"Some people call it his blasphemy."

"But why do you have to go so far back? When was that written?"

"In 1736.[198] You want something more recent?"

"Yes, *monsieur* Bosquet," said the *marquis*, anticipating that laughter would make Zénobe more amenable.

The young man thought for a moment. "How about 1759? *Candide.* After the Lisbon earthquake of 1755, which God apparently sent to punish the city's sinners, the Holy Church organized an auto-da-fé to roast several representative sinners over a slow fire and with full ceremonial pomp in an attempt to expiate the city's wickedness. After the

---

198   In *Examen important de Milord Bolingbroke.*

victims have perished in the purifying flames and the embers are dying down, another temblor razes whatever few buildings were left.

"1763. Voltaire depicts two Italian clergymen reasoning about why they were both castrated in their youth. One of the hapless *abbés* says to the other that this was done so that they could sing in front of the Pope with a clearer voice.[199]

"In *The Defense of My Uncle*, Voltaire writes about the Pope's ultimate ability to dispense with certain rules.[200] The prohibitions against incest may not be broken, unless with the Pope's permission, for a fee, a man may marry his niece. Voltaire knows of a man who was allowed to marry his niece for only 80,000 francs. He also knows of others who went to bed with their nieces for a lot less. In conclusion, it is incontestable that the Pope has through divine right and proper remuneration, the power to dispense with any law.

"1769. Remember Voltaire's epigram on Elie Fréron, the villain who has, of all the priests at the Sorbonne, shown the most rabid intolerance, the most animadversion towards the *philosophes*? Voltaire writes about him,

> *L'autre jour, au fond d'un vallon,*
> *Un serpent piqua Jean Fréron.*
> *Que pensez-vous qu'il arriva?*
> *Ce fut le serpent qui creva.*[201]

"When Voltaire writes against Rousseau, he points out the Genevan's hypocrisies. This fellow writer wrote a play that turned out to be bad, then he goes on to write against all plays. He said that literature corrupts morals; then he gave the public a novel[202] where several passages make the gentle reader blush for portraying a married lady who gives in to her passions for a lover who, while being very willing to jump on top of her, nonetheless loses nothing of his moral rectitude. Rousseau went to Geneva and abjured the Catholic faith, only to come back and live in France. The poor man even composed a French opera,[203] only to write about how bad French opera was. He speaks against cities as being dens of immorality. Where does he live? In Paris. But with such a diseased mind as Rousseau's, Voltaire tells us, it is best not to criticize this escapee from Geneva. Don't even mention him. It is best to ignore him. But how best to ignore a paranoiac who always insists that even this indifference is an act of harm against him?

"Oh, here's another one. In *Questions of Zapata*, Voltaire writes about a humble Spanish priest who sends a bunch of questions to his ecclesiastical superiors, the Junta of Theologicians.[204] For instance, Zapata wants to know why God prohibited Adam from eating of the fruit of knowledge. It seems strange that God gave man the ability to reason and yet He did not encourage him to learn. After all, would He want to be served by an idiot? Another question asks why the New Testament spends so much time giving the genealogy of Jesus, no, *two* genealogies, which, by the way, don't agree with

---

199   From *Dialogue du chapon et de la poularde (Dialogue between the capon and the neutered hen)*.

200   *La Défense de mon oncle*, 1767.

201   The other day in the depths of a valley, / A serpent bit Jean Fréron. / What do you think happened? / It was the serpent that croaked.

202   *Julie, ou la Nouvelle Héloïse*.

203   *Le Devin du village (The Village Soothsayer)*.

204   *Les Questions de Zapata*, 1767.

one another. Why would it matter, asks he, since it's really the genealogy of Joseph, who isn't Jesus' father. Zapata also asks the theologians how much money the three Kings brought to the baby Jesus. After all, they should know this, since they themselves are accustomed to extracting so much money from Kings and their Peoples. And why is the story of the massacre of the innocents so bizarre? Too bad that no Roman historian talks about it. Zapata humbly begs his Junta to shed light on why Jesus never instituted the seven Sacraments, and yet we have seven Sacraments. What about the Pope? Is he infallible[205] when he goes to bed with his mistress, or with his own daughter, or when he comes to dinner with a bottle of wine poisoned for the Cardinal Cornetto?[206] And, for that matter, what about when there are two Popes, each of which anathematizes the other one, which of the two is the infallible one? Finally, Zapata's last question is: Given all the inconsistencies, all the illogical, labyrinthine complexities of the Bible, isn't it much better to simply preach about virtue? Let's attempt to extricate the truth from all these lies and to separate religion from fanaticism; let's teach and practice virtue. Zapata was sweet, charitable, modest, and he was roasted alive in Valladolid in the year of our Lord 1631. Please pray for the soul of our brother Zapata.

"Two days ago, Voltaire writes to a friend, the *chevalier* de Rochefort, in which he says that the preacher of Versailles, Beaumont, would apparently refuse him a Christian burial. Voltaire thinks that unfair, since he would like nothing more than to bury the preacher. In all fairness, Beaumont should owe him the same courtesy."

Thibouville laughed, genuinely caught up in Voltaire's humor, in spite of his ulterior motives where Zénobe was concerned.

Zénobe continued, "In the same letter he says he understands why the priests are so angry with him. He forced them to pay back the patrimony they had taken from Calas' children, and Sirven's children, and Lally's children.[207] Voltaire says it had to be that. They certainly couldn't be angry at him for not observing Lent. 'I am skinnier than any monk in Europe,' he wrote. 'I am more diaphanous than any saint. I resemble Lazarus coming out of his niche.' "

Watching Zénobe tell Voltaire's jokes and seeing his mouth open in laughter to reveal his strong white teeth and his pretty pink tongue proved too much for the *marquis* de Thibouville. Irrational impatience was normally not one of the older man's characteristics, but something about Zénobe's mirth caused an irremediable reaction in Thibouville's otherwise cerebral comportment. The spry *marquis* launched himself like the chameleon launches his sticky tongue and sprang into Zénobe's lap. The *marquis'* mouth landed squarely on Zénobe's before the young man could react. Thibouville's aristocratic tongue felt around Zénobe's upper teeth while his hands knocked off the young man's wig as he grabbed his hair in fistfuls in order to pull his head back against the *bergère.* Zénobe began to struggle but, not wanting to convey feelings of disrespect or ungratefulness, he immediately brought both his arms down again and decided that he had to remain passive and allow the *marquis* de Thibouville to fulfill his volition.

---

205   [From the author] Before any fact-checker takes me to task, I defend myself at this point: Even though the dogma of the Pope's infallibility was not registered until the First Vatican Council of 1869-1870, the idea had been around for a long time. Pope Gregory VII in the year 1075 had already stipulated that the Pope is to be judged by no one and that the Church he guided could never err. I suppose that burning astronomers to death was not a mistake. It was merely a diversion.

206   Voltaire is thinking of Pope Alexander VI.

207   The Church confiscated all property belonging to convicted criminals.

How far the *marquis* would want to go, however, was completely unknowable, but since Zénobe was the prey, he decided to let nature take its course. He offered up his breast to distract the predator from continuing to explore his mouth, which was not a pleasant experience, considering the *marquis'* hard pointy tongue was darting up into Zénobe's palate. Thibouville took the bait. With trembling fingers he unbuttoned Zénobe's vest and then went for the shirt buttons but the loops were too many and too tight, so with a sweep of his arm he tore the shirt open. With buttons flying all around, Zénobe's chest was exposed and the librarian valet saw himself as Prometheus chained to his rock ready to receive the piercing laceration from the eagle's beak.

Thibouville was on the opposite side of the emotional spectrum. The view of the young man's torso was almost too beautiful to bear, and even the look of fear on Zénobe's face intermingled with shame added to the *marquis'* savage intoxication, and he absolutely had to see what was further down. The hair on the young man's chest became a single line going down his stomach pointing towards a place to which the *marquis* needed immediate access or else die.

The belt was undone in a flash, the larger buttons on Zénobe's fly were easier to undo, and the magical place was soon attained. The *marquis* de Thibouville had struck a recompense that was as beautiful as it was awe-inspiring. It was every bit as glorious as he had imagined, only better. With an expression of rapturous anticipation, Thibouville let himself slide to the floor, the better to contemplate Zénobe's twin iliac muscles extending down from his sides into the center of the universe. Thibouville could now no longer have the power to stop himself. Mesmer himself could not have done a better job at magnetizing him. He took the plunge.

Zénobe had expected the stab of an eagle's beak but what he was now receiving was not that bad. He looked at the floor where some of his buttons had landed and mourned his shredded shirt. It was only one of two that he had. How was he going to explain to *monsieur* Maurel? But the expert movements of the *marquis* de Thibouville brought his attention back to the matter at hand, and he realized that André had a thing or two to learn. In spite of himself, he felt transported to a state of frenzy, as the *marquis* took him through a series of novel experiences.

So this is what experience offers. The learning that books offer is invaluable, but the learning that comes from activity and experimentation in the real world is also valid. It is a lot like farming. One can only learn by doing it. Or in this case, by having someone else do it to you. With a mixture of complicated emotions and sensations, Zénobe was brought to the epiphany that the sexual nature of man is completely disembodied from his emotional nature. But because of the confusing character of his present experience, he really couldn't quite grasp the truth of this idea. Was this, then, a verifiable fact, or simply a conjecture based on faulty, or perhaps incomplete, knowledge?

A Caesura However Brief

Early one morning, Voltaire and Zénobe shared a dream. Both awoke with the feeling that the dream was not yet over and that it had spilled over into their wakeful state. A metallic pounding, rhythmic and insistent, had caused Voltaire to dream of a mast with clanking ropes striking it. The old man found he was in an ethereal ship voyaging into uncharted waters, with a sea in front of him that was like a calm mirror, yet the sails were billowing and the vessel glided onward with great speed. In his dream, Voltaire missed his Jura mountains, and wondered what he was doing on a ship. Even though this was a very beautiful ship and he felt calm and peaceful, he remembered that he didn't particularly like the sea. Even asleep, in the middle of a dream, Voltaire's mind started analyzing. If this were a symbol of his final voyage out of this world, why couldn't Morpheus have chosen a caravan through the desert or better yet, a trek through snowy mountain passes with elephants and red sheep laden with rubies, emeralds and sapphires?

Zénobe's dream took the form of a smithy in commotion. Several men were pounding on a sword with hammers, beating it to a fine cutting blade. Other men held Zénobe down on a rustic roughhewn chair the size and shape of a throne. Zénobe knew that the sword was meant for him, and when it was of sufficient sharpness it was to be used to cut off his head. He wasn't struggling against the men holding him down. He realized it was useless to struggle. The less he resisted, the faster the whole thing would go.

When Zénobe woke up he realized that during the night he must have pushed off all his blankets that now lay crumpled on the floor beside his *chaise longue.* He saw that Voltaire already had his eyes open and did not seem happy. The clanging outside the *hôtel* must have been the cause.

Zénobe got up and went to the window. He drew back the curtains and gazed upward.

"There are men on ladders working with a long metal rod," he announced to Voltaire.

"Ah, Villette is having Franklin's lightning rod installed. Not that I am averse at embracing progress, but why did he have to choose such an early hour in which to modernize himself?"

Upstairs, the *marquis* de Villette woke up with a pounding headache and felt spikes being hammered into his temples. In the darkness of his curtained bed, he searched for the cordon to call for assistance and when he found it he pulled on it with violence.

Another floor higher, the *marquis* de Thibouville shot up in bed and yanked on his own cordon. He hadn't been awakened in this way since all the church bells of Paris had announced the death of Louis XV.

Downstairs in the kitchen, *monsieur* Maurel was mortified. Along with the outside pounding, he heard the bells in the summons board clamoring all at the same time, and he immediately sprang into action.

"André, go outside and tell those idiots to stop what they're doing this instant. Sylvie, go to the third floor and inform the guests there that all is well and the noise will cease forthwith. Don't forget *monsieur* de Thibouville's room. As a matter of fact, start with his."

Maurel rushed off to the stairs with Sylvie. "And I shall go alert the master. Zénobe will look after *monsieur* de Voltaire."

But Voltaire needed no looking after. In spite of this morning's rude awakening, Voltaire shook off his portentous dream and told Zénobe, "I want to go on a buggy ride."

Zénobe came over to Voltaire's bedside and smiled at him. "You must be feeling much better."

"Zénobe, my young rascal, I do! I do feel much better. It's like my aches are gone and the pressure in my abdomen has dissipated. Today is Sunday, and you have no visit to the Arsenal. What say you, would you accompany me around town?"

"With pleasure, *monsieur* de Voltaire."

"I think you can drop the *monsieur* and the *particule*, by now, Zénobe. All my friends call me Voltaire."

"*Monsieur* de Voltaire!" said Zénobe with such shock and apprehension, forcefully conveying the meaning that dropping the title and the *particule* could be construed as the epitome of disrespect, that they both laughed. But it was the last time that in private Zénobe called Voltaire *monsieur* de Voltaire.

When Zénobe announced to Maurel his principal guest's desire to go sightseeing, the *maître d'hôtel* threw up his hands in despair.

"Zénobe, I cannot at this moment acquiesce to *monsieur* de Voltaire's command. I am at my wits' end! Go speak with Henri or Philippe. One of them is going to have to drive you. *Monsieur* de Voltaire's coachman drove *monsieur* Wagnière back to Ferney, saying that his master's visit was supposed to have lasted only three weeks and that he had had enough of Paris. *Monsieur le marquis* de Villette's coachman is needed to take *monsieur le marquis* to Passy."

"*Monsieur* Maurel," said Zénobe.

"He'll be bringing *monsieur* Benjamin Franklin back to the *hôtel* de Villette for supper, and I..."

"*Monsieur* Maurel..."

"And I have my hands full what with, what with..."

"*Monsieur* Maurel..."

"What with tea for *monsieur le chevalier* d'Éon who will be visiting us with his friend *monsieur le chevalier* de Saint-George this afternoon..."

"Papa?"

"Yes, Zénobe, my son. What is it?"

"I can drive us."

"Drive whom?"

"I can drive *monsieur* de Voltaire in a carriage ride. Remember, I know my way around horses. I've been itching to ride *monsieur le marquis* de Villette's phaeton. It's fast. We'll use two of *monsieur* de Voltaire's white horses: that should look pretty."

Maurel had forgotten that Zénobe knew about animals. He was also impressed with his feeling for aesthetics.

"But the phaeton is uncovered. *Monsieur* de Voltaire will freeze to death."

"What, with his Louis XV wig and the sable coat which Catherine the Great gave to him and which was made for Russian winters? He'll be snug, I'll make sure of it."

Maurel realized that there was no one on earth more capable of taking care of Voltaire than Zénobe.

"Wear your gentleman's outfit."

"I was intending to. I need my foil with me, just in case an intolerant fanatic decides to play God."

"What do you mean? Oh, my God. Don't even think about that," said Maurel. "Maybe he won't be recognized."

"*Monsieur* de Voltaire not be recognized?" Zénobe answered with a wide smile. "Don't worry, Papa, I'll be very careful."

The phaeton was perfect for riding around town. It could turn around tight corners and could stop on an *écu*.[208] Perched atop the light carriage, they could see all around and enjoy the panorama, and also enjoy the unobstructed view that they knew they were providing to passersby.

The day was clear of drizzle. Even though the sky was covered by an uninterrupted light-gray shroud, the sun's outline could be seen through it, and the rays penetrated well enough to be able to cast shadows.

Voltaire wanted to go see the *place* Louis XV that he had never seen.[209] He also wanted to go see the house he was buying on the rue de Richelieu. Zénobe took him there by way of the Pont Neuf because he wanted Voltaire to see the rue des Platrières where Jean-Jacques was living.

Looking up towards the fifth floor at Rousseau's flat, all Voltaire could do was shake his head and say, "*Le pauvre homme, le pauvre homme.*"

Zénobe wasn't sure he caught the tone of irony that Molière placed in Orgon's "*le pauvre homme.*"[210] Looking at Voltaire he just saw an expression of pity and concern.

But it didn't last long. As soon as he saw the town houses on the rue de Richelieu, Voltaire's face brightened up. They drove past the house that Diderot was buying and stopped in front of Voltaire's future abode.

"Ah, very staid, very staid. That woman," he said, referring to his niece, *madame* Denis, "gives me a lot of trouble, but she certainly knows how to pick a good house."

"Do you wish to go in?" asked Zénobe.

"Why, no, I do not. Does a man wish to make himself acquainted with his future mausoleum?"

Zénobe smiled, thinking of Charles II of Spain who had tried his future coffin on for size. He pressed the horses on.

Voltaire did, however, wish to walk into the *place* Louis XV. He had been told of its grandeur but still seemed impressed as Zénobe helped him up the staircase crossing

---

208   Small gold coin.

209   Today the Place de la Concorde.

210   Zénobe is thinking of the play *Le Tartuffe*, where Orgon pities the man who is taking advantage of him and living quite well at his expense.

the moat and leading up to the octagonal plaza from the quai des Conférences.[211] Louis XV's equestrian statue dominated the grounds. France's previous monarch was dressed as a Roman general looking ahead in a heroic fashion.

"I don't remember his head being so small," said Voltaire as he peered up.

"Well," offered Zénobe, "he didn't require much space for the amount of knowledge he held in it."

Voltaire chuckled. "I think it was Pigalle who finished the statue after Bouchardon died. Maybe he got to do the head. Although, in his defense, he certainly got *my* proportions right.[212] But what a stir he got out of my statue. It was his idea to sculpt me as naked as when I was born. The denizens of morality took it upon themselves to order him to stop. It wasn't until I weighed in and defended the artist's prerogative to his own creation that Pigalle was allowed to finish it. What a fuss. Clothed or not, I was not about to attract young women nor to excite prurient imaginations."

They walked around the statue. Standing like caryatid sentinels at the four corners of the pedestal were the allegorical figures of Peace, Prudence, Force and Justice.

"The horse's ass is very well formed," admired Zénobe.

"You know, some courageous monkey slipped a placard around Louis' head the first night after its inauguration. Let me remember, let me... I found it.

> *Oh! la belle statue! Oh! le beau piédestal!*
> *Les Vertus sont à pied, le vice est à cheval.*[213]

I heard it made Louis so angry," Voltaire said with a hearty laugh.

"I would have been more audacious," Zénobe boasted. "Listen to this.

> *Oh! la belle statue! Oh! le beau piédestal!*
> *Monture et cavalier, lequel est plus royal?*"[214]

Voltaire laughed. "Ah, that's good."

Zénobe felt encouraged. "What do you think of this one?

> *Oh! la belle statue! Oh! le beau piédestal!*
> *Entre l'homme et la bête, dis? Qui est l'animal?*"[215]

The ladies and gentlemen strolling around them could not help overhearing Zénobe's irreverent verses. They couldn't help staring at Zénobe's companion. Swaddled in his monstrous wig and oversized coat, his face practically disappeared from within. Only the two eyes, burning like two embers, shone out. A few of the passersby, intrigued by what they saw and heard, ambled closer to the strange pair.

---

211   Today the quai des Tuileries. In 1778, the whole Plaza was on higher ground and surrounded by walls and a moat. The stairs mentioned in this scene were rendered unnecessary when the area surrounding the Plaza was raised and the moats filled in.

212   Pigalle's statue of Voltaire is today in the Louvre.

213   Oh! the beautiful statue! Oh! the beautiful pedestal / Virtues are on foot, Vice rides a horse.

214   Mount and horseman, which is the more royal?

215   Between man and beast, say, which is the animal?

"Here's another," said Zénobe, who liked this game of combining versification with disdain for the royals.

> *"Oh! la belle statue! Oh! le beau piédestal!*
> *L'être équin est fier, l'être humain est brutal."*[216]

"Ah, yes, that one is good, too!" exclaimed Voltaire, and as soon as he had spoken, a voice in the crowd spoke up.

"It *is* he. It is Voltaire!"

"Voltaire?" someone else called out. "But I heard he had just died!"

Voltaire turned to the voice and said, "Yes, an agonizing death, slow and tortuous, his mind gone before his body was, poor man, and, not knowing what was in his chamber pot and thinking it was food, he ate his own shit! Yes, I've heard those same rumors. But know that Voltaire is not or ever will be a coprophagist. I reserve my shit for others. Besides, I have a *chaise percée.*[217]

The crowd burst out in applause.

"Voltaire is here! Voltaire is here!"

This commotion caused others to approach, and soon there was a big crowd surrounding Voltaire and Zénobe beneath Louis XV.

There was no rabble here, for the *place* Louis XV, like the Jardins des Tuileries directly to the east, was dedicated only to the higher echelons of society. Zénobe felt comfortable because the aristos took their codes of ethics and decorum seriously. Even the few domestics accompanying some of the noble gentlemen and ladies were attired in fine livery and mirrored the exquisite gentility of their masters. Etiquette notwithstanding, the crowd became boisterous because of the nature of the situation. Those who were for Voltaire wished to greet him. Those who thought that Voltaire was the right hand of the Devil realized that this was nonetheless an historic moment in their lives. Many sprang forth to kiss his hands.

"*Monsieur* de Voltaire," yelled a man. "You've been gone far too long from your native city. Your presence among us does us honor…"

The man's voice was interrupted by a woman's. "*Monsieur* de Voltaire, tell us that you are here to stay."

"This is where you belong," said another.

"You are the friend of humankind!"

"The apostle of liberty!"

"The creator of the rights of man!"

A lady's shrill voice began to say, "You have made us proud to be French…" before the mass of voices rose up in noise and confusion.

Everybody who had been on the place Louis XV was now grouped in the middle of it, including the Swiss guards posted at all of the entrances who had by now joined the throng to investigate this most unusual hubbub.

With Voltaire's admirers talking all at once, his detractors found courage to voice their own opinions. When Zénobe started to hear some of their negative comments amidst the clamor, he became alarmed.

"You best go back to Ferney! You'll do less mischief there!"

---

216   The equine being is proud, the human being is brutish.

217   "A pierced chair" or a rudimentary toilet.

"There's a reason the Emperor went out of his way not to visit you."[218]

"There's no place for you here! Go home!"

"The creator of the rights of man? The creator of the death of man!"

"Usurper, anarchist!"

"Antichrist!"

Scuffles broke out among the assembly, and Zénobe's heart was in his throat. He searched for a way out, but there was none. The only direction of escape was up, and he doubted that Voltaire would be able to clamber up Louis XV's horse. Slowly he brought his hand down and wrapped it around the handle of his foil. Voltaire saw his movement and touched him on the arm. He pointed to the pedestal and Zénobe understood that Voltaire wanted his help in stepping up on it. Zénobe gladly obeyed to get him further away from the clutches of the crowd.

As soon as Voltaire was on the pedestal, standing next to Prudence, dwarfed by Louis XV's horse, he raised his arms. The crowd immediately became silent.

"*Messieurs, mesdames*, it is indeed a great pleasure to be among you today in the shadow of our great king, and to be once more in this great city which is, as it has been for centuries, the seat of western civilization."

"To which you have single-handedly added tons," gushed an admirer.

"Ah, I thank you for that, kind *monsieur*. I don't know whether civilization can be measured in weight, but if you speak of books, then perhaps I may concur with you. I myself have written tons, and tons have been written about me. Tons of me have been burned as well, and not too far from here. There, on the steps of the Parlement de Paris, over there at the *place de* Grève, and way over there at the *place* Maubert. My books have been condemned to be lacerated and then burned by the hand of the executioner. My books have been judged to be heretical or blasphemous by those who take it upon themselves to evaluate such matters. One of my books was ordered by the Parlement de Paris to be thrown into the pyre that sent a sixteen-year-old boy to the next world.[219] I sincerely doubt that the lad had ever read it."

"La Barre was a blasphemer!" yelled an apparently pious woman.

"If you think," answered Voltaire, "that the failure to remove one's hat in front of the Holy Sacraments needs to be punished by having your tongue ripped out of your mouth, your right hand amputated, your head separated from your neck, then all these body parts thrown into the flames until only ashes are left, then I would never want you, *madame*, to judge one of my omissions."

"He learned from you not to respect morality and authority," yelled out another voice, this time a seemingly devout man. "He would have corrupted other young people. He was convicted of sedition."

"*Monsieur* de La Barre's official crime was impiety, not sedition. Inform yourself better, before you speak. But you are right about one thing. I do not respect, now or ever, any form of morality and authority based on superstition and fanaticism. You can count on me to continue to trouble the tranquility of your world as I combat against those two diseases of

---

218   A reference to the Austrian Emperor Joseph, Marie Antoinette's brother, who in the summer of 1777 snubbed Voltaire by refraining from visiting him in Ferney. Besides his personal disappointment, Voltaire had to suffer the indignity of his enemies' insults that ensued.

219   The *chevalier* de La Barre in 1766 was arrested for not having doffed his hat during a religious procession in Abbeville. Voltaire's *Dictionnnaire philosophique*, allegedly found among the youth's possessions and presumably the book which had corrupted him, was ordered to be burned along with him.

humanity. I shall continue to fight against that particular lunacy that makes the believers of a religion claim that they have exclusivity of truth and of salvation, and that nonbelievers are their mortal enemies. These fanatics suspend their capacity for reasoning as they justify torture and massacre to rid themselves of their enemies, just because they think themselves superior. They do not even respect logic: they propose to persuade others of their faith by duress and intimidation when their faith teaches them to be gentle, patient, charitable and just. No, I will never accept such malignant behavior. I will always prefer to denounce intolerance and to defend the cause of the victims of that intolerance. I might be the *Don Quichotte* of all those broken on the wheel, of all those hanged, of all those burned at the stake, but my soul will not find any rest until theological discourse is a thing of the past. Men kill over words, and these words, words like transubstantiation, consubstantiation, Purgatory, the infallibility of the Pope, words which describe a God who comes in three pieces, which create and condone rituals of cannibalistic behavior, words like these are nothing but pure invention, figments of a febrile imagination. None of them is found in the Sacred Texts. They have all been created by a corrupt institution whose main principal is to blind its constituents, to hold them cowed and enslaved. All I have ever proposed is to show humanity its follies. The only thing of which I shall ever be intolerant is intolerance itself."

Voltaire looked down on the crowd with anger but with sympathy. The crowd was still. The wrath of an 84-year-old man had rendered them mute.

Voltaire continued to speak. "All I wish for," said he, "is a world where people will no longer tolerate statements such as, 'The total extinction of Protestants in France will not weaken France any more than a bloodletting weakens a well-constituted sick person.'[220] Can you believe it? This sort of thing is published during a time when philosophy has made so many inroads, so much progress? This same writer has said that Protestants comprise one twentieth of the nation! A man of the Church calmly suggests killing millions and millions of Frenchmen, and equates it with the bloodletting of a patient? This same writer says that intolerance is an excellent thing! Because 'it wasn't expressly condemned by Jesus Christ.' Well, Jesus Christ didn't condemn those who would light fires in the four corners of Paris, either; is that a reason to canonize incendiaries? Are we to tolerate, then, fanaticism that becomes increasingly indignant as it sees reason reap some success? Shall we condone intolerance that battles against humanity with ever increasing rage? Shall we let fear, superstition and prejudice hold sway over enlightenment? I think not, *messieurs-dames*, I think not."

Voltaire leaned on Zénobe who helped him jump down from the pedestal. "*Monsieur* de Bosquet, let us continue our sight-seeing. I've seen enough of the place Louis XV. It is vast and majestic and sterile. I would prefer now to go see the Tuileries Gardens. I haven't been there since *madame* du Châtelet and I used to run around in the bushes."

The crowd parted to let them through. Nobody followed them. On the way to the park Voltaire leaned over to Zénobe and whispered, "I hope you don't mind that I have given you the *particule*. I am quite content to have people think you are the bastard son of a king. Your star shall rise one day, my boy, so let's help it along."

"I would rather have people think that I am your son, Voltaire."

"The *marquis* de Villette beat you to that innuendo, Zénobe. But, hear me, you will be my son in that you will continue with my work after I'm gone."

"With all my heart," answered Zénobe.

Voltaire stopped walking in order to peer into Zénobe's eyes.

---

220   From the 1762 publication entitled *L'Accord de la religion et de l'humanité sur l'intolérance* (*Agreement between religion and humanity on intolerance*) attributed to the *abbé* Malvaux.

"Yes, I believe you will," he said. "I believe you will."

When the *marquis* de Thibouville found out from the *maître d'hôtel* that Zénobe had taken Voltaire out for a tour of the city, his pique was great.

"A tour of the city?" he spluttered. "To see that blighted mass of humanity in their unwashed glory?"

"*Monsieur* de Voltaire considers himself the defender of that humanity," said Maurel, as if that alone justified his going on an outing.

Zénobe had of course told Maurel of the *marquis* de Thibouville's sexual overture upon his person and the *maître d'hôtel* had cried himself to sleep later on that night. It was now his life's ambition to thwart this man in every way he possibly could.

"*Monsieur le marquis* de Villette will be dining with several guests this evening."

"Oh, with whom?"

"The *hôtel* de Villette will have the honor of hosting *messieurs* Benjamin Franklin, *le chevalier* de Saint-George, and *madame la chevalière* d'Éon."

"A very colorful array of guests, I might say," said Thibouville. "An American Quaker, a West Indian mulatto, and a Bird of Paradise! When do Voltaire and Bosquet return to the *hôtel* de Villette?"

"Soon, I believe. *Monsieur* de Voltaire's constitution will not allow for an extensive tour of the city."

"Yes, that is most probable," answered the *marquis* with an undertone of annoyance.

"This afternoon they are of a mind to continue with *monsieur* de Voltaire's letter A."

"With *monsieur* de Voltaire's what?"

"His letter A, *monsieur*, in the new dictionary for the *Académie française*."

"Oh! Oh, I believe I should be pleased to help them with that. It would gratify all my longings to collaborate in their endeavor. I shall begin to collect my words this morning. Asinine, for one. How about anoia, now there's a great word."

The *marquis* walked away from Maurel who continued to hear in decreasing volume an enumeration of words beginning with the letter A.

"Artifice. Avidya. Abscond. Arrogant. Antipathetic. Absolutely. Atrocious…"

"*Anus*," thought Maurel to himself.

Zénobe did not bring Voltaire home right away. The old philosopher, who had been known to sow his wild oats in his virile youth, caught the fancy of going to see one of his past flames. Suzanne de Livry had been sending him notes ever since he had arrived in Paris but because of her advanced years and delicate health had not been valiant enough to brave the crowds flocking to the *hôtel* de Villette. Voltaire thought it only chivalrous to go call on her. Zénobe directed his horses to the Marais, to the ancient and elegant home of *madame la marquise* de La Tour du Pin-Gouvernet, Suzanne de Livry of old. Voltaire was unconcerned that *monsieur le marquis*, her husband, might be on the premises.[221] As they approached the *hôtel* de Gouvernet, Voltaire explained to Zénobe that he had wooed Suzanne over sixty years ago, and that after her marriage to her *marquis*, she had closed her door to him. But in honor of nostalgic young love, Voltaire was now willing to forget such an affront. She apparently was willing to forsake propriety, decency and morality, for she had her front door opened wide to allow her old paramour in. If she had ever been a starving actress dying to be cast in one of Voltaire's plays, she was now no longer, at least for the moment, willing to play the role of virtuous widow, for she instructed her valet to skip the *salon* entirely and show her two visitors directly into her antechamber. She rushed in from her boudoir with disheveled hair and in negligée attire. Voltaire, who had begun to run to her with open arms, instead fell abruptly to his knees and yelled, *"Madame!"*

She, too, dropped to her knees and yelled, *"Monsieur!* Is that you, *monsieur* de Voltaire?"

"Is that you, *madame* de Gouvernet? Suzanne?"

He took two steps forward on his knees, and she did the same.

"Oui, Voltaire, *c'est moi!* You don't recognize me?"

"You don't recognize *me*?" Voltaire asked, walking on his knees the rest of the way to her.

"Of course, I recognize you," answered Suzanne, who fell into his embrace. "Let me look at you. Yes, you have the same penetrating gaze. The light in your eyes is still exactly the same as I remember it."

Over her shoulders Voltaire espied a portrait of himself as a youth. "What's that?" he asked, pointing to it.

"That's a portrait of you which I had Largillière paint for me."[222]

"You had my portrait painted for you? My dear Suzanne, what does that mean?"

"It means that I never stopped loving you, my dear Voltaire. You have been with me every morning for breakfast for the past sixty years."

"You weren't worried about the *marquis'* jealousy?"

"Not since 1718, Voltaire! Besides, I only told him that it was a portrait of a family ancestor."

"As if I could be that old or you that young."

"Oh, my dear Voltaire, we are two antiquated souls in decrepit bodies, devoured by time."

When they both made movements as if they wanted to get up, Zénobe had to lend a hand. He simply embraced them both as they embraced each other and raised them up together, the two of them combined weighing less than one regular person.

Some love birds, thought Zénobe as they trembled in his arms.

The emotional strain of love long lost was too much for them. Voltaire left soon afterwards, with Zénobe following him with a package under his arm. The *marquise* de Gouvernet had decided to wrap up Voltaire's portrait as a gift and a remembrance of their shared past. It was *madame* de Villette who absconded with it as soon as she saw it later on that evening.

---

221   Voltaire had obviously not heard that the *marquis* de Gouvernet had died four years previously.

222   This portrait now hangs in the Voltaire Museum at Les Délices in Geneva.

Messieurs les chevaliers d'Éon and de Saint-George came to tea at the *hôtel* de Villette dressed for combat.

It was Maurel who had invited them, in the name of Voltaire, with the expectation that they would linger until supper. Since both were friends of Benjamin Franklin, he suspected that the American would wish for their company in the dining room, and furthermore, Maurel ardently wished that by setting this precedent of having the son of a candlestick maker at the table, that perhaps it would not be construed as outlandish to have master Zénobe, dressed in his gentleman's attire, join the party as well.

By the time Zénobe brought Voltaire back to the *hôtel* de Villette, there was no more time to work on the letter A. They barely had time to remove their coats before *messieurs les chevaliers* d'Éon and de Saint-George arrived.

Zénobe was thankful for this diversion because Voltaire had been very meditative on the way back from his visit to Suzanne de Livry.

The *chevalier* de Saint-George came with his épée and with his violin.

The *chevalière* d'Éon also came with her épée, dressed in an outlandish contraption whose conception and fashioning, one was sure, had nothing to do with *mademoiselle* Rose Bertin, dressmaker to the Queen. It was a strong crossover piece of attire, with black velvet breeches underneath, and which ended mid-calf to enable the *chevalière* to fence unencumbered by a long dress. But over it, to the knees, was an overlay of what would properly be called a short skirt, made of bundles of blue satin interspersed with white. One thought of Venetian dominoes wearing such fashions during Carnival, in one of their most extravagant of congregations. At the torso, d'Éon wore a loose-fitting silvery-white silk blouse with enormous sleeves and with a daring décolletage that uncovered very little cleavage. One look at this apparition and Voltaire's eyes got as big as saucers, especially when the *marquis* de Saint-George, his chocolate-brown face and hands set off in a white wig and a light-gray evening suit, sidled up to d'Éon's side to begin their bout.

The whole household, including the staff, came into the *salon* to observe the combat. *Madame* Denis' hand was at her throat throughout, and the *marquise* de Villette would let out squeals of fright every time one of the foils came close to its mark. Zénobe followed the action with more knowledge now, and his arms and feet would twitch based on his reaction to the movements and thrusts of the combatants. Maurel's eyes glanced at Zénobe as often as they did at the two *chevaliers*.

The bout ended when one of the *chevalière* d'Éon's dainty shoes slipped on the parquet and the *chevalier* de Saint-George hit a bull's-eye between her breasts. *Madame* de Villette buried her face in her hands. D'Éon screamed at the nerve of Saint-George, and then they both burst out in laughter. The whole *salon* exploded in applause and shouts.

Zénobe noticed that Voltaire was clapping his hands like a gleeful little boy.

Then it was the other side of Saint-George that the audience clamored to see. As soon as he had mopped up his face and his breathing had returned to normal, he tucked the violin under his chin and changed from the foil to the bow. He began by playing one of his own compositions, and the ladies present, the *marquise* de Villette, *madame* Denis, and the *chevalière* d'Éon looked up to him as if they were adoring a god.

Such was the scene when the First Electrician walked into the salon with his host the *marquis* de Villette, both of them surprised at this unexpected pleasure, but only the *marquis* unsettled by it.

They quickly sat down in silence and Franklin, like the others, listened in bedazzled rapture. Saint-George's virtuosity and consummate skill as a composer convinced them all that he was the best French musician of their era.[223] Melodious and melancholic at times, it became playfully staccato at others. Sometimes, when the *chevalier*'s fingers were a blur and his music became alarmingly exuberant and the audience thought that his instrument could not possibly take all that abuse heaped on it, the auditors held their breath. Then, when the music subsided and engulfed them in a more tranquil assonant air, *largo* and *sordo*, they let it out again in sighs. During one emotional passage, the three women in the *salon, madame* Denis, the *marquise* de Villette and the *chevalière* d'Éon, seemed ready to shed tears.

It wasn't until the *salon* exploded in applause that *monsieur* Franklin noticed that his favorite *chevalière* was present.

"Ah, *mademoiselle la chevalière*, what a pleasure it is to see you here!" exclaimed Franklin in English.

"The pleasure is all mine, to be sure," said she, also in English. "One wishes one could see you more often, *mister*, but your many responsibilities diplomatic steal you away from us. I know from my first of hand how it is, for when I was minister plenipotentiary in Saint Petersburg, and then in London, leisure was a commodity difficult to taste."

Zénobe looked in wonder at this lady. She may look odd, he thought, but she has so many hidden talents. Her English is so self-assured, and sounds flawless.

The only other person who dropped by and was allowed in was Condorcet, and he was invited to dinner as well, by Voltaire. While Villette seethed quietly about losing control of his household to his *philosophe*, that *philosophe* seemed very happy to keep asking the servants for still another chair to be brought to the table. The last chair was for *monsieur* de Bosquet, who had accompanied Voltaire all day, and whose presence the old man did not wish just yet to relegate to the staff.

As everyone took their places in the dining room, only Maurel realized that these seating arrangements did not suit Villette's plans for the evening, which the *maître d'hôtel* imagined were for the purpose of wooing Benjamin Franklin in the hopes of gaining access to either his grandson or to his secretary. Furthermore, Voltaire's wishes presented something novel for Zénobe and André: the former, seated with the guests, was about to be served by the latter. Maurel hoped André's self-esteem was sturdy enough for this. Neither he nor Zénobe had thought it would survive intact had he known of Thibouville's sexual indiscretion with Zénobe, so they had decided that André would best know nothing about it. They obviously didn't know what the Cordays of Normandy were made of.

The *marquis* de Villette presided at one end of the table, a mostly silent host. The energy of the conversation came from the opposite side where Voltaire sat, flanked by Condorcet and Zénobe. In the middle sat the *chevalière* d'Éon next to Benjamin Franklin, with the *chevalier* de Saint-George facing them. The female contingent, *mesdames* Denis and de Villette, sat at the right and left sides of the *marquis* de Villette, respectively.

The *marquis* de Thibouville remained upstairs in his room, disgusted both by the way the evening had turned out, and by his own dislike of boisterous crowds around tables. He did, however, come out to the banister a couple of times to eavesdrop on the conversation.

---

223   It was the 19th Century with its bourgeois color-sensitivity that buried the *marquis* de Saint-George beneath increasing layers of prejudice and intolerance. That, and the fact that his humanist stance during the Revolution brought him many enemies.

Voltaire gave his fellow diners a synopsis of his afternoon. Everyone agreed, especially *madame* Denis, that his appearance in front of the crowd at the Place Louis XV could have been dangerous, but the old *philosophe* said that crowds are maneuverable when you know how to speak to them.

"Besides, I had my young *protégé* by my side who, paradoxically, is also my *protecteur.*"

"I wholeheartedly agree, *monsieur* de Voltaire," exclaimed the *chevalière* d'Éon. "In the presence of *monsieur* Bosquet, one feels safe and secure."

André, who had just begun to serve the soup, thought to himself that nobody in that room but he knew just how safe and secure one felt to be in Zénobe's arms. When it was Zénobe's turn to be served, Zénobe turned his torso a bit to allow André more room with the tureen. At the same time, Zénobe brought his hand down in order to caress André's knee with the top of his forefinger. Nobody saw this gesture but Maurel.

The next topic during supper was introduced by *mister* Franklin's innocuous observation that Henri IV, the first French monarch of the Bourbon line, had always been a favorite of Voltaire's.[224]

"I have been reading your *Henriade, monsieur* de Voltaire," he said in French, "and I find it stimulating and edifying."

"Ah, that little versification," responded Voltaire. "A work from my youth."

"Published in 1728," offered Zénobe.

"It almost didn't make the light of day," explained Voltaire. "One evening in a fit of discouragement I flung the manuscript into the fire. If it hadn't been for my friend and mentor Hénault, who burned his sleeves while retrieving it from the flames, it would have never been published and I would never have become famous."

"You need not worry," said Condorcet. "Any of your other early publications would have assured, each by itself, your immortality."

Voltaire smiled modestly.

"You liked this fourth Henri well," observed Franklin.

"Indeed I did," said Voltaire. "One of France's great monarchs. He proved that peace is a sign of a strong king, not a weak one, and that peace is good for a country. War always brings strife and calamity, especially wars of expansion. But sadly, a wise king also brings out enemies who wish a return to more bellicose policies."

"And the golden age terminated," commiserated a sad Franklin.

"A shame, and a crime," continued Voltaire. "And also a sin. The regicide Ravaillac was a monk! And a schoolmaster! Ironically enough, his Catholic predecessor, Henri III, was also murdered by a zealot, and a fellow Catholic as well, a dominican monk, a member of the Holy League!"[225]

"One wonders how that can be possible, to have murderers working in the name of a church," said Franklin.

"Oh, it is possible. With the Catholic Church, anything is possible. Henri III's defense of Catholicism was considered far too tepid. His friendship with his distant

---

224   Voltaire's position on Henri IV (Henri de Navarre, born and brought up a Calvinist) had always been clear: it was that king's Edict of Nantes in 1598 that had put a stop to the war between Catholics and Protestants in France. This hiatus did not last, unfortunately, for the revocation of the Edict in 1685 by Louis XIV provoked a new era of conflict. Voltaire had always admired Henri IV as being the author of peace during which the king presided over a period of industry and prosperity, until his assassination by a Catholic fanatic, Ravaillac.

225   *La Sainte Ligue,* an armed faction of the Church at its most rabidly anti-Protestant stance.

cousin Henri de Navarre, a Protestant then, was considered way too dangerous. The Church of Rome is wicked in its self-defense," said Voltaire with an expression that took on a squint of impious sedition.

He continued, "However, all religious considerations aside, I am left to wonder if, more than for his alliance with a Protestant leader, Henri III was not murdered for his dalliance with his *mignons?*"

Mademoiselle d'Éon gave a dainty little cough of surprise.

Zénobe stared wide-eyed at Voltaire.

The *marquis* de Villette rolled his eyes while his wife looked demurely at her wine glass, albeit with a smile.

The *chevalier* de Saint-George began to see why Voltaire had the reputation of being shockingly irreverential.

Only Condorcet and *madame* Denis let out guffaws, the first, because he knew how Voltaire itched to rewrite history, the second because she knew her uncle so well.

"How so?" replied Franklin. "You must excuse me, but I am not aware of Henri III's *mignons*. Who were they? What does that mean, anyway. Minions?"

Condorcet answered that question. "Well, that, too, and there were so many of them, but mostly in the king's personal apartments. I think in your language you say, *darling, dear, dainty, beauty of a delicate kind.*"

"*Beloved, favorite,*" offered d'Éon. "*Beloved favorites!*"

Franklin though he understood. "Ah, *the king's favorites.* Like *madame* de Maintenon for Louis XIV, or *madame* de Pompadour and *madame* du Barry for Louis XV."

"Well," said Condorcet. "Almost, but not quite."

"Henri III's *mignons* were all young men," explained d'Éon matter-of-factly. "And he had them all at once, not one after the other."

"Ah," said Franklin. "Oh. I see."

Zénobe offered a detail. "Agrippa d'Aubigné, the Huguenot writer, called Henri III 'the Man-Queen.'"

"Aha," said Franklin, who could not help darting a furtive glance at the *marquis* de Villette.

Voltaire continued, "The Church saw no daintiness in Henri III's flaunting his sexuality in front of the whole court. Henri III was not as discreet as Frédéric II. Henri would assign high positions to his favorite *mignons*. He would enrich them, to the detriment of the realm's treasury, would romp with them in view of anyone who cared to see. He once took a slew of them to join in a religious procession. The king and his beautiful young men wore sacks of penitence and marched barefoot and bareheaded, flagellating themselves, in unctuous atonement for their sins. The Church fathers were not amused."

"I can see why they wouldn't be," answered Franklin. "That might have presented a problem."

"So when Jacques Clément stabs the king in the middle of the palace, we are left to wonder if the regicide was allowed access to the king in order to put an end to the king's sexual antics, or to put an end to his pro-Calvinist sentiments. Who knows, Henri III might have joined his sister, Marguerite de Valois, in knowing his brother-in-law in, shall we say, a Biblical way?"[226]

---

226   Marguerite de Valois, Henri III's sister, was married to Henri de Navarre.

"It was two for the price of one," concluded d'Éon who was speaking of Henri's two crimes, but since his comment could also work for the two kings in bed together, everybody laughed.

Voltaire stopped laughing. "Henri III's murder was a double crime. It was wrong for both of those motives. Killed for not being intolerant enough, and killed for being too free with his sexuality."

"Just a minute," said Condorcet. "I can understand your ire against the part of religious intolerance. But where is your reasoning in defense of sexual wantonness?"

"Ah, my dear Condor," said Voltaire wistfully. "I wish Diderot were here present to explain. The question boils down to, 'Would God wish his creation, Man, to turn away from carnal pleasure, such pleasure, mind you, to which God in his wisdom made man susceptible?' I am convinced that *Leviticus* got it all wrong! You see, the Sodom episode refers to rape, to sexual domination, not to consensual sex acts between rational adults. Jesus said nothing of anti-physicality.[227] Even the word is wrong. Who invented that silly term? It's all very physical. 'Anti-nature'? Wrong again. Animals mating with members of their own sex is rampant in nature. 'Pederasty'? That might have been the right terminology for certain Greeks where one of the partners might have been young, usually a young slave, but nor for the vast majority of, of... We need a new word here!"

Condorcet suggested one. "How about *homophile*?"[228]

"That will do. In any case, society's condemnation of *homophiles* is just another exercise in intolerance. And another hypocrisy. For it is another mask that virtue wears behind which hide the double twins of evil: cruelty and fanaticism."

"My best dragoons were those who had friends, close, intimate friends, in the regiment," said the *chevalière*. "They were the most ruthless, the most persevering, the least likely to relent in the face of danger."

"Just like the Sacred Band of Thebes," said Condorcet.

"They are inspiring," said the *chevalier* de Saint-George. "I am tempted to compose a military march in their honor."

"Oh, do," pleaded the *chevalière*, "and call it 'the March of the Thebans,' with lots of wind instruments and lots of percussion!"

"Mind you," asserted Voltaire. "I don't mean to put any connection, or separation, between *homophilia* and virtue. A *homophile*'s morality has nothing to do with his sexuality. Take Frédéric II, for instance. As much as I love that monarch, and in spite of all my grievances and all the grudges I hold against him, his preference for young men does not add to or subtract from the fact that he is a tyrant. Enlightened as he might call himself, he is still a tyrant and a bully."

"Is there such a thing as a virtuous despot?" asked Condorcet.

"No," said Voltaire. "But there is such as thing as a virtuous *homophile*."

"But could we please use a different word?" asked the *chevalière* d'Éon. That one reminds me too much of *hémophile*."

"Well, that's fine," responded Voltaire, "we'll come up with one. We'll be better than the English, who still don't have a name for it. 'The crime that has no name,' they still say, those illuminated bastards. 'The sin that shall remain nameless.' Ah, when will people learn?"

---

227   The term for homosexuality at the time.

228   Condorcet's neologism is logical: *homo* from the Greek meaning 'same', and *philo*, meaning 'lover of'.

"That's right," seconded *mademoiselle* d'Éon. "When will people learn? People still have much to learn. The plight of the anit-physicals is misunderstood; so is the plight of women. When will people learn about women on the battlefield? How will they learn that in modern warfare a woman can be just as good a soldier as a man. It's no longer just brute force that is needed, it's also the ability to plan, to outfox your enemy. Anybody can carry a rifle, and anybody can plunge their bayonet into the heart of the enemy. The foil is light as a feather!"

"Oh, but *mademoiselle*," cried out her admirer Benjamin Franklin. "How I would hate to see you in the midst of war. War is full of guts and blood, and that is no place for a lady."

"*Monsieur l'Américain*," said d'Éon with venom upon her lips. "Were I not convinced that your words were said out of concern and love for my person, and that you yourself have been a woman prior to this, I would slit you in half from head to crotch, although," she said with a coy smile, "that is just a figure of speech."

She loved Benjamin Franklin, so she patted his hand to let him know that no physical danger would ever come from her.

The American, and the rest of the party, looked puzzled. Voltaire asked the question burning in everybody's mind. "You said that *monsieur* Franklin was a woman prior to this?"

"Yes, I did, and I will be forever in *monsieur* Franklin's gratitude. But you do not seem to remember, *mister* Franklin?" This last question was in English.

"No, I do not know of what you speak," answered Franklin, also in English. "Can you help me to understand?"

"It was when you were very young and, I imagine, very foolish, but very wise in your youngness and in your foolishness. For several weeks when you were sixteen, you played the role of a woman, a woman called Silence Dogood."

Benjamin Franklin roared in laughter and recognition.

D'Éon continued to explain for everybody else, but in French. "You wrote letters to your brother's newspaper, pretending to be a woman, and you succeeded beyond your wildest dreams. You wore your womanhood like a cloak made for you. You thought like a woman, and expressed yourself like a woman, and made a woman's case, and all of Philadelphia fell under your deception. You really did become a woman, which means that you understand what it is to be a woman."

She patted his hand again, and this time he took it into both of his.

"But let me tell you something, my beautiful friend" *la chevalière* continued, "in amity and in confidence. Louis XV never had a problem with a lady serving him on battlefields or in foreign courts. He trusted my loyalty; I never gave him cause for concern. Well, except for London. But the problems I had in London were all the fault of Beaumarchais. In any case, it is a shame Louis XV died of smallpox, for Louis XVI ordered me back to Versailles, and ordered me to mind my manners, and either to get married, or go into a convent. My government wished me to start having babies or forever to hide my face in a nunnery. That is injustice! That is disservice! That is ingratitude! But as proof of my loyalty to the French monarch, I did visit convents to try them on for size. I even had a list of 'convents to choose' with a dozen or so to consider. I studied what kind of woman I wanted to become, I did research on gender and personality and social roles and kept notebooks with outlines and schemas. But then, as if I could banish myself and live as if in shame, I began to want to live in a 'temple of purity' far from the society of men where d'Éon's name had become a target for humiliation and opprobrium and where d'Éon's body was nothing but a justification for pimps to make money off of.[229] Can you believe it, in London, when, through the newspapers, I challenged Beaumarchais to a duel, it was reported that he responded politely that 'it would be impossible to meet d'Éon anywhere but in a bed.' Then I had to endure vilification by the London press who called me a shameless Amazon, an indecent Diana, an uppity Vesta. They said that the qualities of my sex, discretion, modesty, gentility, were unknown to me. Crowds threw rocks through my windows. These vitriolic misogynist attacks wounded me. Oh, I was dejected, oh, I was depressed, oh, I was demoralized. At the convent, I thought, I would be elevated and exalted among women. There, I could learn much from the sisters' moral courage and virtue. I would enter into a world of meditation and tranquility, the just repose for a well-bred celibate lady, which is not to say that I haven't received attractive offers of marriage. Then, Jean-Jacques Rousseau offered me a vision, a modicum of relief, in living the life of a hermit who eschews the turmoil and duress of society. That's why I went to visit him! All I wanted to do was to express to him my feelings of admiration, of attachment, and of the tender respect that I had vowed to him. And how did he welcome me? That misanthropic antisocial monomaniacal paranoid son of a bitch! If it hadn't been for this young gentleman here, seated among us, and for my other angel who is also here today making sure we are well fed and comfortable, I don't know what would have happened. I might have run him through with my blade! I might have squeezed the life out of him with my bare hands! I might have defenestrated him!"

D'Éon laughed at the thought of Jean-Jacques Rousseau falling six floors to the street below. Nobody else did. They were admiring her big, powerful hands.

"But then I realized what it was that I needed. Entomb myself between cloistered walls? Spend all day reciting the catechism? Reject my potential and turn my back on my nature? No, never. That is why I am preparing myself to go fight the British in America!"

This last was said with a flourish of her arms. Benjamin Franklin nearly choked on his wine.

"I have for this past year," continued the *chevalière*, "been trying very hard and very much to lead a domesticated existence, but the sedentary lifestyle of propriety is going to kill me. It has ruined my muscle tone. My spirit is flagging. After fifty years of activity, how can I be expected to take my repose, to rest on my laurels, to be a refined lady serving tea and *brioches*? Not on your life's blood! I have written to all the king's ministers, to Princes of the Blood, to all the admirals, asking for passage to America. Yes, to America! America, where there is another group that is oppressed, exploited, conquered. The American natives, the Indians, as they are called, those good savages who live in harmony with nature. You, *mister* Franklin, you must speak to John Paul Jones on my behalf. I know that he is a forward-thinking military man. I will prove to him how I will incite our French soldiers crossing the Atlantic to engage in battle, to the full extent. I might even be able to incite the American soldiers once someone teaches me the military vocabulary in English. I will be like the women of ancient Gaul who accompanied their husbands to war. I will inspire the troops to new heights of virility. The warrioress Pallas protected Athens and Joan of Arc fought side by side with her soldiers. You know, my Cross of Saint-Louis was given to me regardless of my sex because of the dangers I incurred, at great risk to life and limb, during battles and sieges where I proved my valiant mettle. My sex didn't matter, for I have the same virtues as a woman that I had as a man. Why should a man's bravery, temerity, and physical

---

229   A reference to Beaumarchais' wagers in London about the sexuality of the *chevalier* d'Éon.

force be virtues to be extolled and deserving of the Cross of Saint-Louis, whereas the same qualities in a woman be considered eccentric, absurd, ridiculous, disgusting and even depraved?

> 'What cruel laws depress the female kind,
> To humble cares and servile tasks confined!
> That haughty man, unrivalled and alone,
> May boast the world of science all his own:
> As barb'rous tyrants, to secure their sway,
> Conclude that ignorance will best obey.'[230]

"No, the woman in me will not retire to a convent to practice modesty, virtue and chastity. I want to be active as a woman. I want yet again to be Captain of the Dragoons, I want to be sent once more to a foreign capital as a spy, and I haven't yet relinquished the wish to be plenipotentiary minister to an important country, just like it all was when people thought that I was a man. Ah, when I was a man. When I was a man, it was acceptable that I create my own destiny. That will not change. I am adamant that it will not change. I shall still create my own destiny, fate has determined that. People might wish to hold me back, they will tie me up with ropes, but the ropes will stretch taut, then the ropes will break. Too bad if they lash out at those standing in the way. Let them pull back. For I go on. I make my own way. The devil take me if I go back. I am without qualms. No irresolution! Cartesian steadfastness!"

The *chevalière* looked around her, and when nobody said anything she continued, "In short, since it is true that the entire life of the *chevalière* d'Éon has been full of acts of courage, wisdom and loyalty, and since it is true that d'Éon has been celebrated in army camps, in diplomatic circles and in the *salons*, it is therefore true that he will know what to do once he's in America."

She looked around the table, gave a dainty little cough, and demurely corrected herself. "That *she* will know what to do once *she's* in America. In America, I will find salvation in the force of my valor, of justice, and of acceptance. In any case, here in France, I cannot go from the glory of freedom to the misery of submission."

It was Condorcet who voiced a doubt. "But what will happen, *mademoiselle*, if you are wrong and the Americans don't want women fighting in their midst?"

"Ah, it will be their loss. I am older and wiser than *monsieur* de Lafayette,[231] [232] and they should want me for I am as valiant as he. As for me, I shall continue trying, for I know that is what's best for me, for I also fight against tyranny and prejudice. I have never repented of my past actions, nor do I foresee repenting of any future ones. I have long been predestined to final impenitence!"

That was something with which Voltaire could identify, and he nodded thoughtfully.

---

230   Elizabeth Tollet, 1724, from *Hypatia*.

231   La Fayette was nineteen when he made a name for himself in the Battle of Saratoga in September, 1777.

232   [From the fact-checker] There seems to be some confusion among the French between La Fayette's heroic actions at the battle of Brandywine, which was a loss for the American insurgents, and the victory at Saratoga, during which La Fayette was still recovering from the wound he received in Brandywine. His valor is under no confusion: it is said that his blood was at such a fever-pitch that he never even felt the Hessian bullet pierce his calf.

"Let me go from impenitence to impertinence, my dear *chevalière* of all Eons and of Thunder.[233] When was it that you decided to become a woman? And how did it come to be that you were ever a man?"

Everybody burned to hear the answer to this question. All eyes turned to her.

"That is simple to answer. I never would have become a woman if it hadn't been for that insufferable busybody Beaumarchais who put up the question of my sexuality to London bookies. He would make money selling his mother if he could. He made a fortune selling me. And I, who had given him my kindness and my trust—and my portrait as well! I even knit socks for him since he was forever complaining of the damp cold. If it hadn't been for him, a supposed friend to whom I had confided, I would have forever been known as a man. But the truth of it all came out, and I now bare my soul. I was born a girl. My father was so disappointed that I was a girl that he had me brought up as a boy. He never regretted doing that. And I never regretted it either."

"So nature is not all when it comes to the formation of one's character; it is society that matters most," observed Condorcet. "As a matter of fact, I would say that society's pressures even rescind, or negate, natural instincts."

"I wouldn't go as far as saying that," said Zénobe.

Everybody looked at *monsieur* de Bosquet.

"How so?" asked Condorcet.

"Nobody in his right mind would consider being, or decide to become, or accept to be turned into, an *homophile*, or an *anthropophile*, to coin another word, which is definitely not a *philanthrope*.[234] Oh, here's another one: an *homosèxe*."

"Why do you say that?" asked Condorcet, who as Voltaire's youngest philosopher friend had the least difficulty with new ideas and taboo subjects.

"Well, why intentionally choose something that is so unpopular, that is so fraught with antipathy, with prejudice, with danger, that by so doing one opens oneself up to all sorts of unhappiness, to insults, to blackmail, to banishment, to unspeakable suffering, and to being burnt at the stake? It seems to me that, free will being equal, an individual would choose to take the common road and live undisturbed, at least in matters of sexual preference. God only knows that one will be picked on because of one's religion, or gender, or left-handedness, or color of hair, or color of skin. Why add to that one's sexuality?"

"I will vouch for that," said the *chevalier* de Saint-George. "At least the part on the color of one's skin."[235]

"You are saying then, master Zénobe," ventured Condorcet, "that people are, or become, *anthropophiles* in spite of themselves?"

"That would be my opinion. Why else would they persevere in something that brings more trouble than it's worth? I mean, wouldn't you choose a wife over being

---

233   Voltaire remembered that the *chevalière* d'Éon was born in the town of Tonnerre, which means thunder.

234   Zénobe's idea for 'a lover of men' isn't bad either: *anthropos* = man; *phile* = lover.

235   [From the author] Let the kind reader remember that when Louis XVI made Saint-George executive conductor of the *Académie royale de musique*, its three principal sopranos wrote a letter to the king to state their unequivocal refusal to receive orders from Saint-George. A fourth singer, Louise Rosalie Dugazon, had Saint-George's baby, but according to some versions of the story, her husband ordered the baby neglected to death. In other versions, the lad, Gustave Dugazon, grew up to have a fine career as a musician. L'Abbé Grégoire had called Saint-George "the black Voltaire" in view of the criticism and humiliations he had to endure.

burnt at the stake? *Monsieur* de Voltaire was speaking of pleasure as a God-given right. God makes no mistakes, so if He gave to Man the gift of pleasure, then it is sinful for Man not to use it. The Church teaches us that pleasure of the flesh is sinful; therefore this teaching would be in error. Pleasure for an *anthropophile* is doubly condemned, for it is doubly shameful. Not only does his act bring pleasure, but it is also considered to be a sin against nature, since it doesn't lead to procreation. We may be philosophical in this matter, but it would be like Giordano Bruno having been burned alive for the pleasure of discovering astronomical truths. Did Bruno die a martyr to science? Then an *anthropophile* who dies in the same manner is a martyr to sexuality. Tell me, would you accept to die in such a terrible manner because of your carnal pleasures? I think not. Only fanatical, irrational people die for what they perceive to be true causes. I will go further: the people who most readily die for their causes are the most fanatical, and therefore the most irrational. This explains why zealots become regicides. They are always caught, and they know they will be caught, and they certainly know that they will face a horrendous way to die, slowly losing pieces of themselves as they watch, their fingers, their tongues, their genitals, their entrails, before being thrown into the flames."

"So the Christians being thrown to the lions were irrational?" asked Condorcet.

"Truly."

"The saints martyred for their beliefs were irrational?"

"Well, the Church fathers who tell us what those saints did are the same ones who tell us what Jesus Christ did. Do you believe them?"

Voltaire spoke up. "Well, well, let no person in this room say that I was the one who corrupted this young person. As God is my witness, he was already like this by the time he came to me. Next, I'll be forced to swallow a cup of hemlock."

"Which Socrates took voluntarily," added Condorcet. "Was he irrational then, because of his willingness to become a martyr?"

Zénobe was at a loss. He realized sheepishly that he would need to hone his philo-sophical and rhetorical skills if he were to take on these giants of science. The conver-sation had come to an abrupt end.

It was André who came to his rescue.

"*Monsieur* Bosquet," he ventured to say as he timidly stood behind Voltaire. "Didn't you tell me that Socrates…"

The *marquis* de Villette raised his head when he heard this unaccustomed voice in the dining room. He was so surprised, he said, and did, nothing.

Maurel, who had been hiding behind the dining room door, thrilled that Zénobe was speaking, now walked briskly in when he heard one of his servants addressing the assembly. Torn between embarrassment as a *maître d'hôtel* and his paternal love for André, he walked up to him in preparation to whisk him gently away, but the *marquis* de Villette raised his hand to stay him.

André noticed nothing of this for he was rather nervous. The conversation around the table had upset him, and he now felt a push to join it. He remembered what his father had always told his children: 'If your conscience tells you to do something, you do it. Your conscience is yours and yours alone, and nobody can take it away from you.'

His conscience had told him to speak up, but now that he was following his conscience's orders, he didn't know very well how to proceed.

"When you told me about Socrates… that Socrates… that is, if I'm not mistaken… you said…"

Voltaire recognized André's discomfort and turning his head around said to him, "Come round, my child, that I may see you. Come on, don't be bashful. Say what you want, we're all friends here. Liberty of thought is the life of the soul. Have you some light to shed on this question? Was Socrates made to die for his *daimonion*, his guiding spirit, which usually was not pointed in the same direction as the rest of Athens, or for having told his friends that there was only one God? Or perhaps you have come up with something altogether new!"

"*Oui, monsieur de Voltaire, merci beaucoup, monsieur.* The other day, when *monsieur* Bosquet was giving me my afternoon lesson, he said that Socrates died for his love, his love of teaching, his love for the youth of Athens, his love of truth and knowledge, of freedom. He also loved par... par..."

"*Parrhesia*," said in unison Voltaire, Condorcet and Zénobe.

"Yes, that's it. *Parrhesia*, free and uninhibited speech, based on tec... uhm..."

"*Techne logon*," said the three.

The young André continued with his line of reasoning. "The art of reasoned discourse. So in order to return to your previous theme, *monsieur* Bosquet, perhaps a person would not be willing to die for pleasures of the flesh, but I think that any person in his right mind would die for love. The reason why the warriors in the Sacred Band of Thebes and the dragoons in *mademoiselle la chevalière*'s regiment had so much success is that they were fighting not just for Thebes, not just for France, but for their loved ones, their beloved. We all have our *mignons*, then, I should say. Even Henri III had his favorite among them. Didn't he build a shrine to Quélus after the *mignon* was killed by the Holy League? I'm sure the king suffered a lot over his friend's death. I read that the king would not let anybody else take care of Quélus as he lay dying of his wounds. To conclude, then, *messieurs, dames*, perhaps I wouldn't be prepared to die for simple pleasure, for that is superficial and does not last long, but I certainly would be willing to die for love."

"Ah!" burst out *la chevalière*, "well said, well said! Come over here, my angel, that I may embrace you once again!"

André did as he was told and gave himself up to d'Éon's Amazonian hug, his face squeezed between a bulging arm muscle and her bosom.

Zénobe looked at his pupil in a new light.

Condorcet said to Voltaire, "At the *place* Louis XV this afternoon, you said that you spoke to the crowd about men killing each other over words. Well, here in our midst this evening we have the example of a brave young man willing to die for a word. 'Love'."

"Oh, posh-tosh," answered Voltaire. "It's what the words represent, you know that. And love is real. All those other words that I mentioned to the crowd this afternoon are not. They're pure invention, created by raving lunatics, that is all. 'Transubstantiation.' All that this word does is prove the impudence of the clergy and the imbecility of the laity for swallowing it. Ha, ha! Just like they swallow the wine and the bread which is said to become the blood and the flesh of God, although they still continue to taste like wine and bread. So there they are, eating and drinking their God, which means of course that they also pass their God out of their digestive system. Words like that are deceitful, redolent of superstition; a hundred times more absurd and more sacrilegious than all those of the ancient Egyptians. But it brings an Italian priest fifteen to twenty millions in profits. No, my dear Condor. 'Love' is not an empty word of pure invention. That one is truly substantive. Oh, 'love', '*love*', now there is a theme worthy of all the poems ever written about it."

For an example, and in honor of Benjamin Franklin, Voltaire turned in polyglottic inspiration to English.

> "'Adieu, dear life! here am I left alone;
> The world is strangely changed since thou art gone.
> Compose thyself to rest, all will be well;
> I'll come to bed as fast as possible.'"[236]

"Why such a morose example?" asked the *chevalier* de Saint-George. "What do you think of this?

> 'Is ecstasy so great! delight so vast!
> That was it lasting, could but nature bear
> The rage of such unsufferable joy.'"[237]

"Oh, I can top that," boasted the *chevalière* d'Éon. "Listen.

> 'What a charming thing's a battle!
> Trumpets sounding, drums a-beating;
> Crack, crick, crack, the cannons rattle,
> Every heart with joy elating.
> With what pleasure are we spying,
> From the front and from the rear,
> Round us in the smoky air,
> Heads and limbs and bullets flying!'"[238]

When her friends looked at her in quizzical glances, she explained, "What? That is love. Love of battle. The poet gave me those verses himself. He's another of society's rejects, for being an *anthro... homo... antiphysique.* He fled London and is now living in Paris."

Voltaire took over. "To get back to a more personal example, here is one of my favorites.

> 'But Cleomira's love can bless,
> And turn t'a grove a wilderness,
> A dungeon to a pleasant place.'"[239]

Everyone laughed, partly because of the words of the poem, but mostly because of the way Voltaire recited them, as if he were the great Lekain intoning the verses of Œdipe.

"You will certainly be ready to greet your fellow litterateurs," said Saint-George.

"What do you mean?" asked the old *philosophe.*

---

236   Jonathan Richardson, 1726.

237   Henry Baker, 1725.

238   Isaac Bickerstaffe, 1770.

239   Samuel Jones, 1714.

"Well, the *chevalière* d'Éon and I are not supposed to say anything, and you must wait for the official invitation, at which you will manage to show great surprise, but we have heard from a trustworthy source that you are to address the forty Immortals at the *Académie française* next Monday the 30th. They will be holding an extraordinary session in your honor."

Voltaire was beaming.

"But that is not all," added d'Éon. "Also in your honor, the Lodge of the Nine Sisters wish to induct you into the Freemasons, you and *mister* Benjamin Franklin."

Voltaire beamed even more. Franklin laughed.

"Well, well," said the modest American. "It seems that we are coming up in the world, *monsieur* de Voltaire."

"It seems to me, too!"

Organ music, which had been faint at first, suddenly made itself heard from outside the *hôtel.*

Madame Denis jumped up. "Oh, it's the *montreur!*"

She rushed off to the front door saying, "Oh, let's see, let's see!"

"The *montreur?*" asked Benjamin Franklin.

"The *montreur de la lanterne magique,*" said the *marquis* de Villette, speaking for the first time that evening.

Benjamin Franklin still didn't know what they were talking about.

"You'll see," said Saint-George. "It's actually quite interesting."

Madame Denis returned to the dining room followed by two men, one playing a hand-held organ, the other carrying a heavy device on his back.

Chairs were hastily moved back, a painting was removed in order to have a blank wall, and the *montreur* set up his *lanterne magique.* It was a contraption with a lens in back of which were placed glass plates with designs of transparent color etched on them, and by the light of a couple of candles burning at one end, threw the image out the other and onto the wall, the result being a life-sized replica of the etching. The group looked at the images in amazement. Besides pictures of ancient mythological figures, Apollo, Vulcan, Icarus and Europa, there were scenes from more contemporary sources, like Watteau and Fragonard. Interspersed with *monsieur* the Sun and *madame* the Moon, were Cupid flying over a pair of lovers, the prodigal son ruining himself with some girls, Persephone in the underworld, Delilah cutting off Samson's hair, Lot's wife turning into a pillar of salt as she looks back on burning Sodom, and, to the joy of all, Benjamin Franklin flying a kite with thunderbolts all around, and Voltaire on a throne as if he were some statue on a pediment, with an arm raised and holding an open book from which emanated rays of light. With the flickering of the candles, the rays seemed to move.

The sounds of astonishment coming from the dining room were too much for the *marquis* de Thibouville. He finally was drawn down by curiosity and was able to see the remaining images of the *lanterne magique,* but his self-imposed isolation and envy kept him from having as much amusement as the others.

Apotheosis

André was not the provincial bumpkin that *messieurs* Maurel and Bosquet seemed to think he was. How could they underestimate him so? Didn't they know that God gave him eyes with which to see and a mind with which to think? He had thought it odd when a few days ago Zénobe had appeared in their little room all the way at the end of the servants' quarters and urinated into their chamber pot. André saw that the head of Zénobe's penis under his prepuce was glistening wet. Afterwards, as he was thinking of that, he remembered that Zénobe had smelled of oranges, and there hadn't been any oranges in the kitchen for months. The following day, André had smelled oranges wafting after the *marquis* de Thibouville as the old fop went from the hallway into the kitchen on his way out the side door. It was a trail plain to smell.

Strange, all of that was strange. But having meant what he said to Voltaire when they were all in the dining room, he realized that love was giving him an improved perception, a sort of new sense, one reserved for Zénobe only, a sense for concern and a sense for any threats to their union. He was on the lookout. With nostrils flaring.

Meantime, he participated in the preparations for Voltaire's triumphant return to the hallowed ground of the *Académie.* It was planned for four o'clock in the afternoon. Afterwards, in view of the philosopher's improved health, Voltaire was to go to the theater to catch his play, whose first, second and fourth acts André had seen on the stage at its première. The rest he had seen during rehearsals at the *hôtel* de Villette. He thought it a good play, filled with passion, guilt, regret and despair. But sometimes he thought that Irène would get into a tizzy over things that she made overly complicated. How come she didn't yearn for calm and happiness? She only looked for tears and turmoil, and everything she said brought a gasp from the audience. What a way to live! Would anything he said bring a gasp from an audience?

The young valet was already anticipating Voltaire's departure from Paris, precisely because it would bring peace and calm back to the *hôtel* de Villette. The boredom of pre-Voltaire days would be welcome after such frenetic activity and long workdays. Besides, André felt that he would never feel bored again. Not with Zénobe around, to give him lessons, to steal a kiss with in the wine cellar, to cuddle up with during the cold nights. That was an adventure that could go on for the rest of his life. He and Zénobe, together forever.

As soon as Voltaire had his fill of all the accolades and commotion, he would go back home, and the house would return to normal. Yes, Voltaire would only be away for the summer and would eventually come back to Paris when his house on the rue de Richelieu was finished, to coincide with the new theater season in the fall. That would give André and Zénobe four months filled with easy days and heavenly nights. Imagining this better future gave André the courage and stamina needed for the rest of Voltaire's stay in Paris. Today the whole household was preparing to send, first to the *Académie française* in the afternoon, and then to the theater in the evening, Voltaire, *madame* Denis, the *marquis* and *marquise* de Villette, and the pompous and priggish *marquis* de Thibouville, who smelled of trouble.

After Villette's coachman drove the felicitous party to their first destination, the household staff of the *hôtel* went out as well. *Monsieur* Maurel had given them the rest of the afternoon and evening off. They hadn't had such a respite since the day before Voltaire and his retinue had arrived. But to be sure that they would all leave the premises, Maurel gave them supplementary funds and the recommendation to go frolic in the cabarets of Montmartre. Only André and Zénobe remained behind. Maurel had other plans for his angels. He lovingly prepared an intimate repast for them, and then went to his own room for a nap, relishing the five or six hours of peace that they had before them. There was plenty of time for his angels to eat, to relax, to luxuriate, to make love, and then to clear off any evidence of their having cavorted.

The drive from the *hôtel* de Villette across the Seine on the Pont Neuf and on to the Louvre took but a few minutes. The walk from the *berline* across the front courtyard to the monstrous front doors of the old palace took half an hour. The two-thousand-strong throng awaiting Voltaire made sure of that. The *marquis* de Thibouville almost ran back into the *berline*, but the crowd parted before them only to close up tight again behind, as if they were being swallowed by a huge and grotesque snake. It took another fifteen agonizing minutes to amble into the main hall and up the stairs. Thibouville had to focus on the back of Voltaire's huge wig and study its curly ringlets in order to stomach the fracas. With his heart racing, he had to grab the *marquise* de Villette's arm in order to obtain added courage. Slowly they made their way up to the first floor. There, in the antechamber of the hall where the *Académie française* held its seances, its members, recognizable by their colorful Renaissance regalia, had congregated to await the coming of their long-exiled fellow member. A few had even spilled out into the hallway. Such an act of honor had never been demonstrated before. Even Emperor Joseph of Austria, Marie Antoinette's brother, had had to walk in unaccompanied, looking a bit lost, into the grandiose chamber where pomp and silence greeted him. With Voltaire, waves of clamor rose and grew with his approaching steps, although the academy members, conscious of their solemn dignity, refrained from shouting or waving their arms about. Still, something caught at their throats, to their surprise, as they realized the importance of this event. The magnificent cries of approval from the crowds was seconded by the academicians welcoming back their prodigal son. Thirty-three of the society's other thirty-nine members had been elected after Voltaire's exile had begun in 1750, and had therefore never seen him seated among them. The roar of acclaim lasted until the ponderous doors were shut. Voltaire was shown to the chair of the perpetual secretary in front of which he made a sign as if to refuse it, but with insistent invitations to the contrary, he finally acceded to the throne. The members took their seats, the other visitors were escorted to a row of chairs by the wall, and Jean le Rond d'Alembert, the *Academie française*'s perpetual secretary, approached the honored guest.

"In view of your exceptional visitation to the august premises of the *Académie française* which have for these past twenty-eight years felt the absence of the echoes of your steps and the resonance of your voice, the members of this institution have voted you to be their perpetual secretary for the duration of your stay in our capital."

Voltaire smiled in toothless modesty. "*Merci beaucoup*," he nodded to the members, "*merci beaucoup*. Such an honor you bestow on me!"

Then, with the old philosopher's friends taking the lead, Condorcet, the *duc* de Richelieu, Jean-François de la Harpe, Jean-François Marmontel, the *comte* de Buffon, *l'abbé* Condillac, and the *marquis* de Voyer d'Argenson de Paulmy (the one whose library was educating Zénobe), and two or three more, offered speeches worthy of Marcus Aurelius in order to commemorate the occasion and to communicate their esteem, respect and admiration to a man who had before his death already achieved the status of a god, and by whose lights newer generations could continue the travail and progress in the pursuit of their goddess, *la philosophie*.

Thibouville thought that he had gone in the space of a few minutes from terror-fraught panic to stultifying boredom, and he couldn't decide which was worse, until he heard, in-between the words of the orators, the crowd outside beckoning to Voltaire. It was a reminder that bad things always lurk in the world.

He was almost asleep by the time Voltaire was asked to address a few words to the assembly. The old man tottered to his feet and woke Thibouville up with his first sentence.

"My dear, respected brothers, fellow members of an institution founded by the *cardinal* de Richelieu almost a century and a half ago, we have a sacred duty to fulfill as stewards of the French language, which we are honor-bound to protect and to perfect, but at the same time, in view of our humanity and imperfectibility, we should be conscious of past sins and omissions that the present members need to expiate."

Except for those who knew Voltaire well, a murmur arose from the others in the hall. As far as they were concerned, they were the epitome of French men of letters, and none could do better, so there could be no sins or omissions.

"Why should we have a guilty conscience, you ask? Well, any institution that never invited one of the best authors of all centuries and of all lands to be part of its brethren, created an unpardonable omission that Jesus Christ would find difficult to pardon. I give you this writer's name. Jean-Baptiste Poquelin. Molière. Why was he never made a member of this hallowed academy? He was brilliant, he was prolific, and his literary creations today still serve to represent humanity's foibles: Harpagon, Tartuffe, Alceste, Scapin, Armande, even *monsieur* Jourdain. Perhaps it was his lowly background, being the son of an upholsterer, which kept him out of this august institution. I blush at the injustice, but if it is true, that he was excluded because of his family background, then we, today, must face this glaring omission and make it right, by the realization, and the formal recognition, that genius and social status have no connection, and that the geniuses of the next generation might even now be trying to claw their way out of the profundities of our cruel and unyielding social hierarchy."

Condorcet, who was already fomenting the revolutionary idea that education should be universally offered to the masses, was the first to applaud Voltaire's comments. A few others joined him. But most remained with hands nailed to their laps.

"The second sin of which I make reference, is to me even more incredible. One of the tasks assigned to the *Académie française* from almost its very inception, was to take responsibility for the compilation and publication of a French dictionary. This task has unfortunately not yet been brought to fruition. Members of this most august fraternity! We must light a fire beneath us. Language is a living thing, changing, multiplying, energizing itself as we speak, because we speak. A dictionary waits for no generation. Each generation owes it to itself to paint a portrait of its language before it's handed over to the next generation. If you will allow me, my niece here has the papers to the first letter of the alphabet. In the time that I've been in Paris, I have taken the opportunity to write out the definitions and usages of words beginning with the letter A. I'm up to A-m, and I should be finished with the rest in the remaining weeks of my stay here. If each of you manages to take responsibility for a letter, even half a letter, we should be finished with this task within a year. By the time I return to Paris in the autumn, I would be willing to take over a P, or an R, even a Q."[240]

The assembly laughed. By the time Voltaire had finished his speech, the members of the academy could hardly wait to run home and begin with their assigned letters. There was glory and immortality in the making of a dictionary. The examples to be used to illustrate the words would come from their best literary works. They would hold the public in awe of their lexicological prowess and would forever be known as the Academicians who had achieved the dictionary for the new generation.

But Voltaire had to run. The path between the Louvre and the Tuileries Palace was short, but the crowd in-between was still overwhelming. To what point they realized only when they went out the Louvre's front courtyard again. The snake was now a sea of humanity, lapping towards them with waves of bodies, thousands of arms reaching up wishing to take Voltaire in its huge embrace. And the noise was deafening. Thibouville collapsed against the doorway and realized that he would never be able to throw himself into that beast, that beseeching, voracious maw whose very papillae were crying out to Voltaire to join them, to join them. Voltaire and his group continued to walk, and Thibouville saw how the papillae reached over to taste Voltaire, to touch him wherever they could, on his arms, on his shoulders, on his head. The papillae followed him like a huge walking mouth. From his vantage point, Thibouville saw the little group arrive at the *berline*, and, after Voltaire, his niece and the two Villettes went in, the horde took control of the white horses, with two or three people sitting on each of them, and with more people clambering up on the roof of the *berline*. Thibouville saw in horror how the fantastic procession began slowly to wend its way to the Tuileries Palace, the *berline* floating away on a swarming sea like a funeral barge on the river Styx.

Thibouville waited until he calmed down and then, after the darkened courtyard was as deserted as the moon, he began to make his way to the Pont Neuf. Over his shoulder, back towards the west, he could still hear the roar of the Furies. The *marquis* was ecstatic that they loved Voltaire, for they could just as easily have torn him apart into his constituent atoms.

---

240   Voltaire was always willing to draw laughter. This last bit, in French (*je voudrais bien m'occuper d'un P, d'un R, ou même d'un Q*), plays with homonym meanings: I would be willing to take over a fart, an air, or even an ass.

Voltaire was not worried, but someone had torn out tufts of ermine fur for a keepsake, and his wig was sitting awry on his head. The gauze placed in the corner for his protection was pulled down to enable him to be seen, and someone cried out that Voltaire's hand was as young and fresh as a young girl's. "It's a miracle!" cried the lucky possessor of the hand, not realizing that in the tumult of the moment he was holding on to the *marquise* de Villette's hand.

The *berline* inched its way to the *Salle des Machines* in the Tuileries Palace, the temporary home of the *Comédie française*, and only when the crowd wished the *berline* to disgorge its occupants was it allowed to do so. Stepping off at the Carousel, Voltaire basked in the glory of their love, smiling like a sage who's come down from the mountain and touching as many hands as he could.

It took half an hour to walk into the theater. Once inside, Voltaire and his three guests were not allowed to sit in *monsieur* de Villette's box. No, a special arrangement had been made, and they were to sit in the box belonging to the gentlemen of the king's bedchamber, on the first row. Amid a deafening roar, Voltaire was placed in the center of the box, with *madame* Denis and the *marquise* de Villette to his sides, and the *marquis* de Villette behind him. Nobody dared go against the choreography of the mob. One of the actors, *monsieur* Brizard, handed *madame* de Villette a crown of laurel, to be placed on the patriarch's head. She stood in order to place it on her adoptive father's wig, but in modesty he removed it, only to have the mob shout out in a tone of disapproval. He instantly replaced it on his head and left it there, and the audience replaced its shouts with such thunderous applause that it sounded like the heavens were about to engulf them all.

On the stage, where the curtains were still closed, the entire cast came out. In unison, they turned towards Voltaire's box and bowed or curtsied to the ground. The crowd's reaction was overwhelming. To the din of shouts and applause was added the thunder of thousands of stamping feet, and the dust of centuries arose from the wooden planks, beams and banisters, suspending an opaque haze into the air. Without the commotion abating for a minute, after half an hour the curtains opened, and the crowd quieted enough for the first few lines of the play to be enunciated, after which the crowd again erupted into riotous clamor. The little figure of Voltaire was at the center of this maelstrom and he pressed his hands together and said, "You are killing me with kindness," but not even *madame* Denis or the *marquise* de Villette could hear him.

The *marquis* de Thibouville was not amused when, after having walked all the way home, he found the door by the side gate locked. He had never seen the *hôtel* de Villette locked up like this. He rattled the door and found it wasn't bolted. Thank Jove the *marquis* de Villette had long ago given him the key, one day when he had extolled Thibouville's personal virtues and his presence at the *hôtel* de Villette as a 'kindred spirit.'

"That was all a lot of rot," Thibouville said to himself out loud as he searched different pockets for his keys, which he eventually found. He crossed the courtyard and found the kitchen door locked as well. He peered into a window and rapped on it with his knuckles, but all was dark inside and there didn't seem to be anyone there.

"That's strange," he observed, again speaking out loud. He had already put his keys away, so he again began searching for them. He found the right key after fumbling in the dark and managed to open the door. Once inside the kitchen, he went to the stove, found a long wooden match, and lit the four candles of a candelabrum. He went to the pantry, looked for a bottle of mead, and poured out a steinful almost to the rim. He enjoyed two long draughts while standing in the pantry, then refilled his stein, one of a dozen that had been a gift to Voltaire from Frederick II, but which Voltaire had given to the *marquis* de Villette since the old man didn't like to drink beer or mead. Then he proceeded across the kitchen and into the hallway, but instead of taking the main staircase, he slipped into a small storage room, put the candelabrum down on a shelf, and undid a hidden latch that opened a secret door at the back of the small room. Since none of the staff even knew of the secret passageways deep in the recesses of the *hôtel* de Villette, no maid or valet had ever had a hand in cleaning them. But the spiders' webs and strange shadows and stale air didn't bother the *marquis* de Thibouville. He felt safe there, ensconced and alone and unobserved. He ascended a staircase whose steps had been reinforced during construction to keep them from creaking. Thibouville would have gone straight up to his own room, but since he had both hands full, he decided it would be easier to come out a floor below, into the *marquis* de Villette's boudoir. Placing the candelabrum on the floor, he used his free hand to unlatch the secret door. When he went in, he saw several lighted candles placed around the room, and thought it strange, for Villette never left lighted candles in his absence. There were a few remaining embers in the fireplace. He went to his favorite *bergère*, and sank deep into it with his mead, and proceeded to enjoy it with solitary delight.

After Zénobe and André had enjoyed *monsieur* Maurel's dinner, *poulets en musette à la Financière*,[241] they had placed the dishes back on their tray and placed the tray out of view in the dumbwaiter. Then they had enjoyed the rest of their Sauternes wine in heavy blue Saint-Louis goblets, taking sips interspersed with long lingering kisses. For the first time, they felt all alone in their lovemaking, not having the sleeping staff in adjoining rooms to worry about. They had so much more room, as well, luxuriating in a bed three times the size of the one they had to share in the back room of the servant's quarters. It had been very nice of *monsieur* Maurel to have lent them the *marquis* de Villette's bedroom for the afternoon. Not that they had ever envied their master's vast wealth, but they were young enough to enjoy vast wealth's accouterments in innocence. They could be impressed, and boast to themselves, and walk around naked in a cocky manner with the braggadocio that comes from fine, expensive things. They even went into the *marquis' garderobe* and tried on some of his shirts and coats, but they were too small for them. Zénobe found a *robe de chambre* that wasn't too narrow for his shoulders, and paraded around in it, regally refilling his glass and André's with more wine. But after a spirited, and vociferous, bout of lovemaking, they had both fallen asleep in each other's arms concealed behind the voluminous curtains of the *marquis* de Villette's big bed.

---

241   Hens cooked inside lambs' bladders.

When the *marquis* de Thibouville walked into the room, they heard not a thing. The *marquis* heard nothing and suspected nothing, except for finding it strange that Villette had left several lighted candles around the room. Perhaps Villette had been in too much of a rush to blow them out. But Maurel should have seen to it that they were snuffed out and the place tidied up. He could see a few cushions on the floor, and even though they bothered him enormously, he was too tired to get up and place them back on the chairs. But what he saw next made him knit his brows in puzzlement. There was something white at the foot of Villette's bed, and hanging off of it, like a cantilevered cushion or shoe, but without any visible means of support. Thibouville wondered what was holding it up, but in spite of his curiosity, he instead took another sip of his mead, which tasted wonderful and was bolstering his tranquility and obliterating his fatigue. As warmth coursed through his veins, he had to fight off the last vestiges of his fright with the many-headed hydra that had taken Voltaire and company away in its maniacal embrace. He hoped that the playwright was safe, and that the play was being performed without a hitch.

The play was being performed, to be sure, but the hitches were so numerous, the interruptions for standing ovations so overwhelming, that hardly anybody was paying attention to the words. Even the actors, when the enthusiasm of the crowd became too great, broke character and bowed and curtsied in reverence to the playwright. *Madame* Vestris in her role of Irène was weeping in a scene where no tears were called for. The evil emperor, who had heretofore bowed to no man, was stooping low before the little old man who was responsible for all of this. Voltaire would send kisses through the air, then hold his heart, then send off more kisses.

No one left the theater. It wasn't until hours later that Versailles found out about this ecstatic welcome given to Voltaire, but a sleepy Louis XVI looked as if he were asking, "Well, why are you telling me this as I'm going to bed?" and Marie Antoinette managed to ask, "Ah, is that possible?" before placing her next bet in a game of faro.

Monsieur Maurel woke up from his nap feeling refreshed but very disoriented. There seemed to be no more light coming in from his window. It felt as if it were late, but he needed to remain in bed for a minute to try to bring his ideas into focus. There was nothing to be worried about, but perhaps it was time to bring André and Zénobe out of the *marquis* de Villette's bedroom and back into his own. The boys probably even had time for a lesson before the theater party came back to the *hôtel.* In Maurel's opinion, these lessons needed to continue, but it wasn't possible to have them every day, what with unforeseen events keeping one, or both, boys away. Sometimes Maurel thought that André viewed himself as inferior to Zénobe, and these lessons would help to rectify that. He was glad that no preparations for supper were going to be necessary. If people were hungry, there was Reblochon cheese and crusty bread, and he himself could whip up an omelette or a crêpe.

He got up and dressed quickly but carefully. He even put on his wig. Walking downstairs in a happy, sleepy haze, he realized the whole house was dark. As soon as he retrieved his two angels from *monsieur le marquis'* bedroom, he would have them go downstairs and light candles in preparation for the arrival of the theater group. In the dark hallway, Maurel walked up to the *marquis'* room and opened the door a crack to peek in. He didn't want to catch André and Zénobe in the middle of something. When he heard no sounds emanating from within the boudoir, he opened the door the rest of the way and walked in.

It wasn't until he was in the middle of the room that he saw an aristocrat sitting on one of the *bergères.* Maurel froze and felt something deep in his gut ignite in a sudden fire. He was all of a sudden wide awake and unable to breathe. The figure on the *bergère* was still, with his head bowed down to his chest. In the flickering light of the candles Maurel couldn't tell who it was. The figure was holding a beer stein in one hand, but seemed to have dozed off.

Where were André and Zénobe? He quickly went to the bed and peeked into the curtains. They were both in there, sound asleep, lying on their sides like two spoons. How was he going to wake them up without waking the person on the *bergère?* Maurel looked at the person's shoes, and recognized that it was the *marquis* de Thibouville. What the devil was he doing in the *marquis* de Villette's bedroom? He must have come back to the *hôtel* early. Whatever happened, the *marquis* couldn't possibly be allowed to discover that there were two servant boys in the master's bedroom, sleeping in the master's bed.

The stein in the *marquis* de Thibouville's hand was in danger of turning and emptying its contents onto the Oriental rug. Maurel had to act quickly.

In two steps he was in front of the sleeping *marquis* and gently prying the stein from his fingers, hoping that this action wouldn't wake him. But it did.

"*Monsieur le marquis* de Thibouville," he said loud enough to wake up the ghosts in the rafters. Or the angels in the room. "What a pleasant surprise to see you here!"

"Yes? Ah! What is it?" asked a befuddled Thibouville.

"It is such a pleasure to see you here, but why aren't you at the theater with the others?"

Thibouville regained his composure, but remained sleepy.

"There were too many people waiting for Voltaire. Thousands. I couldn't, I couldn't do it. Go to the theater, I mean. It was madness. Absolute madness."

Then he stretched his back and remembered the candles.

"Maurel, when I came in here, I saw all of these candles burning all over the place. They should not have been left unattended. And look at those cushions. It's a bordello in here."

Thibouville held out his hand for one of the cushions. Maurel quickly went around the seating area of the boudoir and picked up a few, and gave one to the *marquis* who put it behind his back.

"Where is my stein?"

"Here it is, *monsieur le marquis.*"

Thibouville took it and drained it. There mustn't have been much left.

"Ah," said Maurel. You must have run out. Shall I run to the kitchen and get you some more? Was it mead you were having?"

"No, thank you, Maurel. I think I'll just remain here in quiet repose and wait for Villette."

Maurel almost panicked. "But *monsieur*, you must be tired. Your experience must have been terribly frightening or otherwise you would have accompanied the others to the theater. Shall I escort you to your room?"

"No, no. The mead must have removed the remaining pangs of fear, for I feel quite comfortable now. Look, there's another cushion out of its place."

"Where, *monsieur*?" Maurel could see no other cushions on the floor.

"There, on the bed. It seems ready to fall off."

With his better eyesight Maurel could see it was a foot. It was the foot of one of his angels.

"Ah, *monsieur le marquis* de Villette must have been in a terrible hurry before he left," laughed Maurel. "He doesn't usually leave the premises in such disarray."

"Indeed he does not. That's something we both shared, from the very beginning. A distaste, no, an abhorrence for disorder and uncleanliness. 'Everything has its place,' *Maman* used to say. 'Order is its own reward.' And my favorite, 'Cleanliness is next to godliness.' But that last one belongs to *monsieur* Benjamin Franklin. My mother would have loved him."

Maurel had removed the offending foot and replaced it with one of Villette's robes that he found inside the bed next to his angels. His angels were stark naked. But they were now awake, and frightened to death. Where were their clothes? thought Maurel. Where were the dirty dishes from their dinner?

He continued prattling. "Oh, indeed, ladies simply love *monsieur* Benjamin Franklin. He displays a certain *savoir faire* with them, and they seem to swoon in pleasure at the sight of him. Which is curious, when one realizes that he is not the most handsome man in the kingdom. Wouldn't you think so, *monsieur* de Thibouville?"

Maurel was moving swiftly as he spoke. He whisked away the *robe de chambre* and took the stein to the dumbwaiter. There he saw that André and Zénobe had already stashed away the dirty dishes. He pulled the lever and sent the whole thing down to the kitchen. That left only their clothes. Where had they put the clothes they were wearing?

"Meh," shrugged the *marquis*. "On the contrary. He's rather homely. And so very stout. But he does have that high unparalleled intelligent forehead. And that twinkle in his eye, which makes him resemble a mischievous little boy. He has a nicely delineated philtrum. In the evening, his whiskers seem abundant and manly, not like our sparse French beards that sprout only on our chins. His lower lip is full and sensual, almost as if he were pouting. Hah! I can't believe I am coming to this realization, but I do believe that I wouldn't kick him out of bed. Me, with Benjamin Franklin? Is that not terribly funny?"

"Oh, *monsieur le marquis*, do not make me laugh so!" exclaimed Maurel. "That would indeed be quite a sight. The roly-poly *monsieur* Franklin and yourself, so trim, so well-coiffed, so, so, neat, and balanced in your equilibrium, while he, he, would just roll around the bed, like a loaded die. I would be afraid that he would squash you!"

The *marquis* didn't like the sound of that possibility. Besides, he thought that Maurel was being too familiar, sharing thoughts about him and another man in bed.

"Quite," said Thibouville dryly. "That would be rather annoying."

Maurel bit his lip. He was pretending to put order back into the boudoir, all the time searching for André and Zénobe's attire. Where the deuce had they put their clothes?

Zénobe and André had been awakened by the name of the *marquis* de Thibouville. But it was *monsieur* Maurel who had spoken it. They had thus been roused in alarm, but all they could do was open their eyes in panic. They did not dare twitch any other muscle. They could tell that Maurel was communicating to them that the *marquis* de Thibouville was in the room, had been in the room for a while, from the looks of it. Apparently he had fallen asleep in an armchair and had not seen that they were in bed, hidden behind the bed curtains. It was André's white foot that was hanging off the edge of the bed, and the *marquis* didn't seem to notice that Villette's robe was too dark a color, a reddish brown, to be substituted for the precariously placed cushion. After Maurel pushed André's foot in, he pressed down hard on all the feet he could find to let them know to stay motionless and silent. The boys scrunched up into a ball and dared not breathe.

Monsieur Maurel quickly took the *marquis* de Villette's *robe de chambre* into the *garde-robe*,[242] not to hang it up neatly in the *armoire*, but to throw it on top of the vanity while looking madly around for André's and Zénobe's clothes. They were not there.

He reappeared in the boudoir, and in the pretense of looking for more wayward cushions, got down on his hands and knees and looked under the bed. Nothing.

When Maurel was back on his feet, the *marquis* de Thibouville removed his wig and held it out in his hand. Maurel came over to retrieve it.

"On second thought," said Thibouville, "I think I shall have a bit more mead. My throat still feels so dry."

"*Oui, monsieur le marquis.*"

"And I think I'll stretch out on the bed."

Maurel's heart fell through his stomach.

"Ah," he cried, so loudly that it startled the *marquis*. "The bed… the bed is not made. *Monsieur le marquis* de Villette must have lain in it after Suzanne made it earlier, and the sheets are… rumpled, the bedcover is… is… rumpled. Why don't you stretch out on the *chaise longue* instead? Look, I shall place it by the f-f-fire that I that I that I shall stoke for you. It'll be cozy and snug and I'll fetch a nice woolen blanket and, there! I'll remove your coat and your shoes, *voilà*, and wouldn't you want some warm brandy instead, *monsieur le marquis*?"

Inside the bed, André and Zénobe started to tremble. No, they thought, don't leave the room! And if you do, on your way out, don't close the door!

"Thank you, Maurel, I do feel cozy by the fire, but I think brandy will burn my throat. I think mead is what my throat needs. And my nerves."

Maurel threw another log into the fire and slid the screen in front of it.

"May I feel the *marquis'* forehead to see if he has a fever?"

"You may."

"Ah, my dear *monsieur le marquis*, I do believe you have a slight fever. I should go to bed if it prove to be so and coddle it."

"But I was going to bed until you put me on the *chaise longue*."

"No, no, I mean go to bed in your own bedroom."

---

242   The *garderobe* was a small room behind the boudoir into which were placed an *armoire*, a vanity (a dressing table with a small mirror on top), a *psyché* (a full-length oval mirror hanging on a horizontal swivel), and, for more modern individuals, a *chaise percée*. The *marquis* de Villette liked to think of himself as modern, yet he didn't have a *chaise percée*. Voltaire did, however, as did *madame* Denis.

"No. No. I wish to wait for the *marquis* de Villette. I want to know all the news of their evening at the theater. Maurel, you should have been there. The throng. It was alive. It was a monster. It swept away everything that lay in its path."

Thibouville shuddered.

The monster still wasn't pacified. The play had ended, and still it clamored for more. Nobody could guess what it wanted. The actors had curtsied and bowed until their leg muscles ached. Voltaire's wreath of laurels was losing some of its leaves. Yet the monster rattled the theater as if the deluge itself was falling on the Palais des Tuileries. The roar was deafening, the acclaim overwhelming. It was unrestrained delirium, a voracious hunger for a little old man who had been absent for far too long, and who, unbeknownst to everybody there, symbolized a resolution of all the problems that they had had and were still having. Social problems, religious problems, economical problems, civic problems, legislative problems; the kingdom was broken and the king could not put it back together again. In his stupidity and retrenched religiosity and sclerotic Ancien Régime mentality, he was not even here on this day. None of the Royals was here today, everybody but the king had already seen the play. And guess what, seemed to cry the thundering voices accompanied by the maniacal applause, they were not missed. The only king on hand today, with his simple crown of victory, of democracy, was Voltaire. He was enough. Nevertheless, the mob had not had enough of him. The acclaim lasted and lasted and would not diminish. The actors, who were the only people thinking tonight, had the brilliant idea of leaving the stage for a few minutes and then reappearing, dressed in antique Greek costumes. They wheeled in after them a pedestal covered with a sheet. With great pomp they slowly unveiled what was on the pedestal. It was a bust of Voltaire, borrowed from the Louvre next door. The crowd went mad. More laurel was produced, and another crown was placed to encircle the bald pate of the noble marble. Voltaire stared at his duplicate, his representative, and burst into tears. The tears were sincere and copious and fell heavily down his cheeks. The crowd, too, erupted into tears, and the noise that had engulfed the theater became subdued, as if this weeping which followed the climax was like a light rain following the storm. The mob had had enough of Voltaire at last. It lifted him up in its thousand arms, along with the rest of his party, transferred him gently across the theater, and into the courtyard, and then delivered him with tender love into his carriage. The crowd parted and liberated him into the night. Under the power of the unencumbered white horses the *berline* slowly drove away. The horses' panaches that had been handled by a thousand hands were bent and awry, as bedraggled as the occupants of the vehicle.

Monsieur Maurel could not think of doing anything else to make the *marquis* de Thibouville more comfortable. The *marquis* was reposing on the *chaise longue*, with a blanket tucked in all around him, feeling morally sustained by Maurel who seemed to understand his harrowing experience with the crowd. He didn't always see eye-to-eye with Maurel, who always seemed to take Villette's side, which was proper, after all, yet Thibouville was always appreciative that Maurel was also one of them and understood in a way that most other majordomos seemed not to. One didn't always have to paint the entire picture for Maurel. The *maître d'hôtel* understood intuitively, instantly, in a most uncanny way.

"Thank you, Maurel. I think I'll be wanting my mead now."

"Oui, *monsieur le marquis*, I shall go get it immediately."

Maurel left the *marquis* de Villette's bedroom and closed the door behind him.

Thibouville had been looking into the fire, mesmerized by the flames and burning embers, looking like a row of miniature houses all on fire, but when he looked up into the room again, he caught sight of a most curious irregularity. It put the thrown cushions and unattended candles to shame. This was slovenliness unrestrained. There was, on the back of the door, hanging from the bolt, an array of clothing which, in spite of the fact that the trousers and the shirts were all hanging evenly, nevertheless created such a sight of disarrangement, of unsightliness, that the *marquis* de Thibouville's love of harmony was slighted.

"Villette would never have left those clothes like that, even if he had been in a rush," said Thibouville out loud. "He would have left them draped over the chairs or on the bed."

Too curious to stay put, Thibouville got off his comfortable *chaise longue* and crossed the room to go inspect the offending clothes more closely.

Why, these aren't even Villette's clothes, thought he. Wait a minute. These are servant's clothes. These are the clothes of a valet. Two valets, it seems.

Appalled by this insufferable discovery, Thibouville could not wait for Maurel to return with the mead. He walked over to the bed, and with one of his arms reached within the curtains feeling for the braided summons cord.

"No, please, don't pull it," said a voice from within.

Thibouville nearly fell over backwards.

"What! Who is it?"

Zénobe came out, naked as the day he was born, looking downcast and penitent.

"Zénobe, you nearly killed me with fright!"

"I'm sorry, *monsieur le marquis*. There was no other way to alert you to the fact that I was here."

"Had you given me a few more minutes, I would have surmised it on my own. Where is your partner?"

André slid out of bed and stood shoulder to shoulder with Zénobe.

For the second time within a minute, Thibouville's breath was taken away. He had already seen Zénobe's body, but had not yet had the pleasure of seeing André's. His initial fright was certainly well worth this new scene. His eyes couldn't get enough. Having two beautiful bodies to peruse, to compare, to admire, was heavenly. But he had to think quickly.

"Quick, go put on your clothes. Before Maurel returns."

André and Zénobe did not need insistence. They ran to their clothes and started to put them on.

"Tomorrow I begin to take over your afternoon lessons. After you come back from your fencing lessons, Zénobe, I want you to go fetch André and I want the two of you to come up to my boudoir. You need not tell Maurel. You need not tell anyone. When Maurel gets here, you tell him that I left, using the secret door. If he finds out that I discovered the two of you here, I promise you, so will the *marquis* your master. And he would be very sorry to know that two of his servants were caught, *in flagrante delicto*, by me, using his boudoir, abusing his bed."

The *marquis* de Thibouville was gone in a flash. When *monsieur* Maurel came in he saw his boys dressed and waiting for him by the open door.

"*Monsieur* de Thibouville left by the back door," said Zénobe.

"And we got dressed in a hurry," added André.

Maurel sighed. "That was a close call. It was stupid of me to have set you up in here, but I never dreamed he would come back early. Oh, my heart was pounding. But what a relief! Well, my boys, go downstairs and light the candles and wait for everybody's arrival. Some of the staff are already here. I'll go to *monsieur* de Thibouville's room to give him his mead. Off you go, lads. But, wait a minute. Where were your clothes? I didn't see them anywhere."

Zénobe looked sheepish. "We were lying on top of them. I suppose we couldn't wait to take our clothes off, and they landed pell-mell."

"Ah, my angels. The impatience of youth!" said Maurel before he went off to the third floor to deliver the mead.

Zénobe and André looked at each other, but had no time to brood over what awaited them in Thibouville's bedroom the following afternoon. They didn't have time to talk it over that night either, because André had tasks to do and Zénobe had to help an extremely tired Voltaire to bed. As he gave the old man his nightly dose of medicinal opium, the *philosophe* told him of the events of the evening, and he fell asleep in Zénobe's arms talking about the roar of the crowd and the intensity of his feelings.

Becoming April Fools

Alexander the Great had been considered by the Egyptians to be a living God, and he was allowed to rule over them as he pleased. The only difference between him and Voltaire was that Alexander was thirty years old, and Voltaire was 84. On the day following his apotheosis, this old god was too tired to get out of bed. He was even too tired to work on his dictionary. This god, just like the Real One, didn't have an inextinguishable amount of energy and needed to rest every once in a while.

In the end, everybody came to see Voltaire in his bedroom. All the philosophers, academicians and scientists who wanted to congratulate him on his double celebration of the preceding day came in droves. The *abbé* Gaultier and the *curé* Tersac, the two ecclesiastics most anxious about the state of Voltaire's soul, tried to come in through the side gate, but were rebuffed. They got lost in the mob milling about the quai des Théâtins, a mob as great as it had ever been since the 10th of February. Only one thing was different: this crowd was boisterous, and chants kept breaking out among the multitude: "The writer of *Œdipe*, the writer of *Mérope*, the writer of *Zaïre!*"[243] Also: "*L'homme aux* Calas, *l'homme aux* Sirven, *l'homme aux* Lally!"[244] The people turned their backs on the two men of God, sometimes intentionally jostling them with their shoulders. Dressed in their black garb, the *abbé* and the *curé* were quickly vomited to the outskirts of the crowd, as if the mob were an organism wishing to rid itself of a distasteful foreign object.

Zénobe had all the time in the world today. He left early to go to the Arsenal Library, and while there, tried to think of a way to circumvent the *marquis* de Thibouville's power over André and himself. Blackmail was a powerful force, but he was confident that one of the books in this huge library would be able to throw some light on the subject. He scoured Voltaire's writings against the arbitrary powers of feudal institutions. They helped him realize that the *marquis*, any *marquis*, had powers over him that no state judicial court and no ecclesiastical judge could ever overturn. Some of the arbitrary powers belonging to the king trickled down to the nobility, and even a vassal's life was not as worthy as that of the aristocrat. And a vassal's life could be directed, controlled and dominated by any person possessing a title. A thrice-titled *marquis* could without question send Zénobe and André to hell, if so he wished.

Even if Voltaire had been available for discussion, Zénobe doubted he could have brought up the issue with him. The *marquis* de Thibouville was a guest living under the roof of the *marquis* de Villette, so in a sense, Zénobe would be in conflict with

---

243   These are the titles of Voltaire's most popular plays.

244   These are victims of false justice whose cases were defended by Voltaire.

both of the noblemen, and he didn't wish to put Voltaire in the position of having to choose sides between his servant caretaker and his aristocratic host. Zénobe began to wonder why Voltaire had friendships with Villette and Thibouville in the first place. Two known *homosèxes*? Two very tepid writers? Two mediocre minds? Perhaps it was the two insecure *marquis* who had latched on to Voltaire in order to gain some social confidence. And Voltaire would never have said no to a relationship with an aristocrat. In all practicality, the *aristos* were beneficial to the way the world ran, and the world was run by them. They had purchasing power and always were in the market for more. True, the *marquis* de Villette was only a second-generation aristocrat, but the *marquis* de Thibouville's family dated from 1276 (under their title of Lambert from Normandy), and they held a total of three titles, Lambert, Herbigny and Thibouville. They had money, territory and influence, although this latest scion needed Voltaire's luminous friendship to give his influence a boost.

Zénobe felt despondent, for he didn't know how he was going to confront Thibouville later on that afternoon. He and André were going to have to yield to his whims like two little sheep. And judging from what Thibouville had already required of him, he was sure that André, too, was going to have to submit sexually to the *marquis*, and Zénobe didn't think he would be able to stand seeing André under Thibouville in an act of sexual subservience. Maybe the *marquis* would take each one separately? He felt ashamed that he and André could be the objects of lust to an older man and they could do nothing about it. He was sitting in an armchair with Voltaire's books arranged about him when the *marquis* de Voyer de Paulmy d'Argenson surprised him.

"What, my favorite reader, not reading, and in a brown study?"

Zénobe sprang out of his chair and bowed to d'Argenson.

"Forgive me, *monsieur le marquis*, but I was thinking."

"I could see that. In a very concentrated way, I might add."

D'Argenson removed his gloves and indicated to Zénobe to sit down. The *marquis* sat down as well.

"I just came back from visiting your philosopher friend. He seemed in high spirits. His pompom didn't stop flicking around for a moment. I think he likes all that attention. He deserves it, mind you. He has set us back quite a ways, granted, meaning us, the aristocratic class, but he has certainly set the common people forward. I see you have been perusing his works."

D'Argenson picked up one of Voltaire's books. "Oh, yes, this is where he speaks against Jesuit monks, forced tithes, theological repression and corruption, and the unholy alliance between Church and State."

The *marquis* laughed while glancing through the book. "If only those priests weren't so stupid. They lay themselves open to such criticism. The buying and selling of administrative positions, the addled arbitrariness of their ecclesiastical courts, draconian punishments for simple crimes, the secrecy, the fanaticism, the persecution of nonbelievers, the oppressive coercion of conformity. I could go on and on."

"You could be speaking of aristocratic power as well," Zénobe snapped back.

A startled d'Argenson looked up from the book into Zénobe's eyes, and laughed.

"You are Voltaire's son," he observed.

Zénobe continued, "The buying and selling of noble titles to wealthy commoners; the injustice of forced feudal taxes on their vassals and the nobles themselves being exempt from taxes; the purchase of judges' seats by the highest bidder, and the ability to inherit such seats as if they were a farm in Normandy; the corruption at court; the political repression of anyone who does not agree with the *status quo*; torture in the jails and other penal injustices; the arbitrary powers held by the privileged castes; and the social irresponsibility of the aristocracy in that unholy alliance between Church and State of which you speak. The noble class allows the injustice to go on, and does nothing when individuals are given the death penalty over sins, as opposed to crimes. The State should base its moral compass on truth, and truth stems from science, not religion. Religion wages war on the State, therefore State and religion should be seen as entities which are mutually exclusive."

"I can see how you became Voltaire's *protégé*, my brave young man. But today you speak in a different way. You are no longer discussing in the tone of the social scientist. Today you are bitter and angry, as if you were personally touched by these matters. Tell me, my son, what is wrong? Tell me how I can help you to avenge humanity."

Tears sprang to Zénobe's eyes. The *marquis* d'Argenson was a fellow academician of Voltaire's, a fellow bibliophile, and the fact that he was wearing a superb gentleman's outfit, along with his member regalia of the *Académie française*, did not seem to matter. Wasn't Zénobe himself wearing a superb Swedish gentleman's outfit? Maybe in this case clothes didn't make the men.

"*Monsieur le marquis*, you are very perspicacious for you have identified my worries. I am under the duress of an aristocrat who wishes to use me in a humiliating way, and I don't see any way to get out of it."

The *marquis* d'Argenson had lived a life full of experiences, and he had read many of the novels in his library as well. He understood what Zénobe meant by the word 'duress', although he misidentified the culprit.

"The *marquis* de Villette wishes to make himself master of your body? It was to be expected."

"It is not the *marquis* de Villette, *monsieur.*"

"Who is it then? Is it at the *hôtel* de Villette? Oh, it is the *marquis* de Thibouville!"

Zénobe nodded.

"Ha, ha," laughed d'Argenson. "Either way, you should find sufficient ammunition to use against them, one or the other. Why don't you just tell Voltaire?"

"Oh, no, I couldn't do that. *Monsieur* de Voltaire's new house on the rue de Richelieu won't be ready for a few months and in the meantime he is living at the *hôtel* de Villette. I wouldn't want anything to come between them, Voltaire and Villette I mean. The whole world is watching that house on the quai des Théâtins. I wouldn't want to make trouble for Voltaire."

"Hmm, at the expense of your well-being. Still, I can admire your prudence. Which means, then, that you are going to have to take on Thibouville under your own power, which I can identify as being more than adequate for the task."

"What do you mean, *monsieur*?"

"You are not a helpless little victim. You will use your ability to reason, and you will throw reason to his face. You will let him know that his designs upon your person are unreasonable, and that therefore he will have to cease his interest in you."

"He is threatening to tell the *marquis* de Villette about a... a... an indiscretion I committed."

"And what was that?"

"I used the master's bed to, to... to make love to another servant of the house."

D'Argenson seemed very interested in this last detail.

"And Thibouville caught you. Well, well, blackmail does have its edge, doesn't it? But you, but you! You come to the Library of the Arsenal dressed as a gentleman, and now you are using Villette's very bed in which to make love. Who do you think you are, *monsieur* Bosquet, a privileged scion of the Savoyard monarch?"

This last statement was said with amusement but with such bonhomie and frank admiration that Zénobe could not take exception, and he smiled.

"I would be the Savoyard monarch's regicide before I allowed him to be my father," he said, mustering as much good humor as he could.

"Well, how many princes in history have killed their fathers in order to be kings themselves? That would be nothing new."

With an elegant hand d'Argenson rang a golden bell placed on a table. He said to Zénobe, "We shall have a cup of tea and think about the possible answers you can convey to Thibouville. Something reasonable should put a stop to his advances. Tell me what you know about him."

Zénobe told the *marquis* d'Argenson all he knew about Thibouville, and with the older man's recommended points of action, Zénobe felt confident that he would be able to repel Thibouville with a few well-chosen points of argument. An articulate servant could very well hold his own against a mere *marquis* who may very well have wit, but not the wherewithal to fight against the voice of reason.

"But after our discussion here," said d'Argenson, "you had better go to your fencing lessons, just in case reason doesn't work out."

That afternoon, with André and Zénobe standing at attention in the *marquis* de Thibouville's boudoir, the *marquis* began to exact the price of his blackmail. He started by removing their wigs, and caressing and smelling their hair. Zénobe mulled over one of the *marquis* d'Argenson's lessons: blackmail is successful only when the victim's fear of being discovered in a compromising situation is greater than the fear of the price being extorted.

The *marquis* was caressing their necks. The cocky aristocrat took a fistful of Zénobe's hair, raised it up and started kissing the nape of Zénobe's neck. But when he started to massage André's pectorals Zénobe garnered hs courage and said, "André and I would rather confess our transgression to the *marquis* de Villette rather than suffer your sexual advances."

He had already told André that maybe all Villette would demand as punishment from his two wayward servants would be what Thibouville wanted, so yielding to one master's seduction over another's would be all the same to them. Were Villette to demand a harsher payment, send them away, for instance, Zénobe thought that another master in the house, greater than any of the others, might be interested in using his influence to support the two valets. Moreover, there was now another *marquis*, from the outside, and perhaps even a *duc*, who would have some sway over events and circumstances surrounding *monsieur* de Voltaire's main caretaker. D'Argenson was an influential man, and Richelieu certainly was not enamored of *messieurs les marquis* de Villette and de Thibouville.

Zénobe continued to address Thibouville. "It might also be worthwhile for me to let Voltaire's friends, the *marquis* d'Argenson and the *duc* de Richelieu, know about your antics."

Thibouville twirled Zénobe around to be able to look right into his eyes. "Why you ungrateful little monkey. You could bring letters from the King, dispensations from the Pope and special instructions from the Grand Vizir of Persia, but you would receive no aid in this situation. This is a private matter in a private house."

André's shoulders stooped and his head dropped, but Zénobe stood his ground.

"A house that belongs to the *marquis* de Villette. Perhaps he would not be amused that you would molest two of his servants."

Thibouville smiled with contempt. "He wouldn't care. When I'd be finished with you two, he could have a go at you himself. He and I have shared many experiences in this way. Sometimes we toss a coin to see who'll experience it first."

Zénobe shot back, "He wouldn't like the fact that you already haven't been in the sharing mood with at least one of those experiences."

André glanced at Zénobe.

Thibouville recognized that André was ignorant of his tryst with Zénobe, and realized he could use this as a wedge against them.

He said to André, "That's right, my son. The experience that master Zénobe is talking about is mine with him. Apparently *he* hadn't shared this tidbit with you, either."

André responded, "Do not be preoccupied, *monsieur*, about what intelligence Zénobe has or has not shared with me. I know who my enemy is."

And with that, André placed both hands on Thibouville's chest and shoved with all his might.

"No, André, no!" yelled Zénobe.

Thibouville flew across the room and landed hard on the floor. The momentum almost made him roll backwards on his head, but his flailing arms and legs stopped the motion.

André had worked himself up into a frenzy and ran to the *marquis* sprawled on the floor. He leant down and easily raised him up by the lapels, acting as if were going to give him a thorough thrashing.

Zénobe managed to throw his body between André's and the master's, staring into his friend's eyes like Mesmer looking for the soul's magnetic field.

André stopped his rampage. Zénobe turned around, picked up the *marquis*, and gently dropped him into an armchair.

The *marquis* de Thibouville's face showed such a disarray of expressions that Zénobe could not catch any single one overpowering the others. Confusion, mortification, anger, disbelief, embarrassment, hatred, contempt, humiliation, they all played about his eyes, brows and mouth with such speed and discomfiture that Zénobe decided to let him steep in his own emotions. He turned around to André.

"Only primitive people resort to violence when they are frustrated by their inability to express their feelings."

"But you said that you would be ready to fight a duel with the *marquis* de Thibouville."

"Yes, a duel with words, not with swords!"

"How was I to…"

"You have made things much worse, André, do you realize that?"

A spluttering noise made them both turn around.

Thibouville had regained his composure.

"You," he said to André, "you get out of my boudoir. Now."

André bowed to the *marquis* and left the room in silence.

"Please," began Zénobe.

"You, shut up. I want no more lip from you. You have done enough talking. I have never met a more garrulous, disrespectful and brazen servant. Know that I will do my utmost to have you both dismissed. Now, get out!"

Fury took a hold of Zénobe, but he tried mightily to keep his composure.

"I will get out of your boudoir, *monsieur* de Thibouville. Gladly. I didn't want to be here in the first place. And know that we did succeed in getting your foul hands off of us. You might have the upper hand, *monsieur*, but only because of your social standing. In this unjust society, you are the superior one, but you acquired this superiority through no individual merit, nor through dint of hard work or effort, but just because you inherited it. All you ever had to do to acquire everything you have in this world was to give yourself the trouble of being born!"

Zénobe walked out of the *marquis* de Thibouville's bedroom without even bothering to close the door behind him. He had saved André's honor, and he had redeemed his own. At what cost, at what loss, he did not yet know, but–blood of Christ!–had that felt good![245]

André was dismissed that very afternoon and placed on the diligence leaving for Normandy at 8 o'clock in the evening.

Nothing was told to Voltaire, and his young caretaker was allowed to stay, until another caretaker could be found.

Zénobe was the sorriest servant in Paris that evening. After he had put Voltaire under the covers and snuffed out all but one of the candles, he lay on the *chaise longue* and remained the most awake of sentinels. All night long, all he could think of was André on the stagecoach, traveling farther and farther away from Paris, on the long desolate highways of France.

---

245   (From the author) I take the wind out of the fact-checker's sail by preempting his footnote that, no doubt, would revel in Teutonic glee in its accusation of plagiarism. However, this scene is as it happened. Zénobe later recounted it to the *marquis* d'Argenson, who told his doctor, *le docteur* Bordeu, who told the philosopher Friedrich von Grimm, who told the *marquis* de Saint-Lambert, who told the *marquis* de Laborde (the king's banker), who told *mademoiselle la chevalière* d'Éon, who told Pierre Augustin Caron de Beaumarchais, who kept the scene in his memory until he wrote it down three years later when his character, Figaro, a *valet de chambre*, rails against his master, the *comte* Almaviva, who is not as intelligent as he, nor as assiduous, and yet enjoys the money, power and privilege of his class. "What did you do to have so many advantages?" asks Figaro in the famous monologue of Act V, scene 3, of the *Marriage of Figaro*. "You gave yourself the trouble of being born, nothing more." Zénobe said it first, and, unlike Figaro, he had the courage to say it directly to the offending aristocrat.

Laying the Masonry of a Future Foundation

n the morning of April 1st, such was Voltaire's excessive happiness and wanton energy, that not only did he conceive the insane idea of walking to the Louvre, but in his accelerated state he was also blessedly oblivious to Zénobe's heartache. Even when Maurel walked in, as Zénobe was helping Voltaire with his morning ablutions, the lighthearted philosopher didn't notice the *maître d'hôtel*'s red-rimmed eyes and look of utter despondency.

"I wish to sit in the hallowed chair which belongs to the perpetual secretary of the *Académie française.* I want to lord it up over all those religious types, to let them know that I am, if even for a little while, their superior. Additionally, I need to know if everybody is working diligently on his assigned letter. Where are we, Zénobe, with our A?"

Zénobe had just finished exchanging disconsolate expressions of woe with Maurel, but was quick to answer the philosopher.

"We have completed the A-m's, and we are working simultaneously on the A-n's, A-p's, and A-q's."

"Oh, the A-q's should go fast. It'll go like *aqua* down a hill. Perhaps we can work on those this afternoon. Ah, Maurel. What's the weather like today?"

"Cold and bitter," was the reply.

"Ah, but spring must be in the air. I feel lithe and dainty of step," said Voltaire, twirling around in an ancient dance step to give credence to his words. "Ever since I started taking that medicinal compound of the *duc* de Richelieu's, I feel animated. But he should know, he is as ancient as mud, and as viscous. Ah! Albuminous! Did we do albumin?"

"*Non, monsieur.*"

"Our duty is never done! But let's not work this morning! My wig, my coat. I do wonder, though, why the *duc* de Richelieu told us not to tell doctors Tronchin and Lorry about his miracle elixir. Surely they already know about opium's medicinal value. When I wake up in the morning, I feel refreshed, reinvigorated, as if I were sixty again!"

Voltaire let out a whoop that, in spite of Zénobe's sorrow, made the young man smile.

They were out the door in a flash, leaving Maurel alone to fiddle with the cushions and give free vent to a profusion of heavy tears and profound sighs.

Perhaps walking to the Louvre was not such a good idea, thought Zénobe to himself at first. As soon as they were out the front door of the *hôtel* de Villette, the small group assembled there stuck fast to their heels, and as they moved through the *quai*, their little nucleus collected more and more passersby. Zénobe saw that these people were all Voltaire's admirers. All they looked for was to be close to him and enjoy his presence.

"Oh, my hero, and that of humanity!" exclaimed a lady who had been walking in the opposite direction and in a flash changed course, forcing her servant to do the same. And in a similar vein, a hundred people dropped their errand or their marketing, and the group became a swarm. In the mere block it took to get to the Pont-Royal, the crowd was large enough to take up the full width of the bridge. Those few who refrained from joining the march had to press themselves against the sides of the bridge or clamber onto the light posts to avoid being swept up in the current. The same thing happened on the Carousel side of the Seine, and as the merry throng snaked up to the Port Saint Nicolas towards the Terrasse du Louvre,[246] there were a thousand strong to escort Voltaire to the *Académie française*.

An old soldier from the Seven Years' War with a bad leg saw the throng coming and, as soon as Voltaire had passed by, joined it, and yelled out, "We are your soldiers, *monsieur* de Voltaire, we are your battalion! We are your soldiers of freedom!"

Voltaire called out, "Against what do you fight?"

The old soldier yelled back, "Against the enemies of Reason!"

The people who heard this exchange spread it down the column, and, in a few minutes, the ragtag makeshift army was marching in unison, slowly enough to match Voltaire's unhurried pace, but with a synchronism which amazed everybody, especially those in the march, with the amplified sound of its regularly paced steps. Separately, they were just a coincidental collection of diversified humanity; together they were uniform in the assonance of their steps, and a constant force behind Voltaire.

They found out that Voltaire was visiting the *Académie française*, and they waited for him outside the Louvre in patient rows to be able to escort him back across the river.

The old *philosophe* caught the Academy members completely by surprise. There were only about fifteen of them in the great hall, scattered about in poses of silent meditation, or perhaps asleep, but upon recognizing Voltaire they jumped and scampered about like a lady besieged by sudden visitors, rearranging books and dusting off surfaces with her sleeves.

"What is he doing here? What does he want?" they asked themselves in frantic whispers.

The answer was quite clear when Voltaire plopped himself onto the perpetual secretary's chair and asked to see the minutes of a representative session.

"Which session?" asked Claude François Xavier Millot who, unfortunately, was the latest member to be elected, in 1777, and therefore did not know the protocol to be followed on such an occasion.[247]

"Any session," answered Voltaire. "A session with most of the members present. I know! Make it the session of the morning after my arrival in Paris. That would be..."

Voltaire turned to Zénobe.

---

246   Today the quai François Mitterrand.

247   Millot, author of historical works, and a former Jesuit, was nonetheless friendly with d'Alembert who had supported his election into the Academy. He had been one of only two ecclesiastics who had deigned to come to Voltaire's formal welcome on March 30th.

"February 11th," said Zénobe.

"February 11th," repeated the Academy's junior member. "That would be… Wednesday, February 11th. Here you are, *monsieur* de Voltaire, the minutes to the meeting of Wednesday, February 11th."

"*Merci beaucoup*, my good gentleman," said Voltaire.

He took the sheaf of papers and began to glance through them, every once in a while reshuffling them to make all the page edges straight.

Some of the members slunk to the recesses of the cavernous room, hiding among the bookshelves and keeping silent, for they remembered the Academy's discussion on the day after Voltaire's arrival.

Only Voltaire's chuckles could be heard, and every now and then, with some momentous discovery, he let out a telling utterance, like "uh-huh!" or "ah-ha!" In the end, he put the sheaf of papers down and told Zénobe, "I was very nearly given the cold shoulder! Had certain members had their way, I would have been divested of my membership. That would have established an ignominious precedent, for the only way that members up to now have been able to leave the *Académie française* is in a coffin. But, at least, it would have been Voltaire the cause of another new precedent."

Since the only members present this morning were newly elected (since 1746), Voltaire didn't know any by name. None of his cronies was there, and there certainly wasn't a quorum. But he had a desire to find out if members were working on their letters for the new dictionary. Time was of the essence. For him, anyway. He didn't want to go back to Ferney without knowing that some foundations had been set.

After a moment's hesitation, he called out to no one in particular, "Paper, if you please, ink, and a quill."

When the accouterments had been produced, Voltaire instructed Zénobe to stand behind a beautifully carved scriptorium. The quill's ostrich plume towered over the secretary's head and, when he began to write, danced with elegant grace.

"Apathy. Noun. Apathetic. Adjective. Definition: insensitivity; loss of reaction due to an absence of will, of energy, or of sensation; incuriousness. Examples: The people's apathy upon their king's demise was eclipsed by their antipathy for his successor. After gorging herself with dainty morsels during supper, the lady looked on with apathy at the appetizing desserts laid out for her enjoyment."

"Aphonia," pronounced Voltaire. "Noun. Aphonic. Adjective. Definition: the loss of voice; the inability to emit sounds through the pharynx; extinction of the voice; voiceless, muteness. Examples: The priest's violently vociferous delivery of his sermon left him aphonic for the rest of the day. After a morning spent yelling at his hounds, the hunter's voice was stilled by aphonia in the evening.[248]

As other members came into the chamber, they had the pleasure of observing this unprecedented scene: someone actually working. Word got out, and members who had not planned on putting in an appearance at the Academy on that day, hastily changed plans in order to come around. After the second hour of Voltaire's visit, nearly everyone was there. Voltaire's friend and usual perpetual secretary, d'Alembert, brought his personal secretary with him. They began to work on the letter B. Others produced secretaries, and ere long, a hubbub ensued, with all of the letters but F, G, N and the second half of T represented. Words were pronounced, definitions were rolled out,

---

248   Only aristocrats were allowed to hunt. Poachers, that is, hunters who were commoners, were thrown in jail for a period determined by their lords' pleasure.

examples were created. The participants quickly concluded that the examples could be their most artistic contribution to the Academy's dictionary. It was later decided that their initials would appear at the head of each letter, in order for them to receive proper credit.

For three hours Zénobe scribbled energetically, lost in the work of the lexicon. Around him, the other sages of the Academy worked diligently, scouring their minds for lucid examples of the words they were describing, with pride and pleasure beginning to dawn on their faces.

It was when they were walking home, Voltaire and Zénobe escorted by their multitude, that the young secretary realized the lesson he had just learned. Throwing himself into work could appease his heart temporarily. He couldn't change his or André's fate, but at least he could render it less dolorous by the distraction afforded in labor. In action he would find something to divert his lugubrious thoughts.

Docteur Tronchin, who had not bothered to come to the *hôtel* de Villette in a long while, deigned to visit his patient after he heard of that morning's folly.

"He walked to the Louvre? That does not seem possible," he exclaimed.

Yet when he saw the spry Voltaire that afternoon, he realized he was looking at a new man. Checking his pulse, he felt it strong and determined. He had to report that Voltaire now seemed full of vigor, and his ailments, especially those centered around his abdomen, seemed diminished, and with brow knitted in surprise and incomprehension, the doctor even admitted the possibility of these ailments having completely vanished.

While those around him lauded the wonders of new science, Tronchin kept quiet, for he had done nothing to bring about this astonishing cure, and he doubted that Lorry had in his medical arsenal the necessary wherewithal to produce such miraculous healing.

There were three very miserable people at the *hôtel* de Villette these days. Zénobe was in anguish, but courageous in his fortitude and effort to keep to his schedule, and to maintain his attention to Voltaire and his responsibilities to the household. He also continued gamely with his visits to the Arsenal library and with his fencing lessons.

Maurel was leaden with grief, deadened by depression. For the first time in his life, his administration slackened, and promptness and perfection began to creep out of the daily activities. Not that the expertly-trained servants lingered excessively at their tasks or degenerated into slovenliness, but everything which relied on Maurel's memory suffered. Perhaps the newspapers and mail were no longer delivered with the usual alacrity. Missing ingredients remained missing until the kitchen staff took it upon themselves to send Philippe or Henri to les Halles. The two *marquis'* personal effects took longer to return to their rooms or to be replenished. The *marquis* de Villette noticed his *maître d'hôtel's* look of woe and distraction but did not comment on it. It was he who had ordered André's dismissal but he felt magnanimous that he had refrained from alerting the police to the presence of a miscreant in his home. Servants had been arrested for lesser crimes. Raising a hand against a master was considered a grave–and punishable–offense.

The *marquis* de Thibouville did not notice Maurel's despondency. As a matter of fact, he stopped noticing anything at all, for he was the third person on the premises to be overwhelmingly engulfed in a deep and tragic despair.

Thibouville could barely endure the loss of Zénobe. He now realized that, had he not been so harsh and unyielding to the boys, he would not have lost them. Now, on the few occasions that he and Zénobe interacted, the young man looked directly into his eyes with, with, what was it? Not ferocity, not accusation, either, but with a directness that cut into the *marquis'* core. Gone in the boy's gaze was the usual consideration with which he had heretofore regarded him, his superior. And while the outward signs of respect and submission were still present in Zénobe's physical attitude, Thibouville realized that the esteem and deference he had once enjoyed from Zénobe had now vanished. Zénobe had ceased writing his little play about Voltaire, and Thibouville was afraid that perhaps he would never finish it. Looking into those icy blue eyes which stared back at him with frankness and aplomb, the *marquis* languished in a horrible dilemma: should he avow his error to this youth, relinquish his superiority over a trifle, and, what? confess his feelings for Zénobe? Apologize? Show his weakness? to a servant? He'd rather entrench himself in the silence of aristocratic dignity and feigned apathy, where passions remain unspoken, mute, in a sort of elegant and noble aphonia.

But the basic problem would remain: how to win the boy back? Thibouville was not supposed to have fallen in love with Zénobe! Yet the trembling of his fingers and the fibrillations of his heart whenever Zénobe was present in his room attested to a profound longing in his soul. How could this have happened? He had had age, experience and disdain on his side. But now, a secret rage against the vagaries of fate took hold of him, and he kept to his *chaise longue* and thought hard about the myriad of other possibilities that could have ensued on that fatal day when Zénobe talked back to him and André pushed him to the floor. Thibouville could have taken a different tactic. He could have shown more tact. He could have been grand of spirit and treated the boys with generosity and kindness, so that they would have willingly submitted to his entreaties. Why had he entrenched himself behind aristocratic obtuseness, behind the façade of authoritarian nobility, thereby driving the boys to revolutionary behavior? By his own actions, he had pushed them to rebel. Why? This had never happened before! Usually, the subordinate persons fell into line, with no wayward attitudes. Pliant and reliable had they always been under his tutelage. Why had these two boys been so different?

Such were the thoughts that besieged the hapless *marquis* de Thibouville's troubled mind. He remained indoors and incommunicado with the rest of the household, seeing only Maurel who, by his morose attitude, silently accused him of cruelty at every turn; and hoping to see, if only for brief moments, the beautiful and serious visage of Zénobe, which made him revel agonizingly in his despondency and exacerbate his utter despair, as if the *marquis* himself kept plunging and replunging a dagger into his own heart.

Jean-Baptiste Pigalle, who had already sculpted Voltaire in Ferney, was given the honor by the philosopher's admirers of sculpting him again. As the king's sculptor, Pigalle had to receive special permission from Louis XVI for this commission. Seeing that it was for Voltaire's formal statue that would eventually grace the hallowed halls of the *Académie française*, which was also under the king's jurisdiction, the king, finding no reason to deny this permission, gave it, albeit with an air of indifference, which proved to the court that His Majesty gave Voltaire no high esteem. As a matter of fact, since he had read nothing of Voltaire's, ever, or of any other *philosophe*, French or foreign, he felt no esteem at all for writers of Voltaire's sort. As a devout Christian, he would certainly never demean his faith by reading tracts that might conflict with his beliefs.

Once armed with the royal approval, Pigalle began to call at the *hôtel* de Villette at regular intervals to inspect his subject, take measurements, and begin to sculpt. The sculptor certainly was one to hold the subject in high esteem, for he gave Voltaire an expression of sagacious tranquility, of a beneficent wisdom which imparted to the observer the feeling of calm, of hope, of admiration, and the knowledge that learning, and the results of such learning, were in the best of hands.[249]

Jean-Antoine Houdon also started to call on the *hôtel* de Villette. No one sent him; he came of his own volition. He had heard that Voltaire's health had taken a turn for the better, and he wished to capture that resurgence of energy and brilliance for which Voltaire had forever been known. The fact that his subject was an octogenarian meant that possibly this would be Houdon's last chance of capturing him alive. Houdon did capture that life, that force of energy, of intellect, but simultaneously gave him a half-smile of impish sarcasm, as if Voltaire had just told the viewer a quip of sardonic irreverence or impudent impiety.[250][251]

Pigalle's statue was of a Greek elder statesman, of a Socrates or an Aristotle swathed in Grecian robes. Houdon's bust was of an old friend, leaning over to say something witty, funny, with head tilted to lend an ear to your reaction.

Since both *madame* Denis and the *marquise* de Villette were ever-present in Voltaire's bedroom for these sittings, cackling about purchases for the new house, Zénobe would leave Voltaire's bedroom to go mope elsewhere. One morning, on the seventh day after André's departure, Maurel made a sign with his gaze to let Zénobe know that his presence was required for something out of the ordinary. Judging from Maurel's nervous excitement, Zénobe could tell that this was no mere task to be done, but an alluring event of some sort, and one to keep secret. Zénobe followed Maurel into the kitchen, then into the pantry, but there were voices by the stove and without a word Maurel vacated the kitchen and led Zénobe out the door and across the garden to the servants' quarters. Nobody would be there now. They crossed the first two bedrooms of the low building and into the one all the way at the end, unused now, save for Zénobe's naps. Only there did Maurel, still wordlessly, slip out an envelope from his vest and hand it over to Zénobe. The young man did not immediately recognize the importance of this object, but Maurel's knowing gaze and breathless smile made him understand that this was no ordinary envelope. This was a blissful, delectable missive, a message

---

249   This statue is today in the Hermitage Museum in Saint Petersburg.

250   Houdon's last bust of Voltaire, that is, before the death mask, is today in the National Gallery of Art in Washington, D.C.

251   [From the author] You know, can I please tell this story at my own pace? Why even mention Voltaire's death mask at this point? Voltaire is feeling energized, his health is restored, and everything is great.

heaven-sent. Zénobe looked down upon it, but did not recognize the writing. He realized that he had never seen André's handwriting before. He was seeing a calligraphy that belonged to the person he knew in a most intimate way, and yet that was as new and strange as a recently discovered island in the tropics or a never-before observed planet in the solar system. He looked up with exhilaration towards Maurel, but the *maître d'hôtel* was no longer there.

"*Monsieur* Maurel?" he asked.

He went to the window. Maurel was already traversing the winter garden.

"*Merci, merci, monsieur* Maurel," Zénobe whispered.

He sat down on the edge of the bed. It was his bed, his bed with André. He remembered the first night he ever spent on the premises, hidden in this very bed, under the covers, by a valet of the household. It was this valet, kind and considerate, who would become his lover, his friend, his pupil, his mate. He looked down at the letter. Already, two fat circles had made inky rings around the words of the address.

> *Monsieur* Zénobe Bosquet
> *aux bons soins de Monsieur* Maurel
> à l'hôtel de Villette, quai des Théâtins
> Paris

He realized he was weeping, weeping like he never had in his life, the tears flowing out of him like some inexhaustible source high up in the Savoyard Alps.

Holding the letter away from his falling tears, he undid the wax seal. When he opened up the envelope, he saw that André had not begun the letter on the other side of it, but had put a drawing there instead. Zénobe marveled. He did not know that André could draw. It was a picture of two men sitting at a small secretary, on either side of it. Zénobe recognized it as being the secretary in *monsieur* Maurel's room. One of the men was speaking, with one hand to his heart and the other one flourished in the air. The other man was listening in seemingly rapt attention, an elbow on the secretary and his chin resting in his hand, one foot under the secretary but the other behind him, cocked at an angle as if he were ready to bolt off running. The drawing was done in India ink, same as the writing. There was a caption, Zénobe observed. It read, "The teacher speaks while his pupil listens." Zénobe smiled. He continued to study the drawing, interested in the myriad of small details the artist had included: the ink bottle, the quill on its stand, the desk's drawers, the young men's clothing, Zénobe's wig (André was wigless), their irises. Zénobe's were just circles whereas André's were filled in. This attention to details was impressive.

But Zénobe yearned to read the letter, which consisted of about twenty pages, guessing from the heft of it. André's writing was neat, consistent, without the flourishes evinced in the *marquis* de Villette's or in Voltaire's writing. It showed a light but firm hand, unwavering and sedate. It was a calligraphy that didn't call attention to itself.

Even the letter's salutation was sober: "*Mon cher ami estimé.*" Not that Zénobe was disappointed, but just curious about André not being overly emotive.

from the Corday residence
63 rue de Géole
à côté du Château de Caen
Caen, Normandy
the 3rd of April, 1778

My dear esteemed friend,

I arrived here yesterday without novelty or delay to a wonderful welcome into the bosom of my family who, after my absence of over a year, welcomed me with a year's worth of kisses and embraces. My parents and sister are well, especially Charlotte who has grown up to be a young lady, although a highly inquisitive one. I've had to hide from her in order to write this letter, for she is insistent in her desire to find out about things in the capital. She has already asked me three times to tell her about our visit to the author Jean-Jacques Rousseau and three times I have told her about it, with increasing attention to description of details, just as she has commanded.

Having never seen my parents' new residence, and having never been in the town of Caen, save for a few hours here and there, I am pleased and curious about their new arrangement in the town, although after having been in Paris for so long, Caen seems perhaps not as gay or sophisticated, but at the same time not as noisy and dirty. We do have our local aristocrats, but they would be laughed at by the noblemen and ladies of Paris.

My father, while happy in his new surroundings, is worried about the costs of living in Caen. His farm is still accessible to us, for want of a buyer, and the produce and animals we still get from it go a long way in keeping the family fed. Even some of our neighbors partake of the bounty. Yet keeping up the two places is very difficult for my father, and the salary he receives from his employment in town does not even begin to cover the rent of the house. My mother has had to take in clothing for mending and has had to use her dressmaking skills, which barely pay for the costs of running the farm and paying for the caretaker's services. I told Father that I could take over the day-to-day operations of the farm, and thus save the cost of a caretaker. That, and the money that you and *monsieur* Maurel so generously offered to me but which I shall continue to look upon as a loan, will go a long way in reversing my family's temporary money troubles. One of the problems, according to Father, is that the last few winters have lingered way into spring, thus shortening the planting cycle. That, and the low prices of wheat and other cereals, which Father says is being controlled by the King, who apparently prefers to let wheat rot in warehouses rather than make its way to the people.

Zénobe read rapidly through the next few pages in which André described the town of Caen and his parents' house. He was reading quickly, hoping to get to the part where André spoke of his feelings about having had to quit Paris, and the *hôtel* de Villette. He found that thread on the fifteenth page.

Early this morning I went to visit the old farm. I had forgotten how pleasurable the fresh air of the country is, and how quiet it is. My dear Zénobe, I miss you terribly, I would first have you know that; but I'm happy, or perhaps I should say content, to find again the peace and tranquility of Normandy, with its green, rolling hills. I don't mind saying that I don't miss the *maelstrom* of the *hôtel* de Villette. Remember you taught me that word? The whirlpool near Iceland? I'm glad I didn't go down it like ships and vessels that have gone down to their destruction. Far from the commotion of Paris, I can see now that the capital drags people down in a surge of perpetual motion. I hope you'll be able to escape soon, Zénobe, and you can join me here. Here, it is amazing how one can enjoy simple, natural pleasures which are impossible in Paris. Just the act of feeding the chickens, observing them, seeing them bicker and crowd out the smaller ones from the grain is such amusement. It's so similar in Paris! The henpecking, the unnecessary hostility, the hysterical running around. I was pleased to find Henriette, my favorite hen, still here, still beautiful, still queen of the hens, and still lording over most of the roosters, too. There were too many roosters. I culled some and brought them back with me to town. Mother is making *coq au* Calvados. Its aroma was already filling the air in the kitchen before I ran out to hide from my sister. My mother's cooking is the best. I wish you could come and taste it with me.

My observation that there were too many roosters in the barnyard made me think about, and wonder, why there are so many secretaries at the *hôtel* de Villette. There are more secretaries than maids, than valets, than stable boys. Why does an *hôtel* need so many secretaries? Even you had to lend a hand with secretarial duties, both to *monsieur* de Voltaire and *monsieur* de Villette. What am I writing? I no longer have to call them *monsieur*. You were even secretary to that despicable little man, Thibouville. In the barnyard, he would be the bantam who thinks of himself as the cock of the roost, but who is pecked at, even by the hens.

I know how you would respond. 'The *hôtel* de Villette is now the center of the intellectual universe. Before, there was a division, with a part being centered in Paris, the other part in Ferney. Now with the Patriarch of Ferney here in Paris, the division is made whole. Voltaire is now the logical center. All the other *philosophes* come to see him here. The grand society, they, too, come to show their respect. Versailles has never been the cornerstone of anything, except of gossip, hypocrisy, and tyranny.' About this time, your nostrils would be flaring, your adorable brow would be scrunched up in a most beautiful scowl, your fist would be banging on the table. You continue, 'It's Paris, with its men of science, with its mathematicians and intellectual writers, that has held its honored place as the center of thinking. And know that the real King is here, (your Lord of Reason, I shall baptize him), and we are again become the hub where begins the dissipation of all superstition, illogical thinking, and intolerance. Potsdam, Saint Petersburg, London, Philadelphia, the world entire, realizes that the rue de Beaune is the Sun, and all else the satellites revolving around it.'

So you see, little Zénobe, dear Zénobe, I have learned your lessons well. About this time in your lesson you would have tears in your eyes. 'Voltaire… Voltaire,' you would be saying, in the same tone of voice, with the same tenderness as you would pronounce my own name late at night when we would be in bed together. Who could ever have guessed that I would have as my rival, not that pip-squeak of a *marquis*, that Thibouville aristoshit, but the Lord of Reason himself, *monsieur* de Voltaire? The philosopher won out, he did. You left my bed for his. But Zénobe, please know, I always knew he had been your first love, and that I came second. And I knew that your two loves were very different, and that you owe your love of Voltaire to your father, to yourself, to your unhappy past and to what you have become, and to what you will become in the future. It's a love that you owe to who you are and to what you represent. I know that Voltaire is the voice that incites you to the fight, that gives you energy in the battle against the injustices of the world, the oppression, the cruelty, and I recognize, and approve of, your wish to fight, against the Church, against the Inquisition, against the stupid burden of feudal tyranny—we feel it here in Normandy, too! I understand you when you say that you want to fight against a world that counts genealogy stronger than it does a person's character. I understand, too, when you say that for far too long ecclesiastics and aristocrats have sucked dry the blood of society. Look at what that Thibouville did to us! With one word he has separated us. But I won't let that bother me, for I know that you and I will be together again, one day. And I also know that the day will come when we'll all be equal, equal to pursue our desires and ambitions, with no arbitrary power hanging over us to say that we can't.

Dear Zénobe, I cannot but feel pride in your contribution to this battle. But I feel like your comrade in arms and wish to contribute as well. Even my sister, Charlotte, feels the hostility in the air. A few months ago, a noble lady who lives on our street, had the nerve to call her impertinent. My sister replied, "And you are insolent for identifying in me the pride that in you becomes arrogance." The lady called on the services of the police lieutenant, who did nothing, saying that my sister was entitled to her own opinion, just as the lady was entitled to hers. See, Zénobe? There is hope in our society when the people's opinion is on a par with an aristocratic idiot's.

So, continue with your services to Voltaire. However mundane your tasks might seem, I know that they are important to you, and to him. Even calling on *docteur* Tronchin or *docteur* Lorry, when I was doing it, felt like a responsibility of high diplomacy with universal repercussions. Such is the importance of that old philosopher whom you serve. Forget the two *marquis*. They are of no importance. When

they have hired someone to take over for you, run home to me. I have
a farm! What did your friend say? 'We need to cultivate our garden,'
that's it, right? Well, the garden and I await you.

Your loving friend,
André

Zénobe put the letter to his heart, fell over on the bed, and remained still for a long
while. He ached and ached for his friend. So violent was this ache that he no longer
wept, but rather his voice emitted a low drone that was a reaction to his soul being in
agony. Such was his position still, when Maurel came back, looking for him. Zénobe
had Maurel read the letter, and the two of them remained alone in the room, hugging
and crying for the son of one, the lover of the other.

That night Voltaire asked Zénobe to increase the dose of the *duc* de Richelieu's
medicinal elixir.

"I found out from him what this tincture is," said the old man who was already
wearing his pompom on his head and standing beside his bed. "It is opium diluted in
water and fermented with yeast. He's sent us another vial of this laudanum, and he has
ascertained its multifold uses. It was given to Louis XV for his gangrene when he had
the smallpox..."

Zénobe interrupted him. "Gangrene? You have no gangrene!"

"Thank God that's not one of my ailments, but if part of my body starts to rot away,
I know that this drug will be efficacious for it."

Zénobe helped Voltaire into bed.

"It must be just awful," continued the old man, to watch parts of you slowly slough
off. They say that the stench was unbearable as Louis XV lay dying. All of the perfumes
of Versailles could not wash it out."

With Voltaire comfortably under the covers, Zénobe began the preparation of the
elixir. Two drops carefully counted into his drink. Tonight it was an infusion of basil
which received the drops and which would make Voltaire urinate in an hour and then
leave him in complete bladder repose for the rest of the night.

Voltaire looked on as Zénobe mixed the drops into the tea.

"Why don't you increase the dose for tonight?" said he. "Tomorrow I shall be
accepted into the hallowed halls of the Masons and I will need all my strength. I have
heard from Richelieu that the ceremony is interminable and soporific, so I could really
use the power of those little drops."

Zénobe looked at Voltaire. Richelieu had stipulated two drops in liquid right before
going to bed.

"Just for tonight," replied Voltaire to Zénobe's look of doubt and concern. "The
ceremony is at 11 o'clock in the morning, and it will probably run past my dinnertime,
so how will I have the strength to last from breakfast to supper?"

When Zénobe still hesitated, Voltaire said, "Richelieu told me that this medicine is all the rage, *le dernier cri* of Parisian doctors. Tronchin is a Protestant doctor from Geneva who feels his patients must suffer in dolorous and stoic silence."

Zénobe counted out two more drops, but added more basil tea from the teapot.

"Sugar?" he asked.

"No, no, my son. I'll have it bitter, to appease the somewhat austere demands of my unmerciful physician."

"Lorry is Parisian," said Zénobe as he handed the cup to Voltaire.

"Yes, he is," said Voltaire, then took a long first draught. "But he is of the old school. He doesn't recognize these new medications that come from faraway lands, from Persia and India, where they have been used for eons. We have a lot to learn from those so-called infidels. We also have a lot to learn from the other side of the earth, from the Brazils and the Guatemalas. They have jungles there in which reside a plethora of colorful herbs, of mighty trees, whose bark and roots will add enormously to our pharmacopeia. Nature is a veritable apothecary's shop, and Bougainville and Cook are the courageous new explorers of the future."

Voltaire took another drink of his tea.

"Oh, how this soothes! You should go off on adventures of your own, Zénobe. If I were your age, I should want to travel to America, and learn of exotic new things and live in an exciting new experiment."

Zénobe smiled at him and answered, "Then who would take care of you and make sure you want for nothing?"

"That is true, my son, you take very good care of me, and I want for nothing."

Voltaire held out his arms while the pompom danced over his merry eyes. Zénobe went to him and Voltaire embraced his shoulders and kissed him on the forehead.

"After I'm gone, there'll be plenty of time for you to travel and explore the world. But for now, suffice it to voyage to the rue du Pot-de-Fer and watch me be received by the Freemasons."

Voltaire was already getting sleepy.

"Ha, ha!" he chuckled. "The irony of it all!"

Zénobe asked, "What irony is that?" as he smoothed the sheets over Voltaire's body.

"There on the rue du Pot-de-Fer, between the rues de Mézière and Honoré-Chevalier,[252] just a block away from the Church of Saint-Sulpice, stands the huge *hôtel* Mézière, which Madeleine de Saint-Beuve gave to the Jesuits to house their novices. The same Jesuits, they were, who began my education at the *Collège Louis-le-Grand*, in the classical antiquities, an excellent beginning for a ten-year-old, to be sure, but one that I didn't allow them to finish. During most of my life, the Jesuits were there. But now that very building is used for the different lodges of the Grand Orient.[253] Could there be a better antithesis?"

Voltaire rolled over on his side, his eyelids half closed but not in the least hiding the luster of his eyes. After a moment, he sighed deeply.

"As one gets older, Zénobe, one can stand on a corner of a city street, and in one's imagination one can take a chronological tour of the street's different avatars. Buildings go up, fall, are reconstructed, are enlarged, decay, burn, are razed and something else goes up in its place. At the same time, all around me, people die, are born, grow old,

---

252   On today's rue Bonaparte, northwest of the Jardins du Luxembourg.

253   The *Grand Orient de France* took over the *hôtel* de Mézière in 1776, and incorporated several Masonic lodges, including the *Loge des Neuf Sœurs*, which was the most influential.

die in their turn. Life is a huge assembly of disparate parts and people, lurching jerkily towards an uncertain future, but, as I have always hoped, it is one that improves as it so imperfectly travels, leaving the world, and us, better off than before."

Voltaire fell silent. Zénobe, extinguishing the candles around the room, glanced over at him. He had fallen asleep.

The young man marveled. Even half asleep, Voltaire would say the most beautiful things. Zénobe walked over to the lectern and wrote down Voltaire's words as they still echoed in his heart.

April 7, 1778

The Diffusion of Light

Voltaire's Masonic induction was as grandiose and pompous as the glorious imagination of the hundreds of participants could elaborate. The Venerable Brother of the Lodge of the Nine Sisters, Joseph Jerôme Lefrançais de Lalande,[254] would have undoubtedly preferred a somber, dignified reception for the new apprentice, who, after all, was 84 years old, but everybody else would have none of that.

Brother member Guenin composed new music for the ceremony, and it was energetic and magnificent; brother Caperon conducted it with zeal until his baton cracked in two and he had to finish the composition with the remaining splinter lofted high into the air.[255] Brother de la Dixmerie wrote lyrical verses to accompany the music. He had to shout to be heard above the music.

> "At the very name of the illustrious brother
> Every Mason triumphs today,
> If he received from us the light,
> The world receives it from him."

Hothouse floribunda and racemes of multicolored phalaenopsis garnished the dais, courtesy of George Louis Leclerc, *comte* de Buffon, who, as the director of the Jardin du Roi, had access to the choicest of flowers.[256] The brothers Salantin, Caravoglio, Olivet, Balza and Lurschmidt lent their expertise and sense of aesthetics to the production that left no one of the opinion that the Lodge had skimped or neglected any detail for the exorbitant ceremony of Voltaire's regal introduction as a Masonic neophyte. Even the suave Alexandre Sergheivitch Stroganov was on hand, with his family's fabled sponsorship in research and development of the arts, literatures, history and archeology solidly behind him, and a magnificently gracious, polyglot gallantry in front.

Such was the exuberance of the planning committee that both *madame* Denis and the *marquise* de Villette were invited to attend the event, to the intense grumbling of the more conservative of the brothers who were horrified by the idea of the presence

---

254   Lalande was celebrated for his *Treatise on Astronomy*, published in 1764, with new expanded editions in 1771 and 1792. He was professor emeritus at the *Collège de France* and director of the Paris Observatory. He was also known for enlisting women astronomers.

255   Up until then, the baton was four feet long and was struck on the floor to keep time.

256   This became the Jardin des Plantes after the Revolution, and Buffon made it into a museum and a center of plant research that influenced, among others, Darwin.

of women sullying the ceremony. The only sisters present should be the Nine Muses, not the flesh and blood type. True, the *marquise* was beautiful and could stand in for one of the muses, but the short and dumpy Denis would best have served as a dwarfish caryatid holding up on her stony shoulders the entablature that supported the nine graceful sisters. But there they were, the two important women in Voltaire's life, and they were not quiet. Their hysterical tones of admiration and their theatrical interjections of awe could not be kept down, notwithstanding the commands for them to hush from several of the Masonic brothers. But the females were so used to their constant prattle that nothing could tame the effusions of their circumlocutory tongues.

Zénobe was also granted permission to enter, even though he was not a member mason, nor indeed, a mason of any foreign lodge. But his proximity to Voltaire brought him much favor. Additionally, it was bruited about that, as a Scandinavian gentleman of mysterious provenance, this young but wealthy Swede represented the gratitude of his kindred and kingdom towards the patriarch of the Enlightenment. He had purportedly been sent by Gustave III to provide services to the philosopher. Voltaire had written in 1731 a biography of the Swedish king Charles XII, in which he extolled the virtues of that monarch, asserting that Charles deserved immortality for the good he had done his people, and that Charles was "perhaps the only one of all men, and until now the only one of all kings, who had lived without weakness." This Swede, then, was a sort of gentleman-in-waiting who had given himself body and soul, who had slavishly donated the rest of his life to the sole concern of seeking to bring comfort and care to the French philosopher in his elderly years. None there at the Lodge of the Nine Sisters was able to deny the sanctity of such extreme self-abnegation and all welcomed the young man to the induction ceremony, telling him in admiration that he himself had the wherewithal to become a member of their society one day. Love of service, sympathy for mankind, loyalty and devotion to one who was the iconic friend of all mankind, these virtues would serve to justify his entry into the Freemasons. Those who said it with the most compunction, led by Stroganov, cared not a whit to discover the young man's credentials, but rather were drawn to him by his aristocratic bearing, by the colors of his national dress, and by his beautiful blue eyes which seemed to show mainly one emotion before the ceremony began: quiet concern for his master, François Marie Arouet, *dit* de Voltaire.

The young Swede's ancient master teetered as he was passed from the arms of one Freemason to those of another, making his way towards the center of the ceremony, joined midway by brothers Benjamin Franklin and Antoine Court de Gebelin who brought him up the rest of the way.[257] There, on a raised dais, had been placed Buffon's huge display of exotic flora that very nearly overwhelmed an elongated marble pyramid sitting on a square pedestal. On this pedestal were engraved the words, *Que sont les Sciences et les Arts sans la vertu?*[258]

The Venerable Brother Lalande realized that Voltaire would not be able to stand for the duration of the ceremony, even though it had already been decided that it would be curtailed in length by excluding the part that had to do with justification. Voltaire needed to prove nothing. No one there would deny Voltaire's merit, his benevolence

---

257   Court de Gebelin was a respected linguist who worked with ancient mythologies and wrote volumes on the history of language and writing, and worked on the idea of a universal grammar. His magnum opus, *le Monde primitif analysé et comparé avec le monde moderne*, was published in nine volumes from 1775 to 1784.

258   What are the Sciences and the Arts without virtue?

and his disinterestedness, and all accepted that Voltaire had always been a Mason in spirit and that today's ceremony was merely rectifying a technical omission. However, this wasn't the Nine Sisters' fault; Voltaire had been exiled from Paris for nearly 30 years. It had also been decided beforehand to shorten the ceremony by not including the *épreuves ordinaires* of the new apprentice. This was done for two reasons. Firstly, having an 84-year-old man, as lively or sprightly as he may have been, spend two hours standing, kneeling, lying flat on the ground on his stomach, blindfolded and falling backwards to test his confidence that fellow Freemasons would check his fall, smacked some of a religious ceremony that could perhaps alienate the philosopher, and others of a Mesmerist magneto-electric assembly. Secondly, knowing where Voltaire stood in the scheme of the religious and pseudoscientific worlds, they decided it was best to suppress the most mystical of the rituals of their ceremony. The whole thing was whittled down to about two hours. After a few moments of confusion, a chair was brought up on the dais and offered silently to Voltaire. Voltaire bowed to the person who brought the chair, and then sat down. A crown of laurel was placed on Voltaire's head, startling him.

The Venerable Brother began his speech in front of about two hundred Masons and the two women.

"The sacred duty of the Lodge of the Nine Sisters is dedicated to the culture of sciences, of arts and of letters, and in order to propagate their culture successfully in a temporal and in a spatial sense, we are dedicated to the identification and nomination of the individuals who promulgate said sciences, arts and letters. But since culture needs to touch all men in an equal fashion, it is also our sacred duty to assure the availability of said culture for one and all, and it is therefore our imperative that social injustices be annihilated, and that all humanity be allowed to participate unencumbered in the pursuit of cultural and social progress. What citizen has better than you, oh great Voltaire, served our mother country by shedding light on her duties and on her true interests, while at the same time rendering fanaticism odious and superstition ridiculous, and recalling taste to its true rules, history to its true purpose, laws to their first integrity? We promise to come to the aid of our brothers, and you have been the instigator of a whole population who adores you and who cannot but resound with your acts of generosity. You have raised a temple to the Eternal, and yet, something that was even more worthy, one may see near that temple, a refuge for those who have been banished but who are still favorable to society, and who would otherwise have been rejected by blind and zealous prejudice. Therefore, very dear brother, you were a Freemason long before today, and you fulfilled the duties way before having contracted the obligation here with us this day. Here, then, we present you with the square, which we wear as symbol of the rectitude of our actions; the apron, which represents a laborious life and useful activity; the white gloves, which represent the candor, the innocence and the purity of our actions; the trowel, which serves to hide the defects of our brothers; all of this pertains to your beneficence and to your love of humanity, and which by consequence only serves to express the qualities which distinguish you. We can only add, as we receive you today among our brethren, the tribute of our admiration and our undying gratitude."

Voltaire's hands and arms could barely contain the symbols of Freemasonry. Benjamin Franklin lent a hand to keep everything balanced in his grasp.

Brothers La Dixmerie, Garnier, Grouvelle and Echard each said a few words of elegant and approbatory appreciation, adding the sentiment that *monsieur* de Voltaire provided to society a paragon worthy of emulation.

Then Lalande continued to speak, enumerating every specific example of Voltaire's succor and generosity to those victims of injustice, to those who were broken on the wheel, bone by bone, and who bore unspeakable torture by those who dared to judge them by their own prejudiced standards, those unfortunates who were hanged, hacked, burned and beheaded, by an absolutist Church and an intransigent state which could not tolerate any disunity in their ranks or breaches of conduct by their adherents. Voltaire was the new Atlas, carrying the weight of the world on his shoulders. Only he had to fight against extremism at the same time.

The crowd could not help but break out into sustained cheering and applause.

Lalande concluded his speech by saying, "I give you Voltaire, the harbinger of a new era and the vanquisher of fanaticism!"

Monsieur Franklin helped Voltaire to his feet, and held his symbols of Freemasonry for him. Again the crowd roared. The old man made gestures as if to say he wasn't worthy of so much attention. It only made the crowd roar louder.

A new set of brothers stepped up to the dais to extol their new member. That new member, though, had to be asked to sit down, before he fell down. A chair was brought for Benjamin Franklin as well, and they sat side by side, the two transatlantic brothers who now had a new bond to link them.

The *duc* de Richelieu, Stroganov, Guillotin[259] and the *marquis* de Villette spoke highly of quality after quality and virtue after virtue, of a man who had been born during the reign of Louis XIV, and who had gone past that of Louis XV and now brought to the reign of Louis XVI a new blast of air that swept iniquity in its wake. It was the *marquis* de Villette who mentioned Lally.[260] As the latest victim whose reputation Voltaire had come forth to salvage, this case, said Villette, was still awaiting its dénouement: "As we speak, Lally's family awaits with bated breath to hear what conclusion the Parliament of Paris will pronounce on the matter. Was Lally executed unfairly? Was an innocent man defamed? Shall he be absolved posthumously of all charges and shall his name and reputation be rehabilitated? Shall the Parliament return to Lally's family the money and property that was confiscated from them? Testimony is now being heard, among which are Voltaire's impassioned pleas to extract and dismiss the partial testimony of Lally's superiors who would have the most to lose were Lally to be held innocent of treason. When a scapegoat is needed, the men of power abuse that power, and easily sway public opinion by hiding the true facts, inventing new ones, and delivering up the innocent to then quell the public wrath."

So many nice things were being said about Voltaire that Zénobe missed not having anything with which to write. Looking around, he noticed that in order to make room for the dais and the numerous chairs for the audience, the usual furniture of the hall had been bunched up in one corner, behind the farthest row of the seated Masons. He observed that among the furniture there was a

---

259   Joseph Ignace Guillotin, doctor and professor of anatomy at the Faculté de Paris, will be the one to suggest at the beginning of the Revolution that in cases of capital punishment, humanitarian justice use the decapitation machine which today bears his name. Heretofore, possible death sentences were carried out by hanging, burning, quartering, being broken at the wheel, and strangulation, some of which could take hours and even days. The *guillotine*, besides being swift, was the great equalizer, since every citizen, from peasant to worker, bourgeois to priest, and even to the king and queen, met his or her demise in the same manner.

260   Thomas Arthur, *baron* de Tollendal, *comte* de Lally, executed for treason after having lost the French settlements in India to the British during the Seven Years' War.

scriptorium, although he couldn't see if there were pen, ink and paper on it. He discreetly got up and went to it, and discovered all that he needed to start writing down the wonderful sentiments that were falling fast during this ceremony. Zénobe knew nothing of the total secrecy required by the rules and regulations of the Freemasons, but nobody saw him set up his journal and start taking dictation. The curious thing was, however, that being behind the back row of Masons, he could overhear any stray commentary that was unconcernedly pronounced by them, and thinking those of interest as well, he jotted them down democratically with equal conscientiousness.[261] [262] [263] [264] [265]

This is why, in Zénobe's manuscript, after the statement, "We lay wreaths at the foot of the throne of your immortality," one also finds, "Throne? How à propos. The commoner Arouet becomes king Voltaire, with just a few transpositions of letters.[266]

One also reads the two following enunciations juxtaposed: "I will always implore the Heavens to prolong your life as it is of utmost importance to the Empire of Reason: with you gone, we shall certainly see the triumph of fanatics and fools, as surely as one saw the return of monsters after Hercules died." "Fanatics and monsters? They are truly one and the same. But Hercules and Voltaire pronounced in the same breath? Let the old man have a go at sweeping out the stables of Augeas."

There was also a snippet of poetry:

> "Oh, thou! The Corneille of our age,
> Friend of humanity,
> Father of truth;
> We call thee Philosopher, Sage."

followed by the rather prosaic "Father of truth? Who's the mother, then? Mother Denis?" [*Père de la vérité? Qui en est donc la mère? La mère Denis?*]

---

261   [From the author] I suppose that it is up to me, and not to my so-called fact-checker, to alert the reader to a historical fact that perhaps would be embarrassing for *mein Herr* Dr. Ralph to avow. The paucity of information on the Masonic lodges of Paris, most of which were unfortunately housed in the same building on the rue Bonaparte, is explained by the wholesale destruction and burning of all their archives by the Gestapo during the Occupation. It's a good thing that *monsieur* Bosquet provided an alternate source for the verification of events in this chapter.

262   [From the fact-checker] *Monsieur* Luna seems to cast aspersions over a wide area and in the end be guilty of the very things Voltaire warned us about. Prejudice against a whole people for the acts of some sounds to me gratuitously bellicose, and I shall certainly to the editor complain.

263   [From the editor] The editor refuses to join in childish and unprofessional behavior. Let the facts speak for themselves.

264   [From the literary agent] Please, gentlemen, we are going to press in a matter of days and there is no time for this bickering.

265   [From the French publisher] We have never before been witness to such a contretemps among the constituent collaborators of the publishing process. Airing out our disagreements in such a public way does not in any fashion advance our project. The responsibility of the Nazis notwithstanding, if this unprofessional wrangling is protracted, we shall be obliged to rescind our previous agreement to publish the second and third parts of the *Zénobe* trilogy.

266   Arouet l[e] j[eune] (the young) is the anagram to Voltaire (the u and the v, and the i and the j, being interchangeable in Latin.

Zénobe continued in the same vein for pages, golden-tongued adulation alternating with acerbic criticism.

"Perhaps you are very old, but your heart is still gleaming new!" "But other parts of his body have started to fall off!"

"A man who speaks to all Nations, the friend of Kings, the defender of the unfortunate, the oracle who undertook the task of reigning over the debris of all sects; such a being without doubt astounds, and we today are like an eager crowd which is come from the four corners of the globe to examine closely this phenomenon." "*Phenomenon* is right. Like a tornado or a flood to sweep us all out to sea."

"It is to all of Europe, to the whole world, and not just to our century, but to all of posterity, that the glory of this man belongs. This rare man, this singular man, this unique man, has been responsible for a long succession of brilliant singularities which succeeded each other, without interruption, during the course of his life, and which made of him a man such that the preceding centuries had not yet seen, and which the centuries to come may never see again." "What a breathtaking paradigm … of hyperbole!"

"In spite of a constitution which, in appearance, may seem quite delicate, no man other than he has been both as precocious in his early youth, and as robust and as healthy in his old age. No man has begun his career with such brilliance, nor is ending it with as much glory." "No doubt, he'll exit the stage as he entered it … crawling."

"Let us give homage to this most universal of men who has ever lived, whom no person can contest in the quality of unique man, and whose character of frankness, of impartiality, and of courage shall inspire us to the ends of time!" "Or at least to the succession of Louis XVII!"

Zénobe memorized the profiles of the four fops who made light of Voltaire's accomplishments. He promised himself that they would be the first against whom he would fight duels.

But Voltaire was not the only character that day to elicit criticism. When *madame la marquise* de Villette was introduced, one of the idiots declared, "Oh, what a dainty little morsel [*brioche*] she is! I dare say she's hardly been used, being married to the *marquis* de Villette, she's probably as good as new. I'd reveal a few masonic mysteries for her!"

On Richelieu: "Now there's a gallant man of the world; he's caught the pox in every country in Europe, twice in England." Also: "He uses stimulants to stiffen his resolve."

On Franklin: "What an all-natural man! No wonder *madame* Helvétius refused him. He used to run around with the Indians." "They say he takes air-baths in the nude at night in the garden. Imagine such a sight in the moonlight." " 'What's the best conductor of electricity?' 'Copper?' 'No, platinum. What's the worst conductor of electricity?' 'I give up.' 'Woman. Give her a jolt today and it takes nine months to see the light."

Finally it was time for Voltaire to make a speech. As he tottered to the dais, the whole audience fell silent, and his dry, brittle voice, still impish and remarkably voluble, rang over the crowd.

"I stand before you an old and feeble man who can no longer take care of himself, let alone take care of the world."

His audience conveyed its disagreement with grumbling and elongated murmurs of *Non, non, mais nooooon!*"

"*Si, si,* what I say is true. I must soon conclude my lawsuit against Nature, but it is a proceeding that I, that we all, must in the end lose. But this is a good thing, because each generation, after having tried its hardest, fought its strongest, done its best, must yield to the newer, more empowered generation to carry forth the journey towards that shining star, that Utopia, which hovers everlasting so appealingly over the horizon, where we can see her, reach for her, try to make her our own, try to induce her to stay. She is why we labor, why we sweat and grunt in agonizing frustration, why we persist to our last breath, to undo the inequities all around us, to assure the ideals which should be applied to the common man, for we are all of us common men. To see an injustice fall on any individual, however far from us he dwells, however foreign his case may seem, should enrage us as if it were falling upon us directly. Allowing such injustices to happen in our world, without voicing our dissent, without letting our conscience rise up to a fever pitch, is our tacit agreement for such an injustice one day to fall on our own heads. Our rage against injustice should never be quelled, just because we are not its victims on this day, just because we are for the moment tranquil and comfortable and enjoying the fruits which society has to offer.

"You tell me that *monsieur* Lally is finally getting his due process in court. It is too late to save him, of course, but it is never too late to save future victims of the same inane travesty of justice that demands victims even if there is no one to blame. Blind vengeance on the innocent is no way to run a system of justice. It is as if the maw of a primitive society demands constantly to be fed new sacrifices, and we are no better than those who fling children down the throat of a volcano to appease its eruptions. Lally should not have been executed for having lost Pondicherry for the French. Blame his superiors for having ordered him to defend what was impossible to defend. Killing the scapegoat does not in any way dismiss the truly responsible for their heinous actions, and the guilty are still out there, having been given the possibility to continue with their illogical mentality and brutish calls for somebody to pay for their stupidity.

"There are appearances under which human nature is of an infernal nature, where honest people, while passing by la Grève while an unfortunate is being tortured,[267] order their driver to go faster, and go to the Opera to distract themselves from the awful spectacle that they saw on the way.

"But I stand here before you, too old to do much about anything, and I feel the weight of what has yet to be done. Still, I am happy today, I am very happy, for it is my consolation to see all around me young faces, and I see young arms, and I see that our mission towards that star of Utopia is embodied in strong breasts and kept alive in strong minds. I can see now how all men of good will are Masons without knowing it. I say to you with humility, that I am moved, with emotion, with tenderness, and that I am penetrated with excitement by what I had esteemed perhaps less before I came to witness it. I know now that you at the Lodge of the Nine Sisters join everything that you hold in common with the other societies of the same kind: that of cultivating emulation, and of condemning rivalry; of uniting all its members under a same purpose, and of banishing personal interests and pretensions that could otherwise divide its members. I stand in admiration of the sublime simplicity of your moral code and of your genre of instruction. With humble heart and even humbler spirit, I thank you, for myself, and in the name of Lally, and all those who have been wrenched away from the path to our Utopian star."

The Masons erupted in thunderous applause. Voltaire today was their hero, their model, their shining star. Zénobe noticed that even the four idiots at the back had kept a respectful silence during Voltaire's speech and had also joined the mad clapping and calls of "*hourrah!*"

---

267   The Place de Grève, in front of the Hôtel de Ville, was the preferred place for public executions.

Voltaire did not stay for the banquet, politely extricating himself by mentioning his fatigue and his special diet. A throng escorted him to his carriage, but before he could reach it, an old woman managed to cleave herself into the mob and, while eating a crust of bread, addressed Voltaire.

"I am a bookseller on the quay by the entrance to the Tuileries. *Mon bon monsieur* Voltaire, make me some books. I am a poor woman. Make me some books that I can sell, and soon I will be rich."

Voltaire took a long look at her and replied, "Present yourself at the *hôtel* de Villette tomorrow morning and my secretary here will give you a bundle of books, mine you can have: they are a gift to you. But there will also be some copies of a book written by my secretary here, who is also my literary protégé. You can keep 30% of the profits of those copies, the rest you can bring back to the *hôtel* de Villette to present to him. Agreed?"

"*Oui, mon bon monsieur* Voltaire, agreed. Thank you so very much. Your books will sell all on their own. Your protégé's might need some flogging, but I'll say that it's a book written by the next Voltaire."

Voltaire grinned and nodded his head as they marched on.

That evening, Voltaire remembered to lay out about thirty of his books and asked Zénobe how many copies of *Ibycus* he was planning to entrust to the old bookseller.

"I don't know. How many should I give her?"

"How many do you have left?"

"Fifty or sixty."

"I would give them all to her. They're not selling themselves in your room. She'll be good for the 70%. It's in her interest to continue doing business with you, and she'll come back for more books to sell. The *aristos* will tell you that the common people are lazy and shifty; it is my experience that they are industrious and far more trustworthy than the *aristos*. She'll sell your books better than you ever could yourself. But you won't be keeping that money. You'll be lending it out. When the likes of the *duc* de Lauzun lose their spending money at the gambling tables in the Palais-Royal, they need cash until they can access their bankers."

Zénobe was in amazement as to how easy it was to enter into Voltaire's world of finances. His 70% of 60 volumes became a solution of aristocratic cash flow problems that at 10% kept increasing at a steady pace over the next few years. It was Voltaire's other secretary, Bigex, who taught him how to keep track of his money and how to invest it for maximum profits. It never entered into Zénobe's head that it was the *marquis* de Thibouville's initial outlay that made the publication of *Ibycus* possible. Paying the *marquis* back with some of the profits was never even a formulated thought. He plowed all profits back into the lending business, and his salary as Villette's librarian remained untouched. Zénobe, it turned out, wielded his balance sheet as well as he flourished his foil.

April 15, 1778

The Diffusion of Love

le 15 avril
hôtel de Villette
quai des Théâtins
Paris

My dearest André,

There isn't a line in your letters that doesn't grab at my heart and make me wish you were by my side. There isn't a sentiment of which you write that my heart doesn't share. There isn't a mention of tenderness or a conjuration of sadness on your part that my soul doesn't feel. I, too, suffer from your absence and I still look for you every time I turn a corner or cross a vestibule. My arms reach for you in the middle of the night as I lay sleeping and when I cannot find you, I wake up and remember that you are far away and then I weep bitter tears. I don't know how much longer we'll be apart, but I hope it won't be too long. Our souls are inseparable; they must have each other to survive. Your fears of our separation lasting more than we can bear will prove groundless, I am sure. Still, the brutal machinations of pernicious fate have rendered all happiness impossible. The world is cold and dark without you.

My sole consolation is my dedication to Voltaire. He is, after all, the reason why I came to Paris in the first place. But he still speaks of returning to Ferney. Hardly a day goes by that he doesn't receive supplications from his people, begging him to go back to them, or a letter from Wagnière, beseeching him to leave Paris, for as God is his witness, says the faithful secretary, this Godforsaken place will end up killing him. His villagers have pledged to come all the way to Paris and carry him on their backs if they have to. It is sad to see him torn in two, especially when one realizes that the half that keeps him in Paris, his niece, does not merit his sacrifice. Nor do I see how she merits his feelings. What a typical woman she is, more interested in frocks from Rose Bertin and sallies to the Palais-Royal than in his health! While he works at serious things all day, she goes out with the *marquise* de Villette for socials and concerts. I daresay the *marquise* herself cares more for Voltaire's health. She comes to see him more often than *madame* Denis does.

The *marquis* de Villette also pressures the poor old man to remain in Paris, saying it is the stage of his triumphs, the center of his accolades. He has written some verses and propagated them around Paris. The gist is: feel the guilt, or risk being called an ingrate, if you leave your adoring public. Listen:

> *Quand la ville et la cour vous offrent leur hommage,*
> *Et qu'un peuple enchanté vous porte dans ses bras;*
> *Quand vous voyez devant vos pas*
> *Le respect et l'amour peints sur chaque visage;*
> *Quand des pleurs de tendresse échappés de nos yeux*
> *Ont arrosé votre passage;*
> *Vous voulez nous quitter! et vous fuyez ces lieux*
> *Où l'on adore votre image!*[268]

He goes on and on like that, and then the last two lines are:

> *Soyez témoin de vos succès,*
> *Et jouissez de vos conquêtes!*[269]

Euterpe has certainly tired of hoping to inspire Villette![270] To use some examples of the letter A, Villette is such an arrogant, ambitious ass! When he says that it is imperative that Voltaire remain in Paris, the scene of his triumphs, you must understand that it is really the scene of Villette's pomposity. Everybody is looking in on the *hôtel* de Villette, and the *marquis* feels that he is the center of attention, the idiot. Mark my words, he's going to end up like the frog in the fable. Jealous of the size of the ox, the frog strains and swells up to be as big as the ox, but only succeeds in bursting like a bladder. Villette even plays on Voltaire's vanity: he intimates that the king might soften his stance and receive him at Versailles, like he keeps receiving Benjamin Franklin. Louis invites Franklin over to Versailles for supper! What Villette doesn't tell Voltaire, but I did, is that all it means is that the poor American, as famous and intelligent and talented as he is, is invited into the royal presence only to have the unmitigated pleasure of standing behind the queen's chair to watch them eat. That Austrian bitch keeps calling Franklin 'a son of a candlestick-maker,' as if that had any relevance to his celebrated stature today. Can you see Voltaire standing behind the queen-bitch's chair? I can't. I would accompany him into Versailles and be ready to bash her head in. I'd pick up her knife and cut her throat if she even glanced at Voltaire with contempt. How dare she, she who is as stupid as her feet, who can't even add two and two. How dare they give her so much power when she knows

---

268   When the city and the court offer you their hommage,/And when an enchanted people carry you in their arms;/When you see in front of you/The respect and the love showing on each face;/When tears of tenderness escape from our eyes and sprinkle your passage;/You want to leave us! And you want to flee this place/Where your image is adored!

269   Be a witness of your success,/And enjoy your conquests.

270   Euterpe, the Muse of lyrical poetry.

nothing of the world outside Paris. Oh, she goes out every once in a while to collect peasants who come up to her aesthetic standards, to make them live in her Little Hamlet, to milk her cows and collect her eggs and dance around in these stupid costumes. She lives in a world of her own making, an illusion that she's created to fill her boredom and satisfy her whims.

And Villette is part of that whole system. He'll say anything to benefit his own interests. Every day he thinks of new things to tell Voltaire and entice him to stay. 'Books are available immediately in Paris.' 'It is easier to keep an eye on the construction of the new house if you are here.' 'What about the Academy's dictionary, the letter A, the research to be done, the work to rehabilitate Lally's reputation, your friends who are here, etc., etc.!'

I for one don't know how to feel about Voltaire going back to Ferney. Were I to follow him, I would be even farther away from you. On the one hand, I have become indispensable to him since I can do a lot more than Bigex or the *marquis*' secretary, Requain. I can do research for him, and my knowledge of the Ancients is more complete than that of either Bigex or Requain. Would you believe that our old playwright has started writing a new play? *Agathocle*, it's called. So far he's written half of the first act, and one evening he had Bigex and me taking dictation at lightning-fast speed. Both of us had huge smiles on our faces. How does that old man get all this energy, we wondered. How does his mind work so fast? He is an expert both on human nature and on rhyming couplets, and I'm sure that he could hold an everyday conversation in alexandrine verses. His genius takes my breath away.

In your last letter you asked me how my own writing was faring. Well, it isn't. I haven't written a word since your departure, and every time I see that Thibouville 'aristoshit', as you called him, I want to bash his teeth in. Lately, he's been acting mighty strangely, skulking on the third-floor landing, looking at me with big wet eyes, I suppose trying to imitate Mesmer and ensorcell me or silently entreat me to do his bidding. Does he think that he will move me to pity or disengage my resentment by acting like a doe in a trap? Does he seriously believe that I could forgive him for having separated us and caused us so much sorrow? Apparently you're a better person than I, for I cannot even begin to forgive his draconian reaction to such a puny offense. You didn't even hurt him. Only his self-esteem was harmed, but once again, we need to realize that aristocratic self-esteem must be bought for a heavy price.

Villette certainly isn't helping his aristochum to raise the price of his self-esteem. He has decided that he will not replace me, whatever Thibouville says, although as I see it, Thibouville lately has not been pressing his case that I be sent away. Villette says that I'm in the middle of building his library and he doesn't wish to start with somebody new. It is I who have been having conversations with Wailly, the architect. I know about wood. We're using oak for the shelves and panels. We're using lapis lazuli—can you believe it!—for the decorative columns on either side of the Greek and Latin section. Villette knows that I have become indispensable to him. Moreover, the *marquis* d'Argenson has been speaking to him and extolling my intellectual prowess. It pays to have friends in high places. And let's not forget *mademoiselle* d'Éon who every time she sees me calls me her hero, or d'Alembert, Diderot and Condorcet who all want me to continue taking care of their friend Voltaire, and who would put up a fuss were Villette to get rid of me.

Villette is easily intimidated; he's a *marquis* in name only. His father was wealthy enough to buy a *marquisat*, but neither father nor son carried within him the weight of the belief that he is superior in anything other than monetary value. Oh, Villette thinks he is superior in the domain of Euterpe and publishes every two years a book of poetry, but he is like a fly on Voltaire's toe. Neither Villette, father or son, had the requisite centuries of pride behind him, and only vanity comes through in Villette. Neither did they have the compunction that their escutcheon was worthy in the service of the king, and all that shines through in Villette, the son, is a gleaming façade, which is naught but a cracked carapace and contains only bluff and cockiness.

I have come to the conclusion that poor Villette has been pushed around by the working class in times previous, and I would easily entertain the thought that he rather liked it. For some odd reason, I respect him more for that, and the tepid and tawdry Thibouville loses in the comparison. Maurel has told me tales of Villette, years ago, going into the *cimetière* Père Lachaise to look for young men with rough workman's hands. What Maurel didn't tell me, but I surmise, was that Villette was trying to rectify, at least for a few minutes, the imbalance that exists between the classes. Hiding in a mausoleum, behind a crypt, engaged in some passionate embrace of animalistic lust, Villette ceased to be the superior one, and his temporary partner, the sawyer, or the shoemaker, or whatever he was, was the one to order him around, turn the tables and give him commands. The lower the rank of the stud, the better. A schoolteacher of rhetoric or a jeweler would not be satisfactory. He would have to be a joiner, or a coppersmith, or even better, a *brouetteur*,[271] somebody with energy and physical stamina with dusty clothes and mud-encrusted shoes, to be his ideal accidental lover. I asked Maurel if Villette ever brought any of them home, and he answered aghast, 'No! They would have gotten the furniture dirty!'

Thibouville never had that sense of adventure, of placing himself in proximity to danger. He was no hunter. He never roamed around lugubrious, perilous places, a poacher secretly hunting his lord's game, or a sailor trawling the dark depths for mermen. Rather, he stayed put, to see what fell from the sky, like manna from heaven. You and I must have been a godsend to him. But he lost his chance. There will never be a way for him to regain my sympathy, even to the detriment of my play.

Oh, I almost forgot. Last week, I wrote you about Voltaire's welcome by the Freemasons. This week, it was the turn of the *Académie des Sciences*,

---

271   The worker responsible for the handling of material, usually through the use of a *brouette*, or wheelbarrow, on a construction site.

of which Condorcet is the perpetual secretary. It was more accolades, more speeches of hyperbolic praise, each one more grandiose than the last. In any case, when Benjamin Franklin was invited on the stage to accompany his homologue Voltaire, the audience burst out in thunderous applause. Both Voltaire and Franklin kept bowing and saluting the public, but the public could not get enough. Mind you, experts from the intellectual world of science and mathematics should be more phlegmatic, more circumspect, more reserved, but this bunch went mad, cheering and clapping, stomping their feet, shouting, whistling, jumping on their seats. It was wild, and the two figures looked embarrassed and didn't know what to do in front of such adulation. Finally, they glanced at each other, approached each other, and shook hands. The hall went wilder. The two of them embraced and kissed each other's cheeks. The audience went into paroxysms and gyrations of ecstasy, and I myself was weeping at the sight of these two men, representatives of their continents, symbols of progress, of hope, of the future, and they were there, right in front of us, embracing in friendship and in the sharing of the light of knowledge. I wish you had been there, André, it was such a sight. And afterwards everybody was saying how lucky we were to have witnessed this colossal event.

I must leave you for the time being, André. But I will continue to use this time in the afternoon, the time that was for your lessons, to write to you. I miss our lessons. I miss my handsome student, the one who so diligently prepared his readings and memorized the material. I'm glad you bought Plutarch, Thucydides and Xenophon in Caen. I tell you that it is money well spent. I want you to continue with the Greeks, and one day I hope to introduce you to the Romans. But don't neglect your Montaigne or your Montesquieu, especially your Montesquieu, as the Americans are drawing heavily from him in the production of their state constitutions. Several of these have already been translated and published in Paris, and they're the talk of the town, but not, I imagine, of Versailles.[272]

Your loving friend who misses you every single day, and every single night, especially now that I'm back sleeping in our little bedroom. My heart aches for you.

Your loving Zénobe

---

272   These state constitutions were translated and published anonymously in 1778 as the *Recueil des loix constitutives des colonies angloises* [*Collection of the constitutional laws of the English colonies*]. These translations, dedicated to Benjamin Franklin, are attributed to a friend of Franklin's, Louis Alexandre, *duc* de La Rochefoucault d'Enville, but the possibility has been mentioned that Thomas Jefferson had a hand in it. The problem with the openness of these publications lay in the fact that Louis XVI was aiding the Americans in their efforts to extricate themselves from the yoke of their own king and install a republican government instead. Thus, what was deemed good for the American public was denounced as dangerous for the French one. The French king subsequently prohibited the dissemination of the American state constitutions, which went underground and became all the more popular.

Last Visits

lmost three weeks after André's departure, Zénobe woke up after a nap late in the morning with a pang in his heart, an ache deep at the base of his penis, and in his mouth a hunger for his missing friend's body. The emptiness was palpable, and in his solitude, he yearned with all his might that this suffering be allayed by frenetic labor, hoping that Voltaire the playwright would have many scenes stored in his memory and would have enough material for his secretaries to get cramps in their hands. He wanted to work on Voltaire's play *Agathocle* night and day, or begin the letter B in the dictionary, or complete his own little play, but, unfortunately, the work turned out to be light, not enough even for a single secretary; Bigex was away writing a final manuscript for definitions of words beginning with the letter A, and Requain was taking dictation from Villette in the *marquis'* room. After a few short letters,[273] Voltaire asked to be dressed and he and *mesdames* Denis and Villette went out for social visits and the pleasures of gossip and banter. Zénobe had two hours to fill before having to depart for the Arsenal library and his fencing lessons. He wound up in his little room at the back of the servants' quarters, but the books he chose to fill the void could neither master his idleness nor relieve his distraction. There was turmoil in his soul, an angry impatience, but also a painful yearning, as if a sigh and a sob and a yawp were fighting it out in the middle of his chest along his diaphragm, between his heart and his intestines. Carefully putting his books away, he returned across the garden to the main house, and, deliberately avoiding Maurel, went up the three stories to Thibouville's room where he caught the *marquis* having as desultory an afternoon as he was. Walking past him into the room, he threw himself into the closest armchair, saying nothing, but staring intently into Thibouville's eyes. Zénobe sank down into the chair and opened his knees, throwing his pelvis at a cantilever over the seat. One of his hands went inside his shirt between the buttons, and the other he brought down to pose beside his fly. Thibouville needed no other invitation and flung himself on his knees in front of the young man,

---

273   One of the letters was in response to Jacques Pierre Brissot who had sent to Voltaire a prospectus of his *Théorie des lois criminelles*, an attempt to reform the French criminal system which he criticized as not being unified, and which meted out draconian sentences to relatively unimportant crimes, and which was in desperate need of bringing into the age of Enlightenment. Voltaire responded in a letter dated April 13, 1778, thanking the young man for his zeal and assuring him that his work would be worthy of both philosophy and legislation. "It will contribute to the happiness of men, if it is written with the energy which characterizes its introduction." The next time Brissot will have another audience for his ideas on criminal law will be when he addresses his Revolutionary brothers in 1789, after having actively participated in the events of July 14.

and with a furtive glance of teary gratitude, he undid Zénobe's buttons and for a few minutes gave the young man what he wanted. In spite of the *marquis'* efforts to delay the resolution, the valet kept to a different pace, and the end asserted itself too soon, accompanied by the young man's moans and a guttural clearing of his throat as he arched his neck and dug his head into the back of the chair. After a few moments to calm down, they both lifted their heads simultaneously. When Thibouville began to speak, "I... I...", Zénobe quickly put a forefinger to his own lips. He stood up, stuffed his genitals and shirt back into his breeches and buttoned them up. He was out the door before the startled Thibouville had a chance to get off his knees.

As all the accolades and the ovations continued to be heaped on Voltaire, the clergy became more and more exasperated that their adversary continued, unabated and unapologetic, to flaunt his celebrity and flout the sacredness of their attempts to save his soul. The archbishop Beaumont, angry at his underlings Gaultier and Tersac for not having procured from the philosopher a complete retraction, could only groan before the glory that was being used to deify the audacious leader of an impious sect, the destroyer of religion and the annihilator of morals. He redoubled his efforts at Versailles, sacrificing his valuable time to personally say mass in front of the king and queen, never calling Voltaire by name, but making it clear that a terrible, surreptitious force was among them, that it was attracting more and more adherents to it, all the better to undermine that which they held to be the most sacred, the most holy thing in their society, notably the soothing balm which the Church brought to the people through the saintly words of their Holy Father, his Holiness Pope Pious VI, the successor of Saint Peter and the mouthpiece of Our Lord the Heavenly Father.

Reports of these Sunday sermons reached the *hôtel* de Villette, and with the disappointing certainty that Louis XVI was never going to grant Voltaire an audience, the old philosopher began to prepare for his return to Ferney. He did so with a heavy heart, since *madame* Denis was not planning to accompany him, but would rather wait for his return to Paris later on in the summer, or at the very latest, the beginning of autumn. But for her momentary insanity with de la Harpe, *père*, she had not lived in Paris for twenty-seven years, and she couldn't get her fill of it. The dresses, the wigs, the shoes, the visits to the arcade shops in the Palais-Royal, saying *bonjour* to Denis Diderot who liked to play chess there, and then curtsy to the likes of the *duc* de Richelieu or the *duchesse* de Chartres, accompanied by the *marquise* de Villette who eclipsed everybody else in physical beauty and spiritual charm, and sometimes accompanied by Rose Bertin who would help her acquire baubles and bric-a-brac to enhance her frocks and fill her new house which stood face to face with the *hôtel* de Choiseul.[274] Yes, her uncle would have to go back to Ferney without her. It was his fault all along, for he should have brought

---

274   Étienne François, *duc* de Choiseul, Louis XV's minister of war and foreign affairs during the Seven Years' War, was ignominiously dismissed by the king's mistress, *madame* du Barry, who had been a whore all her life, but whose fabled beauty made people forget her past. Brissot met her by chance in the foyer of the *hôtel* de Villette one afternoon when she was just leaving Voltaire. In spite of her assurances to the contrary, Brissot told her that Voltaire would probably be too busy to see someone the likes of him, and promptly turned tail. Luckily, he had the courage to send Voltaire his *Theorie de lois criminelles*.

his books and precious papers to Paris in the first place, as she had insisted back in February. She wasn't worried about being momentarily separated from Voltaire. He would be well taken care of: Wagnière would be tucking him into bed at night and making sure he received his medications. She would even send the young Zénobe to accompany her uncle to Ferney. After all, he himself was from Savoy, which was just an afternoon's carriage amble away. She had complete confidence in the lad, for she was convinced that he loved her uncle. One morning she had caught Zénobe in bed with Voltaire, keeping him warm. She knew of no other servant who would have done that.

Besides, she thought to herself as she made yet another trip to the house on the rue de Richelieu to check on the progress of the interior cabinetry, there was no possibility of her ever going back to the provinces. She had lived long enough in the middle of nowhere, where actors and actresses had to visit the patriarch of Ferney in order to put on skits for the village, where the nearest stores in Geneva sold nothing but Protestant clothes which were simultaneously hard wearing and ugly, and where the idea of a dainty was a brioche smothered with honey. *Non pas*! She took *madame* de Villette's hand in order better to attack the sweeping staircase that took her up to her boudoir, the largest room in the house, with two antechambers and two huge walk-in armoires, one of which had a false back with a secret passageway which led to the adjoining boudoir. One never knew when a secret passageway would be of use.

Zénobe accompanied Voltaire on an outing, which the old *philosophe* had promised to the *duc* de Richelieu. It was a visit to the *duc* d'Orléans, and his son the *duc* de Chartres, at the Palais-Royal. It was as close as he was going to get to royalty.

Being the king's cousin, the *duc* d'Orléans was torn between two conflicting vectors: proximity to the throne (he was fourth in line should something happen to Louis XVI and his two brothers, the *comtes* de Provence and d'Artois), versus his distaste for the prison that was Versailles. This is why the Palais-Royal had been built by his ancestors in the first place, in the heart of Paris, just north of the Louvre which had been the palace of French kings before Louis XIV moved the court to Versailles. After the fire of 1763, Louis Philippe, *duc* d'Orléans had enlarged and improved the buildings and the grounds. The Palais-Royal was his gift to Parisians, with arcades of elegant shops and cafés, including a marvel called the *Café mécanique* with robotic dumbwaiters which by ingenious means delivered food and drink through the middle of the tables; a theater which rivaled the *Comédie française*; a ballet; a musical ensemble which, since it was directed by the *chevalier* de Saint-George, was even better than the *Académie royale de musique*, and other amenities which Louis XVI was too prudish to even think about, but which, according to the way of thinking of the *duc* d'Orléans and his wife, should belong to any civilized society which took into consideration all aspects of man. Namely, the Palais-Royal included sophisticated sex shops where the *demimondaines*, not prostitutes, were educated, high-class and regularly checked for venereal diseases.

But the Palais-Royal was also the *duc* d'Orléans' gift to himself and to his progeny, for here, at home, they were in the thick of things. *Le tout* Paris came to their compound. His wife, Charlotte Jeanne *marquise* de Montesson, was his ideal helpmate, proud, ambitious, enlightened, seeing the talent in the *chevalier* de Saint-George and not caring one whit about the color of his skin. She had been prohibited by Louis XVI from taking the title of *duchesse* d'Orléans because it had been bruited about that she had caught her husband during a royal hunt: instead of rejoining the run of the hounds, she and the *duc* had taken a respite during which she performed fellatio on him. Thus, with a royal decree that she remain but a morganatic wife, she compensated in other ways, and the Palais-Royal had by 1778 become a wonder of the civilized world. Even Londoners admired it. As for the *duc* d'Orléans, since he was marked by royal disfavor, he thus gained favor from the people of Paris.

Sadly, on the day Voltaire came calling, neither the *duc* nor his son was at home. But the old *philosophe* caught the *duc*'s grandchildren playing in the courtyard with their nannies, and the *duchesse* de Chartres, their mother, quickly came down when Voltaire was announced. She was still wearing her *peignoir* and arranging her hair as she popped into the foyer, excusing her disarray, her husband's absence and the noise of her children's play.

"We're trying to raise them like Rousseau suggests, but sometimes they get carried away, the little ruffians."

"Nonsense," replied Voltaire politely. "The activities of happy little children should never be curtailed. Let them roam, let them explore. Did you nurse them yourself?" he asked, eying her breasts.[275]

"Why, yes, I did, for as long as I could."

"That one there, the one with the quiet air about him. Who is that?"

"That's the *duc* de Valois," answered the mother, proud that Voltaire had singled out her first-born. "He's an observer. He'll watch you for hours."

Madame la duchesse de Chartres took the little prince by the hand and brought him closer to Voltaire.

"Well, *bonjour*," said Voltaire. "How do you do?"

The other children approached the old *philosophe* as well, intrigued by his voluminous coat and wig.

The *duc* de Valois was too shy to say anything, but his brother the *duc* de Montpensier asked Voltaire, "Are you the famous old skeleton?"

Madame de Chartres gave a little squeal and chided her son, saying, "My child, we musn't speak that way of this immortal writer and philosopher. He is celebrated everywhere books are published."

"I have books," ventured forth the *duc* de Valois.

"Ah, so you have books," said Voltaire who took hold of Zénobe's arm in order to kneel in the midst of the children. He took the *duc* de Valois by his little hand and said, "Come here, my child. Let me get a closer look at your face."

The little boy allowed himself to be inspected, his little eyes darting from Voltaire's gaze to that of his mother.

"Yes, yes," concluded Voltaire. "I see a remarkable resemblance here, with the Regent!"[276]

"Oh, how nice," said *madame* de Chartres with a little laugh. "It's very nice for you to say so."

---

275   Before Rousseau, aristocratic women sent their infants to nursemaids in the countryside for a year or two.

276   The Regent was the *duc* de Valois' great-great-grandfather, who in 1715, at the death of Louis XIV, became the acting head of government since Louis XV was too young to rule.

It was time for the children's nap, and Voltaire was invited to follow the family inside into the children's room. Voltaire helped to place the three little princes and two twin princesses on their little beds, and waited while the nannies and *madame* de Chartres sang lullabies.

A sense of peace had come to Voltaire, and he didn't say much on the way to the carriage. He hummed a few of the lullabies on the way back to the quai des Théâtins. He was still singing one when Zénobe gave him his medicine that night. Voltaire was now taking six drops of his elixir before going to bed, and Zénobe was convinced that it was allowing Voltaire to sleep like a baby and wake up refreshed and invigorated in the morning.

> *Bonsoir, madame la Lune,*
> *Que faites-vous donc là?*
> *Je fais mûrir des prunes*
> *Pour tous ces enfants-là.*
>
> *Bonjour, monsieur le Soleil,*
> *Que faites-vous donc là?*
> *Je fais mûrir des groseilles*
> *Pour tous ces enfants-là.*[277]

But for Thibouville there were no soothing ditties, no peace-inducing drugs, no relief to the unrelenting pangs of wretchedness that hounded both his head and heart. The constant self-blame for having ruined his relationship with Zénobe, the estrangement he felt from the *marquis* de Villette, the loneliness of his days and nights, all this marked him with lines of worry and fatigue. The worst was recognition of his own hamartia, of his overzealous pride that had pushed André to the limit. "If only, if only, if only," echoed in Thibouville's head, and he told himself more than once, "I myself have prepared the scenes which I am now living through, just as if I had been the playwright of my own life."

Zénobe's power over him was disconcerting. But now that a pattern had established itself, the *marquis* didn't know how to undo this power. Every time Zénobe came into his boudoir, he lost all sense of volition. Zénobe was the handsomest creature he had ever laid eyes on, and his love for the boy served to justify his acquiescence of Zénobe's brutal treatment. As he serviced the youth, his heart felt like it was going to gallop away; he trembled, he accepted everything that Zénobe wanted. All this transpiring without a word ever being pronounced. Zénobe would take hold of Thibouville's body, move and bend him as if he were an automaton, and every time receive his satisfaction with a mute and brisk exertion that contrasted greatly with the older man's groveling and generous compliance.

---

277   Good evening, madam Moon,/What are you doing here?/I'm ripening the plums for all these children./Good day, mister Sun,/What are you doing here?/I'm ripening the currants/For all these children.

Thibouville couldn't even discuss this with Villette. Firstly, they had never discussed adventures with outside paramours with each other. Secondly, Thibouville was loath to expose to a fellow aristocrat the humiliation of his servility to an inferior. Thirdly, Thibouville knew that Villette was very happy with his librarian. The library was coming along beautifully. There was going to be room for an initial five thousand volumes, and when they knocked down the wall into the adjoining room, *madame* Denis' boudoir, there would be room for five thousand more. If only that woman would go back to Ferney with her uncle, or finish her house on the rue de Richelieu. She could certainly move in while the rest of the house was being worked on. Years ago, Villette had lived in his house while it was under embellishment, although in his case it was to observe the workers as they labored, but in the end, none of them proved worthy or amenable to take up to his (unfinished) boudoir. Thibouville had managed to snag a carpenter, a small man whose black bristles of a beard left a rash on Thibouville's delicate face and neck. But the work was finished in two weeks and the *marquis* never saw him again. This time around, Thibouville would go to the library while Zénobe was away in the afternoon, but the workers were just too ugly, and not refined enough. Thibouville could see that Zénobe was doing a good job as supervisor. The shelving was superior, the crown molding exquisite, and the paneling contained images of Grecian urns and sitting harpies with wings outstretched. The coffered ceiling overhead played with different geometric shapes, but in the center of the room the largest coffer was octagonal, mirroring the octagonal table placed right underneath it. Six sides of this built-in table had shelving for books; the other two had recesses for chairs. This exquisite design was heaven on earth, for the eye was inexorably drawn upwards to the repeated configuration above. In the middle of the octagon in the ceiling was the place where the future chandelier would be hung, and Thibouville could imagine the sumptuousness and the grace of the candelabrum's multiple branches. On the side of the room farthest from the entrance, there were two decorative pillars made entirely of lapis lazuli, and the blue swirls of color in the stone set off the warm honey of the oak panels. It was beautiful, and Thibouville's eyes fell on a repeated motif at the top of each division between the shelving: acanthus leaves sculpted out of oak. He saw that they were such things of beauty that they made his heart ache. Then he went into the pantry in the kitchen to get drunk on mead. The mead brought him a bout of self-pity, hot tears of loneliness, and a thought that all of a sudden announced the possibility of extricating himself from his impossible situation with Zénobe. He latched onto this idea as if it were a dilapidated raft in the middle of an endless ocean, and he were the last floating victim of a devastating shipwreck.

Finding Inspiration

The *duc* d'Orléans and his son the *duc* de Chartres were so disappointed to have missed Voltaire's visit to the Palais-Royal that they sent him gracious missives to thank him profusely, along with dangerous, illegal books to cajole him back.

"Look at this," Voltaire told Zénobe one morning as he was still sitting up in bed, several books arrayed in front of him amidst the tangle of blankets. "If I had been caught with these, it would have meant a new sojourn at the Bastille [*un nouvel embastillement*] for me. At my age, it would be a life sentence."

Zénobe came to inspect the texts, his eyes avidly searching the titles.

"I haven't seen any of these in Panckoucke's reading room," he said.

"Panckoucke's reading room?"

"Yes, the little room in the back where preferred customers can peruse books before purchasing them. It is a very convenient way to choose among books which, as Panckoucke says, he does not possess and which he has never seen."

"Ah, that Panckoucke! He has made so much money off of me that he's purchasing a *château* by the Loire at Onzain.

"I'm sure yours in Ferney is bigger."

"I should certainly hope so! I'm the one who writes the books."

Zénobe was looking at the innocuous-looking tomes as if they were chicken cutlets poached in Calvados, his new favorite dish.

Voltaire looked at him and said, "Oh, to be young again! Go ahead. Take these, they're yours. Fill your mind with dangerous ideas; you've probably already had quite a few of them on your own. Remember though, just because they are seditious, or libelous, or sacrilegious, does not in any way mean that they are true. Revolutionaries create as many fallacies as do the idiots against whom they are fighting, those who happen to be holding on to political and ecclesiastic power. The rebels have to go so far to the other side that they, too, enter into the world of the false, of the deceptive, of the illusory. And if you agree with these writers, check yourself, it might be because you want very badly to believe them, not because their ideas are founded on logic or on truth. Books are weapons, but they do not speak as honestly as a foil or a musket. They are rather like the Trojan horse or a goblet of wine in which dissolved powders lie, ready to infuse the immature mind with honey-tongued secrets that readily turn to acid."

Zénobe picked up one of the books and turned it over in his hand.

"This book can be that dangerous?"

"Of course!"

Zénobe turned to the title page.

"*Te chaînes off slav, slav, slav... ry*," he pronounced badly. "This book is in English!"

"Let me see," said Voltaire.

The old man looked at the title page and read in passable English, "*The Chains of Slavery: A Work Wherein the Clandestine and Villainous attempts to Ruin Liberty are Pointed Out, and the Dreadful Scenes of Despotism Disclosed.* By Jean-Paul Marat.[278] Jean-Paul Marat? That name seems familiar to me. Ah! I think I remember. Wasn't he the man who set Benjamin Franklin's hair, what little he has, on fire? It was in an experiment on the properties of fire. Franklin listened politely, but in the end he did not sanction the science. Last year, this *Maraud* [villain], I mean Marat, insulted me, or so he thought, by calling me 'inconsequential' in a book in which he extolled Rousseau but criticized the other philosophes as being false and superficial. In this same book, he criticized the Ancients as if they were a passel of scatterbrains. He also undertook an attack on Newton's theses. Can you imagine that? Any one who goes so far in his denunciations is not even a revolutionary; he's an anarchist."

Voltaire handed the book back to Zénobe.

"Do you understand English?" he asked.

"Father Anselme taught me some back in Savoy.

> Neither a borrower, nor a lender be;
> For loan oft loses both itself and friend,
> And borrowing dulls the edge of husbandry.
> This above all: to thine own self be true,
> And it must follow, as the night the day,
> Thou canst not then be false to any man."

"Well recited," admired Voltaire. "If only our friends here," he said pointing to the books, "would follow Shakespeare's advice, what a better world this place would be. Everybody speaking the truth, everybody accepting the truth, everybody compromising at the truth. With reason by our side to expose our errors, beauty and happiness would follow.

> For truth is precious and divine,
> Too rich a pearl for carnal swine."[279]

Zénobe asked, "Who said that?"

"An Englishman," answered Voltaire. "I forget who. Oh, no. I remember. Those words were written by a man named Butler, in his very naughty poem *Hudibras*, where he gives hell to the Puritans the way I have given it to the Catholics. He speaks of

> *La vraie église militante,*
> *Qui prêche un pistolet en main,*

---

278   Marat deemed it too dangerous to publish this book in France in 1774, so he translated it and had it published in London instead.

279   Samuel Butler, *Hudibras*, part II, canto II, line 257.

Pour mieux convertir son prochain
À grands coups de sabre augmente.[280]

"Just like Isabel the good Catholic, queen of Spain, who, wherever her representatives went, gave her captives three choices: convert, flee, or die."

"Isn't she the one who sent *Christophe Colomb* to discover the Americas?"

"Aren't you putting the carriage before the horse? Neither the explorer nor the Queen knew beforehand what new worlds would be 'discovered.' Imagine, if you will, how we would feel if inhabitants from another world came to our little Earth and told us we had just been discovered. We know we're here. And if they destroyed most of what they found, well, you'd know how the Americans felt when greedy Europeans got their hands on them. Why does Western man seek to destroy what he has just discovered?"

"Because he wishes to destroy it before he has had a chance to understand it," was Zénobe's reply. "Otherwise, it might prove to be a viable alternative for a way of living, and there can only be one, the one that they already have and believe in."

"Ah, you see what I'm saying? You yourself can write a book such as these. Only, be prepared to fight, flee, or convert. It's a dangerous world out there, and you will find yourself in the Bastille before your book is out of the presses. Now do you see why I've always cultivated the likes of the *duc* de Richelieu and the *duc* d'Orléans? They alone can possess these forbidden books, and they can be influential friends when the need arises. That is also why in my own writing I prefer to take ancient historical subjects where there is no need to defend myself. I can criticize the powers that be all I want; the onus of proving my criticism falls on he who wishes to censor me, and usually this sort of person is too stupid to do it convincingly. Let's get to work, Zénobe, my friend. *Agathocle* is in the process of being born, and I feel like he's emerging full-grown from my head. Perhaps some tea might soothe it."

"You have a headache?" asked Zénobe. He quickly went to the kitchen to prepare the tea himself, enough for five or six cups, very sweet, with a touch of cream and a bit of lemon. On the way out of the kitchen, he crossed paths with Maurel who wore an expression of worry and consternation. Maurel would have wished to speak with him, but Zénobe was in a hurry to get the tea to Voltaire and resume work on *Agathocle*. Besides, ever since André left, Maurel was tediously melancholic, and Zénobe did not need the constant reminder of André's absence. In his rush to get back to Voltaire's room, Zénobe missed clues that perhaps the subject on Maurel's mind was more pressing and possibly about a more immediate matter, so an opportunity was lost.

As Maurel watched Zénobe scurry off, he could only sigh, and hope he'd be able to speak with him later about an imminent alteration to the household's population of secretaries.

---

280   Voltaire's own translation, with a 'corrective reduction,' of *Hudibras*, part I, canto I, lines 192-200: For he was of that stubborn crew/Of errant saints, whom all men grant/To be the true Church Militant;/Such as do build their faith upon/The holy text of pike and gun;/Decide all controversies by/Infallible artillery;/And prove their doctrine orthodox/By apostolic blows and knocks.

The *marquis* de Thibouville had not been raised to wallow in self-pity, to give in voluntarily to self-degradation, or to yield to the other in the battles of love. Yet, he had been caught in a morass of all three, and his life, he felt, was not worth living. He couldn't even call on his traditional friend and lover the *marquis* de Villette who would certainly laugh at him and throw to his face the advantages of their class and how he should be manipulating a peon as he liked and not the other way round.

How had this happened? How did he fall into this habit of having Zénobe, a servant, come into his boudoir, barge in at any time of his choosing, and then expect him, the *marquis* de Thibouville *et* d'Herbigny, to give him prompt and satisfactory service for any whim or caprice that the young man had decided in a most unilateral fashion? One night, the *marquis* was already asleep, and yet the young man came in and unashamedly poked him in the face with his erect penis. A brutal awakening, yes, but why had he been swept up in the exhilaration of the moment and latched on to that turgid member as if he were lost in some desert and it were pointing north? Oh, devilish attitude in an angelic countenance, how thou doth smiled as I took in the spasmodic pointer, and made it point straight to me, straight into me, to show me the way to my own humiliation and doom. How have I made thee into my master, and the world turn topsy-turvy? How didst thou make me the one to kneel in front of you?

"I, kneeling, waiting on someone?" the *marquis* asked himself, aghast after about two weeks of this new mode of comportment of Zénobe's. "I was not brought up for this! I cannot sit here day after day, alone in my room, waiting for this, this, this servant boy to come to me and without a word plant himself on a chair or on the bed and expect me to perform acts that are in no way accompanied by a willingness to reciprocate. This is not just."

Of course the *marquis* could not comprehend that this was indeed justice, and justice well deserved, according to Zénobe's viewpoint. It was punishment meted out to the one who had left him bereft and pining for his lover. Every day he suffered from André's absence, so almost every day he went into the *marquis*' boudoir, without asking, to pay him back for his malfeasance. It was a punishment he was enjoying, for he could see on the *marquis*' face the battle raging between his savage carnal pleasure and his precious aristocratic self-esteem.

But on the afternoon when all this ended, as Zénobe quietly slipped into Thibouville's boudoir, he was surprised to hear an unknown voice in the room, and when he turned around, he was shocked to see a boy, a young man, standing in front of the *marquis* de Thibouville who was sitting by the fire in Zénobe's favorite *bergère*, drinking coffee and seemingly engaged in conversation with the young man.

"Ah, this is Zénobe Bosquet," said Thibouville, "Voltaire's attendant, the *marquis* de Villette's librarian, and my sometime protégé. He goes in through so many doors in this house that every once in a while he forgets his place and doesn't wait to be invited in. Good afternoon, Zénobe. Approach, I want you to meet *madame* de Villette's new secretary, André Laurent, whom we procured—"

"You mean we don't have enough secretaries in this house?" interrupted Zénobe, as the new lad flinched but simultaneously shot back a glance of curiosity at this young man who dared walk into an aristocrat's personal room without an iota of decorum, sobriety or deference.

"Your name is André?" asked Zénobe.

"*Oui, monsieur*," said the boy, bowing. "André Laurent, from Gascogne," he said, with the thick accent of Gascogne.

"You don't have to bow to him, you know," said Thibouville. "The gentleman's outfit which he wears, or part of it, today, is just for show, a disguise. He is really just like you, only he hails from the country of Savoy."

"I could tell he was from somewhere else because of his accent," said André Laurent.

"My accent?" asked Zénobe.

"Why, yes," agreed Thibouville. "One finds it difficult to identify it as Swiss French, like that of Jean Jacques Rousseau, or more like a Val d'Aoste accent mixed with a dose of Piémontais. Sounds lilting, does it not?"

"*Oui, monsieur*, it sounds exotic," said André Laurent.

"Well, I don't know about exotic," said the *marquis*. "Perhaps rustic. In any case, Zénobe, André will be an employee of *monsieur* de Villette, so all accouterments which he will need can be put on the *marquis*' account. Uniform, writing implements, oh, I don't know. Whatever he needs."

"Shouldn't you be talking to *monsieur* Maurel about this?"

"He already knows. It has been decided that you shall train André, since you are the *marquis*' librarian—"

"But I am also Voltaire's secretary."

"Well, yes, but the poor man won't be writing forever. I wager that soon he won't be needing your secretarial duties as much as he has in the past. You will therefore take on André's instruction. By the way, he won't be needing any supplementary education for he has a solid background in the classics. He is a graduate of the *Collège Louis-le-Grand.* Ah! The same college that *monsieur* de Voltaire attended. What a coincidence, *n'est-ce pas*? So off you go, young men. Report to *monsieur* Maurel who will see to it about having a uniform made for you, and, and, and *et cetera*. Pray now, go."

Zénobe went immediately to look for Maurel, followed several paces back by the new secretary trying hard to keep up. When Zénobe found Maurel downstairs, he spluttered a few unintelligible words and peremptorily started to take off.

"What did you say?" asked Maurel.

"Oh, I'm sorry, it's my Savoyard accent. I said, here's the new employee for *madame la marquise* de Villette, the new André [*le nouvel* André]." Then he left.

Maurel looked after him with an expression of sympathy and concern. He would have wanted to warn him in advance that the new employee would also be sharing his little bedroom at the back of the servants' quarters.

Upstairs, the *marquis* de Thibouville was still sitting in his armchair, both hands pressed to his mouth in the position of prayer. The tears suspended tremulously in his eyes overflowed and ran copiously down his cheeks.

The whole of this week, Voltaire made numerous outings, most of them accompanied by Zénobe. Four working sessions at the *Académie française*, a visit to the *Comédie française* to see a performance of his 1736 tragedy *Alzire*; three visits to the *duc* d'Orléans, another ceremonial session at the *Académie des sciences*; and personal visits to his old friends *madame* du Deffand, *madame* de Suard, *madame* Necker, and sittings for his sculptor Houdon. One early morning visit was to *docteur* Tronchin to thank him for being his doctor and not yet having got tired of his perennial patient. If Tronchin sounded gruff about being awakened at nine o'clock in the morning, he was positively livid when afterwards he tried to leave to begin his rounds and saw that a crowd of 400 people had gathered by his front door to impede his departure.

Voltaire and Zénobe also advanced on *Agathocle*, the new play that was going to take Paris by storm. They were in the middle of Act III, when Agathocle, the tyrant of Syracuse, bent with age and the constant worry of governing the recalcitrant population of Sicily, is readying to hand over the reins of power to his favorite son, Polycrate, whom he admires for being even more ruthless than himself. Polycrate loves a girl, Ydace, whom he makes his prisoner when she doesn't love him back. It is with Agathocle's second son, Argide, who has received a liberal education in Greece and is thus enlightened and virtuous, that Ydace would rather be. The atmosphere is heavy with presentiment, with the doom of one of the brothers fast approaching. It will be a fratricidal duel which will have to kill one of them off.

"Which one to delete?" asked Voltaire.

"Well, what's the historical fact? Which one of the two survived?"

"Damned if I can remember. Those books are all in Ferney."

"Well, if Polycrate wins out, Sicily will be in for one more generation of brutal and arbitrary government. It sounds like it was Agathocle who inspired Machiavelli."

"Machiavelli had many models."

"If Argide wins, then there is hope that a new, more gentle prince will lead his people out of barbarism."

"Yes, but do you think that Agathocle will bear to see the murder of his favorite son go unpunished? Better to have his line come to an end than allow the kind-hearted and enlightened Argide to take over for him. According to Agathocle, Argide is too soft, he'll let the country go to ruin, he'll allow their enemies to invade and annihilate the whole country."

"There's nothing like fomenting fear to convince the populace of the necessity of cruel and belligerent tactics. Besides, he'll marry Ydace as well."

"Oh, Ydace, Ydace, I want to make her sweet, innocent, kind. For inspiration, I'm using the personality of *Belle et bonne*, you know."

"I had that impression."

"Let's work on her now. What shall she say when she realizes that the two brothers are going to fight it out to the death?"

"She should probably faint."

"Let's not make her entirely helpless. Let's put in some of *madame* Denis' stamina into *Belle et bonne*'s portrait."

"Oh, Voltaire, I don't have the imagination for that." A sob had mysteriously interposed itself in the middle of Zénobe's sentence, surprising him with the profundity of his affection for André.

"Yes, I see what you mean. *Madame* Denis gives new meaning to obstinacy. Well, no matter. Ydace will find strength in the love she has for Argide. Love always gives strength. Has your young life not taught you that yet?"

"I believe it is a lesson that my destiny is teaching me at present."

"Ah, my boy, come here and let me embrace you. Don't look so glum. You will soon be seeing your beloved André. It's not like he's at the other end of the earth. On a horse at a gallop, you can be with him in two days. I couldn't do that anymore, but you certainly can."

"But I'm not going to leave you now when work is going so well on *Agathocle*. You are inspired, and the *Comédie française* is already saying that this play will be even better than *Irène*."

"I dare believe it is so. *Irène* had too many godfathers. This one has only two, you and I."

Zénobe beamed, and took up the plume with a flourish.

"Ydace, you were saying," said the young man. "Ydace will find the strength she needs from within her love for André... I mean, Argide. Let's open the doors to those feelings, and give Ydace the courage to continue loving, to continue hoping, for Venus has given her, and us, a great gift. To know that one belongs to someone, and that that person belongs to you, gives you a mooring in life, a confirmation that one is not useless, and a force, a life force flows from that. My love for André, my love for *monsieur* Maurel, my love for you, all give me courage and I would fight a thousand duels for the three of you."

"Ah, perfect, *mon cher* Zénobe. See how love envelops you and energizes you. But let's not give Ydace so much courage. She's a Carthaginian woman, only one step above a French woman, not counting the Amazonian *chevalière* d'Éon, so she cannot be that courageous."

"But still, a little impassioned, maybe?"

"That is plausible and will make her more likable. Yes, I like that!"

They continued writing several scenes in which Ydace appeared. When the play was finally performed, as a posthumous homage to Voltaire a year and a day after his death, on May 31st, 1779, it was well received by the critics, and judging by the crowd that crammed the *Comédie française*, their simultaneous tears and cries of joy proved that Voltaire had gotten it just right.

That night Zénobe went to bed dead tired. But he had gotten into the habit of reading a few articles of the *Encyclopédie* before he went to sleep, so he kept his candle lit, and after he undressed, he dragged the huge tome with him to bed. As soon as he sat on the cushion he realized with a start that there was somebody already there. The heavy book fell on his toe. Zénobe cussed in pain. André Laurent made a startled cry of distress and sat up, asking if it was time to wake up already.

"Damn!" whispered Zénobe. "What the devil are you doing here?"

"This is where *monsieur* Maurel said I was to sleep. He told me that I'd be sharing your bed. Didn't he tell you, too?"

"Not a word. And I don't want another word from you either. This won't do. You go there," said Zénobe, pointing to the floor.

"On the f-f-loor?" asked André Laurent.

"That's right. And take these." He heaved a pillow and a blanket towards him, and André Laurent slipped buttocks first to the floor. Without a word he fluffed his pillow in a most piteous way and covered himself with the blanket as if trying to cover his shame.

Zénobe, still in a huff, propped up his book to catch most of the candlelight and proceeded to read his articles. But after about fifteen or twenty minutes, fatigue overcame him, and he closed his book and placed it on the chair besides the bed that served for this purpose. He blew out the candle.

In the dark after a few minutes, he realized it was very cold. He sighed. He turned and looked over the edge of the other side of the bed, but he couldn't see the boy.

"*Le nouvel* André?" Zénobe whispered.

"*Oui, monsieur?*" was the return.

"Get back in bed."

"*Merci beaucoup, monsieur.*"

André Laurent lost no time, and tried to remain as far over to the side so as not to disturb Zénobe.

A few minutes later, André Laurent asked in a timid voice, "Are you weeping, *monsieur?*"

Zénobe answered, "Go to sleep."

Stimulants and Soporifics

In order to finish the fifth act of *Agathocle,* Voltaire needed extraordinary means of support. He found it in twenty-five to thirty cups of tea, all before noon. He wished to finish the play before he left for Ferney, and he wanted to depart for Ferney as soon as possible in order to come back to Paris as soon as possible.

"Maybe nobody will even notice that I'm gone," he said brightly.

Zénobe quickly dispelled that illusion with a look of exaggerated incredulity.

"The newspapers are all giving daily reports about you, about the people who visit you at the *hôtel* de Villette, about the people whom you go out to visit. You and Benjamin Franklin are on everybody's tongues, and your disappearance for even a few weeks would not go unnoticed."

"We could get a double who would stand in for me."

"Whom do you propose? *Monsieur* Maurel? Me?"

"How about *monsieur* de Thibouville? He and I have been friends for a long time; he would do this little favor for me."

"You'll first have to overpower his self-conceit; otherwise he might object to playing the role of an octogenarian."

"Oh, we'll cover him up with my wig and plenty of powder."

"He's not witty. Nobody will believe he is you."

"Poor thing, witty he's never been. But he could have a bout of laryngitis."

"You were bleeding buckets out your mouth and nose and *docteur* Tronchin had forbidden you to speak, but to what avail?"

"I was suffering greatly from my restrictive aphonia."

"Well, from where I stood it didn't seem so restrictive."

Voltaire sighed.

"It is difficult to shut me up. But ever since I was a child, because I was always smaller and weaker than the other boys, and sickly, from the moment of my birth, words were all I had to escape their pranks and save my skin. I quickly learned the power of words, just as I quickly learned people's reactions to words. There, in a nutshell, you have my entire life. So, in effect, you can say that words are my action; I write in order to act."

"And by so doing," offered Zénobe, "you make people react. And many of them would want your voice stilled. But they will not be successful, so long as I'm by your side."

"Oh, my boy, my voice will be stilled soon enough, by a power greater than any human's. But do not worry, for the voice I represent, the voice of Reason, will be taken up by younger, more energetic people. Like you, for instance."

"I shall always strive to honor that voice. But you have people like the *marquis* de Villette, who in his opinion is already your literary heir."

"That's quite all right. I let him pilfer my works in order to present my material in a new way. There's no harm in that. It's still a continuation of my work."

"Except that his purpose is for his own personal glorification, not for the selflessness of your work, which is to help humankind."

"But still, his heart's in the right place. At least he doesn't work on the side of the censors, and he doesn't stand with the malicious religious crowd, and he cares not a whit about his aristocratic credentials."

"Because he cares only for the wealth behind them. You know, he's not planning to read the tiniest part of the books I've been procuring for his library."

Zénobe realized suddenly that Voltaire was bent over at a strange angle, with a hand on his lower abdomen.

"Voltaire, are you in pain?"

"The drops of that magic elixir must have worn off. I need to empty my bladder; let's see if nature obliges. Help me up, my boy."

Zénobe helped Voltaire to put his feet on the floor while half-sitting on the side of the bed. He brought his chamber pot to him and held it for him while he tried to urinate. This exercise, which was repeated several times a day and night, was usually one of frustration, but today it was also fraught with pain. At one moment Voltaire held on tightly to Zénobe's wrist, until he finally expelled a liquid that alarmed them both. In addition to the usual blood in his urine, there was also a component that looked like egg whites glistening and swirling in the bloody liquid.

"That's new!" cried out Voltaire. "We must write to Tronchin and have him come over right away. Save that for him," he instructed, indicating the contents of the chamber pot.

Zénobe was ready for dictation in an instant.

> "The old invalid of the Villette Palace asks his savior at the Royal
> Palace if an albuminous discharge in the urine, accompanied with the
> usual strangury and the usual blood in the urine, could not signify
> hydropsy, which runs in my family. The patient would not be upset to
> be reassured by a little word from Asklepios Tronchin.[281]
> His very humble and very obliging servant,
>
> Voltaire."

Le nouvel André was sent to take the note to Tronchin, and a return message came back immediately saying that if the discharge was clear, there was no need to worry. Another message was sent to the doctor. The new André was once again the messenger.

> "The poor sick person tenderly thanks *monsieur* Tronchin. He is filled
> with the most loving gratitude, as well as the most profound esteem.
> He dares hope, in spite of his eighty-four years, that he will owe him
> still a few more days of life."

---

281   Asklepios was the Greek god of Medicine.

Zénobe went back to taking dictation for *Agathocle*, but Voltaire was interrupted by the arrival of *madame* Denis who held a letter aloft written by the *abbé* Gaultier.

"What shall we tell him? He keeps coming by every day and we've run out of excuses as to why you cannot see him."

"Well, tell him," Voltaire said impatiently, "tell him that I'm dying!"

"But that's precisely why he persists in coming every day. He says that there's no time to lose. You must repent, and recant, and confess."

"Oh, he should be satisfied with my profession of faith."

"What shall we tell him?"

"Tell him that I shall respond to his letter, after I've read it, and that I shall request his presence when I'm feeling better, and if I am not feeling any better, then it must be because I've taken a turn for the worse, which means that I will require his presence all the more."

"So what you mean," said *madame* Denis, is that you're not well enough to see him, but you're also not sick enough."

Voltaire smiled his toothless grin.

Madame Denis looked towards the heavens like a martyred saint, but she couldn't help smiling either. After she was gone, it was the *marquis* de Villette's turn. He, too, came into Voltaire's bedroom brandishing a letter.

"Look what they're saying about you! Have people no shame? They say you have gone mad, that you have the Devil in you, that you are a rabid dog and that you are in agony about dying and going to hell."

Voltaire turned to Zénobe and said, "Well, that's a letter I don't wish to read. And to Villette he said, "My friend, my friend, don't fret so. People have been saying the damnedest things about me since I wrote my first play at the age of seventeen. Then it was that I had received my talent from a pact with the Devil. Later it was that I was the Antichrist himself. Now that I am at the end of a long, successful and prosperous career, of course they're going to say that the Devil was my helper. Tell them what I've always told them: I've never said a single word against God; all my vituperation has been aimed at man-made religion, with all its superstitious and illogical, pernicious dogma. It's the dogma I've always fought against. Now, leave me alone, and if they don't understand, send them all to the Devil!"

Docteur Lorry came in before the *marquis* de Villette had left, and when the doctor observed Voltaire in an altered state and understood that it was Villette who was the cause of it, he gently tried to push Villette out the door, saying, "*Monsieur, monsieur*, you are killing him."

Villette exploded in ire about being manhandled by a mere doctor, and the ensuing argument was voluble and contagious. Zénobe got caught up in the acrimony and yelled out, "*Messieurs*, if you please, *messieurs*, there is an old man in need of rest here, so cease your dispute or carry it outside."

With Voltaire in the room, Zénobe's statement could not be construed as illogical, yet Villette chafed at having a subordinate give him directives. But when Zénobe opened the door, the only thing for the aristocrat to do was to storm out. Lorry gave Zénobe a look of disdain, but remained in the room. *Madame* Denis had heard the ruckus from the kitchen, and she came back into Voltaire's room accompanied by an alarmed *monsieur* Maurel, but Zénobe instructed them that all was now well, and that *docteur* Lorry needed to auscultate his patient. He shut the door in their faces.

Lorry was not a better or a worse doctor than Tronchin, just different, but in view of Voltaire's many symptoms, his only act was the one that Tronchin would have opted for as well: he bled him for five minutes. After he left, Voltaire begged Zénobe for a few more drops of the magical elixir. He got four then, and four in the afternoon, after he had drunk a few more cups of tea.

Once again, Zénobe could barely keep his eyes open during his evening reading. In spite of the fact that he was reading a prohibited book, it proved no more interesting than any other. He put it down and blew out the candle and promptly fell asleep.

He awoke during the night with his arm around André's torso. The new boy's hair was under his nose and he could smell its scent, so different from his own André's hair. In spite of the fact that Zénobe would have sworn to be not at all interested in the new André, he was now fully roused from sleep, and the idea of a completely new person in his bed seemed to excite him. He removed his arm from over the new André, turned his back to him, and after a few minutes, he lit the candle and resumed his reading, hoping that the soporific text would quell both his ardor and his guilt.

He of course had not written the old André the news of the new André, nor especially of the fact that they were sharing a bed. Without questioning or examining this omission, Zénobe thought it prudent not to worry his André about the day-to-day activities in the Villette household. He did, however, keep him apprised of the status of Voltaire's health. He certainly didn't say a word to the old André, nor even to Maurel, when he started making love to the new André. It started simply, at first. Just a couple of grinding motions, through their long johns—that's all it took for Zénobe to achieve resolution. After that, it became more ritualized, but *le nouvel* André was too passive, too uninterested in Zénobe's needs, and he also had this annoying habit of pretending to fall back asleep afterwards, even if it was in the morning right before they had to get up. Zénobe realized that there was no love involved here, hardly any emotion at all. It was just an opportunity that Nature was using to relieve pressure, for sometimes the pressure could surely build up. It was just Nature, asking to be let out. He identified it as a natural extension of his onanism, and, in spite of the horrific books he had read on the subject, written by eminent doctors who all seemed to contradict one another, he was convinced that *immoderata seminis profusio*, or excessive seminal emissions, would not terminate in apoplexy, epilepsy, loss of vision or hearing or memory, paralysis, gout, heat in the liver and kidneys, pain in the membranes of the brain, indolence, lassitude, or a continuous rotational movement of his testicles inside his scrotum. Nature was a difficult mistress to penetrate and She held on to her secrets so tightly that it would take much effort and perseverance to uncover them, but he knew, in this particular case, that She in her glorious wisdom would not torture one of her creatures for dissipating his animal fluids. He knew that this was one more attempt by those in power to frighten and subdue, under a blanket of legitimized science, those gullible enough to accept these pseudo-lessons that, in the end, went against Nature. He knew better. He was above this fray, for he could see the manipulations of Church and State. In the interconnections of Law and Science, in the countless interstices of what was Legal and what was deemed Natural, he could see the face of Morality, and he could see that this imposing impassive face was just as ridiculous and arbitrary as the belief that he could fritter away his health and stamina just by ejaculating his semen in between the new André's thighs.

The End is Nigh

Both doctors Tronchin and Lorry had forbidden Voltaire to take any stimulants, and Voltaire was finally convinced by their wisdom. On the morning following the drinking binge of tea, Voltaire woke up with a wail, startling members of the household awake and causing Maurel to go to the servants' quarters to wake everybody up an hour earlier than usual.

In five minutes Zénobe was washed and dressed. Followed by Maurel, he rushed into Voltaire's bedroom. There they found *mesdames* Denis and Villette in their *peignoirs* hovering over the patient's bed.

"*Ah, le voilà*," said *madame* Denis, glancing at Zénobe. "We should never have allowed Zénobe to leave my uncle's bed at night."

"But he was sleeping so well," anguished the *marquise.*

Zénobe looked at Voltaire who was still in bed under the covers, his hands lying protectively over his lower abdomen. The old man gazed at Zénobe with supplication and fear.

Zénobe stood by the open door and said, "Everybody, leave. You may return in a few minutes."

His tone, although decisive, was given in an emotion filled with concern for the patient, and the two ladies did not take any umbrage, but Maurel found a need to attempt to soften the force of Zénobe's naked imperative.

"We'll let you know as soon as you can come back in, *mesdames*, if you please. Thank you, you are so kind."

Before they left, Zénobe had already helped Voltaire up and had the chamber pot in place.

"Ah, my dear Zénobe," said Voltaire. "Ah, my dear Maurel. Thank you both for coming to my aid. Tronchin, is he coming?"

"Both doctors Tronchin and Lorry are being alerted," answered Maurel. "It is to be hoped that they will come promptly."

"Concentrate, please, Voltaire," said Zénobe.

"Nothing's coming out," said Voltaire. "And my bladder feels like it's ready to burst. Ah! How it hurts!"

Zénobe moved his free hand to Voltaire's lower abdomen and tried gently to push down as if he were about to milk a cow, but Voltaire protested at the lightest touch.

"Oh, no, no, I can't stand it. It hurts too much!"

Zénobe gave the chamber pot to Maurel to hold, and then used both hands to elongate and squeeze Voltaire's penis. Many times in Savoy had he faced recalcitrant cows, and he was trying to put that knowledge to use.

"Push out," he said to Voltaire. "Apply pressure, as hard as you can."

Voltaire pushed and cried out in pain. "It is not poss—"

"Push as if your life depended on it, because it does. You have to push this urine out; it cannot stay inside you. Now push, push hard."

Voltaire pushed and groaned while Zénobe manipulated his penis in different ways, but it wasn't until he cupped one of his hands under the base of Voltaire's testicles and lifted them up that something seemed to give, and a yellowish substance, the same consistency of the previous day's egg whites, burst out into the chamber pot. Then a weak stream of yellowish urine, streaked with red, began to dribble down.

"Oh, oh, oh, oh," said Voltaire in a relief which came from the very center of his being.

Zénobe gently put Voltaire back into bed and laid both hands on his chest, as if keeping him from rising, or keeping his soul from leaving.

"Thank you, my dear Zénobe. That one was hard, too hard for me alone."

Zénobe burst out in tears, his hands still on Voltaire's chest.

"Oh, no, my boy, don't weep, don't weep. I feel better now. Just a little bit nauseous, but that agonizing pain is gone. Thanks to you. Here, sit by my side. Maurel, can you go get a cup of tea? Not for me, but for my true friend here. One knows who one's true friends are, who have held on to one's penis while one tries to piss. *Voilà!*" he said, as Zénobe laughed. "That's a true friend."

Docteur Lorry wrote back saying that he didn't wish to return to a house where the hired help told him what to do. Tronchin didn't come until late morning. By then, Voltaire had grown more nauseous and had no appetite for food or drink.

"You have now spent all of your income and are living only on your principal, and believe me, there's hardly any principal left," were Tronchin's words of wisdom. "And what is this?" the doctor asked, picking up a vial of blue glass that Zénobe had carelessly left on the bedside table earlier that morning.

When Voltaire said nothing but acted sheepish, Zénobe answered the doctor's question.

"It is an elixir given us by the *duc* de Richelieu, *monsieur le docteur.*"

"Oh, God, what is it?" he asked, unstopping the bottle to smell the contents. "Oh, dear Lord, it's laudanum, isn't it?"

"I believe so," answered Zénobe.

"It relieves the pain I feel in my abdomen," said Voltaire.

"It will also relieve you of your life, if you are not careful. What is your intake of it?"

"Two drops at night, in some liquid."

Zénobe did not dare give the more accurate account, which was now up to eight or ten drops a day.

"In your nightcap, I'm sure of it," retorted Tronchin. Oh, *monsieur* de Voltaire, *monsieur* de Voltaire, you should have gone back to Ferney when I first warned you."

"I'm going as soon as I can; I need to be back in time to meet with the members of the *Académie française* in a month, to make sure that all the letters are being written. Are you aware? For the alphabet. Do you know what the Academicians said to me at the end of our last meeting? I had enjoined them to finish with speed this most sacred effort of ours, to create a new dictionary which mirrors our time, and I then gave a toast, 'To the French alphabet, gentlemen!' And they responded, 'To French letters!'"

Tronchin didn't even answer. He didn't like the look of the contents of Voltaire's chamber pot. Who had the time for witty Academicians' banter? Certainly not he! He had no time for this old patient of his who didn't do anything he was instructed to do.

He was more accustomed to patients who treated his every enunciation as if they were commandments by Moses brought down from the mountain. Still, he duly auscultated his patient, perhaps a bit too gruffly, but he did find a hard mass in Voltaire's lower abdomen, which apparently caused him exceedingly acute pain. There was nothing he could do. Having found out that Lorry had bled the patient on the previous day, he refrained from doing it today. The pressure was in his urine, the bladder and the kidneys, not in his blood or in any of his other bodily humors, although maybe his spleen might also be affected.

Voltaire was exhausted after *docteur* Tronchin's examination. He fell asleep shortly thereafter, and Zénobe was told that he could go to his afternoon appointments. In the lingering disarray of the morning's alarm, Zénobe did not think to reclaim the bottle of laudanum that *docteur* Tronchin had put back on the bedside table, hidden from view behind all sorts of medical accouterments, towels and a large green bottle of unguent.

At the library of the Arsenal, Zénobe tried hard to find Voltaire's symptoms in medical books, but the best description he could match was in a chapter of diseases of the bladder and urinary tract, under a subheading of cancer of the prostate, and its prognosis was too pessimistic for Zénobe to be able to tolerate. He looked for other possibilities but there were none to be found. He went to his fencing lesson in despair, but the physical exertion soon forced him to concentrate on his lunges and parries, and a new movement, *la botte longue*, which made him sweat, required him to stretch as far as possible with all his weight on his left leg, and La Boëssière instructed him that he should pretend to skewer the setting sun. His victim would be caught by surprise, not realizing that anybody could stretch that far that quickly. In a few minutes he succeeded in capturing both speed and reach, even though during a few of his tries he lunged so far out that he lost his balance and ended up sprawled on the floor.

Afterwards, Zénobe realized that he had been in a trance due to the force of concentration. During the two hours of his exercises, he had not thought even once of the events going on at the *hôtel* de Villette. Once outside on the rue Saint-Honoré, however, he was impatient to return home and broke into a trot.

Everything in Voltaire's room was as he had left it. The *philosophe* was still fast asleep. *Madame* Denis and the *marquise* de Villette had asked for a carriage and horses and were out of the house. Maurel had told Zénobe that Voltaire had suffered another bout of pain, but that the pain had gone away and he had fallen back asleep. Zénobe sat on the *chaise longue* to make himself comfortable for the next few hours until supper time, wondering if Voltaire were going to want to eat. But just as he was picking up a book he intended to peruse, he caught a glint of something shiny on the floor by Voltaire's bed. Zénobe moved his head to the left and to the right, like an owl, he thought, then his whole torso side to side, in order to get a better fix on the unidentified object, but he only succeeded in confirming that there were several separate objects that glistened in unison. He got up to satisfy his curiosity, and as he approached the shiny things, his heart sank and his stomach and diaphragm felt a flash of fire. He knelt on the floor and picked up a few shards of blue glass, and the glass stopper now chipped on one side.

"Oh no, oh no, oh no," Zénobe repeated, patting the floor to make sure there was moisture there, wondering in panic how long it could take laudanum to evaporate. But the floor was completely dry. Zénobe checked the bed, but the sheets and blankets were dry as well. He threw the sheets and blankets off of the patient and patted Voltaire from neck to knees, and there was no damp spot to indicate that the bottle had fallen on him before it rolled to the floor and broke. Next he checked the towels on the table.

They were dry. Everything was dry, blood of Christ, everything was dry. But he began anew to check the bed sheets once more just to make sure.

It was at this moment that d'Alembert came into the room. The *philosophes*, Voltaire's friends, could still visit as they pleased, and Maurel had allowed the mathematician to go to Voltaire's room by himself. Zénobe didn't hear the door open.

"What's wrong, Zénobe? What's frightening you so? Maurel said Voltaire was sleeping?"

Zénobe glanced over. "Oh, *monsieur* d'Alembert, I can't find it, I can't find it. I'm about to go mad."

D'Alembert touched Voltaire's chest. He detected no movement. He bent down to listen to the old man's breathing.

Zénobe beside him was now paralyzed with fear.

D'Alembert said to Zénobe, "Go get me a mirror. Quickly!"

Zénobe went to Voltaire's toilette table and came back with a mirror which d'Alembert snatched from his hands. Placing it under Voltaire's nostrils and bending over, he saw breath condensing on it.

"He's alive," he said. "Tell me, what's wrong?"

Zénobe answered, showing d'Alembert the remains of the broken bottle. "I can't find the rest of Voltaire's laudanum, you know, the *duc* de Richelieu's magic elixir. There was half a bottle left. He's supposed to take only drops at a time. But he was left unattended. In his pain he must have taken the rest of the bottle all at once. I cannot see where it could have spilled."

D'Alembert took hold of Zénobe's arm. "Go get Tronchin and Lorry. Make it fast."

Zénobe shot off like a cannon. He told Maurel that he would go get Tronchin himself, and to send the new André for Lorry.

Maurel said, "The *phaeton* is in the courtyard. Use it."

Tronchin was at the *hôtel* de Villette in ten minutes.

D'Alembert showed Tronchin the shards. "The bottle is broken. We don't know if Voltaire drank the rest of the potion."

"My God, he's killed himself," cried Tronchin. He pulled the covers off of the patient and unceremoniously pressed on Voltaire's lower abdomen.

Zénobe stepped forward in alarm and started to shout, "Don't do that!" but d'Alembert held him back.

"Don't worry, *messieurs*. I'm not hurting him. But that should have been painful enough to wake up a hundred devils. I can assure you, he took the rest of the laudanum. After what I told him this morning! He is irresponsible, recalcitrant, he is the most, most stubborn man I have ever seen!"

D'Alembert stood up for his friend. "That is what made him a great success and a great philosopher."

"It is also what is now going to make him dead," said the doctor.

Tronchin let out a guttural interjection of frustration, and said, "There's nothing we can do now, but wait. If the laudanum is going to kill him, at least he'll go in peace. You know, earlier today he said that he wished to return to Ferney as soon as possible in order to be back in Paris within a month. I bit my tongue then, but I cannot do it any longer. He doesn't have a month left to live. And now, he may not last the rest of the evening."

Lorry came in and the two doctors consulted in low voices in a corner of the room. While they were so occupied, Zénobe came to d'Alembert, streaks of tears on his cheeks.

"It is my fault that Voltaire drank the rest of the laudanum. I was the one who left the bottle within his reach. I didn't think of it, I didn't see it…"

D'Alembert sighed. "It's no use thinking about the things that we can no longer change. But consider the fact that you're not the only person looking after Voltaire. His niece could have put the bottle away. The *marquise* de Villette, Maurel, even *docteur* Tronchin could have confiscated the bottle. But none did. I had in mind to visit Voltaire earlier this afternoon, but a visitor held me up. We are all guilty, then. Moreover, Voltaire knew what he was doing; he is an intelligent man. If he did it on purpose, then none of us can judge what he did, for we were not feeling the pain that he was going through. If he did it accidentally, then he was just trying to assuage that pain, which, be it unbearable, would drive many others to a careless mistake. The only thing we can do now is see him through the night. I shall stay with you and we shall both take care of our friend. I can only thank you for the care and concern that you have shown him up to now. Nobody could have done any better."

Zénobe's tears had started to flow again, thinking that Voltaire had preferred suicide to pain. But now they flowed out of gratitude to d'Alembert, for his kindness, and for his lesson on reasoning.

The house was quiet until the *marquis* and *marquise* de Villette returned from their social visits with *madame* Denis who went into hysterics and shouted for the confessor. The *abbé* Gaultier came after midnight, but threw his hands up in despair. "What do you want me to do at this stage? You should have called me when he was still conscious. I have been coming by every single day, sometimes twice a day! There's nothing I can do now. How is he going to recant like this?"

Madame Denis said tearfully, "Can't you give him Extreme Unction?"

"And his confession? What about his confession?"

"Didn't he give that to you already?"

"Oh, you philosopher types. You understand nothing of the sacraments! He has to make his genuine contrition known! Without that, there is nothing I can do."

Gaultier took Voltaire's arm and patted his hand as if hoping to wake him up.

"He looks like he's dead already."

Gaultier dropped Voltaire's hand and told *madame* Denis, giving his back to d'Alembert and Zénobe, "Come fetch me tomorrow when he's awake. If he's awake."

With that, he turned on his heels, making his cassock flare outwards like the robe of a whirling Dervish, and he walked away.

After he had left, d'Alembert looked at Zénobe and said, "How I hate that little man."

Madame Denis jumped to defend her position. "But what if?"

D'Alembert answered, "But what if what?"

"What if the last rites will make my uncle's soul go to heaven?"

D'Alembert's lines on his face expressed an emotion halfway between amusement and weariness. He threw up his palms and said, "There is nothing I can do."

Madame Denis felt, rather than knew, that this last was meant for her. She pretended to tidy up around Voltaire's bed.

As the hours ticked slowly by, the individuals in Voltaire's boudoir started to disappear. The doctors were first, leaving shortly before 1 o'clock in the morning. The *marquis* de Villette was next, followed by *monsieur* Maurel, then *mesdames* Denis and de Villette two hours later. D'Alembert and Zénobe were the only ones to remain. The philosopher gave Zénobe the *chaise longue*, and he himself took the *bergère*. The two dozed lightly while waiting for their friend to either wake up, or to give up the ghost, as the case might be.

Prometheus Bound

Voltaire did not wake up on the following morning. He did not wake up the following day at all. He did not wake up until late in the afternoon of the second day. The light through the window was already dying when the old philosopher opened his eyes and immediately began to cry out in agony.

Zénobe was there, to console him, and to coax his obdurate urine out of his painfully distended bladder. A bedraggled d'Alembert, along with Diderot and Condorcet, both of whom had been in Voltaire's boudoir since morning, witnessed Zénobe's ministrations as they helped balance the old man on the side of the bed. The urine expelled in jerky dribbles was thick, bloody and clearly suppurative. The discharged pus smelled foul, and Zénobe threw a towel over the chamber pot in an attempt to reduce the smell.

The household was alerted and *madame* Denis rushed in with the *marquise* de Villette. By the time Maurel came in with some chicken broth, the patient had fallen back asleep. The *marquis* de Villette walked in and had to put a perfumed handkerchief daintily to his nose. He stayed only long enough to greet the philosophers, glancing nervously at the old man in the bed. He cited having to meet his architect and left promptly.

The inevitable Gaultier came in a few minutes later.

"Why didn't you keep him awake long enough for him to be able to communicate with me?" he asked *madame* Denis, trembling with frustration in his cassock.

Since nobody answered the question, it was Zénobe who spoke up.

"The effort of pissing took all his energy away."

"Well, he's going to have to come up with the effort to express his profession of faith."

"He's already done that if you care to see it for yourself. It's on every page of his writings."

"Yes, in his writings where he espouses irreligiosity, heresy, atheism—"

"He is no atheist. Either you haven't read his works or you've read them very badly."

"Where he insults Church leaders, cherished saints… Why, he treats Joan of Arc as—"

"As the warmongering whore she was. Mass murderess, lunatic, hypocrite, killing her fellow Christians as if they were Muslims. This is what your church lauds. What intemperate hypocrites you all are; the founder of your church extolled compassion, love, forgiveness and peace for one's neighbors, but you preach from every pulpit in stentorian voices full of hate, violence, hostility, and slaughter. Your armature is contrived to repel and annihilate others, even those who are innocent of any crime, for you do not discriminate between crimes of action and crimes of thought. You would kill me just for what I am thinking."

Zénobe's raised voice alerted Voltaire's three friends to the growing argument in the bedroom.

"I see that you are a partisan of the *philosophes* and that your soul has gone the way of Voltaire's," the *abbé* Gaultier said to Zénobe. "As for Voltaire's body, *monsieur le curé de* Saint-Sulpice,[282] under orders of the archbishop of Paris, will refuse to grant him sepulcher on hallowed ground, if he doesn't–"

"We don't need your sepulcher on hallowed ground," said Zénobe to the *abbé* Gaultier. "We shall build a huge funerary pyre to Voltaire on the Place de Grève, which has seen its share of burnings, and, like in the days of the heroes of old, we shall follow the ancient rite of cremating his body. Then we shall take his ashes and scatter them over all the altars of all your churches in Paris, so that people will see that philosophy only does good for men, and that philosophy seeks to keep men from killing each other, whereas theology only produces intolerance and incites men to slit each other's throats."

D'Alembert reached for Zénobe's arm but the boy, who had noticed a silver aspergillum in one of the priest's hands, had one more thing to tell the envoy of God.

"You can keep your hallowed ground! Anything that a priest consecrates is repulsive to God. Holy water is fictitious, just like the rest of your beliefs!"

Gaultier looked like he was going to pounce on Zénobe and beat him on the head with his aspergillum. D'Alembert, Diderot and Condorcet pushed Zénobe behind them and confronted the clergyman's ire.

"See what you are responsible for?" cried out the man of God. "For the perdition of souls, for turning boys away from the right path. Rest assured that I will report this display of blasphemy to the *curé* of Saint-Sulpice. What is that young man's name?"

Diderot answered, "His name is of no importance, and you shall report no such thing to anybody unless you want the three of us writing letters to the Pope and to all the Crowned Heads of Europe about how you French ecclesiastics continue to hound and assail indefensible youths for their opinions."

Diderot threw out his hands in desperation. "Was La Barre not enough? No, *monsieur l'abbé*, you will not harm a single hair on the head of this boy. Furthermore, I will repeat to you what this young man just told you: Voltaire is no atheist. He is a deist. I should know, for I am an atheist."

Gaultier crossed himself three times.

"Oh, dear Lord, how can I do Thy work in such a den of iniquity? I am surrounded by unrepentant sinners, but know that I will strive to bring to Thee, oh God, the soul of Voltaire."

Gaultier began to back out of the room.

"You shall repent, sinners. Beware. The moment of your death is fast approaching, and your exile from Heaven will remain an eternal exile, for you shall never return to the presence of the Mighty One Who created you. Yours will be like the destitution of Saul, for he was guilty of infidelity towards our Lord."

D'Alembert laughed. "Infidelity? For having spared the life of his enemy's king, after having followed the rest of God's instructions to kill them all, including women and children? If disobedience to God means having a conscience and sparing one life, at least one life, then I'd rather be forsaken by God myself."

---

282 *L'abbé* Faydit de Tersac.

Gaultier crossed himself three times more. He realized he could not speak in front of the philosophers. They always had an answer for everything. He quietly slipped out the door.

A weak voice spoke from the bed, startling everybody. Voltaire was awake.

"What did you say, *mon oncle*?" asked *madame* Denis.

Voltaire spoke feebly. "I do not want to be thrown into the city dump. The dogs will get to me."

D'Alembert came up to the bed and bent over Voltaire.

"Do not worry, old friend. We all of us will not allow that to happen."

He turned to *madame* Denis and asked, "I believe you have a cousin, son of your uncle's sister, who is a priest?"

"No, he's not my cousin. He's my brother. Alexandre Jean Mignot. He's an abbot at the Abbey of Scellières in Champagne."

"I seem to remember," said d'Alembert, "that he was a military man before that."

"Yes he was, for a few years. He was a lieutenant in the infantry. But when that didn't work out well for him, he entered the Seminary."

"Well, it's time to call him to Paris. We're going to need all his skills as an infantry-man and as an abbot. We need to remove Voltaire from the clutches of the clergy, who will have the power to do whatever they please if we do nothing. It's time that Voltaire went back home to Ferney."

Zénobe had much work to do. With the frantic preparations to send Voltaire to Ferney, along with the emotions involved in knowing that he would accompany the old man on the long trip, added to the excitement and danger involved in fomenting machinations against the Roman Catholic Church, Zénobe was of a benevolent mind when the *marquis* de Thibouville wrote him a note, which Maurel delivered to the young man with an expression of worry mixed with fatalism.

"He wants to see you before you go," Maurel explained.

Zénobe tore open the letter, which was addressed to «*Monsieur* Zénobe de Bosquet». He read it out loud to Maurel.

"*Monsieur de Thibouville kindly requests the honor of monsieur de Bosquet's presence for tea in his apartment this afternoon. He wishes the young gentleman to know that this request is given solely in the name of friendship and in no way will create complexities which might impinge on the young gentleman's freedom or volition. Monsieur de Bosquet is not, and will not be, under any duress.*"

Zénobe looked up at Maurel who awaited an oral response to take back to the *marquis*.

"It sounds as if he means no harm," said Zénobe. "I'll be able to handle him."

Maurel's look of concern let Zénobe know that the older man thought otherwise.

"No, it's true. And I won't even use physical force were I to find it necessary to extricate myself from a difficult situation. Tell him I'll be there."

Monsieur de Thibouville poured out the tea himself, after graciously having asked Zénobe to sit on the *bergère* closest to the fireplace.

"I suppose you were surprised to receive my invitation," he asked.

"A little, *monsieur.*"

"Well, I know you have been chosen to accompany Voltaire back to Ferney, and I didn't want you to leave without first extending my apologies to you for having caused you grief in the past."

Zénobe's eyes grew big with surprise.

"I treated you like a servant," continued Thibouville, "which I now know that you are not."

The *marquis* handed Zénobe a cup of tea. "Cream? Sugar?"

Zénobe said, "Thank you, yes, please."

"You came into this house like a thunderbolt from the sky, and immediately your role was multiplied into varied and sundry manifestations, which differed depending on whom you asked. To Villette you were definitely a servant, but not in any single capacity, functioning now as a valet, now as a doorman, then as a messenger, and then as a librarian, sometimes even as a coachman. To Maurel you were no servant, just like he doesn't consider himself to be a mere *maître d'hôtel.* No, he's the brains of this household, and you became his protégé, and he your mentor. To Voltaire you were a secretary, a fellow writer, a companion with whom to share multilingual conversations on classical literature. Then you were his nurse, his sentry, and now his friend."

Thibouville sat down on the other *bergère* and took a sip of his tea, preoccupied about what he was to say next.

"To me, Zénobe de Bosquet, you were a servant, at first, because I did not then know you. I treated you like someone whom I could manipulate and rule over. I thought I would be able to direct you, and you would comply. In my addled state—for you did addle me, Zénobe—I thought I could lead you on with promises of publishing your writings, of cajoling you, not with money—that's Villette's way—but with the offer of having your books come to fruition because I know the hopes that we writers harbor. We want the world to read us, to realize that our thoughts hold interest, artistry and wisdom. We want the world to see what is in our hearts, and we want to touch the heart of the world. We want to be known and remembered, and if possible, loved.

"But I did not realize that you did not have the heart, or the mind, of a servant. And I should have known this, given the way that Voltaire took you on so readily, yes, as a secretary, but mainly as a confidant. I did not respect your freedom or your dignity. And it is for that omission that I now wish to offer you my humble apology. Zénobe, will you ever forgive me?"

Zénobe recognized that what this triple-titled aristocrat had just done was of a magnitude of difficulty tantamount to a king kneeling to one of his subjects.

"*Monsieur,* what you have just told me, I am convinced, is heartfelt. As such, I must forgive you, for you seem to have given the matter much thought, and to have used reasoning to come up with your conclusions. You also were as a mentor to me, and I see that you continue to be so. And I'm sure that André will see it in his heart to forgive you as well when I have written him of our conversation."

"About André," said Thibouville. "Would you like us to send for him? To have him return to Paris?"

Zénobe hesitated. What would André do in Paris while he himself would be in Ferney? Besides, André was happier in Normandy, getting ready for the spring growing season, spending time with his family.

"I don't know how much time I'll be spending in Ferney. Perhaps it would be wiser to wait," he said to Thibouville.

The *marquis* smiled, thinking that Zénobe didn't trust him with André. But he accepted that fact, as he swallowed hard.

"Will you, will you return to Paris after... after..."

"After Voltaire is dead?"

"He might yet live for years."

"I don't know. He is eating next to nothing. He has gotten so weak. The trip to Ferney will put a severe strain on him."

Thibouville tried to smile. "He's resilient. He has been on his deathbed many times before."

"That was to prove to the world how harmless he was, how unthreatening. A spindly little man, who would go unnoticed far, far away from the centers of civilization. He spent his whole life dying, one foot out the door, imminently incorporeal."

"To give false hope to his enemies."

"To recede from view, from life, all the more to garner his strength and spirit for his writings."

"Which were more dangerous, more threatening than whole armies."

"But lately he has shown no interest in writing. His last letters were, in effect, adieus to Frédéric and Catherine. A couple of notes were to finalize the purchase of the house on the rue de Richelieu."

"What about *Agathocle*?"

"He finished that last week. So, too, with the letter A. His last word, which came to him as I tried to get more flame from the fire, was *attiser*.[283] I realize now that this word best sums up what he did all his life. Provoke people, get them to realize, by sticking and prodding them, that to have the light you must shake society up."

"He was our Prometheus," said Thibouville quietly.

Zénobe smiled.

"Look," said the *marquis*, changing the subject. "I have a present for you."

He handed Zénobe a book.

"It was difficult to get. You know how these contraband books are. But I know you've taken more than a passing interest in *monsieur* Franklin and in his newborn country."

It was another copy of the constitutions of the United Provinces of America, but Zénobe didn't have the heart to tell the *marquis* that he already had one, and that he had read it! Indeed, he had memorized parts of it, through no special effort on his part, just that the material was so obviously, righteously true, that it ingrained itself into his thoughts and would not leave his mind. With the book in his hand opened to the title page, Zénobe smiled and looked up at the *marquis*.

---

283   To poke a fire, stir up, and, in the figurative sense, to fan the flames.

"*Nous regardons,*" he said, "*comme incontestables et évidentes par elles-mêmes les vérités suivantes; que tous les hommes ont été crées égaux: qu'ils ont été doués par le Créateur de certains droits inaliénables; que parmi ces droits on doit placer au premier rang la vie, la liberté et la recherche du bonheur.*"[284]

"I'm not surprised," said Thibouville, "that you're already in the know. Those are powerful words."

"That they are," said Zénobe, putting the book next to his heart. "Thank you, *monsieur* de Thibouville, for the present."

"You are very welcome," said the *marquis.* "It is quite à propos. I was the England to your America."

Zénobe laughed, the merriment in his blue eyes sending a jolt of electricity down Thibouville's spine.

"Yes," said Zénobe. "Your taxation was oppressive, and your actions tyrannous."

They both laughed.

"Friends?" asked the *marquis* de Thibouville.

"Friends," answered Zénobe.

When Maurel asked Zénobe later what had transpired in Thibouville's room, Zénobe replied warmly, "We became friends, equal in every way. A *marquis* from Paris and a country bumpkin from the depths of Savoy, we meet on equal footing, we are worth the same, and our mutual welfare is our shared concern."

"And what is that?"

"Why, it's to bring everybody else up to that equal footing. All of France, all of Savoy, all of Europe."

"It sounds like a lot of work still needs to be done."

"Absolutely. A great revolution. To sweep the old ways out and the new ways in."

"What, are you a revolutionary?" asked Maurel in feigned shock.

"Yes, I am, but so is Thibouville. He has to be, since he now accepts my new stature."

"What new stature?"

"He called me *monsieur* Zénobe *de* Bosquet," said Zénobe, emphasizing the aristocratic *particule* «de».

"Well, I shall call you *monsieur* Zénobe *de* Bosquet *de* Savoie. Does that make me a revolutionary?"

"You have always been a revolutionary, dear Maurel," said Zénobe embracing him. "You were the one who showed me how to turn the world topsy-turvy."

Maurel held on to Zénobe while he patted him on the back. That was the best compliment anybody had ever paid him in his whole life.

A few days later, Villette ordered Voltaire out of his *hôtel,* along with all his medical pharmacopoeia, accouterments and chamber pots, syrups, phials and dirty towels, saying that "a pestilential miasma" was permeating the rest of the house. He also forbade his

---

284   We view as incontestable and self-evident the following truths; that all men have been created equal: that they have been endowed by the Creator with certain inalienable rights; that among these rights one should place among the most important life, liberty and the pursuit of happiness.

wife, at first, from going to see him, but when the *marquise* complained vociferously—for the first time in her life—he backed down and allowed her to go see him for half-hours at a time. The real reason for all these precautions was never known to anyone but his wife. Now that she was pregnant, he was afraid that sickroom vapors would adversely affect her or the health of the fetus. He wanted to take no chances. Besides, nobody was being allowed in to see Voltaire anyway, save for his friends the *philosophes*, and he didn't like to sit with them, so why should his wife sit with them? None of them was as warm and deferential to him as Voltaire had been. They didn't appreciate classical poetry the way Voltaire had. Their set of references was in the fields of mathematics and physics, not in poetry and history. Diderot spoke a lot about art, but it wasn't enough for the *marquis* de Villette, who therefore stayed away from Voltaire's sick room.

Villette would go out on visits, and the *marquise* would traverse the courtyard and stay with Voltaire for as long as she pleased.

The old patient had been transferred into Zénobe's room in the servants' quarters. But Voltaire was not in any condition to mind having exchanged his mirrors and paneling for a much smaller and humbler room. Zénobe thought it would have been better to lay Voltaire out in the stable, for the sake of the religious. Why should Jesus Christ be the only one to have had that advantage?

The plan was to make the old man well enough for his trip to Ferney. The doctors would not give their permission for the trip until Voltaire was eating a little and moving his bowels. Apparently, Voltaire's bowels had plans to stay in Paris, for they were not moving for anything.

Nor was Voltaire eating, or even remotely interested in eating. Sometimes he kept down a bit of chicken broth or beef consommé. Most of the time, he felt nauseous. Once, Thibouville brought him a small glass of mead, citing its miraculous properties, with volcanic results. Zénobe cut up some boiled Normand apples, smashed them with a fork and added honey. Voltaire liked that.

Madame Denis had made a new friend, a retired captain and former dragoon, Nicolas Toupet Vivier, and she seemed to spend a lot of time with him in the now empty *salon*. It was Captain Vivier who would drive her to see the progress on the house on the rue de Richelieu.

Madame Denis' brother, *l'abbé* Mignot, came to the rue de Beaune and spoke with Gaultier and Tersac. The Archbishop Christophe de Beaumont was unwilling to compromise, as is the wont of the religious, seeing how they appraise everything in absolutes. Voltaire would not, could never, receive a Christian burial if he remained unapologetic for a lifetime of insults to the Church. However, if Voltaire wished to leave Paris, he was free to go. Beaumont sent word through his underlings that he would truly prefer to see Voltaire return whence he came.

Any day now, the trip would take place. Daily the travel preparations were enacted early in the morning, the horses readied, the provisions refreshed. But the doctors Tronchin and Lorry would withhold their permission. The patient was too weak.

To Zénobe's eye, the patient could only get weaker. He was not eating, and his pain was sapping any remaining strength. There were days when Voltaire's skin felt alarmingly hot. His throat was always parched, and he asked to suck on pieces of ice. Zénobe would sprinkle them with crushed sugar before he gave them to him.

Zénobe spent a lot of time reading to Voltaire, although it was difficult to know if he was awake and listening. Every once in a while, Voltaire would make a request. Virgil's *Eclogues*, Horace's *Epistles*, and Ariosto's *Orlando furioso*, were favorites, and

Zénobe would glance over and see Voltaire's lips moving silently in tandem with the words he was speaking out loud, as if he were praying. Once, in the middle of the scene where Orlando goes mad, Zénobe had to pause to swallow. Immediately, Voltaire's silent orison became audible, and he finished the stanza on his own.

> *Poichè allargare il freno al dolor puote*
> *Che resta solo senza altrui rispetto*
> *Giù dagli occhi rigando per le gote*
> *Sparge un fiume di lacrime sul petto.*[285]

---

285   Because he who is alone, with no one to consider, may give the reins to his grief, from his eyes he pours a stream of tears that flow down his cheeks to his breast.

The Diaphanous Philosopher

Two women were hired by Tersac, the *curé* of Saint-Sulpice, to sit by Voltaire's new bedside in Zénobe's tiny servant's room and listen to every word he said. They were to report immediately should they hear the moribund communicate any interest in speaking with either Tersac or his underling *l'abbé* Gaultier. They should write down any words said against, or in favor of the Church, especially any words concerning Her Holy Sacraments, namely Final Confession and the Last Rites. Only *madame* Denis knew about this arrangement, since she was the one to approve it, and she failed to tell anyone else at the *hôtel* de Villette. Zénobe was surprised and annoyed by the cumbersome presence of these two women in his little bedroom, but there was nothing he could do about it. He was particularly irritated when he caught one of them taking a peek at a book he had left on his table. Thank God it wasn't a particularly irreverent book, but still, he thought, she had no business going through his affairs. When he complained about her nosiness, she answered that she was merely trying to find out if Voltaire was its author.

"Ah, you want to see Voltaire's books? Here, take a look at these."

He brought out a few tomes, including the *Dictionnaire philosophique portatif* that had been on the Index since its publication in 1764. Catching sight of the title, the two women crossed themselves and leaned back away from the book.

"I'll leave them for you here, in case you get bored."

Zénobe could only at first tolerate the presence of the two, until the third afternoon they were there, when he came back from a quick errand and saw that Voltaire's chamber pot had been upset and had wet the floorboards.

"What happened?" he asked.

"Voltaire used his own urine to splash on his face," said one of them. "He has lost his mind."

"Why didn't you ask for fresh water?"

"There wasn't anyone around."

"You could have gone to the house to find someone."

"That's not our responsibility. We are not nurses."

"No, nor are you Christians, either!" Zénobe yelled. "I'm sure you call yourselves Christians, but there's nothing resembling Christ in your attitude. You are monsters, the least like Jesus Christ as any to be found in Christendom. I am not a Christian, and you are not likely to attract me to your religion by your actions, but you shall definitely repel me from it, for I do not want to be like you. You have no charity, no sympathy, no humanity.”

Zénobe went to check his water pitcher.

“There is water here! Why didn’t you give him this water?” Zénobe was trembling with ire.

“We are not the servants of this *philosophe*,” sniffed one, with the word *philosophe* pronounced as one might say *heathen*, or *devil worshipper.* “We are here merely as witnesses to his final words and deeds.”

Zénobe approached the two and they pulled back. His voice was hoarse.

“You are spies, that’s what you are. You are the Church’s paid harlots, a pair of Judases who for a few shekels will make sure that Voltaire leaves this world without the succor and salvation that Jesus Christ promised. I have no power to throw you out of here like the offal that you are, but if you so much as touch the person of this *philosophe*, who is a thousand times better than you are, more charitable, more human than you could ever dream of being, if you touch anything of his, I will see to it personally that I and I alone will be the witness to your own final words and deeds.”

His hand closed into a fist on the pommel of his foil made his meaning quite clear. From under surly brows they both gave him the evil eye, superstitious as they were, which he ignored as he dampened a towel to place on Voltaire’s burning cheeks and neck. The old man opened his eyes and recognized Zénobe.

“*Mon fils*,” he managed to say. “My son, I’m dying of thirst.”

Zénobe poured water into a glass and held up Voltaire’s head to help him drink.

“I’m burning up,” said the old man.

“He already feels the fires of hell,” offered one of the women.

Zénobe turned to her and said, “It’s the fever he feels, you stupid ignorant bitch!”

The vituperation he shot at her with his eyes was enough to quell her religious ardor. She looked down at her hands.

When d’Alembert and Condorcet came to visit the patient an hour later, the two women were forced to give up their seats for them and stand in a corner. They listened avidly to everything that was said, which was mainly on the subject of how to make the patient more comfortable. They left around ten that night to go report directly to Tersac before the *curé* went to bed.

Zénobe went to report to Maurel, to tell him that so long as those two women remained in Voltaire’s room, he would not be leaving it for anything in the world. Maurel made sure that any household business for which Zénobe’s presence was desired was postponed or delegated to either Philippe or Henri. Thibouville was forced to come to the sick room if he wanted to see Zénobe. Villette’s library made no inroads, and Villette became upset, but he couldn’t make Maurel budge, and he couldn’t garner the courage to come to the room where a man was dying, something that his wife did three or four times a day.

On May 26th, d’Alembert rushed to Voltaire’s bedside to present some happy news. Trophime Gérard de Lally-Tollendal had received the decision of *Parlement* to reverse his father's condemnation. Henceforth, General Lally would not be known as a traitor. It was too late to bring him back from the dead, but at least his reputation, as well as his family's honor, was restored. His son would be able to hold his head high. Voltaire's mouth opened wide in a toothless smile and he made gestures to be raised on his pillows. Zénobe helped him to sit up.

"Dictation," said the old man.

Zénobe rushed to get the writing implements, crawling over the black crones to get to the table without so much as an "*Excuzez-moi.*"

Voltaire spoke falteringly.

"The dying man resuscitates upon learning the great news; he kisses tenderly *monsieur* de Lally. He sees that the king is the defender of justice; he will die happy."

After Voltaire signed it as best he could, the letter was sent off to Lally. Voltaire asked Zénobe to write out on another sheet of paper in large letters the following words: "On the 26th of May, the judicial murder committed by the Parliament upon General Lally was avenged by the King's Council." He then had Zénobe nail the sheet of paper to the wall where he could see it and touch it.

These were to be the last words Voltaire wrote.

Zénobe saw his master weakening. He continued to read aloud to him, not because he thought he was listening, but more to aggrieve the sensibilities of the two women who sat like two black vultures watching over Voltaire's final moments on earth. He managed to find books, by Voltaire and others, excoriating the Church for her unclean hands in the massacre of Protestants, in the murder of Jews, in the crimes of the Inquisition, in the intimidation and torture and assassination of men of science. He read with an unwavering voice about the extermination of the Albigenses; the Saint Bartholomew's Day massacre; the burning at the stake of Giordano Bruno; the ghastly execution of the simple-minded Damiens, the would-be regicide of Louis XV, whose torture was halted every time he fainted so that he could be revived anew as his body was cut off piece by piece. Other books told of the long litany of errors and horrors perpetrated by the so-called infallible Popes, who led lives of dissipation, immorality, murder, incest, pillage, warmongering, and who did not deserve to be called followers of Christ. It was a feast of crimes, a banquet of sins, an orgy of hellacious iniquity, all done under the name of God, in His service, for His worship. The followers of Saint Peter had much to answer for. Concomitantly, Zénobe read excerpts from books and journals extolling the new morality based, not on religion, but on philosophy, like Mercier's account of Voltaire's induction into the Freemasons, ironically in the building that used to house the Jesuits.[286]

> Oh, change! Oh, instability of human things! Who would have
> said that the lodges of the Freemasons would one day be established

---

286   Louis Sébastien Mercier has left us wonderful contemporary accounts of everyday life in the second half of the Eighteenth century. These include *Tableau de Paris* (*Picture of Paris*), and a curious book on futurism, *L'an 2440 ou Rêve s'il en fut jamais* (*The Year 2440 or Dream if There Ever Was One*).

on the very street, in the very building, of the Jesuit's Seminary, in the same halls where they argued about theology; that the Grand Orient would succeed the Company of Jesus; that the philosophical lodge of the Nine Sisters would one day occupy the meditation room of the children of Loyola.

When I as a Mason see the vaulted ceilings that are inaccessible to the rays of the sun, I believe I can see those shadowy Jesuit ghosts huddling in the dark, flashing furious and desperate glances at me. And in this place, I saw brother Voltaire enter, to the sound of musical instruments, into the very hall where he had been so often theologically maligned. This is how the grand Architect of the universe wanted it: Voltaire was praised for having fought fanaticism and superstition for over sixty years; for having slain the monster which others had just but wounded.

Oh, Jesuits! Would you have ever guessed any of this? You were the obstinate enemies of the soothing light of philosophy; and philosophers now enjoy being in the space that once belonged to you, delighted with your rapid fall! Freemasons, leaning on the foundation of charity, of tolerance, of universal generosity, will still remain, while your name will no longer evoke anything but a persecuting egoism!

Zénobe continued to regale the two ladies with anti-religious texts, and when there weren't enough texts at hand, he made up his own, pretending to read from books, but inventing as he went along, creating new illustrations of the cruelty, of the inanity, of the savagery of the Church, inspired by his own experiences in Savoy where the ecclesiastics joined the aristocrats in keeping the populace imprisoned in their feudal chains and unable to rise above the poverty and the slavery that was their place according to God.

"If God wishes to keep the vast majority of humanity in eternal suffering, then He is an evil God. But perhaps this deity is just an invention created by the wicked, depraved, degenerate priests, to strike fear into the hearts of men, and to keep them appeased and downtrodden. *Écrasez l'Infâme! Écrasez l'Infâme! Écrasez l'Infâme!*"

The two women sent by the Church to be witnesses to Voltaire's last days on earth grew afraid of the young man who harbored so much hate for religion, and who called the religious such epithets as to leave them trembling for their safety. They sat low in their seats and dared not breathe too heavily.

Black was the color of religion, lackluster, grim, sinister, and it had invaded Zénobe's little room, early in the morning of May 29th. Besides the two women spies, there were also the *curé* Tersac and the *abbé* Gaultier, all in their heavy opaque robes, and they stood around beholding the sleeping Voltaire like the sentries of death, and they were come to whisk him away into their Underworld.

Zénobe, who was still in his sleep clothes, quickly stepped into the next room where the servants had not even been aware that the four ghouls had crept through. He told a sleepy Suzanne to go get Maurel. Coming back into the room, Zénobe squared his shoulders and faced these representatives of the Church with a courage and stoicism that would have made Voltaire proud and Thibouville's heart melt.

"This is my room, *messieurs*. Please allow me to get dressed."

Tersac made a gesture to Zénobe allowing him to proceed. As Zénobe put on his clothes, Tersac asked him, "Has Voltaire been waking up?"

"Yes, he does wake up, to drink some water, or when I place damp towels on his face to cool his fever. Sometimes he wakes up when I'm reading to him."

"I've heard about your reading. You've been scaring my two nuns [*mes deux religieuses*] with your prohibited texts."

Zénobe was amazed that the two women were nuns. How could nuns, of all people, be so cruel, so intentionally inhumane?

Tersac continued, "Once this business with Voltaire is over, know that Gaultier and I, under the auspices of the Church of the Holy Inquisition and under the tutelage of the Archbishop of Paris, have the intention of pursuing you for your willful impiety. We'd like to make an example of you to show other young men that this attitude of disrespect which has so well trickled down from Voltaire to you, can have no place in our society. You are like a bookworm in a Bible, chomping away, digging tunnels in the Sacred Text and undermining the word of God."

"*Eh bien, monsieur*, the bookworm doesn't know how to read, and it believes the Sacred Text to be as delicious as any other."

"Ah, you find it amusing, what I say to you. I who am being frank and sober, you return to me flippancy and disrespect."

"I regard you and yours, *monsieur*, with all the respect you deserve."

Zénobe was putting on his breeches at that point, and he raised them up to his waist with a quick and forceful movement.

"But you see," Zénobe continued, "this tendency has trickled down to me from Voltaire, and it is a tendency of which I am extremely proud. It is what you religious types are in so desperate a need. You need to laugh at yourselves more and not take yourselves so seriously. I mean, I for one don't take you seriously, and I laugh at you most of the time, because that which you represent, that which you have constructed, is already so full of holes that no serious thinking person could possibly believe one iota of what you say."

The two nuns gasped as Gaultier turned to Tersac and said, "You see, he's so brazen that he does not even try to hide his blasphemy from you. This is what I've had to take from this, this, this person all along. One would think that in your presence he would be more circumspect."

"*Messieurs*," said Zénobe, "everything I just told you I would say to the face of your archbishop Beaumont. He, who is higher up the ecclesiastic echelon, needs to hear it even more than you. So reason has it that the Pope himself needs to know that his Church is riddled with worm galleries in the basement, which threaten to bring his entire edifice to the ground."

"You yourself are treading on dangerous ground," answered the *curé* of Saint-Sulpice.

He was a young man, younger than Gaultier, but his exalted position gave him a bearing equal to that of any aristocratic fop, and he moved his black robe with the long bulging sleeves in as regal a manner as possible.

"You will get your comeuppance, young man. Not now, since we don't have the time for the likes of you, but soon. Have trust in the Church about that, and especially in me."

Zénobe was about to reply when Maurel walked into the room.

"I am so sorry, *monsieur le curé* and *monsieur l'abbé*," he said, "that I was not on hand to greet you this morning.

"It's of no consequence," replied Tersac. "We have the key to the gate. We've had it since the widow of the *Président* Bernière lived here. It is our jurisdiction, so we don't need to inconvenience anybody in the main house."

"But *messieurs*, it is no inconvenience at all," continued Maurel. "I assure you, it is no inconvenience at all. Shall I get you some coffee or tea?"

"Perhaps later," said Tersac. "At the moment we wish to speak with Voltaire."

Turning to Zénobe, Tersac instructed him to wake Voltaire up.

Maurel looked at Zénobe, pleading him with his eyes to do as he was told.

Zénobe took a compress from his wash basin, wrung it out, and placed it on Voltaire's forehead and cheeks.

Voltaire opened his eyes.

"Ah, my dear Zénobe. Is it late? Are you going to sleep now?"

"No, *monsieur*. It is dawn. I've just awakened. But I'm sorry to have to tell you that you have two very insistent visitors who wish to speak with you."

With that, he stepped away from the bed to allow the two priests to approach.

In the grand scheme of things, in the exuberant flow of the generations, in the life and death of millions, what is the importance of one human life? A little girl dies of a fever in her village in Africa, and only her immediate family, perhaps the neighbors, take note. A young man is burned at the stake in the main city square in France, a throng is attracted who picnic during the horrible scene, but only that young man's family and close friends will moan and weep.

Such ran the letter that Zénobe was to write to André later on that day. Ever since the visit of the two meddlesome priests—aren't all priests meddlesome, meddling into private affairs that should not be their business!—Zénobe was feeling despondent. How can two proponents of a religion sit in judgment of another man's morality when it has been proven time and time again that the whole institution of the Church is immoral, intrinsically immoral. When men are placed in positions of superiority, where they are told, indeed beseeched, to sit in judgment over the rest, the system of morality over which they rule becomes, in their hands, corrupted. The rules of such a system come to be applied only to the others, and never to themselves. They are unapproachable in their high seats, and they alone can commit the most heinous crimes and remain unjudged. They alone can deputize whole castes of society to do the same as they, to judge their subordinates, and to remain aloft free from accusation or adjudication. Thus do the Church and the Government work in cahoots to maintain their power, a power that they will not relinquish until it is wrested from their cold, dead hands.

But these last thoughts Zénobe did not place in his letter to André. Instead, he wrote:

> But there's a man dying now, of whom everybody is aware, and whose passing will be moaned and wept over by millions. For he is the man who noticed that young girl dying in Africa, dying because of an illness that for a pittance could have been averted, had her parents and village known of the science behind the medicine. The boy burned at the stake, too, met his death over some silly superstition that stipulates that men must remove their head cover while women must put it on in the presence of some inconsequential wafers. This is the man who recognized the injustices of our society that is far, very far, from being perfect. His loss is not going to be felt just by his family and close friends. The whole world will notice it, and all of society will realize that his dream must be kept alive, otherwise we fall back into the Medieval world of biblical punishment and unenlightened existence.

The *curé* de Tersac placed his head close to Voltaire's and spoke loudly to him, as if the old man were blind and deaf.

"*Monsieur* de Voltaire, *monsieur* de Voltaire! Can you hear me?"

"Yes," answered Voltaire. "Who is this?"

"I am *l'abbé* Faydit de Tersac, the *curé* of Saint-Sulpice. I am come this morning to hear your confession and to negotiate your signed retraction. Today, I'm going to procure either your soul or your body."

Zénobe laughed. "You have got to be in jest," he said to Tersac.

Maurel walked over to his firebrand protégé, but Zénobe staved him off with a hand.

"As you can see for yourself, *monsieur*, Voltaire's body is in no condition to be interred, and as for his soul, well, as for his soul, ever since the man took opium we're not sure what it's become."

"*Monsieur*," Tersac said to Maurel. "Could you please remove this young man forthwith from the premises? The *abbé* Gaultier and I have serious work to do."

"*Oui, monsieur l'abbé*," said Maurel.

The *maître d'hôtel* grabbed Zénobe by the arm and dragged him outside the room. Zénobe was about to protest, but Maurel was insistent and spoke from the heart, but also from the mind.

"You must go get d'Alembert, Diderot and Condorcet and anybody else you can think of. You can't do this by yourself, Zénobe."

Zénobe weighed Maurel's words and found them to be logical and true. He went to the men's servant room and told the three men there, Henri, Philippe and the new André, to go round up all the philosophers in the surrounding area, up to a league away.

"We'll show these men of God who is stronger. Battle lines have been drawn. It is us or them. And in the very center of this war, there is Voltaire."

It was a battle worthy of the Valkyries, of Mars, of the Franks who overthrew the other hordes of Barbarians to settle in *la douce* France. It was Clovis, and Charlemagne, and William the Conqueror, defending territory and annexing lands, and grabbing villages and whole countries to the detriment of the enemy. Only here, today, it was a War of Words, a Clash of Ideas, of philosophy against religion, and the soldier enemies were expressions and phrases catapulting volleys of thought to the other side, arrows of ideas and cannonballs of brainstorms, detonations of concepts and principles.

But the opposing sides were mismatched. The volleys hurled by the philosophers were uttered through the convincing voice of Reason, whereas the weaponry which the priests preferred was palaver and circumlocutions based on the illusory and the miraculous, and ultimately anchored on a false premise, on a flimsy pretense, on a flagrant deception: the supposed sanctity and authority of the Bible.

Condorcet was the first *philosophe* to walk into Voltaire's sick room. Tersac was in the midst of yelling to Voltaire that the archbishop was not going to grant him sepulcher on holy ground and that he, Tersac, would not accept this time any meager concessions from Voltaire.

Condorcet's voice startled both Tersac and Gaultier.

"*Monsieur* de Tersac, from the front door of this building I can hear that you are in the possession of a stentorian voice, which I daresay goes quite well with your imperious fanaticism. Hounding a sick old man the way you are, well, you should be ashamed of yourself."

"The one who should be ashamed of himself here is this very man lying on his deathbed. He should consider that he's about to meet his maker with a soul still sullied with sin and corrupted by unrepentant intransigence. It is I who work here in the thankless task of cleansing Voltaire's soul to prepare it for the afterlife."

Condorcet scoffed. "You couldn't care less about Voltaire's soul. Quite the contrary; you would prefer that it go directly to hell. You just want to use him as an example for your empty-minded religious types. You want a scapegoat, a hugely visible, well-known and celebrated scapegoat, whom you can show to the populace and say, 'You see, here goes a sinner, but not an insignificant sinner; a monumental sinner, and even he repented in the face of inevitable death.' The illogical part of all of this, is that we're quibbling about things which don't even exist: first of all, there is no God, and second, there is no soul. Furthermore, there is no hell."

Tersac was aghast, but he recovered quickly, saying, "In that case, your friend will not mind being thrown into the city dump."

"You are right about that," conceded Condorcet. "Intrinsically, Voltaire should not mind being thrown into the city dump. But you forget two things: that the body does exist, and that we humans have attached a sentimental quality on it, especially if the body in question is our own. I do not want to think of my body after my death being torn up by marauding dogs, nor do I particularly enjoy the idea of being devoured by vermin, even if it's in a dry cozy mausoleum. But I'll take the latter any day, because I prefer remaining in one piece and I prefer the calm and repose of the mausoleum, and I particularly enjoy the thought that after I'm gone, I'll still be receiving visitors every once in a while who come to grieve over me at that mausoleum. In any case, you do not have to worry about Voltaire ever more, for we, his friends and family, shall see to his final wishes and to his care and comfort."

"I am afraid I cannot do that, *monsieur.* Voltaire is the declared enemy of the Christian religion, and as such, being a public sinner, he must have a public death and a public burial, however that may play itself out."

D'Alembert appeared.

Condorcet continued to speak with Tersac. "Voltaire does not belong to you. He belongs to us, those of us who love him and wish to care for him."

"Voltaire was a Christian, he was baptized as a Christian," was Tersac's last word on the subject. "Therefore he belongs to the Church."

D'Alembert spoke up. "*Monsieur* de Tersac, why do you show the zeal of a seminarian? I know of a priest, a bit older and more experienced than you, the *curé* of Saint-Etienne-du-Mont, who has informed me that he is ready and willing to inter Voltaire in his church, between Racine and Pascal."

There was a sort of twitter that came from Voltaire's bed. Everyone turned to look at the sick old man, surprised that he had been following the conversation.

Zénobe put a hand on the old man's forehead. "What was that?" he asked.

"Between Racine and Pascal?" Voltaire asked in a weak voice. "Please, put me next to the great Racine, and leave Pascal out of this."

Zénobe, d'Alembert and Condorcet laughed. Racine who had glorified classical heathen stories in his first immortal tragedies was a worthy tomb mate, but the unctuous, chest-beating, guilt-ridden Catholic Pascal was a *cadaver non gratus.*

D'Alembert had more news for Tersac.

"The minister Amelot and the police lieutenant Lenoir have both personally informed me that they would prefer not to see the Church refuse sepulcher, so as not to cause a scandal."

"They have no jurisdiction here in these religious matters," shot back Tersac. "Besides, the scandal has already been caused, and he was the one who caused it."

An accusatory forefinger designated the bedridden *philosophe.*

"I beg to differ, on both counts," answered d'Alembert. "All this drama is taking place in Paris, and it is Amelot and Lenoir's municipal jurisdiction. What? Did you think that the laws of this city count for nothing?"

" 'Render to Caesar the things that are Caesar's, and to God the things that are God's.' " quoted Tersac.

"Right," said d'Alembert. "You, then, take his soul, and we shall take his body. This is an agreement with which we can all live, is this not so?" he asked, looking at Condorcet for approval.

"But you don't believe in the existence of the soul! You are giving nothing up!" said the frustrated Tersac.

"But you believe in it, you think it of supreme importance. So, take it. It's yours. We concede it."

Diderot walked in.

The priests were outnumbered.

"Dear Lord," Gaultier whispered up to God, "why dost Thou allow philosophy to run rampant upon this, Thy world?"

"For the same reason, he allows religion to run rampant all over the world," said d'Alembert. "Man is all alone in the universe, and he makes of existence whatever sense he can. And for eons he has invented a string of fallacies to be able to answer two intrinsic questions, 'Who made me?' and 'What am I doing here?' But the greatest of fallacies, and the first, is that the Bible represents the Word of God and its authors were inspired by God. I propose to you that the bible is just a book written by writers who were crazed by their belief in supernatural events and who, in order to inveigle their followers, would deliver them into the depths of fear with their words."

Tersac turned his mesmerist gaze to d'Alembert, as if searching for the mathematician's soul through the windows of his eyes.

"One day you will see the error of your ways," said the priest to the philosopher. "For you see, error [*la faute*] is the symptom of a malady of the soul. Just the way a medical doctor is accustomed to recognize physical illness, we can discern the soul's illness. But you, and your brethren—" Here, Tersac looked into the eyes of each of the philosophers in turn, including Zénobe's. "You and your brethren refuse to see that your soul is affected, and infected, by a deep-reaching illness. You cannot see it! No remedy from the Divine Text can reach it, no balm from all the exhortations in the world can shift it, no punishment can oust it. You are like the lost sheep, who must remain lost in order for it not to contaminate the rest of the flock. Your hard hearts in the end have meant your spiritual demise."

Tersac swept up an arm across Voltaire's bed as if to denote that their soul would forever remain earthbound.

"But now," Tersac continued. "You must allow us to do what we must do. I pray for your patience as we try to save your brother's soul."

It was Zénobe who responded, non-verbally, using the same hand gesture which Tersac had used when the priest had allowed the servant to get dressed, an impatient 'Get on with it, boy, and what does that have to do with us?'

Tersac and Gaultier turned their attention to Voltaire.

"Do you believe in the divinity of Jesus Christ?" asked *l'abbé* Gaultier of the sick man.

Voltaire didn't hear the priest, or if he did, he did not deign answer.

Tersac said, "Since in his works the divinity of Jesus Christ is strongly attacked, I believe I can assure myself on this point of belief."

Zénobe, again putting his hand on Voltaire's forehead, said, "Here is *monsieur l'abbé* Gaultier, your confessor, who is speaking to you."

Voltaire opened his eyes.

"*Monsieur l'abbé* Gaultier! My confessor! Please give him my compliments."

It was Tersac's turn to ask the question. "Let me do it," he told Gaultier, almost knocking him back.

"*Monsieur*, do you recognize the divinity of Jesus Christ?"

The old man brought up one of his hands and pushed sideways against the priest's skullcap.

"In the name of God, *monsieur*, don't speak to me of that man, and let me die in peace."

Tersac had had it. "His mind is gone," he said, and in an impatient gesture dusted off his skullcap as if it had been defiled. "Gaultier! *Mesdames*! Let us depart!"

The four black blots moved in single file and left the room.

Zénobe said loudly enough to be heard by the exiting priests and nuns, "Upon my soul, I hope we don't have to see the likes of those again."

D'Alembert said, "They won't be back."

Voltaire got up on an elbow, but then fell back on his pillow.

"I'm a dying man, then."

Zénobe went to the water pitcher and poured a glass from it. He helped Voltaire take a few sips.

Mesdames Denis and de Villette rushed into the sickroom, in their *peignoirs*, followed by *monsieur* de Thibouville who was fully dressed.

"*Mon oncle!*"

"*Mon père!*"

"*Mon ami!*"

They crowded around the bed.

"We thought…" said *madame* Denis, unable to finish her sentence.

"No," said d'Alembert. "The priests were here to extract a confession and a recantation."

"Did they get it?" asked *madame* Denis with hope on her expression.

"Of course they didn't. Voltaire's reputation is safe."

"His reputation!" cried the niece. "What about his funeral?"

Zénobe spoke up. "*Madame!* Could you please have this conversation outside? Your uncle needs his rest if he wishes to get better."

Madame Denis said, "Of course. It's just that I wanted to tell you that *monsieur* Mesmer has agreed to come look at the patient."

The four *philosophes* looked at *madame* Denis as if she had lost her mind.

D'Alembert spoke up for all of them. "You, of course, have the final word, but it is our consensus that this Mesmer is a charlatan. He uses other people's scientific discoveries to create a façade that takes in the gullible, but behind which there is empty gibberish and magician's illusions. You will be wasting your time, and your money."

Zénobe needed to speak. "Mesmer is as useless as those priests were."

Diderot said, "Bluntly spoken, but, sadly, true."

Madame Denis looked at all of them, and burst into tears.

"If only Wagnière were here!"

As she was being led back into the main house, Zénobe spoke softly to himself, "Stupid woman. She was the one to send Wagnière away!"

He remained alone with Voltaire, cooling him off with damp compresses while the old man slept.

In the late afternoon, two of Voltaire's nephews, *l'abbé* Alexandre Jean Mignot of the abbey of Scellières, and Alexandre d'Hornoy, a lawyer (and who was really a great-nephew), came to the *hôtel* de Villette and, together with the philosophers, created a plan to foil the archbishop and his intransigent soldiers. They were to remove the prize that the Church so desperately wanted and whisk him away from Paris. Only the nephews were to accompany him on this, his last trip; and, of course, Zénobe. The young man from Savoy had, of all the residents of the *hôtel* de Villette, persistently shown his love and his loyalty for the old man. Besides, the young man had promised everybody that he would not rest until Voltaire was safely entombed, wherever that may be.

They were sure to have the involuntary support of the newspapers, since Louis XVI had decreed that no publication write about the last days of the life, and the eventual death, of Voltaire. In his usual manner to try to make difficult things go away, Louis was doing his very best to ignore this piddling problem. What he did not fathom, because his mind was so shallow and his imagination was so impotent, was that everybody in Paris, nay, in the whole country, in the whole continent, was entirely focused on this little old man about to breathe his last sigh.

That afternoon Zénobe wrote a last letter to André, informing him of the plan. He wouldn't be able to write him another letter for a very long time.

Condorcet came to the servants' quarters to tell Zénobe that he best stay out of Paris for as long as he could. He had heard that the priests of Paris were preparing a case against *monsieur* Zénobe Bosquet. They wanted to make it a very public prosecution, to occur on the heels of the impious Voltaire being thrown out like garbage into the city dump. Condorcet put a hand on Zénobe's shoulder. It would be better if the priests didn't know of his whereabouts. Could he go back to Savoy?

No, he couldn't. But he could certainly go to Normandy where a friend awaited him in a farm close to–

"No, don't tell me. Don't tell anyone. It is best if no one knows. And don't write any letters. They could be opened, you could be found out. The Church is powerful, with spies everywhere. Anybody would be willing to turn you in for a favorable opinion from his god, or for a good word from his confessor."

Condorcet gave Zénobe a purse filled with coin.

"This is from d'Alembert, Diderot and myself. It is in deep gratitude for taking care of Voltaire while we cannot do it, and for being the courageous lad that you are. Would that I be as courageous during my time of need."

Zénobe watched Condorcet walk back across the garden to the main house.

"He is the man who will take over for Voltaire," thought Zénobe. It was easy to tell. As the youngest of all of Voltaire's friends, it was Condorcet who was poised to carry on with Voltaire's ideas and projects.

But then, so was he, Zénobe. He gladly volunteered to continue with Voltaire's progeny. He felt he had enough experience now to take on the likes of Victor-Amédée and Louis, and George, and all the idiot kings of the world, not to mention the likes of the archbishop and the pope and all the idiot priests of the world, as well. For a young person, such far-reaching plans were imaginable, and to him, who was burgeoning with energy and vigor and unburdened with experience and caution, such plans were feasible. Reasonable, even.

Too bad Zénobe's volition was like a leaf in a tornado. The inimical foes of philosophy and science had their sights on him, and their tyranny would not be allayed until Zénobe was in pieces and his ashes scattered to the winds. For his part, Zénobe could not realize that he would end up going to Russia, and that he would not see André again for a long, long time.

A Place to Rest

After the priests' departure, everybody else took their leave as well. Most probably they went home to rest, since this visit had taken place at dawn, and disagreeable things seem much more incommodious early in the morning. Only *mesdames* Denis and de Villette came by every two hours or so, bringing with them *messieurs* Mignot and d'Hornoy, the two nephews, to stand or pace in the sick room for ten or fifteen minutes. The rest of the time, Zénobe was there alone. *Monsieur* Maurel brought food and drink for Zénobe and flavored ice for Voltaire to suck on.

Zénobe read. In all the desperate moments of his young life, Zénobe had always read. The presence of a book in his hand made him tranquil and, slipping away into the world that the book offered, dissipated his worries and cleared his head enough to enable him to think better. It occurred frequently as well, that he would find a solution to real-life problems in the pages he was reading, even if the subject of the text had nothing to do with his situation. Zénobe found that there were always connections, myriads of connections, some intended and some accidental, between what was written, and what was lived. As a matter of fact, he felt that his own life was unrolling as if there were some giant scroll in the heavens, transporting him along a timeline and narrating the events of his life, nay, causing the events of his life.[287][288]

He wished he could look in on this lifeline and help edit it. He didn't feel like a marionette of fate, yet he felt the pull of destiny, for in the past four months, he had lived through an amazing set of events which could not have happened if he hadn't been at the right place at the right time.

And what about this book that he happened to have open on his lap this day on this very afternoon? Was it announcing some future event in his life? Was it a preview, a foretelling of some sort? It sounded improbable, for he was reading Voltaire's thoughts

---

287   [From the author] Before the fact-checker takes me to task, I must write the following: Zénobe could not have possibly read Diderot's *Jacques le fataliste* in which there is mention of this giant scroll in the sky, for the simple reason that Diderot was in the process of writing it in 1778. Perhaps Zénobe overheard the philosopher mention the detail to one of his friends. Perhaps Diderot overheard Zénobe speaking about it to Voltaire. Perhaps the idea was already in the air. Perhaps they arrived at the idea independently of each other.

288   [From the editor] I am afraid that Professor Ralph has resigned from the remainder of his fact-finding duties. This being the last chapter, I shall do my best to take over his responsibility. But let the reader take note, this is not my forte, and he would do well to verify the events depicted in this chapter through the works of historians.

on the revolutions in India,[289] where the philosopher asserted that the white man was repeating the same mistakes on the subcontinent that he had made in the Americas.

> European people discovered America only to devastate it, and to sprinkle it with blood. Those vast domains, and all those wars fought to maintain them, were the fruit of the avidity of merchants, as well as the ambition of our sovereigns.
>
> It is to furnish spices for the tables of our bourgeois in Paris, in London, and in other big cities; it is to bring more diamonds to them than the queens of old ever wore; it is to infect their noses with a disgusting powder; to have their fill of certain useless liquors; it is for these things that an immense commerce, sprang up and that in order to sustain such commerce wars are fought.
>
> ... And now we are doing the same exact thing in India. We have made their lands desolate and we have shed much blood over it. We have shown how much we surpass the inhabitants in courage, but also in maliciousness, and how much we are inferior to them in wisdom.

Zénobe could not help wondering if he would ever set foot in India, or in the Americas. After what Condorcet had told him, he was ready to leave France and go forth to other lands and there broadcast Voltaire's ideas. He could see himself as the hero who would wrest back the liberty that the poor native inhabitants of America and India had lost with the coming of the European. With the tacit agreement of the priests who accompanied them on their boats, the Europeans had enslaved whole peoples just so that some lady in Europe could have coffee and sugar in the morning, and tea and snuff in the afternoon.

Still deep in his reverie, Zénobe looked up from his book to imagine himself as the European liberator who would reestablish equilibrium in the world, when he saw Voltaire with his eyes open and looking at him.

"Voltaire!" Zénobe cried out, letting his book fall to the floor as he sprang up. "Voltaire, you're awake!"

"My son," Voltaire said. "I cannot feel, I cannot feel..."

"Yes, Voltaire, what is it?"

"... my legs," said the old man, exhausted.

Zénobe gave him some water.

"Thank you, my son..."

Zénobe could barely hear him.

"... Thank you for all you have done for me."

"Of course, Voltaire. I love you. I would do anything for you."

Zénobe held Voltaire's hand and then bent down to kiss him on the forehead. He saw one of his tears fall on the old man's forehead. Taking a damp compress he patted Voltaire's face with it. He realized all of a sudden that Voltaire's fever was gone. Joy and hope sprang up within his chest. Maybe the old man would pull through, once again.

---

289   *Fragments sur quelques révolutions dans l'Inde, et sur la mort du comte de Lalli*, published in 1773.

He was a survivor, a fighter, frail and insubstantial as he was, he was going to come back from the brink again and again.

Zénobe wanted to speak to Voltaire about India, but the old philosopher was tired and had closed his eyes. He didn't respond to Zénobe's questions.

Voltaire slept through his niece and nephews' next two visits, but woke up again briefly that evening around 8 o'clock while Maurel was there. Zénobe was peeing in the chamber pot, but he heard Voltaire say something to Maurel.

As soon as he could, he rushed to *monsieur* Maurel to ask him what Voltaire had said.

Tears were streaming down Maurel's cheeks.

"He said, he said, '*Adieu, mon cher* Maurel, I'm dying.'"

Maurel and Zénobe embraced.

Voltaire went back to sleep. His breathing, calm and rhythmic, stopped around 11 o'clock that night, May 30th.

The two closest women in Voltaire's life, his niece, *madame* Denis, and his adopted daughter, *Belle et bonne*, were weeping Madeleines, as was *monsieur* de Thibouville who realized that he was about to lose Zénobe as well. *Madame* Denis embraced Zénobe, thanking him for all that he had done for her uncle, and for all that he still had to do.

Zénobe could answer her only with a deep sob as he tried to keep himself from losing his composure, although the tears fell freely from his eyes.

It is hard, it is hard, he said to himself, to remain strong, to remain reasonable in this time of unbearable pain. My friend is gone, my friend is gone, my guide, my teacher, forever gone. I'll never see him anymore. I'll never hear his endearing laugh, his funny comments. He'll never again recite poetry to me. He'll never again have me take dictation. His jokes, his thoughts… It's all finished, and I want to follow him where he's going, even if it's a dark and lonely void.

While everyone grieved around him, he went to the book he had been reading, and held it close to his chest.

The neighborhood apothecary was called, as was the surgeon who was to do the autopsy, a *docteur* Try, aided by an assistant, a *monsieur* Burard. A death mask was done, for the sculptors. The apothecary, *monsieur* Mitouard, who served as the embalmer, asked to keep the brain, and the *marquis* de Villette sent word that he wished to keep the heart.

Zénobe left the room before any of that occurred. He remained in the kitchen with *monsieur* Maurel and all of the servants. Sylvie prepared supper for them, and also the food that Zénobe was to take with him on his trip.

Madame Denis came to Zénobe to give him letters for Wagnière. One of them was from Catherine the Great of Russia. Voltaire's niece told him that the Empress wished to buy Voltaire's library. She, being the universal heiress of Voltaire's possessions, had agreed to sell to Catherine not just the library but Voltaire's manuscripts as well.

Zénobe looked at *madame* Denis with astonished incredulity, but her heart was so full of grief that she did not notice.

Zénobe could not believe that this woman could so calmly divest herself of such a treasure. Sell Voltaire's library, dispose of Voltaire's unpublished manuscripts, as easily said and done as she would sell last season's frippery.

Voltaire was placed sitting up in his blue carriage with the golden stars, pulled by his six white horses. The gauze that had been there to protect his frail desiccated body was now placed around him to prop him up. His huge wig covered the scar done to his cranium. To any observer, Voltaire was going out for a sightseeing promenade, in spite of the fact that the carriage left at 4 o'clock in the morning. Zénobe sat across from him. As he had promised *madame* Denis, indeed, as he had sworn to himself and to the life that flowed in his veins, he would not leave her uncle's side until he was safely entombed, out of harm's way, where he could not be touched by the priests and used as an example of what would happen to an enemy of the Church. Zénobe was the military archangel Michael sent down to accept Voltaire's body and deliver him to his place of eternal repose. After all, Voltaire was the new Roland, courageous in spirit, resolute of action, valiant in the face of unrelenting threats, the new martyr-paragon for a new age. Zénobe was dressed in his full Swedish dragoon's uniform, and he was wearing two foils, his own and the one André was forced to leave behind. He was ready.

Voltaire's two nephews had already left around 2 o'clock in the morning to make things ready in Scellières. *L'abbé* Mignot was the commanding monk of the tiny abbey of Scellières, which belonged to the order of the Cîteaux, and which was composed of only two members, Mignot himself, and one other, the *prieur* by the name of *dom* Potherat de Corbières, who had already consented to receive the body for temporary repository in the vault of his church. Under the cover of darkness, as if they were the envoys of a dark lord, Voltaire's nephews and a faithful servant were meant to wander on desolate roads in search of a final resting place for the patriarch of the Enlightenment.

But first, Zénobe had to take leave of the Villette household, and in particular, he had to say good-bye to Maurel.

The staff bid tender adieus to the boy and told him to come back when it was safe for him to do so. Without anybody seeing what he did, Thibouville thrust a heavy purse into one of Zénobe's pockets and fled to his boudoir to weep inconsolably. Maurel was braver. Even though his lower lip all the way down to his chin was trembling uncontrollably, the inborn dignity of this *maître d'hôtel* made him unwavering in his stance and in his statements to Zénobe.

"You are the son I never had. With you go my dreams, my hopes, and such a huge part of my life that I don't know how I will be able to continue. I will be a mere automaton until you come back to me."

Zénobe, the younger man and thus the one least in control of his emotions, let his go in a torrent of grief. But he managed to say to Maurel what was deep in his heart.

"I lost my father, and now I don't want to lose you. I need you to tell me how to get on in the world, how to dress, how to behave. I have so very many lessons still to learn and that you need to teach me. I promise that I'll be back, and I'll bring André with me. I'm sure you will manage to convince the *marquis* de Villette to accept us back into his household."

"Ah, yes, my son," answered Maurel. "But as guests. You shall both return as guests."

Zénobe had to go. He jumped into the carriage, the door was closed, and the horses took off into the night.

Among the many things that were said of that night, the detail that Voltaire's servant was weeping in grief as he left the *hôtel* de Villette was altered by the philosopher's enemies to say that he was wailing in fear because Voltaire's autopsied body was falling apart and things were oozing out and an expression due to the preliminary agonies of hell was congealed on the cadaver's face. These were lies, told by, and spread far and wide, by priests of the Holy Roman Church.[290] Nothing could have been further from the truth. *Docteur* Try and the apothecary had done their job well, and Voltaire was, under his clothes and wig, wrapped up tighter than a mummy. Even the jolts in the roadway did not undo the bandages. As for his expression, Voltaire looked like he was asleep. So peaceful did he look that Zénobe felt comfortable enough to fall asleep himself, for after such a night, and in anticipation of the day to follow, he was convinced that the reasonable thing to do was rest.

With the help of Voltaire's friends, thanks to their connections in all areas of the social hierarchy, including the higher ecclesiastical orders, it was found out what the archbishop of Paris was plotting. With the waning of Voltaire's life, Beaumont had written three letters to the bishop of Annecy to have him forbid the *curé* of Ferney from burying Voltaire and from performing any sort of funeral service for him in his parish. From Annecy, in increasing concentric circles, other parishes similarly received their orders. But this territory, although huge, only went as far west as Lyon, as far south as Grenoble, and as far north as Besançon. To the east, of course, was Switzerland and Protestant territory, and those infidels could do whatever the hell they wanted with Voltaire should he fall into their hands. To be sure, the Catholics were confident that the Calvinists would not want Voltaire anyway, for Voltaire had managed during the length of his long life to insult all religions. His philosopher friends knew that to Voltaire, fanaticism was an infection that crossed all lines, and that the contagion did not stop at territorial borders.

As Beaumont smiled with satisfaction in Versailles, enjoying the thought of a dying Voltaire wandering aimlessly across provinces in search of a final place of repose, the priests could take their own repose. How satisfying. Parisians, who had welcomed the antichrist with such fervent enthusiasm, would have their precious icon snatched from their profane embrace, never to know if he was buried in a ditch somewhere beside a lonely roadway, or thrown into a river or a lake.

The rumors that Voltaire had already died, and that his mortal remains had suddenly made an appearance in Champagne, created a disturbance in Beaumont's world, and a new flurry of activity ensued, with new letters and new sanctions going out to chase after the thorn in the side of the Church. These new instructions forbade any member of the clergy of the Catholic and Apostolic Church, anywhere in its huge territories, from granting a plot of land for Voltaire's burial. Messengers were sent on fleet horses to the whole province of Champagne, down to the tiniest chapel, with instructions to apprehend Voltaire, dead or alive, and with force, if necessary, wrest him away from any claimants, and to return him forthwith to the archbishopric of Paris.

---

290   [From the author] The proof of this is in the bibliographical record. Look up any page from a religious source on the Internet and you will find Voltaire dying an atrocious death, hounded by unseen demons, clamoring for forgiveness and recanting his whole oeuvre.

By the time Zénobe woke up it was bright morning. They were still rolling through the Champagne countryside with fields and hamlets and vineyards rushing past. He was hungry, so he opened up Sylvie's package of food. There he found bread, cheese, sausages, hard-boiled eggs, fruits, and a bottle of wine. But the fact that he would be eating alone, that he wouldn't need to share his meal with Voltaire, sent heavy tears falling down his cheeks. He chewed his food slowly, all the while looking at Voltaire. The *philosophe* still seemed to be asleep although his skin in the light of the late-morning sun looked glassy. Voltaire, my friend and master, thought Zénobe. How intelligent he still looks. But the thoughts in that great mind have been stilled, and the world will be a poorer place for it. The world has lost its conscience.

Zénobe glanced at that world unfurling outside. They wouldn't be stopping for anything, except to rest the horses, until they had reached Scellières. He rummaged in his sack until he found the book he had been reading the day before. Slowly, the vineyards and farmyards of Champagne gave way to cardamom plantations and tea fields, cows became elephants, and French peasants turned into Indians who were half naked and wore white headdresses while strange birds flew by filling the air with even stranger calls.

But part of that must have been a dream, for Zénobe had fallen asleep late in the afternoon. The absence of movement woke him up, and when he glanced up he saw a dilapidated church in the background, and two very worried gentlemen, *messieurs* Mignot and d'Hornoy, running up to the carriage.

All that evening Zénobe did not leave Voltaire's side. Only when the philosopher was laid to rest in a white wooden coffin that was then placed on a bier, did Zénobe feel comfortable enough to join Voltaire's two nephews for supper. *L'abbé* Mignot had invited the priests of the neighboring towns of Romilly and Nogent to come and pray for his uncle, and they came, not knowing who this uncle was and knowing even less of the Parisian religious authorities' exigencies imposed on this uncle's burial. The identity of the deceased was known soon enough, but the ban on funerary services would not be known for another twelve hours.

The vigil for Voltaire lasted all night long. Zénobe's grief kept him awake, as did the continuous croaking of frogs. Scellières was not far from a swampy area created by the annual spring flooding of the Seine, and the calls of the spring amphibians was as unrelenting as it was merciless. The thick walls of the ancient church did nothing to impede the chorus; Zénobe could see holes between the roof and the walls and around some of the windows. A vine was sending its tendrils to probe inside the church.

It was disappointing to accept this disintegrating environment for Voltaire's earthly repose. Newton had been entombed in Westminster Abbey during a ceremony filled with much pomp and pride and he was placed in a magnificent mausoleum worthy of his greatness. Here, Voltaire was going to be put underneath a dingy flagstone of the uneven floor of a provincial church that was falling apart. Instead of the Royal Choir singing elegies to the man of science while accompanied by a full orchestra, here there was a pitiable handful of country priests chanting *a cappella* the usual vespers of the dead, accompanied only by the vigorous vocalizations of the slimy residents of the nearby marsh. Still, it wasn't the city dump. And it wasn't forever. The plan was eventually to remove Voltaire's remains and take them to Ferney, where they belonged, in his tomb, which stood half inside and half outside the little chapel he had built.

Mignot and d'Hornoy fell asleep in their chairs, but Zénobe felt a dread that at any time envoys from Paris could show up to stop the vigil. He wished the priests could bury Voltaire immediately, but he realized the process was embedded in centuries of tradition and nothing would be able to sway the priests to vary their customs. There, in the obscurity of the swirling smoke from the incense, Zénobe thought of the darkness in which the Church hoped to maintain its people. *Do not see the light! Do not see the truth!* The Church wanted to keep the truth hidden, the truth that Science wanted to reveal. Science was a liberating force, but the Church wished jealously to keep its power over people, and thus waged war on Science. The Church would never relinquish its hold over the people. The Church was the enemy of Science. And therefore, Zénobe was the enemy of the Church. But he was not the enemy of the people, even though he anguished over those who could accept the lies and be content with rituals and nonsense. He was the friend of the people, as Voltaire had been his whole life. The people had to be liberated even though they didn't know they had been enslaved.

This Unholy Church, which looked nothing like the one St. Peter had established at the beginning, had its jealous claws on everything. Voltaire's friends and family couldn't even find a place to bury him that was worthy of his accomplishments, of his brilliance. And his funeral should have taken place with the participation of his thousands of admirers. The monarch and that bitch of his wife should have come to kneel in front of his sarcophagus to mark the end of a splendid life. The archbishop of Paris should have given a worthy eulogy hours long to praise the *philosophe*, to laud the Lord of Reason, who was better than either the monarch or the archbishop.

But there were signs of hope, here in this moldering abbey of Scellières. If this broken-down church could be but a symbol of the degenerating theological edifice, then the days of the Church were numbered. The building was yielding to entropy. Repairs could not keep up with the relentless attack of nature, and centuries of seasons had cracked the walls and made the ceiling sag. The balustrades and the candelabras were rusted, and the whole place smelled of mustiness and decay that even the incense could not blot out, just like the incantations of the priests could not drown out the singing of the frogs in the marshes.

The coming of the dawn put an end to both the amphibian and the human choirs. They were replaced by more clergy, bringing with them eulogists, choirboys, cross- and candle bearers, a beadle, a boy responsible for the thurible, a couple of deacons, and the gravediggers. The few villagers who had heard something also started to show up, and in the end, by the time the actual funeral began, there were about sixty people congregated inside the crumbling church. Each of the six priests present said mass. Voltaire's coffin was slowly lowered into the hole in the floor, and the heavy flagstone was dragged over it. Zénobe could not tell the stone apart from the others, so he carefully counted the number of stones there were from the sides and from the transept, so that in the future he would be able to recognize which stone was Voltaire's. The funeral over, everybody left. Voltaire's nephews returned to Paris in the philosopher's carriage.

With their bereavement and lack of sleep, they forgot all about Zénobe's existence. But the *marquis* de Villette's librarian couldn't go back to Paris anyway. The rabid priests would get to him quite easily there. He had to go elsewhere.

But where was he to go? He was in desperate need to see his beloved André. But there was something else that was pressing, and which he owed to Voltaire.

Weary and lonely, he left the grounds of the Scellières abbey that looked like they had been abandoned for years. Under a clear and sunny sky, as he approached the banks of the Seine, he heard splashing and screams coming from the water. Alarmed, he directed his gaze to the commotion and saw a circle of boys gamboling and diving into the water. A couple of them were playing with inflated pig's bladders, taking them down below the surface and releasing them whereupon they rose quickly and bounced over the water where the other boys waited to snatch them away. There was laughter and the sprays of water shone brilliantly in the morning sun.

Zénobe realized that Benjamin Franklin's recommendation of aquatic activities as a diversion and a healthy pastime was being disseminated among the general population, and this was glorious. There need be no fear of immersing oneself in rivers and lakes. The thoughts and opinions of the era's luminaries were being adopted, by children, no less. Philosophy was being made accessible to all. Each generation, if it heeded the Voice of Reason, would strip itself of contrived prejudice and superstitions. Each generation would be an improvement on the last. Zénobe had to devote himself to continuing Voltaire's work, for it would take more than a few generations to discard all the stupid notions that society harbored. That all societies harbored. This was work that he could undertake, for it would be a noble endeavor and he would be able to see successful results swiftly. This notion served to dispel his gloomy spirits somewhat as did the sight of the sun's rays falling on the bathing boys' naked skin. He looked up to the sky and closed his eyes feeling the sun's warmth on his face. He could hear the shrill squeals of the youths and he could tell that their voices were just about ready to change.

He remembered from Voltaire's *Fragments sur quelques révolutions dans l'Inde* about another river, the Ganges, in whose sacred waters the Hindus bathed and paid homage to their ancestors. "The waters that bathed and refreshed the body could do as much for the soul," wrote Voltaire.[291] Ebb and flow, Zénobe thought, ebb and flow. The current moves on and takes us indifferently along with it. When he opened his eyes again, he saw the river meandering into the distance.

"Do I have a soul?" asked Zénobe within himself. "Is there something within me that could be construed as a soul? Is this the life force that wounds me now, that with anguish and torment tears me apart? On the one hand, I wish to be reunited with André, to receive his balm and kindness, to seek solace in his arms while I grieve for Voltaire. But on the other, I must go to Ferney and assure for future generations that all of Voltaire's writings will survive. And poor Wagnière still doesn't know that Voltaire is no more."

In desolation, Zénobe walked along the banks of the river. His reverie continued: Here is the Seine. Here is the Seine that leads to Paris. But the water in Romilly is clearer, fresher and, Zénobe mused, more innocent, for it had not yet been sullied by the refuse and corruption of that putrefactive city. He wondered if he would ever see Paris again. What would his destiny be as time continued its ineluctable flow towards the future? He could quite easily climb onto a floating log or into a basket of papyrus and flow downstream to Paris. But he knew that he could not do that.

---

291   *"Ses eaux [du Gange] qui lavaient et rafraîchissaient le corps, en pussent faire autant pour l'âme."*

He walked the few leagues to Romilly where he rented a room for the rest of the day and that night. He needed to rest. And he wanted to finish the rest of Voltaire's book.

In the morning he would buy a horse. Wherever he went, he faced many leagues of travel before he would be able to rest again. Had it been possible, he would have written a letter to André explaining why he couldn't go just now to Normandy. But Condorcet had warned him about writing letters. He had to turn his attention to another place, to Ferney. Somebody had to go warn Wagnière what *madame* Denis was planning to do with Voltaire's library, including the manuscripts. Zénobe and Wagnière would have a lot of work to do if they wanted to transcribe these texts to keep them safe, to keep them together. They couldn't allow these precious works to travel all the way to Russia without documenting them first. A thousand things could go wrong between Ferney and Saint Petersburg. In his imagination he saw religious zealots getting a hold of them and burning them in a pyre. He saw Frédéric II interposing his royal will as he and Wagnière crossed his lands. He would censure the writings, just as surely as Catherine II would, too. He could see the travelers being attacked by marauders, and the thousands of papers being scattered to the winds, landing on the trees and in the rivers, flying off to oblivion. Zénobe shuddered.

Once in Ferney, he would have Wagnière write a letter to Maurel, who in turn would let André know what was going on. He hoped André would understand what an important task he was undertaking. It was nothing less than protecting Voltaire's legacy.

That night, he finished reading Voltaire's *Revolutions in India*. It was one of the philosopher's more somber works in which there wasn't much room for levity. He learned about Vishnapor, and the Brahmins, and of their terrestrial paradise, and of the barbarities exercised by Europeans on the most humane people on earth, of the cruelty of the French and the English and the Portuguese, of their division and despoilment of India. He also learned why it all mattered to him, halfway around the world.

Voltaire's voice came to Zénobe's memory. "If I allow an injustice to occur halfway around the world without adding my voice to condemn it, without making an effort to stop it, then it is my tacit agreement for such an injustice one day to fall on my own head, or on the head of someone I love."

India was far, far away. Just the same, Zénobe grew angry that men should use violence to subjugate others who had learned to live in peace.

Epilogue: The Coming Revolutionary Fervor

Dr. Benjamin Franklin will be elected "venerable" of the Lodge of the Nine Sisters a year after Voltaire's death on May 12, 1779. During the ceremony two eulogies will be read, one for Montaigne, by La Dixmerie, and the other for Voltaire, by Carbon de Flins des Oliviers. Upon his return to Philadelphia after the American Revolution, Franklin will participate in the Constitutional Convention (May, 1787) and shortly thereafter, will begin working on what he considers the Constitution's greatest failure: the liberation of the slaves. In the meantime, the pain caused by gout and kidney stones is alleviated somewhat by small doses of laudanum, but, unlike Voltaire, he will never increase the amount. Towards the end, Benjamin Franklin's doubts about the divinity of Jesus Christ will be of no business to anyone but himself: "I think it needless to busy myself with it now, where I expect soon an opportunity of knowing the truth with less trouble."

Dr. Edward Bancroft, after having acted as Benjamin Franklin's private secretary in Passy, will return to London, marry an English lady, and settle down in England. He will die in London in 1821. Before his death, he will have made a fortune selling clothes dyed with a process invented by him, and will have obtained an Act of Parliament to secure to himself sole rights of said process, whereby the sap of a certain species of oak, that when mixed with iron, produces a yellow color, applicable to wood, linen, silk, and the new very popular material, cotton. It won't be until 70 years after his death, when the papers of Lord Stormont, ambassador to France, and Paul Wentworth, head of the British Secret Service, are released to public scrutiny in 1891, that it will be found out that Edward Bancroft was a spy in the employ of the British government, and, thanks to him, everything that went on in the offices of the American diplomats in Passy was made known within a week to George III.

Jean-Jacques Rousseau dies a little over a month after Voltaire, on July 2, 1778. He and Thérèse will have left Paris to enjoy the cool countryside retreat of his friend, the *marquis* René Louis de Girardin, at Ermenonville. He will die suddenly of a brain hemorrhage after an early morning walk on the grounds, while he and Thérèse are seated discussing the payment of the locksmith. Thérèse will survive him until 1801.

Jean Le Rond d'Alembert won't die until 1783. Voltaire had recommended to his care the 24 letters of the alphabet, but he won't be able to bring the 38 other Academicians to finish the task of the new Dictionary. A new edition will not be published until 1798. Voltaire's chair in the Academy, number 33, will be filled in 1778 by Jean-François Ducis, the secretary of the king's brother, the *comte* de Provence. Ducis' speech of acceptance will be written by the *abbé* de Radonvilliers, since Ducis felt "uncomfortable with prose." ["*Il ne se sentait pas à l'aise dans la prose.*"] Neither the king, nor any of his siblings, would have been able to recognize talent, or lack thereof, in the field of Letters, since none of them had ever read a book.

Denis Diderot's death follows in the year after d'Alembert's, in 1784. His novel, *Jacques le fataliste et son maître*, which he was writing in 1778, will not be published until 1796 although a partial translation into German will be published in 1785. Many of his other works will be published posthumously as well, since their publication during his lifetime would have made his life impossible to live in view of the oppression from Church and State. This includes his *Mémoires*, where one finds the following sentence about Voltaire: "*Quand il y aurait un Christ, je vous assure que Voltaire serait sauvé.*" [Were there to be a Christ, I assure you that Voltaire would be saved.]

Frederick II, King of Prussia, will order a solemn mass in the Catholic church of Berlin, which will be attended by all the members of all his academies, to mourn the passing of Voltaire. In Paris, despite the efforts of some members of the French Academy and the Academy of Sciences, no such commemoration will be allowed. Frédéric, in his Eulogy of Voltaire, will talk about the "*prêtres imbéciles de Paris.*"

Catherine II, Empress of Russia, goes into mourning. She will buy from *madame* Denis Voltaire's complete library, and will have a facsimile of the château of Ferney built in Czarekoselo, the construction of which will be overseen by Wagnière. She will write to *madame* Denis, "*Personne avant lui n'écrivait comme lui; à la race future, il servira d'exemple et d'écueil.*" [Nobody before him wrote like he did; for the future race, he will serve as an example and a stumbling block.]

Her political descendants will inaugurate with great pomp a new Voltaire hall at the National Library of Saint-Petersburg in the spring of 2003.

Voltaire's primary secretary, **Jean-Louis Wagnière** will be devastated by the death of his master. Voltaire had once written to him, "*Je ne peux me passer ni de vous, ni de mes livres.*" [I cannot do without either you or my books.] Wagnière will forever blame *madame* Denis and the *marquis* de Villette for having caused Voltaire's death by not returning him quickly to Ferney. He will spend the rest of his days writing a book about it, accusatory in tone, *Mémoires sur Voltaire*, which becomes a bestseller when it's finally published years after his death, in 1826. The year after Voltaire's death, in 1779, Wagnière accompanies Voltaire's library to Russia. Before his own death in 1802, Wagnière will have been the mayor of Ferney during the turbulent years of the Revolution.

Charles-Joseph Panckoucke, the publisher, had become wealthy, mostly by selling banned books by Voltaire. After Voltaire's death, Panckoucke will attempt single-handedly to publish his complete works, but because of the breadth and danger of such an enterprise, he will enlist Beaumarchais' help, to whom he will eventually yield the whole project. After Voltaire's death, Panckoucke becomes the first press tycoon, his presses working night and day to produce the *Mercure de France*, the *Gazette de France*, and the *Moniteur universel.*

Pierre Augustin Caron de Beaumarchais will take over from Panckoucke the enormous compilation of Voltaire's complete works, which will finally be published between 1784 and 1789 in the château fort of Kehl, right over the German border from Strasbourg. This enterprise will ruin Beaumarchais financially, having taken ten years of his life and 3 million francs of his money.

When the Revolutionaries, right before the September Massacres of 1792, raid Beaumarchais' mansion on the boulevard Saint-Antoine, which was a few minutes' walk from the destroyed Bastille, they will not find him at home, since he will have taken flight a few seconds before through his secret subterranean exit, but they will find a few hundred unsold sets of Voltaire's complete works in the cellar.

Jean Antoine Nicolas de Caritat, marquis de Condorcet, "Condor," the junior member of Voltaire's group of philosophical followers, will write a biography of his master, *Vie de Voltaire*, which will be published in 1784 in the 70th volume of the Kehl edition of Voltaire's complete works. He will also organize the works and the correspondence of the edition, as well as provide editorial commentary. In 1788, along with the *marquis* de Lafayette and the lawyer Jacques-Pierre Brissot, the same Brissot whom Zénobe will accompany to America, Condorcet will found the French antislavery group *"Les Amis des Noirs"*. He will also become an advocate for the rights of women.

Antoine Court de Gébelin, the Mason who helped induct Voltaire into the Lodge of the Nine Sisters, will be accidentally killed on May 10, 1784 during an electromagnetic seance with Mesmer. While being treated for dropsy, the electrical charge during the experiment will cause an arrhythmia that will eventually stop his heart. A newspaper of the day will carry the headline, "M. Court de Gébelin has just died, cured of dropsy by Mesmer's animal magnetism." The king will direct the *Académie des sciences* to hold an investigation on animal magnetism. In the committee will be Franklin, Bailly (the future revolutionary mayor of Paris), and Lavoisier, the chemist. They will conclude that even though Mesmer's science was erroneous and dangerously so, and that Mesmer himself was nothing but a charlatan, the whole of the proceedings was perhaps not entirely devoid of a reason for scientific inquiry. Their conclusion will be as follows: "Magnetism will not have been totally useless to the science which condemns it; it is one more fact to be consigned to the history of errors of the human mind, and a great experiment on the power of the imagination."

Posterity also remembers Court de Gébelin for his interest and efforts on behalf of cartomancy (the Tarot); he will be considered as the father of occultism, due to his interest in hermeneutics.

Louis François Armand de Vignerot du Plessis, duc de Richelieu, Friend of Voltaire for 60 years, who played "hero" to Voltaire's "poet," and whom as protector of the arts, Voltaire found indispensable, was much appreciated by Louis XV for having introduced *madame* du Barry to His Royal Highness. The duke made attempts to soften Louis XVI's stance against Voltaire, to no avail. His offer of opium to Voltaire was done with the kindest intentions; he would never have thought that his old friend would have increased the dosage.

The Archbishop of Paris, Christophe de Beaumont, failed in his attempt to deprive Voltaire of a safe, dry, comfortable grave; he also failed in his efforts to have the old philosopher's works suppressed and his memory expunged from the world. When the archbishop dies in 1781 at the age of 79, his funeral procession will consist of 500 poor people at the head of the march, followed by 72 orphans, the brothers of the orders of the Capucins, the Cordeliers, the Frères Prêcheurs, the monks of the Rosaire, the Augustins, the Carares, the priests of the Scapulaire, clerics and other assorted clergymen. The coffin, borne on a splendid catafalque, will be followed by hundreds of Swiss guards, officers and prelates, with the ducal crown and the pastoral cross held aloft on mourning cushions. Bringing up the rear of the procession will be 30 archbishops, followed by the aristocratic Beaumont family, escorted by 50 valets in double file, holding torches in their hands. The somber march will proceed from the archbishop's palace to Notre Dame de Paris, where after a sumptuous mass and eulogies galore, Beaumont will be laid to rest in the family crypt in the chapel erected to Saint John and Saint Mary Madeleine. During the Revolution, Beaumont's remains, along with centuries of the ecclesiastical dead from all the churches of Paris, will be broken out of their tombs and scattered around Paris or thrown into the Seine.

Jean-Josèph Faydit de Tersac, *curé* of Saint-Sulpice, felt a weight after Voltaire's death, genuinely disappointed that he was not able to save Voltaire's soul. Having been *curé* of his church since only the previous year, he continues to throw himself zealously into other sorts of good works, including improvements to the church buildings and the square in front of it. Because of him, the church will receive new baptismal founts, a huge organ, eight new bells, a statute of the Virgin Mary by Pigalle, a new pulpit designed by Wailly, and minor interior and exterior decoration. Tersac continues his work to improve the lives of the poor. Exhausted by such moil, the priest decides to take the waters of the Nivernais, but he succumbs to mortal fatigue on August 14, 1788, just a few days before his 49th year.

It was the chaplain of the Hospital of the Incurables, *l'abbé* **Louis Laurent Gaultier** who, by zeal alone, and without consulting the ecclesiastical hierarchy, had attempted to save Voltaire's soul. It was he, therefore, who was forever blamed by his superiors for having botched the job. Disowned by the archbishop of Paris and the curate of his diocese, Gaultier will never get another chance to convert a soul as big as Voltaire's. He will, however, receive honors posthumously, when in 1926 pope Pious XI has him beatified for, among other things, having been a victim of the September Massacres of 1792.

Dom Potherat de Corbières, the *prieur* of the Abbey of Scellières will get into enormous trouble for having buried Voltaire. He will be dismissed from his post and relegated to an inferior position elsewhere, in spite of his continued contention that as prior he could only have refused a Christian burial to someone who had been excommunicated, which Voltaire clearly had not been. In any case, he will not miss his leaky abbey and its swampy grounds. Furthermore, he never would have had enough money to buy a cushier position in a more attractive abbey.

Charles-Michel, *marquis* du Plessis-Villette, Voltaire's host in Paris, will keep his guest's heart in a golden coffer, which he will place in Voltaire's bedroom in Ferney, with the "epitaph" "Voltaire's heart is here, but his spirit is everywhere." When he sells the château in 1785, the golden coffer is sold along with it, and the buyer inherits the headache involved in the numerous pilgrims who wish to go bask in front of the philosopher's heart. Too bad that the heart had already returned to Paris in 1783, where it remained at the *hôtel* de Villette, under the care of the *marquise.*

Villette will be an active participant in the French Revolution. His biggest moment will come when, in full view of the National Assembly, he will ostentatiously burn his Letters of Nobility, which had cost his father a huge sum of money to buy from Louis XV. With this symbolic and typically histrionic gesture, Villette, no longer a *marquis*, but rather Charles Villette, citizen, becomes the equal of members of the Third Estate. They, however, never quite accept him as one of their own, never forgetting the indiscreet follies of his youth.

Reine Philiberte Rouph de Varicourt, *marquise* de Villette, *Belle et bonne* to Voltaire, in spite of her proximity to a dying man, will proceed to have a good pregnancy and will be delivered of a beautiful, healthy daughter. In 1792, a son will follow, baptized with the name of Voltaire-Villette. For the rest of her life, the *marquise* will enjoy the lauds that a grateful public will lavishly bestow on her because of her love and concern for her adoptive father, Voltaire.

Ferney, Voltaire's château and village, today called Ferney-Voltaire, started out in 1759, the year Voltaire bought them, as a shabby provincial mansion in dire need of repairs, and a collection of 41 hovels and isolated farmhouses whose godforsaken inhabitants eked out a living from the swampy land and from a derelict tile factory. By 1778, Ferney the château had been enlarged, embellished and improved, and the village had grown a hundred-fold and had become a place suitable not just for farmers but also for masons, goldsmiths, watchmakers, clock makers, assorted artisans in pottery and tile-making, an architect (Voltaire's, a *monsieur* Racle), a surgeon, a baker, a butcher, and silk-makers who sustained the cultivation of mulberry trees and the raising of silkworms. Swamps had been drained, streets paved, a post office created, even a small theater built, ornate and comfortable. Voltaire also had installed in 1776 on the public square a beautiful fountain to bring potable water to the villagers.

If Ferney was on the grand tour of Europe, it must have surely been because of the great Voltaire, but at the same time travelers came to gaze upon a community wrought by the Enlightenment, a sort of principality of the Age of Reason, where Catholics and Protestants lived together in tolerance and in harmony.

Voltaire's niece, **Marie Louise Mignot Denis**, having inherited a lot of money and a lot of real estate, to say nothing of future earnings gained from Voltaire's publications, becomes a very wealthy woman, and very much sought after. In 1778 she sells Ferney to the *marquis* de Villette and Voltaire's library to the Empress of Russia Catherine II.

She will be consoled of the loss of her uncle by the formidable presence of a former dragoon, a Captain du Vivier, who will become the lucky groom in 1780, and who will help her to spend the inheritance at an aristocratic rate. In the end, there will be nothing to leave to the remaining relatives of the Arouet and Mignot families.

Henri Lambert d'Herbigny, *marquis* de Thibouville, will be saddened by Voltaire's death, but will be desolated by Zénobe's departure. When Villette informs him that the *marquise* de Villette is pregnant, Thibouville decides that it is time to visit his ancestral lands in Normandy. He will visit André in Caen about a month after Voltaire's death, in the hopes that Zénobe will already have gotten there after the philosopher's funeral in Champagne, but will be disappointed. He will be there when André receives a letter from *monsieur* Maurel from which they both learn that Zénobe is in Russia.

Thibouville will travel less and less to Paris, finding the city *hoi polloi* increasingly uppity and thoroughly dead common, but whenever he is in the city, he will never fail to use his connections to gauge the Church's case of prosecution against Zénobe Bosquet.

Thibouville dies in Rouen on June 16, 1784.

Jacques-Henri Maurel, the *maître d'hôtel* in the service of the *marquis* de Villette, will no longer go to the provinces to retrieve handsome boys for his master's perusal, citing the *marquis'* age and position in society which do not lend themselves to trivial bouts of concupiscence. Maurel himself will find a modicum of happiness when he marches into a relationship with a Revolutionary of note.

At Voltaire's death, **Marie-Jean-Baptiste Zénobe Bosquet** would have been surprised to know that he soon would travel to Russia, to accompany Wagnière and Voltaire's library to Catherine II's court. In so doing, Voltaire's oldest secretary together with his newest will see to it that their master's literary corpus, just like his library, will not be dismembered, but rather will hold together in preparation for the definitive edition of his complete works, including thousands and thousands of his letters.

Furthermore, who could have but known that Voltaire's suggestion to Zénobe that he travel and have adventures in America would have planted the seed that would germinate in 1788? When the future revolutionary Jacques-Pierre Brissot decides to leave for the newly established country of the United States of America, he needs a secretary. Zénobe, who is still being pursued by the Church for sins against God and crimes against the State, is only too happy to comply. Leaving André behind in Normandy, Zénobe and Brissot tour America and get their fill of American republicanism, enthusiasm and hope. By the time they return to Paris in 1789, it will be just in time for the gathering storm of the French Revolution.

André Corday will wait patiently while Zénobe travels to Saint Petersburg. He will wait, once again, for the return of Zénobe from America. His love for him will never diminish, which is why he will be with Zénobe when the young revolutionary gets caught up in the politics of the Terror in 1793.

André's sister, **Charlotte Corday**, will be admitted in 1781 to the Abbaye des Dames in Caen where she will be a student pensioner until February of 1791. In 1793, in the midst of the Terror, Charlotte will travel to Paris, buy a knife with a 6-inch blade at a cutler's in the arcades of the Palais-Royal, and seek an audience with Jean-Paul Marat, the Revolutionary, whom she blames in general for the gratuitous violence of the Revolution and in particular for the September Massacres of the preceding year. She will stab him while he is in his bath. For this political assassination, Charlotte will be guillotined on July 17, 1793.

The New André, **André Laurent**, remains in the employ of the *marquis* de Villette for a few more years, until he gets a better position as preceptor of the children of an aristocratic family who live in the neighborhood of Saint-Germain. His path will cross Zénobe's a few times, when Zénobe returns to Paris with André Corday right before the Revolution. Zénobe will feel embarrassment… no, regret, that he ever made love to the Nouvel André, and perhaps concern, when he identifies in the Nouvel André feelings of nostalgia and tenderness. It is true, le Nouvel André comes to the sad realization as Zénobe becomes more and more involved in Revolutionary activities, that he had had in Zénobe, if only for a fleeting moment, the love of his life.

Another of Zénobe's previous lovers, **Yolande Martine Gabrielle de Polastron, *marquise* de Polignac**, whom Zénobe hated with passion, but with slightly less passion managed to make love to her, continued her meteoric rise in the esteem of the Queen who lavishly bestowed such gifts on her that the detractors of the aristocracy had ample ammunition with which to evince the profligacy of the court. In 1780 Marie Antoinette used her influence, once again, on her husband the King to grant the Polignacs the status of *duc* and *duchesse*, and in 1782 the Queen made Gabrielle *gouvernante des enfants de France*, raising her already substantial stipend, giving her twice as many rooms in Versailles as any other aristocrat, and granting her one of the pastoral cottages in the *Hameau de la reine*, the Queen's rendition of a rustic village bucolically laid out in glorious isolation on the grounds of the royal palace.

Interestingly, *madame* de Polignac will not have forgotten her brief tryst with the cute little peasant boy from Savoie. (To her credit, she never knew that Zénobe was a peasant.) When she sees him again during the emerging machinations of the revolutionary machine, she is not loath to renew her sentimental attachment to the young man, now grown in confidence, stature and valor. She will be the key to his entry at Versailles.

After the events of July 14, 1789, the whole of the Polignac family will be among the first to abandon both their royal quarters and their sovereign benefactors. True, Gabrielle will keep up a steady correspondence with the Queen, promising her undying love and eternal regard for her, until the Queen is no longer allowed to read letters. Coincidentally, or perhaps tellingly, *madame* de Polignac will die shortly after the beheading of her cherished Queen. Was it heartbreak that led her to her end, or was it guilt for the fortune squandered upon her person and upon her clan, and thus acceptance of her personal role in one of the causes of the French Revolution? Whatever the case, she was still dazzlingly beautiful when she died, and forever more she was known as the incarnate symbol of the death of the French aristocracy.

After having been rescued from a convent by Diderot and taken to the *hôtel* de Villette as a maid, **Suzanne** will remain in the employ of *monsieur* and *madame* de Villette. The Revolution will affect her as well, or rather, as badly, as the other servants, and, with the death of the *marquis* in 1793, will scatter them into different directions.

Voltaire's travels and hectic pace will not halt after his death. On July 11, 1791, on the third year of the Revolution which he helped to propagate, the Revolutionaries will bring back his remains from Scellières into Paris, with great pomp and seriousness, passing by all the addresses of his triumphs, by the French Academy in the Louvre, by the French Theater in the Tuileries Palace, by the *hôtel* de Villette on the quai des Théâtins which thereafter will become known as the quai Voltaire, before bearing Voltaire to the Panthéon, the resting place of all national heroes and the new manifestation of the Church of Sainte Geneviève, the patron saint of Paris.

Rousseau's body will also be treated to this honor, and today, in the crypts beneath the rotunda of the old church, their two mausoleums are forever confronting each other, separated only by the main hallway.

When Voltaire had died initially, the *marquis* de Villette had appropriated his heart, which was the central piece of a shrine he kept at the château of Ferney. His brain had been kept by the apothecary, *monsieur* Mitouard, who embalmed him. During the funeral march through Paris, somebody made off with one of Voltaire's toes. In 1814, supposedly, ultra-Royalist sympathizers, blaming Voltaire and Rousseau for the Revolution (*'C'est la faute à Voltaire, c'est la faute à Rousseau!'*; It's Voltaire's fault, it's Rousseau's fault!), crept into the crypt of the two philosophers in the middle of the night in the month of May, 1814, stole the two cadavers, and carefully shut the tombs again. The two philosophers were then thrown into the city dump. Nothing of this midnight robbery was known until the Second Empire under Napoleon III in 1864, and the Emperor himself had the crypts opened: nothing was found inside. This, however, does not coincide with the results of an inquest made in 1878, under the auspices of the first president of the Third Republic, Louis Jules Trochu, which certified that each of the two coffins contained a skeleton.

Voltaire's heart will be kept by the son of the *marquis* and *marquise* de Villette, who will donate it to Napoléon III. The Emperor will have it placed in the Bibliothèque Impériale, today the Bibliothèque Nationale de France in Paris, where it remains to this day.

Voltaire's brain was kept by the apothecary Mitouard until his death. Mitouard's son will offer it to the Government of the Directoire, which refuses it. In 1830, it will be offered to the new monarch Louis-Philippe I, one of the children whom Voltaire visited in the Palais-Royal in 1778, but who will also refuse it. In 1858, the heir of Mitourard's son will offer it to the *Académie française*, which also refuses it. In 1870, an old unmarried demoiselle of the Mitouard family bequeaths Voltaire's brain to an employee of the Mitouard pharmacy on the rue Coquillère, a *monsieur* de La Brosse, who dies intestate five years later. His possession are sold off and dispersed, and Voltaire's seat of reason disappears from the historical record.

Antoine René de Voyer d'Argenson, *marquis* de Paulmy, the former keeper of the Royal Arsenal who became a librarian, will not forget the young radical Bosquet who had access to his books for a period of time right before the death of Voltaire. When Zénobe returns to Paris, he will look up his fellow bibliophile and will continue to avail himself of the thousands of books in the Arsenal Library. By the time of the *marquis'* death in 1787, Zénobe will be ready to leave the bookish life, and go from reading about adventures to actively pursuing them, first in America, then in Revolutionary France. Still, his heart will ache when d'Argenson's library is sold to the *comte* d'Artois, the king's brother, who in no way deserves it.

Joseph Bologne, chevalier de Saint-George, the virtuoso violinist, incomparable composer, and master of fencing, will become a captain of the National Guard, which is to be responsible for the defense of the country in the depths of a Revolution within and simultaneously at war with her enemies without. He will acquit himself of national service with respect and grudging admiration, but at his death in 1799 his body will not be entombed with other national heroes in the Panthéon. It is unclear exactly where his body lays. Furthermore, General Bonaparte, first Consul of the First French Republic, has Saint-George's works burned, and has slavery reinstated in the French Antilles in 1802.

Texier de La Boëssière and **Antoine de La Boëssière**, *père et fils*, will continue to hold the most prestigious fencing academy in Europe. The Revolution will only increase their student enrollment. La Boëssière, *fils* will publish in 1818 the definitive book on fencing, *Traité de l'art des armes, Éloge de l'épée,* which is consulted even to this day.

Charles Geneviève Louis Auguste André Thimothée d'Éon de Beaumont, called the *chevalière* d'Éon, will flee France during the Revolution and seek exile, like hundreds of her aristocratic brethren, in London. She will have first offered in 1792 to the National Assembly her patriotic services as leader of a military unit of Amazons, but to no avail. The remains of her fortune will not last long, and her pension will die along with the French monarchy. In 1796 she will be forced to share a flat at no. 26 New Wilman Street with a friend, Mrs. Cole, another lady in financial distress. The two of them will live together, in respectful poverty until one fine spring day in 1810, Mary discovers *mademoiselle* d'Éon dead in her bed. Around her, scattered about the room on the furniture and hanging on the walls, remain the musty remnants of her heyday as Captain of the Dragoons. However, her Saint Louis medal is still pinned to her bodice, the bodice of her faded threadbare nightgown.

Since *mademoiselle* d'Éon was no anonymous person, an autopsy will be performed. A Dr. Copeland, accompanied by a dozen other English gentlemen, an esteemed group which includes surgeons, lawyers, and a journalist, will conduct said autopsy, and its findings will be followed in print by the avid readers of all the London newspapers. During the autopsy it will be found that the *chevalière*'s anatomy showed all the proper parts, without disfigurement, without stuntedness or deficiency or blending of any kind, that established without a doubt the veracity of her true sex: *mademoiselle* d'Éon was a man.

She will be buried in Middlesex.

Monsieur le professeur **Roy Luna**, *dix-huitiémiste* and unapologetic Voltairean, will continue teaching and forming young minds. He will continue, in subsequent volumes, the story of Zénobe and André, seeing them through the decade before the Revolution (volume 2: 1778-1789), and then during the Revolution itself (volume 3: 1789-1794). Zénobe's Americanization during his trip to the newly established country as secretary to the future Revolutionary Jacques-Pierre Brissot, will be of particular interest, as well as the fatal events of the Terror in 1793, when the Revolution starts to eat its own children.

Herr **Dr. Theophilus Ralph**, historian, even though he did not see eye to eye with the author during this, the first volume of Professor Luna's trilogy on the decade leading up to the French Revolution, will be persuaded to continue collaborating on the two subsequent tomes not only as fact-checker, but also as a sort of deflator of the hyperbole to which *monsieur* Luna is inexorably attracted. Like the alter ego of a split personality, *Herr* Ralph will thankfully be present to shepherd the voice of Reason along reasonable parameters, to repudiate inexactness of historicity, and to facilitate for the reader the perplexing arcana of the past.

A word about the typeface used in this novel: The Baskerville font, designed by John Baskerville of Birmingham in 1754, was bought in 1779 by the Société Littéraire Typographique, Beaumarchais' enterprise, in order to publish the Kehl edition of Voltaire's complete works. During the French Revolution it will be used by the presses of the *Gazette Nationale*. Baskerville's detractors claimed that the typeface was so stark that it damaged the retina. Benjamin Franklin, however, whom Baskerville met in 1758, admired it greatly. Franklin, who was the same age as Baskerville, would visit him in Birmingham and stay in his home. Baskerville, too, never bothered to marry his common-law wife.

An atheist, Baskerville refused to be buried in hallowed ground, stipulating in his will that he be buried in his back yard.

The last word belongs to Voltaire:

«*Le doute n'est pas une condition agréable, mais la certitude est absurde.*»
"Doubt is not a pleasant condition, but certitude is absurd."

Photo by Mark P. Young

A professor of French language and literature, Roy Luna is an expert in the history and culture of France, particularly the 18th Century, that most tumultuous and game-changing epoch. Luna's fascination with history brings a unique perspective to the *Lord of Reason*, the first novel in a trilogy of works that explores that ambiguous boundary between historical episode and fictional imaginings. *Monsieur* Luna resides in Miami.

Dr. Theophilus Ralph, professor of history and historiography, serves as the voice of conscience within the *Lord of Reason*. Ostensibly the novel's "fact-checker," *Herr* Dr. Ralph is in point of fact its "crossing guard," policing the interpenetrating space between fiction and history that *Lord of Reason* dramatizes. Dr. Ralph divides his time between Westphalia and Aquitaine, and is sometimes considered – by those who know him best – to be a work of fiction, himself.

* 9 7 8 0 9 9 6 7 0 3 1 0 9 *